A COURT AFFAIR

EMILY PURDY

AVON

This novel is entirely a work of fiction.
The names, characters and incidents portrayed in it are
the work of the author's imagination. Any resemblance to
actual persons, living or dead, events or localities is
entirely coincidental.

AVON
A division of HarperCollins*Publishers*
77–85 Fulham Palace Road,
London W6 8JB

www.harpercollins.co.uk

A Paperback Original 2012
1

First published in Great Britain by
HarperCollins*Publishers* 2012

A catalogue record for this book is
available from the British Library

ISBN-13: 978-1-84756-344-6

Set in Simoncini Garamond by Palimpsest Book Production Limited,
Falkirk, Stirlingshire

Printed and bound in Great Britain by
Clays Ltd, St Ives plc

FSC™ is a non-profit international organisation established to promote
the responsible management of the world's forests. Products carrying the
FSC label are independently certified to assure consumers that they come
from forests that are managed to meet the social, economic and
ecological needs of present and future generations,
and other controlled sources.

Find out more about HarperCollins and the environment at
www.harpercollins.co.uk/green

A COURT AFFAIR

By the same author:

THE TUDOR WIFE
MARY AND ELIZABETH

Carnal marriages begin in joy but end in sorrow.

—Sir William Cecil commenting on
the marriage of Robert Dudley and Amy Robsart

Amy Robsart Dudley
and
Queen Elizabeth I

I used to think of her. She used to think of me.

PROLOGUE

Elizabeth

The Church of Our Lady in Oxford
Sunday, September 22, 1560

I told Kat to fetch a chair and be my dragon, to sit outside my bed-chamber door and guard my lair after I was gone.

"Let no man or woman cross my threshold and enter here. Say I have a black and red *beast* of a headache, and any who dare disturb my rest do so at their own peril," I instructed as, one by one, the regal layers of pearl-and-jewel-encrusted, gold-embroidered, white-brocaded satin tumbled to the floor, followed by the cumbersome farthingale, stays as stiff as armour, rustling layers of starched petticoats, bejewelled ribbon garters, and the silk stockings Robert bought me, specially ordered from Spain by the score—twenty pairs at a time, in a typically extravagant gesture—and, lastly, like a bridal veil, a shift of cobweb lawn thin enough to read a book through if the light were good and the ink black enough.

With all my court finery pooled around my naked feet, the jewels on my discarded gown seeming to float like ruby red and sapphire blue flowers upon a froth of rich cream, I stood straight and breathed deeply, stretching my arms high above my head. If Robert had seen me thus, he would no doubt have compared me to Aphrodite emerging newborn and naked from the surf. But I could not think about that now; I could not think about Robert. I took another deep breath before stepping out of the rich, luxurious fabric froth and trading it all for a shirt of unbleached linen and the plain brown leather and cloth of a common man's clothes.

I ignored Kat's concerned queries and anxious pleas as I sat and pulled on the high leather riding boots while she circled and flapped around me like a bird futilely squawking and batting its wings in a gilt-barred cage, pinning my hair up tightly even as she implored me not to do this foolish, insane, and dangerous thing.

The moment my telltale flame-coloured tresses were tucked out of sight beneath a brown cloth cap, I stood and imperiously waved her aside, cutting off Kat's chatter like a headsman's axe with one flourish of my long-fingered, marble white hand. And, in the stark silence that followed, I snatched up the leather gloves and riding crop and headed for the secret door and stairs that descended into my private garden, where I so often walked in the mornings still wearing my nightgown before I girded myself in queenly regalia to face the business of the day, the heavy responsibility of ruling the realm, and feeling, sometimes, like one lone woman against the whole world.

I hugged tightly to the wall as my booted feet felt carefully for each one of the stone steps in the dim and close torchlit stairway. *A staircase,* my mind kept repeating. *It all ended with a staircase. By mishap or murder, it all ended with a staircase.*

A common hired barge waited for me upon the river, then a horse, a fleet bay stallion, muscular and lean, yet another gift from Robert. It was a dangerous and heady sensation to be out in the world anonymous and alone. I, the Queen of England, unencumbered by escorts, chaperones, and guards, was making my way as a lone woman, disguised in male attire, on a secret pilgrimage. *Anything* could happen. I could be set upon by a gang of ruffians or thieves; I could be murdered, or, if my sex was discovered, raped, then left for dead in a ditch, or, my identity unknown or disbelieved if I proclaimed it, forced to live out my days catering to the lusts of men as a prisoner in a bawdy house. Every step I took was fraught with danger, but we were old friends, danger and I; danger of one kind or another had dogged my steps since the day I was born. Safety was a stranger and a state more illusory than real to me. I had outlived the shifting moods and murderous rages of my father, and even when my own sister wished me dead and futilely and painstakingly sifted the haystack to find a shiny silver needle of guilt with which to condemn me, still I managed to prevail and preserve my life.

I was alive, but another woman was dead—a life for a life. She had died alone and unloved with no one to protect her from danger, to keep Death at the hands of cruel Fate, her own desperation, fatal mischance, or all too human villainy, at bay. That was the reason for my solitary journey; that was why I had stripped myself of my royal persona and raiment and was riding hard to Oxford in a pouring rain that cloaked my sorrow as silent tears coursed down my face.

I was in time to see the funeral procession pass. Mourners, and those just curious to catch a glimpse, lined the roadside and stood bareheaded in the pounding rain, the men clasping their caps over their hearts.

I closed my eyes and thought of Amy, weeping and raging, pounding her fists upon the mattress of the bed she should have been sharing with her husband in a home of her own instead of sleeping in alone as a perpetual houseguest of some obliging friend or gentleman retainer of Robert's, eager to do the high-and-mighty lord, the Queen's Master of the Horse and rumoured paramour, a favour by providing lodgings for his unwanted and inconvenient wife. How she must have *hated* me and raged against the unfairness of it all: at the cancer marring the pink and white perfection of her breast and stealing her life away, sapping her vitality and strength like an ugly, bloated, blood-hungry leech that could never be sated until her heart ceased to beat; at the husband, once so in love with her, who desired her death and might even have schemed to hasten it, so he could have another who came with a crown as her dowry; and at the woman—the Queen—she thought had stolen the love of her life away. She had every reason to be angry, bitter, and afraid, and to hate me.

When the embalmers opened the body of my father's first queen, the proud and indomitable Catherine of Aragon, they found her heart locked in the ugly black embrace of a cancerous tumour. Some took it as a sign that the woman who had used her last reserve of strength to write to my father, *Lastly, I vow that my eyes desire you above all things,* had actually died of a broken heart. Was

Amy's deadly malady of the breast also physical proof of the pain inside it, a visible manifestation of the broken heart of a woman mortally wounded when Cupid's arrow was forcibly pulled out? If that were true, the gossip and rumours were right: we—Robert and I—*had* murdered Amy. Robert had pulled the arrow out, carelessly and callously, leaving her alone to suffer and bleed, while he gave his love to me. And I, a selfish and vain woman, exulting in the freedom and new-come power to control my own destiny, eager for passion without strings, had accepted it, like an offering of tribute and desire laid at the feet of an alabaster goddess.

The black plumes crowning the staves carried by the men who walked before and aft the coffin hung limp and bedraggled, beaten down by the rain, like squiggles of black ink running down a wet page, like the tearstained letters Amy used to send her husband. The eight-and-twenty men—one for each year of Amy's life—who walked in solemn procession, two by two, down that long and winding road, escorting Amy to her final rest, wore long, hooded black robes. I shivered, remembering the letter I had once found on Robert's floor, crumpled into a ball on the hearth. He had flung it at the fire in a fit of annoyance but had missed. He hadn't cared enough to disturb himself and rise from his chair and cross the room to pick it up and feed it to the flames. Instead, he had left it lying there, where any, whether they be servant, queen, or spy in the Spanish Ambassador's pay, might pick it up and read those smeared, hysterical words scrawled frantically across tearstained pages about a phantom friar who haunted Cumnor Place in a grey robe with a cowl that hid his face—*the face of Death!*—in blackest shadows no human eye or light could pierce. *I know I have seen Death,* Amy had insisted. *He is stalking me!*

Now, as the church bells tolled mournfully, robed men with hoods that hid their faces in black shadows carried Amy to her tomb on a grey and gloomy day when even the sky wept. The coffin was leaden and heavy, and they took turns shouldering it, those who had borne the burden falling back to walk in seamless step whilst others took their places beneath its weight; it was all done as precisely as military manoeuvres, as perfectly choreographed as a court masque, with not a single stumble or misstep. What little family she had and the women and servants who had borne her company at Cumnor followed the casket, a few of them weeping copiously and volubly, the others enjoying the notoriety of being, however slightly and momentarily, at the centre of a maelstrom of raging scandal. Each of them was outfitted in new mourning clothes paid for by the absent widower, who remained closeted in his milk white mansion at Kew, feeling sorry for himself instead of grieving for the wife whose so-convenient death he now realised was a grave inconvenience. And a choir of solemn-faced little boys in white surplices brought up the rear, clutching their black-bound songbooks and singing dolefully.

At the black-draped, candlelit Church of Our Lady, as the boy choir sang, the coffin was opened and draped with black sarcenet fringed with gold and black silk, surrounded by candles and mounted escutcheons supporting the Dudleys' bear and ragged staff, and Robert's personal emblem of oak leaves and acorns, and Amy lay in state, to be entombed in the chancel on the morrow.

The Doctor of Divinity, Dr Babington, a round little man with a bald pate ringed by a fringe of grey, and lopsided spectacles slipping from his nose, then came forth to preach his sermon, "Blessed are they who die in the Lord," but few bothered to listen and instead sat in the pews or stood in the back with their heads bent together, gossiping about how Lady Dudley had met her death, by villainy or mischance or, "God save her," her own desperation, and the fact that her absent husband was rumoured to have spent the astounding sum of £2,000 on this splendid funeral, and that not counting the cost of his own mourning garb, which was said to be the very epitome of elegance. But there was a gasp and a lingering, horrified pause when Dr Babington misspoke and recommended to our memories "this virtuous lady so pitifully *slain*". He stood there for a moment with his mouth quivering and agape. "Oh, merciful Heaven, did I *really* say *that*?" he gasped before he hastily continued and completed his sermon in a babbling rush, his face highly flushed as he stumbled and tripped over the rest of the words as though his own poor tongue were falling down a staircase, going from bad to worse with each bump and thump. Then the mourners came forward, in solemn procession, to pause for a moment by the coffin and pay their last respects to Lady Dudley. For those who needed more than a moment, Robert had thoughtfully provided a pair of impressive—and no doubt expensive—mourning stools fringed in Venice gold and black silk and upholstered in quilted black velvet, placed at the head and foot of the coffin, so that any who wished to might sit and mourn in comfort.

As the mourners filed out, to go and feast at the nearby college and honour Lady Dudley's memory, a plump, greying woman—she reminded me of my own dear old governess, Kat Ashley—her round, wizened face red and swollen from crying, lingered to lovingly lay a bouquet of buttercups upon the coffin before she buried her face in her hands and, her shoulders shaking convulsively with loud, racking sobs, turned away and followed the others out. "Mrs Pirto," I heard someone in the crowd say, identifying her as Amy's maid, who had "loved her lady well and dearly and been with her her whole life long".

When the church was quite deserted, I steeled myself, squared my shoulders, and approached the black-draped bier, supremely conscious of the sound of my booted footsteps upon the stone floor; no matter how softly I tried to tread, they rang like a tocsin in my ears, and more than once I glanced guiltily back over my shoulder as though I were committing some crime by coming here. I knew I was the *last* person Amy would have wanted or expected to come; she would have thought I came to gloat over her coffin, to bask in my triumph, now that she was dead and Robert was free to marry me.

Tall white tapers, arranged like a crescent moon, stood behind the coffin. Had someone known that Amy was always nervous of the dark, afraid of the encroaching shadows and what they might hide, and ordered the candles placed there as a comforting gesture just for her, or was this merely thought a becoming touch, or done for the simple sake of providing light?

Burnished golden curls, perfectly arranged, gleamed in the candlelight, framing her pale face, white as the candle wax. A wreath of silken buttercups crowned those perfect curls; real ones would have soon wilted and withered away within the coffin. Ashes to ashes, dust to dust; so it is in the end for all that lives, from buttercups to beautiful girls too young to die. Who had fashioned that wreath of yellow silk flowers and her hair into those perfect curls? Surely it must have been the devoted Mrs Pirto. I could picture her, near-blinded by grief, sitting by the fire, tears dripping down onto the gnarled and thick-veined hands that laboriously cut and stitched silken semblances of the yellow flowers that had always been Amy's favourite as a final act of love. Amy loved buttercups; I remembered that from her wedding day, when she had carried a great bouquet of them and worn a crown of them upon her head and had them embroidered in gold upon the creamy satin field of her gown, the very one she wore now. Amy was going to her grave in her wedding gown. Mayhap in death, I prayed, she would find a love better and more worthy of her than she ever found in life.

"Love," I softly mused aloud, "so kind to some, so cruel to others." That fickleness was one of Life's harsh realities that blessed some and damned others.

She was much and sadly altered, though the times I had gazed upon her were scant—a mere three times, twice up close and once from afar—and the difference was startling to behold. The first time I saw her, on her wedding day, I thought this petite, plump, buxom blonde would soon be as round as she was tall with all the children she would bear. I thought surely to hear that she was pregnant every year. With her full breasts and round hips, she looked ripe for motherhood, born for breeding. But it was not to be. Amy Robsart had prospered neither as a wife nor as a woman; even the joys and consolations of motherhood had been denied her. And now she lay pale, wan, and wasted in her coffin, cancer had consumed her curves, and Life and Love's cruelties had taken all the rest. This was a woman whose hopes and dreams had died long before she did.

Her wedding day—that beautiful June day—had been the happiest day of Amy's life. And I had been there to bear witness to it. I had seen the joy alive and sparkling in her blue green eyes, and the radiant smile of pure delight that lit up her face, the love and trust that shone from her, like a sunbeam, every time she looked at Robert. It had felt like an intrusion, almost, to witness it, and I had felt something else: the hard emerald bite of envy when I looked at the bridal couple, resenting them—resenting Amy, to be more honest and precise—for something I could never have and wasn't sure I even wanted. Watching her, I had felt a tug-o'-war within my soul; part of me wanted to be her, yet another part of me obstinately pulled back, remembering my mother's warning, urgently spoken the last time I saw her, *"Never surrender!"* and in my memory's eye at the foot of my bed the ghost of Tom Seymour, winking and grinning lasciviously, his cock pointing adamantly out at me from between the folds of his brocade dressing gown, before he leapt and pounced on me, the giggling, giddy girl I used to be, writhing and revelling in my newly awakened sensuality.

Now Amy lay in her coffin. The future that had seemed so golden had turned out to be as false as the trinkets the peddlers at the country fairs sold to the gullible, touting them as genuine gold and gems, though they were in truth but glass and tin from which the gold paint would all too soon flake to reveal the base metal beneath. All that glitters is not gold.

Her hands were folded across the bodice of her gold-lace-garnished wedding gown. The vast golden profusion of buttercups embroidered all over the cream-coloured satin seemed to sway as if caressed by a gentle breeze, an illusion wrought by the play of the candles' flickering flames upon the gilded threads, tricking out their shimmer, causing them to appear to dance. How sad that the flowers on Amy's gown seemed to live when she herself lay dead.

Someone—Mrs Pirto's loving hands?—had filled in the low, square bodice with a high-collared yoke of rich, creamy lace veined with gold and topped by a tiny gold frilled ruff to support her broken neck and hold it properly in place. If I looked closely, I could just discern the white bandages beneath, wound tightly—too tightly for life—lending further support to that frail, shattered neck. And, as another remembrance of the happiest day of her life, someone had tied around her waist the frilly lace-, pearl-, and ribbon-festooned apron she had worn over her brocaded satin gown. I could picture Mrs Pirto leaning down as she dressed her lady for the last time, stroking that pale face, tenderly kissing the cold brow, and whispering in a tear-choked voice, "Take only the happy memories with you, my sweet, and leave all the rest behind."

Amy's hands, I noticed then, were nude and nail-bitten, gnawed painfully down to the quick; they must have throbbed and bled. Robert would not want to waste jewels upon the dead; to him that would be the same as throwing them into the Thames. Even the golden oak leaf and amber acorn betrothal ring had vanished, just like the love it had once symbolised. Where had it gone? I shuddered and hoped fervently never to find it on my pillow or presented to me in a velvet box.

It wasn't right; Amy, who so loved pretty things and delighted in the latest fashions—Robert complained that she ordered as many as fourteen new gowns a year—*should* have something more than lace and flowers, even if they were silken and embroidered.

I took off my gloves and stared down at my hands, perfect, gleaming nails on long white fingers sparkling with diamonds her husband had given me. In my haste, I had forgotten to remove my rings. All save the gold and onyx coronation ring that had wedded me to England were gifts from Robert; he stroked my vanity like a cat and loved to cover my hands with cold jewels and hot kisses.

She really *should* have something! I started to remove my rings, but then I remembered that Amy didn't like diamonds. I could hear Robert's voice cruelly mocking her, calling her a fool, insisting that *every* woman *loves* diamonds and would sell her soul for them, adopting a high-pitched, timorous, quavering parody of a woman's voice, parroting words Amy had once spoken, likening diamonds to "tears frozen in time". Yet somehow now it seemed most apt; Amy herself, at only eight-and-twenty, had become a tear frozen in time.

I took the rings from my hands and, one by one, put them onto the thin, cold, death-stiffened fingers, knowing all the while that not all the diamonds in the world could make up for all the tears that Robert and I had caused this woman to shed. And she had shed tears aplenty—oceans and oceans of tears. She had been drowning in tears for two years at least, perhaps even longer. Robert's love had died long before Amy did. Love is cruel; it kills its victims slowly.

I gave a dead woman a fortune in diamonds, but not even I, the all-powerful Elizabeth of England, could give her back her life or undo the hurt I had caused her. Robert had married her in a flight of youthful fancy fuelled by hot-blooded young lust, a fit of impulsive passion for a pretty country lass of rustic, pure, unvarnished, fresh-faced charm, lacking the hard, sophisticated polish and rapier-sharp or flippant wit of the bejewelled silk-, satin-, and velvet-clad ladies of the court with all their exotic perfumes, ostrich plumes, intricate coiffures of coils, curls, and braids, artfully plucked brows, rouged lips, and painted faces, a woman he went to bed in love with and woke up to find he had nothing in common with. Robert came to resent and blame her for the rash act that had bound him to her. Though he was quite a prize for a squire's daughter, as a duke's son he could have found himself a far better dowered and pedigreed bride, as his father, brothers, and friends had all tried to tell the deaf-to-reason, love-struck lad of seventeen who was determined to listen to the bulging and throbbing need inside his codpiece rather than good common sense. Robert had married in haste and repented at leisure. And his kindness, often doled out as a careless afterthought, eventually turned cruel as, more and more, he repented his youthful folly, and because of me, a woman he wanted but could not have, a woman who could, if she would, make him king but wanted him only in her own way and would not wear the ring of a subservient wife or bow to any man as her master. Robert thought he could change my mind, and others feared he would, and Amy, like an innocent child wandering into the midst of a raging battlefield, got caught in the cross fire.

I had wanted to protect Amy, though I doubt any would believe that if they knew. And for that I cannot fault them; if I weren't me, I wouldn't believe it either. My failure was a secret I kept locked up inside my heart in my private lockbox of regrets. I could not save Amy from a marriage where love was only in one heart, not in two, and I could not save Amy from cancer, her husband's ambition, or my own cruel, coquettish caprice that kept me dangling myself before Robert as a prize almost within his grasp, which he could even at times hold in his arms and kiss and caress but could never truly win. I played with him like a cat does with dead things, the way I toyed with all my suitors; Robert was unique only in that I loved him. But even though I loved him, I had no illusions about him. My love for Robert, in spite of what others thought, was *never* blind; I always saw him as sharply and clearly as if I were blessed with a hawk's keen and piercing sight. Life long ago taught me not to idealise Love; I leave that to the poets and ballad singers. I learned the hard lessons taught by Love's illusions long ago; I was scarcely out of my cradle before the lessons began. My father and his six wives, amongst them my mother and cousin, whose lives ended upon the scaffold; my stepfather, Tom Seymour, that handsome and fool-hardy rogue who bounded into my bedchamber each morning to tickle and play and teach me anatomy in an infinitely more intimate way than is printed in books; my poor, mad, deluded, love-starved sister, pining her life away for want of Spanish Philip; and my cold and imperious Spanish brother-in-law, who courted and caressed me behind his wife's back, hung my neck with jewels, and even had a tiny peep-hole drilled so he could watch me in my bath and as I dressed and undressed and availed myself of my chamber pot—they were all *excellent* teachers, and all my life I have been an apt pupil, and education doesn't begin and end in the schoolroom.

I will always love Robert Dudley; he has been my best friend since I was eight years old, and would be—if I let him—my ardent lover and husband; but there is something he worships and adores more than England's Virgin Queen—Ambition is his guiding star. I've seen men ruined before by this elusive, tantalising, sparkling star that they spend their whole lives chasing after, leaping and grasping for, sometimes snaring a little stardust but more often crashing empty-handed back down to earth. And Robert, for all his fine qualities—his smouldering dark eyes, his heart-melting, knee-weakening smile, towering height, handsome horseman's legs, and hands both gentle and firm, callous and soft, his intelligence, charm, wit, and passion, his showmanship and debonair flair on the tennis court, dance floor, and tiltyard, his supreme confidence and courage riding to the hunt or charging into battle, his feats of daring at the gambling tables—is still Ambition's catamite and fool.

My eyes are not starry-blind with love for him; romance doesn't soften and tint everything all rosy pink and beautiful for me. I love Robert, but I see him for what he is, and, though I love, I often do not like. There is ice beneath the fire, steel beneath the softness, and the hard armour of cruelty beneath the plush velvet cloak of kindness. I have often wondered if I were a mere woman—a squire's daughter perhaps, just like Amy, instead of England's Queen—would his passion for me have ever flared so high or burned so brightly and constantly? I think not. Or perhaps it is merely that I have lost the ability to believe in anyone's sincerity. I trust no one; I cannot afford to. I am a queen before I am a woman, England *always* comes before Elizabeth, and though there are times when my passions flame high and I resent and rage against Fate, I will *not* bankrupt my soul or my realm by giving too much of myself to the *wrong* people. My subjects as a whole always come before any individual, and that includes myself. Though I am the Virgin Queen, I regard myself as the mother of many.

There's something in Robert's blood he inherited from his father and grandfather that makes him willing to do *anything,* and risk *everything,* to rise the highest and shine the brightest, to eclipse even Ambition's own lustre and luminescence. But all that glitters is not gold. My mother once spoke those very words to my father when he asked why she preferred the doltish Harry Percy, who was, I have heard, as clumsy as a newborn foal, to the more elegant, polished, and cocksure men of the court.

Robert and I, we are the scandal of the civilised world. There are many who would wager all that they possess that I would have him for my husband and no other. I have at times indeed spoken such words myself to confound and cloud the issue of my refusal to marry; the more perplexed and puzzled my suitors are, the better I like it. Even my cousin, the Queen of Scots, has been heard to quip that the Queen's Master of the Horse murdered his wife to make room for her in his bed. Well, let the gaggles of gossipmongers wager all they wish—*they will lose!* I let them think that, but it was all part of the merry dance and mad whirl that always kept them guessing and wondering as so many men vied for my hand; but though the dance must of necessity go on, it must slow now to a stately pavane from a galloping galliard. I am Elizabeth of England, mistress with no master; I call the tunes, and my musicians play them, and my courtiers dance to them; and so it has ever been and always will be until the day I die. There will be no King Robert I of England, or a king by any other name, in *my* lifetime!

I reached out and gently straightened a ruffle of lace on Amy's wedding apron and tweaked a silk bow, adjusting the sunny yellow ribbon streamers and the strands and loops of tiny seed pearls until they lay just right. I could still smell the lavender and rosemary from when the apron had been lovingly packed away, no doubt with dreams of the daughter Amy longed to have, and of tying it around her waist, with a mother's love and kiss, on her own wedding day. A dream sadly fated never to come true.

At least Robert had not begrudged her her lace. Amy loved lace; she said it was "like wearing snowflakes that don't melt". I hadn't actually heard her say it, only Robert's cruel parody when he slapped his hand against the tailor, Mr Edney's, bill, loudly complaining, "Lace, lace, and more lace!" Laughing at and belittling her. Robert left her alone in the country, foisting her off on his friends instead of giving her a home of her own and children, while he danced attendance on the Queen of England, showered her with jewels, lost hundreds of pounds at cards and dice, spent excessively on his own ornate wardrobe and lavishly laden table, and was known to every moneylender in London, yet he begrudged his wife a few lengths of lace. That was one of the times when I did not like the man I loved.

Sometimes I sent Amy lace and other pretty baubles, trinkets, and tokens in Robert's name—a bolt of bright blue silk the colour of bluebells; a pretty white silk headdress edged with silver braid and embroidered with violets and pinks; a Venetian looking glass framed in enamelled flowers; and dusky-rose-coloured gloves fringed with gold and embroidered with bright pink rosebuds for her birthday. I *knew* he would not deny the gifts; he would rather be worshipped like a gilded god, basking in her humble, loving gratitude, even if it were for a gift he had not actually given. I know something of this too. I am the living embodiment of chaste Diana, the Virgin Queen, a secular Holy Virgin; I am worshipped and adored, the subject of poetry and songs. It would be all too easy to let this adulation go to my head like strong wine, and though some may think I have done just that, I have not, for I also know that no one sits easily upon a throne; for all its gilded, jewel-encrusted glory, it is as insecure as a high, rickety stool with one leg shorter than the rest, and no crown fits so firmly that it cannot be knocked or tumble off. The higher the pedestal, the farther the fall; no one who rises to power should *ever* forget that.

Amy's little notes of love and gratitude were proof Robert could point to that he had always been a good husband. And always I would ponder the perversity that it is often the lot of womankind to give our love to those who are unworthy of it, like my sister, who destroyed herself all for love of Spanish Philip. We do it, I think, because we fear that if we withhold our love, we may never find a

truly worthy recipient for it, so with the largesse of a rich philan-
thropist we give the precious gold of our affection away rather than
be miserable misers and hoard it. What good does a fortune do a
spinster on her deathbed? Better to have lived well and spent it.
And so we do, we spend our love, though very seldom wisely, and
many of us die paupers for it.

Amy's love of lace—"like wearing snowflakes that don't melt"—
was just one more of those little titbits Robert's tongue had casually
let fall, scornfully, mockingly, or exasperatedly dropped over the
years, which my mind had gathered up. As I stood there gazing
down at her in her coffin, I staggered under the realisation that
perhaps I, Amy's glittering and much resented diamond-and-pearl-
encrusted-alabaster-tower-of-confidence-strength-and-pride rival,
the woman, the Queen, who all the world thought had stolen her
husband's love away from her, had known and understood Amy
better than her own husband ever had throughout their ten years
of marriage, from the first stirrings of the wolf of lust hiding under
the sheep's clothing of love, to the death of that lovely illusion, and
the loneliness and hurt, the estrangement, indifference, and callousness that came afterwards.

Robert wanted something he couldn't have, something that was
not his right—my crown, to rule England. And I was guilty of the
same, of wanting something I couldn't have, that I had no right to,
something that didn't belong to me. I wanted a handsome, fun, virile man whose company I could revel and delight in, someone
whom I could be free and just be me with, to just be Bess with, not
Queen Elizabeth, someone who could never truly hold and chain
and enslave me in the bonds of holy wedlock. I wanted to be free,
but I wanted love, passion, and excitement; I wanted a lover, not a
husband, and certainly not an ambitious schemer after my throne. I
had known and loved Robert Dudley since I was eight years old,
and I eagerly let myself believe his assurances that he and Amy
were estranged, that the love betwixt them had long ago died; I
didn't think to look, to inquire, whether there was truth or lies behind his words. And even if I had, would I have released him,
would I have let him go? My head says yes, but my heart says no.
And a woman lies dead because of this game Robert and I have
been playing with each other, this taut and tense flirtation, a wild

dance, a chase, but at the end . . . only Death has made a conquest, a helpless and innocent bystander who unwisely but all too well also loved Robert Dudley, and with more right than I had to, as she was his lawful wife.

We are—we were—a triangle, with Robert at the apex and Amy and I on the sides, but at the bottom, I like to think two arms, two hands, stretched out to form that short, straight line. If I had been kinder and reached out an understanding hand to you, Amy, would you have reached out and taken it, or would you have bitterly, angrily, or fearfully pushed it away? Now, when it is too late to make amends, I want so much to stand before you, a living, breathing woman, not a cold, dead corpse, and touch your chin, to stop its trembling, look into your eyes, glistening like rare blue green jewels beneath the tears, and say, "You don't have to be afraid of me, Amy; you never did." Could I, if I had it to do over again, in all my glittering, regal, emerald green jealous, possessive pride have done that, and could you, timid, hurt, afraid, sick, and lonely, simmering—and rightfully so—with resentment, have believed and accepted? That is yet one more mystery the answer to which we may never know, just like how you met Death and how He came to leave you lying broken at the foot of that staircase. Did He hurl you down violently or lay you down gently? Will we *ever* know?

∾ 1 ∾

Amy Robsart Dudley

Cumnor Place, Berkshire, near Oxford
Sunday, September 8, 1560

The hot bath feels heavenly—the billowing clouds of steam caress my face as they rise, like warm and comforting angels' wings—but it has also sapped my strength. I feel light-headed, and a little dizzy and faint, with a persistent fear of falling should I dare attempt to stand. Part of me wants to give up, to surrender to the desire for sleep that never leaves me now, to lay myself down in the arms of Lethargy and never rise again. Now, each time I sleep, I feel as if I am floating out to sea, and the tether that binds my boat to the shore is stretching farther, growing frailer, and fraying more and more. Sometimes it scares me, and sometimes I don't even care; I turn my back to the shore, stare straight ahead, and face the horizon boldly, ready to drift away and leave all my pains and woes behind me. Nausea stirs deep inside my stomach, like a serpent slowly uncoiling and waking grumpily from its slumber, just enough to make me aware of it but not so urgent as to send me grasping for the basin that is now never beyond my reach. But I say nothing of this to dear Mrs Pirto, who has attended me faithfully and lovingly for all of my eight-and-twenty years, as a nursemaid turned lady's maid turned nurse again; it would only distress her, and she worries so about me; my failed marriage and failing health are the cause of most of the lines on that kind and careworn face and have turned her ebony hair to pewter and dingy silver.

From my bath I can see the sky, black and starless, through the high, arched windows, yet one more reminder that monks once made their home at Cumnor, for two hundred years or more, before King Henry ordered the dissolution of the monasteries and cast their cloistered inhabitants out to fend for themselves in a confusing and frightening, often unkind world. Before Cumnor fell into private hands, my spacious apartment was divided up into several stark and tiny monks' cells furnished with only the bare necessities—a hard-as-a-board cot to sleep upon, with a chamber pot hidden underneath, and a crucifix looking down on its occupant from high upon the wall, to remind him that God is *always* watching us. Sometimes I fancy that I can still see their faint outlines, like the ghosts of those banished crosses haunting their former home. In spite of myself, I smile and blush a little at the thought that a monk's cot might even have sat right here where I sit now, naked in my bath.

No doubt to the simple country folk hereabouts it seems like the height of extravagant folly or absurdity—like the French king's mistress bathing in a tub filled with crushed strawberries to preserve her famous beauty—my rising when it is still as black as tar outside to take my bath. Many already think me a woman of a strange mind. But it's a soothing and peculiar kind of peace, to sit in a candlelit bath while most of the world still sleeps, and I like it, and even though I am naked, I feel less vulnerable somehow. I like the quiet solitude of sitting in my bath, luxuriating in its warmth undisturbed, before the sunrise and the busy bustle of the day begins, hours before there are voices downstairs and outside the windows, the clatter of cart wheels and horses' hooves in the courtyard, the laughing, joyfully raised voices of children playing, servants calling to one another, and footsteps and chatter in the Long Gallery outside my room where I used to walk up and down before I became so weak, and below stairs the gossip of servants and the crash and clang of kitchen pots. Though Cumnor is in reality four separate households under a shared roof, and I keep to myself most of the time, the other ladies who lodge here are more social creatures than I, and each thinks that *she* is the queen bee here, and over this entire hive reigns. There is the ancient Mrs Owen, the

mother of Cumnor's owner, Dr George Owen, who, like the mouse
who bravely pulled a thorn from the lion's paw, received it as a reward for his attendance on King Henry's sore and seeping leg; and
the plainspoken, sometimes tart-tongued Mrs Forster, wife of Sir
Anthony Forster, my husband's treasurer, who holds the current
lease on Cumnor; and his mistress, the widow Mrs Oddingsells,
one of those rare women who seem to grow more attractive and alluring as they age. My servants dart about Cumnor like busy bees
doing whatever they are told to do regardless of who gives the commands; sometimes they don't even have time for me, they are so
busy doing Mrs Owens's, Mrs Oddingsells's, or Mrs Forster's
bidding. But I let it go; I am too tired to complain, it would take
more strength than it is worth, and I just don't care any more. Besides, I like being here with only Pirto to attend me, free from the
fear that some well-intentioned or curious maidservant will come
knocking and catch a glimpse of my pain-racked body and ruined
left breast when Pirto opens the door, or will even boldly cross the
threshold and ogle me, while pretending not to, so she can tell the
others what she has seen, as she delivers a stack of fresh linens or a
package from my husband containing a pretty piece of apparel to
lift my spirits, or the latest doctor's or witch's brew calculated to restore my health or more likely hasten me to my grave if I were fool
enough to drink it. With rumours rife in London and spreading
throughout the land, and even across the sea, that Robert and his
royal paramour mean to poison me, I would be a fool to let any potion he sent cross my lips. But the colours are pretty, and I sometimes set the glass bottles on my windowsill so that when the sun
strikes them just right, rays of amber, ruby, emerald, and lemon
light shoot into my room like a rainbow to fight the clammy gloom
of Cumnor's grey stone walls and floors.

Outside my windows the sky is as dark as black velvet, with not
a star in sight to provide even a pinprick of diamond-white light,
and the silver coin of the moon has been spent. It's strange, but before the cancer burrowed into or erupted out of my breast,
whichever description fits it best, I never realised how dark it is before the dawn. It frightens me yet at the same time makes me feel *so*
grateful and glad to be safe and warm inside my room with numerous candles all about, beside a comforting fire that crackles with

flames that move and sway and leap like dancers in red, yellow, and orange costumes, instead of wandering lost, stumbling and staggering blindly, out there in the dark, feeling likely to jump out of my skin at every noise, whether it be a rustle of branches in the breeze, the hoot of an owl, the trill of a night bird, or the howl of a beast. The thought of being enfolded by darkness *terrifies* me and makes me shiver despite the warmth of my fireside bath. I am *so* afraid that that is what death will be like. What if Heaven is only a comforting myth, a fairy story to reassure the faithful, to instil hope instead of horror, peace instead of panic, calm instead of a frenzy to cram full and make each moment count? What if death is really the permanent cessation of light and an eternal reign of darkness, like being wrapped round and round and suffocated in a bolt of heavy black velvet, unable to breathe or see or move, locked in stultifying black stillness forevermore?

Sometimes I dream that I awake in black-velvet darkness to feel a pair of strong hands about my throat intent on squeezing the life out of me. It's funny in a way, I used to be so afraid of the city, the country used to seem such a safe haven to me, and London with all its crime, bustle, and brawls the epitome of danger, yet now I realise, secluded here in the country, that if anyone came meaning harm to me, if they chose their moment well, no one would hear me scream. I know now that I was wrong to insist on solitude. If anyone should come to me with murder in mind, I have colluded in my own demise, I have made it easier; all a killer has to do is wait and choose his moment well, and Justice will turn a blind eye.

Hot tears fill my eyes and threaten to spill over as I gasp and shiver. Gazing at me with deep concern, Pirto starts to speak, but I shake my head and reassuringly murmur, "It's all right, Pirto. Come." I force a smile. "Let's wash my hair now. I want to look my best today!"

I mustn't spoil dear Pirto's day; up until the last moment she must think this is one of my good days, and I am excited about going to the fair.

I close my eyes and lean back as she ladles warm water onto my head and begins to massage my scalp and, from root to tip, to work in a special chamomile and lemon blend to make my hip-length yellow hair shine like straw miraculously spun into curls of living gold, as though King Midas himself had touched my head. "Harvest gold"—years ago my husband dubbed its colour as he lay upon me in a bed of buttercups by the river, our favourite trysting spot, playing with my sun-streaked hair, stroking and fanning it out above and about my head like rays of the sun, likening it to a bountiful wheat harvest flourishing proudly beneath the sun that daily bestowed a thousand kisses upon it. "Hair with a lustre that puts gold to shame," he said, then kissed my face and declared that my cheeks were "as pink as the sweet roses of May". He has such a way with words, my husband; his letters used to make me melt like butter left out under the hot summer sun. Does he lie by the fire with Elizabeth and fan her red hair out around her head whilst in poetic words comparing it to the dancing, crackling flames, I wonder? Does he make her melt too? And is she fool enough like I was to love, trust, and believe him?

I sigh and breathe deeply of the lemons' tart tang and the fresh, clean smell of the chamomile, a combination at once soothing and invigorating. I wonder if this was made from chamomile I helped gather before I became too ill. I can't help but smile at the memory of my former self standing young and strong amongst the sun-kissed flowers with a straw hat crowning my wild, wayward hair to keep my fair skin from freckling or worse—Robert would be *horrified* if he came riding up for a visit and found his wife burned as red as a boiled crayfish or looking like "The Nut-Brown Maid" stepped out of her song—with a basket slung over the crook of my arm, and my skirts tucked up to my knees, and the grass tickling my bare ankles and toes.

I was *never* sick a day in my life before this disease! I used to be a strong, happy, country lass, pretty, pink-cheeked, and smiling, brimming over with health and vigour. Not rawboned, big, and brawny like a blacksmith in petticoats, but hale and hearty, round and rosy, not like a fashionable, porcelain-skinned lady of the court who would like the world to think that she is as delicate and fragile as an eggshell, a treasure to be handled with the utmost care lest it shatter beneath the slightest pressure. I sometimes think that the *real* tragedy of my marriage is that for Robert the novelty of what I was paled against the reality of what I wasn't.

As soon as it is light enough outside to see, everyone will be stirring, alive with excitement and anticipation, fidgeting through their chores and the church service at St Michael's like children eager to go outside and play. Today the Fair of Our Lady opens in Abingdon. I have given all my servants leave to attend and cajoled the other ladies to do the same, to make this Sunday not just a holy day but a holiday, a *happy* day. I want them all to do what I cannot—to forget their cares and woes, and frolic, laugh at the antics of the jugglers, acrobats, dancing dogs, puppet shows, and clowns, to dance and sing, have their fortunes told, ask a question of "The Learned Pig", gape in wonderment at the living oddities like the two-headed sheep, test their strength and skill and win a prize for their sweetheart, and glut themselves on cider and cake until their bellies feel fit to burst, and spend their hard-earned pennies on trinkets and frivolities from the peddlers who follow the fair like fleas after a dog.

My servants have been *so good* to me, putting up with all my pains and whims, all my tears and fears, my melancholy and maudlin fancies—if they *really* are fancies. There are times when I am not sure any more what is real and what isn't. I know it is what they are paid to do, but it is no fun or easy task attending a sick woman, breathing in the stink and stale air of the sickroom, the endless changing of pus-stained dressings, laundering sweat-sodden bedsheets and night shifts, emptying basins and chamber pots, carrying in trays of nourishing broth that like as not will be carried out again untouched or nearly so, the applications of ointments to flesh that is at once alive and festering with disease and pain yet also decaying, dying right before any eyes that dare look upon it, whether it be in curiosity, revulsion, compassion, or necessity.

Death put His mark on my breast, and it is now spreading throughout my body. Sometimes I fancy I can *feel* it swimming through my veins like a school of tiny fish. And soon He will take my life as well. Death will take my heart in His hand and *squeeze* it until it ceases to beat and lies squashed, broken, and bleeding in the palm of His hand, both merciless and merciful at the same time.

My mind is already giving way. Already there are fissures through which fantasy and suspicion seep in and become hopelessly blended with my reason, and the resulting mixture is not pleasing to anyone, least of all me. It frustrates and bewilders me to always have to stop and wonder and ask myself, and sometimes even to swallow my pride and ask others, if something truly happened or if I only dreamt or imagined it. I used to be a woman with a calm and steady, sensible mind, possessed of good country common sense, dependable and reliable. Despite my very feminine love of fashions and finery, I was *never* a woman who could be called frivolous or featherbrained.

I used to be the chatelaine of my father's estate. My mother was a rich widow who never had much interest in such things. She preferred the life of a pampered invalid, lounging her life away in bed, propped up against a mountain of pillows, munching sweetmeats, gossiping with the friends and family who came calling, and showing off one or another of her pretty lace-trimmed caps and bed gowns, so I took charge of the household as soon as I was old enough. I kept account of 3,000 sheep—the lambing, the shearing, the wool sales, those animals sold for mutton at market—I tallied the profits and the losses and kept account of the barley crop, the yield from our famed apple orchard and other fruit trees, the berry picking, the brewing of cider and ale, the salting of meat for winter, the milk, butter, and cream from our cool stone dairy, the honey from the hives, the distillery where we made our own perfumes and medicines and dried herbs and flower petals for sachets and potpourri to sweeten our rooms and the chests where we stored our clothes and bed linens; I oversaw the larder and wine cellar and made sure they were always well stocked, with plenty to eat and drink, barrels of dried fruits and salted meats, and jams and jellies to delight us with summer fruits in wintertime. I supervised the laundry and candle-making, planned the meals with our cook, and dispensed charity, packing and giving out baskets of food, clothing, and medicines to the poor, ailing, and elderly. I rode out daily to inspect the fields, orchards, and pastures. I used to be able to do it *all*! Father used to say I was a paragon of efficiency!

But now . . . Now there is no work for me to do even if I were able. Now I sit in the homes of strangers as a gracious, idle, and ailing houseguest with too much time on my hands and weighing heavily upon my mind. I was brought up to believe that idle hands are the Devil's tool, but I think that is equally true of an idle mind.

Rumours, fears, and fancies prey on me, they bite deeply like fanged monsters, and I can no longer distract myself and stave them off with work as I used to do. It is not just my body that is failing. Now my mind is a mass of contradictions—I think or say one thing and then another, I veer from the highest heights of hope to the deepest pit of dark despair, one moment joy rules my life, then, in a finger snap, I am fury incarnate or drowning in deep blue doldrums; I grasp greedily at life yet long for death, I fight to survive and then sink down, ready to yield, admit defeat, and surrender. I've lost control of my own mind, and I don't know what I want any more when I used to be *so* certain. I've strayed so far from the woman I was and the woman I always meant and wanted to be. I've lost my way, and now it is too late to remedy my course, to stop, stand still, get my bearings, and think, turn back to the crossroads of Fate and choose a different path. As my father would say: "You've made your bed, Amy my lass, and now you have to lie in it!"

Some rumours already claim that I am a madwoman kept chained in an attic for my own good and the safety of others and that loyal Pirto is not my maid turned nurse but actually my keeper.

"Poor Robert!" those who hear the rumours—both the ones that tell the truth and the ones that lie—must say and sigh as they dolefully shake their heads and pat his shoulder or back sympathetically if they are acquainted with him well enough to take such liberties with his person. Under the circumstances, even those who dislike him—and there are a great many who do—cannot begrudge him his extravagances and pleasures. Eight-and-twenty is far too young to be burdened with such a wife, they no doubt think or even say outright. "Poor Robert" indeed! Healthy, handsome, virile, strong, and vigorous Robert, riding like the wind and dancing the night away, his ambitions blazing like a comet so bright, they almost turn night into day, spending every waking hour fawning over and flattering the Queen, paying poets to write her sonnets he can sign his own name to, gambling as if gold were as common as shit and all he has to do is squat down over a pot to get more, racking up debts buying her costly gifts—silk stockings by the score and an emerald that would have paid for us to have a *real* home of our own if such had been his desire—and dreaming of the day when he will be free of me to marry her and become King Robert I of England.

It's always "Poor Robert!" *never* "Poor Amy!" though eight-and-twenty is far too young to be burdened with the fatal canker of cancer in her once-beautiful breast, to live every day locked in a brutal, unbreakable embrace of pain that can only be numbed by a powerful powder of opium poppies mixed into strong wine that brings strange dreams, both sleeping and waking, that hopelessly muddles fact and fiction in her poor, befuddled brain, to live every moment knowing that her days are numbered and ever dwindling, and in such pain that she often falls upon her knees and prays to God to deliver her from her desperation. Yes, "Poor Robert" indeed! Dancing the volta with the Queen and showering kisses onto her perfect alabaster breasts; rolling silk stockings up or down her long, fair legs; flaunting his prowess on the tennis court and in the saddle; riding to the hunt or against an opponent in the tiltyard; and sitting on the Queen's Council to arrogantly contradict the wise Sir William Cecil because he resents the trust that exists between the Queen and the Secretary of State. Robert wants to reign supreme! If Cecil said black were white, Robert would bang his fists down hard upon the table and shout, "Nay, it is *green*!" then pout and sulk with a face as dark as a storm cloud if Her Majesty chose to take Cecil's word over his. Such is my husband's life. "Poor Robert" indeed; he is the one *truly* deserving of sympathy, *not me*! If I were dead, he would be free, he would be King, but my weak and waning body stands between him and his Destiny. *Poor Robert! How the heavens must weep for him!*

Dried chamomile bobs about my breasts, but I don't look down; this disease has already killed my vanity and murdered all the delight my body ever gave to me. I sometimes wonder if it has been visited upon me as a punishment for my vanity, the pride and pleasure I once took in baring and flaunting my breasts before my husband to entice and excite him and enflame his lust. Whenever Pirto helps me dress and undress, I keep the candles at a distance and my eyes fixed straight ahead. I *never* look down, even though I know ignoring it will not make it go away. I tried that when I first discovered the inwardly turned dimple that later pointed outward in an emphatic and angry lump that demanded my attention and could not be ignored. I shun the looking glass now and drape it in black velvet as if I were already dead and this were a house in mourning. But even though I avoid looking, I know *exactly* what I would see if I did. My right breast perfect and plump, like a creamy custard crowned with a cherry pink nipple, the left marred, mottled, swollen, and florid, with an ugly, oozing lump but half a thumb's span from my nipple, as if it were my nipple's ugly, grossly deformed twin, a grotesquerie made to nurse Death's pet imp. Sometimes I dream that he is there, a wicked little gargoyle, a tiny bilious green and black sulphur-stinking devil, dainty only in his size, with pointy ears and a forked tail, glowing red eyes, and needle-sharp fangs he sinks with ravenous relish into the lump to suckle and suck the life out of me and make me either scream out in agony or fall fainting and breathless to the floor, defenceless against the onslaught of pain his suckling brings. I used to dream of someday having a baby, a little girl with my golden curls or Robert's dark ones, to nurse at my breast, but instead I have this evil imp called Cancer to suck from me, and instead of good and wholesome mother's milk my nipple leaks a foul discharge, sometimes milky in further mockery of my dreams, other times tinged pink by my blood to remind me of the pink dresses and hair ribbons I would have given the little girl I know now I will never carry under my heart, feeling her flutter and kick inside the warm, safe nest of my womb.

The swelling extends beneath my left arm so that I feel always tender and sore there. I try to carry myself carefully, as if I were a woman fashioned from the finest Venetian glass, but often, out of habit, a lifetime of moving freely without thought or worry, I forget. It has happened so many times that hearing me gasp and cry out has become commonplace; those about me have heard it so often that the maids seldom even look up from their work, or Mrs Forster and Mrs Oddingsells from their game of cards or backgammon, and Mrs Owen, who as the wife of one doctor and the mother of another, one might have expected a show of compassion from, has become immune to human suffering. At such times I fancy I could run stark naked shrieking like a banshee through the house with my hair on fire, and no one would even look up.

The candlelight is kind to me, for which I am grateful, as I am for any kindness that is given me. Lately the disease has lent a yellow tint to my skin and the whites of my eyes—jaundice. But in the kind, flattering light of the candles it isn't obvious; it is the harsh, unsparingly honest light of the sun that cruelly gives my secret away and shows the world that I am like a woman made of straw, brittle and yellow from the top of my head to the tips of my toes, and everyone waits with bated breaths for the inevitable day when I will break, like a piece of dry straw snapped in two.

"All right, love?" Pirto asks as she finishes rinsing my hair.

I nod and smile. "Just dreaming of cinnamon cakes and apple cider, Pirto; they remind me of home, and the cider made from the apples from Father's orchards at Syderstone. I remember how we used to celebrate the harvest, with dancing and apple bobbing and a great feast with every dish made with apples—every single one, even an apple in the roast pig's mouth! And hair ribbons, Pirto!" I flash an even brighter smile and half turn round in my bath. I stubbornly ignore the protesting pain, sharp and grinding, at the base of my spine that makes my breath catch, though I hastily hide that, quickly turning it into a sigh of eager excitement instead. For Pirto, I pretend I am once again that giddy young girl she used to know, excited about a day at the fair. "They're *sure* to have hair ribbons at the fair, aren't they, Pirto? I've a fancy for buttercup yellow, maiden's blush pink, and Our Lady's blue."

"Indeed they are, pet, to be sure, they will!" Pirto beams back at me. I can tell it does her heart good to see me like this—excited and looking forward to something, even a rustic and rollicking country fair.

"And apple green and cherry red! I want My Lord to see me with a rainbow of ribbons streaming down my back when he comes to visit me!" I add, still smiling, as the pain gives my spine another brutal twist, like a master torturer manning the rack to make his victim howl and beg for mercy and divulge her most deeply guarded secrets.

"Aye, love." Pirto nods excitedly. "And if we can find one in primrose pink, it will match the new dress you've ordered from Mr Edney just *grand,* it will!"

"We must look out for one, then," I say, the smile frozen on my face as the pain causes pearls of sweat to bead my brow as it twists round in the small of my back like a spring wound dangerously tight until it threatens to break. "Oh, I do hope Mr Edney finishes my new gown in time—dusky rose velvet embroidered with bright pink roses with the collar fringed in gold, like the one on the russet taffeta he made for me. I ordered it to match the gloves My Lord sent me for my birthday. *Surely* that is a sign that he *still* cares for me, Pirto? If he did not care, he would not have taken the time to choose something so pretty that he knew would please me so much. I want to wear it for him with the gloves when he comes to me. And *surely* he will come *soon*; the court is not very far . . . Windsor Castle is only half a day's ride away. Only half a day . . ." I sigh. "Half a day!"

The thought of the husband I still love *so much,* even though I know I should not, and long to see even though with all this talk of poison and murder he now frightens me, fills me with such sorrow that the tears I have fought to hold back for so long threaten to overwhelm and drown me from within if I do not let them out. *Why* do I still love him when he no longer loves me? *Why* do I still strive to win back a love long gone? *Why* do I desire a man who has shattered all the trust that ever lay between us, just as he has dashed all my hopes and destroyed all my dreams? He has even tried to murder me. And yet . . . my head says no, but my heart cries yes, and even as I fear and hate, I still love and long. Life will never be the same as it was again, this I know, but of the dream I cannot let go. Right or wrong, I *still* love him.

"Come, the sheet now, Pirto." I swallow back the tears and force myself to smile as I nod towards it, draped over the back of a chair to warm before the fire. "I will get out now and sit by the fire while you comb my hair."

I grit my teeth and brace myself to stand up. But stand I must, and stand I will. Summoning all my strength, steeling myself against the pain that I know will flare beneath my arm and explode like fireworks within my chest, I bite my bottom lip and, with Pirto hovering anxiously beside me holding up the drying sheet, ready to wrap me in it, I lever myself up. It takes everything I have not to scream and to fight back the faintness that threatens to knock me off my feet, and the unrelenting pain twisting agonisingly in the small of my back. It feels as though a little dog were sewn inside me friskily chasing his tail round and round and bumping my spine at every turn, then rounding on it in sudden fury for getting in the way and spoiling his play. But I succeed and step triumphantly from the tub, straight into Pirto's outstretched arms that wait to wrap me in the sheet. It is just a simple white linen sheet, no longer fit for use on a bed but perfectly fine for drying off with after a bath, and yet, as she drapes it round me, I am struck by the sudden horrific notion that it is not a sheet at all but a shroud, and it's all I can do not to tear it from me, give way to tears, scream the house down, and curse God for the unfairness of it all.

"I'll not have a shroud," I say suddenly to Pirto, blurting it out before I can stop myself. "When I die, bury me in my wedding gown."

"Now, none of that grim, melancholy talk, Miss Amy," Pirto gently chides me as if I were still a little girl. "You're to have a good time at the fair today and think naught but happy thoughts!"

"Yes, Pirto," I nod and smile and say obediently as I let her lead me to sit beside the fire. She helps me to gently lower myself onto a padded stool, with a quilted purple velvet cushion as plump as the juiciest plum, then comes to stand behind me and begins to draw the comb through the wet yellow waves of my hair. Carved into the stone of the great fireplace, angels and demons fight their eternal battle, mirroring the war that rages between my heart and head, and the skirmish inside my mind as dreams and reality grapple for supremacy when the medicine blurs the boundary between the two.

I close my eyes and dream of groves of sun-kissed lemon trees and chamomile blossoms swaying in the breeze and the pink-cheeked, barefoot hoyden I used to be, running wild and free, before the chains of cancer enslaved, slowed, and weighted me. Oh, how I wish I could be her again, even if it were just for *one* more day! I would live it to the fullest and make every moment count! To kick Pain in the bum and tell him to clear off and leave me be until the stroke o' midnight! I miss the Amy I used to be. Even before I banished the looking glass from my life, I no longer recognised the pale, thin wraithlike woman with the dark-shadowed, pain-glazed eyes who stared back at me. That was *not* the Amy I knew! That was not the Amy I was inside, and not the Amy Robert Dudley fell in love with ten years ago.

I sit and drowse and dream by the fire as my hair dries into a wealth of spun gold curls; then Pirto gently breaks my reverie. "It is time to be dressing you now, love," she says. She helps me to rise as I grimace and brace myself against the deafening though silent scream that only I can hear that my spine unleashes inside of me.

Will a day come, I wonder, when it will stop screaming and simply snap in the ultimate protestation against my defiance of the pain? Though numbness may seem like a blessing at times, not being able to move at all or feel anything fills me with such fear, I think I will drown in it. Sometimes I think I feel too much, but to live and feel nothing at all is a living death and absolutely terrifies me.

Gently, Pirto eases the sheet from my shoulders. I know what comes next and lift my chin and obstinately stare straight ahead, focusing on the inky blackness outside my window; even though I fear losing my soul in darkness, it is still better than looking down and seeing the rot and ruin of my flesh. Although I have only just bathed, already the fetid stink of decay wafts up to my nostrils as the lump begins to weep ugly tears. It isn't right, it isn't fair; a body shouldn't decay until *after* death! Although some people are not very particular about cleanliness and bathing, I have always been, yet, no matter how much I bathe, no matter what perfume I wear, the stench of death *always* hovers about me, seeping from my breast.

From the corner of my eye a movement distracts me. I turn and catch Pirto reaching for the big cork-stoppered earthenware jar that holds a special blend of powders that Dr Biancospino left for me. When mixed with water, it becomes a thick paste of lime, hemlock, and belladonna that, with the deft brushstrokes of a master artist, the exotic foreign doctor used to paint my breast with, creating hope where there was none before, and whitewashing the ugliness of mottled and festering red flesh and charred-looking dead black tissue. When it dried, it hardened so that my breast appeared to have turned to white marble, as though Pygmalion's Galatea were starting to turn back into a statue after having lived, for the brief span allotted her by the gods, as a flesh and blood woman.

I remember that story. Years ago, in the early days of our marriage, when I saw him more often, Robert used to write poetry and sometimes make clever remarks with classical allusions, but I never understood what he meant. Seeing my puzzled face, he would frown, deplore my ignorance, and sometimes even shout at me or stomp out, grumbling that talking to me was about as sensible as trying to hold a conversation with the sheep. I asked my old swain, my first sweetheart, Ned Flowerdew, who succeeded his father as my father's steward, to send to London for a book of mythology for

me, something simple and easy to understand, writ for a child new
to the subject perhaps. And each and every night while I waited for
my husband to come back to me, I would sit by the fire, with my father dozing nearby in his chair, and my cats, Onyx and Custard,
curled up next to me, and read the stories of the Greek and Roman
gods and goddesses, my tongue tripping and tangling as I tried to
sound out their peculiar names. But it was too little too late. By the
time I knew who Aphrodite, Persephone, Artemis, and Athena
were, Robert was already kneeling at the feet of the flame-haired
Tudor goddess he worshipped and adored with all his ambitious
passion, praying for his regal reward.

"Not that one!" I cry out, startling Pirto so that she jumps and
nearly drops the jar. "The other one—the sticky one that looks like
honey the wise-woman sent."

Confusion and uncertainty furrow dear Pirto's brow. "But I
thought . . ."

"No, Pirto, no," I plead as tears pool in my eyes and cause a qua-
ver in my voice. And, seeing the tears that threaten to spill over, Pirto
sighs as she, reluctantly, puts the jar back and reaches for the other,
the one she thinks, perhaps rightly so, is more chicanery than cure.

The truth is, I don't trust anyone any more, not even myself. I
didn't trust Dr Biancospino when he first came to me; like most
"ill-bred country folk", as Robert would no doubt disdainfully call
us, I believed the lurid tales I had heard of the Italians and their skill
at concocting and administering deadly poisons, stories of poison-
doused gloves and gowns, and fiendish poisoners so adept at their
nefarious craft, they could poison but a single side of a knife and sit
down and boldly share a repast with their victim that would end in
death for only one of them. I was so afraid he had been sent to kill
me. He was like no one I had ever met before. An air of mystery
hung about him, as exotic and peculiar as his accent and the blend
of Italian and Arabic blood that flowed beneath his olive skin. He
would only say that he had been sent by someone who wished me
well and whom I had no cause to fear, someone who had heard all
the disturbing rumours about my health and my husband's intentions and wanted only for me to get well and have the best of care,
free from the worry and suspicion of harm masquerading in the
guise of medicine.

"This is a sincere and well-intentioned gift, else I would not be here, my lady," he assured me.

He would only confirm that it was not my husband who had sent him, but the name of the person who had he would never reveal; he was sworn to secrecy.

"Madame, I have come to make you well if I can, not to play at guessing games," he would smilingly chide me when I tried to guess my mysterious well-wisher's name.

Then, in spite of myself, I began to trust him. He was able to do more for me than any English doctor or wise-woman I had seen. And, deep in my heart, as if it were buried alive, that trust kept fighting to claw its way back out of the premature grave I had consigned it to. Then the plain-wrapped parcel arrived from London, with no name writ upon it, nor could the courier tell me who it was from. Inside was a big leather-bound book, its worn gilt edges gleaming seemingly with malice. It was a long and learned, detailed and thorough, tome all about poisons, written by my Italian-Arab physician—Dr Kristofer Biancospino. When I read it, I felt the blood freeze inside my veins. There were horrors within its pages that *still* give me nightmares! And, stuck amongst its pages, like a bloodstain marring the creamy vellum, was a lone strand of long red hair that told me *exactly* who had sent it—my rival, my enemy—the Queen, Elizabeth. But my mind was too afraid and befuddled; I could not figure out if she meant to warn or merely frighten me, scare me into doing what I indeed did—send Dr Biancospino away so Death could regain the ground that He had lost while I was under that skilled physician's care.

After I received the book of poisons with his name, Dr Kristofer Biancospino, on the title page, and a tale of terror, a litany of suffering, dispassionately detailed on every page thereafter, I would have no more of him or the medicines he gave me, some of which I knew to contain the deadly plants he wrote about—monkshood, mandrake, hemlock, thornapple, henbane, and belladonna, the deadly nightshade that has nothing to do with beauty despite its name, though I have heard it said that the Italian ladies dare to use it in their cosmetics and even put drops of it in their eyes to make their pupils larger, but I shudder at the thought of doing either. I think sometimes women go *too* far in their pursuit of beauty.

Again and again he came to my door, begging to come in, to just sit and talk with me, but I hardened my heart and barred my door against him and refused to answer the letters he sent. Right or wrong, I let myself become afraid of the one person who could help me.

Even now, on the table beside my bed—in the pretty little heart-shaped trinket box lined in rose pink velvet that Robert won for me in a game of skill, throwing coloured wooden balls through a hoop, at a country fair when we were courting—his last letter lay folded into a tight square, containing—if I were brave enough to take it— one last chance to save my life. A gamble, a risk, a life-and-death wager I might win or lose, he told me frankly, showing his respect for me by telling me the truth unvarnished, just as he had done when he first described this daring and dangerous procedure to me, but a *chance* that no English doctor, whether quack or from the College of Physicians, or even the Queen's own doctor himself, could offer me, an operation nigh as excruciating and brutal as the hanging, drawing, and quartering condemned traitors were subjected to, but one, though it skirted death by a hairsbreadth, that *might,* if God were willing, save my life and let me live to be an old woman with silver hair and grandchildren. But the time to think had almost passed; today I *must* decide. It was now or never.

That was why I wanted to be alone today while the others were having a fine, merry time at the fair, to think, to ponder, with no distractions of any kind, to look back and decide whether I wanted to go forward, whether my life was worth saving now that I had lost everything that mattered. I had lost my husband's love, as well as his presence, and the cancer had already destroyed my beauty, and the operation that might cure it would complete the destruction and leave me disfigured in such a way that no man, least of all my fastidious Robert, would ever want me again. What man would ever look with desire upon a woman with an ugly, scarred, and gutted crater where her breast, full, creamy, pink-tipped, and tempting, used to be?

After she returns from the fair, I will send Pirto to the inn with my answer, and Dr Biancospino will either stay or go on his way depending upon my answer, whether it comes in the form of stony, distrustful silence or words writ upon paper; I know that he will wait, and hope, for me for one more day. And I will use that day well, to weigh life against death.

I close my eyes and swallow back my tears as Pirto gently dabs away the milky discharge leaking from my nipple and coats it, and the ugly, oozing lump alongside it, with the honeylike ointment with the sharp, acrid scent and the caustic, biting tingle the old woman—wise, witch, or charlatan? I do not pretend to know which one she is—made for me. Only when the whole unsightly, sticky mess is covered over with a fresh linen dressing do I open my eyes again. The sky is starting to lighten, and outside my window, high above the trees in the park, I can see the spire of St Michael's, the morning sun glinting on it as lightly as a lover's kiss as he steals away with the coming of dawn after a passionate night.

A small smile plays across my lips as Pirto anoints me with the perfume I used to distil myself, my own special blend made from the pink roses of Norfolk and sweet honeysuckles. Which will last longer, this last vial of scent captured and bottled from my father's garden or my life? I have become such a maudlin, melancholy woman! I am too young to be so bitter! Such lemon-and-crabapple tartness is better suited to a woman much further along in years, *decades* older than I, a woman stoop-backed, wrinkled, and grey-haired who has lost her teeth and everyone she ever loved, or never had anyone at all. I press a hand to my forehead and sigh. I *hate* what I have become!

Carefully, slowly I raise my arms, and Pirto gently slips a shift of fine white lawn over my head, and it billows down easily about me, unimpeded by curves, concealing the now frail and wasted figure Robert used to describe as "luscious", playfully sinking his teeth into my breast, buttock, or hip as if it were a ripe and juicy peach. Gone is the round and rosy Amy he used to love.

Though I have no need of them now—this disease has melted away so much of my flesh, the full, buxom, rounded curves, hips, and bum, and flattened the little round hint of a belly that *longed* to swell with the promise of a baby nesting inside—I insist that Pirto fetch my stays from the chest at the foot of my bed, so prettily embroidered with bright yellow buttercups, and lace me up tightly, even though it ignites a lightning storm of pain rippling across my ribs and up and down my spine. Pain plays my spine like the ivory keys of a virginal, but I don't care; I want to be perfectly dressed today. I want to look like Lady Dudley, Robert's wife, *should* look.

Then come the petticoats, starched and crisp. I want my skirts to billow and rustle; I want to have full, feminine hips again, even if it is just an illusion. And then the gown, a glossy satin the colour of high-polished oak, festooned with frills of golden lace, and embroidered all over with green and gold oak leaves and amber acorns— my husband's personal emblem.

Though everyone knows it is a play on the Latin word for his name, *robur,* which means *oak,* only I know this device once had another, more intimate and loving, meaning. Perhaps even Robert himself has forgotten, but *I* remember the day we stood in the drizzling rain huddled together in our cloaks beneath a mighty oak overlooking the crumbling ruins of Syderstone, fallen into decay and disrepair, too sprawling and expensive to keep up, the lands gone to seed and weed, overtaken by thistles and grazing sheep with burrs studding their woolly coats. Robert promised me that he, as my husband, would be like a mighty oak unto me, to shelter and protect me all the days of my life, and these acorns represented the many children we would have. Syderstone would rise again, he swore, and be a *greater, grander* estate than it had ever been before. He would double—nay, *quadruple!*—the size of our flock, and he would breed and train horses that would be famed throughout the land and even abroad. And, best of all, the halls of Syderstone would ring with the joyous laughter of our children playing. My husband was one of thirteen children, though five of them had died before they reached the age of ten, and, as we held our hands together, cupping a shared handful of acorns, we both dreamed that each tiny acorn represented a child that would someday grace our nursery. We both wanted a large family, "the more the merrier," we smiled and agreed. And with a broad sweep of his arm at Syderstone, he vowed that we would have an avenue of oaks leading to the house, a new sapling planted each time my womb quickened with a new life, and we would bring our children out and show them their own special tree, planted the day they first stirred inside of me. Oh, it was a *beautiful, grand, wonderful* dream!

But not all dreams come true, and there were so many promises that he didn't keep. There were never any children, not even one, to fill our nursery; we never even had a nursery. And there was no avenue of oaks. Syderstone still lies in ruins, the sheep still munch thistles, and the burrs still snag their coats, but someone else owns it all now. Robert sold it—to pay off his gambling debts and buy lavish gifts for the Queen, the one who holds his future in the palm of her hand, the one who can make him a pauper or a prince upon a moment's whim. And though he might be a mighty oak, he does *not* shelter and protect me. *It isn't fair!* If Robert can afford to hang the Queen's hair with diamonds, he can afford to put a roof of my own over my head to shelter me; it's as simple as that. I needn't spend my days as a constant guest in the homes of others but never the proud chatelaine of my own domain. And he certainly does not protect me; even in the rustic wilds of England the rumours still find me. Divorce, poison, murder, madness, adultery! I've heard them all. My father would weep and spin like a chicken roasting on a spit in his grave if he knew that his daughter had become the centre of such a lurid, raging scandal, her name being bandied about like a bawdy woman's in every alehouse in England.

I cross the shadowy room and go to sit upon my bed, made fresh by dear Pirto while I rested in my bath, enveloped by soothing clouds of steam. A sad smile flits across my face, like a pebble skimming a pond, as my hand caresses the apple green and gold brocade coverlet woven with a pattern of apples and apple blossoms and trimmed with frills of golden lace. Apples remind me of the happy years of my childhood spent at Syderstone before it became unfit to inhabit and we moved, a good, long but brisk, invigorating walk away, to my mother's more elegant abode, Stanfield Hall. I love apples, everything about them—their colours, their smell, their taste, especially that first juicy, crisp bite, whether it be tart or sweet.

Pirto comes and kneels before me to put on my shoes and stockings, tying the satin garters into pretty bows just below my knees and easing my feet into the dainty brown velvet slippers sewn with tiny amber and gold beads. I always loved to go barefoot whenever I could. I loved the freedom and the feel of the grass, or wood or stone, rough or smooth, chilled or sun-baked, beneath my bare feet. Robert used to send me velvet and satin slippers, a dozen or more pairs at a time, as a silent signal of his disapproval, but I never let that stop me; I gave up too many other things for Robert.

When Pirto starts to gather my hair up, I stop her. "No, the pins make my head ache. Leave it free." This is my one and only concession to comfort—a proper married lady wears her hair pinned up, while a maiden leaves hers unbound—but no one will see. Pirto, however, still thinks I mean to go out today, to church and afterwards the fair.

At times it seems too great an effort and a silly charade. I love Pirto, but I am the lady, and she is my servant, and it is not for me to placate her. I could have done without all these tedious preparations and put on my night shift and taken to my bed, unencumbered by corset and the stiff and rustling confines of petticoats and gown, garters, stockings, and shoes, all the accoutrements of a lady, but for some reason I don't quite understand, it is important to me to be dressed today, to not lounge about languid and loose as a concubine in a sultan's harem.

"As you wish, love," Pirto agrees and gently sets the gold-braided satin hood that matches my gown upon my head, fastening the strap and adding just a couple of pins, placing them carefully, anxious not to cause me any more pain. "There now." She smoothes the cascade of golden curls streaming down my back. "All ready now, you are, pet, except for your purse, though you'll not be needing it just yet, but I have it ready—it's there upon the desk."

"Not quite ready yet, Pirto." I smile. "I want my necklace. The special one My Lord gave me when he still loved me."

"Aye, I know the one." She nods and brings forth from my jewel coffer a rich and heavy necklace of golden oak leaves and amber acorns that matches the betrothal ring I have worn on my left hand since the day Robert put it on my finger when I was a green girl of seventeen brimming over with hopes and dreams. I could not imagine then a world in which Robert would cease to love me. Even now, I like being clothed and jewelled in Robert's oak leaves and acorns; like cattle wearing its master's brand, I am *still* his wife, even if he wishes otherwise; *I* still remember, even when all he wants to do is forget. I *am* Lady Amy Dudley, Lord Robert's wife, and I will *never* surrender that until Death takes it from me. *With this ring I thee wed. Until death do us part.* My affections are not frivolous and fickle despite the changeable nature often ascribed to my sex; when I stood beside Robert on our wedding day to make our vows, I spoke from my heart and meant *every* word.

"Will you lie down for a bit, love?" Pirto hovers anxiously beside me.

"No." I shake my head. "It will muss my gown. Help me to my chair please, Pirto."

It is the most comfortable, beautiful, cheerful chair imaginable, so inviting that it often tempts me from my bed, which is good and exactly as it should be, Dr Biancospino said when I told him. It was the last present my husband sent to me. Such thoughtfulness surely proves that, somewhere, deep in his heart, despite his outward show of indifference, he *must still* care for me. It is upholstered in the most vibrant, rich emerald green all embroidered with bright, beautiful flowers, their petals, leaves, and stems accented with threads of gold and silver. When I sit in it, it is like sinking down into a bed of wildflowers. It always makes me smile. It is so wonderfully, heavenly soft. Sometimes, when I am so sick that I think I will never leave my bed again, I gaze across the room at it, and I am drawn to it. I want to reach out and touch the pinks and daffodils; their leaves seem to beckon to me, to coax a smile from me, and I cannot resist the urge to rise and sit in it—it is *too* powerful to ignore.

As Pirto bustles about the room, putting things right after my bath, I sit and watch the dawn break over the park, where the pond catches the sun's reflection. Mrs Forster's children will be out looking for frogs in their Sunday best if their mother and nurse don't keep a sharp eye on them. I smile at the thought, I can so well imagine it; it's a scene I have seen before and laughed at until it hurt so much, I cried.

As my hand caresses the bright flowers embroidered on the well-padded green arm of my chair, I gaze down upon my betrothal ring, and in that amber acorn, caught like little flecks and flotsam in the golden sap, I can see the happy, joyful days when I was strong, happy, and beloved by the man I can never forget, the one who made me believe all my dreams would come true, and that there *really* was a happily ever after . . .

❧ 2 ❧

Amy Robsart Dudley

Stanfield Hall, near Wymondham, in Norfolk
August 1549–April 1550

I remember the first time I saw Robert Dudley. Sometimes one look, one glance, is enough. Though many, perhaps even I now, would scoff at my youth—I was only new-turned seventeen—that August day I *knew* I had met my destiny.

I sat beside the river, lazy and languid in a bed of nodding yellow buttercups, almost one of them myself in my yellow gown, with my golden curls tumbling down, wiggling my bare toes, with an apron full of apples in my lap. I was daydreaming, building castles in the blue sky and white clouds, pretending that I was a princess, dreaming of the day my prince would come. Suddenly the whinny of a horse startled me and blew all the dreams right out of my head. I leapt up and spun round, the apples falling from my lap, tumbling and rolling every which way. That was when I saw him—Robert, Lord Robert Dudley, my prince in a shining silver breastplate, mounted on a night black steed.

A playful smile twitched and tugged at his lips, and his dark eyes danced as they took my measure, eyeing me up and down as I stood there spellbound at the sight of him. His silver breastplate flashed in the sun, dazzling my eyes, nearly blinding me when he reached up to doff his purple velvet cap, adorned with a sprightly peacock feather. He tethered his horse to a nearby tree and came to me, this dumbstruck, barefoot, country lass gawking and gaping at him, and gallantly knelt to retrieve the fallen fruit around my feet. I had never seen anyone quite like him before, and my knees gave way, and I sank down, back into the buttercups, with him.

Smiling broadly, he asked my name.

"Amy," I said, and to this day I don't know how I managed to utter it, he left me so dazed and breathless.

"Beloved!" He breathed the meaning of my name in a way that was like a caress to me, savouring each syllable upon his lips as if they were the most delicious morsels he had ever tasted.

With a boyish grin, he took from his belt a dagger with its hilt studded with sapphire and emerald cabochons, like blue and green bubbles, and from my lap where he had laid them, he selected an apple, his fingers gently, lingeringly brushing my thigh through my skirts and making my cheeks burn as if the blood beneath my skin had suddenly burst into flames. It was love, I would later tell myself, burning like a fever that would in time consume me.

As the peeling fell away in one long, curling ribbon, he smiled and asked of me:

"Do you country girls still play at that old game of tossing the apple peelings over your shoulder to see how they fall and discern in their shape the initial of your bridegroom-to-be?"

"At times we do, My Lord." I blushed to admit it. It seemed now, when this elegant young man spoke of it, such a childish and silly game.

"Go on, then." He passed the apple peeling to me and jerked his head back over his shoulder to indicate that I should toss it over mine. "Let's see how it falls."

With a merry little laugh bubbling up from my breast, I did as he asked and tossed it over my shoulder.

"Hmm . . ." The handsome stranger tilted his head and tapped his chin thoughtfully as we both turned and scrutinised the peeling. "It *could* be a *D,* yet . . . that little flourish there at the bottom . . . it just *might* be an *R* instead, but . . ." His face brightened as he turned to flash the full brilliance of his pearl-bright smile at me. "Either way, whether it's *R,* or whether it's *D,* it's me." He swept me a half bow. "Robert Dudley, that's my name!"

And before I knew what was happening, he had pulled me into his arms and was kissing me, rolling me onto my back, pressing the weight of his body onto mine as his hand reached down and gathered up my skirts to rove beneath.

With a startled cry, I pushed him away and leapt to my feet and bolted away, my heart pounding so hard and fast as I ran, I could hear it in my ears. It was as if it had split into two pieces, two separate hearts, and both had floated up out of my chest to become lodged, to beat hard and fast like little drums, inside my ears. I ran all the way back to Stanfield Hall.

The servants looked up, startled, as I burst through the kitchen door. But I didn't tarry. I didn't stop running until I was safe behind my bedroom door, where I collapsed in a fit of giggling upon my bed. He must have thought me some light-skirted milkmaid whom any man could tumble; imagine his surprise were he ever to discover that I was Sir John Robsart's daughter, and one of the richest heiresses in Norfolk! I convulsed in gales of gleeful laughter at the thought of it. If not a milkmaid, maybe he thought me a humble shepherdess, never guessing that I was sole heiress to a flock of 3,000 fine sheep. Oh, how it made me laugh! I knew I should be, but I wasn't offended, though I was not the sort of girl to allow a man to take liberties; I had only been kissed once before, a chaste and hasty peck on the lips, light as a feather, from young Ned Flowerdew when we bumped into each other while dancing round the Maypole at the fair, each of us clinging to one of the long, gaily coloured streamers. Red-faced and sheepish, we laughed together and hastily rejoined the other dancers weaving round and round the Maypole in the intricate series of steps, and no more was ever said about it.

I *never* dreamed I would see him again, this Robert Dudley. Why should he linger hereabouts? It was obvious he was one of the men, the thousands of soldiers, who had been sent to put down Kett's Rebellion, the outburst of furious protest that had erupted over the enclosure of common grazing land and had fast gotten out of hand, boiling over to the extent that the frail boy-king, Edward VI, had to send out troops to quell it.

I was drowsing on my bed, dreaming of Robert Dudley's playful smile and dancing dark eyes, and the warm weight of his body on top of mine, with my new kitten, Custard, a fat, cream-coloured ball of fluff, curled up beside me, when my mother burst in. It was one of the rare times she was up and out of bed, so I knew something momentous must have occurred. She came in all aflutter, gesturing with her hands as if they were a pair of anxious butterflies, to tell me that the Earl of Warwick and two of his sons—"two fine, handsome sons, Amy, and neither of them yet married!"—were doing us the *very* great honour of lodging with us tonight, then breathlessly went on to say that I must look my best when I came downstairs to dine. Thereupon she turned away from me and fell to arguing with Pirto about what I should wear.

Mother was set upon the new silver-trimmed milk-and-water gown. White with the barest hint of blue, it was the colour of the moment in London, but Pirto thought it much too pallid and was adamant that I needed something bolder and brighter to show off my golden curls and blue green eyes to best advantage.

While they bickered back and forth, Mother never once wavering in her support of milk-and-water, as Pirto suggested one robust, jewel-bright hue after another, I took from a chest an apple green satin gown embroidered all over with white meadow daisies, their centres like little yellow suns, and brazen red ribbons that playfully crisscrossed the bodice and came together in a flirtatious bow when they reached the top—a pert little flirt of red satin that *begged* to be toyed with and untied. Next I found a bright cherry red taffeta petticoat and under-sleeves dotted with seed pearls and dainty gold beads, and a pair of cheerful and bold red stockings, and went to stand before my looking glass, humming as I held the ensemble up against me.

I *never* worried about such things then; I *always* knew my own mind with complete and utter certainty. I *never* worried or prevaricated, doubted or second-guessed myself. I was as far from nervous as we were from the Emperor of China's palace. I was just me—Amy Robsart—and I did whatever felt right for me to do. I never worried about what other people might think of me. "You wear your confidence like a queen wears her crown, Amy, my lass," Father used to always say of me with a broad, beaming smile and a hearty nod of approval.

I smiled as, behind me, my mother wagged an emphatic finger

in Pirto's face and insisted, "No, no, Pirto, I tell you the milk-and-water gown is much more refined!"

"Aye, My Lady," Pirto nodded, wagging her finger right back in Mother's face, "that may well be, but *I* tell *you* it's too subdued; Mistress Amy's beauty needs a bolder colour to set it off best! Now a nice, robust red . . ."

I laughed and, hugging my gown, pale and bold hues perfectly married, against me, I pranced and spun, dancing around them, then kissed them each upon the cheek, making them both smile at me. *That* was the Amy I used to be!

When I saw him again, I nearly fell straight into his arms. I was at the top of the stairs, with my head in the clouds, about to come down with not a thought in my head about what my feet were doing, as he was bounding up them, as easy, confident, and graceful as a young tomcat strutting on the prowl. I gasped in surprise and stumbled, my foot missing the next step and losing its slipper. He caught me before I fell, and from the safety of his arms, I watched my little black shoe tumble down to the bottom of the stairs. Closing my eyes, I murmured a quick prayer of thanks. That could *so* easily have been *me* falling downstairs, my bones and head banging and jarring against every step.

He clutched me close. Without the metal breastplate, I could feel how muscular and firm his chest was, and he could feel the soft fullness of my breasts.

"Safe in my arms . . . *beloved*!" he whispered, his breath hot against my face as his lips grazed my blush-scorched cheek and slid down to my neck. "You should be more careful, Buttercup"—that was the first time he ever called me that dear, special name—"this is far too beautiful a neck to break."

Then, with a smile, he put me from him, holding me at arm's length, gazing at me in a sort of dazed wonderment; then he blinked, gave his head a little shake as if to clear it, and pressed a kiss onto my brow before he turned and bounded down to retrieve my slipper. He was back in a trice, kneeling on the stairs before me to lift the hem of my gown, and, encircling my ankle in a caressing hand, he boldly bent to press a kiss onto my foot, before he put my shoe back where it belonged.

"I like a lass who is as bold as brass and dares to wear red stockings!" He grinned up at me, then stood and folded my arm through his.

"You thought me a light-skirt today, the kind of maid any man may tumble," I said, frowning a little in mock rebuke as, arm-in-arm, we continued down to the Great Hall to dine.

"Such a woman as any man may tumble can hardly be called a *maid* in the *true* sense of the word." He smiled at me. "All I know is that you struck me like the first sunbeam does a man coming out of a dark cave, and I wanted to be close to you, to bask in your golden beauty and be warmed by you. And when you ran away from me, your little naked feet were like a pair of white doves flying away from me, and I wished with all my heart that I were a hawk so I could soar and pounce and bring you back to me"—he paused, turned me in his arms, and pressed me close to his chest again— "back into my arms again, Amy . . . *beloved*!" And, again, he kissed me in a way that lit such a burning, raging fever in my blood, I thought it would scald me senseless.

Such was the way that Robert courted me; he left me breathless and burning and too dazzled and dumb to speak. He must have at times thought me a pretty mute or a starry-eyed simpleton with nary a brain in my skull. It seems to me now, upon reflection, that only after we were married did I really learn to speak; it was as if wedlock untied the knots in my tongue.

The bed of buttercups by the river became our trysting place. We used to lie there and kiss, caress, hold each other, and dream of the life we would make together, the golden future that awaited us as husband and wife. I imagined the future unfurling before us like a road paved with gold, glowing brilliantly in the sun, which we would walk down together hand-in-hand, confident, brave, and sure in our love, to face whatever lay before us, come what may. And one day he fastened round my neck an amber heart, the rich golden colour of honey, suspended from a cord of braided black silk. "Here is my heart, beloved," he said, "so that even when we are apart, you will know my heart is always with you. And as these flecks and leaves and tiny creatures, these little bits of nature's flotsam, are caught, captured, frozen in time forevermore inside it, so shall my love for you remain always as true and ardent as it is at this very moment; let this token stand as surety for my eternal, undying love."

Lying back in our bed of buttery yellow blossoms, watching the clouds drift by, Robert told me of his dream to breed and train his beloved horses, vowing that he would become famous throughout the world for the perfection in both appearance and disposition of his mounts. "Someday," he boasted, as if he could see the future unfolding in the clouds above us, "all the crowned heads of the world will vie to have my horses in their stables; every king, queen, prince, and princess, even the Emperor of China and the Sultan of Turkey, will want *my* horses!"

He came to me whenever he could, galloping back to Norfolk, thundering down the road to sweep me up in his arms and hold and caress me again, forsaking London and the court just for me. And I would come running out to meet him, pink-cheeked and breathless, scampering through the wildflowers, my hair streaming out wild behind me. "Ah, here comes my wild harvest-gold filly!" Robert would laughingly declare as he watched me race towards him to throw myself into his arms. And together we would loll back in our bed of buttercups by the riverside, and he would hold me in his arms, and we would watch the clouds drift, and dream of the wonderful life we would make together.

I was *amazed* that he wanted me. Robert Dudley had been raised a veritable prince, sharing nurseries and schoolrooms with King Henry's children. His father, the mighty Earl of Warwick, was the king in deed, though Edward VI was the king in name. Even at seventeen, though his sword was but newly blooded in his first battle, Robert was already a suave and practised seducer, well versed in the allure and mysteries of women. Elegant court beauties, who painted their faces as white as consumptives with blood red lips and lounged about in a perpetual swoon, never lifting anything heavier than a fan, and rough, hardworking servant girls with strong shoulders and callous hands but no fine manners or learning, had all been pierced by his fleshly sword. He could have had anyone, and yet . . . he wanted *me, me—Amy Robsart*! I doubted whether I was worthy of him. He was the Earl of Warwick's son, and I was a squire's daughter, best suited to be another squire's wife, a country chatelaine presiding over a hardworking landed estate, not a grand lady like those at court, but he wanted *me*! When I tried to talk to him about it, he just laughed at me. "Are you trying to talk me out of it, little fool?" he asked teasingly, and he hugged me tightly and kissed the tip of my nose.

He said I was like good, wholesome custard, with a touch of pretty garnish, like raisins or saffron or a dash of sprinkled cinnamon, not elaborate marzipan and spun-sugar subtleties, confectionery turned art, like the ladies of the court. I was a pure, country-bred beauty, a *true* English rose, not some exotic, easily wilted, hothouse flower. I was fresh, clean air, blue skies, sunshine, and acres of green grass to their close, over-ripe, and perfumed chambers, tapestried walls, and Turkey carpets. My words were sweet, plainspoken, and true, not barbed and double-edged, honeyed words filled with hidden, sometimes poisonous, meanings, or all done up in flowery parcels with the true meaning concealed inside the poetry. He said he loved my pure, unvarnished charm. I was natural and real; I had no sleek and deceptive veneer of sophistication, no studied, artful airs. "You wear no mask. Your life is no masquerade. When I look at you, I see the *real* you, the *real* Amy, not a pretty painted façade that is false and ugly when it is laid bare and washed clean of paint, and I love what I see. With Amy Robsart seeing *is* believing!"

But I doubted that his father, the high-and-mighty Earl of Warwick, would be swayed by all this talk of love. It was only common sense that he would want a greater, grander match for his son, even a fifth one like Robert. And then I did something that still shames me. I was *desperate* not to lose him; there was no one else in the world like Robert, and I loved him so much, I couldn't bear to let him go, to think of him with another who loved him less or not at all but whose pedigree and education were better than mine. And so I surrendered. I lay down and let him lift my skirts; it was the only *sure* way to defeat common sense and worldly realities and let true love prevail. Or maybe it was merely that I was too weak to resist the heat of his hands burning through the cloth of my gown, cupping my breasts, and the kisses that made me feel more alive than I ever had before and that made me tilt my head back, like a hungry baby bird ravenous for the nourishment of his kisses. When pleasure met pain, and my maiden's blood watered the roots of the buttercups, I knew that he was mine. I was Sir John Robsart's daughter, his only legitimate heir, sole heiress to his lands, estates, flocks, and fortune, not some poor little milkmaid whose father would accept a purse as compensation for his daughter's lost virtue and be grateful for it, tug his forelock, and say, "Thank you, kind sir."

Afterwards, still wrapped in Robert's arms, I trembled and wept, afraid, but not sorry, for what we had just done. What if I conceived a child? But Robert smiled his easy smile and laughed his ready laugh and kissed me from my brow to my belly, teasing my navel with his tongue and doling out great, smacking kisses all over my stomach, making me laugh in spite of myself. He assured me that he wanted me and our baby—if we had indeed just made one—and he wanted all the many babies we would go on to make in our long life together. We made love again, then tenderly tidied each other, washing each other with a kerchief dipped into the river, and smoothing and fastening each other's clothes; then, hand-in-hand, pausing often to kiss, we walked back to Stanfield Hall and into my father's study so that Robert could ask him for my hand in marriage.

My father was a *wonderful,* jolly man, stocky and sturdy, with a head of untamable iron grey curls, and cheeks like the famed apples from his orchards. He loved me as no one ever did before or ever would again. From the moment I came into this world until the mind that knew and loved me so well abandoned his body as a snail does a shell and left behind a dazed wanderer, a stranger even unto himself, I was his pride and joy. I was most aptly named *Beloved.*

I was born when he had given up hope of ever having a child of his own to love, nurture, and teach. Arthur, my half brother, was baseborn, the result of a drunken tumble with "a conniving, black-haired witch of a tavern wench", when he was a young man and too foolish to know how many cups were too many. Father paid generously for Arthur's care, but his mother would not relinquish him, and Father never saw his son unless a need for money brought him and his mother with their greedy palms outstretched to his door. And Arthur grew up an ignorant wastrel frittering his time away in a tavern, rather than as a squire's son learning how to manage an estate; he sneered and turned his back on a chance to better himself. Content to be a ne'er-do-well, he never really cared about Father, only his money, and only when he had need of it.

When he married her, my mother, Elizabeth Scott Appleyard, was the proud widow of Sir Roger Appleyard. She had already borne four children—two uppity girls, Anna and Frances, who always treated me like manure sullying their satin shoes, and a pair of pompous boys, John and Philip, who thought the sun rose and set solely for their sake. She thought that that part of her life was well behind her, when I came along, unexpectedly, and, I think, as a most unwelcome surprise. Knowing that every man desires a son, she hoped to bear a boy and be done with birthing once and for all. But I was a girl, and my birthing damaged her inside, dislodging her womb from its proper place, causing her much discomfort until the end of her days and giving her an excuse to permanently abstain from any further marital relations and spend the rest of her life as a pampered invalid in pretty lace-trimmed caps and robes with a comfit box always at her side. Everyone expected Father to be disappointed, to curse and rage as King Henry VIII had done when first Catherine of Aragon and then Anne Boleyn failed to give him a son, but my father took one look at me and breathed the word *"Beloved!"* and thus named me Amy.

That very day he wrote proudly inside his prayer book: *Amy Robsart, beloved daughter of John Robsart, knight, was born on the 7th day of June in the Blessed Year of Our Lord 1532.*

He petted, indulged, and spoiled me like no other child, as if I were indeed a princess, and longed for my happiness above all else. So now, when I was of an age and of a mind to marry, he could not bear to deny me, though he had grave qualms about the man I had chosen to be my husband.

"But you barely know each other!" again and again he protested, worry ploughing deep furrows into his brow. He urged us to tarry a year, or two, or even more. Four-and-twenty, he said, was thought by many to be the ideal age for a man to marry, to have sown his wild oats and seasoned his mind so that he was able to govern himself and make the *right* decision when choosing a wife, not a hasty pick led by hot blood and a pointing prick. But neither of us could bear it; we were seventeen, and to wait even a year seemed like an eternity. We were in love and impatient to start living our life together.

My lips trembled, and tears filled my eyes. Robert gave my hand a reassuring squeeze and stepped forward before my tears could overflow onto the accounts ledger lying open on Father's desk.

"Sir, we love each other truly," he said. "Getting to know each other will be a joy and an adventure, like unearthing buried treasure each day of our life together. Each new discovery will be a priceless, precious jewel," he promised my father as he gallantly raised my hand to his lips and kissed it, then pressed it over his heart.

And my father was won over by the sight of tears glimmering in my blue green eyes and Robert's eloquent and impassioned words, though I know in his heart worry would ever dog him like his faithful hound Rex.

I understand far better now than I did then; Father thought by marrying Robert I was wading in over my head, and he was afraid I was going to drown. The *one* time in my life when I should have listened and been guided by my father's advice, I turned my back and ignored his wisdom. But I would not realise my mistake until the waters were already closing over my head. My only comfort is that Father, as much as I miss him, did not live to see the bitter fruits our hasty and impetuous union have reaped, the sourness that was left behind after the sweet passion died. It is a dismal harvest, with the fruits of young love all blackened and blotched; diseased and spurned, they tempt no one. I am glad he did not live to see what I have come to. It would have broken his heart to see the child he named "Beloved" unloved, unwanted, and dying, while my husband dallies with the highest lady in the land and dreams of wearing a golden crown, dancing while he waits for me to die; for Robert my cancer will correct the mistake he made when he was a lusty lad of seventeen. My end will be Robert's new beginning. Sometimes I dream of him and Elizabeth dancing with joyous abandon upon my grave, and I wake up with my whole body aching as if their dancing feet had actually trampled and bruised me, and Pirto has to dose me against the pain that makes every bit of my body feel as if it were screaming.

Even on the very morning of my wedding day the following summer, Father was still trying to save me from myself, to arm Reason with a sword that would vanquish Lust. "First love is rarely evergreen love, my dear," he warned as he stroked my hair and pressed a kiss onto my brow. "Bide at home a while longer with me, lass," he cajoled. "Wait, and you'll see, something'll come along that is better, *far better,* for you than Robert Dudley."

But with tears in my eyes I turned to him and said simply, "Father, I love him." And there was an end to all discussion. Within the hour I was kneeling beside Robert at the altar, my heart swelling nigh to bursting with love, believing all my dreams were coming true, that this was just the first step of the many we would walk together . . .

❦ 3 ❦

Amy Robsart Dudley

Cumnor Place, Berkshire, near Oxford
Sunday, September 8, 1560

"What is it, love?" Pirto, her face all concern, asks, tugging gently at my sleeve as she kneels beside me. "You look so sad! Is it the pain again?"

"I'm all right, Pirto," I sigh with a wan, halfhearted little smile, "but I shall not go to the fair today. No, no"—I stop the protests forming on her lips—"you and the others go, and have a *good* time today. I insist, I will hear no argument. Take my purse, and bring me back some cakes and cider and hair ribbons—a whole rainbow of hair ribbons. Spend whatever you like, and tell me all about it when you come back tonight. Do this for me as you love me, Pirto. I have a sudden craving for solitude. I can't really explain it, but I want to be all by myself in a quiet house, where I can truly hear myself think and listen to what my mind is saying. *Please!*" I take both her hands in mine. "There is *so* little anyone can do for me now, but you *can* do *this*."

"My Lady, I like not to leave you alone . . ." Pirto frowns, and the lines on her face seem to bite a little deeper.

"It is just for *one* day, Pirto, one peaceful day, and I shall be fine," I promise her. "*Please,* do this *one* thing for me! And tell the others to go—*make* them go if you must—but just give me this one quiet Sunday all to myself."

Pirto sighs and gives in, as I know she will. "Very well, My Lady!" Then, with a creak of her aged knees, she stands and begins bustling about, sending down to the kitchen for a platter of food, covered so that the sight and smell of it will not sicken me, just to be there in the event my appetite should awake and stir its sluggish self, and bringing medicines, water, wine, a basin, and ginger suckets to combat the nausea, and putting them all on the table beside my chair so that I will have anything I might need within ready reach. And also, at my request, she brings the pretty red and gold enamelled comfit box filled with sweet and sour cherry suckets Tommy Blount brought me last time he rode out from London. Though I cannot bring myself to eat them—my stomach raises a sword of threatening protest each time I think to try one—I love looking at them, the candied cherries glowing in neat rows like a jeweller's tray of round, perfect cabochon rubies, waiting for me to make a selection.

Voices raised in argument outside my door suddenly penetrate my reverie, and, even though Pirto hastens out to try to quiet them, I lever myself up and follow her out into the Long Gallery, where watery sun pours in through the gabled windows to pool upon the cold stone floor, trying vainly to warm it, like an ardent lover wooing an icy maid.

"But what nonsense is this?" Mrs Oddingsells demands, fluttering the note I had sent late the night before to be given to her upon arising. Her bosom heaves in such a mighty and zealous show of hypocritical outrage that I fear her breasts will burst like two cannonballs from her too-tightly-laced mulberry silk bodice, and I step back lest I suffer a blackened eye. "Sunday is the Lord's Day, Lady Dudley, and *all* God-fearing people should be at home and at their prayers and reading their Bibles, not gallivanting at the fair! And certainly it is no day for gentlefolk like us to mingle with the sort of low, common people who are likely to frequent a fair upon a Sunday; no doubt they will be very loud and vulgar and given to drunken and lewd disport and excess!" She wrinkles her nose as if the very thought of such folk conjures up a stink as powerful as a cart heaped high with rotten eggs.

Her false façade of morality makes me so mad, I want to tell her that if she is so worried about offending the Lord, she shouldn't be wearing her bodices cut so low, but I'm too tired, and it's more trouble than it's worth to stand there bickering like hens who all want the only cock in the henhouse, so I let it go.

"Humph!" Mrs Forster sniffs, and she gives a smart tug to her new goose-turd green and yellow bodice and tucks a stray wisp of hair back beneath her lace-bordered white linen cap. "Put on airs and play pious as you will, Lizzy Oddingsells, but *I* have been going to country fairs all my life, many upon a Sunday, and enjoyed them every one, and my blood is just as good as yours is, if not better, and you'll burn in Hell just the same whether you go to the fair or stay home with a whole stack of Bibles—for being my husband's *whore*!" And with those words and a flounce of her green and yellow skirts, she's off with her nose in the air to gather her children and prepare them for a day at the fair, determined to enjoy herself all the more to spite Mrs Oddingsells, and I know that for many days to come she will bubble like a pot boiling over every chance she gets about what a fine time she had at the fair while some falsely pious hypocrites with jumped-up notions about themselves stayed at home.

"Mrs Oddingsells is right. Sunday is the Lord's Day"—like a judge, the grey-haired and grey-clad Mrs Owen solemnly weighs in, gravely intoning the words as if each one were as heavy as a granite boulder—"and a day meant for contemplation and prayer. After church I shall return to my chamber and spend the day quietly with my Bible."

"But you *must* go!" I insist, turning first to one and then to the other, fighting the urge to fall on my knees and actually *beg* them. Mrs Owen, I could bear—I know she would not bother me—but I do not want Mrs Oddingsells about. I want peace and quiet and privacy, not prying eyes and forced companionship when I would have none. And I know that if she stays home, forced to make do with her own company, Mrs Oddingsells will soon be *so* bored that she will gladly suffer *any* company, even mine; that woman would sit down and drink a tankard with Satan himself if it would save her from being alone half an hour. "I promise, you will have a good time, and there is no harm in it! I have been to many a fair on Sunday, and my soul has suffered no harm from it! And it is not nearly so rough and rowdy as you imagine; the common folk are jolly and good, and most are well-behaved."

Mrs Owen turns and sweeps her glacial grey eyes over me in a glance so cold, it makes me shiver. Her voice drips with disdain when she begins to speak to me. "You are mortally ill and abandoned by your husband, Lady Dudley, a man who leaves you alone to die of an incurable and agonisingly painful disease while he goes to court to dance and fornicate with the Queen. And, when last I looked, my fine lady, your name was not on the lease to Cumnor, nor is your lord's. You have no home of your own and are merely a guest in this house, so what makes you think that you can give orders here, or to presume that God is *not* punishing you with your suffering for some transgression you have committed, mayhap even all those fairs you have attended on Sundays?"

I gasp and reel back as if she had just struck me. If Pirto had not caught me, I surely would have fallen flat. I stare back at her, aghast, with tears of anger and surprise welling in my eyes. My chin quivers, but, as is often the case with me, I feel myself helpless and tongue-tied in the face of such bluntness and cruelty.

Ignoring me, Mrs Oddingsells turns to Mrs Owen and asks if perchance she would like to dine with her.

"Perhaps you would like to dine with me instead, Lizzy?" Mrs Owen counters with an invitation of her own. "My cook is preparing a fine suckling pig stuffed with apples and pears and raisins. The *dear* woman spoils me so; but it is far too rich and full a repast for a lonely old woman like me."

"Gladly!" Mrs Oddingsells beams. "Many thanks, Mrs Owen; you are an angel in disguise who has come down to earth to shower blessings upon me!"

"And perhaps later we might have a game of cards?" Mrs Owen suggests as, arm-in-arm, they turn and start to walk away, down the Long Gallery, heading for the stairs. "Though since it is Sunday, all the winnings must go into the church's poor box, of course."

"Of course!" Mrs Oddingsells readily agrees. "I would not have it any other way! I would not feel right even touching a deck of cards on a Sunday unless some poor soul were to reap some benefit from it. Win or lose, I know I shall have helped some poor soul in need."

"You are welcome to join us, of course, Lady Dudley," Mrs Owen calls back over her shoulder. "If you find solitude weighs too heavily upon you, you will know where to find us. You know, Lizzy, I am not the superstitious sort," I hear her say in a confiding tone as, arm-in-arm like the oldest, dearest friends, they walk away from me, "but my maid is, and she told me that Tom, the miller's son, saw the Black Man." At her words my skin crawls, and I can't help but think of my husband's sinister henchman, Sir Richard Verney. "Yes"—Mrs Owen nods as she continues her tale—"the Devil himself, in human form, by moonlight at the crossroads last night, out looking for desperate souls to sign their name in blood inside his big black book; it's all ignorant country folderol of course, but just the same, I should not like to tempt fate by going to the fair today . . ."

I pale at her words, and my knees buckle and shake, and Pirto has to put her arm around my waist to steady me.

"I don't think it was the Devil at all," I say after Mrs Owen and Mrs Oddingsells have gone, as I sag weakly against her. "I think the Black Man is Death, and He is coming for me, mayhap even in the guise of Sir Richard Verney."

"Now, now, pet," Pirto gently chides, "'tis no such thing at all, merely superstitious nonsense, just like Mrs Owen said. But are you *sure* you would not like me to stay with you? I don't like to leave you alone when you're so distressed," she adds as, rubbing my back, she shepherds me back into my room and helps settle me in my chair again. "I've been to enough fairs in my lifetime, so 'tis no sacrifice at all."

"Dear Pirto." I reach out and stroke her wizened cheek, so like the faces of the poppets we used to make from dried apples when I was a little girl. "Thank you, but I *want* you to go; I want you to enjoy this fair for me. I want one more fair before Death closes my eyes forever, but I have not the strength to go myself, so you go, for me, for both of us. Let your eyes drink in every detail, and bring me apple cider and cinnamon cakes, and ribbons for my hair, and sit here with me tonight when you come back and tell me all about it."

"Aye, that I will, though I hate to leave you even for a day, love,"

Pirto says, stroking my hair and pressing a kiss onto my brow before she leaves me.

"I'll bring you a bit o' gingerbread back as well, love," she says brightly, just before she closes the door. "That'll tempt your appetite—you always did love it so—and the ginger'll settle your stomach and keep the nausea down."

I breathe a sigh of relief when I hear the heavy front door close behind them all, followed by the clatter of hooves and wheels in the courtyard. With a deep, shuddering sigh, I let the pretence fall away from me as I lean back in my chair, holding tightly to the arms, digging my fingers into the embroidered flowers, gasping, with tears rolling freely down my face, as a pain, like a lance driven all the way through me, pierces my breast and rings like a shrill, echoing bell up and down my spine and across my ribs, and Death gives my heart a little warning squeeze, toying with me, teasing me, like a braggart showing me what he can do. I wait until it has passed; then slowly, carefully, I raise myself from my chair and go to the shelf where the medicines are kept, all except the ones my husband sends.

A pain shoots along the length of my arm as I reach up for the bottle I want. A sunbeam streaming in through the window catches it as I lift it down, causing the dark liquid to glow like the richest amber, agleam with honey and crimson lights. When he sent his last letter to me, Dr Biancospino also sent this. If I choose to let my illness take its natural course, he wrote, when the end is nigh and the pain at its most excruciating, this will ease me into the arms of Death, and I will think Him merciful then, not cruel to take my life away when I am only eight years past twenty, with my hair still gold instead of silver. I should never have doubted Dr Biancospino; he was, I think, the only one who ever told me the truth laid bare, ugly and naked, not falsely painted to make it look pretty. And what if this bottle does contain one or more of those deadly ingredients described in his book of poisons? It was not given me out of malice, and it was meant to be saved, to be used only to drive pain away from my deathbed; it is not a tonic to sip every day like the lime and orange water Mrs Owen recommended.

Boldly, defiantly, I uncork the bottle and take a sip, grimacing at the bitter, burning taste. It should be mixed with wine, or have sugar added, to make it more palatable and sweet, the pasted paper label says, written in Dr Biancospino's elegant script, but, yet again, I am deaf to reason and ignore good and sound advice, acting again as if I alone know better. Mayhap I do, and mayhap I don't. Today I'm too tired to care and quibble about it. Just a sip to ease my pain and prove my trust; what harm can it do? If I fall down dead, it is just the inevitable come sooner rather than later.

I turn to my altar, thinking I would like to pray; it *is* Sunday after all, and it seems only right that even though I am not in church that I should talk to God just the same. Every day I pray for Him to deliver me from my desperation. I jump and nearly drop the bottle, my heart beats fast, and the familiar pain impales my breast, for there is the grey friar who haunts Cumnor Place, kneeling before my little altar, his head solemnly bowed, hidden deep in the dark shadows of his cowl so that I cannot see his face, his hands clasped tightly, wrapped with a dangling rosary of polished wooden beads and a swaying silver crucifix upon which Jesus Christ hangs in perpetual mute agony, nailed to the cross and crowned with thorns.

Slowly—I am in a defiant mood today—like one warily approaching a dangerous beast, like a wounded lion or slumbering tiger, I go to the phantom friar and carefully ease myself down to kneel beside him. The air about him is icy and pierces through my many layers of clothes, making me feel as if I were wandering naked and lost in a world made entirely out of snow. But I defy the icy blast. I have been afraid of him for far too long. I accept his presence now and no longer scream or try to evade and hide from him.

"Have I drunk Death?" For the first time I speak to him, my voice faint and all aquiver, like lute strings plucked by nervous fingers, as I set the bottle down upon the altar, like an offering. It glows and gleams in the candlelight as if it were lit from within by a fiery ember that, defying all reason, continues to emit a red glow even though, submerged in liquid, it should have gone right out. But the friar gives no answer and goes on with his prayers as if he has not even heard or noticed me kneeling beside him.

"Who were you in life?" I persist, though he continues to ignore me. "What was your name? Did you struggle with the desires of the flesh that bedevil most men? Or did you embrace the cloistered life? Was it something you came to willingly? Did it bring you peace? Were you happy? Or was it a struggle to honour your vows? Did you rebel and fight against yourself your whole life long or meekly accept and resign yourself to your fate? Was your life a success, or a failure like mine? There *must* be a reason your ghost still walks! Were you walled up alive for some grievous sin? Did you love a nun, or a great lady, or a peasant girl perhaps and plant your seed inside her? Were you caught trying to abscond to France to start a new life with her? Or did you take your own life? The servants tell such wild and lurid stories; I don't know which, if any, to believe. Did you do something *so* terrible, *so* unforgivable, that the gates of Heaven are barred to you, and your spirit is damned to walk the earth forever? Is there no absolution, no atonement, that will bring you rest?"

But the ghostly grey friar is not inclined to divulge his secrets to me, and, intent upon his prayers, he ignores me, but I am used to that.

"The Queen wants my husband, and my husband wants the Queen, and to wear a golden crown and call himself King Robert I of England, and only my life stands between the fulfilment of all their desires," I confess to him. This is no lurid fancy; this is fact all England knows, and only those who wish to be kind and comfort me lie and say it isn't so.

Our lives—Elizabeth's and mine—are a strange reversal of Fate. Usually it is the mistress's lot to live hidden away in the shadows of a man's life, while the wife walks proudly in the sun in a place of honour at his side. But Robert's mistress rules the realm and basks always in the glorious, bright sun of pride and adoration, while I, his wife, languish forgotten and ignored in rustic obscurity, consigned and banished to oblivion, in one country house or another owned by those who wish to ingratiate themselves to Robert and the Queen.

Housing Lord Robert's ailing and unwanted wife has become a coin to barter for and pay back favours. Sometimes I wonder which one of these "gentlemen" who house me will be the one to betray me, to ensure my death beneath their roof, that this inconvenient guest does not survive their hospitality, and bravely bear the stigma and the scandal and suspicion that will darken their character, and their doorstep, forever after, like Judas for thirty pieces of silver, with the Queen's profile minted on each coin and doled out from Robert's coffers. Sir William Hyde? Sir Richard Verney? Sir Anthony Forster? Just lately Robert has written to say that the Hydes have agreed to have me back again. They were so glad, so relieved, to see me go before; I wonder what he has promised them. I'm to leave Cumnor and go back to lodge with them for a spell, then back to Compton Verney, before I return to Cumnor again. Thus has Robert ordered my life. I'm to go back and forth like a shuttlecock between these three houses. Whose doorstep will be stained with my blood? Whose threshold will be forever shadowed by that black, funereal pall? Which one will the Judas be?

If not one of them, there is always Robert's minion, his poor country cousin, sweet young Tommy Blount, with his freckled face, mass of ginger curls, and shy but ready, endearing smile, always so eager to please and bursting with a young man's zest for life and tireless, unflagging vigour. He seems to spend all his time on the road as Robert's courier, galloping hither and yon, back and forth between the court and wherever Robert sends him on one errand or another. He reminds me so much of the boy my husband used to be, only without Robert's cocksure confidence, elegance, and bold sophistication. But I dare not trust even Tommy, a young man who looks at me with desire obvious in his eyes and words poised on his lips that he dare not say. Time has taught me that a sweet nature can be false or fade, especially when a man bows down to the golden goddess of Ambition. And Tommy, honoured to be favoured by such a great lord, is my husband's loyal and trusted servant and kinsman, so I dare not trust him; succumbing to that temptation could very well be fatal for me.

How will my husband set the deed down in his accounts ledger, I wonder. What innocuous expense will disguise my death? Will my blood be covered up with fluffy white wool, or will my corpse be hidden in a barrel of apples?

The candlelight catches my betrothal ring, causing the golden oak leaf to glitter, and the amber acorn glows like a dollop of honey flecked with shifting glints of rich red, fiery orange, and shimmering gold, just like the memory of a beautiful sunset we once shared standing under the mighty old oak overlooking Syderstone, imprisoned inside this amber acorn. Sometimes nowadays it feels too heavy for my hand, like my end of the shackles and chains of the wedlock that hold Robert and me together. Sometimes I want to just undo the lock and let the chains fall and set us both free. I'm so tired of it all, the pain and misery and living in fear. *Pride goeth before a fall,* the Scriptures say; now I want to let that obstinate pride in being Lady Amy Dudley, Lord Robert's wife, fall from me before I myself fall, pulled down by a weight I can no longer bear. I just want to let go of it all, even though I'm afraid of falling, but I'm also tired of holding on, and tired of being afraid.

"O My Father," I pray, "if it be possible, let this cup pass from me; nevertheless, not as I will, but as Thou will."

What a strange toy my mind has become! Even as I desire death, I long for life! It is as if these two contrary desires are locked in perpetual battle within me. One moment the desire for death gains and holds a sword to the throat of life; then the next the longing for life pushes back, parries the sword, and seems poised to be the victor; but within an instant it all changes, again and again and again, so that I, who used to be *so* certain, now never know what I *really* want any more. I am losing my mind; it is becoming a stranger to me! I am so afraid I am going mad!

I rise and leave the phantom friar to his prayers. But first I reach out my hand—though I don't quite dare to touch him—and feel the icy prickle on my trembling fingertips as they hover just above his diaphanous grey sleeve. "I'm sorry," I tell him. "I was wrong to be afraid of you. I have far more cause to fear the living than I do the dead." Then I cross myself—there is no one here to see, and the old Catholic ways bring me comfort, and I'm not sure which is the *right* religion any more, may God forgive me. As I rise, I utter a silent prayer that God will grant the ghostly friar absolution for whatever denies him his eternal rest and keeps his soul trapped and earthbound within the clammy walls of Cumnor.

Across the room my husband's proud and insolent face stares out at me with piercing dark eyes that smoulder with impatience and freeze my soul from within a gilded picture frame ornately carved with acorns and oak leaves and the Dudley coat-of-arms with the bear and ragged staff at each corner, as though once was not enough and it must be pounded into the beholder's brain that he is looking at an illustrious scion from the House of Dudley.

This is how I know my husband now—from his portraits.

Handsome and haughty, as proud as Lucifer, he strikes a princely pose, like a king-in-waiting. Arrogant and condescending, in his gold-and-pearl-embellished amber brocade doublet, with an oval, diamond-framed enamelled miniature of the Queen hanging from a jewelled chain about his neck, showing the world where his heart lies. But to my eyes that chain is a very short, jewelled leash that tethers him to Her Majesty just like what he has become—her pampered and petted, much favoured lapdog, one who just might turn and bite the hand that feeds him someday or else strangle himself with his own leash.

Remembering what he was like when I first knew and loved him, I cannot help but hate what he has become, and my heart mourns and weeps without cease for that lost love and the soul he has gambled, lost, and damned with his vainglorious ambition. He stands there so proud and lofty with his hands upon his hips, one of them lightly caressing the jewelled hilt of his sword in a subtle warning that he would not hesitate to fight anyone who dared provoke or challenge him. The wild, rumpled black curls have been cropped and tamed beneath a plumed black velvet cap. Gone is the wild, untamable Gypsy; he has donned the vestments of respectability and left a staid and proper gentleman behind in his stead. And gone also is the easy grace I remember; he looks so stiff, so uncomfortable and rigid, as he stands there so erect, head high, shoulders back, his neck encased, like a broken limb, in a high collar that holds it like a splint, his cheeks cushioned by a small white ruff. His eyes and mouth are so hard now, I no longer recognise them. Even his hands, which used to be so gentle and tender with me, seem more likely to strike a blow or strangle than caress me now.

This is a portrait of a vain and cruel, self-consumed man with no regard for anyone else, a far cry from the kind, eager, passionate boy I fell in love with ten years ago. Had the man in this portrait come courting me, I would have shrunk from him; he would have roused only fear and uneasiness in me, not captured my heart and lit a fire inside me that made me feel as if I were melting every time his dark eyes turned my way. If this man had come to Stanfield Hall instead of the charming, winsome boy he used to be, I am sure I would have kept to my room until this insolent and disdainful creature—with the cold, hard, dark eyes that seem to freeze and burn me at the same time, and the forked, Devil-dark beard hanging from his chin—had gone away again, and I would have breathed a deep sigh of relief to see the back and, hopefully, the last of him.

I miss the Robert I fell in love with. Sometimes I dream I rise from my bed and slit the portrait down the middle, and he, the clean-shaven boy with the dark, tousled curls and ready, winning smile comes bounding out to take me in his arms, cover my face with kisses, and sweep me up and carry me out to make love in a bed of buttercups again. But I know if I were to slit the canvas, my dagger would find only the hard stone wall beneath. The Robert I loved so much, and who I thought loved me, is gone forever; instead, within his skin resides a stranger, a cold, imperious, commanding man who shuns and disdains the sweet simplicity of a country buttercup for the regal red and white Tudor rose instead.

I wanted so much for him to love me and be proud of me, but, I know now, I was doomed to failure from the start.

I know I should, but somehow I can't let go of the dream—I just can't! My dream came true, I lived a love all girls dream about but rarely find, and then I lost it. I'm not even sure how or when it died; it just slipped away from me. I tried so hard to bring it back, as if I were digging in my heels and pulling with all my might upon its coat tails, but the Robert I loved and the life we led together simply slipped the sleeves and left me holding an empty coat, to spend the rest of my lonely life trying to deny and run away from the truth that they were gone forever, and desperately seeking a way to woo and win them back.

Gazing upon Robert's portrait only saddens me, so I turn away from it and go and gently ease myself down onto my bed, taking another sip from the medicine bottle before placing it carefully on the table beside me. At times I am of a mind to have Robert's portrait taken down and moved elsewhere. Sometimes I even yearn for the fleeting, momentary satisfaction of seeing it burned or chopped into kindling. Only the knowledge that the servants would surely gossip, and, when word reached London, as it inevitably would, an angry letter from Robert would soon follow—only that stays my tongue from giving the necessary orders.

I *hate* the way his eyes seem to follow me, so impatient, hard, and hateful, as if he were wishing that I would hurry up and die. The man in that portrait I do not think would hesitate a moment to send an assassin to hasten me to my grave. That is a man who would freely spend his gold to buy poisons to send to me or persuade a physician to undertake my cure but bring about my death instead. This is a portrait of a man who loves only himself; even the woman whose likeness hangs about his neck is only a means to an end.

Sometimes I wonder if Robert has fooled her too. Does he make her feel like a weak-kneed woman of wax melting under the hot sun of gaze, burning lips, and the ardent, skilful hands that know *exactly* how and where to touch, the deft fingers that seek out and stroke the most intimate and sensitive places? I was Love's blind fool; I trusted and believed and gave him my heart, body, and soul, and all the best of me; I married him. Will Elizabeth Tudor do the same? Or does my own bitterness cast a shadow and unjust suspicion on both of them? Is it *true* love betwixt Robert and the Queen? Am I, after all, just a youthful error, a foolish mistake that with my death will be remedied, undone and erased, to give true love the chance it lost through rash, young, and lusty folly?

Robert has become very much his father's son. John Dudley, Earl of Warwick, Duke of Northumberland, would be proud to see his son standing so near the throne, and the woman who sits upon it head over bum in love with him. It was always his ambition to play kingmaker and become the founder of a great royal dynasty. But with Robert, I thought that, as a fifth son, the hardness had been buffed smooth, the sharp edges rounded and softened, and the ambition that coursed through his veins diluted. I thought happiness was enough for Robert, that he had turned his back on fame and glory and wanted only a simple life with me, breeding horses and filling our nursery with as many children as we could have, and presiding over our flocks, fields, and apple orchards. I thought Robert was different.

I remember the day Robert's father, the Earl of Warwick as he was then, sought me out . . .

❧ 4 ❧

Amy Robsart Dudley

Stanfield Hall, near Wymondham, in Norfolk
April 1550

I was in the dairy, with my hair bunched up carelessly beneath a white ruffled cap, wearing a faded old blue cloth gown with an apron tied over it, my sleeves rolled up to my elbows, and my hems pinned up to my knees. The stone floor was deliciously cool and smooth, like silk gone solid, beneath my bare feet, and I was laughing and gossiping with the milkmaids as I took my turn at a churn, just as if I were one of them and not Sir John Robsart's daughter.

The Earl eyed me up and down, then shook his head and sighed, *"Poor Robert!"*

Of course, I did not know then that I was fated to perpetually arouse pity for my husband.

My father-in-law-to-be bade me come out and walk with him. The silence hung heavily between us like a velvet curtain on the hottest summer day, and I felt as if I were walking alongside the Devil, there was such an aura of cruelty and power about him. But he was my beloved's father, so I *must* try to win his good regard.

"I am sorry you catch me, Sir, at a time when I am so unkempt and ill-prepared to receive visitors," I said, blushing and flustered, my tongue tripping clumsily over the words and no doubt making me seem more crude, ignorant, and rustic.

As we walked along, I rolled down my sleeves and tucked a stray lock of hair back inside my cap while debating whether I should stop and unpin my hems to let my skirts fall down to cover my bare shins and feet. I had a pair of comfortable old leather and wood clogs, but in my haste I had left them lying outside the dairy.

"I have always taken a more active role in running my father's estates than perhaps a grand man like you would consider fitting," I half-apologetically explained, though in truth I was not the least bit sorry. I *loved* being a part of it all and having a hand in it, not standing idly by like a court lady with her nose in the air or a pomander ball smelling of oranges and cloves pressed to it. I *never* failed to feel a sense of wonder as I watched things come into being, from the birthing of a new calf to making a loaf of bread or churning butter; each time was like witnessing a little miracle to me.

"For all your timidity, you are direct, lass," the Earl of Warwick said with a grudging admiration. He stopped and turned to face me. "Shall I in turn be direct with you?"

"Please do, sir." I nodded. "I would account it a very great favour if you would. If you've something to say, just say it, I always say—don't hide it under a bushel of pretty words so I have to dig and search for it."

"You might not think it so great a favour after you have heard what I have to say," he cautioned. "Shall I continue?" And at my nod he did. "Though he is my fifth son, Robert has always been my favourite, so I am of a mind to indulge him and let him have his way, even though I think it is the *wrong* way. And he wants you; he thinks and talks of nothing but you. I think he is making a grave mistake and will rue my generosity one day, when he finds that your fresh-faced rustic charm, plain speech, and earthy common sense are no match for the sophistication and wit of the highbred ladies of the court, as he inevitably will. Even so, I am inclined to let him have you. I had other plans—great plans—for Robert, but I have other sons, and if Robert would wed and bed a country squire's daughter and sink instead of rise in the world"—he shrugged and gave me a glance that was at once pitying and scornful—"so be it. But, I warn you, Mistress Amy, it will be *you* who will bear the blame and pay for it when Robert realises and repents his mistake.

Are you *sure* you want to do this? You'd fare far better as Robert's mistress than you ever will as his wife, my girl—I would bet the Crown jewels upon it. And if you're willing to trade the role of mistress for that of wife, you'll not find the Dudleys ungenerous—you and any bastards you bear will be well provided for, and I'm sure there'll be a husband for you someday, someone who will suit you far better than Robert."

"Thank you for your concern, Sir." I drew myself up stiffly. "But I love Robert, and he loves me, and whatever the future holds, we will face it together, as man and wife united, and none but God shall ever tear us apart!" I avowed, confident and proud. "I am sorry you find me lacking and do not think me a fit match for your son and worthy of the name of Dudley. But Robert loves me and thinks I am good enough to be his wife, to bear his name and be the mother of his *legitimately* born children, and that is good enough for me, with or without your approval. Now, if you will excuse me, I am needed in the dairy." I turned and, with my head held high, as if I were every bit as good as those haughty and imperious highborn court ladies, I walked with great dignity back into the dairy to help pour the milk into the great shallow pans to cool for cream, another of God's sweet little wonders.

I didn't show my fear, but inside I never stopped fretting and trembling, and even though I knew long before my wedding gown was finished that I did not carry Robert's child, I never told him, and he never asked. Maybe it didn't matter? Or maybe he was wise enough in the ways of women's bodies to know that his seed had not taken root inside me? But I couldn't bring myself to broach the subject. I feared that knowing that there was no babe to bind us might make him think again and reconsider and forsake me, and that I could not bear. Now—when it is far too late—I know that was wrong of me; I should have been honest and hoped for the best, trusted in God and Fate.

"And none but God shall ever tear us apart!" I was *so* confident and sure of myself at seventeen. I marvel at it now. The Amy I was then and need to be now is lost to me when I need her confidence, courage, and strength most of all. I spoke those words with such

utter certainty; I *never* for an instant doubted them. Each syllable rang true and clear, like a triumphal peal of church bells, in my head and heart. I trusted Robert and fully believed that the bow of love that bound us together would never be untied save by the hand of God when the hour came for one of us to die.

✑ 5 ✑

Amy Robsart Dudley

Syderstone Manor in Norfolk
June 4, 1550

The first time I saw Elizabeth Tudor was on my wedding day. June 4, 1550—that was the happiest day of my life. We celebrated our marriage in the clover-and-daisy-dotted meadow at Syderstone, with the breeze-caressed buttercups nodding their approval and the bluebells swaying as if they were indeed bells ringing with joy for us.

Despite the manor's crumbling, ramshackle appearance, the young King Edward and his court came to see us wed. We had benches and trestles set out to serve them fresh milk and Father's famous cider, and many dishes made with apples, just like our wonderful harvest feasts. And at the centre of it all was a great, towering, spiced apple cake nigh as tall as me, with nuts, raisins, and little chunks of apples baked into the batter, all covered with frothy waves of cream, dusted with cinnamon, and decorated with red, gold, and green marzipan apples. And some clever person from the royal kitchens, who must have been like a magician with confectionery, had made gilded candy lace that we could actually eat to adorn the cake that *exactly* matched the golden lace on my gown. Lace spun of sugar, what a *marvellous* thing indeed; I *never* even imagined that there could be such a thing!

I wanted everyone to have something. I did not want a soul to go away empty-handed that day. I wanted to share my happiness with them all, and for everyone to have a token to remember this day by, something that would make them smile every time they looked at it. And, though they were at a trestle table set far apart from our royal and highborn guests, there was a roasted pig with an apple in his mouth, apple cider, custard, tarts, and cake for the common folk. And my father personally gave each one a shiny new penny in a little blue green velvet pouch "the same colour as my Amy's eyes!" he boasted proudly of the specially dyed velvet. And everyone, highborn or low, was given a sprig of gilded rosemary tied with a blue silk ribbon as a wedding favour, and a new pin, which I gave out myself from a pincushion made to look like a pomegranate, the fruit of fertility. The men, as was the custom, wore these favours upon their hats, while the women pinned theirs onto their sleeves or bodices.

And there was another trestle table set up, draped in gold-fringed white linen, to display our wedding presents. There were gifts of gold and silver plate, all of it most ornate. Tall, weighty salt cellars in a variety of shapes like castles high on mountaintops, and one with a mermaid resting on a rock, dispassionately watching a sailor drown in the sea below her, drawn to his death by her song. Spoons with ornamental handles topped with animals, from the ordinary, everyday sort like rabbits, horses, and leaping fish, to fanciful beasts of legend such as unicorns and dragons, crests for both our families, including the Dudleys' bear and ragged staff, and also some with gilded acorns and oak leaves as Robert's personal emblem, and beautiful damsels with flowing hair, and a similar set with mermaids instead, and even a set topped with golden apples and another with silver sheep from my father. I don't think I ever saw so many spoons in my whole life! And there were all sorts of vessels made of beautifully enamelled and glazed pottery, so that our cupboards would house a rainbow. And fine Venetian glassware, including a set of jewel-coloured cups and bowls—ruby, emerald, amethyst, and sapphire—each with a silver cover and swirls of silver gilt painted upon the glass. And, my favourite of all the gifts, a complete table service made of Venetian Ice Glass. I had never heard of such a thing. I remember when I first opened the straw-stuffed crate, I gave a long and loud wail of dismay—I thought it all cracked and broken—until Robert laughed at me, hugged me, and kissed my cheek. "Everything is as it should be, my silly little chick; it is the fashion," he said, and he went on to explain how, as the glass was being blown, the glassmakers rolled it over cold water to produce cracks that made it look as though it were actually made of ice. I was simply *amazed* by it! And, after I understood, whenever I reached out to touch it, I half expected to find it cold and wet like ice just beginning to melt. I thought they were the cleverest, most beautiful glasses I had ever seen, and I could not wait to see them upon our table, to host my first grand banquet as a wife, with our table fully laden with a fine meal and all these beautiful things; already I was planning the menu in my dreams.

There were also gifts of linen for our household, cushions of velvet and damask, and rich fabrics for us to have made into clothing, gifts of jewellery, and costly and rare perfumes in ornately carved crystal bottles. There were even games, including beautifully inlaid chess, draughts, and backgammon sets, even one made entirely of crystal and silver, decks of beautifully painted playing cards, some embellished with real silver and gold paint, and, my personal favourite, a Fox and Geese game board with little ivory geese and a fox carved out of carnelian. And there were musical instruments— richly adorned virginals with ivory keys and painted panels, and lutes inlaid with mother-of-pearl—and pretty gilt and enamelled boxes to hold all manner of things like comfits, documents, jewellery, and playing cards. There were even a set of exquisitely carved crossbows, great and small, perfect for a lord and lady to hunt together, and a pair of beautiful trained falcons with a keeper to attend them—"a big, handsome, docile fellow trained to serve both a lord *and* a lady, if such is desired," the giver explained with a wink, though I wasn't sure why. Some gave us books filled with humorous or wise homilies about marriage, volumes of advice on being a good housewife, and venery, which Robert told me was a fancy word for hunting; there were books of Scripture and song, and even a beautifully embellished book writ in Italian that Robert whispered in my ear was filled with fun and bawdy stories that, if I were good and "buxom and bonair in bed and at board" as a bride should be, he would translate and read to me in bed at night to enhance our pleasure. Some of the guests even gave us Turkey carpets and tapestries; my favourite had a beautiful, golden-haired maiden petting a unicorn as he trustingly laid his noble head in her lap.

It was a truly *astounding* array; I had never expected even half so much, but the Dudleys were an important family—the power behind the throne, some might even go so far as to say—so many went to *great,* even extravagant, lengths to impress so that they might be remembered for the lavishness of their gifts, should they ever need a favour from the Dudleys someday.

And there were gifts from the royal family as well. King Edward sent us a life-sized portrait of himself to hang in a place of honour in our home and a big black-bound copy of his Book of Common Prayer. His elder sister, the pious Princess Mary, sent us a gold-fringed embroidered hanging of damned souls writhing in Hell, being tormented by flames and leering, pitchfork-wielding demons, to adorn our chapel. And the Princess Elizabeth sent us a cunning little clockwork device, a small gold and silver cart on wheels with pretty pink enamelled and mother-of-pearl roses, that, when wound, would travel the length of our table and, when a little tap was turned, would dribble rosewater for our guests to wash their fingers. I had never seen the like of it before, and, just like a child, I kept winding it again and again to watch it roll, until Robert laughed and bade me stop, else I wear it out before it ever had a chance to grace our table.

I walked across the meadow that day as a barefoot bride in a frothy, fanciful rendition of a milkmaid's garb, a gown that blended court elegance with country charm in creamy brocaded satin festooned with golden lace and embroidered all over with gilt butter-cups, with a dainty lace apron trimmed with silken ribbons and seed pearls. I wore my golden curls in a careless, carefree tumble cascading down my back, crowned with a wreath of buttercups, the customary gilded rosemary, and gold-lace butterflies whose wings moved ever so slightly in the breeze and shimmered with diamond dust, and long ribbon streamers trailing down my back. And I wore a heavy necklace of golden oak leaves and amber acorns that matched the betrothal ring on my finger, the one folk said contained a vein that ran to meet the heart, like a pair of lovers running to embrace and kiss one another. And in my hand I carried a great bouquet of buttercups, their stems tied together with gold ribbon and frothy white lace. Sweet little barefoot pageboys in white silk raiments with rainbows of long silken ribbons streaming from their sleeves ran alongside me, and little girls in white dresses, with wreaths of gilded rosemary and wildflowers crowning their free-flowing hair, carrying trays of golden honey cakes baked full of red currants, raisins, and nuts to share with our guests, and musicians in merry motley satin stitched together with gold capered and danced around me, serenading my every step.

Blissfully happy, I walked in a dream with pink clouds of love swirling round my head. I was *so* happy, so light of step, I felt as if I were floating, my feet never once touched the ground. I can't even remember the green grass tickling my toes that day, the way it always did, or the hard-packed earth beneath my soles, or even the cool, smooth wood and stone floors inside the manor house; I have not one single memory of feeling solid ground beneath my feet that entire day.

I went out amongst our guests with a gilded wooden yoke about my shoulders, carved with cherubs, garlands of flowers, and frol-icking sheep and goats, from which hung two gilded pails, and served them delicious cold milk from our dairy. And Pirto, smiling as proudly as if she were my own mother in her new spring green damask gown, followed alongside me with a big gilded tray of spe-cially made clay cups fashioned and painted to look just like a woman's full, bountiful breast. These were a souvenir, a special wedding favour, for our noble guests to take home with them and keep to remember this day by, and to wish us all luck, happiness, and fertility. Some years ago, my father had met a man, a scholar of ancient lore, at a wool fair who had told him a story about cups moulded from the perfect breasts of Helen of Troy. The tale caught Father's fancy, and he never forgot it and vowed that I should have such cups made for my wedding day, and I knew it pleased him much to see his promise fulfilled. Though some seemed startled and even embarrassed when presented with these most unusual cups, I didn't care; the smile on Father's face was worth more than all the cups in the world to me.

I served the King first, as he was the guest of honour, though when I knelt before him with a tentative smile, timidly offering up milk in one of the special cups to him, he never once smiled. Instead, he sat there stiff-backed in his bower of white roses, evergreen boughs, and softly fluttering gold lace and creamy satin bows and streamers, glowering at me, with his mouth a firm, straight-across line, his eyes as hard as blue-veined marble, and his arms folded across the chest of his cream and gold doublet as if he were impatient to have done with all this and take his leave. He seemed so solemn and stern for a boy of twelve, as if he did not even know what the word *fun* meant. He should have been romping and running, playing, bobbing for apples, and tossing them about with boys of his own age, jumping and tumbling in the hay, or going fishing and dangling his bare toes in the river, not sitting there all bitter and grim as a gouty old grandfather who has outlived all life's pleasures and everyone he ever held dear. I fully expected the hair beneath his cream and gold plumed cap to be grey instead of ruddy-fair; it was as though he had been born old, and God had not blessed him with the gift of good humour.

Quaking with fear that I had unknowingly done something to offend him, I backed away, with tears brimming in my eyes, but Robert hugged me tightly against his elaborate oak leaf, acorn, ivy, and yellow gillyflower embroidered chest, and kissed my cheek and told me not to be afraid, such was just Edward's way.

"He may be King of England, but that doesn't stop him from being a self-righteous little prig, and as cold as the Devil's prick," he whispered in my ear, giving the lobe a playful little nibble that made my knees tremble unseen beneath my skirts. "And I, for one—and the *most* important one, if I do say so myself—*love* my buttercup bride. And it's just as well that Edward isn't impressed, for I will have no man for my rival, not even a king. Remember that, Lady Dudley, when I take you to court and you are formally presented, and you will do just fine; you'll carry yourself as proudly as the grandest lady, knowing that you are *all* mine."

At his words, my face lit up with joy, and I threw my arms around his neck, standing up, straining on my tippy-toes, and covered his face with kisses. I was *so* eager to be alone with him! Even though the revelry had scarcely begun, the King was not the only one to want it over and done; I wanted to be with my husband in the curtained privacy of our bridal bed with all our finery stripped away, leaving only warm, naked skin and hands and lips eager to explore, caress, and kiss. But duty beckoned, and I must resume serving the milk and meeting and making welcome our guests, so many of whom were complete strangers to me. And I fear I gave offence to many, for, as I did not know them even by their lofty names, they seemed annoyed by the blankness in my eyes, my tentative, uncertain smiles, and my clumsy, faltering attempts to make conversation with them. But they were all smiles for Robert, and he moved amongst them with the utmost confidence and easy grace. I will have to do better, I told myself sternly. I must not disappoint him; I must school myself and become the woman Lady Dudley *should* be, a worthy consort for my husband, not a pig-ignorant Norfolk squire's daughter he will always be ashamed of.

I was serving the milk when I first saw *her*. I instantly froze, stricken by that horrible realisation one feels when one has accidentally trod upon a serpent hidden in the grass, at first sight of that tall, taper-slim woman, as white as the pearls around her throat, her vivid scarlet hair the only spot of colour about her. Her dark eyes seemed to hammer nails into me, and I felt my heart jolt inside my breast. She was so cool, so supremely regal and poised, I shivered, and for a moment I think I actually believed she had the power to call down rain to ruin my wedding day and banish the golden sunshine that warmed this happy day and shone down so brightly upon me. I was afraid the milk in my gilded pails would curdle beneath her gaze. I couldn't rightly tell if she hated me or if she just envied me.

Of course I knew who she was—the Princess Elizabeth. I'd heard titbits of tattle about her, that she was fresh from a scandal, a frolic with her stepfather, the Lord Admiral Sir Thomas Seymour, that went too far and led to their both being disgraced and the Admiral losing his head on Tower Hill, leaving Elizabeth with a besmirched reputation that she tried to whitewash by wearing virgin-white gowns dripping with pearls and living a quiet life. All around me people whispered behind their hands and darted swift glances at her stomach. Though it was as flat as a board beneath the tightly-laced white satin stomacher, rumours had long been rife that she had been with child by the Lord Admiral; some even said it had been born, delivered by a midwife brought blindfolded into her lying-in chamber, and foully murdered by being thrown alive, kicking and wailing, into a fireplace. She seemed so brittle and hard, tense and wary, that I couldn't believe the rumours were true and that she had ever cast caution and decorum to the winds and let herself go with a man, or that she had ever loved Tom Seymour, or anyone at all. She seemed entirely too cold, frozen too solid, to ever be melted by the flames of passion. That flaming red hair was deceptive; I felt certain there was a core of solid ice and steel inside Elizabeth.

I forced myself to approach and offer her a cup of milk. She refused it with a wave of her hand, but when I started to back away, she reached out and took my face between her cold, long-fingered white hands and stared at me as if she meant to suck out my soul with her eyes, like a cat on a baby's chest, stealing its breath as it lay sleeping. She studied me so intently, searching my face, but I don't know what she was looking for. She never said one word to me. And then, just as suddenly, she released me and turned away to converse with a plump, grey-haired little dumpling of a woman who waddled like a duck when she walked and whom the Princess called Kat—that must have been her governess, who had also been implicated in the Seymour scandal. And I was left standing there shivering as though a goose had just walked over my grave. She scared me, though I was at a loss to explain why, and had I tried, I know I would have been thought quite silly.

Later on while we all sat merry with our tankards and ate our fill of apple cake, the men decided to have some sport. There was to be a joust in which they sought not to unhorse each other but to impale upon the sharpened tip of a spear a goose with a lacy gold bow tied about her neck. When I realised what they were about, I burst into tears; I wanted no blood spilled upon my wedding day, and I ran out amongst the men, already mounted on their horses, and caught the goose up in a protective embrace, hugging her tightly against my breast. I would not release her until Father himself came and gently took her from me, dried my tears, and swore the goose would not be harmed but would live out her natural life unharmed, pampered like a beloved pet. Then he called for the musicians to play, and for us to have dancing instead, even as the men still grumbled and lamented their spoiled sport, ruined by a silly, soft-hearted girl who would shed a bucket of tears over a plump goose that cried out for roasting. But Robert dismounted and drew me closely against his chest, kissed me, and declared he loved me all the more for it. "No goose-down pillow is softer than my Amy's heart," he said, and later, when he engaged an artist to paint a portrait of me in my wedding gown, he ordered the beribboned goose painted in, standing beside me and eating from my hand.

And then, at long last, as the sun was sinking like a great orange too heavy for the sky to hold up any longer, the time came to put the bridal couple to bed. Amidst much bawdy jesting and singing and showers of flowers, sweetmeats, and herbs, my stepbrother John Appleyard and my dear old swain, Ned Flowerdew, swept me up onto their shoulders, as two of Robert's brothers, John and Ambrose, did the same to him and, in a torchlit procession, carried us inside the manor. At the top of the stairs, I untied the ribbons that bound the stems of my bouquet of buttercups and flung them high into the air, laughing delightedly, as hands reached up to catch them. I only wished there were enough; I wanted everyone to have a flower. Then they carried us to our bridal chamber, where, on opposite sides of the room, modestly shielded by guests of the proper gender, we were divested of our wedding finery.

After they had stripped me bare, a bevy of giggling girls and smiling matrons stood facing one another in two rows alongside the bed and formed themselves into a human passageway, lifting their arms and joining hands to create an arched roof. And I, blushing rose-red and hugging my arms over my jiggling breasts, ran naked, clad only in my unbound hair and crown of buttercups, through the tunnel they made for me and leapt under the covers to join Robert, whose friends had already performed the same service for him. I felt the warmth of his naked thigh press mine as we leaned to kiss; then I pulled the covers up high, clutching them tightly about me as everyone clapped and cheered and raised their cups to drink one last toast to us.

We drank a loving cup, a special brew of warm red wine mixed with milk, egg yolks, sugar, and spices, to give us "strength and vigour for the night's passionate exertions", those about us teased, and everyone applauded when we had drained it to the dregs. And then they drew the bed-curtains and left us alone. But just before the curtains closed at the foot of the bed, I caught a glimpse of the Princess Elizabeth watching us, her dark eyes narrowed and intent, her long, slender white fingers twirling a buttercup by its stem. And again I shivered as if I could feel those very fingers closing murderously around my neck, squeezing the life out of me.

I turned to Robert to seek refuge in his warmth and found him staring straight at her, until she dropped the buttercup and, with an abrupt and angry tug, jerked the curtains shut, then slammed the door behind her in such a way that the sound must have rung throughout the manor. She was like a human cannon packed with gunpowder, and the tiniest spark would make her explode, and I was deathly afraid that somehow I was that spark. I wanted to talk to Robert about it, to ask him why it should be so—what had I done?—but some inner instinct warned me to keep silent, and I was too afraid to defy it.

I slipped my arms about Robert's neck and laid my head upon his shoulder, but I found his body rock-hard and tense. The silence that had so suddenly replaced the merry, good-natured ribaldry hung heavy and awkward about us, and I felt so afraid, though for the life of me I couldn't explain why. I felt Robert's hands upon my waist, and I started to relax and allow a smile to form upon my lips, but it died midway as he put me from him, wrenched open the curtains, and leapt from the bed. Naked, he stalked across the room and, not even bothering to pour it into a goblet first, drank long and deeply from the flagon of wine that had been left for us. I grew alarmed as I watched a ribbon of red wine dribble down his chest, like a crimson snake winding its way through black grass, yet still he drank as if his thirst could never be quenched. Then, just as suddenly, he flung the flagon into the fireplace, where it shattered, and, like a lion attacking a trembling and helpless lamb, sprang at me from the foot of the bed and pinned me flat beneath him, grabbing my wrists, leaving bruises where his fingers pressed, as he held my arms above my head.

I cried out when I felt his savage thrust. He was rougher with me than he had ever been before and ignored me when I begged him to be gentler, as he had been when we coupled in our bed of buttercups. I knew he *must* be angry with me, but I didn't know why; I also knew that asking would only make it worse.

Later, when I lay sobbing, huddled and hugging my pillow with my back to him, he kissed my shoulders and stroked my hair and spoke softly, blaming it all upon the wine, but I knew it was something more than that, and I felt certain it had to do with Elizabeth.

He coaxed me to sit up, saying he had a present for me. To spare me any embarrassment upon the morrow, when all would expect to see the sheet we had coupled upon hung up to proudly display the dried red rose petal stain of my vanquished maidenhood, he took his jewel-hilted dagger and made a tiny cut to his chest, right over his heart, so that it would be his heart's blood masquerading as my maiden's blood that stained our sheets and saved me from dishonour. For the rest of his life he would bear a little scar there, just over his heart, that would be our secret that only we two, husband and wife, would know; that tiny raised white line upon the bronzed beauty of his chest that my tongue would seek out so many times to tease and trace would be a precious remembrance of our wedding night. And then he took me in his arms again and loved me so gently that I cried. And I fell asleep after with my head upon his chest, listening to his heart beat, like a lullaby, singing me to sleep.

The next morning while I was still asleep, my husband rose early to hunt. I lay abed for a long time, lazily savouring the fact that I was now a married woman, a wife, and, God willing, soon to be a mother, caressing my little round belly and wondering if it had already become a warm nest for our baby to grow in. When I rose, I noticed that my husband had left our chamber in some disarray; clothing lay strewn about the floor and protruding from beneath the lid of his big oak travelling chest, carved with his initials and coat-of-arms, the Dudleys' great bear and ragged staff, and beautifully bordered with acorns and oak leaves. I instantly set about tidying it, gathering up garments from the floor, and, observing the crumpled and wadded disarray inside, I scooped everything out of the chest, thinking to do my duty as a wife and put it all right, everything perfectly placed and folded, all pristine, perfect, and neat, and later amongst the folds I would put little bags of sweet-smelling herbs tied with blue silk ribbons, as that was my husband's favourite colour. As I lifted out the last linen shirt, something clattered against the bottom—a small rectangle-shaped portrait framed in black enamel and pearls.

I instantly recognised the haughty and imperious young woman who stared back at me from beneath the feathered brim of her round, pearl-studded black velvet hat, with her hair caught up like a pair of plump, fresh-baked buns on each side of her head protruding from a caul of pearls. It was the Princess Elizabeth in a black velvet riding habit worked with gold embroidery all down the front and around the hems, with its tight, close-fitting sleeves studded with an elaborate lattice pattern of pearls. But what struck me most was her hand murderously clutching her gloves as if they were a neck she wished to break.

I remembered the look that had passed between her and Robert last night as she stood at the foot of our marriage bed and began to tremble violently as tears overflowed my eyes. Feeling of a sudden ill, I dropped the portrait back into the chest as if it burned me and bunched up all the clothes my arms could hold and crammed them back inside the chest and slammed the lid shut. Perhaps I should have confronted Robert when he came back, asked or said something, but every time I tried, fear tied my tongue in knots, and the words just would not come out. I suppose I was afraid that knowing would be even worse than not knowing. But every time I glanced at that chest, knowing that portrait was hidden away inside it, I felt a surge of blind terror that made the breath catch in my throat and my vision dim and at the same time dance with jewel-coloured sparks like gems sewn on black velvet. I didn't know then that that flame-haired princess would ignite such a blaze of passion and ambition in my husband's soul that it would reduce all my hopes and dreams to ashes.

Amy Robsart Dudley

Cumnor Place, Berkshire, near Oxford
Sunday, September 8, 1560

As hot tears roll down my face, I reach for the medicine bottle and take another calming sip. What a *strange* sensation it brings! As if I were floating above myself, above the pain, like the notes of a song hovering above just-plucked and still-vibrating lute strings. I have the most peculiar feeling of being outside myself, and behind myself, as if each time I move, I have to pause and wait a moment for my body to catch up with my soul. Or is it the other way around, and my mind that must rush to catch up with my body? What a curious notion! I am filled with the oddest fancies! I can't help but laugh, even though it makes me feel as if Death were playing my ribs like the ivory keys of a virginal, but the medicine numbs it, and there is that strange delaying sensation; even though Death's fingers strike the keys, the sound of the notes lags behind a moment or two. I take another sip, and the chords of pain are muted even more, as if I have run too far away to hear them as more than a distant, wind-borne melody. The pain is my fool now, and I am not the fool of my pain. I giggle and take another sip of that amber liquid, and now I don't even mind the bitter taste that burns my throat as it courses down; I *welcome* it as if it were my saviour. Salvation in a bottle, the nostrum peddlers should call this magic brew! And after another sip I lie back on my bed, close my eyes, and let my mind wander where it will . . .

When last I visited the crumbling, overgrown ruins of Syderstone, though they were no longer my own, I put on my wedding gown and went out, barefoot, with my hair all a-tumble down my back, and walked across the meadow, just as I had on my wedding day, picking myself a bouquet of buttercups as I went. What a strange sight the sheep must have thought me as they fled baa-ing before me, pausing oft to look back and stare before they fell to munching clover and thistles again. I know it sounds silly, but I wanted to see what it would be like, how it would feel, to see if by wearing my wedding gown again I could magically recapture even a *little* of the joy of that day, as if an echo of it might linger, hovering in the air like a butterfly, and I could run after it and catch it in my hands. I am a silly, fanciful creature, I know. And the dress made no difference at all. Wearing it again brought me only sorrow; it had become a symbol of tarnished hopes and dead and broken dreams that could never be revived or repaired. Nothing turned out the way I thought it would. I perched upon the old, moss-festooned stone where the shepherd sometimes sat and buried my face in my hands and wept. Both my parents were gone to their graves, and my stepbrothers and sisters all had their own busy lives, with homes and families of their own and no time or care to spare for me and my troubles. The adored darling, the spoiled beloved, now had nothing. There was no one to love and adore her any more, not even a home to call her own, she had lost her highborn husband to the Queen, and cancer was slowly stealing her life away.

The dress remained the same, but the woman who wore it had changed; it now hung loose upon my frame, and every dream that eager, smiling, happy, young bride had had that day when she walked across the meadow to serve milk to her guests in cups shaped like breasts had come to nothing or gone horribly, nightmarishly wrong. I wanted to run backward, racing, hurtling, across time, and catch hold of that hopeful young girl on the threshold of the church, draped with evergreen boughs and bows and ribbons of gold and cream, and *beg* her not to marry Robert Dudley. To slap and shake some sense into her if I must, and let her gaze fill upon me and know what her life would become if she persisted. I would even tear open my bodice and let her see the ravages of this disease, the ugly, seeping wound left by the worm of sorrow burrowing deeply into my breast, for I truly believe my sadness opened the door to let this disease into my life. But I knew that, even if I could, that confident, headstrong seventeen-year-old I used to be would merely laugh in my face, toss her blond curls, and shrug off my urgently grasping hands, along with my dire warnings of doom and gloom, and tell me that none but God would ever tear her and her beloved Robert apart. She would turn her back on me and, with her head held high, walk proudly up to the altar and take his hand in marriage, just as she did when her wise old father warned her just before she passed through the arched portal beneath the evergreen boughs, "First love is rarely evergreen love, my dear." The Amy I used to be would *never* have listened to the Amy I am now. It's folly to even think so.

❧ 7 ❧

Amy Robsart Dudley

Hemsby-by-the-Sea, near Great Yarmouth
June 1550

We honeymooned at Hemsby Castle, by the sea. That quaint sandy-gold stone box hugged by ardent ivy, rugged, weathered yellow stones and green vines clinging together like lovers, was my new father-in-law's gift to us, the deed presented on our wedding day in a pretty gold, enamelled, and jewelled box fashioned to look exactly like the seaside castle. He also gave us lands that had once belonged to the priory of Coxford, where we might build a house someday, but these I would never see; at some point Robert sold them without telling me.

Hemsby sat high on the cliffs near Great Yarmouth, overlooking the sea, with a long, spiralling, sandy lane lined with stones leading down to the beach, which Robert and I would race down nigh every day to splash and play and love each other in the chilly, salty surf. He loved to tickle me; his fingers would dance nimbly over my belly, roving down to my sex, making me gasp, giggle, and writhe in pure delight.

I could see the grey sea, the rolling waves crested in frothy white, like feisty old dowagers in lacy caps, from our bedchamber window. I used to sit and watch it, lost in a dream, for hours, with Robert's love like a shawl draped about my shoulders to keep me warm. There was even a seagull who learned to come to the window whenever he saw me there to be fed from my hand, and I always saved titbits from our table for him. Robert laughed and said the gull was "clearly a woman's bird", as it struck a haughty stance and would not deign to accept even the most tempting morsels from Robert's hand. Which was strange, as animals and children alike always adored Robert; he was a *wonder* with horses and seemed to know, as if he were one himself, what they were thinking and feeling and, when affrighted, what they were scared of and how best to soothe them. Yet my seagull turned up his beak and would have nothing to do with Robert.

I remember the day we arrived, Robert bade the servants, who followed with our luggage in a cart, to see to everything and, with me in the saddle before him, nestled back against his chest, galloped down to the beach. He swung himself from the saddle, lifted me down, slapped the horse's rump and left it free to run, and stripped off his clothes, letting them fall where they would, and plunged headfirst into the sea.

I stood and watched him, my heart beating wild and fast, as if I lived only to love and be loved by him, and this was what I had been made for. Then he stood, laughing, as he shook the salty spray from his black curls, and, with water dripping down his hard, handsome, sun-bronzed body in salty rivulets, his erect cock bobbing against its nest of short, wiry black curls, he came towards me with a determined look in his dark eyes. In that moment he was a man who knew *exactly* what he wanted—*me*!

I giggled and began to run, but he caught my sleeve, spun me round, quickly unfastened the gold-braid frogs, eased the russet velvet jacket from my shoulders, and let the wind snatch it from his fingers. And then, with salty kisses up and down my throat, he removed my shirt of fine white linen, laughing as the breeze caught it and sent it skipping and billowing down the beach. Had it been dark, any who chanced to see might have thought it a ghost and started a tale about a restless spirit roaming the shore in search of a lost love. As he led me down to the sea, Robert left my leather stays, russet velvet skirt, and petticoats lying where they fell, laughing as my sheer cobweb lawn shift was caught up and carried away by the wind like a dancing cloud.

He laid me down where I could hear the sea in my ear—"like a pink seashell," Robert whispered as his warm lips grazed and nibbled the lobe—and he made love to me, matching me smile for smile, laugh for laugh, as I squealed in surprised delight at the feel of the cool surf caressing my naked skin, and the mad, wanton feel of making love on a beach wearing nothing but my black wool stockings and brown leather riding boots. I laughed when I lifted my legs to wrap tightly around him and heard the golden buckles on my boots jingle as if they were also laughing from the wild and wanton thrill of it all. I *loved* this carefree, wild, raw, mad feeling of love and lust mingling on the sandy shore, the warmth of our passionately coupling bodies and the cold kiss of the sea, and the freedom to forget everything and just be us—Robert and Amy, a man and a woman, husband and wife, in love.

Afterwards, as we lay entwined in the wet sand, being caressed by the cold waves and salty breeze, with my wet hair clinging to us like golden seaweed, Robert told me that the Goddess of Love, Aphrodite, had been born from the surf, and, perhaps, he said, gently kissing my lips, our child would be too, born of the love we had just made, clinging together in the cold, salty surf.

Those were such happy days, perhaps the happiest days of our marriage and my life. I remember us walking hand-in-hand upon the beach, the wind whipping and tugging my hair and skirts in such a frenzy that I feared I would be ripped bald and bare-skinned by those invisible grasping fingers, but I was so happy the whole time, I never stopped smiling, and I laughed more then than I ever did in my whole life.

We collected pretty shells to adorn our mantel, and Robert promised he would order a cabinet of glass made to display them in. He even made a sketch of it, with notes alongside describing the pretty gilded woodwork with blue, green, and white enamelled waves and pink enamelled seashells, and bare-breasted mermaids with "harvest gold hair" just like mine. And someday, he said, we would sit together and tell our children about the shells we had collected. Every year, he promised, we would go back to Hemsby for another seaside honeymoon and collect more shells to put inside our cabinet. Oh, how I dreamed of those days to come, when we would sit with our children, the babies on our laps and the older ones clustered around us, and see their eager little hands carefully cradling the shells, their eyes bright and open wide with wonderment at the beauty of God's gifts from the sea that would always serve as a reminder of the strange little creatures that had once made their home inside them.

We pretended we were castaways, stranded on a deserted island, inhabited only by the two of us, and we swam and ran naked, wild and free, like savages, up and down the beach, and fell down and coupled where we pleased. And at night we cooked our meals of fish and oysters over a fire Robert built with driftwood while we huddled together, letting the fire and each other's nakedness warm us against the deliciously cool sea air. He found a pearl in one of the oysters he gathered—a big, funny-shaped, silvery grey and white thing, like a thumb with a swollen tip. "Like a fellow who has cut his thumb with a knife while trying to pry open an oyster shell," Robert quipped, sucking his own injured thumb. Despite its peculiar shape, I *loved* it, and Robert would later have it cunningly set so I could wear it either as a pendant or a ring.

And every day, before we left the beach and made our way up the winding path back to the castle, meandering, watching the stars come out, first we stood on the golden sand, Robert behind me, his arms about me, and watched the sun set, like a ball of fire sinking slowly into the sea.

Robert carved horses and mermaids out of driftwood, and even a baby and a cradle for it, and we argued playfully about whether the driftwood baby was a boy or a girl until Robert carved another with a prominent but petite phallus that made us both roll in the sand and howl with laughter until my husband silenced me by offering me his own member to suckle like a greedy infant, kneeling there stark naked in the sand with my hair whipping wild about me, tugged by the wind as if it too would be my lover and sought to woo me away from Robert, but he was *everything* I ever dreamed of or wanted, and the only one for me.

One day when the tide left a special gift for us, a flat pebble, nigh heart-shaped and the deep brown red of dried blood, worn smooth by the sea's caresses, he carved our names, encircled by a heart and bound by a lovers' knot, upon it and swore that we would keep it always. We would use it as a paperweight, he decided, and keep it on our desk, and whenever one of us sat down to write letters or with the accounts ledger we would always have this memento right there to make us smile at the blissful memories it conjured of the two of us frolicking and loving on the beach at Hemsby.

And once, to my delight, using a stick he found lying on the beach, Robert fought a duel with an irate blue green crab that did an angry dance, clacking its claws in the air like a Spanish dancer's castanets. I laughed until tears rolled down my face and my sides ached as I clung to my beloved's arm, the two of us leaping back as one as the crab advanced, snapping its pincers at our bare toes. Robert wanted to cook and eat it, but I implored him, "No, let it live," and Robert kissed me and gave in. Back then, he still loved his "tenderhearted buttercup bride who pleads for the lives of geese and crabs".

❧ 8 ❧

Amy Robsart Dudley

Cumnor Place, Berkshire, near Oxford
Sunday, September 8, 1560

I have no illusions now that, if I were to do the same today, I wouldn't end up alone, crying in the bedroom all night, and the crab would be flung into a pot of boiling water, then onto Robert's plate. He would have no compassion, no tenderness, no mercy for either of us.

It seems a whole lifetime ago now, as if I am a withered and ancient crone looking back on the fond days of her girlhood, not a mere ten years. It breaks my heart all over again to look back over the years and see it all gone so wrong, all the honey sweetness of our love turned to vile and sour vinegar, and so soon; I often marvel at how little a time our love—the time when we were *both* in love—lasted.

Hemsby seems little more than a dream now, a fairy tale, a magical time like King Arthur's Camelot; all that is left of it now are memories and the ornamental box the deed was gifted to us in. All the pretty shells were packed away in a box; I've moved so often since, I don't know where they are now—like our love, they got lost along the way. As for the castle itself, Robert sold it, to pay off his gambling debts, or buy gifts for Elizabeth, or help pay her expenses when she was in disfavour, or perhaps to pay his tailor when he declared he would not make another garment for Robert until the bill was settled, or buy yet more horses; the money came and went *so* fast, it was there and gone again, like a flash of silver white lightning, vivid and bright against the night sky. My mind was never quick enough to keep up with it and follow where it went. And that was the way Robert liked it; he preferred that on this subject my mind should always remain a darkened muddle, a dingy mud puddle rather than a crystal clear spring. "You have your pretties and a roof over your head, my angel," he would say, kissing my cheek. "Best to leave it at that; I have men in my pay to balance the books and dole out the coins. No need for *you* to spend your days squinting and wrinkling your pretty brow over the ledgers when you could be embroidering roses on the hems of your petticoats instead. And you *know* how much I like that, knowing that I am the only man to see them, and these rosy buds," he would add, then bend his head to nuzzle and kiss my nipples and fly all facts and figures right out of my head on passion's wings.

✤ 9 ✤

Amy Robsart Dudley

Hemsby-by-the-Sea, near Great Yarmouth
Summer's End, 1550

And then the day came—as I knew it must—when he had to go, back to London and the court, and leave me. I begged him on my knees to take me with him, even though the thought of it scared me sick. I clung to him and trembled and wept. But Robert said that since the King was still in his minority and too young for marriage, the presence of women was frowned upon. Men were not encouraged to bring their wives and daughters to court except to celebrate holidays and other festive occasions; not even the King's sisters were allowed to lodge there except for during their brief and rare visits. But he promised he would send for me soon, for a brief visit, to have me presented, and I must see to having a new gown made, so that when he summoned me, there would be no delay over feminine fripperies. And this would give me something to do, Robert said, something fun and diverting, for he knew how I delighted in pretty clothes. It would give me something to look forward to and would help ease my loneliness and the sharp pain of missing him.

I didn't know it then, but it was a sign of things to come, the first stitch in a pattern, and the first of many such absences when I would be left alone with only servants or strangers to keep me company. It would be my fate to spend most of my marriage parted from and pining for my husband, to wait and want in vain.

Before he left me, he bade an artist come and capture my likeness. Robert wanted a miniature to wear over his heart and lay on the table beside his bed every night so that my face would be the first thing he saw upon awaking and the last he gazed upon when he put out the candle and closed his eyes at night. He would order the frame set with a bail at the top so he could wear it on a ribbon or a chain about his neck while he went about his business, and I could know that, in this way, I was always with him. Touched by his words, spoken as we prepared for bed, I took some of my hair ribbons from the carved wooden box upon my dressing table and sat down by the fire to braid them to make a satin chain for him.

"Buttercup yellow for my favourite flower, and the bed of buttercups by the river where we first made love, spring green for the grass beneath us, and blue for the sky above us," I said.

Robert went to my dressing table and selected another ribbon and, with a kiss, handed it to me. "And pink for these two rosebuds I love to caress and kiss so much and watch as they bloom beneath my fingers and lips from the palest pink to the rosiest," he said, reaching down to caress my nipples through the sheer linen of my shift. And then the satin braid fell forgotten to the floor, to be finished on the morrow, as he knelt before me and drew me down to make love on the hearth.

Much to my surprise, the artist was a *woman*!—a bright-eyed, merry little Flemish woman who wore her flaxen hair in an intricate pattern of lacquered and beribboned braids that made my eyes dizzy trying to follow and work out where they ended and began. I was *astounded*; I had been expecting a man. I know it sounds silly, but I did not know there was such a thing as a female artist. I thought all artists were men, as though one must possess a phallus to wield a paintbrush.

Tears sprang to my eyes as Robert chided me on my lack of manners, for "behaving like a gape-jawed peasant", as he stepped past me to greet our guest, gallantly bowing over her hand and apologising for his wife's "conspicuous lack of manners", assuring her that "we are not *all* country bumpkins beneath this roof".

But she laughed and smiled good-naturedly. Gently, she put her hand under my chin and closed my mouth.

"This is far too pretty a jaw to risk bruising by letting it hit the floor. Nor would you like to swallow a fly—a candy would be sweeter," she said in her charmingly accented English. And, just as if I were indeed a child, she opened a pretty comfit box that hung from a braided cord at her waist and popped a honeyed sweetmeat into my mouth, then showed me the miniature of her little son, Tobias, which she had painted on the lid.

Her name was Lavinia Teerlinc, and she specialised in miniature portraits, which she painted with the most delicate little brushes I had ever seen. Watching her dainty hands expertly wield them made my own hands seem as big and clumsy as bear claws. I was *fascinated* to hear her tell of her work, the techniques she had learned from her father, and the pigments she ground and mixed herself. There was a costly but beautiful blue made from lapis lazuli that she liked to use as the background for all her portraits, "as a sort of signature without words," she explained, a deep, vibrant green derived from crushed malachite, and a red that came from ground insects that also produced the cochineal the court ladies liked to rouge their cheeks with. She showed me the long string of beads of malachite and lapis she always kept somewhere about her person, so that should she find herself in desperate need of either the precious blue or exquisite green, she would simply remove and grind and mix some of the beads to produce the desired colour.

I thought it all such a breathtaking marvel, and I spent hours poring over the sketches and painted miniatures, both complete and in progress, that she had brought along with her, asking questions about them, and how the colours were made and the particular shades achieved, and about the people whose likenesses had been captured by her gifted hands and elfin brushes. I'm sure I must have made quite a pest of myself asking so many questions, but she smiled and assured me that this was not so, and she hoped her son would evince the same curiosity and enthusiasm when he was old enough.

I was as nervous as could be about having my picture painted, but Lavinia put me right at ease, telling me stories as I sat for her about her life and travels and all the people she had met and painted along the way. She told me the story of how she had left her home in Belgium and come to England, after Hans Holbein died and left the Tudor court bereft of his brilliance, to become "the paintress" to His Majesty King Henry VIII at "the stupendous sum of £40 per annum. More than even the great Holbein himself was paid!"

The "regal mountain", as she called King Henry, who had grown quite bloated and fat in his later years, had doted upon his new court painter and called her his "Flemish Fairy" because she and her work were so dainty, exquisite, and magical. He had told her more than once that if he were not so old and his legs not so bad, he would have her sit upon his knee.

She had painted all his children, from the precious heir Edward, whom the King called his "golden boy" and beamed like the sun upon, to the pious and dour Catholic spinster Mary, and the vibrant, flame-haired Elizabeth, whom Lavinia clearly liked best from the way her face lit up when she spoke of her. "That one, she will be the light of the world, I predict," Lavinia declared. "I would bet my last paintbrush upon it!" From her descriptions, I discovered that she had painted the portrait of the Princess my husband kept hidden inside his trunk, buried beneath his linen shirts.

"At the risk of speaking treason," Lavinia confided, "she is King Harry's *true* heir, *not* the boy; if he were cloven instead of crested between his legs, no one would think that"—she snapped her fingers—"of him; a cock does not a great monarch make!" She had even painted all three of the King's nieces, the Grey sisters: woebegone Lady Jane, whose books were her only pleasure, a quiet little mouse who turned into a fierce lion at the mention of the Protestant religion; pert, pretty flirt Katherine, whose eyes danced and skirts swayed and sashayed at the sight of anything in breeches, eager to make men's hearts her baubles; and, though she had neither been asked nor paid to do so, little Mary, the hunchbacked dwarf who was kept hidden away as an embarrassment by her ashamed and angry parents. Lavinia had painted her as a kindness, so the little girl would not feel left out. "Little things can be pretty too," she had said as she handed the child her miniature and been rewarded with the rare, fleeting ghost of a smile from little Lady Mary Grey. And she had even sketched a design for a dress that draped and flowed in back to make the hump that disfigured the little girl's spine appear less noticeable, telling her, "When you have new dresses made, show this to your dressmaker and tell her to make the back just so. Perhaps the dark purple of a plum in velvet?" she suggested, which would be both "regal and flattering" to the fair-haired child.

She painted first a miniature, since time was pressing and Robert wanted to take my likeness away with him.

I chose a sombre but fashionable gown of glossy satin that appeared in some lights black and in others the deepest, darkest blue. It had a square bodice edged with a wide band of thick, raised gold embroidery that bared my shoulders and showed just a hint of my cobweb lawn shift bordered with a row of tiny black embroidered gillyflowers. My satin under-sleeves and petticoat were the colour of cream, trimmed with a rich froth of golden lace and embroidered all over with gilt buttercups. Though neither sleeves nor skirts would show in the miniature, it made me feel good to wear them, as they reminded me of my wedding gown, which I would soon don again for a full-length portrait.

Around my neck I doubled a long, sparkling strand of deep blue sapphire and diamond blossoms set in gold that my father had bought me on a long-ago trip to London, the one and only time I had been there, when I was five years old. And upon my bodice I pinned the brooch he had also bought for me that day, despite my mother's purse-lipped disapproval, when I had taken a fancy to it. It was such a curious thing, an ornate textured gold circle, rather like an antique coin or a round shield perhaps, set with a carved black onyx head of Julius Caesar with his prominent nose and laurel-crowned brow in profile. It was still a great favourite of mine, and I wore it often. As I prepared for my portrait, I used the brooch to pin a spray of yellow gillyflowers, the emblem of marriage and fidelity, and some oak leaves and a cluster of acorns to my bodice, beautifully framing the brooch. Even if my name were never put upon it, I wanted everyone who beheld my likeness to know when they saw those oak leaves, acorns, and gillyflowers that I belonged to Robert and would love him, loyal and true, heart, body, and soul, until the day I died and, if God were willing, for all eternity afterwards.

I wanted everyone who thought Robert had married beneath him to see that I could hold my own against all those lofty, elegant, highborn ladies of the court, that the squire's daughter could pose for a portrait every bit as good as theirs. And if mine were ever mixed amongst theirs and a stranger from a foreign land asked to pick which one did not belong, he would not single me out like a leper.

Lavinia came into my room as I was dressing. When she saw me with my hair down, she pleaded with me to leave it so, so taken was she by the cascade of harvest gold curls rippling down to my hips. But I was stubborn and said no and had Pirto part it down the centre and braid and pin it up smooth and tight, as if I were daring even one tiny curl to escape, and fasten over it a white satin French hood edged in gold braid with a long black silk veil in back. I was a wife now and proud of it; I wanted to flaunt it, to revel and glory in it, like a pig wallowing in muck; I wanted everyone who saw my picture to know that they were looking at a married woman. I had even asked Lavinia to paint me with my hand up, resting on my bodice, to show off my betrothal ring, but she gently dissuaded me that this was not the done thing and would only detract from the beauty of my brooch, and that the gillyflowers coupled with my husband's oak leaves and acorns made the point well enough.

Though I did not want to be mistaken for an unmarried girl, a virgin maiden with her hair unbound, even though in truth I preferred to wear it thus, hanging free without pins poking and stabbing my scalp and making my head ache, I could not bear to disappoint Lavinia, and after each session of posing for the miniature I would take out the pins and shake my hair out and give her leave to sketch me if she pleased. She would later sketch me in a pensive pose, looking out the window, waiting for Robert to come home, and again sitting on the window seat wearing a bright smile upon my face as I dangled a string for my cats—fat, fluffy Custard and sleek black Onyx, whom I'd found as a mewling, half-starved kitten, like a blot of ink spilled upon the clean white snow, with her ribs poking out and her tail broken and bleeding. I had bound it up myself to set the bones, but it had mended a trifle crookedly.

The day before Robert rode away to London, I put on my wedding gown to begin posing for the full-length portrait. I had just finished dressing when Robert walked unexpectedly into the room. I had thought him gone for the day, but he had come back to retrieve a letter he had forgotten, and my face lit up at the sight of him. Lavinia snatched up a stick of charcoal and began to sketch wildly, feverishly trying to capture the true and naked love she saw upon my face.

"This," she would later say when she showed the rough and hasty sketch to me, "is the *real* Amy. This is what a bride *should* look like if we were not such mercenary people who make marriage a business like wool or any other trade all about goods and profits."

The finished painting would be as different from the usual staid and formal wedding portraits as night from day—"a woman in love, not just a lady showing off her wedding gown," Lavinia would proudly say.

I described the meadow at Syderstone, and she painted me there, walking barefoot in love and sunshine, with a big bouquet of buttercups in my hand and wreathing my wild, tumbled-down hair. And, at Robert's request, made the night before he left, as we sat beside the fire after supper and he regaled her with the tale of how I had saved the goose's life, she painted the goose in beside me, with a golden bow about her neck, eating from my hand.

"This is my masterpiece," Lavinia declared when we at last stood before the finished portrait.

Robert had already been weeks away by then, and I wished fervently that he could see that happy painted girl who seemed poised to step out of the golden frame as if she were about to walk right into the arms of the man she loved. That love, that longing, showed clearly upon her face.

"That's me," I marvelled as I stood before it, my hand rising up tentatively, then falling back down, not quite daring to reach out and touch it lest I smear the paint. "That's how I feel inside! Oh, *thank you,* Lavinia, *thank you*! Now the feeling will live forever. Should it ever start to fade, all I will need to do is look at this portrait, and it will all come rushing back again. *Thank you!*"

I liked it far better than the miniature Robert had taken with him, galloping off wearing it over his heart under his riding leathers upon the braided satin chain I had made for him from my hair ribbons. I thought the young woman captured against the azure

ground looked far too solemn and grave, as though she were inclined to melancholy, as if her eyes and lips were a stranger to
smiles and laughter. "Is that *really* me?" I bit my tongue lest I say it
aloud and Lavinia see how disappointed I was and think the failure
was hers, when it was in truth all mine. Without my habitual smile,
I thought my nose appeared a trifle too large and my mouth too
small, almost as if it were pursed in disapproval. And my eyes
looked oddly vacant, flat, more blue grey than blue green, and entirely lacking their accustomed vivacity and sparkle. I looked so cold,
so aloof and chilly, and that was a *great* shame, when I was in truth so
warm and friendly; I was a little shy, that's true, but I was not unap-
proachable; I wanted everyone to like me. I feared that anyone
Robert might show it to would come away thinking him encumbered
by a dull and grim wife whose bed was as cold as the grave.

Now, when it was too late to change it, the elegant dark gown
seemed a poor choice, far too funereal, and I wished I had worn the
maiden's blush pink or the sky blue or apple green, or even one of
several gowns I owned in my favourite buttercup yellow. I was a sentimental young bride, and my trousseau brimmed over with exquisite gowns embroidered, woven, and figured with hearts, flowers,
and lovers' knots. I even had a white gown sumptuously embroidered in red and pink silks with cupids and hearts and flying arrows. I should have worn something like that, something that
showed who I *really* was, that was true to the giddy young girl who
walked on pink perfumed clouds of love, not the staid and elegant
lady I was trying to be. I should not have tried to impress, for in
doing so I had made my face a stranger even to myself, who was accustomed to seeing it every day in the looking glass. Even Pirto,
when she saw it, furrowed her brow and asked, "But where's your
smile, pet? You don't look half like yourself without it!"

If I were superstitious, I would think the face in the portrait was
a portent of the sad and sombre woman I would become.

When the larger portrait was finished, Lavinia had to pack up
her paints and return to court; she had many commissions awaiting
her and could not tarry, and I was left alone again, with only the
servants to bear me company. Robert, though I wrote him many
anxious and yearning letters, was vague and evasive about when he
would return, and when he would send for me to visit him he sim-

ply could not—or would not—say. I spent my days walking list-lessly upon the sandy beach, alone, with the grey waves crashing and the gulls circling overhead, sometimes pausing to pick up a shell, remembering all the joyous hours we had spent there, frolick-ing and loving. It made my loneliness even harder to bear.

A fortnight later, unable to bear it a moment longer, I leapt from my lonely bed in the middle of the night and shook Pirto awake and bade her, "Pack my things at once; we're going home to Stan-field Hall!"

At my parents' home I would at least be among familiar faces, and there was work I could be doing. I would no longer be the idle, pitiful bride the servants and common folk at Hemsby whispered about walking the beach alone with her hair billowing in the wind, pining for her husband in a windblown white gown embroidered with gold lovers' knots. They said the sight of me reminded them of a ghost, and I wondered if such would someday be my fate, that my lonely shade would return one day to walk the beach for all eter-nity, waiting for Robert to come back to me. I shuddered at the thought and even had nightmares about it and prayed it was not an omen; I wanted to rest in peace when I died, not continue to exist as an anguished spirit doomed to walk the earth forevermore with-out peace or rest; to me that was like being damned, another ver-sion of Hell, only without the flames and demons. And resuming my old duties as chatelaine was a far better way to occupy my time than weeping and yearning and letting fearful fancies about the beautiful ladies at court, who would not scruple to flash their most beguiling smiles and gaze at Robert with invitations in their eyes, rob me of my sleep and peace of mind. So I packed up my things and went home to my parents.

❧ 10 ❧

Amy Robsart Dudley

Stanfield Hall, near Wymondham, in Norfolk
and
Syderstone Manor in Norfolk
September 1550–May 1553

Nearly three years crept slowly past, like a snail on a pane of glass, with the tense and tedious waiting relieved by only brief and hurried visits from Robert. He always came bearing gifts, as though he thought worldly goods could atone for his absence. But his preoccupied smile and distracted eyes told me that even though his body was, his mind wasn't *truly* there with me. He was there like a whirlwind and then gone again, and I was left dizzy and reeling in his wake.

He was *never* there for holidays. They always had such great need of him at court, he said, but he always sent gifts—lavish, costly gifts for everyone, even the servants—but he never came himself; the King, and his father, were counting on him to help organise the Yuletide revels. So in muted sorrow, trying to smile and not let my tears rain on everyone else's pleasure, each year I celebrated the Twelve Days of Christmas and toasted in the New Year without my husband beside me.

Father and I went back to Syderstone—a draughty ruin though it was, and becoming less habitable every year—for our traditional New Year's ritual. Muffled in our furs and warmest woollens, and with all our servants and workers and their families gathered around us in the snow-blanketed orchard, we set a great fire blazing, and Cook brewed up a bubbling cauldron of Lambswool—a special blend of beer flavoured with roasted apples, ginger, nutmeg, and sugar, so named for the white froth that floated on top—and ladled out cups of the steaming brew to us all. And as the church bell tolled the midnight hour, we toasted the apple trees and sang carols to them, thanking them for the fruit they had given us and hoping that their winter nakedness would soon be clothed with fine green leaves and, later, beautiful, fragrant pink and white blossoms, then fat, ripe, rosy fruit. Then the musicians played, and we danced and drank Lambswool and ate gingerbread until the sun came up, and we all staggered home and fell into our beds to sleep half the day away.

And in June, after the shearing was finished, we held a celebration with music and dancing and served our people apple cider and sweet wafers baked to a golden crisp inside special irons that imprinted upon each side a design of a sheep in full woolly coat ringed by a border of Syderstone's famous apples. We always let them have cream, as much as they pleased, to dip the wafers in. That was a *real* treat for them, as most had to use the cream from their own cow for making butter and cheese, so this was a sweet luxury indeed, and it made my heart glad to see the happy smiles it brought to their faces. But in my heart I ached because Robert was never there to share the fun and joy with me. Even as I smiled and clapped my hands as we watched the morris dancers, fire-eaters, acrobats, and jugglers, I could not help feeling his absence and longing to have him there with me. And when we went out at midnight, singing and skipping and still sipping cider as we made our way to the top of the hill and there packed a cartwheel all around with straw and set it alight and rolled it down, hoping it would reach the bottom before it went out, for that foretold a bountiful harvest, I wished with all my heart that he were there and that the revelry would end in love, with me in my husband's arms, and not with me alone, restless and yearning, in my lonely bed.

And he was never there to take part in the Candlestick Branle we danced every year in the Great Hall on All Hallows' Eve, sometimes slow, solemn, and stately, other times rollicking, fast-paced, and lively, passing lighted candlesticks from hand to hand as we danced in a line and, like a lady's intricately braided coiffure, wove complicated formations, while my father, and the others who were not taking part in the dance, watched from the gallery above or standing high upon the stairs.

But there were good times too, even though they were few and far between and grew more so with each year that passed as Robert's absences grew more prolonged and his visits ever briefer. Eventually they dwindled to a hasty handful strewn throughout the year that seemed to be hello and goodbye all in the blink of an eye.

Once he sent me some jewelled grapes to wear in my hair, beautiful clusters of smooth, round amethyst and emerald grapes with silver leaves set with sparkling diamond dewdrops. They were so pretty, so special, and unique! And when he sent me word that he was coming, I was ready. When he started to bound up the stairs, sweaty and smelling of horses, sweat, leather, and spice, I was there at the top waiting for him with the jewelled grapes in my hair, wearing a new gown of gooseberry green silk with a kirtle and under-sleeves of wine-coloured silk embroidered with silver vines hung with green and gold grapes. Without a word—there was no need for any—Robert swept me up in his arms and carried me to our chamber and straight to our bed. We didn't leave it until long after the sun came up the next day.

But the next evening, when he sat late by the fire, and I came in my shift, sheer like a clinging cobweb covering my body, with my hair unbound, to lay my head upon his knee, he just sat there, staring broodingly into the flames, as if his mind were miles and miles away. I could not help but wonder who it was he saw dancing in those entrancing flames. Was it the flame-haired Elizabeth? Did the crackling, rippling, swaying, leaping, grasping flames remind him of her, shining like the brightest bonfire, dancing in an orange and yellow gown with her hair a flaming mass about her shoulders, flying out as she leapt and spun round and round? I was *certain* of it, but I bit my tongue and said nothing. I didn't want to ruin the rare and peaceful bliss and shatter it with an argument. I wanted kisses and caresses, not raised voices and quarrelsome words. So I knelt down and laid my head in his lap, but when his hand moved to absently stroke my hair, I wondered if in his mind it was red instead of golden. Does she do this with him? I wondered. And the pleasures we shared together in bed, did he give and take the same with her? Was I special in *any* way, was there anything he did with me that was ours alone, or did I share all with Elizabeth, or, even worse, did I only get the crumbs from her plate? I didn't know, and I wasn't sure I wanted to. I wasn't sure which would hurt more—knowing for certain or the questions that clawed at my mind, like raging, hungry lions that I tried, sometimes successfully, other times not, to quiet and subdue and send retreating with a crack of my whip, but they were *always* there, sometimes growling low, other times roaring deafeningly, *demanding* to be heard, to have their curiosity fed and sated.

When Custard had her yearly litter of kittens, even though I marvelled and caught my breath at each tiny mewling, squirming body, so small I could hold it in the palm of my hand, I felt the shadow of sorrow hanging over me. I *yearned* to be a mother. But how could I conceive when my husband was away and had so little time for me? There was always one excuse or another to keep him away or prevent him from sending for me. Even as the proud mother brought each kitten to me and laid it in my lap, and I petted and praised her and profusely admired her babies, I envied her, even though she was a cat. And while Custard lay in her basket by the fire and nursed her little brood, I would take Onyx, who had, like me, never conceived, onto my lap and stroke her sleek black fur and listen to her purr, and smile through my tears; the kittens were such a bittersweet sight, they did my heart good and hurt it all at the same time.

I would stay at Stanfield Hall so long that many would forget that I was a married woman, and they, along with those who did not know about my marriage, would call me Amy Robsart, as if it had never happened at all. Even I at times thought it was all a lovely dream that had vanished upon my waking. I had to look at the ring on my left hand to remind myself that I had the right to call myself a wife at all. The name Amy Dudley, or *Lady* Dudley, seemed foreign to my lips and ears; when I heard it spoken, it always took a few moments for me to realise that it was me they were talking about or speaking to. *Robsart* felt right and natural; *Dudley* made me feel like I was a pretender, claiming a name that wasn't

rightly my own. A few times I even caught myself about to introduce myself as Amy Robsart instead of Dudley, and I would grow
flustered and red in the face as my tongue tripped clumsily over the
syllables, trying to sort them out and speak my name aright, and
the whole time I felt like a fool, and sometimes, if I saw pity in the
other person's eyes, I felt angry, at myself and Robert too. Maybe I
had flown in the face of Fate, and I was never meant to be Lady
Dudley at all. Maybe I was never meant to have any other name or
be anyone other than Amy Robsart.

Fear began to take a fierce hold of me; I could not outrun it or
shake it off. No matter how hard I tried to lose myself in my work,
its fangs and claws bit deeply and left scars and wounds that never
truly healed. I would feel it in my heart, in my head, keeping me
awake at night, gnawing my nerves until they were bleeding raw
and leaving me so sensitive that I would cry at the least little thing.
There were many days when, after tossing and turning in my big
and lonely bed all night, I could not rise and would spend the day
sleeping and weeping in bed. But more often than not I forced myself to rise, even though it meant I came downstairs with dark-
circled eyes, leaden steps, and a dull mind. I would follow the
sheep out to graze, sit myself down on a stone, bury my face in my
hands, and weep. But the fear held fast; I couldn't cry or drive it
out. It festered and became a part of me until I could not remember what it felt like to live without it.

I watched Mother Nature change her gowns each season. Drap-
ing herself in the white ermine and diamond frost of winter, then
doffing the cold, sumptuous white for bright, floral-sprigged
spring, then upon a sudden whim changing into sunny yellow to
drowse and sweat each day away beneath the brim of an old straw
hat with the sun beating down upon its brim, then primping like a
lady who can't decide between all the crackling, crisp brown,
bronze, gold, orange, russet, tawny, yellow, and red taffeta gowns
draped over the branches, so she tries them all on one by one,
yanking them down, throwing the discarded dresses on the ground,
and leaving the trees naked and bare before reverting to white and
ermine again. I could feel Robert slipping further and further away
from me, but I was powerless to make him stop and stay; every time
I saw him, he seemed more distant and remote, as if he were stand-

ing on the tip-top of a tall mountain and I were stranded far below, cupping my hands around my mouth and shouting or else jumping up and down and waving my arms, trying desperately to get his attention. But all I did was in vain; he ignored me.

And he never sent for me. Though the idea of being presented at court both terrified and excited me, when I wrote and asked when, there was always some excuse to tarry, and *later* and *not now* were words I soon became all too familiar with. Where I was concerned, my husband was never one for pinning down dates and sticking to them; on the rare times when he did give a definite one, he was more likely than not to forget and never appear; something more important *always* came up.

The first year, I had Mr Edney make a *beautiful* silver-embroidered icy blue gown trimmed with silver lace and sewn so thickly with crystals that the silk looked like water shimmering under ice, with white fur to trim the graceful bell sleeves. And Father gave me a beautiful necklace of opals to wear with it. But I never got to wear it as I curtsied before the King.

The next year I decided something brighter would be better, and I chose a pretty pink that reminded me of how rosy my cheeks used to be, and I had the sleeves furred with a tawny gold that looked wonderful with my hair. I never wore that gown for the King either.

The third year brought another dress—a buttercup yellow damask, worn with a petticoat and sleeves of pale green, the colour of new shoots emerging from the earth after the winter thaw. King Edward never saw me in that gown either.

After that, I stopped hoping. I could not bear to look my tailor in the eye and speak of my being presented at court; I no longer believed Robert's *later* would ever come.

I still wore the pretty dresses, just not for the King or my husband; I wore them for myself and tried to forget the occasion they had been intended for and not to let my mind dwell on the disappointments or keep tally of all the times my husband let me down. The disappointments had begun to outnumber the delights, and the broken promises far surpassed the ones that had been kept. I *hated* myself for hoping every time Robert said or wrote something that made me believe I had something to look forward to, but I wanted *so* much to believe, yet almost every time I let myself, he let me down again. I *hated* myself for giving him the power to do this to me. Every time he did, I was *furious* with myself for allowing hope to blossom like a flower inside my breast, even though I knew all too well that Robert was more likely than not to trample and crush it or pluck it and give it to another.

To make matters worse, I rarely knew when he would arrive on one of his rare and infrequent visits. And I would see the disdain curling his lips into an ugly sneer beneath the new silky black moustache he was growing even though I hated it, and the haughty, annoyed contempt in his eyes when he found me out in the sun with my feet bare and my skirts pinned up, an old straw hat on my wild, tumbled-down hair, my face flushed, with sweat beading my brow, and dark, wet stains spreading beneath the arms of my old faded blue cloth gown, standing waist-deep in the barley crop or supervising the shearing of the sheep, with Ned Flowerdew at my side with a ledger, which we both bent our heads over, keeping tally of the wool sacks. While my father, now grown feeble in his steps and increasingly hazy in his head, though he was at times still his dear, old self, was carried out in a chair to sit in the shade and watch.

There were other times when someone would rush to bring me word of Robert's arrival, and I would go running out to greet him, just the way I used to when we were courting, scampering through the green grass and rainbow of wildflowers, a barefoot hoyden with my skirts tucked up, with a basket brimming with the berries I had been picking slung over my arm, and stains about my lips and on my apron and fingers. My fastidious husband in his elegant clothes, with gold braid and buttons even on his riding leathers, would recoil, cringing as if the mere sight of me might soil him.

At the sight of him, I seemed to live again, and I would be so overcome with happiness that I would run to him and try to fling myself into the arms that used to reach out, open wide, to enfold me, only to smack up against the hard wall of his chest instead, with the smile and glad-hearted laughter dying on my lips, as I looked up to see him frowning down at me as tears of hurt filled my eyes.

The damage was done, and forever afterwards whenever Robert looked at me, I could tell that he was still seeing that boisterous, barefoot, berry-stained bumpkin running towards him, pink-cheeked and breathless, with her hat flying off and her hair streaming out wild behind her. The image was seared into his mind forever, and I could never change it. Even perfumed and pretty in rose-coloured silk, with pearls about my throat, and my hair gleaming in perfect golden curls with pink roses and pearls, still he could never forget the berry-stained, barefoot bumpkin.

Yet I found that if I spent my days idle, dressed in gorgeous array like a fine lady with an overabundance of leisure, sitting anxiously by the window, hoping and wishing that he would come galloping up the road, my embroidery, or the book I was studying as I endeavoured to better myself lying forgotten on my lap, the weight of sorrow was like a stone about my neck, dragging me down to drown. The waiting, the hoping, yearning, and worrying were just *too* much for me to sit idly and bear. I had been raised to believe that idle hands were the Devil's tool. I needed to be up and about, busy inside and out, and there were moments, I found, when, caught up in the busy bustle of the day, I could *almost* forget. I would be helping gather cider apples, or salt down meat for the coming winter—though Pirto would later scold me for the toll the salt took upon my hands, leaving them coarse and red and in sore need of long soaks and rubbing in soothing creams to make them soft again—or standing shoulder to shoulder with the servants before a wooden trough wielding a wooden hammer to mash the black, rotted crabapples to make verjus for the pickling, and I would of a sudden start up, like a child bolting awake in bed at the crash of nearby thunder shattering the perfect quiet of a still night, at the realisation that whole *hours* had passed without a single thought of Robert intruding upon my mind. Those were my best days, though they became my worst if Robert came riding up unexpectedly.

I liked it far better when he arrived after dark, after the household had already gone to bed, and found me waiting for him, naked beneath the sheets with my hair spilling across the pillows. "My gold and pink alabaster angel," Robert always used to call me then, in a whisper dripping with lust. And though I had many beautiful night shifts, bed gowns, and robes, from the most delicate cobwebby pink or white lace to sumptuous jewel-hued velvets trimmed with gold or silver adornments, I always slept naked, knowing that were Robert to come in and pull back the sheets, he would *never* be disappointed in me and would come eagerly into the arms I held out for him. Those were the times when he was *so* loving and passionate, so like the boy who had come to woo me, that the flame of hope leapt high within me, to burn, unwavering and steady, until the moment came—as it always did—when he would douse the flames with cold words that made light of his ardour, dismissing it all with a wave of his hand, dampening the ecstasy with excuses that he had gotten carried away, spoken rashly in the heat of passion, and that no man should be blamed for that. He never realised—or maybe he just did not care?—though I tried *so hard* to tell him, to make him understand, that each time he did this made it harder for me to trust and believe him. If his mind was likely to change in the cold light of morning or two days, two weeks, or even two months hence, how could I possibly know what to believe? He left my mind dizzy and reeling in a constant state of confusion and uncertainty, as though I were playing Blindman's Buff and grasping for the truth. And though I always hoped and wanted with all my heart to believe, his words lost weight with me until all his passion and promises became as light as feathers that would waft away upon the slightest breeze.

I knew *something* had changed one day during the second year when he came to visit me. Clinging to his arm, I so happily escorted him upstairs and, proud and excited, showed him the rich new set of brocade bedclothes—coverlet, curtains, and canopy—I had had made for my—our—bed, thousands of yellow buttercups in perpetual bloom upon a ground of spring green, "as a remembrance of the day we first made love," I explained, pressing my body against his in a way that I hoped conveyed how much I would like him to lower me onto the bed.

With an exasperated sigh, Robert shrugged free of me and strode across the room and sat down by the fire and began to tug off his muddy boots.

"I don't need a remembrance, Amy!" he snarled, slamming his boot down, causing the silver spurs to rattle and bits of mud to flake off onto the fur rug, and then beginning on the other. "I am not likely to forget the seventeen-year-old boy I used to be, thinking with my cock instead of with my head! I should have just tumbled you in a haystack and been done with it, but . . ." With an angry sigh he flopped back in his chair, seething like an angry bull, and closed his eyes. His hands curled tightly round the arms of the chair, the knuckles shaking and standing out white, as if he was fighting hard to restrain himself from some act of violence. Then he sighed deeply and opened his eyes. "You got your gold ring, Amy, so be content with that, and cease prattling to me about remembering things that are best forgotten. Incidentally, I *loathe* buttercups; they are such a *common* little flower."

My head felt light enough to float away, as if it were a weathercock caught in a strong and violent wind, and I couldn't catch my breath, I felt as if he had just kicked me in the stomach. I felt icy and aflame all at the same time. And I couldn't see! There were all these dark and coloured sparks floating before my eyes, obscuring my vision, and I feared I was being struck blind by terror. But I couldn't speak, I couldn't tell Robert what I was feeling, what was happening to me; it was as if a door had slammed inside my throat, barring the jumble of confused words from coming out. When Robert saw my lips trembling and the tears spilling down my face, he swore loudly and snatched up his boots again and stormed out, slamming the door behind him.

Later that night, alone in my bed, when I was huddled up with the covers pulled high above my head, still weeping, though my eyes and throat were a swollen, sore misery, he would come to me with kisses and a bolt of blue silk the colour of a robin's egg, and lengths of pretty, sunny yellow lace and matching embroidery silk to make a fine new gown, and tell me that he was sorry, he had only spoken out of anger over something I could never understand that was "nothing to worry your pretty head about". And he rolled me over onto my back, covered me with kisses, and made such passionate, tender love to me that I was soon persuaded that he hadn't really meant it and that he truly did love me, that it had been nothing more than a show of temper, he had been taking out his frustration upon the most convenient person, the one he said he trusted to see him at his worst and best, like an angry fist that I had stepped in front of and caught a blow not intended for me.

The next morning, when I woke, he was gone, back to London,

but he sent back to me a bolt of buttercup yellow brocade with the flowers I loved so figured golden in the weave, and a ring in a green velvet box—a buttercup made of sparkling yellow gems, with a note, ardently inscribed in bold black ink in my husband's handsome script with graceful and elegant curlicues and flourishes trimming the black letters like pretty lace:

I Love My Buttercup Bride!

And I let myself be lulled into believing that everything really was all right, though in my heart I knew it wasn't.

Even though these outbursts of anger followed by tender, passionate reconciliations in bed became a disturbing refrain repeated often during his visits, I let myself believe. I shut my eyes to the truth that they really settled nothing, that they were merely a means to turn off my tears and free Robert from seeing and hearing the consequences of his temper, that they were a way to render me docile and smiling for the few days we would spend together, to make life more peaceful and pleasing for Robert until, feeling he had done his duty, he could gallop back to London again as fast as his horse could carry him.

When I heard that his father had deeded him Saxlingham Manor near Holt, my hopes briefly surged back to life. I thought it meant a proper home for us, but Robert preferred to lease it out rather than live there, and he eventually sold it, all without my ever setting eyes upon it.

Having the loving good grace not to say "I told you so," Father even tried to bring him back, to keep him home with me and away from the court, so that we might settle down and have the children I longed for. He arranged to have Robert made a knight of the shire, and, now that his health was declining, shared with him his own honours—the Lieutenancy of the county and joint stewardship and constabulary of Castle Rising in Norfolk. But these rustic honours paled against being a Gentleman of King Edward's Privy Chamber, Honorary Carver at the King's Table, and Master of the Buckhounds, with its responsibilities of breeding, training, and tending the royal hunting hounds, organising the hunting parties, and keeping the deer parks well stocked. None of which I could share, and so I was left alone, trying to fill up my life with things to do, all the while pining for my husband and missing him sorely.

My lengthy stay at Stanfield Hall ended abruptly one warm April afternoon when Robert burst into the kitchen, dusty and sweating in his riding leathers, giving us all such a fright the way he rushed in. He had caught me unaware again and found me laughing and gossiping with Cook and the kitchen maids, just as if I were one of them, standing there flush-faced, with my hair carelessly pinned, my sleeves rolled up, and my apron stained with colourful splotches, surrounded by great bubbling cauldrons of jewel-coloured fruits—the strawberries, apricots, cherries, both sour and sweet, gooseberries, peaches, quinces, plums, apples, currants, raspberries, and pears I had myself helped pick. We had been busy for days making the jams and jellies that would delight us all winter when sweet red strawberries smeared on a piece of bread would feel like a slice of Heaven, paradise in your mouth, as luxurious to the tongue as a length of red velvet on bare skin.

The spoon in my hand clattered to the floor, and I, with a startled cry that quickly turned to one of pure delight, started to run to fling myself into his arms, but he froze me with a look.

Hurt, I stopped in my tracks and self-consciously brushed back some wild wisps of hair clinging wetly to my brow and untied my apron and balled it up and thrust it at the nearest maid.

"We were just making our jams and jellies for the winter, so we can have fruit," I explained, nodding towards the boiling cauldrons. "Look at them, Robert—aren't they pretty? Like liquid jewels, the colours are. Did you ever see an emerald a finer hue than our mint jelly?" I pointed to the row of jars sealed earlier that morning and lined up on the table.

"But they are *not* jewels," Robert said, with a hard, deep frown. "You cannot wear them except as unsightly stains upon your apron, and they have no value except for their taste and the pennies that could be earned should you sell them at market; therefore, any *slight* similarity between jewels, jellies, and jams is *completely* irrelevant. It is absurd you should even think it!"

"I-I'm s-sorry, Robert," I said softly, and I hung my head, staring down at the crude wooden and leather clogs I wore in the kitchen and outside on muddy days, shamed that I had displeased my husband and that he had rebuked me before the servants.

"Come upstairs, Amy"—Robert started for the door—"*after* you have tidied yourself and made yourself look as my wife *should* look. Then we will talk."

And meekly I nodded. "Yes, Robert."

As I was leaving, Cook caught my hand and gave it a comforting squeeze.

"Don't you believe 'im, Miss Amy. They *are* pretty, whether 'is lordship thinks so or no. An' as for m'self, I'd much rather 'ave a bit o' bread with cherry jam slathered thick 'pon it than a ruby any winter's day when the cherries aren't there to be plucked off the trees, but a ruby, if you've the money an' the use for it, is there all the year round, so I'm inclined to think the cherries more precious than the stone, even though it do sparkle pretty. And you're *beautiful* just as you are, an' we all think so!" And at her words the other servants chimed in, "Aye, that we do, Miss Amy!"

I smiled back at her and squeezed her hand, then, smiling and nodding my thanks at them all, as my husband impatiently called to me again—"Amy, are you coming?"—I gathered up my skirts and bolted up the stairs, thus provoking him to complain about the way my clogs clattered and order me to "take those ugly things off—a woman shouldn't clatter like a horse when she runs, not that a *real* lady has any cause to run at all", and "they are not fit shoes for a gentlewoman to wear, only a peasant whose only other choice is to wrap her feet in rags or go barefoot".

"Yes, Robert!" I nodded breathlessly as I caught up with him on the landing.

Obediently, I stepped out of my clogs, tripping as I did so, and I had to grab hold of the banister to keep myself from tumbling bum over pate down the stairs.

Murmuring beneath his breath exasperated words about my clumsiness, Robert unsheathed his dagger, and my heart leapt from my breast into my throat as he came towards me. For a moment I was afraid he was going to *stab* me! But then, he bent over and, using the blade of his dagger, lifted first one, and then the other, of my clogs and, opening the window that let light stream onto the landing, cast them out "like the rubbish they are!" Then, as he sheathed his dagger, he asked if I had thought to tell Cook to send up hot water for me to bathe, since "a lady shouldn't stink as though she had been slaving in a hot kitchen all day", he said pointedly, and I shamefacedly bowed my head and hugged my arms across my breasts, tucking my fists beneath my arms and hoping he hadn't seen the dark, damp stains blossoming beneath my armpits.

"Yes, Robert!" I nodded, though in truth I hadn't said a word to Cook or anyone about a bath; it just seemed wiser to agree. I would have to have a quiet word with Pirto and ask her to see to it.

With Pirto's help, I splashed hurriedly through my bath and anxiously doused myself with rose perfume, spilling a goodly amount from the bottle in my haste. My nerves were humming like bees whose hive has been disturbed, and I was near to tears trying to decide what gown would best please my husband. I had already been laced into one and was halfway to the door before I turned back and bade Pirto unlace me, weeping despairingly as she did so that though it was so very pretty, the dusky rose damask might displease him by reminding him of dirt and grime. I just didn't know any more; in my desperation to please him I sometimes felt quite silly. In the end, I finally settled on a rich cream satin embroidered with gold lovers' knots profusely trimmed with golden lace. Then Pirto fastened a necklace of gold hearts around my neck, and I stumbled and tripped my way into a pair of gold slippers. And, with my still-damp hair caught up at the sides with ivory and amber combs, and the length of it rippling down my back to dry, I rushed breathlessly into the adjoining room to see my husband and give him a proper wifely greeting.

When I burst in, poised to hurl myself into his arms and cover his face with kisses, Robert's valet, Tamworth, was just helping him finish dressing, while another pair of servants were carrying a tub out, taking care to move slowly and not let the water slosh out over the sides. To my dismay, I saw that they were fresh riding clothes that my husband was wearing, and a new pair of high-polished leather boots were on his feet.

With not one word about my improved appearance, he began, "My brother Guildford is being married in late May. It will look strange if my wife does not attend, so, no tears or arguments, Amy, to London you shall ride."

"A wedding! A big family wedding! Oh, Robert, how exciting! What great fun we shall have!" I cried, clasping my hands to my heart as happy memories of my own wedding came flooding back and momentarily blotted out my fear of going to the great big noisy and crowded city. "Who is the girl? Are they in love? Is she pretty? Has he known her very long?" One by one the excited questions tumbled out of me.

Robert held up his hand to silence me.

"The bride-to-be is the Lady Jane Grey, and she is pretty enough, I suppose, if one likes the quiet, melancholy type, though too much of a scholar in petticoats for most men's taste, I think. Fifteen years old with pale skin, marred by freckles, brown eyes, chestnut hair, slumps her shoulders and stares at the floor unless she is corrected and told to stand up straight and hold her head up, timid and whisper-voiced, almost afraid to speak, except in the schoolroom or amongst other scholars—then she is bold enough, perhaps overly so," he summed her up, and by his dismissive, disdainful tone, I could tell he did not like her.

"But she is the King's cousin and in line for the throne; *that* is the important thing. This is a *very* important marriage, Amy, and the Dudleys shall profit well by it. Who knows but one day Guildford and Jane's children may be kings and queens. We are on the threshold of founding a new dynasty that may someday supplant the Tudors as England's ruling family—*that* is what matters. Love has nothing to do with it, so do not behave like a silly goose and come to London prattling about love, Amy; no one will think well of you for it, you will only make yourself appear lowbred and ridiculous, and it will only confirm the beliefs of many that I have married beneath me. And we don't want that, do we?"

He held up his hand to stay me as my lips began to tremble. "I do not say these things to hurt you, Amy, only to educate you, to help you understand and acquit yourself accordingly, since you are not accustomed to the ways of the nobility and court. Love rarely has a role to play in marriage. Love is a game, a sport, the stuff of poetry, legends, and songs; it has nothing really to do with *real* life. You *do* understand that, don't you?"

But instead of waiting for me to answer, he nodded towards a plump purse sitting on the desk atop a book.

"I've left coin enough to equip you with suitable garb, jewels too. If you need more, buy whatever is necessary and send the bill to my man Forster, and he shall take care of it, but do not bother me about fripperies and whether I like this or that; you are my wife, and no London tailor would *dare* make you look unworthy of that honour if he values his reputation; one word from me in the right ear, and he would be ruined forever. And choose well, cost be damned. I want everyone to see what a beautiful wife I have so that perhaps they will change their minds and think I have not done so badly after all. There *must* be *nothing* of the country bumpkin about you. To that end, I have also left you a book of etiquette; study it well." He nodded again at the desk. "Doubtless you will find that there are many words in it that you do not understand; they are difficult to avoid, but that cannot be remedied at this late date. If you find that it is too much for you, ask Ned Flowerdew to arrange to have the schoolmaster in to help you, since your father no longer can—his age and infirmity have robbed him of his mind, so the village idiot now has more wit than the squire—or perhaps your mother can assist if it does not interfere with her lying in bed eating bonbons and complaining about her aches and pains all day. And I have arranged to have a dancing master spend a fortnight here. I expect you to profit well by his stay and practise with him all you can, every day; even when your feet hurt, remind yourself that he will not be here forever, and get up and practise some more. He will teach you all the latest dances and make sure you are up to par on the old ones; my wife must be seen to elegantly acquit her-self at every dance, slow and fast, new and old; I'll not have it said that she is only fit to leap and kick up her heels in country jigs and reels. And have a new gown made for Mrs Pirto, plain black velvet as befits a proper lady's maid, and tell her that if she *must* smile, then learn to do it with her mouth closed—her teeth are ugly. I will send a proper escort to fetch you when it's time. A litter, I think, will be best—I don't want you to fall off a horse and break your neck, or an arm or a leg; crooked limbs and limps are unsightly, es-pecially in a female; every move a lady makes should be filled with grace."

As he spoke these last words, he was pulling on his gloves, and Tamworth was holding out his riding crop and feathered hat to him; then, circling Robert with a brush one last time to make sure no stray hairs or dust marred the deep brown velvet and leather, he gave a nod of approval.

"But you just arrived!" I cried. "Surely you're not . . . you *can't* be . . . leaving?"

Robert brushed a brusque kiss across my cheek. "I cannot stay. My father needs me in London. There is much to be done and little time to do it in; I was merely passing by on an errand for him and thought I would stop in and tell you personally instead of sending a letter. Since you are always writing telling me how much you long to see me, I thought this would please you better. Too much perfume." He wrinkled his nose and pulled away from me. "Go and wash, Amy—you smell like a French whore! Do not fail me, Amy; you must be *perfect. Perfect!* If you are not, do not look to come to London again; I will leave you here in the country for the rest of your life to rot!"

I rushed after him and caught his arm.

"Why did you marry me if I was not good enough for you?" I demanded, hating myself for the way my lips and voice shook and the tears that filled my eyes.

"I haven't time for this now!" Robert impatiently thrust me from him and headed for the stairs. "Christ's blood, there's not a sight on earth or in Heaven or Hell even half so vexing as a woman's tears!"

And then he was gone. I sank down by the fire, though its warmth paled against the warmth of the embraces I had hoped to enjoy. Part of me wished he had indeed sent a letter; even a curt little short one would not have been so cruel as this brief, brutally blunt meeting. I looked at the purse of coins and the etiquette book he had left on the desk for me, and suddenly I wished he were still standing there and I had the courage to leap up and hurl them both at his head. Tears spilled from my eyes as I realised I could not remember the last time I had heard my husband say, "I love you." This visit, he had not said one nice thing to me at all.

* * *

I tried to lose myself in the flurry of preparations and the ordering and fitting of new gowns, though the very thought of travelling to London filled me with terror. Robert had wanted us to be married there, but I had carried on and cried so that in the end he gave in and let me have my way, though he insisted on making my big country wedding as grand as it could be. I had not been to London since I was a little girl of five, and the noise, stink, and crowds of babbling, shouting, rushing people, so different from anything I had known in the country, so frightened me that I cried and cried, even after the momentary distraction of the jeweller's shop and the purchase of a pretty yellow songbird in a tiny gilded cage, until Father, fearing that I would make myself sick, cut our visit short and took me home with all haste. I'd not been back since and had no desire to go. Any goods I wanted could easily be sent, and the court held no allure for me; unlike most young girls, I'd never harboured dreams of serving as a lady-in-waiting and far preferred the life of a country chatelaine. But I knew I *must* do this; I must not disappoint my husband. I must go to London and do him proud and show everyone who thought that he had married beneath him that I was a lady and not a disgrace to the Dudley name.

Mr Edney, my tailor, came down from London, bringing with him some of the most beautiful fabrics I had ever seen, with his head overflowing with ideas about the gowns he would create for me. There was a bright glossy satin the colour of a ripe peach, which he proposed to embroider all over with yellow roses; and a silver-shot brocade of blue grey woven with dainty flowers that he would have his seamstresses accent with seed pearls and tiny diamond and sapphire brilliants; and a new damask of the most delicate flesh colour lightly suffused with pink that he called lady's blush—"not nearly as deep a pink as maiden's blush," he explained, holding the two colours up side by side so I could see the difference. And, of course, there would be French hoods, and slippers, fans, stockings, cloaks, and gloves to match each gown. And jewels—Mr Edney assured me that appropriate gems would be provided to match every gown; he would see to it personally that "each gown and the jewels that go with it are like a marriage made in Heaven!" Then he unfurled a glossy forest green satin already embroidered in thick gold with an elaborate pattern of pinecones and pomegranates, which he envisioned worn over a cloth-of-gold petticoat and matching under-sleeves, and my bare neck hung with emeralds of the deepest, most peerless green. And to contrast with it—"like the moon and the sun," Mr Edney said—a gown of pale willow green silk embroidered with silver artichokes that opened over a petticoat of silver. He also brought along a new colour to show me; it was called horseflesh, a bronzy brown colour with just the faintest undertone of pink, to be tricked out by a kirtle of bold, bright pink, he enthused as he unfurled the fabrics and held them up to show me. "Being such a lover of horses," he said, "Sir Robert is certain to adore it and you in it! Dare I say it, My Lady? Do not wear this gown if you need to rise early the morning after, else everyone will know by your face that you passed a night with very little sleep, being—dare I say it?—ridden hard and fast." And, just so I would have something more flamboyant, should the need arise, he designed a gown of peacock blue satin and a vivid green of a hue he called virli with the longest train I had ever worn, the whole of it adorned with peacock feathers and lace all a-sparkle with jet beads and diamond dust, with a headdress of swaying peacock feathers, as well as a mask and a peacock feather fan, just in case I attended a masked ball while in London, as such a dramatic gown would be perfect for it. And, for travel, something more subdued was called for, but elegant nonetheless, and so he outfitted me with a full skirt and flaring jacket of rat grey velvet, with grey pearl buttons and just a hint of silver lace and embroidery, a silver net to contain my hair, and silver-fringed grey leather gloves and matching tasselled ankle boots, and, as the crowning touch, a little round feathered hat with several strands of grey pearls that looped becomingly beneath my chin, though I didn't like to say, lest it hurt his feelings, that their clacking and swaying was *extremely* vexing. And, lastly, a trim, gold-buttoned riding habit and feathered hat of brassel red, a shade reminiscent of rust, just in case I should want to ride. The gold buttons Mr Edney chose for me were heart-shaped, and that made me smile, and there was a gold lovers' knot clasp set with garnets to hold the spray of tawny speckled feathers on my hat.

Mr Edney and I always had such fun together; he was such a bubbly, bright, gossipy little man who loved pretty clothes just as much as a woman did. Sometimes, in fact, I seemed to forget that he was indeed a man; it was *so* easy to talk to and confide in him. With a fringe of grey-peppered dark hair around his bald pate, he looked more like a monk, a short, portly priest one was accustomed to give one's confession, than one of London's most avidly sought-after tailors, but his apple cheeks and ready smile chased all illusions of priestly solemnity away. And he was so *very* kind! And each gown he made was a work of art; he never threw something together like "slap, dash, and it's done!" He wanted every garment to be perfect in every way for the woman who wore it. One had to only give him an idea, to say one word, like *butterflies,* and his imagination would take flight, and the results would be as marvellous as a stitched and sewn miracle to behold.

But of all the gowns Mr Edney ever made for me—and there were a great many—my favourite was by far a sea green and white silk confection of a gown embroidered with silver and gold seashells that reminded me of those precious weeks at Hemsby when Robert and I were newly married; there was even a pattern of scallop shells in the silver and gold lace that trimmed it. And, to further increase my delight, there was also a shell pink petticoat and under-sleeves embroidered with gold cockleshells that I might also wear with it when I liked. The three colours—the sea green, shell pink, and white—complemented each other beautifully. And a jeweller, working closely with Mr Edney—they seemed to be great friends and in London even shared rooms together above their adjoining shops—provided me with ropes of pearls interspersed with gold cockleshells to wear with it. I was *so* excited. I had thought my trousseau would be the first and last time I would ever have so many new and beautiful gowns at one time, but these . . . they were almost like a second trousseau, and I could not wait for Robert to see me in them!

❧ 11 ❧

Amy Robsart Dudley

Durham House in the Strand, London
May 1553

I was sick with fear all the way to London. Many times I had to call "Halt!" to the bearers and lean from the litter while Pirto held back my hair while I vomited onto the side of the road or else leapt from the conveyance and ran behind some bushes to hastily hitch up my skirts lest I soil them as the bottom fell out of my stomach.

As we entered the city, I huddled quivering behind the curtains, clinging fearfully to Pirto, who did her best to calm me. I was always supremely conscious of the numerous dangers that lurked outside the curtains, of the noise and the ugly smells, the peddlers shouting out their wares, and the cutpurses, beggars, and bawds who made nightmares fill my head even though I was wide awake in broad daylight.

Through it all Pirto stroked my hair as I lay with my head on her lap, whispering over and over, "It's all right, love, Pirto's here; no harm shall come to you."

As we neared our destination, I sat up and dried my tears as Pirto put right my hair, catching it up in the silver and grey pearl net, and set my hat in place. I peeked nervously out at the world outside the litter's curtains. I could never understand how anyone could want to live in London. How could they prefer the din, bustle, and stink of the city to the clean, fresh air, blue skies, and green grass that rivalled even the finest emerald of the country? And the wildflowers, bright, living jewels, not hard, glittering gems and the cold, unmelting ice of diamonds that the ladies and gentlemen of the court prized so. I never did see any gem so vivid and vibrant as a daffodil or an amethyst even half so regal a purple as a violet or a pearl as perfect as a snowdrop. Just the thought of them made me homesick. I loved to lie amidst the flowers; I found more comfort there than in any feather bed, perfumed linen sheets, and velvet coverlet. To lie in a bed of flowers was to rest in Mother Nature's bridal bower.

When I arrived at Durham House, the Dudleys' stately London town house, prominently situated in the Strand, and walked past the fierce pair of grey stone bears standing upright clutching ragged staves that flanked the front steps, I was a bundle of nerves but loosely bound together. I felt as if the tiniest touch or the barest breeze might make me fall apart; just one breath and I would be like ashes in the wind. I feared the very steps would slip away from beneath my feet as I mounted them, deeming me unworthy to set foot on them. I felt like a cinder-begrimed scullery maid in tattered rags and dirty feet about to walk into a court ball where everyone was in shimmering silks and lustrous satins ablaze with jewels. I knew I did not belong here and that, no matter how hard I tried, I was destined to disappoint those who dwelled inside.

Robert's favourite sister, Mary, and his mother greeted me coolly but kindly, stiffly embracing me so as not to crush their fine gowns and kissing me on each cheek, though their lips scarcely touched my skin. It left me feeling like a leper, as if they thought the very touch of me could taint them.

Before we could progress any farther, or I could be shown to my room, I beheld an astonishing sight. Two men appeared at the top of the stairs. One was obviously a servant, grey-haired and clad in the Dudley blue livery with an embroidered badge of a bear clutching a ragged staff on his sleeve. The other was a breathtaking young Adonis, aged about seventeen, who glowed like the very sun itself, resplendent in a gold brocade dressing gown with big diamond-centred rosettes on the toes of his golden slippers, his golden hair tied up in curling rags. The servant held a large silver platter of what appeared to be candied figs, syrupy and sweet, generously dusted with sugar crystals.

"You idiot!" the petulant young sun god shrieked, striking the platter from underneath so that, standing below stairs, I suddenly found myself being pelted by a shower of candied figs. "These are *candied* figs, you fool! My complexion demands the milk of *green* figs to look its best! And how dare you serve me on silver? I demand the best! I must have gold! Gold for Guildford! *Gold!*" He stamped his foot down hard upon the servant's toes. Then he threw back his head and bellowed, *"MOTHER!"* in a voice so loud and shrill that it pierced my eardrums like a pin until I feared they would go *pop!*

"Yes, dear!" In a breathless rush Lady Dudley gathered up her skirts and was up the stairs and at his side in a trice, panting and holding her side as though her stays pinched.

I just stood and stared as if I had been stricken dumb as a pair of serving maids silently appeared and knelt to clean up the sticky mess of figs from the floor around me. So this was Guildford, Robert's youngest and soon-to-be-married brother.

"This man is incompetent!" Guildford jabbed an accusing finger at his servant. "I *demand* that he be dismissed at once, thrown out into the street without pay. And don't you *dare* give him a good reference. I wouldn't recommend him to serve gruel to condemned prisoners! I want a new valet!"

Turning to the valet with an apologetic smile, Lady Dudley began, "You heard my son, John . . ."

"George, ma'am," the valet corrected. "I believe the man who held this post before me was called John."

"No, it was Thomas," Mary called up helpfully. "John was the one before him, right after Mark."

"I don't care what his name is!" Guildford snapped. "Where's Father? I *must* have a new valet at once—someone who knows how to wait upon a great lord. This man does not even know how to serve a plate of figs correctly!"

"Your father is at court, dear," Lady Dudley gently explained, lovingly stroking Guildford's brow as if she were trying to smooth away the mutinous scowl that made him at once to be both a beauty and a beast. "The poor King is very ill . . ."

Guildford's face lit up with interest. "If the King dies, can I have his valet?"

"I don't see why not," Lady Dudley declared. "I think that is an *excellent* idea. The man will surely want employment . . . but, for now, my darling boy, let us make do as best we can with Michael . . ."

"George, ma'am," the valet corrected.

"All right, Mother." Guildford heaved a sigh worthy of a mar- tyr. "Well? Don't just stand there gaping, you nitwit! Get me some figs! *Green* figs! Then you can squeeze the milk from them and massage my face with it. But first, go draw my bath!" And with those words he spun round and stalked away, presumably back to his room.

"Yes, My Lord." The valet heaved a sigh and followed him like a man on his way to the gallows. "And for your bath, will you be wantin' the asses' milk or the crushed strawberries mixed with rosewater?"

"The asses' milk, you ass!" Guildford screamed as he slammed the door.

"You must excuse Guildford," Lady Dudley said as she de- scended the stairs again, "he's just nervous. He's always been rather delicate, and he is such a sensitive boy, and he's never been a bride- groom before. My little golden bird is nervous about flying the nest!"

"Is . . . Is . . . h-he . . . Is he *always* like that?" I stammered.

"Whatever do you mean?" I was startled to hear my husband's voice and spun round, stumbling over my own feet and nearly falling, to discover him and his father standing behind me. Appar- ently they had come in whilst I was watching the scene above. "When servants do not perform their duties properly, one must reprimand them. Surely you know that, Amy?"

"My dear daughter-in-law," the Earl of Warwick, now styled the Duke of Northumberland, began in a tone that made it quite clear that I was not at all dear to him, "are you aware that there are *stains* on your dress? And is that . . . *sugar* on your shoulders? Robert, you should instruct your wife that this is London, not the country, and she must make every effort not to appear slovenly and un- kempt; people notice such things, and they do not forget. Dudleys do not marry slatterns. And Dudley women either born or joined to us by marriage do not appear in public with stains upon their clothes."

I glanced down at my rat grey velvet travelling dress and saw to my dismay that the brown syrup used to coat the sweet figs had left dribbling stains all down my bodice and skirt like a series of smeared blots and smaller dots.

"I . . . I'm s-sorry," I stammered with tears welling in my eyes. "Y-your s-son . . . G-G-Guildford . . . the f-figs . . . h-he . . ." I endeavoured to explain, blushing hotly as I felt Robert's hand fastidiously brushing the sugar crystals from my shoulders and disdainfully plucking a stray fig from the nest of white and grey plumes atop my hat.

"How very thoughtful of Guildford!" the Duke exclaimed, smiling at the thought of his youngest son as he led the way into the parlour. "But, my dear"—he turned anxiously to his wife—"you *must* instruct Guildford to let the servants serve refreshments to our guests. I know he wants to be a gracious host, but that is what they are here for."

"Yes, dear." Lady Dudley, always a dutiful wife, obediently nodded. "But you *know* how Guildford is . . ."

"Yes." The Duke nodded. "He is such a kind, thoughtful, generous boy . . ."

Seeing my astonishment—I couldn't believe my ears—Lady Dudley hastened to explain, "Of course we love all our children, but . . . Guildford is the youngest, and we all dote upon him so!"

At that moment, Guildford, still in his gold dressing gown and curling rags, apparently having put off his bath and slathering his face with fig milk for the moment, strode in as grand as an emperor with his much-harassed manservant trailing after him like a royal trainbearer.

"Father, is the King dead yet? I need a new valet! What are you standing there for?" He turned suddenly to his servant, stamping on the poor fellow's toes again. "I'm hungry; fetch me some figs! *Now!*"

"Yes, My Lord," the weary servant sighed, and moments later, as Guildford was busy petitioning his father to have the King's valet for his own if the King died, the man returned with a gold platter heaped high with green figs.

"Are you trying to make me ill? Are you trying to kill me? Don't bother to deny it—I *know* you are!" Guildford rounded furiously on the poor fellow. "I can't eat these! They're *green*! I want candied figs, and I want them *now*!" And with that he struck the golden platter from below and, once again, figs went flying everywhere.

Before I knew what I was doing, the words were flying out of my mouth. "Are you all blind and deaf or just insane? Guildford is the most hateful, rude, spoiled, obnoxious, and ungrateful boy I have *ever* seen in my life! I would not talk to a dog the way he does to his manservant! If he were my son, I would wallop him with a broomstick and send him to sleep in the cellar and dine on naught but table scraps until he learned to keep a civil tongue and behave like a gentleman!"

Lady Dudley gave a cry and wilted against her husband in a half swoon while Mary, Robert, and their father all stared at me as if I had suddenly turned green, and, had Guildford's eyes been daggers, they would most assuredly have cut me into mincemeat.

It was the much-put-upon valet who broke the silence. "Amen to that, even if I'm horsewhipped for sayin' so! God save you, ma'am"—he bowed to me—"that is the most honest and sensible thing I've heard anyone in this house say the whole week I've been here. No need to throw me out, My Lady"—he bowed to Lady Dudley—"I know where the door is." And, so saying, he turned his back on us all and walked out, whereupon Guildford shattered the stunned silence by bursting into tears.

"You *can't* leave me! You *can't*! What will I do without a valet? How will I live? If I don't have a valet, I *know* I shall die! These curl rags are too tight; they make my head ache, and I can't take them out myself!" And with that declaration he flung himself weeping onto the fireside settle and buried his face in the crimson velvet cushions, weeping as though he had just lost the love of his life. I was appalled. I had never seen a boy of any age carry on so, and this one, at seventeen, was accounted a man.

"Now, darling, don't cry!" Lady Dudley pleaded as she rushed to embrace him. "Mother and sister Mary will take the hateful curl rags out to ease poor Guildford's head, and we shall get you a new valet . . ."

"I want the King's valet!" Guildford screamed.

"Now, son"—the Duke hurried to his side, to comfortingly pat his back—"the King is *very* ill right now and needs his valet, but . . ."

"*I don't care!* I shall be ill myself if I don't get the King's valet, and then I shall die, and it will be as though the sun has gone out of all your lives, and then you will be sorry you were all so mean to me! No one loves me! She"—he stabbed an accusing finger at me, causing everyone to turn and stare at me—"thinks I should be walloped with a broomstick!"

"Now see what you have done!" Lady Dudley rounded on me with fury blazing in her eyes like fire from a dragon's mouth. "You have upset Guildford!" The way she pronounced those words, one would have thought I had committed bloody murder right there in the parlour.

"Robert," the Duke said with a severe frown, "your wife is nothing but a troublemaker. Walloping Guildford with a broomstick indeed! Such may be the ignorant and ill-bred way things are done in the country, but not in London, and not by civilised, highborn people like us! And Guildford is such a delicate, sensitive boy . . ."

"Robert, don't just stand there," Lady Dudley said urgently as she bent over the prone and sobbing form of her youngest and dearest child, stroking his back. "Take your fastest horse and fetch Dr Carstairs. And, for God's sake—*hurry*! And get an apothecary too! The poor dear will make himself ill if he goes on like this! Oh, Guildford, Guildford, my dearest, darling boy, *please* don't cry! No one wants you to be walloped with a broomstick, and no one ever shall do such a horrid thing as long as either I, or your father, or any of your brothers, has a breath left in their body! We all love you and would lay down our lives rather than see a hair on your head harmed!"

As Robert strode past me, hastening for the stables, he flashed me an angry glare. "You've not even been here an hour, and you've already made my brother ill and offended my parents!"

As he left, his elder brother Ambrose walked in, drawn no doubt by Guildford's sobbing. "What ails Guildford now?" he asked as though such scenes were very much commonplace. "Did he lose another valet?"

"Ambrose, thank God you are here! Guildford is *very* upset—

yes, his valet has left him—*again!*—and that *dreadful,* lowbred girl from the country Robert so foolishly married thinks Guildford should be walloped with a broomstick and made to sleep in a cellar and dine—if you can call it dining—off table scraps! *Table scraps!* Oh, my *darling* boy!" She clutched Guildford protectively against her bosom. "Mary"—she turned suddenly to her daughter—"there is your lute on the window seat. Sing that song about the old maid; you know how it always amuses Guildford. And, Ambrose, do some cartwheels or flips or something—you know how Guildford *adores* acrobats and tumblers."

"But, Mother . . ." Ambrose began to protest, gesturing down at his rich court clothes, which anyone could see were ill-suited for that sort of thing, but he was sharply rebuked by his father, who shouted at him to do as his mother said.

And so Mary took up her lute and began to sing, over and over again, the maddeningly repetitious tune:

> *"There was an old maid who was forty,*
> *As rich as Croesus was she,*
> *And every swain*
> *Who came courting*
> *She would shoo out her door*
> *As she sang:*
> *'Oh, fie, fie, fie!*
> *I'll live an old maid till I die!*
> *Oh, fie, fie, fie!*
> *I'll live an old maid till I die!"*

And as she sang, Ambrose reluctantly did cartwheels and flips back and forth across the room in his sky blue and silver, diamond, pearl, and satin-beribboned court attire, while Guildford's mother and father bent over him, Lady Dudley endeavouring to calm him with soothing words, kisses, and caresses, and the Duke with more restrained pats upon his back. Both urged him to sit up and watch Ambrose's antics and sing along, and, to encourage him, they loudly joined in the song.

I just couldn't bear it a moment longer and, in tears, with my head hung low, crept out and, not knowing where to go, sank down on the bottom step and wept as I waited for my husband to come home while Guildford continued to sob and scream lamentations that put all our eardrums in peril and would have put a banshee to shame, and his parents and sister sang out with great gusto:

> *"Oh, fie, fie, fie!*
> *I'll live an old maid till I die!*
> *Oh, fie, fie, fie!*
> *I'll live an old maid till I die!"*

Poor Jane Grey! I thought. Though I had yet to clap eyes on her, I pitied her already; I would not wish such a bridegroom as Guildford upon my worst enemy. Unless she died young or was endowed with a remarkably placid manner that cast a calming spell over Guildford, she was likely to spend the rest of her life singing silly songs and turning cartwheels in the parlour to soothe her husband's tears and savage temper. If she were blessed with understanding parents, she would do far better to heed the words of the song and chase Guildford away, even if it meant living an old maid till she died. I wouldn't be in that young lady's shoes for a kingdom, I told myself as in the parlour Guildford keened like a banshee and his parents and sister boisterously burst forth with yet another chorus of "I'll Live an Old Maid Till I Die!"

That night in bed I awaited Robert, naked and inviting, with my golden hair spilling across the pillows and my body laid bare and ready for his embrace. But when he came, he merely nudged my hip to push me over onto the other side of the bed. He spoke not a word—*not one single word!*—and turned a cold back to me. I knew by his silence that I had greatly displeased him. Even when I reached out a hand to stroke that hard, unyielding back, expecting to find it as cold as a wall of ice, he jerked away from me, and when I dared to try again, to stroke lightly that stiff spine, he turned and dealt my hand a fierce slap. I turned away then, buried my face in my pillow to stifle my sobs, lest the sound of them disturb Robert, and cried myself to sleep.

I knew then, no matter what I did, no matter what I said, it would never be good enough, and I would always be found wanting. Even if I memorised every etiquette book from start to finish and comported myself as gracefully as a queen, correct and perfect in every way, still the Dudley family, and amongst them the one I loved best, would find some fault with me. I would *never* be good enough for them.

Even when, in my sleep, I turned to him, wanting to drape my body around his, to curve round him as if we were two spoons stored in a drawer, Robert woke me by shoving me away so hard, my brow banged the edge of the table beside the bed, causing me to wake with a startled and pained cry and send the heavy silver candlestick clattering onto the floor, so Robert had to scold me for making enough noise to rouse the whole house and the dead as well. And when I appeared at the table to break my fast the next morning with my eyes red, swollen, and bleary and a red gouge upon my forehead and a bruise upon my hand, I had to listen to the Dudley family talk around me, as if I were not even there, about how country women let themselves go and did not care about appearances the way highborn ladies did. Though they said they pitied such creatures, they spoke with scorn and used the words *stupid* and *slatternly, ignorant* and *unkempt* so many times that I lost count. I wanted to bolt from my chair and run all the way back to Norfolk and not stop running until I was safe inside Stanfield Hall again, but when I leapt up, upsetting the marmalade in my flustered haste, and started for the door, Robert's hand shot out to grasp my wrist, twisting it painfully. As he forced me back into my chair, he hissed into my ear: "Sit down, Amy, you're making a spectacle of yourself!" And then there was more talk of uncouth manners and a lack of decorum as a maid came in to clean up the marmalade, and my tears dripped into my cup to further water down my breakfast ale, and I gently clasped my throbbing wrist.

"Your wife wants discipline, Robert," said the Duke of Northumberland.

"This filly is yet a bit wild," my husband admitted, comparing me to a horse, "but, never fear, Father, I'll soon break her and teach her who her master is."

"Aye." The Duke nodded. "I've no doubt you'll soon have her docile and eating out of your hand. You've a way with horses and women, Robert"—he nodded approvingly—"and know how to use it; you know best when to use the whip and spurs and when to spare them."

I couldn't even raise my eyes to look at the array of unfriendly faces staring at me; all I could do was sit there, staring down, cradling my hurt wrist, and silently weeping into my ale until the Duke of Northumberland rose to signal that the meal was finished and we could all quit the table.

Rather than spend a day with Robert's mother and sisters, listening to them gossiping about people I didn't know and finding fault with me as we plied our needles, I claimed to feel unwell and stayed in bed all day. Nor did I come down for dinner or supper either. I had Pirto undress me and put out the candles, and in my shift I cowered under the covers, pulling them up high above my head, and hid from my in-laws. And even though it greatly vexed him when he came, expecting to find me elegantly gowned and ready to accompany him downstairs, I told Robert I was far too sick to sit up and could not bear to even look at a morsel of food, claiming it must be the London air or something I had eaten that had made me ill, though the latter he took as an insult to his mother's table and said he would not "emulate my bad manners by telling her so".

Thus I passed each day up until right before the wedding, hiding in my room, cowardly feigning illness, though it led Robert's family to dismiss me as "a useless thing" and meant all my beautiful new gowns, intended to dazzle and impress my in-laws and their fine friends, were all for naught—"a splendid waste of money!" Robert declared them—but I just could not bear to face all those hostile faces that branded me so unsuitable and unworthy to take my rightful place amongst them at my husband's side. Even my husband's eyes burned me, and his tongue spat out scornful, scorching words every time he spoke to or of me. And that—the solid wall of disdain he readily and willingly joined his family in building against me, the lowly outsider who thought the golden ring on her left hand was enough to make her one of them—that is what hurt me most of all. I thought Robert was the one person I could count on to be on my side, to encourage, defend, comfort, and support me; I thought his love would keep me safe. Finding out how wrong I was was like a hammer's blow to my heart.

The night before the wedding, Robert came into the room and ripped the covers off me and ordered me to get up or else he would take his riding crop to my back and flay my hide off. I leapt trembling from the bed and stood shivering before him in my shift. He barked at Pirto to get out my gowns and lay them on the bed so he could inspect them; he would choose what I would wear on the morrow, as it was the only way to be certain I did not disgrace him.

One by one, he rejected them, always finding some fault with them—"too gaudy," "too pale," "too bright," "too sentimental," "too whimsical," "too complicated; that pattern will make any who beholds it cross-eyed or else drive them mad trying to puzzle it out," "too bland," "too plain," "too prim," "ugly as a monkey's arse," "too common," "that colour hasn't been worn in London since last year; if I were a woman and that was the last dress I owned, I would go to my grave naked rather than be buried in it!"; "too whorish; with that neckline, you're ready to walk the streets of London—you might as well stick a banner on your arse that says *Fuck me!*" and so forth, never sparing me, despite my tears and hurt and appalled exclamations. Not a one of my new dresses seemed to please him. *Not even one!* Not even my precious seashell-embroidered dress, though I had hoped it would stir happy memories in his heart and make him turn to me, kind and loving once more, just as he had been at Hemsby. At last, with an irritated sigh, he flicked his riding crop at the willow green silk extravagantly embroidered with silver artichokes and said I might as well wear that one, and pearls and emeralds with it, and the silver slippers, and then he walked out. Even the splendid array of gowns made for me by one of London's finest tailors could not render me pleasing in my husband's eyes! In a mixture of anger and despair, I swept all the dresses onto the floor and flung myself weeping onto the bed.

Later, I rose unsteadily, picked up the dress Robert had chosen, and, hugging it against my body, went to stand before the looking glass. Through my tear-swollen eyes I peered anxiously at myself, staring hard, trying to see myself as others saw me. How had I changed? How had I altered from the girl who used to delight Robert and make his eyes light up until a smile seemed to be the only expression he ever wore upon his face? What had happened to the girl he used to kiss and caress and call his "Buttercup Bride" and tickle and tease because she was so tenderhearted she could not bear to see even a crab or a goose die? What had I done wrong? What had brought my marriage to this low and sorry state? I wished with all my heart that I knew, and then I might, somehow, some way, correct my mistake before it was too late and bring Robert back to me, kind and loving just as he used to be. I was trying *so hard* to be what he wanted me to be, but I didn't know how to be anyone else but me. And I was being me when he fell in love with me, so why was I no longer good enough?

The next morning when I arose to don my wedding clothes, I felt a bubble of rebelliousness suddenly burst inside of me. I flung aside the green and silver gown and ordered Pirto to bring the vibrant peach satin one festooned with yellow lace and embroidered with a wealth of yellow roses. I had loved that gown from my first sight of it and always planned to wear it to the wedding. Then, with my head held high, clad in the gown that I had chosen for myself, I boldly walked towards the door. But as my hand was reaching out to open it, my steps faltered, and I felt a shrill and sharp pang of alarm. What if the gown really was all wrong? What if it stood out as too bright and garish? What if Robert really did know best? The doubt that assailed me now was as violent as the rebelliousness I had felt earlier and made my stomach churn with cowardice and uncertainty. And instead of opening the door, my trembling hands reached behind me to frantically fumble and claw at my laces as I cried for poor, bewildered Pirto to "hurry and get me out of this!" and to "bring the green and silver gown My Lord chose for me; he surely must know best!"

When Robert came in, I was standing morosely before the looking glass, frowning as Pirto finished lacing me, inwardly cursing my cowardice and repenting my decision to change gowns and to let Robert win. Would the peach and yellow dress *really* have been *so* very wrong? It was ever so pretty! He waited until Pirto was finished and then stepped behind me and unclasped the opulent, shimmering ropes of pearls and emeralds from about my throat and tossed them aside, onto the unmade bed, as if they were nothing more than tin and glass trinkets country swains bought their sweethearts at the fair instead of a fortune in precious gems, and replaced them with a necklace of diamond artichokes to match the silver ones embroidered on my gown.

"What's the matter?" Robert asked, looking over my shoulder at my glum expression. "Don't you like it? When I give a woman diamonds, I expect her eyes to light up to rival their sparkle!"

"I never did care much for diamonds," I reluctantly admitted, for better or worse choosing the truth over a lie. "They seem so cold and hard, like . . . ice that never melts, or . . . tears frozen in time."

Robert threw back his head and laughed. "I never heard anything so absurd in my life! 'Ice that doesn't melt! Tears frozen in time!'" He brayed with laughter. "Oh, Amy! Don't be a fool; *every* woman *loves* diamonds; most would sell their soul for them!"

"*Really?*" I was surprised to hear it and turned to look him full in the face, to see his nod of affirmation for myself, not merely a reflection over my shoulder in the glass. "You're serious? You're not just teasing me? Well, then," I said with a shrug and a sigh and a little shake of my head, "they must account their souls of very little value if they would sell them so cheaply. Pretty though they are in their way, they're just sparkly rocks, Robert."

"*Sparkly rocks!* This from the woman who says lace is like wearing snowflakes that don't melt." Robert laughed and good-humouredly kissed my cheek whilst inwardly I sighed, relieved to hear his laughter instead of a barrage of vexed and angry words. "You dear, sweet fool! If married life doesn't suit you, you can always earn your bread and board as a jester; you've nigh made me split my breeches laughing! Sparkly rocks indeed! Oh, that *is* funny!"

Once he had recovered from his attack of teary-eyed, breeches-splitting mirth, he smiled and kissed me again, his hands reaching round to gently cup my breasts as he pressed his body against mine, letting me feel his desire. "Tonight," he whispered, his lips hotly grazing my ear, making me shiver at the delicious, melting sensation that still, even after all these years, made my knees tremble, "we shall relive our wedding night."

I shivered again, this time not from desire, as I wondered if Robert had forgotten or remembered all too well the bruising violence with which he had first taken me that night. I felt of a sudden so cold and sad. Most women would be in a tizzy of anticipation had a husband they married for love whispered such tender words in their ear. Most would not have to worry whether he was rewriting history and remembering that night, and himself, in a better, much kinder light, or if he liked well enough to remember it exactly as it had been.

And then he kissed my cheek again. "Don't be too long, you silly goose," he whispered, giving my ear a playful nip, then, with a fond and indulgent peck on my cheek and a pat on my bottom, he started for the door, still chuckling to himself, still scoffing at my ridiculous notions about diamonds. "Sparkly rocks! Ice that doesn't melt! Tears frozen in time!"

At the door he turned back. "Shoes, Amy!" he said, pointing at my bare toes peeping out from beneath the hem of my green and silver gown. "The silver slippers, don't forget."

"Yes, Robert." I nodded and forced a smile, as Pirto hastened to fetch them. Somehow, in my flustered flurry over what to wear, I had forgotten all about my feet, and Pirto had too, and had I indeed gone downstairs in the peach gown, I might not have realised my feet were bare until it was too late.

"For the life of me," Robert sighed, shaking his head as he drew the door shut behind him, "I'll never understand why a woman who owns three large chests filled with the most beautiful shoes would ever want to go barefoot."

As I turned back to the looking glass, I could still hear the faint echo of his laughter upon the stairs as he again repeated my observations about diamonds. Was it really all *that* funny? Of a sudden I felt gripped by a rising panic. Was there something *really* wrong with me, the way I thought, the things I did and said? What if there was, and I was the only one who didn't know it? Was I *really* making a fool of myself and Robert?

Nervously, I queried Pirto about it, giving voice to my concerns to the only person I knew would not scoff at, dismiss, and belittle me.

"Pirto, is there something wrong with me? I try *so* hard, but . . . I don't think or behave like Robert thinks I should . . ."

"If you mean like the highborn folk we've encountered here, I'd say thank and praise God for it; you've a deal more sense than any of them, pet!" Pirto said as she rolled a green stocking up my leg and tied the white silk garter just below my knee.

Pirto looked up and smiled at me from where she knelt helping me ease my feet into the new—and just a little too tight—silver slippers.

"Stuff and nonsense! You're right as rain, Miss Amy!" She smiled up at me as she smoothed my skirts down. "And I don't care"—she snapped her fingers smartly as she stood up—"what Lord Robert says to the contrary!"

"Oh, Pirto!" I hugged her.

She kissed my cheek and reached out to adjust the angle of my French hood, then gave me a nod of approval. "Off you go, then!"

That Whitsunday was to be a triple wedding, a grand show with three gold and silver brides and grooms. The King was too ill to attend, but he graciously sent fine and costly fabrics of silver and gold and precious gems to clothe all three bridal couples. The chapel of Durham House was decked from floor to ceiling with great shimmering sheets of red and gold tinsel cloth that reflected the light of thousands of tall white wax tapers.

And in the Great Hall there were new Turkey carpets with fantastical designs, swirls and arabesques, vines, flowers, and animals woven in rich colours that fascinated the eye. There was also a series of six tapestries worked in brightly coloured wools and silks shimmering with silver and gold threads illustrating the tale of Patient Griselda and its overpowering theme of wifely obedience and submission. Robert proudly informed me that he had personally chosen them and that he had paid—or overpaid, in my opinion— £2,000 for them.

Someday, he said, they would adorn the walls of our own home. He went on to paint a picture with words for me of the tapestries hanging in the Long Gallery and us sitting by the fire with our family, me sewing and Robert reading aloud from Chaucer the very tale told in the tapestries to instruct our sons and daughters; he hoped by then he could point to me and say, "There—in the form of your mother—Griselda lives and breathes!" He kissed my cheek and daringly, though we were surrounded on all sides by wedding guests, reached down to pat my bottom through my full skirts and said he might even let me take them home with me and hang them where I could look at them each day and meditate upon the story. For one who could not read very well, Robert said, these tapestries were a fine picture book on how to be the perfect wife; even a child or a simpleton could follow the story just by looking at them.

I looked at the tapestry depicting Griselda, golden-haired and blue-eyed, rather like a less buxom and voluptuous me, clad only in her shift, kneeling humbly in the dust at her regal, resplendently apparelled husband's feet, as though he were a bejewelled altar meant to be worshipped, as, nose in the air as if she stank and pointing adamantly away from him, at the gate and winding road beyond, he turned her out of his kingdom to make way for a new bride, one of more lofty rank and pedigree far more worthy of himself than the poor and humble peasant maiden he had lifted up to high estate when he had chosen her to be his wife.

The sight of those tapestries made me sick at my stomach, and I dearly hoped Robert would forget about sending them home with me. I didn't want them near me. I would sooner have my life bled out by a surgeon's lancet than spend every day having my eyes bombarded by images of a woman who would let her children be taken away to be slain and herself turned out in her shift to make way for another woman, all without a murmur of protest—no tears, no fight, no argument, just an amiable smile and an "as you will, My Lord!" That wasn't me, but I was afraid that these tapestries were Robert's way of telling me that that was what he wanted me to be, that he wanted his own amiable and smiling "I would lay down my life if it would make you happy" Griselda waiting at home for him, never crossing, contradicting, or questioning him.

I shook myself out of my reverie, banishing Griselda from the kingdom of my thoughts. The wedding was about to begin.

Though I had been told all three marriages were arranged, I hoped nonetheless that the wedding would be a joyous occasion, that duty would blossom into love, and the couples would find true happiness together.

But the Lady Jane Grey, who would have been a *great* beauty if she ever smiled, wore an expression as dark and stormy as a thundercloud and dripped tears like rain; one would have thought she was going to her execution instead of the altar. The poor little thing seemed so weighed down by her ornate gold and silver brocade gown, thickly encrusted with diamonds and pearls, that more than once I saw her mother pinch and slap and scold her for being as slow as treacle. I remembered how light and frothy my own wedding gown had felt despite the rich, embroidered fabric and gold lace, and how I felt as if I were walking on air. It made me want to rush over and gather up the heavy train and help that poor little girl, but, knowing how in the eyes of the Dudleys I could do nothing right, I didn't dare, and to this day I regret it and wish that I had.

Her younger sister, the Lady Katherine Grey, however, was *radiant*. Though only twelve years old, she was a pert and pretty little thing, all bouncy auburn curls and dancing eyes that seemed smitten already with her bridegroom, the handsome young Lord Herbert, the Earl of Pembroke's son. By the way they looked at each other I could tell, having been an impatient young bride myself, that they were longing to be put to bed together. I said as much to Robert, hoping to remind him of how we had felt on our own wedding day, but I gave a great cry of dismay on the young couple's behalf when he told me that this was not to be, that, for the time being, none of the marriages would be consummated. Robert's father thought it best to delay for reasons he was, at the moment, not prepared to disclose; he was keeping his cards close against his chest.

The third bride, another Catherine, also aged twelve, was Robert's youngest sister, and she and her bridegroom, Lord Hastings, gave no sign of amorous attraction but were cordial to each other and dutiful to their parents' wishes.

Of them all, it was the Lady Jane I most pitied, especially when Guildford walked in, pausing dramatically, framed in the doorway like a living portrait, so that everyone might bask in the sun of his radiant golden beauty, as he stood there arrayed in a splendid ivory doublet lavishly embroidered with yellow gillyflowers and swirls of gold and green vines sewn with diamonds and pearls. Each golden curl upon his head was a work of art, perfectly coiffed with not a hair out of place. When he at last began to move forward, graceful as a dancer, his liveried manservant, the latest in a long line of valets, followed solemnly three steps behind, carrying Guildford's white plumed satin hat adorned with jewelled yellow gillyflowers upon a gold tasselled cushion as if it were a king's crown.

"Methinks the groom is prettier than the bride," an elderly lady gowned in pear-coloured damask trimmed with sable standing next to me declared. "A tasty morsel!" she added, smacking and licking her lips, even though Guildford was young enough to be her grandson.

"Someone can have the prettiest face in the world and still be ugly," I replied, speaking my mind without stopping to think how it sounded. I was, after all, a member of the Dudley family by marriage, so I should not be criticising my brother-in-law, and the fact that I was doing so, quite candidly, in words no one could misinterpret, and to a complete stranger at his own wedding, only compounded my fault.

"You are Lord Robert's wife?" the woman asked, raising to her eye a jewelled peering glass that hung from a chain of diamonds about her waist. Squinting hard as she peered through the crystal at me, she looked me up and down several times. "You're pretty enough, but the tongue wants schooling. *Never* speak your mind, my dear—better to say the opposite. A lie will take you further than the truth any day of the week, even Sunday."

"I understand"—I nodded politely—"sincerity is not the fashion."

"My dear, there is no such thing!" this dispenser of grandmotherly advice proclaimed. "At least not in London or at court. There is no falser face than the one that dons the mask of sincerity!"

"I think that rather sad," I ventured. "I don't know that I want to live in a world where I cannot believe in anyone's sincerity."

With a nod of her head and a knowing smile, she patted my arm. "Better you stay in the country, then, my little dairymaid; let Lord Robert attend to matters at court while you tend the cows instead."

I was stung by her words and turned away and let myself be swept up in the grandeur of the ceremony. Lady Jane, in her ornate gold gown and silver kirtle and under-sleeves, stood with Guildford upon a dais, raised higher than the other two couples as they were the most important, while below them on either side, the two Katherines, one with her head in the clouds, the other completely down to earth, wore silver gowns over golden kirtles and sleeves, and their bridegrooms wore silver-shot grey satin doublets sewn with pearls and diamonds so as not to outshine the white, gold, green, and yellow glory that was Guildford Dudley. Of the six young people standing before the altar, I thought only three of them were in love—Katherine Grey and Lord Herbert, and Guildford Dudley with himself. I later heard that Lord Herbert's wedding clothes had originally been blue studded with sapphires, but an hour before the wedding Guildford had locked himself in his room and refused to come out unless the handsome youth changed into something more subdued, which had occasioned a frantic consultation with a tailor.

At the banquet that followed I was dumbstruck. I stopped in my tracks and stood there, silent, slack-jawed, and staring at the sight before me until Robert pinched my arm and hissed into my ear not to make a fool of him by acting like I had never been to a wedding banquet before. He grabbed my arm and, feigning good cheer and flashing smiles to those about us, led me to sit at the great trestle table beside him. The serving maids were all clad in diaphanous, flowing silver, lavender, and palest rose gowns, like classical nymphs, with wreaths of gilded rosemary and ribbons crowning their unbound hair, and the musicians in the gallery above also wore silver and gold cut in diamond shapes all sewn together like patchwork. And the food! There must have been at least two hundred different dishes, all served on golden plates, and each one like a work of art, as though it had been arranged to pose for its portrait and wanted to look its best.

At the centre of it all was the most amazing, gigantic salad I had ever seen. It sat on a gilt-embellished blue marble pedestal table all its own, with two fountains flanking it flowing with red and white wine. The great bowl that contained it was made of gilded marzipan shaped like a giant scallop shell, and it was filled with all manner of salad greens—lettuce, both purple and green varieties, spinach, scallions, mint, cabbage, parsley, seaweed, chives, red sage, samphire, purslane, skirrets, endives, red dock, watercress, parsnips, sea holly, and violet leaves, and I thought I even spied some nettles, dandelions, and ivy in the mix. And there was a whole rainbow of sugared flowers arranged so that they seemed to float upon the leaves.

There were deep purple violets, marigolds, daisies, yellow cowslips, feverfew, meadowsweet, heart's ease pansies, and pink, red, yellow, and white roses. And there were carrots in three colours, radishes, and turnips carved like fishes, great and small, I even spied a couple of turnip sharks, and there were currants, raisins, blanched almonds, strawberry, lemon, and orange slices, dainty little pickles, chunks of apple, grapes both red and white, cauliflower, raspberries, rhubarb, asparagus, dates, candied mallow root, bean pods, peppers, cucumber slices, eggs, onions, olives, capers, and snippets of toasted bread, and just about everything under the sun one could ever think to toss into a salad. And there were arranged around it a few smaller fountains that flowed with salad oil, vinegar, and other dressings. At each side of the great scallop bowl, posed as if it were leaping out of the salad sea, was a big blue and silver fish, so lifelike I thought they were real, but they were actually sculpted out of marzipan, and the droplets of water sparkling on their scales and fins were actually sugar. And out of the midst of it all rose an ornate blue, green, and gold marzipan pedestal upon which sat three bare-breasted marzipan mermaids, their faces and hair exquisitely rendered likenesses of the three brides. And behind their bare backs a second pedestal rose even higher, and, at the very top, standing inside a gilded scallop shell, like a male version of Aphrodite, born from the sea, stood a marzipan likeness of Guildford Dudley in all his golden-haired naked glory with a small golden cockleshell covering his privy parts. And, kneeling, one on each side of him, as if to worship him, were the two other, darker-haired bridegrooms, their nakedness veiled by pale blue and green marzipan draperies, for none, it was clear, must ever outshine Guildford.

As the banquet progressed, the marzipan mermaids became an occasion of great lewdness amongst the young men who clamoured, balancing upon one another's shoulders or teetering atop chairs whilst their fellows held their ankles lest they topple into the salad, to lick and nibble and suck at the candy breasts until all semblance of a woman's bosom had melted away and they were flat-chested as little girls more suited to the nursery than the marriage bed.

But there was something awry with that great big wonderful salad, as awesome as it was for the eye to behold; it made everyone who ate of it green-faced and sick from both ends, so that there was a stampede and even fistfights for every privy, pot, and basin in Durham House that began when Guildford snatched up a great golden basin heaped high with boiled red crayfish and flung them onto his startled bride. And then, as the Lady Jane was disentangling crayfish claws from her long chestnut hair and plucking them from out of her bodice, he leaned over the table, thrust his head into the basin, and vomited.

With my husband groaning and green-faced on our bed, hugging his bloated, aching belly, and my in-laws all laid low but nonetheless dragging themselves and their basins to rally round Guildford's bedside as he screamed like one in mortal agony, I discovered that here was something I *could* do. Pirto and I pinned up our long, flowing sleeves and tied on aprons over our new gowns and set to work mixing up and ladling out great batches of celery tonic to calm the nerves and cool the fevers of those who were ailing, and handing out ginger suckets to fight down the nausea, sugared aniseeds and, for those who preferred them, quinces to aid their digestion, and dosing them with spoonfuls of mint syrup, conserve of roses, and a balm of wormwood and mint to settle the aching, angry tempest raging in their bellies. In between ministering to the sick, we had a jolly time in the kitchen. None of the servants had eaten of the salad, and after so many had sickened from it, none wanted the leavings, so we passed round trays of mincemeat tarts and gingerbread and baked apples sprinkled with cinnamon and sugar in the great stone fireplace, and sang songs and told stories, and no one looked down upon or thought badly of me at all; it was the *best* time I had the whole time I was at Durham House.

When I left the kitchen and went upstairs to look in on Robert again, I remembered that I had seen naught of Lady Jane and thought to tap on her door and see how she fared.

"Come!" she called, and I opened the door to see the elaborate gold and silver wedding gown thrown, reeking of crayfish, with its laces torn, in a great, glittering heap in the middle of the floor, along with a few stray crayfish that had been caught in its folds, while the slight, black-gowned figure of Lady Jane, her glorious chestnut hair severely pulled back and pinned under a plain black

French hood, curled up on the window seat, nonchalantly munching a pear, her head bent over a book.

"I just came to see if you were unwell and might need anything." I nodded down at my basket of remedies.

"No." She shook her head, barely bothering to look up from her book. "While I cannot honestly say that I am well, I did not partake of the salad, so . . ." Her words trailed off as she turned the page.

Her rude indifference irked me, and I snapped, "There are a great many ill, you know, including your husband, both your parents, and all your in-laws; you might have come and helped us tend the sick instead of burying your nose in a book and leaving all the work for others to do!"

For the first time since I had come into the room, Jane lifted her head and looked at me with a chilling stare that froze my blood and made the nape of my neck prickle. "Why should I help those I hate?" she asked in a voice as smooth as glass.

"Well, it's the kind thing to do!" I exclaimed. "For all your studying of the Bible—I'm told you can read it in Latin and Greek and are studying ancient Hebrew so you can read it in that language too—you might try living by its teachings instead of just memorising the words and debating over their meanings! But"—I sighed and threw up my hands—"please yourself. You will anyway!" And I turned and left her.

As I continued on my way to check on Robert, I heard a groaning from an alcove hidden behind a gold-fringed red velvet arras and went to give what aid I could. But when I pulled it aside, I saw that the couple there was in no need of my assistance and more likely to resent my intrusion. For there were Katherine Grey and Lord Herbert, he with his back to me, and she with her skirts up and her bodice down, clinging to him, with her arms wrapped tightly around his neck and her legs around his hips, plainly defying the Duke of Northumberland's edict that none of the marriages was to be consummated for the time being.

Seeing me, Katherine squealed and unwound from her beloved as he spun round guiltily to face me.

"Please don't tell!" Katherine pleaded as she hastily pulled her gown up over her breasts and smoothed down her skirts.

"Please!" begged her hot-faced bridegroom as he fumbled and struggled to lace up his codpiece.

"Of course I won't!" I assured them. "It seems to me that someone should get some joy out of this day!" And, with a smile, I let the arras fall back into place and left them to their pleasure.

Two days later I departed Durham House, alone but for Pirto and my entourage of liveried servants brandishing the Dudley banner of bear and ragged staff. And bringing up the rear, behind the cart laden with my trunks of mostly unworn finery, lumbered a second cart, with the tapestries of Patient Griselda carefully rolled up and wrapped in linen sheets with sachets of herbs to keep the moths away. Robert had personally supervised their packing. He even made a point of sending along a serving woman charged with the sole task of caring for them, as he doubted there was anyone at Stanfield Hall who was suitable, forgetting that we had many fine tapestries and not a one of them had been reduced to a moth-eaten rag. He paced back and forth and swore up and down that backs would be flayed if the tapestries suffered any damage upon the journey or after they arrived.

He was still preoccupied with seeing the tapestries safely loaded onto the cart when I bid him farewell, and he merely brushed a quick kiss across my cheek, then was off to cuff the ear of a lad who nearly dropped one end of the tapestry he was helping carry across the courtyard.

Though I hated to say goodbye to my husband and felt as if I were being sent away in disgrace, as a punishment, like a naughty child who had misbehaved, a part of me was heartily glad to quit the Dudley abode. There was no more talk about presenting me at court, especially now that the King was so ill. Robert seemed to have forgotten all about it, and I hadn't the courage, or the desire, to remind him. I knew full certain now that this life was not for me.

This time, after we had left the noisy, stinking, crowd-choked city behind us, I called a halt to the procession of outriders, guards, servants, and carts, and leapt out of the litter, smiling, as nimble and spry as ever, and called for a horse. I suddenly wanted to ride. I wanted to be out of the stultifying confines of the litter, as well as the Dudley household, and feel free, and breathe—just breathe— the clean, fresh, country air with the sun on my face and the wind in my hair. I tore the cap and net off my head, tossed them to Pirto, letting the pins fall down into the dusty road, and shook out my hair, rumpling it and running my fingers through it, shaking my head hard this way and that, like a wet dog just emerged from the river, loving the wild abandon of it. And, startling the groom who came to help me to mount, I swung my leg over the saddle to ride astride rather than sidesaddle as becomes a fine lady. I dug my heels into the piebald's sides and galloped off, laughing and waving back at my dumbstruck entourage.

I was going home where I belonged. I was only sorry that it wasn't at my husband's side. I thought we belonged together, but Robert disagreed, and in a marriage it is the husband's word that carries the weight and is like unto law. I understood by his gift of the tapestries that Robert wanted Patient Griselda for a wife, and he had either mistaken Amy Robsart for her or thought he could press her into that mould, like the confectioners did to make figures out of marzipan—that the Amy he married would go docile and trusting into the mould just as he wanted her to and come out as Griselda. But he was *wrong*!

❧ 12 ❧

Amy Robsart Dudley

Stanfield Hall, near Wymondham, in Norfolk
July 1553

I did not see my husband again until July. I was in the kitchen, gossiping and having a laugh with Cook and the maids. I had the sleeves of another old gown—the pink one I had gotten stained with paint—pinned up and was mixing a bowl of spiced batter to coat a roast in while Cook readied it for the spit, when he burst in, taking us all by surprise. He snatched the bowl right out of my hands and flung it at the wall, sending shards of green-glazed pottery and batter flying everywhere; then he wrenched the spoon from my hand and tossed that away too, and ripped the apron from me with such force that it tore underneath the waistband and I was left with the strings still knotted round my waist and frayed threads dangling down in front as he grabbed my hand and dragged me upstairs where his wife belonged, scarcely even stopping when I stumbled and banged my knees upon the stone stairs.

"Christ's blood, Amy, you're clumsy as a tot in leading strings when it comes to stairs!" he snapped as I hastily righted myself, and he gave my hand an impatient tug, nigh pulling my arm from its socket by the way it felt, and I knew I would have to ask Pirto to rub it with liniment before I went to bed that night, else it would pain me like the Devil on the morrow.

Upstairs in the privacy of my bedchamber, while I removed the remnants of the torn apron and tidied my hair and quickly shed my gown and covered myself with a pretty yellow damask dressing gown as Robert barked at me to "take that filthy rag off; just looking at it makes my eyes sore!" Robert poured himself a goblet of wine and raged like a caged lion, pacing back and forth before the unlit fireplace.

"It should have been me!" he cried, both petulant and passionate, before bolting down an overflowing goblet of red wine, then refilling it and draining it by half in one gulp. "It should have been King Robert I, *not* King Guildford I! My little brother has stolen *my* crown, and *you*"—he levelled an accusing finger at me—"*you* cheated me of my destiny, *you* tricked me into marrying you, and now, because of *you,* I'll *never* be King!"

Stung by the venom in his words, I was half afraid to ask, yet I forced myself to stammer, "B-But, R-R-Robert, I . . . I don't understand; wh-what are you talking about? H-How could you b-be King or G-Guildford either?"

"Of course *you* don't understand; *you never* do!" Robert spat the words at me as he refilled his goblet again. Each word was like a slap in the face to me, and, in truth, I thought blows would have been kinder; they would have only stung and smarted for a little while, and after a few days the bruises would heal, but the words would burrow into my memory and make a home for themselves there from whence they could come out whenever they pleased or were summoned forth to hurt me all over again. "Do you *ever* understand *anything*? God's teeth, what did I ever do to deserve to be married to a simpleton like you? Why do you think Guildford married Jane? The King is dead, though it's not to be announced yet, so tell no one; only Father and a few others know. Before he died, Edward wrote a new will; Father propped him up in bed and helped him sign it; he was so weak, he could scarcely hold the quill. Mary and Elizabeth are out—we'll not have Catholic Mary on the throne—England's a Protestant country now, and all the Papists can go hang or drown!—and Elizabeth will brook no master; not even Father can control her—so Jane is in. She'll do what's good for her or else . . . She has felt the sting of the whip before—her parents have seen to that—so she *knows*! She shall be proclaimed Queen in

London very shortly, and Guildford shall be King of England. If I had married Jane instead of you, I would be King Robert I of England! Oh, *why, why* did I not listen to my father?" He tore at his hair as he paced back and forth before me. "He tried to stop me, but I would have you against all reason; I in my young man's lust knew better than any! *God damn you!* May He curse and rot you from the inside out for what you've done to me!" He paused to fill his goblet again, but halfway to his mouth he changed his mind and hurled it at me. And though I put up my arms to shield my face, I was still spattered with wine, and my lovely yellow dressing gown was ruined, stained with red blotches like blood that would never wash out.

When I put my arms down, he was already on the stairs, boot heels clattering, spurs jangling, leaving me as suddenly as he had come. "Never mind about ordering a dress for the coronation," he shouted back over his shoulder. "No one wants you in London. You can stay here in the country and rot for all eternity for all I care! At least that way you'll not embarrass me!"

I later learned that he was off, riding hard at the head of an army of five hundred men, to capture the Princess Mary before she could proclaim herself Queen and rally the people round her to claim the throne that was hers by right. But at this he failed. The reign of Queen Jane lasted just nine days. And when Mary took the throne and set the prisoners from her late brother's reign free, there were plenty more to take their places in the Tower of London, including all the Dudley sons, their father, and the unwilling usurper, the luckless Lady Jane, who I heard even as the crown was being forced onto her head tried to push it away, sobbing, "It is not my right!"

As all England celebrated the ascension of Queen Mary, I was sick with worry about my husband. Hellish, blood-drenched dreams of horror, of Robert chained up in a dark dungeon and undergoing fiendish tortures, screaming like a damned soul for mercy as his nails were ripped out, or mounting the scaffold and having his head struck off, disturbed my rest at night, and even if I attempted to steal a nap during the day, still they tormented me. It seemed every time I closed my eyes, I saw my husband's severed head with his neck dripping blood, while his clouded eyes stared sightlessly into space, dead to the world with no emotion or light of life to light them.

The whole Dudley clan were branded traitors, and it was a most fortunate thing indeed that I had a safe and welcoming home with my parents, for all the Dudley estates and lands were confiscated by the Crown. Even quaint little Hemsby Castle, where Robert and I had loved and frolicked in the sea, was confiscated by Queen Mary.

❧ 13 ❧

Amy Robsart Dudley

London
August 1553–October 1554

It took *all* my courage to return to London, but I *had* to see him, to know if he was all right. I clung to Pirto and cowered behind the curtains of our litter as the stench of death and rotting flesh overpowered us. Pirto pressed a pomander ball of oranges and cloves against my nose and urged me to "breathe deeply, love, breathe deeply, close your eyes, and don't think about what's outside". But I couldn't help it. Bodies of executed traitors hung like rotten fruit from gibbets on every street corner. They terrified me; their ghoulish faces haunted my dreams. I felt suffocated in the city, the way the houses leaned towards one another across the narrow streets, nigh blotting out the sun, and the danger of being drenched in filth as housewives tossed the contents of their chamber pots out the upstairs windows with only a careless cry of warning that scarcely allowed any time to avoid a nasty, fetid drenching.

When I disembarked from the litter, teetering on the high-soled wooden pattens I wore strapped to my feet to protect my slippers from being soiled by the filthy streets, and struggling with the weight of the large basket I clutched protectively against me, dirty little hands of rag-clad children reached out to tug at my skirts and heart as they pleaded for pennies. Pirto had to beat them back to clear a path for me. But I couldn't say no to such sad faces, and I reached into my purse and drew out a handful of coins.

"Toss them down, My Lady, toss them down!" Pirto cried as they clamoured about me, jumping up and down and standing on tiptoe, shoving and jostling as they strained to reach up and snatch the money from my hand. And, though it seemed such a contemptuous gesture, I did as Pirto said and threw the pennies onto the ground. The children instantly abandoned me and pounced on them.

The breath caught in my throat as I gazed up at the Tower. It was such a terrifying place, grim grey on the outside and blood-drenched within. It was as if just standing outside of it I could feel all the suffering that had gone on within its walls, and I didn't want to go on, I didn't want to go in. Under my arms, I felt the sweat soak through my gown and trickle down my sides and back, and I felt so ashamed, knowing that the laundress would see these stains as emblems of my cowardice, and I *hated* myself for it. After all, I was not the one who was a prisoner in the Tower, I could come and go as I pleased—Queen Mary had issued an order allowing me and Ambrose's wife to visit and tarry with our husbands whenever we liked—and there was not a scaffold being built below my window as an ever-present reminder that each day might be my last. But Robert *was* inside, and such was the grim reality he lived with every day and lay down with every night, and I, as a dutiful wife, must go to him. I must be brave for his sake and not let fear keep me from his side.

I forced myself to breathe deeply, reminding myself that I was a grown woman one year past twenty and not a little child. "You *can* do this!" I said with a confidence I didn't quite feel, as I squared my shoulders and, gripping tightly the basket of comforts I had brought with me, passed through the portal of that Hell of human misery.

"*Please,* God," I prayed fervently, "don't let me fail Robert, don't let me disappoint him yet again."

To my immense relief, he was not lodged in a dungeon at all, nor was he shackled, and his person had not suffered any atrocities that I could see. He shared a good-sized cell with his brothers, and, to my surprise, they even had a few luxuries—there were books, decks of cards, a chess set, a lute, a set of ivory-keyed virginals, and even a pair of tennis rackets—and the remains of a generous meal replete with a round of cheese and a large bowl of apples sat upon the table. The apples I would later learn were for the porcupines; the brothers were allowed to visit the Tower's menagerie, and Robert had taken a fancy to the porcupines and delighted in feeding them apples. There were velvet coverlets upon the pair of large canopied four-poster beds that the brothers shared, sleeping two to a bed, and the mattresses and pillows looked plump and inviting instead of threadbare and crawling with fleas as I had imagined prison bedding to be. There was even a spotted hunting hound whose name I knew to be Hugo lying by the fire lazily wagging his tail, and they even had Robert's faithful valet, Mr Tamworth, to attend them. Nor did they lack for fine clothes either, judging from the sloppy array half hanging out of an open trunk at the foot of each bed, though what need a man in prison had for claret-coloured satin with gold piping upon the seams or velvet the colour of perry wine, I really could not fathom. There were even, draped across the backs of the fireside chairs, four fine-furred velvet dressing gowns in rich, jewel-hued colours and matching slippers with gilt threads, jewels, or tassels twinkling on the toes.

The Dudley brothers were occupying themselves by carving the family crest and their names onto the stone wall to leave behind as a souvenir of their stay in the Tower. When I entered, they were all in their shirtsleeves and breeches, hard at work, painstaking and precise as men unaccustomed to such labours and intent on getting it right. Ambrose and John were working on the bear and ragged staff, and Robert was carving a fancy border of acorns and oak leaves, while Guildford was making himself a wreath of gillyflowers. He showed me where he had already carved *JANE,* "the name of the one whose fault it is that we are all imprisoned here," he explained as John and Ambrose fell upon my basket like greedy children, tossing aside the warm woollen stockings, gloves, and blankets, and carefully wrapped bottles of medicine I had brought, and going straight for the goodies—the sugar wafers, candied and sugared nuts and fruits, spice comfits, cream-filled pastries, fruit suckets, tarts, and cakes. I had even, just to be kind, brought some candied figs for Guildford, though I sincerely hoped he would not throw them at me. To my relief, he did not, and instead popped one into his mouth and after thoughtfully chewing and swallowing pronounced it "tolerably good".

"You see, Madame, your husband has become a stonemason." Robert flashed me a reassuring smile as he showed me his work, which was indeed fine, as was everything my husband did.

Before the words were entirely out of his mouth, I was across the room, hugging him tightly, burrowing against his chest as if I were holding on for dear life.

"Robert, oh, Robert," I kept saying over and over until he put me from him, observing that my conversation was woefully repetitious and lacking in originality.

"Robert does not have a witty wife!" Guildford chortled.

And then, to my surprise, though we were not alone, my husband swept me up in his arms and carried me to one of the beds.

"Robert!" I protested. "Your brothers are here—they will see us!"

But he just shrugged as he laid me down and climbed on top of me.

"There are no virgins here to offend or shock," he said, and he proceeded to have his way with me.

Thankfully, he left me dressed and merely lifted my skirts, and his body over mine kept his brothers from seeing overmuch of me, but, from over his shoulder, I could see them watching us as they munched the pastries and nudged and whispered to one another, laughing, smirking, and winking, and even sometimes calling out words of encouragement or advice to Robert. I shut my eyes and swallowed hard when I felt the sickness rising up inside me.

When it was over, as John, Ambrose, and Guildford applauded their brother, calling out, "Fine show, Robert, fine show!" he clambered off me and took several bows before he fastened his codpiece.

I bolted from the bed and ran straight for the door, hammering hard upon the thick wood and crying for the gaoler to let me out. I couldn't bear to stay and try to pretend that nothing had happened; I couldn't bear their eyes on me. I wanted to fly at Robert, scream and curse him, and demand, how could he do that to me? Take me like a common bawd, a woman hired from the streets, there before his brothers. He cared *nothing* for my feelings or my dignity!

"Come again tomorrow, and bring more candy!" Guildford called after me as I fled with my face burning red with shame. "And some lemon and chamomile for my hair; if I stay in prison too long, it will turn as dark as Robert's!"

"Well, there are worse tragedies!" I heard the eldest, John, sharply retort, as I rounded the corner.

I wept and clung to Pirto all the way back to Camberwell, where we were staying with some of my mother's people, my cousins, the Scotts, at their fine town house. Once safely back inside I tearfully waved aside their polite and concerned queries, unable to speak for the tears clogging my throat, stifling the words in a knotted jumble, and nothing would do but for me to have a hot bath and go straight to bed.

After that, I made my visits to the Tower as brief and seldom as I could. Though it shamed and hurt me to desert my husband, what he had done, and might do again, shamed and hurt me more. I knew that, as a man, Robert had needs, and as my husband, he had rights, and that it was my duty to submit and obey, but whenever I thought of going to the Tower, I would, in my mind, see myself back on that bed again, looking over his shoulder and seeing John, Ambrose, and Guildford winking, smirking, and laughing as they passed between them a jar of strawberry preserves and another of cream to dip the crispy sweet wafers in as they ogled us as if we were a public show they had paid their pennies to see. The thought of enduring that again made me sick. There were many times when I dressed myself and prepared to set out, only to turn back at the last moment when queasiness and faintness overwhelmed me on my cousins' threshold, and the coachman had to be paid for his futile journey, and I helped back to bed.

"Whoever would have thought she would be so fastidious?" Guildford said of me another time when Robert reached for me and would have taken me to the bed, but I demurred, lowering my eyes and implying that I was unwell with my monthly courses. "*Everyone knows* country folk rut like animals and don't care who sees them!" But I wouldn't give in, and I didn't care what Guild-ford thought of me.

On a late August morning I stood beside my husband and his brothers at the back of St Peter ad Vincula, the Tower's chapel, under which the bones of the condemned mouldered, and watched as their father—who had, in a failed endeavour to save himself, converted to Catholicism—celebrated Mass. Before he was led out to die upon the scaffold, Queen Mary had granted him the privi-lege of hearing Mass and to confess and be shriven of his sins by her own priest.

"Truly I profess before you that the plague that is upon us now is that we have erred from the true faith these sixteen years," the humbled and fallen Duke of Northumberland proclaimed, still hoping to the last for a reprieve.

Huddled together despite the summer heat, we watched as the man who had once been the power behind the throne and fancied himself a kingmaker, the almost founder of a new royal dynasty, be-trayed everything he believed in to try to save himself. But it was all for nothing.

From the scaffold, he tried to save his sons. With his dying speech he begged Queen Mary for forgiveness and implored her to be kind and merciful to his children, "considering that they went by my commandment, who am their father, and not of their own free will". And then he laid his head upon the block, the axe fell, and he died as I shut my eyes and cowered against Robert's chest, jumping when I heard the heavy axe thud down.

Afterwards, back in his cell, Robert threw me onto the bed again. This time, though he was rough and hurt me, I did not protest. I closed my eyes tightly against his brothers' lewd smirks and stares, and when I felt my husband's hot tears drip down between my breasts, I held him even closer, as his hard flesh pounded and bruised my softness, and let my body give him whatever comfort it could.

In February, I forced myself to be brave and bent my head against the brutal, icy wind and rode to London again.

But I chose the wrong day to go visiting. I found myself caught up in a crowd from which I could not fight my way free. The press of their bodies pushed me forward, battering me against those surrounding me even as I tried to break free, until I found myself staring right up at the scaffold.

Clad in crow black with her shoulders and neck bare, I saw Lady Jane standing with her head bent over a small black book, then handing it aside and tremulously speaking her last words. And I bore witness to the macabre parody of Blindman's Buff that followed when she knelt, blindfolded, and groped helplessly for the block before she found it and laid her head upon it. And though I shut my eyes tightly, I heard the axe come down, the crunch and crack as it broke through skin and bone.

Screaming like a madwoman, striking out at those who surrounded me, slapping, kicking, and scratching, desperate to get free, not caring who my nails clawed or whose shins I bruised, I finally managed to clear a path for me and ran screaming all the way to Robert's cell and threw myself weeping into his arms, begging him to hold me tightly and never let me go again.

As I clung to him, shaking and sobbing, I managed to blurt out what I had seen. Robert had also seen it looking from his window high above. He had watched it alone, Ambrose and John having been moved recently to another cell. And, though he had not seen him die, as Guildford was bound for Tower Hill, not Tower Green, twice he had seen his youngest brother pass below his window. The first time, he had walked pale-faced, trying so hard to be brave and hold himself proud, even though his chin and lips did mightily quiver, clad in sombrely rich, elegant black velvet embroidered with burnished gold roses and trimmed with frills of golden lace, with not one golden curl out of place. The second time, he rode in a cart, a broken, lifeless corpse, naked—the executioner had claimed Guildford's clothes as part of his fee—carelessly wrapped in a blood-soaked sheet, thrown on straw to sop up the blood and keep it from staining the wood.

Robert had no comfort to give me, and, in truth, I should have been the one to give it. But I did not, and failed yet again as a wife. *He* was the one who had just lost a brother, not I. He thrust me away and rounded on me in a fury, speaking harsh words, shaking and slapping me, ordering me to compose myself; all the tears and hysterics in the world would not bring Guildford and Jane back, nor would they save him from following in their footsteps if Queen Mary so decreed it.

Later, when I had regained some semblance of calm, half-frightened back to my senses by my husband's slaps, I went to him again as he stood with his back to me, still staring from that same window. I put my arms around him and laid my smarting cheek against his back.

"Are you still sorry that Guildford stole your destiny, that you were not the one to marry Jane?" I asked.

"You little fool!" Robert spun round and shoved me away so forcefully that I fell hard onto the stone floor. "If it had been me, it might all have been a different story with a different end! They were a pair of weaklings and fools, he for his vanity and she for her books. Neither of them had it in them to rule; it was inevitable that they would be crushed. They hadn't a dollop of *my* bravery and strength! But I was *born* to be King; it is written in the stars, that is my destiny!"

And he turned his back to me again, and I, knowing that it was wiser not to provoke him again, left him to his thoughts instead, with a pinch of grief for Guildford simmering, like salt, in the rich stew of his ambitions.

The second time I saw Elizabeth Tudor, I was hurrying in to visit my husband with a special treat for him, one I hoped would brighten his day and make him smile—a large sack bursting full of walnuts—when I chanced to look up. I saw the flame-haired Princess, who was now the prisoner of her own sister, accused of conspiring with the Protestant rebels to steal her throne. She was standing on the wall-walk, her black cloak flapping about her like the wings of the ravens that circled above, her vivid hair whipping in the wind. She stood there motionless, staring down at me, her face a hard, inscrutable white mask, like one carved of marble. I shivered, feeling like, as we said in the country, "a goose just walked over my grave," and I bent my head and hurried on my way.

Looking back, I think that was when their affair began, when both of them lived in fear, as prisoners beneath the shadow of the axe, wondering if each day would be their last, if each sunrise and sunset they witnessed would be the last one they would ever see. When you know Death is looking over your shoulder, sometimes you throw yourself full force at Life, determined to dig your fingers in and grasp as hard, and hold as tightly, and get as much as you can from it, and savour *all* the delights and pleasures it has to offer. I know that now, but by the time I found it out, I was too tired and timid to grab.

I found Robert pacing restlessly about his cell. I could feel the tension and anger emanating from him like heat from a roaring fire. He was like a caged beast. I so feared his roar and bite that, had he not heard the gaoler unlock the door and announce me, I would have been sorely tempted to turn around and quietly tiptoe back out and come again another day. I should have expected what came next. Robert flung the sack of walnuts at the wall. It burst, sending the nuts that were his favourite clattering and scattering everywhere. Then he kicked a footstool with all his might into the wall, where it exploded into kindling, and then he flung a chair after it. I put my arms up to shield my face from the flying debris. I loved my husband so much, but at times like this, he *frightened* me.

"My father and brother are dead, and *you* bring me walnuts!" he bellowed at me. *"Walnuts!"* he spat contemptuously.

I backed away from him, fighting down the urge to raise my hands to shield my face again. I didn't know whether he was going to strike me, but I didn't want to give him any ideas either, and I was afraid that if I acted like I feared the blows, that would only be inviting them.

Timorously, I told him that I had written a letter to Queen Mary, begging for an audience, so that I might go on my knees before her and plead for his life.

"God's blood, Amy!" Robert roared, slamming his fist into the wall, then turning round and walking away from me, running his fingers through his thick hair, tugging it, even as blood dripped from his knuckles. He swung round suddenly and dealt his writing desk a savage kick that left it lying on its side, shy one gilded leg. *"Why* can you not leave well enough alone? Go back to the country, and leave such things to my mother; you will only say the wrong

thing, and that will indeed be the death of me! My mother knows how to do things *right*! Your country-bumpkin ignorance will be the death of me yet!"

"As you wish!" I blurted through a great, bursting bubble of sobbing, and, turning my back, though he already knew I was crying, I ran out. I wept all the way back to my cousins' town house in Camberwell. I was crying so hard that I quite overpaid the coachman, and he doffed his bedraggled plumed cap and smiled and bowed my sobbing form all the way up the steps to the front door as though I were the Queen of England myself.

With tear-blinded eyes, I helped Pirto pack my things, throwing them into the trunks any which way, not caring if my gowns wrinkled or if anything broke, and set out for Stanfield Hall at first light the next morning. I was out in the courtyard whilst the sky was still dark, pacing back and forth and stamping my feet with impatience, waiting for the sun to rise so we could be off. I knew I was running away, and it would look as though I were abandoning my husband, but I didn't care; he didn't want me there, and I didn't want to stay where I wasn't wanted.

I wanted *so much* to help my husband, to save him if I could, and he didn't even think I was good enough to go on my knees before the Queen and plead for his life. He thought I would commit some terrible blunder that would seal his doom! How could he think I would ever do *anything* to hurt him? The Queen was a woman, and a woman in love, if the rumours spoke truth, infatuated with a portrait of a Spanish prince she longed to marry. *Surely* if I knelt before her and spoke from my heart, she would understand. But, even though he was locked away in prison, I had not the courage to defy my husband's wishes, so I crept away, like a whipped and whimpering dog with its tail tucked between its legs, and left my husband's fate in the hands of my most capable mother-in-law.

❧ 14 ❧

Amy Robsart Dudley

Stanfield Hall, near Wymondham, in Norfolk
and
Syderstone Manor in Norfolk
November 1554–November 1558

Though he lost his father and Guildford to the headsman's axe and would lose his youngest surviving brother, Henry, right before his eyes to a cannonball at the Siege of St Quentin in Calais, and John to gaol fever, and his mother likewise to a fever, but the last smiling on her deathbed, happy in the knowledge that she had succeeded in securing a pardon for her surviving sons, Robert would save himself by swallowing his pride, changing his colours like one of those peculiar lizards that can change the hue of their skin to suit their surroundings, and crawling on his knees and grovelling before Queen Mary.

With tears in his eyes, his hand upon his heart, and a gold crucifix studded with garnets and diamonds about his throat, he *swore* that he had *always* been true to *her* and no other sovereign, but he had been raised and had always endeavoured to be a loyal and obedient son to his father—as all children are taught from the cradle to be—and thus he had followed his father's commands, though in his heart he raged and rebelled against them, knowing that Mary was the true and lawful Queen of England.

"When I was sent to capture Your Majesty, my failure to do so was intentional, not some accident of fate or blunder," he lied shamelessly.

And the Queen, as women were ever wont to do with Robert, let herself believe him. But it was *all* a lie. Behind her back, Robert mocked Mary as "a pathetic old maid" and "the greatest fool who ever wore petticoats"; he laughed at her dreams of love, her desire to be a wife and mother; just because she was naïve and no longer young or pretty, he thought she was a fool for hoping, wanting, and dreaming. "That is one woman who should thank her lucky star that she was born royal; otherwise, no man would look twice at her, much less wed and bed her!" he avowed. I thought him *very* cruel.

And then began the grand deception. Just like a couple of chameleons—that's the name of the lizard I mean—we must change our colours to save our skin. Robert sent for the jeweller and ordered a number of large jewelled crucifixes of both silver and gold, the more ornate and elaborate the better, and hung them about my neck and his own. He ordered rosaries for us of pearls and precious polished jewel beads and had our feet shod and our hands gloved in the finest and most beautifully embellished Spanish leather. He fastened beneath my skirts a cone-shaped Spanish farthingale and about my waist a long chain from which a little gilt and bejewelled book with beautifully painted and gilded pages hung. The words were in Latin, so like gibberish to me, they might have been a witch's curse or a recipe for laundry soap for all I knew, but Robert told me to read it anyway and *always* make a point of saying what *great* comfort it brought me. He also instructed that if any great or influential personages were about, I should let myself be seen embroidering an altar cloth. He strode about in fine, gold-fringed, jewelled, and embroidered blood red Spanish array, with rubies sparkling on his spurs, like blood red centres of a pair of golden suns, and nodded in approval as Mr Edney decked me out in a gown of sunny yellow satin embroidered and fringed in vivid red, so much that I looked as though I were dripping blood. And as he ordered ornaments for our chapel and embroidered vestments for the priest, the embroidered hanging Mary had sent us as a wedding gift was frantically sought and dug out of a box in the attic at Stanfield Hall and dusted off and hung in a place of honour for all to see. But it was all a grand, elaborate fiction, calculated to win favour with the sovereign, because Mary had won, and we must stay on the winning side.

Talk of having me presented at court was revived, and a sparkling purple tinsel gown trimmed with diamonds and beautiful silver point lace was ordered to be "made with all haste" by Mr Edney. But the thought of all the eyes of the court watching me, so critical and condescending, mocking me and laughing at me behind their hands and fans as I stood alone and curtsied before the Queen, made me *so* sick with terror that I begged to be excused. I was sorely afraid that I would commit some grievous blunder, that I would trip over my own feet or tangle them in my skirts and fall flat on my bum. I had nightmares aplenty in which I did just that or, worse, where I started to speak, but only gibberish or crude and rude vulgarity or vomit came spewing out of my mouth, or a great belch, or else I broke wind as loud as cannon fire, the humiliating sound echoing throughout the stillness of the vast presence chamber before the pointed fingers and convulsive laughter began, or that I was so nervous that I lost control of my bladder and left a yellow puddle right there at the foot of the Queen's throne. I would start awake with my face wet with tears and my whole body quaking, fearing that the dreams might be a portent, a sign of things to come.

In the end, Robert relented and decided it was all for the best that I stay where I was. He rode back to court alone, leaving me and my new purple gown in the country. "Wear it for the chickens, Amy," Robert said scathingly before he banged the lid of the chest shut upon it, with the same finality as closing a coffin. "I am sure that they and the cows and the sheep and pigs will be quite impressed, and when you walk past, you will dazzle the eyes of every peasant, and they will fall to their knees and praise God, thinking that a princess walks amongst them."

I knew that he was very disappointed in me. Robert and I, we always seemed to let each other down now in one way or another. I loved him *so much,* and I wanted to please him dearly, but at the same time I knew I would never make a courtier's wife, and I would rather disappoint my husband in the quietness of the country than before the eyes of the entire court. I would rather my disgrace be a private one.

To further prove his loyalty, Robert faithfully served Queen Mary's much-detested Spanish bridegroom. And when Prince Philip made war against the French in Calais, my husband acted as personal messenger, conveying the Queen's love letters to her consort, and his cold and brief replies back to her. Ever one to see an opportunity and seize it, when it was a spoken message instead of written words that he carried back to Her Majesty, with deft skill Robert embroidered it, weaving in words of love that made the Queen's haggard, careworn face light up. She blossomed like a rose after every such message Robert brought her. One time, Her Majesty was *so* grateful that she took Robert's arm and led him into her private chapel to hear Mass kneeling beside her and afterwards gave him a gift of £100 for "bringing my languishing, lovelorn heart back to life again, pulsing with the life's blood of hope and true love".

Robert was still mocking, still laughing, over her words when he lost every penny of that money in a card game and, to be in ready funds again and satisfy his debts, had to borrow at an absurd rate of interest from a London moneylender. He was in so thick with them, I later learned, to satisfy a £5 debt to his late mother's apothecary he was left indebted to a Mr Borrowe, a most aptly named moneylender, for £20 in interest on top of the original sum. I never did understand my husband's financial dealings; to me they were all a tangled, knotted disarray I never could sort out. When he arranged to take over a manor called Hales Owen that had originally gone to his brother Ambrose by their late mother's will, my heart leapt and gladdened. I thought it meant a home for us, but neither Robert nor I ever did set foot there, and somehow Robert ended up in debt to Ambrose for £800 and to his Uncle Andrew for £300, and responsible for all his late mother's debts, a generous stipend of £50 per annum to his sister Catherine, and Hales Owen was mortgaged to the hilt to his own treasurer, Mr Forster, as recompense for various loans, only to be leased right back to Robert, who then sold it not once but *twice,* first to a Mr Tuckey and then

to a Mr Lyttleton for £2,000 from the first and £3,000 from the latter. My mind still cannot grasp it, nor do I know where the money
went, but I feel as certain as certain can be that there was some chicanery at the heart of it.

Queen Mary next sent Robert back to Calais on her fastest ship
with a basket full of Prince Philip's favourite meat pies, fresh and
hot from the palace oven. Robert swore he would guard them with
his life, painting a picture with words of himself bravely defending
the basket of pies, keeping the hungry sailors and starving citizens
of Calais who were drawn by their enticing aroma at bay with the
point of his sword. Nothing, with a hand over his heart he assured
the poor, lovesick Queen, would give him greater pleasure than to
kneel at Prince Philip's feet and present these pies to him with his
wife's loving words and, perchance, have the honour of watching
him savour each bite so that he might, upon his return, kneel before
"The Queen of My Heart" and tell her of the pleasure her gift had
given her beloved, and the pleasure he himself had derived from
being the messenger entrusted with this "gift to nourish love".
What nonsense and cruel, self-serving lies it all was! It hurt my
heart then, and still does now, to contemplate my husband's cruelty. And as far as the pies were concerned, Robert did no such
thing. I think he ate them himself; he later pronounced them "fit
for a prince", and how else would he have known that if he had not
tasted them?

The whole time Robert was supposedly playing "Love's Messenger" and "Cupid's Emissary", as he poetically described himself, he simply cut through the sentimental treacle and told Prince
Philip only what he needed to know and saved the sugary word
confections he concocted for Queen Mary, reassuring her that
though her husband's letters were brief and blunt, such was the
way of most Spanish men in their correspondence, but the words
that Philip spoke about his wife were "infinitely—and dare I say intimately?—more tender", and left the Queen swooning back
against the velvet cushions of her chair, clasping her heart, believing that Philip kept her miniature beside his bed so it would be the
last thing his eyes saw every night and the first they opened to each
morning.

And when he learned that Prince Philip was an ardent admirer of Venetian Ice Glass, nothing would do but for Robert to give him our own vast set, my favourite, much-treasured wedding gift that had never even been used, never had the chance to grace our own table, over which I presided proudly as Robert's wife. Instead, I got to watch—"to supervise", Robert said—the servants as they packed it all with great care into crates filled with straw, and took it in carts, driven no faster than a walk, all the way to London, where they carried it gently, as if each crate were a cradle containing a royal prince, aboard a ship that would then convey it to Philip's palace in Spain.

Thus Robert found favour with both sovereigns, and his star was on the rise again. The attainder against the Dudleys was reversed, and all property, including Hemsby-by-the-Sea, was returned. But we would never go there again; though in those days I still continued to hope, in truth he never had any intention of returning to the place where we had spent the happiest days of our marriage. I would later learn he sold it and sent the money to the Princess Elizabeth, "so she doesn't forget who her *real* friends are". At those words I almost laughed in his face; Robert was a real friend to no one but himself, and sometimes I thought he would even betray himself for thirty pieces of silver. One day, I was certain, he would aim too high, fly too close to the sun, and see all his dreams of grandeur burned to a cinder; he would crash and burn from everything to nothing.

In the dark days of Mary's reign, when the burning of heretics showed England and its monarch in such an ugly light, a blaze that illuminated the murder of hundreds of innocent people, Elizabeth became like a prayer to the English, a candle burning bright and steady at the heart of a fearsome storm.

And Robert, like a hawk diving to fasten its beak and talons on the sparrow of opportunity, became—in secret of course, lest Queen Mary find out and send him back to the Tower again—her most ardent supporter and sent her gifts and money whenever he could to feather his nest to make it comfortable for the next reign.

He wrote and bade me sell the wool, even if it were at a loss, and I did, foolishly thinking he had sore need of the money for his own sake. But he gave *every* penny of it—*all* £200—to her! I was with him when he sent it; it was one of those rare times when he was at home with me, and I saw what he wrote: *I would gladly lose my life if that would be of any service to you or procure your liberty*. Robert dismissed it as mere gallantry, chivalry, the kind of thing men said all the time to royal and lofty ladies, and berated me for "being too great a simpleton to know about such things", that it was the way of the world, and men who wanted to advance themselves and rise high had to know how to flatter the right people with pretty words about love and loyalty. I didn't bother to contradict him; arguing with Robert always left me feeling so tired and befuddled, as if he had opened up my head and poured thick glue inside it. He *always* had an answer, an explanation, that always made me feel at fault and inferior.

I noticed that he didn't sign the note. That told me that Elizabeth would recognise his hand; Robert was not about to risk his gift being credited to the wrong person.

When I protested, he pulled away from me, slapping my fingers from his sleeve.

"Don't be such a simpleton, Amy," he snapped. "Any dunce knows that if you want to soar, you bind yourself to a shooting star, and Elizabeth is a star—England's *brightest* star! That flame-haired Tudor wench will bring such a light to England, she will outshine all Catholic Mary's burnings!"

With her marriage to Prince Philip and persecution of Protestants, Mary's star was falling fast, but Elizabeth's was rising just as rapidly. Even those bound to the stake, dying in mortal agony, whispered her name with their last breaths as if it were a prayer, as if she alone could save England. What faith they all put in that red-haired girl! I never could understand it. What had she done to make them all believe in her so much, to fill their hearts with such hope? But when I asked him, Robert snorted and said it was more trouble than it was worth to try to explain it to me; I wouldn't understand. And perhaps I wouldn't. I never did understand the magic and allure of Elizabeth; I just knew she possessed a rare and special power, perhaps it was simply true majesty, a power unique to those meant to become kings and queens.

On the rare occasions when he came to me at Stanfield Hall, I *begged* Robert on my knees to stay away from court, to forget it all and stay with me. I was sorely afraid he would be killed in Calais as his brother Henry had been, or else become a victim of the poor, mad Queen's delusions and end on the scaffold or at the stake, for though he dressed in fine and elaborate Spanish fashions and played the faithful Catholic, kneeling devoutly in chapel and never being seen without a jewelled crucifix about his neck and his rosary on show and often in his hand, Robert remained in secret a staunch Protestant, and I lived in fear his deception and secret support of Elizabeth would be discovered.

I reminded him of all the things he had once said to me, how we would restore Syderstone to its full splendour and our children's laughter would ring throughout its halls, while Robert became famed far and wide for his fine, magnificent horses. But now Robert laughed in my face and scoffed at his own dreams, claiming that he had gotten carried away, that the country was no place for a man like him, that when he had spoken of these things, he had thought they were the most he could achieve, the best that he could hope for, he was despondent and trying to make the best of things and putting on a brave face for me. But things were different now. Fate had shown him a different and better path, one that led to wealth, fame, and glory, not a dull and humdrum existence as a country squire breeding horses and overseeing the shearing and the selling of the wool, and the barley and apple harvests; Robert Dudley was meant for greater and grander things. "Just because I married beneath me, that doesn't mean I am going to let you drag me down as low as you are, to crawl on my belly in the dust," he said to me. "Just because you lack the wit and ambition to rise in the world, I'll not stay at the bottom to bear you company. I intend to climb *very* high indeed, to *claw* my way to the top, and I don't care who I have to hurt, step on, kick down, and clamber over to get there!"

Every time he spoke such words, I felt a pain in my chest like a stab clean through my heart; they wounded so, I felt I was likely to bleed to death.

"I thought you married me because you loved me," I said quietly, with my head hung low beneath the weight of sorrow.

"We were both *so* young!" Robert sighed, and I could feel him seething at the memory of what his youthful fancy had cost him. "Only seventeen! Oh, what a *fool* I was, to ruin my life for so little so young!" he bemoaned and bewailed his fate. "Lust overcame Reason when I needed Reason most of all".

"Lust, *not* love?" I asked.

"Lust," he repeated firmly in an adamant voice that left no doubt, staring me straight in the eye so I would know there was no mistaking what he meant or whom he blamed for it.

It broke my heart to hear him speak thus, and whenever I could, I would flee from his words, find some excuse to quit his presence. Robert always let me go; why should he have me stay? It was clear he did not want me and there was much he blamed me for. Though I do not think I did wrong—except by not openly declaring there was no baby growing inside me to bind us. I married the man I loved; how was I to know his love was false and that he would in but a few years' time regret it? I wished the love I still felt for him were strong enough to make a difference. But Robert was now mired deeply in worldly ambition and had no desire to be pulled free of the muck of courtly intrigue. And there was no place for me in that world; I didn't belong at court.

Every night that he was with me, as we prepared for bed, I would feel, as if I were too close to a simmering pot, him stewing with impatience, and I feared the moment when his anger would boil over and burn me.

"If I were at court, my evening would just be beginning!" he would sometimes say, the words snapping like whips, as he banged his fist down on my dressing table, the desk, or mantel or aimed a kick at the fragrant apple logs in the grate. Going to bed with me was no longer something he looked forward to, a time he counted the hours up to, as it had been when he was an eager new bridegroom. Robert now saw only the fact that we were going to bed at an hour he considered far too early, not the delights that awaited him there and were his for the asking and *always* gladly given if only he would turn to me. But that was no longer enough for him. He wanted something that was beyond my power to give him. He wanted a glittering, exciting, perilous life filled with pageantry and excess lived on the knife's edge of danger. How could my sincere love and open, welcoming arms and warm, ready body ever compare or compete with that?

So I let him go. I had to. I was powerless to stop him; it was like trying to hold back and harness the wind. To me the court was a bewildering game of chess, but it was the game Robert wanted to play, the life he wanted to live. So while my husband played both sides to make sure he came out a winner, I stayed at Stanfield Hall, but even without Robert there was heartbreak within its walls.

My father had grown as helpless as a tot, and, worst of all, a dense fog enshrouded his mind, and most of the time he no longer knew the daughter he had named "Beloved"; now I was just "the pretty lass who brings me flowers and feeds me my soup and porridge every day". Every time he saw me, it was as if we were meeting for the first time; there was always a welcoming smile and lively curiosity but no recognition in his eyes, and I had to introduce myself, to tell him the name that he himself had given me.

And though his old, time-battered, stained and faded prayer book lay always on the table beside his bed, and he took great comfort in holding it and having me read aloud from it, the inscription he had himself written on the day of my birth—*Amy Robsart, beloved daughter of John Robsart, knight, was born on the 7th day of June in the Blessed Year of Our Lord 1532*—no longer meant anything to him. He didn't realise it had been his own hand that had written these words or know who the people therein named were; his own name as well as my own were now strangers foreign to him.

Robert had no sympathy; he saw only that my father had "turned idiot" and exclaimed in vexation and contempt, "He's no use to me now!" as though my father's influence as a landowner and great man amongst the Norfolk gentry, Justice of the Peace, and former Sheriff, and what honours he might procure for or share with his son-in-law were *all* that mattered. I wept, but Robert didn't care; he turned his back on me, and his eyes and his steps firmly towards the court. Father and I were of no use or interest to him any more.

Sometimes, to my shame, for it only dug deeper furrows into his brow and sorely confused and distressed my father, I broke down in tears and sobbed because he did not know me. "It's *me, your Amy,* Father! You *must* remember me—you *must*! You're the *only* one who ever truly loved me! And I *need* that love more than ever now; *please* don't you abandon me too! I *need* you!" But by the next time he saw me, he would have already forgotten my fit of despair and weeping and would be asking me my name again, eager to "make the acquaintance of such a pretty lass".

But a trace of his old wisdom still remained, like a seed planted very, very deep in the soil of his mind, and sometimes he would make some apt observation, such as, "Your eyes are so sad, even though your lips are trying hard to keep smiling." And many a time he would ask me, "Why are you not married yet, a pretty lass like you?" How could I break his heart and tell him the sorry truth about my marriage, one I had made against his better judgment? Even though he would forget it within moments, how could I for even an instant break the heart of the only one who ever truly loved me? So I just shrugged my shoulders and smiled and said I hoped someday to find a man who would love me even half as much as my dear father did. That pleased him, and he would always smile, pat my hand, and say, "You're a good lass, and your father's a lucky man, and so will be the man who marries you." And I was *so* glad that someone saw some good in me, someone thought me worthy, that it was all I could do not to weep and fall down on my knees and kiss his hands in humble, loving gratitude.

When my stepsisters—Anna and Frances—came round to sit and gossip and sew and pass the comfit box around with Mother as she held court in her bedroom each afternoon in her lace cap and one or another of her pretty damask bed gowns, they were full of advice on what I should and should not do. It was *always,* "If I were you, Amy, I would . . ." They were *always so* quick to tell me how I was at fault, to make me feel that I could do nothing right. They boasted proudly about how they managed their own husbands quite nicely and, even though the men did not realise it, bent them to their own will. "A clever woman *knows* how to manage a man," Anna said. And Frances agreed, "*Any* woman can be a wife, but it takes brains to be a *good* one and not let your husband get the better of you, to put your own ideas into his head and make him think they were his all along and praise him to the skies for having thought of it." Yet whenever Robert came for one of his rare visits, they treated him like a king, fawning over him, scurrying about to satisfy his least little whim or want, and curtsied so low, they nearly banged their noses on the floor; in their eyes he could do no wrong, and the fault was entirely my own. "She's so far beneath him," I once heard Frances say and Mother and Anna agree. Even my own mother thought I wasn't good enough for Robert.

Why was everyone, including Robert, so quick to forget that he had come a-courting *me,* that he had sought *me* out? We were in love when we married, at least I *believed* we were—*we, not just me!*—and though I can in the end only speak for myself, I *know* that with *all* my heart I loved Robert Dudley. How was I, at only seventeen, and in love for the first and only time in my life, supposed to know that it wasn't real? And why was all the blame heaped upon my shoulders to bear and all the pity and sympathy given Robert? *Why? Why?*

He was not with me when my father died. There was no one there to hold me, except Pirto, when, with a cheery smile and a song on my lips, I went in to bring him his breakfast tray. It was my birthday, and even though I knew he would not remember it, I had prepared a special breakfast for us with a small apple and raisin cake sprinkled with cinnamon for us to share. And I wore the pretty pink dress he always smiled at the sight of, taking it for new each time and telling me how pretty I was, teasingly asking if I was wearing it for my sweetheart. "Indeed I am!" I would always say, and I would hug and kiss him. "I am wearing it for my *best* sweetheart!" When I found his life had fled, my knees collapsed, and I fell down by his bed, shaking my head, quaking and sobbing "No!" over and over again. I bathed his cold, lifeless hand with the warmth of my tears, begging him to come back to me, willing the warmth of my tears to restore life to that cold, dead flesh, wishing with all my heart to feel him stir and his other hand to reach out to caress my hair and to hear his voice, just one more time, speaking kind and comforting words, full of a love that was *still* there, rooted deep, even though he had forgotten it. Pirto found me thus, and when she tried to tell me he was gone and I must come away, I clung to him and wept all the more, begging and sobbing, "Don't say it, Pirto! Don't say it, and then it won't be true!" I don't know how she ever managed to lead me away.

The next thing I remember is being gowned and veiled in black, hugging his prayer book tightly against my heart and walking at the head of the long, solemn procession, leading the mourners and Ned Flowerdew and the other seven men who bore the big leaded coffin to the church. My eyes were so swollen and bleary from cry-ing, I half feared I would stray from the road and fall into a ditch. I remember laying a bouquet of buttercups and a lock of my hair tied with one of my blue silk hair ribbons on Father's chest and bending to kiss him goodbye before the lid was shut. And then, it was like a coffin lid was being closed upon me, and I fainted dead away. Ned Flowerdew, I was afterwards told, carried me in his arms all the way back to Stanfield Hall and upstairs to lay me on my bed.

Robert wrote that it was all for the best. It was, he said, "a mercy", that my father's last years were like having a baby perpetu-ally trapped in an old man's body, and instead of weeping I should rejoice that he had been "set free from this undignified and de-meaning existence". He said that it was one of life's great tragedies when a man's body outlived his mind.

Though I saw the truth in my husband's words, I found little comfort in them, and I wept and mourned my father without my husband's arms to hold me. My father's love had been the only pure, true, and lasting love I had known in my life, and, even though his memory was gone, *I* remembered. And while he lived, Father was my living reminder of that love, but now that he was gone . . . that love was also dead and buried, and there was no one left to love me.

Nor was Robert with me the following spring when my mother died. The doctor said there had never been anything really wrong with her, that other women suffered the same dislodgement of the womb that had accompanied my birth and went on to live happy and normal lives with only minimal discomfort, but she had taken with great zeal to the role of a pampered invalid and had indulged herself to death. "Lying in bed eating sweets and wondering 'What will I wear next?' can hardly be termed healthy living," the doctor declared without a drop of sympathy.

As I had no claim to Stanfield Hall—it was, along with my mother's other property from her first marriage, my stepbrother John's rightful inheritance—I withdrew to dear, decrepit old Syderstone.

To my surprise, Robert arrived soon afterwards, leading a lively but nervous snow white filly prancing along wilfully, tossing her silky mane, behind him. I thought she was the prettiest horse I had ever seen, but when I reached out to pet her, Robert slapped my hand down with his riding crop, raising a stinging welt on the back of my hand, and ordered me to never again come within ten paces of her. He said she was being schooled for a *very* special owner, and he would brook no interference from me. "You will *not* spoil this, Amy," he said firmly, slapping his riding crop down onto the flat of his leather-gloved palm. "By Christ and all His saints, you will *not* ruin *this*!" So I kept my distance, though every day from my bed-chamber window I watched Robert putting the pretty white horse through her paces. He took greater pains with her than I had ever seen him take over any other horse, he put her through her paces with a gentle but masterful hand, he petted and pampered her, feeding her apples and carrots and bits of sugar, and making sure her white coat shone like glossy satin and her mane and tail like the purest white silk. And he would go out and spend the whole night in the stable with her if that nervous beauty gave the least sign of feeling sickly.

Later, he lined up all the dairymaids and servant girls and, walking up and down before them several times, like a general reviewing his troops, eyed each one slowly up and down before he finally chose one—a tall and slender-as-a-river-reed, auburn-haired girl named Mollie—to assist him in turning the white horse into the perfect lady's mount.

I confess, I was hurt by his choice. Why did he not choose me, his own wife? I knew how to ride. Many a time he had ridden out with me keeping pace with him on my sweet brown mare Nut-Brown Maid, and he well knew, having seen for himself, that I was a competent horsewoman who had never taken a serious tumble and could hold my own in the saddle. And if it was a matter of breeding, I was more of a lady than Mollie, I was Sir John Robsart's daughter, and though I was not as polished and grand as the diamond-bright ladies of the court, I was not a milkmaid born of peasant stock or on the wrong side of the blanket either.

Many a time I disobeyed Robert's edict and crept too near, anxiously wondering if there was a more carnal reason behind his choice. And if, perchance, he caught a glimpse of me, he would fly into a rage and chase me off, brandishing his whip, causing Mollie and the stableboys to smirk and titter as I fled from the barrage of insults my husband hurled after me.

One night in our bedchamber I confronted him, with accusations and tears, accusing him of being unfaithful, of betraying me with Mollie.

I had seen the way he held her close and they pressed their bodies together as he lifted her down from the saddle. The way her arms stayed about his neck and he clasped her tiny waist. If it had been all business, surely he would have kept his distance and set her feet on the ground much sooner; there was no reason at all for them to linger in a lovers' embrace. And there was no rational reason to do with riding lessons that would excuse her burrowing her bosom against his chest, or Robert's pressing his loins against hers like that. Nor could I see any need for him to reach under her skirts whilst she was in the saddle. None had ever dared such when I was learning to ride, and I, like many a maid, had had a handsome riding master who made my girlish heart flutter. I might be jealous— aye, that's true—but I was *not* a fool!

But Robert merely laughed in my face. "If I want to tumble an ignorant country bumpkin who is as stupid as a pumpkin, why should I look elsewhere when I am already married to one? Why should I set my sights even lower? That would be like fucking a halfpenny whore with no teeth and the pox on top of a dung heap!"

I flinched away from him; I *hated* it when he talked like that, using such *ugly, vulgar* words. When they came out of his mouth, so sharp and angry like arrows, they made him ugly too.

"Then why did you choose Mollie?" I demanded, still smarting from the words that stung my heart like a lash.

His words really could be as cruel as a whip. In my heart, I still clung stubbornly to the memory of the boy he had been, so exuberant and kind, even as I wept for the man he had become. Yet the hope never died that the sweet boy would triumph over the cruel man and emerge from this hard shell with its elegant enamel and fashionable veneer he had created for himself and glossed with the varnish of ambition. Even I knew that softness and vulnerability were fatal if one aspired to rise high at court. Time and again I implored him to "forget it all when you're with me", to break the shell and let his *true* self roam free, to give himself, and us, a respite from that hard pretence. But Robert would always shrug me off and claim not to know what I was talking about. "You talk non-sense," he would tell me. "Unfortunately it is the only language you are fluent in."

Robert blew like a bull, clearly annoyed at having to explain something to someone he considered a simpleton. "If you really *must* know, she best resembles in build the one I am preparing the horse for. She is tall, not short, and her hips are as slender as a boy's, not full and round." He put his hands on mine, clasping their curves through my skirts, digging in hard. "And her breasts don't jiggle like a pudding when she walks and rides." As he spoke, he glanced down at my bosom. "So don't carry on like it's a slight against you, because it isn't, Amy. I know you are more of a lady than Mollie is. But you *cannot* understand how *important* this is! *Everything must be perfect!*"

Then he bent his head, kissed the creamy mounds of my breasts above my bodice, and hoisted my skirts, making me forget the cruel words with the nimble ministrations of his fingers, nuzzling my neck and laughing softly as I squirmed and sighed in his arms, and then he bent me, facedown across our bed, and loved me hard, like a stallion mounting a mare.

Yet when next Robert stayed the night in the stables, I crept out with a platter and tankard and an extra blanket, thinking only to be kind and see to my husband's comfort and perhaps tempt him into inviting me to stay the night with him. My knees were trembling a little at the thought of making merry with him in the hay of a horse stall, when I heard Mollie's high, shrill giggling and, mingling with it, my husband's low, throaty laughter, followed by a series of cries, sighs, grunts, and groans that betrayed *exactly* what they were about, and it had *nothing* to do with nursing a colicky horse.

Softly, I sat the platter and tankard down outside the door, and, feeling suddenly chilled to the marrow, I wrapped the blanket round my shoulders and returned to the house. Though we both knew that I knew, when I next saw my husband, he said nothing of it beyond thanking me for the refreshments I had so thoughtfully left outside the stable door, and neither, to my shame, did I; I meekly accepted his thanks and left it at that. I screamed and wept and raged inside my soul, when I should have done so aloud. I should have banged my fists upon his chest and confronted him, but, like a coward, I kept silent and tried to ignore it and pretend it wasn't true. All men strayed and dallied—it was "the way of the world", I had heard my mother and stepsisters say many a time when they talked amongst themselves—so why should I expect Robert to be any different?

So I said nothing. Instead, the next night when he sat by the fire, seeming so morose and gloomy as he watched the flames, I came and knelt before him with a tray upon which sat two small bowls of custard and a plate of apple tarts with a generous helping of cinnamon baked in and great dollops of cream on top. I was hoping he would remember. The last time I had knelt before my husband with such a repast, he had laid me bare upon the bed and upended the bowls of custard over my breasts and licked them clean, until my nipples were revealed, glistening like cherries, and after we loved, we lay together and fed each other the apple tarts.

Robert merely glanced at the tray and then at me and shook his head before he turned his eyes back to the flames.

"You overindulge yourself with sweets, Amy. You should learn to control yourself; you are getting fat," he said.

I gave a wounded cry and sat back on my heels, crestfallen, still clutching the tray. Robert had always loved my curves, the fullness of my breasts, bum, and hips. Was he now comparing me and finding me wanting beside the tall and slender Elizabeth?

"Once upon a time never comes again, does it, Robert?" I asked softly, sadly.

"What?" He turned and stared hard at me, his annoyance unveiled.

"I was just remembering the way we were, how happy we used to be. Don't you remember the last time I brought us custard and apple tarts?" I asked hopefully.

"Of course I do," Robert said in a voice sharp and crisp. "I am unlikely to forget a night I spent crouching over a chamber pot with a torturous, griping bellyache when I would much rather have been in bed asleep."

"Liar!" I cried out impetuously, forgetting myself, for what he

was saying wasn't true at all, I remembered; it had been one of the happiest nights of my life! "We made love, and you—"

Before I could finish, Robert's booted foot flew out and kicked the tray from underneath, and I found myself sprawling flat on the floor with custard, crumbled tarts, and broken pottery all over my face and chest.

"I am your husband!" Robert roared as he towered over me. "Don't you *dare* call me a liar!" he added as he stormed out the door.

Where he slept that night I never knew for certain, but I could easily guess.

Although it is pointless and does no good, sometimes we can't help looking back upon our lives and trying to pinpoint the precise moment when it all went wrong. For me it happened on November 17, 1558, a day when frost still lay upon the ground, and the trees stretched their branches up to the sky in naked supplication, begging for new green leaves to clothe them.

While Robert and I lay together, warm in our bed, naked skin to naked skin, nestled tightly and bundled beneath the blankets to ward off the nip of November, Queen Mary was breathing her last, wasting away for want of her Spanish prince. Poor Queen, I sometimes thought to myself, how it must hurt her to know that the people who had once loved her were now praying for her to die to make way for another, the one they saw as the flame-haired beacon of hope, her very own sister—Elizabeth.

We bolted awake to the ringing of church bells. I snatched up my night shift from the floor where Robert had thrown it the night before.

"Praise God, Bloody Mary is no more!" Robert crowed as he sprang out of bed and ripped off his nightshirt and flung it high in the air. "She's dead! Dead at last! God has answered our prayers and sent us our Elizabeth! Elizabeth is now Queen! I must go to her! Help me dress!"

I tried to do as he asked, but I only got in the way.

Fear flooded my heart as I watched him running about, snatching up and just as quickly throwing down various garments. Once, he turned to me holding up two doublets and asked whether the forest green velvet was too sombre or the mulberry velvet too gay, but before I could answer, he had flung them both away, pronouncing me useless as he did so, and snatched up a multihued velvet one that looked like a sombre version of a fool's motley, a patchwork of deep red, gold, green, and blue.

I reached out and caught hold of his arm, but Robert slapped my hand away. "Little fool, let go of me; I go to make my fortune!"

All haste and frantic jubilation, his face aglow with the most radiant smile I had ever seen on him, Robert was so anxious to be off that he didn't even sit down to pull on his boots but tugged them on by hopping first on one foot and then the other. I had never seen him so happy before. Without a backward glance at me, he raced downstairs, taking the steps two and three at a time in great, leaping strides.

I ran after him, calling out to him, begging him to wait, and making quite a pitiful spectacle of myself before the servants' startled eyes. The pease-porridge kersey gown I had hastily thrown on gaped open in back and drooped from my shoulders so that I had to constantly pull it back up, and I had thrust my bare feet into the first shoes I could find—a pair of fancy raspberry satin slippers with diamond-encrusted berries on the toes—and my hair was a wild, sleep-rumpled mess flying every which way like a storm-swept haystack.

But Robert ignored me, hell-bent on reaching Elizabeth at Hatfield, to remind her who her *real* friends were, and he was deaf to my cries. My importance had been diminishing for quite some time, and now, with a plunging sensation in my stomach, I felt it hit rock bottom. Henceforth, Elizabeth would always be first, and I would always be last.

Out in the courtyard, even as I slipped on the ice and fell, skinning my hands and knees, Robert leapt nimbly into the saddle of a black stallion, to which the proud white beauty was tethered by a lead.

As he galloped off along the road, I ran after him, shouting his name, waving my arms, blood trickling from my scraped palms, but he never once looked back.

Defeated, I stood there in the road and cried and cried, with the tears turning to ice upon my cheeks, and my gown slipping from my shoulders until it was hanging loose and limp about my waist and the slush making a sodden mess of my expensive slippers. I stood and watched until he was completely out of sight. Then Pirto was there, red-faced and panting from running, like a dragon belching frosty clouds of air instead of fire, to decently pull up my gown and drape a fur-lined cloak about my shoulders and gently lead me back inside.

"He didn't even kiss me goodbye," I whispered before I fell weeping into her arms, sobbing as the shattered shards of my heart drove deeper into my breast.

That was the day I truly lost my husband. Though his body came back to me from time to time, the Robert I loved left me forever that day, he never came back to me, and the tears I shed that day fell on the grave of Hope.

As the beautiful snow white horse raced Robert's ebony steed along the road, I noticed that she wore a saddle of silver set with diamonds and edged with ermine. That saddle was empty, but I knew it would not be for long . . .

✖ 15 ✖

Elizabeth

Hatfield House in Hertfordshire
November 17, 1558

As I stood beneath the frost-spangled branches of the majestic old oak in the park at Hatfield, my white skirt being tugged by the chill fingers of November, the Earls of Arundel and Throckmorton knelt at my feet and, with hands over their hearts, watched as I solemnly slid the weighty gold and onyx coronation ring onto my finger, as though it were a wedding ring. At that moment, I felt touched by the hand of God. "This is the Lord's doing, and it is marvellous in our eyes!" I declared, my heart filling each word. I felt such a sense of awe and wonderment. I came face to face with Destiny that day and saw it bow to me. All my life I had walked side by side, often even hand-in-hand, with Danger, and yet God, and the wits He gave me, had always stepped between, often at the last instant, to divert the fatal blow and preserve my life. Now I *knew* why. Before, it had always been a hope and a dream, a feeling rich with conviction, but now it was *real*! I was England's Queen!

I hoped in Heaven my mother, Anne Boleyn, was having the last laugh as she smiled down on me. She had promised my father a prince, a future king for England, and had died because she had failed. And the prince his next wife, Jane Seymour, had given him had also failed. Edward had died a young and pale, watered-down imitation of our father and left little mark on England. And my sister, Mary, when her time came, had turned the people's love to bitter black ashes when she burned the Protestants she deemed heretics. As I gazed up at the grey sky through the dark lattice of frost-laden branches glittering in the weak November sun, I promised my mother, and my father, that in me they would see a monarch, a sovereign, such as England had never known before. And though some might see my sex as a weakness, a detriment, before I left this world I would prove them all mistaken. My weak and slender woman's body was the witch's cauldron in which were combined the bold audacity of Anne Boleyn and the might and majesty of Henry VIII, and that was a magical and potent brew. In me, England would find a pillar of strength, not sugar or salt; I would not buckle in the heat, melt in the rain, or crack in the cold. I would not fail! I had already learned to never show weakness, except when it served me to bait a trap with feminine frailty. And never to show fear, nothing that could be used against me, to make me seem like a sheep onto which any hungry wolf might pounce, to never let my heart control my mind, and that confidence, real or feigned, is vital, the key ingredient, if one would hold and keep the reins of power firmly in hand and call the tunes everyone dances to. In order to be obeyed, one must act as if they expect and will accept nothing less.

Then Robert, my dashing, black-haired, dark-eyed Gypsy, my best friend from childhood, was there, bowing to me from astride a great black stallion, leading a dazzling white horse, a graceful and elegant beauty, at once strong and delicately formed, fluid and white as milk, already saddled in silver and ermine in readiness for me. He made both horses dip their heads and forelegs and bow to me, and I smiled and laughed and clapped my hands in pure delight. I went to pet the horse, the slush of sodden and brown fallen leaves squelching beneath the thin soles of my white satin slippers. Robin held out his hand to me, and I took it. Then I was in the saddle, and we were riding like the wind across the park. I felt the wind's icy fingers in my hair and tugging at my billowing white skirts, pulling as though it were trying to restrain me, to slow me down or hold me back, but I laughed defiantly and urged the white beauty beneath me to gallop faster. I was *free*! Free, fearless, and five-and-twenty, and no one could hold or gainsay me! For the first time I fully understood what the words *drunk with power* truly meant, and I knew it was up to me to water down the wine and not let it addle my brain and corrupt me. Drunkards *always* come to a bad end, and I would not be one of them; I could not, now that England was mine. I had a sacred duty, one I had been born to fulfil, and failure was not an option I would ever consider. I had defiantly swept that card from the table, and none would ever dare pick it up and lay it back before me.

As we rode back to the house, the dear, familiar, turreted, red-brick manor where I had spent most of my childhood, I saw the austere, black-clad figure of my good and loyal friend Sir William Cecil waiting for me in the winter-barren knot garden, and I waved to him. Though he had served my brother and sister, Cecil had always discreetly given me his shrewd and sage advice. He had long since proved both his loyalty and his worth, and I meant to honour him now by appointing him my Secretary of State, a position akin to being the monarch's right hand, the man who knows all and has his finger in every pie.

Laughing, I reined my horse in, my hair a wild and windblown mess billowing about my shoulders like a spreading flame. I was trying to smooth and tame it when Robert came to lift me down.

He held me close—some might have even said *too* close—for a long moment and, blowing my hair back from my ear, grazed it with his lips, making me feel at once hot and cold as he whispered, "I will come to you tonight . . ."

I laughed and nimbly spun away from him, light-headed and lightheartedly dancing away from him in a swirl of wind-tugged white skirts.

"Yes, Rob, do, and we shall celebrate—the fulfilment of my destiny and your appointment as my Master of the Horse, for I cannot think of anyone I would rather have beside me when I ride out. And I know I could not have a better man overseeing my stables; you understand horses as if you were one yourself. I must have fine horses, Rob, the very best—spirited, prancing beauties and hunters whose energy will not flag before mine does—and I am trusting you to find them for me."

And as he fell to his knees, with his hastily doffed velvet cap over his heart, the white plume billowing up to tickle his chin, I laughed, giddy as a moonstruck maid, and ran to meet Cecil.

He paused on the gravelled path and reverently knelt before me.

"Nay, old friend, do not kneel! Rise, my good Master Secretary!" I cried, reaching out to help him.

Cecil started in surprise, but I had seen that he struggled with his stiff and painful knees, a sad harbinger of the rheumatism that would in time become the bane of his existence and eventually, as he aged, cripple him. Though only eight years past thirty, Cecil was one of those men who seemed to have been born old: his back was stooped from the many years he had spent hunched over a desk, first as a young scholar labouring at his studies and then in the service of the Tudors; his brow was deeply lined, and there were wrinkles about his eyes; and grey strands already far outnumbered the brown in his still thick hair and beard.

"Majesty, you do me *great* honour," he said.

"And you do me great service, Cecil, and, I trust, will continue to take such pains for me and England. I have this judgment of you—that you will not be corrupted by any manner of flattery and gifts, that you will be faithful to me and to England, and that you will, without respect to my private inclinations and will, give me whatever counsel you think best, even if it will displease or anger me, and that if you know of anything that should be said to me in secret, that you shall do so without fail. And, henceforth," I added with a smile to break the solemnity, "I pardon your poor knees from kneeling. Sit or stand as you will, I know you respect and honour me, and my eyes need no demonstration of it."

He took my hand and bowed over it. "*Always*, Majesty, I will serve you faithfully until the day I die."

"As I—as we—shall serve England, my friend," I replied. "Come, walk with me." I took his arm. "We must discuss the appointments for my Council . . ."

"And this vexing question of religion, Majesty—I fear it is *most* pressing," Cecil interjected, as though he had read the words printed on the parchment of my mind.

"I've no desire to make windows of men's souls, Cecil, but we *must* strive for outward conformity. Officially, we are a Protestant nation. All services shall henceforth be read in English, so that *all* my people may understand them, and, *officially*"—I emphasised the word—"the Mass and Elevation of the Host must, in due course, be banned, but those who desire it, myself included, shall have candles and adornments, music and vestments to honour God and beautify their worship. Let those who wish it have their Masses and Latin litanies in private, but if they do not outwardly conform and regularly attend Protestant services, they must pay a fine. How my people worship Our Heavenly Father is their own business, as long as they are loyal to me as their earthly sovereign. I shall decree three days of mourning for my sister, and she shall be buried in the full Catholic rite, as I know she would have wished, but let it be given out at once that there is to be no retaliation against or molestation of priests, Catholics, or sacred places to avenge the atrocities of her reign. We go forward, Cecil, not back."

"A wise course, Your Majesty," Cecil nodded, "but I fear that if the Pope excommunicates you, both your person and throne will be in extreme peril from the Catholic sovereigns of France and Spain. England cannot afford a war, the Treasury is empty, our army and navy are threadbare, our fortifications crumbling, and—"

I held up my hand to silence him. "I am five-and-twenty and fairly comely, am I not, Cecil?"

"Aye, Majesty, and if you would marry *sooner* rather than later, not only would you secure the succession—you are, Madame, the last true Tudor—your husband would not only be able to share the cares, labours, and fatigues of ruling but also enrich our coffers and strengthen our defences."

"While it is true that I cannot impregnate myself and thus give England an heir, Cecil, all the rest I *can* do just as well as any man, mayhap even better. At the moment, I am more concerned with nurturing my kingdom and making it strong than I am with motherhood of the more traditional sort. And I will not make my own shroud by naming as my successor one who already lives and can pose a threat to me. I remember all too well how even as my sister lived, people plotted and conspired to have me, or one of the other claimants, take her throne. Already there are murmurs that my cousins the Scottish Catholic queen, Mary Stuart, or Katherine Grey here in England have a better claim to my throne than I do.

But I will *not* stand by and watch those murmurs grow from a whisper to a scream; if I were to uphold one's claim over the other's, there would not even be time for me to finish stitching that shroud before I had to wear it." Cecil opened his mouth to protest, but I continued as though he hadn't. "As for the French and the Spanish . . . well, as I was saying, Cecil, I am five-and-twenty and fairly comely, if I do say so myself, and I daresay we shall soon be entertaining suitors from both nations, though I must not forget that my sister lost the affection of her people when she took a foreigner for her husband. And there are things I could tell you about my former brother-in-law that might make you blush, dear Cecil, but I shall spare you, as they are the sort of things that should remain a woman's secret."

"I have heard it said that, despite being married to Your Majesty's sister, he was quite smitten with you," Cecil ventured delicately.

"That's a discreet way of wording it, Cecil"—I nodded—"and I warrant we shall see the proof of it very soon. And no doubt the French have a duke or two who will soon come a-wooing. As the Austrians say, why make war when you can obtain what you desire by marrying? It's strictly a matter of economy—it is far cheaper both in cost of money and in lives. Meanwhile, maintain our ambassador in Rome; we must remain on cordial terms with His Holiness for the time being, and"—I heaved a dramatic sigh and pressed a hand to my heart—"grief over my late sister and awe at finding myself so newly risen to such an exalted position has *quite* overwhelmed me and prevents me from making any *drastic* alterations to our government for the time being." Then, quick as a wink, I laughed and flashed Cecil a smile. "Being a woman has its advantages, Cecil, and I intend to make the most of every one of them."

Cecil smiled back at me. "Aye, Majesty, I do not doubt it."

"Oh, look!" I drew his attention to a tall, dark-haired man elegantly but sombrely attired in deep brown velvet with gold-edged ruff and cuffs and a short velvet cloak swinging smartly from his shoulders coming towards us. "Here comes the Spanish Ambassador now! Come, Cecil, we must greet the Comte de Feria. I am sure he brings us good tidings of his master, and, unless I am very much mistaken, that looks like a box for a necklace tucked beneath his arm."

"Majesty"—Cecil smiled and shook his head, chuckling in amusement—"you are the only woman I know who can spy a diamond necklace hidden in a box under a man's cloak across the length of a pleasure garden."

"*Not* diamonds, Cecil." I adamantly shook my head. "For me Philip would choose a stone of a much warmer colour, rubies, perhaps, to match his hot blood, to remind me of that scorching Spanish sizzle, or emeralds, perhaps, to speak of the constancy of his affections and his jealousy of any other man who might dare compete with him on the tiltyard of love where my hand in marriage is the ultimate prize."

After the obligatory greetings had been exchanged, and condolences for Mary and congratulations for myself offered, Ambassador de Feria, still on his knees, begged to present me with a small token of his master's continued affection, and he opened the box to reveal a long golden necklace set with more than a dozen large rubies sparkling like newly spilt blood.

"It's *beautiful!*" I breathed with due expression of my awe—I am a woman, and we do like our finery after all. "Señor de Feria, please convey my most bountiful thanks to your master, and assure him I like his gift well. Whenever I wear it, I shall think of him, and . . . tell him . . ." I modestly averted my eyes for a moment before I boldly raised them and continued. ". . . tell him that Elizabeth well remembers a day she spent in the forest with Philip; he will, I have no doubt, know *exactly* which day I mean."

"With the utmost pleasure shall I convey Your Majesty's message to His Highness." De Feria smiled. "And may I be so presumptuously bold as to express—for His Highness, of course, as well as for myself, his most dutiful servant, and *your* servant, Madame—the hope that you shall spend another equally pleasant day in the woods together *very* soon?"

It was all I could do not to laugh out loud, remembering the day Philip had stripped me to my waist and slammed my back against a tree, begging me to marry him even as his wife, my poor, mad, deluded sister, still lived and laboured to expel a phantom child from her womb, but I maintained my composure and serenely nodded. "You may; I would be *most* remiss to discourage you—I mean, of course, him—Philip," I added, attaching a little sigh to his name and letting my eyes grow soft as though with tender, loving memory. "As a queen, alas, I cannot wear my crown upon my heart, but I know, were I to take Philip as my husband, my heart would not be parched by a loveless, passionless marriage."

"Oh, Madame, *never* fear that!" de Feria exclaimed. "The passion between you and my royal master would scorch and burn the world and leave all whose lives are devoid of love as green as emeralds with envy!"

"Yes." I nodded. "Philip did once liken us to Antony and Cleopatra—a successful version of the pair, of course, without failure and suicide at the end."

"Indeed, Madame." De Feria nodded assiduously. "You have it within your power to make all your dreams, and my master's dreams, come true, if you will only say yes and hold out your hand."

I smiled and held out my hand for de Feria to kiss, to signal that our interview was over. "Perhaps," I purred. "Only, at the moment, I am so overcome, so *overwhelmed* by the rapid and tremendous wave of changes that have swept me up that I cannot let my heart gallop ahead of my mind, even if it would run right into the arms of a certain person," I added with a meaningful glance down at the ruby necklace.

As de Feria, smiling broadly, bowed repeatedly before he turned and walked away, I said in an aside to Cecil, "Hope springs eternal, Cecil. It is a *most* stubbornly determined and resolute swimmer, always bobbing right back up to the surface, even when the sharks snap around it or the current endeavours to pull it down. It very rarely sinks to the bottom like a stone or succumbs to death by drowning, and we must keep it alive in the hearts of my suitors for as long as possible. You were saying something about the Treasury being empty, Cecil?" With a last admiring look at the magnificent ruby necklace I decisively snapped the lid shut and handed the box to Cecil. "This should add a few coins to our coffers. But first, have it replicated with glass stones or whatever serves best; only see that it is done well enough to fool the Spanish Ambassador, as I must wear it from time to time, so that he can report back to Philip that he has seen me wearing it. There will be time enough for real gems later, but now England has greater need of them than I do. And above all, see that it is done *discreetly*; it would not bode well for us if word were to leak out that Elizabeth of England was wearing glass gems and had pawned the King of Spain's precious rubies. We cannot expose our weakness and vulnerability, or they will be upon us like wolves on a newborn lamb."

"Madame"—Cecil smiled at me in marked admiration—"you are a *marvel*! And never fear; I shall see to it personally. When all is finished, the Count de Feria may stand directly before you with a quizzing glass at his eye and not know the difference."

"Thank you, Cecil." I took his arm again as I smilingly accepted his compliment. "I hope I may always astonish you all. God preserve me from the day when my people can read me like a child's hornbook. Now, about the Council, I shall keep some of Mary's, of course, ones who are good Englishmen before they are good Catholics, but we shall infuse the Council with new blood, and blend the old with new . . ." And we continued our stroll around the denuded garden, our footsteps crunching the gravel, as we discussed matters of immediate importance to the realm.

That night in my bedchamber I found myself possessed of a boundless energy. Even as Kat undressed me and helped me into my white linen nightgown, I could not stand still; I was still wide awake and had not the least desire for sleep. Though it would have been unseemly to do so, as I had decreed three days of mourning for Mary, I was sorely tempted to summon musicians and some fun young people to dance with me. "I could dance all night and still be just as nimble on my feet come cock's crow!" I said to Kat, who just shook her head and smiled indulgently as, humming to myself, I whirled and spun, kicked and leapt all around the room, my bare feet flying like fearless doves through the intricate and boisterous steps.

"Robert!" I breathed when I heard a soft tap upon the door. He had said he would come, and now I would have someone to dance with me. And, ignoring Kat's protests that it was unseemly to entertain a man alone in my bedchamber, I laughed and ran to throw wide the door and drag him in to dance with me.

He came in his nightclothes—a rich wine velvet dressing gown ornamented all down the front with gold frogs and tassels worn over a long white linen nightshirt with matching tasselled and embroidered velvet slippers. And he was carrying a fresh loaf of white bread and a jar of strawberry jam.

"I thought Your Majesty might like to partake of a midnight picnic," he said with a smile.

"Oh, Rob, how well you know me!" I cried, and I pulled him farther into the room. "But come, put those things aside for now. I want to dance and dance—tonight I wouldn't mind dancing with the Pope or the Devil or even Philip of Spain himself!"

"Your wish is my command!" Robert said gallantly as he unhesitatingly swept me up into his arms, swung me around, high in the air, making my hair whip and swing through the air, and my nightgown bell and sway about my limbs, and then led me back and forth and round and round in the most joyous, boisterous gavotte, ending with a kiss at the end as we fell together onto the big feather bed, ignoring Kat's pursed-lipped disapproval as she took a seat by the fire, folded her arms across her chest, and stubbornly refused to budge and leave me alone with Lord Robert. Our danger-spiced dealings with Tom Seymour had left my dear Kat more a cautious rather than a curious cat.

Robert bounced up to retrieve the bread and jam, then came back and flopped down beside me. And, like naughty children, we feasted, laughing and licking our fingers.

"This is *delicious*!" I declared of the jam. I picked up the jar and studied the script on the label, the word *Strawberry* written in wavering, hesitant, uncertain letters that sprawled wide across the label as though a child had written it. Only much later, when I saw her letters, would I realise that it was Amy's hand, that she loved to gather berries and help in the kitchen when they made jellies and jams.

"I shall see that my cook is appointed to your kitchens; she shall be the first of *many* jewels I give my gracious queen, who rules my heart as she does this realm," Robert said with fluid gallantry, taking my hand, covering it with kisses, and licking and sucking away the jam that lingered on my fingertips.

He pressed me back onto the bed and began fanning my hair out across the pillows, saying it was like "flames of red silk", but when his lips covered mine, and the press of his body and his kisses became too ardent, I pushed him away and, covering my nervousness with laughter and hoping that my nightgown hid my quivering knees, went to my writing desk and pulled out the chair.

"What are you doing?" Robert asked, leaning on his elbow and eyeing me curiously. "Come back to bed!" He patted the mattress beside him.

"I am writing a letter to your wife," I said, as I selected a quill and pulled forward a sheet of paper. "I want to ask her to serve as one of my ladies. Your position as Master of the Horse will require you to be constantly at my side, and . . ."

"*Please* don't do that," Robert said, frowning and serious, as he came to my side and plucked the quill from my hand.

"But why not?" I asked. "She will surely be very lonely without you."

Robert shrugged. "She has the cats."

"*Cats?*" I exclaimed, laughing and incredulous. "Being a woman myself, though, granted, an unmarried one, I think I can say with a fair amount of certainty that cats, however sweet and loving and amusing they are, are hardly a fit substitute for a beloved husband."

"She will not come and will not like for you to ask her. She is afraid of London and the court and will cry and make herself sick, fearing that her refusal will offend you or that you will be angry and send guards to force her to come anyway," Robert explained, looking very distressed and glum. "Her coming would bring no happiness to either of us. We are estranged."

"And embittered too, I see." I nodded, crumpling the letter I had started to write in my hand.

"Amy was a mistake of my youth, better put behind me, better left in the country, which she likes far better than the city. She is content, Elizabeth; she will understand the requirements of my position and not begrudge me, or you, the time we spend together, I assure you. There is no love lost between us; it all died long ago. It never *really* was love. My place is at *your* side, Elizabeth." He knelt and took my hand and pressed it to his lips. "You know it, and I know it; do not send me away, and do not rub salt in my wounds by talking of my wife, who is better left forgotten. She doesn't want me, and I don't want her—only you!" He kissed my hand again.

"Very well, Robin," I said softly, as I nodded, but my mind was very far away, remembering his wedding day, when I had stood beside Kat and watched the loving couple and wondered aloud, "What will be left for them after the lust pales?" Now I knew the answer—regrets and bitterness for both of them. I knew Amy was a country girl at heart; I had seen with my own eyes how much she loved it and how ill at ease she seemed with the high and nobly born people who had come from London and the court to attend her wedding. Perhaps she truly was content with her life, to dwell in the country with her pets. I hoped so. I remembered the golden-haired girl with the rosy pink cheeks, irrepressible smile, and the bright blue green eyes, in her grandiose rendition of a milkmaid's garb, and her crown and bouquet of buttercups, and her bare feet. She had one of the most *beautiful* smiles I had ever seen. Such a pure and loving radiance shone like a sunbeam from her that day, I *hated* to think of her frowning and weeping, spending her days and nights submerged in melancholy, with the warm, happy sunshine of her life replaced with night black darkness and bleak, cold, rainy-day greyness.

Robert's arms were about my waist again, and his warm lips were nuzzling my cheek. "Come back to bed," he whispered. "Oh, Bess, I have waited *so* long . . ."

I put him from me with a commanding hand as firm as steel. "If you are tired, go to your own bed, My Lord. Kat! Show Lord Robert to the door if he cannot find it himself, and let no one else trouble me this night. It's late, and I have much to do on the morrow and all the other morrows to come! Good night, Robert!"

But I slept scarcely at all that night. Whenever I would close my eyes, the phantom shade of my stepfather, Thomas Seymour, would come to caress and fondle the body whose lusts I so insistently denied and to tauntingly sing his courting song of "Cakes and Ale".

I gave her Cakes and I gave her Ale,
I gave her Sack and Sherry;
I kist her once and I kist her twice,
And we were wondrous merry!

I gave her Beads and Bracelets fine,
I gave her Gold down derry.
I thought she was afear'd till she stroked my Beard
And we were wondrous merry!

Merry my Heart, merry my Cock,
Merry my Spright.
Merry my hey down derry.
I kist her once and I kist her twice,
And we were wondrous merry!

Even with my hands clutched tightly over my ears, pressing with all my might, tossing and turning in my bed, moaning and groaning as though I had the bellyache, *still* that maddening song plagued me, and the memory of how he had once kissed and caressed me; and in my dreams, as he did so, his image blurred and merged with Robert's until at times the two seemed almost one.

At last I bolted from my bed with an anguished cry and ran to my desk to spend the last dark hours before the dawn perusing the papers Cecil had left for me. If I could not sleep, I would work; England had need of me, more so than my body had of carnal pleasure and the disillusion and disappointment that followed hard on its heels thereafter.

"Never surrender!" my mother had once whispered adamantly into my ear, with such urgent emphasis that the words had been burned, branded, into my brain forever. My mother had learned there is sometimes a very fine line between winning and losing. And she had learned the great and terrible price all womankind pays for letting a man straddle, master, and break her, and giving him the power of life and death over her. With the lance of flesh between his thighs, an inept midwife, the fever that often burns out a woman's life following childbirth, a French executioner's sword, an English headsman's axe, or the might and rage of his bare hands, surrendering to a man gives him the power to destroy her.

"*Never surrender!*" I repeated as I bent over my desk. "*Never surrender!*" I already knew what it was like to dance in the arms of danger and to lie down with it, weak-kneed and burning with the fever of lust between my thighs; Tom Seymour had taught me well, and I had seen in the panoply of those who had come and gone throughout my life—my father and his six wives, my sister and her Spanish bridegroom—the pain, and the price to be paid for letting passion have free rein. And I didn't want to spend any more of myself.

"*Never surrender!*" I whispered again, and I resumed reading reports on the state of my newly inherited kingdom. I knew that, in England, I had found a lover who would never forsake or disappoint me, and our love would never die, wane, or turn bitter, even if the passions of my body must be denied. England was well worth the price; it was mine, and I was going to keep it. I would let no man take it from me; my England would not be forfeited to a husband as my dowry. I looked up and caught my reflection in the darkened window glass. "I am mistress here and will have no master!" I said proudly, and tossed my hair back. Then I banished all distracting thoughts of lust and its consequences from my mind and gave myself fully to my work—to England.

❧ 16 ❧

Elizabeth

Whitehall Palace, London
December 1558–January 1559

We celebrated the Twelve Days of Christmas and the New Year at Whitehall. Robert, zealously diving into his duties as Master of the Horse with a headfirst plunge, never let a day be dull or dreary. From the moment I rose until I laid my head down on the pillow well after midnight, all was fun and splendour. There were lavish banquets, masques and plays, music and dancing, and jousts and tournaments. And gifts—*always* gifts—a plethora of presents from favour-seeking courtiers, fond friends, would-be suitors, and foreign ambassadors playing at matchmaker on behalf of their royal masters.

"They all want me!" I cried, jubilantly spinning around, with the replica of Philip's rubies about my neck; a fine, well-tamed, hooded falcon from the Duke of Prussia perched upon my leather-gauntleted wrist, flapping its wings, causing the little golden bells on its jesses to jingle, startled by my display of exuberance; a sapphire as big as a carbuncle on my right hand from the elderly but nonetheless ardent Earl of Arundel; an emerald bracelet on the same wrist from the Earl of Shrewsbury, whom I affectionately called Gooseberry for the colour of his eyes and his short, round figure; a most becoming feathered hat sitting at a rakish tilt atop my gold-and-pearl-netted hair from the debonair Sir William Pickering; and a cloak of sumptuous sables draped about my shoulders so long it swept the floor behind me, the last from Prince Eric of Sweden.

Robert caught me in his arms and took the bird from me and called abruptly for its handler to take it to the mews and be gone.

"When you were a little girl of eight," he began, with a fond, indulgent smile and a twinkle in his dark eyes, "you told me—and quite adamantly too, I remember—that you would *never* marry."

"And I never will." I pulled free of him. "I have not forgotten."

"But you are Queen now," Robert persisted, "and you must, the succession . . ."

"Oh, Robert, leave off!" I cried peevishly, slipping my arm through a sable muff with a great starburst of diamonds pinned upon it, another gift from Eric of Sweden. "*Please,* not you too!" I pouted. "Marriage, marriage, marriage—I hear *nothing* but, from Cecil, and the whole of my Council, from my ladies, from the foreign ambassadors, from my people. Everyone wants to know who I will marry and when I will marry. All of you want to see me wedded and bedded with a baby in the cradle and another in my belly on the way, to give England an heir and a spare, and I say to you all— *Never!* I would sooner be a nun than a wife!"

Robert came and slipped his arms around me again, pressing his lips against my neck.

"Do you remember what I said when you, as a determined little girl of eight, told me that you would never marry?" he asked.

"Aye." I smiled. "You said you would remind me of it when you danced with me on my wedding day."

All seriousness now, Robert took my hand, still draped with the Swedish prince's sable muff, the diamonds flashing in the light that poured in through the diamond-paned windows, as he solemnly knelt before me. He gazed up at me for a long moment and then, most earnestly, implored, "Let it be when you dance with me on *our* wedding day that I remind you of your childish words."

"*Our* wedding day?" I repeated, pulling away from him. "But, My Lord Robert"—I took shelter in formality—"there cannot be such a day for us, as you have a wife already, living happily in the country, or so you tell me."

"Elizabeth, *my* Bess." Robert caught my hand again and pressed it to his lips, then held it tightly, determined never to let go of me. "You are Queen now, and Supreme Governor of the Church of England, a title your mighty sire created when, like a man driving his fist through granite, he persevered and changed the world to divorce his wife to wed your mother. Amy is not Catherine of Aragon; she's a country lass of no consequence, too timid and ignorant to fight or oppose us. All you need do is—"

"No!" I yanked my hand away. "Do not presume to speak to me of this again, Robert. Put all such thoughts from your mind if you wish to retain my favour, for I assure you, I can take away *all* that I have given you. As I have raised you, so can I lower you—my father once spoke similar words to my mother, when he had tired of her, and his eye had already turned to another—and I speak them to you now. I will not abuse my power thus, to satisfy a carnal lust; even if I desired to marry, I would not do it. Leave me now!" I turned my back on him and strode across the room to stand before the great marble fireplace in stony, stormy silence, tapping my nails against the blue-veined marble mantel.

"If it had not been for such a carnal lust being strong and overpowering enough to change the world, *you* never would have been born!" Robert shouted at me.

I snatched a bronze figure of a phoenix rising from the mantel and flung it at him, but Robert neatly dodged it.

"And if our desire is not strong enough for you to grant me a divorce, to right a wrong I committed in my foolish, lust-mad youth, our son will never be born!" he continued. "And England will be denied a king as great as the late Harry!"

"So be it!" I said simply, and I slammed through the door of my bedchamber, barking an order at Kat to bar the door and let no one enter.

But I could never stay angry at Robert for long. On Twelfth Night, when I went into my bedchamber to dress for the evening's entertainments, I found lying upon my bed, its full skirt spread out like a fan, an evergreen velvet gown with its bodice and petticoat latticed in gold embroidery and pearls, and a stiffened collar of beautiful gold lace, like exquisite golden filigree, that stood up to frame my face. There was also a pair of gold-embroidered green velvet slippers twinkling with emeralds, and even green silk ribbon garters to hold my stockings up. There was a net of gold to contain my hair and pins tipped with emeralds and diamonds, an array of emerald rings for my fingers, and a beautiful necklace of deep green stones, the very colour of evergreen boughs.

When I was dressed and about to leave my apartments, Robert appeared on the threshold, kneeling before me, clothed all in evergreen velvet and cloth-of-silver twinkling with the green fire of emeralds and the icy sparkle of diamonds. Suddenly he reached boldly beneath my gown, even as Kat and my other ladies gasped aloud, shocked at Lord Robert's touching the Queen of England so presumptuously. But Robert was undeterred. Smiling roguishly, the movement of his arms causing my taffeta petticoats to rustle, he untied my left garter and rolled my woollen stocking down, swiftly removing my slipper before he peeled it over my toe. From his doublet he took a handful of black silk, and, with a flourish of his hand, he unfurled it. "Silk!" he announced before he proceeded to slip the stocking over my toe, and slowly, caressingly, roll it up my leg, then tie my garter below my knee. Then he did the same with my right leg, first stripping it of wool, then sheathing it in silk.

"Mmm . . ." I sighed rapturously, closing my eyes as I luxuriated in the feel of silk—and Robert's warm hands—on my bare skin. "How *fine* they are, how *exquisite*! Henceforth I shall wear no other stockings but silk!"

"And I shall dedicate myself to keeping Your Majesty well supplied with them. Never shall wool again touch these shapely alabaster limbs!" he vowed. Then, pressing my discarded woollen stockings to his lips and tucking them inside his doublet as "a love token", he rose and took my arm and led me down to the Great Hall, where he had arranged a *very* special performance for me.

Large, well-stuffed evergreen velvet cushions tasselled in silver and silver brocade ones tasselled in green silk had been strewn about the floor for me and my court to sit upon, and with boughs of evergreen tied with silver ribbons and hung with silver tinsel, and a white velvet carpet sprinkled with diamond dust that flashed in the light of hundreds of tall white wax tapers, Robert had created a winter wonderland for us. And before us had been erected a stage, mounted on wheels so it might later be rolled out to make room for dancing, curtained in green velvet fringed with silver.

Musicians masquerading as holly bushes, their green livery— even their hats, hose, and boots—sewn all over with what appeared to be real holly branches replete with prickly leaves and red berries, came to stand below the stage. After they had bowed to me, grimacing and stifling cries of surprise and pain as the holly thorns pierced them, they began to play a song I knew well, for my own father had written it.

As the music began, Robert bowed over my hand and backed away from me, until he was standing before us all, framed by the musicians and rows of white tapers. Then, his eyes never once leaving my face, he began to sing in a fine tenor voice:

> *"Green groweth the holly, so doth the ivy.*
> *Though winter blasts blow never so high,*
> *Green groweth the holly.*
>
> *As the holly groweth green*
> *And never changes hue,*
> *So I am, and ever hath been,*
> *Unto my lady true.*
>
> *As the holly groweth green,*
> *With ivy all alone*
> *When flowers cannot be seen*
> *And greenwood leaves be gone.*
>
> *Now unto my lady*
> *Promise to her I make:*
> *From all others only*
> *To her I me betake.*
>
> *Green groweth the holly, so doth the ivy.*
> *Though winter blasts blow never so high,*
> *Green groweth the holly."*

When the song ended, he knelt, swiftly doffing his white-plumed green velvet cap and holding it over his heart as he ardently declared to me, "Eternal and evergreen shall ever be my love for you!"

Then he clapped his hands, and two young pageboys, a pair of angelic children, each with a mop of golden curls, shivering, all but naked in a white loincloth with golden wings tied to his back, came running, one to me, the other to Robert, with a silver tray upon which sat a golden goblet wrought with an ornate and intricate design of hearts and lovers' knots.

Loud and bold, Robert said, "Let us drink a toast to undying love!" and he raised his cup to me.

I smiled wanly at him over the rim as I took a polite sip of the red wine. I also had heard the story of how my father had sung "The Holly" to my mother, and how she, years later, in disgrace, had sung it back to him, as a reminder he conveniently ignored as he turned his back on her and gave his hand to Jane Seymour.

"There is more, my Queen, *much* more," Robert said, gesturing to the stage, as he came and lolled on the cushions beside me, taking my hand, kissing it, and playing with my rings, pointedly ignoring the many who frowned and murmured at the lax formality and careless familiarity Lord Robert displayed in the Queen's company, comporting himself as though he were my equal or even my superior in rank. "He carries himself like a king," many said of my dear Gypsy. It was one of the reasons I so delighted in his company; he was so natural, so free and easy, and sometimes even made me forget myself.

"Robert"—I turned to regard him fully—"would you love me the same if I were not Queen?"

"But you *are* Queen!" Robert smiled back at me as he bounded up, brushing a quick kiss onto my cheek, and ran towards the stage and plunged behind the green velvet curtain.

"Yes, Robert," I nodded and said softly, a shade bitterly, to myself, since he was no longer there to hear me. "I *am* Queen."

The curtain opened to reveal a painted scene of a castle high atop a hill and Robert standing, arrogant and grand, in ermine-furred purple robes and a jewelled crown, before a huddled mass of grovelling peasants, kneeling bareheaded before him, clasping their caps over their hearts as they gazed up at him with soulful, imploring eyes.

Kneeling at the fore, right at Robert's feet, his springy ginger curls standing up every which way, was my dear Gooseberry, the Earl of Shrewsbury. Blushing and bashful and looking as round as a berry himself, he nervously cleared his throat and began to stammer a speech, his voice at times cracking and rising to a higher, more nasal, pitch before it fell again as he droned through Chaucer's words, with no more passion and feeling than a rather dull-witted child reciting the alphabet. He was imploring the great lord to marry and secure the future of his kingdom and the happiness of his people. As he spoke, he gradually turned on his knees, until he was fully facing me as he recited:

> "But bow your neck beneath that blessed yoke
> Of sovereignty and not of hard service,
> The which men call espousal or wedlock;
> And pray think, lord, among your thoughts so wise,
> How our days pass and each in different guise;
> For though we sleep or wake or roam or ride,
> Time flies, and for no man will it abide.
> And though your time of green youth flowers as yet,
> Age creeps in always, silent as a stone;
> Death threatens every age, nor will forget
> For any state, and there escapes him none:
> And just as surely as we know, each one,
> That we shall die, uncertain are we all
> What day it is when death shall on us fall.
> Accept then of us, lord, the true intent,
> That never yet refused you your behest,
> And we will, lord, if you will give consent,
> Choose you a wife without delay, at least,
> Born of the noblest blood and the greatest
> Of all this land, so that it ought to seem
> Honour to God and you, as we shall deem.
> Deliver us from all our constant dread
> And take yourself a wife, for High God's sake;
> For if it so befell, which God forbid,
> That by your death your noble line should break
> And that a strange successor should come take

Your heritage, woe that we were alive!
Wherefore we pray you speedily to wive."

By the end of his speech, poor Gooseberry's face was as red as a beet, and his nervous fingers had shredded his cloth cap until he was holding nothing but a tattered handful of brown cloth strips.

At the far right of the stage a movement at the back of the massed peasantry caught my eye. A barefoot, red-haired wench whose breasts jutted immodestly high above her low white linen bodice and tightly laced black stomacher stood, swaying her nut brown fustian skirt with a basket of daisies swinging from her hand. It could be no other than my cousin—Lettice Knollys, the granddaughter of my mother's sister, Mary Boleyn. Only sixteen, Lettice was a flirty little minx so taken with her recently acquired bosom that she flaunted her breasts as if they were God's greatest gift to mankind. There were many who said there was a remarkable resemblance between us, in our colouring and features, though Lettice's hair was a shade or two darker than my own. Perhaps, from a distance, some might be fooled; *if* her gown weren't cut as low as a tavern slut's and she weren't slouching over to give the men a better view, some *might* be fooled. She reminded me far more of another cousin—my foolish and wanton young stepmother, Katherine Howard. Lettice was like a taller, slimmer version of poor, hapless Kat; she had exuded the same raw sensuality as Lettice did, and it had cost her her head when she dared cuckold my father with his favourite body servant.

Abruptly, I stood up, bringing the performance to a sudden halt as the rest of the court hurriedly scrambled up after me in a great rustling of clothes.

"The performance is over," I announced. "I've no desire to see Griselda stripped down to her shift by a man who is not worthy of her love and devotion, much less such perverse obedience," I added, no doubt leaving most of the men disappointed that they would not be treated to the indecent spectacle of Lettice Knollys wiggling out of her dress, though it left little enough to the imagination to start with; she obviously wasn't wearing a single petticoat beneath that skirt.

"Better to be a beggar-maid and single than a queen and mar-

ried!" I cried as I spun in an indignant flurry of green velvet skirts
and headed for the door with my ladies hurrying after me.

Everyone wanted me to marry! Even the schoolboys at Eton
had sent me a book they had made filled with Latin verses imploring me to marry with all haste so that all might rejoice to have a little Henry in the royal nursery who would grow up to be a great
king and England's saviour someday.

On the threshold I halted and turned back to face my court and
the dismayed performers, frowning and flustered on the stage, and
poor Gooseberry, who looked very near to tears.

Always keep them guessing, that was my philosophy; just when
they think they've found their balance, give them a push, and leave
them staggering and flailing!

With an airy little laugh and a flutter of my fan, I called out,
"Gooseberry!" beckoning to the Earl of Shrewsbury as if he were a
lapdog. "I've a fancy to take a turn in the garden, to see the frost
glittering on the trees like diamonds in the moonlight; will you accompany me?"

"N-N-Nothing c-c-could g-g-give me gr-gr-greater p-p-plea-
sure, Y-Your M-M-Majesty!" he managed to stammer, falling off
the edge of the stage as he took a step towards me. But, undaunted,
he quickly righted himself, shook himself off, and ran to kiss my
hand as though it were the most precious and sacred holy relic.

As I linked my arm through his, I glanced back over my shoulder. "And . . . I think . . . Sir William Pickering"—I smiled and
nodded at the tall, suave, slender diplomat newly returned from
the French court with bold grey streaks at his temples marring the
ebony blackness of his hair and lending him an air of distinction
that made many a feminine heart flutter—"should join us, and . . ."
My eyes darted playfully about the Great Hall as all the men
watched me with bated breath and eyes that pleaded, *"Please pick
me!"* ". . . the Earl of Arundel," I concluded as I flashed a smile at
the potbellied conservative and quietly Catholic old greybeard,
"looks as though he could use a bracing blast of winter-fresh air."

And with a merry trill of laughter I walked out as they hastened
to join me, Gooseberry holding tightly to my left arm, determined
not to relinquish it, as Pickering and Arundel vied to take my right.
With a last backward glance I saw Robert standing alone on the

stage in his false crown and royal robes, looking as though he would like nothing better than to draw his dagger and bury it to the hilt in the backs of each of the three gentlemen I had chosen.

Even my dear Gypsy must be kept in his place. His presumptuous airs had already made him despised, and he must never think that my favour was all his alone. The next morning, I refused to see him at all. I invited Sir William Pickering to breakfast with me, though I was still in my nightgown, and spent five whole hours closeted alone with him, enjoying his conversation and lively gossip about the French court. He had such a fine speaking voice, he could make even the dullest document sound as pleasant as poetry. And when I emerged from my chamber, bundled into the Swedish Prince's sables, my arm linked through Pickering's, talking and laughing as though we were old, dear friends, I sent for Gooseberry and Arundel and invited them to go out in my barge with us. At the very last moment I included Robert in the invitation, but I soon sent him ashore to buy roasted chestnuts for us, and then I had him sit with the musicians and sing to us. "Sing for your supper!" I laughingly commanded. And when he finished his grudgingly sung love song, I laughed and tossed him a chestnut, which he made no attempt to catch and let fall to the floor as he stared up at me with a smouldering glare, itself as hot as a chestnut just taken from the fire. But I only laughed all the more and gave myself up fully to the combined attentions of Gooseberry, Pickering, and Arundel.

That evening I shunned Robert's lavish entertainments and spent a quiet evening listening to Gooseberry trip and stammer through a volume of poetry. And all the court was left to wonder, and the foreign ambassadors grew more worried with every day that passed as I seemed to favour these three Englishmen over any of the royal and titled foreigners who sought my hand. Did this mean England would soon have a homegrown king? The betting had already begun. And Kat, who had grown most disapproving in her old age, had frowningly informed me that Arundel had ordered himself a splendid new wardrobe and distributed upwards of £2,000 amongst my ladies to encourage them to speak well of him, whilst Gooseberry had attempted to buy their allegiance with jewels. And the debonair Pickering, gossips reported, had taken to dining in lordly fashion, seated alone at his table while musicians played. He and Arundel had even nearly clashed swords over who had the right to pass through a doorway first.

As I went about with all three of them, every time I saw Robert glowering at us, I would throw back my head, laugh, and exclaim, "I don't know which one of you gentlemen I like best! I just can't make up my mind! Oh, if only I could marry all three of you, how happy we would be!"

I just loved keeping everyone guessing! With no father, brother, or uncle to force my hand, I could play the game *exactly* as I pleased, and oh, how I *loved* playing it, and I never wanted to stop; there was *nothing* more exciting or empowering than being the most avidly courted and desired woman in the whole of Europe.

17

Elizabeth

As tradition dictated, I must return to the Tower of London to lodge there, in the royal apartments, before my coronation. This time I entered in triumph, in pearl-encrusted purple velvet and ermine, with my head held high.

" 'Tis a rare feat," I said proudly as I passed through the gate, pausing to wave heartily at the throngs of cheering people, "for one who was once a prisoner here to return in triumph! O Lord Almighty and Everlasting God," I said fervently as my people quieted to hear me speak, "I give Thee most hearty and humble thanks that Thou hast been so merciful unto me as to spare me to behold this joyful day. Some have fallen from being princes of this land to be prisoners in this place, whereas I am raised from once having been a prisoner here to become a prince of this land!" And with another wave, I passed fearlessly through the portal I once feared as the threshold leading to my death.

With a gasp of surprise I recognised the rotund figure kneeling humbly, waiting to greet me.

"Rise, Sir Gaoler!" I cried out in impetuous delight, as Sir Henry Bedingfield, who had once been tasked with keeping me under house arrest, struggled to his feet, looking more fat and florid than ever, and so awed and shamed by the memories of that time tugging at him like little demons on his coattails that he could not even meet my eyes.

"God forgive you the past, as I do," I said readily, as I reached out to gently lay my hands, richly gloved in purple velvet sewn with pearls, upon his arms. "Do you remember what I promised you when we last parted?"

"Y-Yes, Your Majesty," he said, nodding, daring a smile, "indeed I do."

"Well, it *still* holds true," I affirmed. "Whenever I have one whom I require to be most straitly and securely kept, I shall send them to you, my *dear* Sir Huff and Puff." I patted his plump apple red cheek fondly as I passed him by with a smile and, with my ladies and guards hurrying after me, continued to the royal apartments.

But I was restless in the Tower; I could not bear to sit still. I felt the need to retrace my steps, to revisit the past, now that it could not harm me. I walked alone, for I could not bear to be crowded, to be dogged by following footsteps or curious, questioning eyes, along the snow-blanketed lead wall-walk between the Beauchamp Tower and the Bell Tower, where I, as a prisoner, had been allowed to take my daily exercise. Fearlessly and boldly now, through a veil of lightly falling snow, I stared down at the Green, where my mother, and so many others, had died, confident and secure for the *first* time in my life that such would *never* be my fate. I gasped as I felt a pair of arms steal around my waist and warm lips nuzzling my ear.

"Did I not say to you, the last time we walked here and watched the ravens circling above the heads we despaired of keeping, 'Have patience, Bess. Someday, we too shall soar and fly free as the birds in the sky'?"

I felt his hands rising slowly from my waist, his palms travelling up over the firm, tightly laced purple velvet stomacher of my gown as I sighed, shut my eyes, and leaned back against his strong, hard chest. His thumbs lightly grazed the undersides of my breasts, as I answered, my voice low and tremulous with the rising desire I was trying so hard to trample back down, "Aye, Rob, you did."

"You see, I was right," he said, as his lips again found my ear and his hands rose to boldly, fully cup my breasts.

Instantly I pulled away from him and spun around to face him, my cloak flapping in the winter wind as pearls of snow beaded our heads and clothes.

"Yes, you were." I nodded. "And so we are—*free*!" I flung my head back and my arms wide and cried up at the ravens, "Free as the birds in the sky! *Free! Free! Free!*"

"*Free!*" Robert joined his voice with mine. "*Free!*" we shouted. Then, laughing, he took me in his arms again and began to dance me down the wall-walk, back to his old cell.

Sagging against the thick wooden door, I let him kiss me. I succumbed to the wild desire burning like a flame inside me and let him caress me. I shut my eyes and, just for a moment, let myself forget everything and just be a woman, not a queen.

"Let us meet here tonight," he whispered as his fingers moved deftly beneath my skirts. "We shall feed each other cakes and drink a loving cup and then become one as we were destined to be. It is written in the stars, you know; we were born the very same day and hour, not as twins but because we were meant to be lovers, to be together, like this." He kissed me again, and his fingers probed deeper. "Dr Dee has cast our horoscopes. I can show you . . ."

But I didn't hear him; a ghostly voice that haunted my mind was singing of cakes and ale again. I went as stiff as a suit of armour in Robert's arms, but he didn't seem to notice and went on kissing me and whispering hot, persuasive, and encouraging words in my ear. But I wasn't listening; I was remembering another man, another handsome, bearded, dark-eyed rogue who had awakened my body even as my mind cried out, "*Danger!*" and a beloved voice from the past urgently whispered, "*Never surrender!*"

I pushed him from me. "Another time, Rob," I said shakily as I hurried briskly away, my knees trembling beneath my skirts as I tried to run, and my whole body burning as if lit from within by a raging fever despite the falling snow.

I tried to avoid him. I sent him on errands to keep him at a distance, but he always came swiftly back. I tried to put walls between us, but he kept hurdling over them, leaping nimbly, dodging my every attempt at evasion. No door could keep him out; he seemed to slip through the keyholes like mist, to be always there, where he could train upon me a piercing, unwavering gaze, deadly as an arrow to the heart, blazing and burning with desire, like a toothache I could not ignore. He left me always feeling torn, as though wild horses, bound to my limbs, tugged and tore at me. I felt my body melting into a hot puddle of lust at the sight or thought of him, whilst my mind tried to drench the inferno with ice water, to bring the wild horses to heel and free me from the bonds of a passion that wanted to run, rage, and burn unimpeded. And in my dreams, the handsome fellow who stared at me, cock in hand, from the foot of the bed before he climbed slowly up the length of my body, was two men—Tom Seymour and Robert Dudley— merging and blending together until they seemed almost one, and I woke, crying out, to find my nightgown clutched tightly between my thighs and warm and wet with lust and sweat. And I knew God was testing me once again, to see how well I had learned my lesson, and Passion was mocking me, challenging me, to deny and save myself if I could, if only I had the will to withstand it.

The day before my coronation, as I was having the final fitting of my gown, he came to me.

I stood there, nervous and erect, my body feeling as taut as a too tightly strung lute string, amidst the sewing women, gowned in golden brocade with a raised pattern of silver that brought out the gold in my hair, brushed out and worn loose and flowing like a virgin maiden's about my shoulders and down my back. My wary eyes never left him as he circled me like a shark swimming around a drowning sailor, devouring me with his eyes.

"Out!" He suddenly clapped his hands and spoke that single word in a tone that was meant to be obeyed. And they, women accustomed since birth to taking orders from men, did not hesitate or even look to me, their Queen, for permission, but meekly scurried out.

When the door closed behind them and we were alone, he swept me up into his arms and carried me to the bed and there laid me down gently. And I felt the length of his body stretched against mine.

"I have dreamt of this day for a *very* long time," he said as he fanned my hair out across the pillows, as though my head were the sun and my tresses its radiant red gold rays. He bent and pressed a kiss onto each of my breasts, heaving above the low, square-cut bodice. "The day when I would at long last make love to a queen, the Queen of my heart."

I gave a great sigh, and my arms went up to embrace him, and I felt my petticoats growing damp and hot between my thighs as he lay upon me.

"You are *mine*," he whispered as he rained hot kisses down on me, as through my half-lidded eyes I watched the snow fall outside the diamond-paned windows. A part of me wished I could run stark naked out into it to cool the fever of lust that raged within me, driving my body to give in, to surrender to the urgent hardness pressed against me and the firm, commanding, exploring hands that were even then lifting my skirts. "You are *mine*," he whispered again, *"all mine!"*

"No!" With such force that he tumbled from the bed and cracked his elbow upon the stone floor, I shoved him from me as I scrambled across the bed and ran to the window as if it alone offered my salvation. I was as flushed and breathless as if it were the hottest summer day as I flung wide the window, not even caring if the glass cracked against the wall, and thrust my head out. I hung there, my nails grinding, cracking, as I dug them against the stone sill, the wind seizing, tugging, and whipping my hair in a wild frenzy about my head, as the snow pelted down, and I gasped as though I had been holding my breath far too long, until my lungs were near to bursting. The air burned and cooled at the same time. I shut my eyes and tried to coax my reason back, like trying to lure a starving bird, outside pecking in the snow, to come near, to perch upon the windowsill for some breadcrumbs, even though it spies a cat curled beside the fire.

"Elizabeth." I stiffened at Robert's touch. His hands were on my shoulders, and he was pulling me back in, closing the window, and trying to smooth and tame my wild, wind-whipped hair with his caressing hands. "There is nothing to be afraid of," he said, adopting a patient yet patronising tone, as if I were a simpleton or a child. "Come back to bed, and let me show you . . ."

"No!" I slapped his hands down. I strode past him to the door

and flung it wide and bellowed for the sewing women to come back in. "Who is King of England?" I demanded of them.

They furrowed their brows and gave me a puzzled stare. "Why, there is no king," they answered. "Your Majesty is Queen of England."

"Precisely!" I exclaimed. "There is no king, *I* am Queen of England, *I* rule here, *not* Lord Robert nor any other man, and *I* did *not* give you leave to withdraw!"

Most humbly they apologised, falling on their knees before me, some with tears in their eyes, begging forgiveness, giving every assurance that they had not intended to offend me.

"You are forgiven," I said, "*but,*" I added adamantly, "see that it does not happen again. Now, come"—I smiled—"let us finish this gown. Just because our nerves are fraying does not mean we should leave our seams to unravel." And I stepped back up onto the little wooden stool again to resume the fitting. "Lord Robert," I said coolly, without turning to look at him, "you may go. This is women's business, and you are not needed or wanted here."

As he left, I watched the women kneeling at my feet, searching for some sign, fearing that they could somehow see or smell the lust upon me. I breathed deeply and lifted my head and stared straight at the wall ahead of me and wondered why a war must always rage within me. For other women life seemed so much simpler, but I wasn't one of them. I wanted more, but I also wanted less. Would I *ever* find the right balance, the proper portions, that would allow me to live my life content, to be both a woman and a queen, filled and fulfilled, happy and complete? Often, I lay awake in bed at night, restless in both my body and my mind, waiting for sleep, with thoughts flapping like bats inside my brain, wild and frantic. At those times, I felt *so* alone, as though I were fighting, rebelling, against the whole world, swelling, overflowing the mould I was supposed to fit and neatly fill. I wanted love, I wanted passion, but I wanted it *my* way. I wanted to control the burn, I didn't want to be enslaved and devoured by it, consumed by fear, to lose myself and everything I held dear within the flames, and be saddled and bridled, stabled and broken, by the man who rode and roused me. I *must* be sole mistress of my life, and of England; I could brook no master, and master was the role every man thought he was born to play. And with my crown as a glittering prize to be snatched and crammed onto his own head, what man could resist being not just master of his own household but of a whole kingdom as well? Thus would any man I married take from me what I valued most; he would reduce me to a figurehead of the nation, a queen consort, instead of the queen in her own right I was born to be. If I took a husband, his decisions would always hold sway, he would always have the final say, and the whole world would be deaf to my opinions. Even when the pain of loneliness stabbed me hard and the tears pricked my eyes, I must remind myself a cold and lonely bed was better than a life lived in the dominating shadow of someone who had stolen my right and destiny away from me by putting a golden ring onto my finger and reducing my crown to just another pretty headdress with no real meaning. I, Elizabeth, Elizabeth I, *Semper Eadem,* that was my fate, to *be always one.*

January 15, 1559—that was my coronation day, a day that will always shine in my memory as the happiest, warmest, brightest day of my life, even though the sky was in truth as grey as pewter and the snow drifted down upon us. I remember well that frosty morning we left the Tower, to progress slowly through the streets of London, to Westminster Abbey, with speeches and pageants and singing choirs along the way.

As I gave Robert my hand to assist me as I started to climb into my litter, while Kat fussed with the cumbersome, heavy folds of my long, ermine-trimmed gold and silver brocade train, a full three and-twenty yards long, the lions in the Tower menagerie suddenly gave a tremendous roar.

I paused and, raising my eyes to Heaven, uttered a solemn and most heartfelt prayer:

"O Almighty and Everlasting God, I give Thee most hearty and humble thanks, Thou hast dealt as wonderfully and as mercifully with me as Thou didst with Daniel, whom Thou delivered out of the lions' den."

Those near enough to hear applauded and cried out their blessings and "God save Your Majesty!" and I nodded and smiled my thanks as I waved back at them.

As I gave Robert my hand again, I gazed before me, at the scarlet-liveried trumpeters, their golden instruments glistening in the weak winter sun, and my heralds, bearing silken banners, then back at my long and splendid retinue that would follow my litter and snake slowly through the streets like a great jewelled serpent for my people to behold. My golden litter was upholstered in gold brocade to match my gown, and there were four yeomen guards poised to lift it, liveried in red and black embroidered in gold with my initials, *ER,* Elizabeth Regina, and red and white Tudor roses. Next a groom stood patiently holding the reins of Robert's black horse, and the white one, my horse, which he would lead, its scarlet and gold jewelled and gold-fringed saddle symbolically empty. Next came my ladies, all gowned in crimson velvet with sleeves of cloth-of-gold, then the gentlemen of my court in crimson velvet doublets with gold sleeves and rows of gold buttons down the front, each with a jaunty white plume on his crimson velvet cap, and their legs sheathed in crimson hose, all of them, male and female, mounted on fine horses chosen by Robert and caparisoned in red and gold, their saddles cushioned in quilted crimson velvet. And behind them the men of my Council in gilded chariots, resplendent in their ceremonial robes and weighty gold chains of office. Even my household servants had new clothes; there was a red dress for my laundress, and my fools danced and capered to delight the crowd in new suits of orange and purple motley with tiny gold bells sewn along the seams and on their caps and sceptres. And my guards and archers were all in shiny and splendid array, everything polished to a high shine; even their ceremonial battle-axes gleamed with fresh gilt.

Despite the solemnity of the occasion and the heaviness of my clothes and the jewels that weighed me down, sapphires dark as the midnight sky, rubies as luscious and round as sweet, candied cherries, and pearls, both rounds and teardrops as pale as the full moon, set in heavy gold about my throat, shoulders, and waist, I felt featherlight and free. I knew it would not be easy, but I welcomed and embraced all the burdens that came with the crown. Though my form looked frail, inside I was filled with a coursing strength, and though there would be times when I felt weak and weary, it would *always* be there when I, and England, had need of it.

As I settled into my litter, and Kat fussed with my full skirts, Robert said that in my golden gown with my hair unbound, rippling down about my shoulders, I looked like the sun itself, "bright and blazing, nigh blinding in its radiant glory".

"Thank you, Robin." I smiled. "And though I do sit," I said as I shifted my position upon the brocaded cushions, "I hope you mean a rising sun rather than a setting one."

"Aye." Robert smiled. "God grant that many, many years shall pass before this *glorious* sun ever sets."

A light snow had begun to fall, and Kat hurried forward with an ermine lap rug, poised to drape it over my knees, lamenting that it was such a shame to cover the dress; the people always took a keen interest in such things and would be eager to see what their new sovereign was wearing on this most special day.

"Leave it off." I gently pushed it away. "The love of my people shall keep me as warm as a roasted chestnut this day."

Then we were off in a fanfare of blaring trumpets and flapping gold-fringed silk banners. And though I had been cheered and blessed by crowds many a time in my late sister's reign, never before had I known such love; it was like luxuriating in a steam-caressing hot bath, whilst outside the window the snow was falling. I saw the love in the eyes of every man, woman, and child and heard it pouring from their lips, in their tears, and every smile and wave, in every cry of "God save the Queen!" and "God bless Your Majesty!" I waved and called back to them, "Thank you, my good people! God save you all! I thank you with all my heart!" and hoped they could hear my love in every word. Though there were barriers to keep them back, to prevent their impeding the procession or anyone being harmed or trampled by it, their arms reached out, straining, as if they would embrace me, and I felt as if they did. Some even dared vault or crawl beneath the barricades and run to me, to present me with little tokens, bunches of herbs tied with string or ribbon or the few paltry flowers they could find in wintertime, and some housewives even brought me cakes they had baked. One old woman offered me a sprig of rosemary, and I pressed it carefully into my English Bible, which lay upon my lap, promising her that I would treasure it always, as a remembrance of this day. Rosemary was always present at weddings—the bride and her maids often wore it in their hair, woven into crowns, or carried in bouquets—so it seemed so right, so *very* fitting, that I should be given this sprig of rosemary on the day I bound myself to England like a bride to her husband. In my heart, my coronation day was also my wedding day.

Every bell in London was ringing for me that day. And choirs sang with joyous fervour. There were gilded and decorated triumphal arches for us to pass under, and from the windows of the houses overlooking the street people leaned and waved and called down to me, tossed handfuls of herbs or flower petals down, and unfurled banners they had made.

At times the procession paused so that pretty children might recite speeches to me or my people stage little plays and *tableaux-vivants*. One depicted the whole Tudor dynasty, with costumed wax and wooden effigies, each one rising from the centre of a red and white Tudor rose. And for the first time I saw my mother, Anne Boleyn, honoured, standing beside my father. And I myself, gowned in gold, stood on the highest pedestal of all, as though I were blossoming out of the heart of a Tudor rose and shining, like the sun, down upon them all. And another pageant, staged outside St Paul's Cathedral, where Latin scholars praised my wisdom and learning, depicted me as another Deborah, the brave woman who had restored the House of Israel and "had been sent by God to rule His people for forty years".

At the Eleanor Cross in Cheapside the Lord Mayor of London awaited me in his ermine-edged crimson robes to present me with a purse containing the traditional 1,000 gold marks the City always gave the new monarch. The crowd fell to a respectful hush as I stood up to speak:

"I thank my Lord Mayor, his brethren, and you all. And whereas your request is that I should continue your good lady and Queen, be ye well assured that I will be as good unto you as ever queen was to her people. No will in me can lack. And be thou well persuaded, that for the safety and peace of you all, I will not spare, if need be, to spend my blood. God thank you all!"

The cheers and cries that greeted my words were deafening, but no music could ever have been sweeter to my ears or touched my heart more.

At Westminster Abbey, I dismounted from my litter, taking the hand Robert held out to me, and I slowly traversed the blue velvet carpet that had been laid down for me, all the way to the altar. Standing at the top of the steps before the great doors, I raised my hands, gesturing for my people to fall silent, and spoke to them from my heart:

"Be ye well assured that I will stand your good Queen. I wish neither prosperity nor safety for myself, only for our common good."

I spied an old man weeping by the door, and I went and laid a hand upon his arm. "I warrant that it is for gladness that you weep?" I smiled.

"Aye, Your Majesty!" he cried, and he dropped to his knees to press the hem of my robe to his lips.

I touched the top of his head and thanked and blessed him before I gently pulled my robe away and continued into the abbey, whilst behind me the people fell like starving wolves onto the blue velvet carpet I had trod upon, tearing it up, with teeth and nails, to take home as a treasured souvenir.

The ceremony inside passed as a golden blur, lit by hundreds of candles, spoken in both English and Latin, to please Protestants and Catholics alike. And Cecil knelt, despite the pain in his knees, and held my English Bible as I laid my hand upon it and solemnly spoke my coronation oath. I remember the fishy stink of the oil used to anoint my head and breast and the *wonderful* weight of the crown when it was at last put upon my head, a responsibility I welcomed and was ready to bear, and the fulfilling manner in which the weighty golden orb filled my hand, so heavy I feared I might drop it but knew in my heart I never would, and the way my fingers closed around the jewelled sceptre in such a firm grip, symbolic of my determination never to let go, and the heavy gold and onyx coronation ring upon my finger, right where a wedding ring belonged, as a sacred covenant, wedding me to England, the one lover I desired most, who would *never* disillusion or disappoint me; this *really* was a love that would last and withstand every test of Time.

As I stepped outside into the late-afternoon sun, to show myself to my people in full royal regalia, with the crown on my head and the sceptre and orb in my hands, the blare of the trumpets, the tolling of the bells, and the jubilant cries and cheering of my people nigh deafened my ears, and I knew this joyful noise would ring forever in my heart. Whenever I felt weak or weary, this memory would give me the strength to go on.

As I walked slowly towards Westminster Hall, where my coronation banquet would be celebrated, treading upon the few stray, straggling threads that covered the cold ground where once a blue carpet had been, my people fell to their knees and reverently reached out fingertips to touch my skirts and trailing robe, and behind me, as I briefly glanced back, I saw many bow their heads down and kiss where my feet had touched the ground, and tears welled in my eyes, blinding me so that I saw all as a colourful moving blur through a wavering, watery curtain. *God help me to be the Queen they deserve!* I prayed with all my heart.

"Remember old King Henry the Eighth!" an old man in the crowd cried, and my lips spread in a broad smile. I was my father's daughter, and I vowed that when I was an old woman whose Tudor red tresses had faded to grey and the time came for me to close my eyes on the world forever, I would leave behind an England greater than my father had ever known. Poor, weak, little Edward, and mad, deluded, lovelorn, and brainsick Mary had each failed to be a worthy successor to our father's throne and memory, and now it was my turn, and, with God's grace, I, the last Tudor, the princess who had sorely disappointed our father by not being a prince, would show the world that disappointment had been misplaced, that *here,* in this frail female form, was Great Harry's true and worthy successor, and, through me, my mother would also be redeemed. Though she had given birth to a daughter instead of a son, time would reveal that she had *not* failed; I would prove that what many thought was her greatest failure was instead her greatest triumph.

Though the banquet, one continuous, dizzying round of delicious dishes, music, and dancing, lasted until dawn, shortly after midnight I rose from my chair at the high table, beneath the canopy of estate, and toasted my nobility, wishing them good health and thanking them for the pains they had taken on my behalf, and then withdrew to my bedchamber.

I dismissed my ladies. I told them to go, dance and make merry, or to sleep in their beds; I wanted to be alone. But I wasn't alone.

And I knew I wouldn't be. Robert was there, waiting for me. I let him undress me, luxuriating in his touch, as he bared my skin, setting it free from my grand but heavy, cumbersome raiments, sighing under his hands as he rubbed the red marks my stays had left. I let him carry me, naked, to the great purple velvet and gold-fringed bed, its canopy supported by great, fierce, carved and gilded lions, claws and fangs bared, poised ready to pounce on us, and there ease me with his lips and hands. But when he took my hand and placed it on his bulging codpiece, I merely smiled, gave it a pat, and told him to go home to his wife.

"Leave me. I am tired and wish to sleep," I said, and I rolled over onto my side and pulled the covers up and shut my eyes. I smiled at the sound of his footsteps and the curses he muttered beneath his breath and the slam of the door behind him, and I drifted off to sleep, intoxicated by my power to control men, those who thought God and Nature had decreed that it should be the other way around.

❧ 18 ❧

Amy Robsart Dudley

London
Sunday, January 15, 1559

Robert wrote and bade me come to London for Elizabeth's coronation, to the grand town house owned by his uncle; he said I would be more comfortable there than with him at court or lodging with my cousins, the Scotts, in Camberwell. Nothing I could say would persuade him that I would rather be with him. He would not change his mind and let me come to court; he said he was too busy and hadn't time to play nursemaid to my nerves or schoolmaster to correct my backward, blundering ways. So I packed up the magnificent purple tinsel and silver lace gown I had intended for my presentation to Queen Mary, reasoning that it would do just as well for her sister's coronation, and sat down with Cook and painstakingly wrote out our recipe for strawberry jam, which Robert had most urgently requested for his own cook, cautioning me not to dare to come to London without it, and then to London I went.

I was in my bedchamber, with Pirto and my tailor, dear Mr Edney, and his apprentice, when my husband walked in.

"*No, No, No!*" Robert bellowed, stamping his feet, his hands going up as if to tear the hair from his head. "*That* is the *Spanish* style! Do you want to proclaim to the whole world that you are Catholic and true to the memory of Mary?"

"But, Robert, I am not a Catholic. I was only pretending when you told me to!" I crinkled my brow at his outburst and glanced down at my gown, trying to discover what was so wrong with it. "I am not wearing a crucifix or rosary, and this is the grandest gown I own, and, I thought, since it was made to wear for one queen, it would do just as well for another. And the fashions have not changed so drastically that—"

"*You!*" Ignoring me, Robert pointed at Mr Edney. "Make her presentable, or I promise, no one of any means will ever hire you even to make their shroud—you'll end your days sewing shifts and shirts for the poor." And then he was gone, slamming the door behind him.

"Oh, Mr Edney!" I wailed with tears filling my eyes as I turned to him. "He should not have been so unkind to you—I am so sorry! The dress is beautiful, *really*. I . . . I am sorry my husband does not like it! It is my fault . . . I should have realised . . . I should have known that it would not do and ordered something new, and now . . ." I sank down sobbing onto the side of my bed. "Now it is too late—the coronation is tomorrow!"

"There, there, sweeting, don't you worry." Mr Edney knelt before me and with his own handkerchief dried my tears. "We'll fix it! Just a snip here and a tuck there, and no one will *ever* know it was made in the Spanish fashion. Yours is not the first angry husband I've encountered, and I daresay he will not be the last. And with being appointed Her Majesty's Master of the Horse—a great and grave responsibility that is indeed—it is only natural that his lordship's nerves should be a-fraying at the seams. But with your beauty and my needle we'll give him a sight to make him proud! Come now." He raised me to my feet and led me to a small stool positioned before the full-length looking glass. "Step up here, and let me see how best to work my magic!"

By the time Robert returned later that evening, Mr Edney had transformed the gown, and there was not a trace of Spain about it, and it was *still* the most magnificent I had ever owned, and I felt confident that I could hold my own amongst all the grand, highborn ladies of the court on the morrow when I took my seat in Westminster Abbey. Robert was *delighted*; he was all smiles and compliments as he twirled me around so he could fully admire my gown. To my immense delight—and relief—he could not find a single fault with it.

He took me in his arms and danced me all around the room in a lively galliard, sweeping me up in his arms, lifting me high, my skirts swaying like a ringing bell, as he spun me round and round. I smiled and laughed and clung to him. I felt happy and alive. Dancing in my husband's arms, I felt like one returned from the grave to the land of the living. It had been so *very* long since we had danced together and I had felt such joy, I had almost forgotten what it was like.

Like a cockerel strutting to impress me, Robert performed a series of leaps and turns, and I threw back my head and, laughing and carefree, began to circle the room from the opposite end, spinning round and round, doing spirited leaps and kicks of my own, until we met, and I was in his arms again, crushed tightly against his chest, as he showered me with praise and kisses and lifted me high in the air and spun me as I laughed in dizzy joy. Then Mr Edney, familiar with the ways of the court, held a big yellow silk tassel up high for Robert to display his skill at high kicks. I clapped my hands and called "Bravo!" each time the toe of Robert's boot made the tassel bounce and sway. Then Robert caught me up in his arms again and spun me until we collapsed together, dizzy and laughing, on the bed.

My husband kissed me then with a passion I thought long dead. As he bent his head to plant a kiss onto each of my breasts, flushed and heaving above the low-cut bodice, he bade Mr Edney, his apprentice, and Pirto to withdraw and leave us. Even as the door closed behind them, he gently rolled me over onto my stomach and unlaced my gown, then lifted my skirts and untied and drew the stiffened farthingale and layered taffeta petticoats down over my hips. He turned me round and kissed me again as he carefully eased away my gown, taking great care not to crumple or tear it. He even rose and went to drape it over the back of a chair. Then he was back on the bed with me, and I was in his arms again. He made such tender, passionate, gentle yet ardent love to me that I was reminded of the days we spent at Hemsby-by-the-Sea when we were newly wed. I *gloried* in the warmth and weight of his body over mine, skin against skin, and the feel of his lips and hands that assured me I was wanted and admired, and the hot skin that told me that my husband was on fire with desire for me. I clung to him and cried out my passion and love for him; it was *so* intense, I felt likely to die of it. And as I fell asleep with my head on his chest, my ear to his heart, listening to it beat, like a love song and a lullaby in my ear, just for me, I prayed fervently that this would be a new beginning for us.

But it turned out that my gown would be wasted yet again. I would only glimpse the coronation procession from afar and would not set foot in Westminster Abbey at all and thus see nothing of the crowning ceremony. I would watch what little of it I could see leaning from my window high above, not seated with the noble and privileged guests as Robert had promised me.

When I came downstairs, smiling and ready in my shimmering purple gown, the colour like frosted lilacs, with my shoulders and face framed with stiffened silver lace, Robert took my hand and led me into the parlour. Sitting side by side, facing each other on the fireside settle, he quietly told me that I would be watching the procession from my bedchamber window; he feared that the crush inside the abbey and the press of the crowd outside, all the shouting and grasping hands, would be too much for me. I was not accustomed to such spectacles, he said, and his active role in the ceremony and organising the pageantry would not allow him to be at my side to comfort and protect me, and Pirto alone, he judged, would not be sufficient, and he could not spare any of his men— not even one—to guard and escort me. He assured me that I wouldn't be missing much; indeed many would think me the more fortunate, as the ceremony inside the abbey would be lengthy and drawn out and dreadfully dull. The procession, he insisted, was the best part, and I would have a wonderful view of that, far better than being pressed and jostled by the masses behind the barricades on the crowded streets, having my toes trod upon and the rabble shouting from all sides around me, and the cutpurses were sure to be out in vast numbers preying on the distracted revellers. And, taking me in his arms again and holding me close just like he had the night before, and lavishing my lips and throat with kisses, he promised that as he passed below my window, he would look up and blow a kiss to me.

Looking from a window above—that was the third time I saw Elizabeth Tudor. Surrounded on all sides by public jubilation, heartfelt cheers, adoration, and the fanfare of gleaming golden trumpets, she was majestically gowned in opulent gold brocade with an ornate raised pattern of silver and cloaked in ermine as befits a queen, and laden with sapphires, rubies, and pearls, with her flame-hued hair flowing free like a virgin's as she was carried through the streets in a magnificent golden litter borne by footmen clad in crimson liveries. The people wept and cried and reached out their hands as if they *longed* to touch and embrace her; some even broke from behind the barricades and ran to present her with humble offerings, simple little gifts, which she accepted as if they were the most precious things in the world to her, worth far more than jewels and furs.

Robert rode behind her, richly clad, like a king himself, in crimson velvet and ermine, mounted upon a regal, high-stepping ebony steed, and behind him, just like the day when he galloped off to Hatfield, was the white horse, a spirited, prancing, milk white beauty who showed not a sign of nervousness that I, from my high perch, could discern at being in the midst of all this bright, noisy, crowded pageantry. My husband carried himself just like a king; all that was missing was a gold and bejewelled crown upon his head.

The whole time I had him in my sights, as the procession passed slowly beneath my window, he *never* took his eyes off *her*. Once, he even presumed to ride forward to take her hand, lean over it, and press it to his lips, letting them linger long against the pale white flesh. I felt then the most overwhelming sense of dread and panic; it made me dizzy and faint, and I found it very hard to breathe. Panting, trying to draw a deep enough breath in my tightly laced, stiffly boned bodice, I grasped hard the windowsill, feeling the rough, gritty bite of the stone against my palms, fearing that I might pitch forward, toppling over it, into the street below, to lie broken and crumpled in the new Queen's path, to be crushed and trampled by the horses.

I prayed with all my heart that he would remember his promise and look up and blow a kiss to me. But he never did. He had eyes and kisses *only* for Elizabeth, and none to spare for me, his loyal and loving wife. I was *nothing* compared to her.

All about me people were rejoicing, shouting and singing out their love for Elizabeth, blessing her, wishing her a long life, and thanking God for bringing her to the throne, but I alone, I think, *hated* her. When she had all this love showered upon her, why must she also have Robert's? I needed him more!

What had seemed like a new beginning was actually the end. Robert was no longer mine; he belonged to another now, one with whom I could never compete, one whose wishes, commands, and capricious whims would always come first, one to whom he would never say no. Elizabeth could give him the world, make all his dreams come true, but all I could give him was my love, and that was not enough. What was my love compared to the glittering gold temptation of a crown? I already knew the answer—*nothing!*

I sat up all night in my glittering purple and silver gown waiting for him. But he never came. As the sun set, I thought of him making merry at the coronation banquet, to which I had not been invited. I pictured him seated at the Queen's side and dancing the night away with her, holding her close, boldly caressing her bodice when he lifted her high during the volta, and perhaps even daring to let his lips graze her neck as he lowered her, her body pressed tightly against his until her feet touched the ground again, and, even then, lingering for a moment or two longer.

I watched the sun rise through the diamond-shaped panes of my window and wondered where he was and on whose pillow he had laid his head that night. I didn't touch the breakfast tray Pirto brought for me and shook my head at her attempts to coax me to change into something more comfortable, or to at least let her unleash my hair from the silver net sewn with amethysts and pearls and to loosen my armour-stiff stays. But I wanted Robert to see me again in the gown that had reawakened his long-dormant passion. I wanted it to happen again, to be the woman he wanted, not just one whose conveniently available body he made use of from time to time.

It was well past noon when I finally heard his boots upon the stairs. He had barely crossed the threshold before I was there, kneeling at his feet like a supplicant, grasping his hands, looking up at him with tears spangling my lashes, begging him not to abandon and forsake me.

Robert raised me to my feet and gathered me up in his arms and carried me to the big velvet-cushioned chair beside the fire. With me nestled upon his lap, clinging tightly to him, begging him like a child, nearly incoherent with tears and fears, to never let me go, Robert tried his best to calm me. He said I was tired—we both were—and should go to bed, but first, he would like to read a story to me, just the way he used to do.

"Oh, yes, oh, thank you, Robert, I would like that so much!" I cried, smiling through my tears, which were already starting to dry at the memory of the many times during the early days of our marriage when we would curl up together with a book and my husband would read me tales like *Guy of Warwick,* or stories of King Arthur and his Knights of the Round Table, or Robin Hood and his band of Merry Men, bawdy Italian tales which he translated for me himself, and Chaucer's *Canterbury Tales.* Which one would it be this time? My mind was dancing, awhirl with tales of adventure and romance.

"First we must make ready for bed," Robert said as his skilful fingers swiftly divested me of my gown, stripping me down to nothing but my cobweb lawn shift. He removed my dainty silver slippers, untied my purple satin garters, and rolled down my stockings, and I held my breath for a moment and trembled for fear that he would be repulsed by the roughness and calluses that were the unattractive result of the pleasure of going barefoot every spring and summer of my life, but he said nothing of them. Then he plucked the pins from my hair, cast aside the net, and combed his fingers through the harvest gold waves as they flowed down past my hips. Then it was my turn to undress him, though my fingers were nervous and clumsy and fumbled overlong over the golden buttons and aiglets and laces until, at last, he stood before me clad in only his gold-bordered white shirt. He took my hand, kissed it, and led me to bed.

Once we were settled, with him propped high against a mound of pillows, and my head was on his shoulder, Robert drew the three-branched candelabrum closer and took a book from the bed-side table. I saw from the gilt letters on its spine that it was *The Canterbury Tales.*

"I chose this story just for you, Amy; I have wanted to read it to you for a long time, but I have been waiting, saving it, for just the right moment. And now that my life has changed with my new appointment at court, that moment has *finally* come."

I pressed a kiss onto the side of my husband's neck and nestled closer. "Begin at once then, my love. For you to have wanted and waited so long, it must be a *very* special tale indeed."

Robert opened the book to a page he had marked with a red satin ribbon.

My heart sank like a stone, plummeting from a great height, as if it had been dropped from a clifftop into the sea, when I realised it was "The Clerk's Tale" of Patient Griselda that my husband was reading to me.

Slowly, as if he wanted each word to sink in, he read me the tale of that stout-hearted and eternally obedient and devoted peasant woman raised to royal estate when the monarch chose her to be his bride, who patiently endured and passed each one of the cruel tests her husband set for her, even when she thought her own children taken away and slain upon his orders, and herself being turned out clad only in her shift and bare feet to make way for a new royal bride. Sometimes he would pause, indicate with his finger a certain passage, and pass the book to me and say, "Now you read to me." And I heard myself saying things like: "Never in word or thought shall I ever disobey you," and "I would gladly die that it might please you," as Robert nodded and favoured me with an encouraging smile.

When the tale was finished, and Robert had set the book aside, he asked me what I thought of the story.

"Men like this Walter are unkind," I said, for how could a man with even a glimmer of kindness in his heart treat his wife thus? It was such a cruel game he played, a game where her head, heart, body, and even the children she bore him were tokens, pawns, made even crueller because only Walter himself knew that it was a game they were playing, while loving, trusting, and loyal Griselda took it all as truth. She paid the price for believing in her husband.

"I don't believe she could have been happy despite what the story-teller says; for every public smile she must have wept a whole ocean of tears in private," I said. "She must have felt as if she lived her life walking always on ground that might at any moment start to move and shake violently beneath her feet, fighting to always keep her balance and keep smiling and not let anyone see her fear."

Robert sighed and shook his head and said I had missed the point entirely, but we would work to remedy my ignorance later, but now he was too tired and wished only to sleep. But first there was something else he must tell me: I was to go and stay with Mr William Hyde and his family at their fine new mansion house—built in the new style rather than an old moated manor made of blocks of stone with arched or arrow-slit windows—in Throcking, a peaceful little hamlet in Hertfordshire.

"But why can I not stay with you?" I demanded.

"You're a country girl born and bred, Amy. You'll not be happy in the city or at court—it's a whole other world, Buttercup! And my Buttercup Bride cannot thrive without sunshine, blue skies, fresh air, and green grass; she would wither and die shut up within the walls of a crowded palace. All the etiquette and ceremony would chafe you raw. It is a world where a single mistake can ruin you forever; people have long memories, and the walls have eyes and ears. There is always someone ready to smile to your face, then turn around and talk about you behind your back or stab you in it. You'll be happier in the country, and I will come to visit you as often as I can. In fact, it will be easier for me to visit you at the Hydes'; you'll be nearer there than you would have been at Syderstone or any of the other manors your father left you."

"But, Robert, I want to be *with* you, not just nearer!" I cried. "I can learn to be the lady you want me to be—I *know* I can! I want us to be together—*that* is what matters most to me! I don't want us to drift apart until we are like two strangers and there's nothing left holding us together; as it is, every year it feels like the knot that binds us together grows looser."

"Come now, Buttercup, be sensible." Robert took me in his arms and kissed my cheek. "You don't want to ruin my chances, do you?"

"Ruin your chances?" I repeated. "But how should I do that?"

"Wives are not welcome at Elizabeth's court," Robert explained. "Elizabeth is a vain and selfish woman who demands to be worshipped and adored like a goddess; she needs to command a man's *full* attention, and those who make her think she must share them with a wife or a mistress do not prosper."

"You mean *you* wish to pretend that you are not married," I said. "I think, Robert, the truth is that you are ashamed of me, and that you are bored and tired of me."

"Now you're speaking nonsense again, and fluently too!" Robert reproved me. "I am merely telling you how things are, educating you in the ways of the court. It is Elizabeth who wants to pretend, not I! And I am not the only man who must be parted from his wife to please her!"

"Then be brave enough to be different, Robert," I insisted. "Make a stand and show her and the world that you love your wife and want her at your side where she belongs!"

"And wave farewell to everything I have worked so hard for? Do you *know* what you are asking me to give up, Amy, and what it will mean to you? Do you really want an angry and embittered husband who sits all day by the fire nursing his regrets and blaming *you* for ruining his chances, while his love for you withers and dies until it is turned to solid, hard black hate? Do you *really* want that?"

"No, but . . ." I began.

"No buts, Amy." Robert smacked a kiss onto my lips. "You're for the country, I'm for the court, and Elizabeth's for England! That's the way it has to be if we are all to prosper. Elizabeth holds my future in the palm of her hand, and she knows it, and with her favour I can rise high and become the greatest man in the land. Don't hold me back, Buttercup, unless, of course, you *want* to sink into poverty and a bitter, loveless marriage; it's entirely up to you, my love." He took my hands in his, kissed each one, then held them together, forming a cup of my two palms. "My fate is in these two little hands!"

"Very well!" I sighed and gave in. "But *must* I go to the Hydes'? I don't even know them! Why can I not go back to Syderstone instead? Even if it is farther away, it is still my home, and I know it and the people well, so I will not be as lonely as I would be plunked down amongst strangers. *Surely* I am worth riding a *little* farther to visit me?"

"Oh, Amy, do be practical!" Robert snapped. "You *cannot* go to Syderstone because it's falling down, and it is not a fit place for my wife to reside. If I let you continue in such a decrepit and ramshackle abode, people will talk; they will think I don't care about you. Do you want people to gossip and think ill of me? They will say that while I lodge beneath a gilded ceiling, my wife is left to shiver under one that lets the rain in and where the wind whistles the walls down. Besides"—he hesitated, but only for a moment— "it has been sold, so you cannot stay there any more; it is no longer *your* home. Doubtlessly it will be demolished and used for pasturelands or to build a new house if the new owner has sufficient means."

"Sold! Sold?" I leapt out of bed and spun round to face him. *"Syderstone has been sold?* But it *can't* be! It's *my* home! I grew up there! You said that we would restore it, make it as fine a manor as it ever was, or even grander, and our children would grow up there! You *promised*, Robert, *you promised*!"

"Oh, Amy, will you not let it rest? Why do you keep on and on? Once you get something into your head, you *never* let go! You just don't know when to stop, do you? Even when it's for your own good, *still* you keep on dredging up the past! When I spoke those words, I was young and foolish; I was being passionate, not practical, and I got carried away," Robert excused himself, shrugging it off as if it were nothing at all. "I was just dreaming aloud! Can you not understand that? You were young then too, and surely that foolish head of yours has harboured its share of outlandish dreams that you knew, even as you dreamed them, would never *really* come true. Restoring Syderstone simply is not practical. It would break us. The expense would be *enormous*. Even if we had the money— which we don't—it would bankrupt us. And it is not conveniently located to suit my needs; it is too far from the court."

"But it was my home, Robert—I grew up there!" I sobbed. "You had no right!"

"I am your husband, so I have *every* right to dispose of *my* property as *I* please—your inheritance became *my* inheritance when we married—and it pleased me to sell a house that was nothing but a burden to me and for which I had no use. It was nothing but an encumbrance! But cry all you want." Robert shrugged. "Only do so where I can't hear you. I need my sleep." He rolled over onto his side and pulled the covers up higher. "But there's really no point in weeping; it won't change anything." He yawned. "Syderstone is gone, and you must accept it."

"I didn't even have the chance to say goodbye," I said softly.

"Oh, come now!" Robert snorted. "Saying goodbye to a *house*? *Really,* Amy, at times you are the very meaning of *absurd*—you make that word come to life and breathe!"

"But the furniture, and my things . . ." I persisted.

"There's nothing there of any value!" Robert exclaimed. "As for your personal things, I assure you, anything worth saving will be awaiting you at Throcking. And I've arranged to have your cats sent there too—that fat, fluffy one and the silly black one with the crooked tail—so you shan't lack for company with them to baby and croon over."

"Thank you, Robert. I don't know what I would do without Onyx and Custard—they are indeed like babies to me—but *I* should have been the one to decide. *I* should have been the one to . . . to . . ." I buried my face in my hands and broke down in tears.

"There wasn't time for that!" Robert peevishly exclaimed. "Besides, the men I assigned to do it are most capable and not the sort to be swayed by sentimentality, like you are; they think with their heads, *not* with their hearts! If I had left the matter to *you,* it would not have been concluded by Doomsday, and the new owner would have had me in the law courts because of your dallying; then what would I do? I can't give his money back; I've already spent it! I am sorry to say it of my own wife, Amy, but you asked, and so I have to answer, and, though it saddens me to say it, you are just not competent and efficient enough to be entrusted with such a task. If I let you do it, you would be weeping over every spoon, cup, and candlestick and clinging like a lover to every stick of furniture."

"That is not true!" I sobbed. "I know Syderstone better than anyone, so none would be more suited to the task than I! And I have been managing large households since I was but a girl!"

"That is hardly the same thing!" Robert retorted. "Managing a house and dismantling a house are two *very* different things!"

"Well, if I cannot go to Syderstone, my father left me three other manors—Bircham Newton and Greater Bircham in Norfolk, and Bulkham Manor in Suffolk," I reminded him. "Could I not go to one of them instead? I know they are much smaller, but I would much prefer that to living amongst strangers. I want my own home, Robert, to be surrounded by my own things, and people I know, not to be a guest in someone else's house, partaking of their bed and board, having to sit and be gracious with no work to do except embroidery. I want my *own* home and work to do to keep me busy so the loneliness of missing you doesn't drive me mad!"

"I have told you before, and I tell you again now, you *must* accept that you are the wife of a great man and conduct yourself as such; no more churning butter in the dairy, picking fruit, and working alongside the servants as if you were one of them. We shall have a fine country house later, when my position at court is more established; then I will find a country house worthy of me, or else I shall build one when I know I can afford to, but it will have to wait until then, for I shall have nothing but the best. I shall accept nothing less, and if that means waiting until there is more gold in our coffers, then you must be content to wait. And, for now, you will have to go to Mr Hyde's, and I don't want to hear another word about it! I've already arranged it; your things are doubtlessly being packed and sent to Throcking as we speak. And you don't want to appear ungracious or ungrateful, do you? *That* would reflect *very* badly upon me, and I will *not* have such things said of my wife; Lady Dudley must *always* comport herself as a *perfect* lady, like an etiquette book sprung to life in female form. I will tolerate *nothing* less, and I warn you now, it shall not go well for you if I hear differently. Besides, you cannot go to Bircham Newton, Greater Bircham, or Bulkham; they have been sold as well, and you know you are not wanted at Stanfield Hall now that your stepbrother and his family have set up house there. Oh, and the sheep are all gone as well, so you needn't start talking any wild nonsense about becoming a shepherdess and going to live with the flock, taking shelter in a cave upon cold nights and when it rains. Nor can you make your home in an apple tree like a bird in a nest; the orchards have been sold as well. Now, no more tears and absurdity, Amy. Come to bed. We both need our rest. And you've really *nothing* to fear. You will have a whole wing—the best one, of course—and you will like the Hydes, and they will like you if they wish to continue to enjoy my favour; one word from me in the right ear, and they are ruined, and they know it."

"I never thought I would come to this," I said in quiet defeat as I climbed back into bed, "that people would like me only because they were obliged or paid to, and not for myself."

Robert sighed deeply and rolled over in bed, turning his back to me. "You *really* are the most ridiculous creature! You know *nothing* of the ways of the world! Now draw the bed-curtains, then lie down, and think about the story we just read until you fall asleep! I had hoped it would prove instructive, but you're so dull and dense, I see I shall have to think of another way to make its lessons sink in. Your mother taught you nothing, obviously!"

Those were the last words my husband said to me, spoken as if he were issuing orders to an army of foot soldiers, as he snuffed out the candles and laid his head back down. And, obedient as Griselda, I obeyed. What good would it do to fight him? My childhood home and inheritance were already gone, sold, before I even knew it; I never even had a chance to say goodbye. I had taken it for granted that I would be coming back. I thought of the servants, the common folk who lived round about, who worked our land and tended our orchards and sheep, and always had a smile and a kind word for me. They would think I didn't care! To think that I would never see them again, that I had left them without a goodbye. And I would never again walk amongst the flocks of woolly sheep and hear them baa-ing or sink my teeth into a Syderstone apple—it broke my heart.

Tears trickled down my cheeks, and in my mind I disobeyed my husband. I spared not a thought for Patient Griselda and fell asleep thinking only of Syderstone, the only *real* home I had ever known. Stanfield Hall had always been my mother's—it was always understood that it would go to her son, my stepbrother, John Appleyard—but Syderstone had always been Father's and mine. Even as it crumbled, our love for it never died.

I always dreamed of teaching my children—sons and daughters—everything I knew about managing a landed estate, of teaching my girls to be the perfect chatelaines, and my sons never to be wastrels who cared little and left all in the hands of their steward, and of sharing our traditions with them. I used to dream of taking my children out, wrapped up warmly against the cold, singing carols as we trudged through the snow to serenade the apple trees and drink a toast to their good health when the clock struck midnight to welcome the New Year; and of presiding proudly, with my children at my side, over our wonderful harvest celebrations, watching them taste, for the first time, each delicious dish made from our very own apples, and seeing them clapping their hands and bouncing on their toes, eager to join in the high-spirited country dances, and taking their part in the Candlestick Branles we danced on All Hallows' Eve; and of watching them wading through the golden fields of barley, growing taller each year, and having them beside me at the shearing celebrations after the sheep were shorn nude and the wool sacks packed, and we all drank apple cider and feasted on crisp golden wafers and rich, sweet cream as a special, and most luxurious, treat for our workers. Now it was all just a dream that would *never* come true, and one that I needed to stop dreaming, for I knew each time I did would break my heart all over again.

With the late-afternoon light blocked out by the blue velvet bed-curtains, my tear-filled eyes turned resentfully, burning and accusing, to Robert's naked shoulder as he slept soundly beside me, apparently at peace with himself and what he had done. No worries disturbed *his* rest! How could he do this to me? How could he take my dreams away? Make my past a bittersweet memory that would bring tears to my eyes and an ache to my heart every time I looked back, and deprive me, and the children I yearned to bear, of the future I had envisioned—a good and wholesome life in which we preserved our traditions, and even though we lived in a grand manor, it was also a home, a *real* home, not just a house where we ate our meals, entertained guests, and laid our heads at night. I wanted that life for myself and my family so badly, I could taste it, just like that first crisp, delicious, juicy bite of a Syderstone apple, but now, because of Robert, it could never be. How could he do it? How could he take it all away from me? All my hopes and dreams gone, banished and vanished without a qualm or a care! And without even consulting me! He only told me afterwards, when it was already done and too late to change anything.

"I can *never* forgive you for this! *Never!*" I whispered to his bare shoulder, even though I knew, had he been awake and able to answer, Robert would have said I was being sentimental, absurd, and foolish, thinking with my heart instead of with my head. But I didn't care; I was being me. I didn't know how or want to be anyone else.

19

Amy Robsart Dudley

William Hyde's Mansion House in Throcking, Hertfordshire
January–March 1559

Robert personally escorted me to Mr Hyde's house. We travelled in grand style, escorted by my husband's ever-increasing retinue of liveried retainers, all proud to wear the Dudleys' bear and ragged staff blazoned on their blue velvet sleeve and to carry arms in case any dared threaten or insult their lord and master. Some of them I had heard were rather unsavoury characters, rough men about whom rumours of rape, murder, and robbery swirled, but my husband apparently had no qualms about having such about him. There had even been talk of brawls and tussles between them and the liveried retainers of some of the great noblemen at court who, for one reason or another, disliked and opposed Robert. He made such a show of our progress along the country roads that I was surprised there were not heralds blaring trumpets and minstrels singing our praises afore us and children scattering rose petals for our horses to walk upon.

As we rode along, side by side in silence, all we passed doffed their caps and fell to their knees. Whenever this happened, my cheeks flamed, and I ducked my head until we had passed them. It just didn't feel right; to me it felt like putting on airs, as if I were pretending to be someone I wasn't and taking something that was not my right. But Robert didn't seem troubled by such notions; he sat straight and proud in the saddle, accepting it all as if it were his due, with his head held high as if it supported a phantom crown.

"They know they are in the presence of greatness," he said to me once, with a self-satisfied smile.

I stared straight ahead and had to keep swallowing hard to keep my tears from getting the better of me. I couldn't even look at Robert without the tears welling up afresh, and hurt and blame blazing from my eyes like fingers of frost and flame. For this reason, I had Pirto fasten a veil to my hat and kept it down over my face all the way to Throcking. I told Robert it was to protect my complexion from the frosty air that burned even as it chilled, and I did not want to arrive at the Hydes' with my nose bright red and my eyes streaming, and he seemed content to believe the lie and said that he was happy to see that, for once, I was displaying some common sense.

The house was indeed a fine one, bold redbrick plopped down in the middle of a daisy-dotted meadow, though there were carefully cultivated pleasure gardens replete with a fishpond in back. And, just a ways down the road a bit, was the little church of the Holy Trinity.

Fortunately, I did not have to face the Hydes straightaway. Mrs Hyde was with child and "feeling a trifle sick and having a lie-down", the steward said, and Mr Hyde had had some business come up that prevented him from being there to greet us personally. We were shown to the left wing of the house, where I was to lodge, by the pleasant, smiling-faced steward who was so chatty and effusive, I could not help but like him. I thought it might be fun to talk to him later and learn the local gossip; if I had to stay here, I thought I really should make an effort. But Robert dismissed him quickly, saying he deplored such forwardness and familiarity in servants and that country people were notoriously lax about such matters.

Much to my dismay, I found my bedchamber hung all around with the Griselda tapestries. I had hoped Robert had forgotten them or would take them with him to London. There was a pretty little silver gilt writing desk inlaid with mother-of-pearl and turquoise positioned before the window to catch the best light, with a silver inkwell, a quantity of quills, and a child's copybook at the ready atop it, arranged just as if they were waiting for me, along with Robert's copy of *The Canterbury Tales,* the start of Griselda's story still marked with the red satin ribbon.

"To practise your penmanship," Robert explained.

Even before I had a chance to take off my gloves and hat, he was there at the desk showing these things to me, lecturing me like a schoolmaster.

"You read tolerably well, though with much hesitancy and uncertainty and without any grace; you falter often and trip over the words. But your penmanship is *atrocious*; you sign your name like an old woman with palsied hands and failing sight. Every day I want you to sit at this desk for two solid hours—I have given orders that no one is to interrupt you unless the house is on fire—and copy "The Clerk's Tale" into this copybook as many times as you can until it is filled from cover to cover. When you have filled the entire book, you may send it to me. But do not wait to hear from me; go on with your work and begin at once upon another." He opened a drawer to show me that it was filled with at least a dozen more copybooks. "When you are down to the last one, tell Mr Hyde, and he will provide you with more. And every morning when you awake, I want you to lie in bed and contemplate these tapestries, and think about the story you have been copying, and do the same whenever you feel compelled to pester me with letters asking when I am coming to visit you. I will come when I can, not a moment sooner. I hope you understand that asking will only annoy me and will not bring me to you a moment sooner."

I was *so* angry, I wanted to fly at him, kick his shins, pummel him with my fists, and rake my nails down that handsome face, I wanted to fling the inkwell at his head and tear the copybooks and even that beautifully bound book apart. But the hurt went deeper than my anger, deeper than actions. And instead, even though I *hated* myself for doing it, I could only nod and hang my head and murmur, "Yes, Robert." Then I asked if I might lie down. "I am not feeling well," I said delicately with downcast eyes, hoping Robert would take that to mean I was ill with the onset of my courses.

He gave his consent—"but just this once," he stipulated, saying that he would make my excuses to the Hydes, but I must not make a habit of shunning their company. "Remember, Amy," he said, "you must not be rude to your hosts and make them think you find their company irksome and unwelcome—even if it is. Some people," he continued, "equate a reserved and solitary nature with snobbishness, and I will *not* have that said of *my* wife; Lady Dudley must *always* be a kind and gracious lady who is a credit to her lord." Then he summoned his valet, Mr Tamworth, and set about washing and changing his clothes, making ready to dine with the Hydes.

When he was gone back downstairs, I stripped down to my shift and pulled the covers up over my head and curled up on my side, crying for all that I had lost, inwardly raging against all the false hope my husband had given me throughout all our years together. I had hoped so very much for a new beginning, a fresh start, another chance for us to love as we once had, but now I was homeless and banished and had lost my husband to his ambitions and the only woman who could fulfil them—Elizabeth. I was, just like Griselda, being turned out in disgrace so that another woman could take my place. And I had a feeling, a deep, fearsome foreboding inside me, gnawing at me, and giving me no respite or mercy, that, unlike Griselda's story, mine would not end happily.

My eyes found the tapestry, the last in the series, in which Griselda is reunited with the daughter and son she thought slain and discovers that she is not to be replaced after all, and is restored to her fine clothes, jewells, and her husband's loving embrace. As I gazed upon that tapestry, I wept all the more. I didn't believe in happy endings any more. That's why people loved stories so, I realised in that instant, because they found in them what was missing from their own lives, the things they knew, no matter how much or how hard they might hope and dream and scheme, they would never have.

Robert stayed late downstairs, drinking far into the night with William Hyde. I awoke to the feel of his body on top of mine, his fingers fumbling, clumsy with drink as he lifted my shift, and his breath sour with wine. I was not ready when he pushed inside, and he hurt me, but he ignored my tears and pleas. When he was done, he rolled off me, heavy as a log, and fell at once into a deep sleep.

I awoke the next morning alone, feeling raw, sore, and aching between my legs, and a trifle bewildered at waking up in a strange place. I had to remind myself where I was. As I gazed about the room, I realised that the small travelling chest Robert had brought with him was gone, and there was nothing of his left within the room. I bolted out of bed, snatched up my shift, and pulled it over my head as I ran to the window. I was just in time to see him turning onto the road, heading back to London, at a fast gallop, followed by his retainers.

The door opened behind me, and then Pirto was there, enfolding me in her arms and looking as if she was about to weep too.

"Oh, my lady!" she said as she held me close and stroked my back.

"He should not have gone without saying goodbye!" I sobbed. "Heaven knows when I shall see him again!"

The next day, though I did not feel like leaving my bed—I had a feverish and aching head and knew I presented a sorry sight with my eyes still all swollen and red—I forced myself, lest I offend my hosts, to descend the stairs and sit and sew with Mrs Hyde in the parlour.

When I opened my sewing basket, I found, nestled like an egg inside a nest of colourful embroidery silks, a note from my husband.

> *When your script improves sufficiently, embroider these words upon a cushion for me, inside a great heart made of smaller hearts, lovers' knots, and flowers. Embroider the words in deep red, as if they were written with your own heart's blood, and put your soul into every stitch so that when I gaze upon it, I will <u>know</u> that you mean <u>every</u> word.*

Below it was a verse, words Chaucer had assigned to Patient Griselda:

> *"There is nothing, God so my soul save,*
> *Pleasant to you that doth displease me.*
> *There is nothing on earth that I desire to own,*
> *Nothing I fear to lose, save you alone."*

"My husband is not a kind man," I said softly, forgetting myself and speaking the words aloud, then gasping when I realised that I had done so.

"What's that, my dear?" Mrs Hyde cocked her head over her embroidery. Cupping her hand around her ear, she apologetically explained, "I'm afraid you will need to speak a little louder. Since the last baby I am a trifle deaf. The doctor cannot explain it, nor can the midwife; it's quite a mystery, and a *most* vexing one."

I breathed a brief prayer of thanks that Mrs Hyde had not heard me aright and forced myself to smile as I folded the note and tucked it beneath the coloured silks. Then, like a dutiful and devoted wife made in the mould of Griselda, I said in a clear voice loud enough for Mrs Hyde to hear, "My husband is such a kind man."

"Oh, yes, indeed he is!" Mrs Hyde enthused. "The *very* soul of kindness! Oh, Lady Dudley, you are the *most* fortunate woman alive, to be married to such a man!" She clasped a hand to her heart and looked fit to swoon in rapture as she piled praise upon Robert. "So kind, so thoughtful, so courteous, so brave, and charming! There cannot be a handsomer man in *all* of England! And such a fine voice—I never have a whit of trouble understanding Lord Robert! Oh, and the stories he told last night at supper! I feared I would burst my stays, I was laughing so hard! He is such a clever, witty man! And he can sing and recite poetry too! And he is *so* considerate! Do you know, my dear, last night he drew up a footstool and sat at my feet with my sewing basket on his lap, handing me whatever I needed as I sewed, and so humbly implored me to look after you, flattering me that while he could not ask me to be like a mother to you, as I am not old enough"—she laughed delightedly and patted her grey-peppered curls—"but perhaps he might presume to ask me to be like a sister to you. He *begged* me to take good care of you, and I could hear his worry for you in *every* word! Oh, what a considerate and loving husband he is—you are *so* blessed to have him, my dear! He moved me to tears, and I *swore* upon my life that I would care for you as if you were my very own daughter and my own sister as well. And I will, Lady Dudley, I will. I cannot *bear* to even contemplate disappointing such a *marvellous, magnificent* man! My husband and I have already decided to name this child I am carrying"—she patted the bulge beneath her loose gown of pink brocade—"Dudley, even if it is a girl!"

I nodded and forced myself to smile. "I understand, Mrs Hyde, that disappointing Robert can feel like a crime. I thank you for all your kindness," I added, just to be polite; then I bent my head over the doublet I was embroidering with forget-me-nots as a gift to send to Robert.

And so I settled down to a life of waiting. Glum and morose, I would sit beside a window, with my hands either idle, listlessly embroidering, or dutifully wielding a quill, endlessly filling a child's copybook with the tale of Patient Griselda, and all the time my heart would hope and yearn and burn with longing and the green flames of jealousy fed by my fears and hot, angry tears. And there were other days when I was so prostrated by tears that I could not even get out of bed and would lie all day with my cats, taking what comfort I could from holding their warm, furry bodies and hearing them purr.

Every time I heard horses' hooves, on the dirt road or the gravelled path leading up to the house, hope would leap from my heart into my eyes, and my lips would spread in an eager, expectant smile that would slowly die as the riders passed on by or turned out not to be Robert or one of his men bearing a letter for me.

And each day as twilight fell, my hopes would also plummet as one more day passed without a sign of Robert. I tried *very* hard not to pester and plague him with queries about when he would come to see me, but I wanted him so much. In his letters, Robert always said vaguely that he would come "soon", but something would always come up to prevent or delay his coming. It was as if I was the last and least important item on his list, the most expendable, and the first to cross off and discard in favour of other, more important people and things. And, like a demon, a ballad of longing for one's absent love that had been popular in Queen Mary's reign—it was said some had sung it as a cruel taunt while she was pining for Prince Philip—began to haunt me, and I could not get it out of my mind. It was as if a phantom singer had invaded my brain, hiding in dark, quiet corners, where I could never turn her out, endlessly singing the same doleful refrain:

Complain, my lute, complain on him
That stays so long away;
He promised to be here ere this,
But still unkind doth stay.
But now the proverb true I find,
Once out of sight then out of mind.

No, no, no! My mind rebelled against the verse. That is *not* the way it is—out of sight, yes, but *not* out of mind, rather, *always* on my mind, *always*! I think of him all night and day! Even though he seldom spares a thought for me, I am *always* thinking of him, *always* wanting and longing for him! And surely *she*—my rival, the Queen—must think of me. She often crosses the threshold of my mind, an imperious visitor who should be an honoured guest but who has taken the one thing I valued most. But, out of courtesy and deference to her royal blood, I cannot confront her as I would any common rival; I can only endure the trespass and thievery, wearing a false smile, politely, as if she had come and admired a prettily painted porcelain plate in my cupboard and I had taken the hint and graciously presented it to her with my compliments. Because she is the Queen, I cannot fight her. And it is not a plate she wants—that I could bear—it is my husband!

I was trying *so* hard to hold on to my husband, to remind him of how we used to be and the love that once pulsed and thrived like a living thing with a heart of its own beating between us. I couldn't bear to believe that love was dead and gone forever. I kept trying to bring it back to life, like a necromancer casting a spell to resurrect the dead. But the enchantment I tried—and failed—to cast was a rich, golden, and loving one, born out of the depths of my soul, not dark and sinister. The spell I tried to cast over him was not witchcraft; it was the wiles of a woman who, though disillusioned with her husband, was still *desperately* and wholeheartedly in love with him.

Sometimes Robert sent tokens, little gifts, delivered by one of those rough and surly men who wore his livery, pretty little things like buttons made of Spanish gold, velvet slippers, silk stockings, and lengths of lace, linen, and silk. But, despite their richness, they were poor recompense for his absence.

"Forget it all when you are with me!" I begged and beseeched the rare times when he was there with me, as I had so many times before, often on my knees, clinging to him, desperately trying to pull him back to me whenever his mind strayed back to the glittering world he had left behind in London.

"But I don't want to forget!" Robert always said angrily, pushing or pulling away from me. "And I won't forget! It is my life, Amy! I am not a country squire content to stay at home with his country-bumpkin bride and sit by the fire! A *real* lady, a *highborn* lady accustomed to life at court, would understand that her husband's attendance upon the Queen and retaining her favour is as vital to his success and good fortune as breath is to living. She would not make the *slightest* difficulty or murmur even *one* word of complaint; she would understand and encourage him and never hinder him in *any* way. But *you* can't understand that, and if I brought you to court, you would only blunder and bumble and embarrass and disgrace me. I could no more take you to court than I could Mollie the milkmaid!"

Now it was no longer "our" life but "his" life and "my" life, two separate lives, not one joined together by holy wedlock. The lock had been sprung, either picked or broken, and Robert was glad of it, glad to be set free, like a prisoner released from gaol revelling and rejoicing in his freedom.

And the loving words grew as rare as his visits. Once, he marched furious-faced into the parlour, grasped my arm, his fingers digging deeply into the soft flesh, and marched me into Mr Hyde's study and shut the door behind us, even as he smiled and made his excuses to Mrs Hyde, who sat back swooning against the green velvet cushions of the fireside settle, her hand pressed over her heart, felled by his charm, with her embroidery fallen forgotten to the floor to be dragged away by the cat. He had come, "taking valuable and precious time away from pressing business at court," to chastise me over "my profligate spending on such an ordinary, mundane item as candles".

Mr and Mrs Hyde were so honoured to have me—Lord Robert's wife—to lodge with them that they had on more than one occasion implored me to treat their home as if it were my very own and to do exactly as I pleased. Though I could not bring myself to interfere in household management, to usurp Mrs Hyde's place as mistress and chatelaine; even though I *longed* for such work to distract me, I did not want to incur her resentment and that of the servants. But I did ask that every day at dusk a candle be lit in each window of all the public rooms that faced onto the road, as well as in my bedchamber, and that they be kept burning until the first light of dawn so that, should My Lord be on his way to me, he would find the house aglow with a warm and inviting welcome that would make him smile and spur his mount onward and speed himself into my arms. Often, I would go out and walk into the gloaming, and, from a little hillock nearby, watch the candles being lit and let them guide me back to the house. As I walked along the avenue lined with chestnut trees, I would imagine myself a weary traveller, like my husband, being guided by those candles like tiny beckoning fingers of flames urging me ever nearer to a pair of empty arms that ached to hold me. And I would pause and look up as the stars came out and wish upon their twinkling brightness that my husband would come soon.

But when he came, all he did was brandish the bill for the candles in my face, smack it against his palm, and complain about my foolishness and this "ludicrous expenditure", and ask if it were my intent to make of him a laughingstock.

Stammering, wringing my hands, and teetering on the verge of tears, I tried to explain, to tell him how much I loved him, that I meant only to give him a warm welcome, to make the house look inviting if perchance he arrived after dark. But he only snorted and dismissively, derisively, waved aside my heartfelt words, exclaiming, "That is the most ludicrous thing I have *ever* heard! I am Lord Robert Dudley, the Queen's Master of the Horse, and *any* house in England would make me welcome and be *honoured* to have me within its walls, and I don't need a candle burning in every window to tell me so!"

Pacing before me, he said I had humiliated him and caused him no end of trouble. When he first saw the bill, he had thought there might be an error, that Mr Hyde had miscalculated or become distracted and mistakenly written the wrong number down; thus, he had his treasurer, Mr Forster, query Mr Hyde about the matter. Jewels and fine clothes, lavish furnishings, foods I had a craving for and that made my table look rich, like gilded marzipan, sugar sculptures, candied fruit, or a roasted peacock or swan dressed in its fine feathers—any sort of luxury that made a grand show that impressed others and made life more pleasurable, he could well understand—but £8 spent on *candles*? "Do you realise, Amy, that working men are fortunate to earn as much in a year?" he demanded. And regarding the fact that they had been left burning from dusk till dawn, Robert could only say, "If I were you, Amy, I would get down on my knees and thank God the house did not catch fire; for I'll not bankrupt myself to buy another man a new house, even if my wife is the fool who set the old one ablaze!"

With a long, exasperated sigh he thrust the bill inside his amber doublet. "Pray word of this does not spread, Amy, else everyone will think you a madwoman, and in truth I cannot blame them. £8 squandered on *candles*—what a *ridiculous* expense! I've half a mind not to pay it! No more candles in the windows, Amy," he said over his shoulder as he strode out. "And if perchance I do ride up after dark and see candles in the windows, you'll feel the warmth of my wrath, and then you'll wish I hadn't come at all instead of 'welcoming' me."

"Yes, Robert." I sighed and hung my head and sank down onto the window seat, defeated yet again and feeling of a sudden tired of even trying. *You cannot win,* a tiny little voice in the back of my head said. And I knew it spoke the truth. But to stop trying . . . to me that was the same as dying. I *had* to keep trying, fighting this futile and oh, so wearying fight, and hoping that I would discover a way to win back his love.

But he came to me that night, and he was passionate, and made me believe our quarrel was all forgotten, just another misunderstanding, as all lovers are apt to have from time to time. He said he would come again in February if he could, on St Valentine's Day perhaps, for that was a day meant for lovers, the day when the birds chose their mates. I was in his arms when he said it, our naked limbs entwined, and my head resting on his chest, listening to the beat of his heart as he stroked and played with my hair, twining it round his fingertips, admiring its golden shimmer in the candlelight. I was so happy that I kissed him, and Robert used his warm, ardent body to roll me over onto my back again.

* * *

On St Valentine's Day I was up with the sun, though I was so eager and excited, I had barely slept the night before. I sang as I bathed, and Pirto washed my hair with our special blend of lemons and chamomile. I was all smiles as I sat by the fire, my cheeks rosy and pink, and it was all I could do to sit still. I wanted to leap up and run down the road until I met Robert. As I waited for my hair to dry, I rubbed the whole of me with a sweet-smelling lotion I had made from the roses that grew in such pretty pink profusion at Syderstone, and I dreamed of Robert's hands caressing my naked skin. Then I had Pirto dress me in a new gown of vivid robin's egg blue satin that opened to reveal a kirtle of cream-coloured satin embroidered with branches that stretched across the front on which pairs of birds perched, nestled lovingly, and Mr Edney had cunningly fashioned little nests for them out of coils of gold braid and filled them with speckled turquoise eggs. I loved it. I was in raptures when I first saw it and even hugged and kissed Mr Edney and gave gifts of candy and coins to his apprentice boy and embroidery women. It was such a fun, clever design, and I couldn't wait for Robert to see it. I could barely sit still—I wanted to run and sing and dance—as Pirto brushed my hair until it cascaded down my back in a mass of curls that shone like spun gold. I was so eager to be outside waiting for my beloved, walking, watching the birds and the road for any sign of Robert, that Pirto had to chase after me with a shawl, for the air still had a sharp nip of chill in it.

I walked and waited and hoped all day. Every time I heard hoofbeats, my heart jounced in time with them, singing in step with them, dreaming that at any moment my beloved would come galloping up, sweep me up into his arms, and carry me away to make love in a bed of wildflowers, just like he used to. But he never came, nor sent a letter or even a gift, not even the tiniest trinket, trifle, or token to let me know he was thinking of me, because he was *not* thinking of me; he had forgotten me yet again.

I watched the sunset, and then I gave up, and with heavy steps and an even heavier heart, and my shawl, fallen from one shoulder, dragging on the ground, I went back inside as the darkness descended and the air turned even colder. I was almost late for supper.

Later, seated at the table, even though I dreaded to hear the answer, I asked Mrs Hyde how Valentine's Day was celebrated at court.

She told me that all the ladies wrote their names down on dainty slips of paper and put them into a bowl, and then the gentlemen reached in—"like drawing lots, my dear!"—and gave a gift to the lady whose name they chose. "Pretty little things that a lady might fancy—a bit of silk, lace, or gilded braid to trim a gown, a brooch, or a silk flower for her to wear, an ivory comb for her hair, a figurine to adorn the mantel in her room, or a book of poesy perhaps." And, of course, there would be a banquet, "no doubt presided over by a great Cupid sculpted out of sugar and marzipan," and there would be all sorts of dishes that were said to "encourage love to flourish". And there was a dance, "a sort of gavotte, only a kissing game set to music," Mrs Hyde continued, oblivious to my distress, as with each word I travelled further away from peace of mind. "And there will be a masque, of course, something to do with love, with the Queen at the centre of it all, like the Goddess of Love all men bow down to worship. And this year, since England has a new Queen, and a young and beautiful one at that"—Mrs Hyde nodded knowingly—"I think every man at court will choose her to be his Valentine and woo her with a gift. Already they say there are sonnets enough to 'The Fair Eliza' to fill a whole library, floor to ceiling, with books."

Abruptly I let my spoon clatter onto my plate and stood up, claiming I felt all of a sudden unwell, and I fled upstairs to my room. I could not bear to let the Hydes see me weep.

That night I dreamt of the Queen dressed as a bee, the queen of the hive, all in yellow and black stripes, glittering with hard, icy diamonds, with a golden crown perched atop her flame-coloured curls, and gauzy, shimmering, wire-stiffened wings on her back. Haughty and majestic, she was surrounded by a circle of men, from beardless youths to bald-pated greybeards, all of them costumed as black and yellow bees. They danced in an ever tightening circle around her, jostling and clamouring just to be near her, each holding out an offering—jewelled necklaces, ropes of pearls, brooches, earrings, bracelets, rings, jewels to adorn her hair, velvet-lined caskets filled with loose gems, muffs and cloaks of ermine, sable, or fox, beautiful crystal bottles filled with exotic perfumes, fringed and embroidered gloves to show off those vain, long-fingered hands, bolts of rich fabric, velvet slippers, or golden and silver ones, with jewels on the toes that would twinkle when she danced, reams of lace and braid to trim her gowns, gifts of gold and silver plate, musical instruments inlaid with mother-of-pearl or ivory, fancy saddles, jewelled or fringed, for her horses, Turkish carpets, tapestries, paintings, and statuary to adorn her chambers, and sonnets and songs praising her beauty, grace, and majesty that they raised their voices to recite or sing, vying to be heard over the others who were doing the same.

And then there was Robert, crashing through the circle of her admirers, astride a big black horse, sending the besotted bee-men and their gifts scattering, tumbling, and rolling. He was clad like the others in the black and yellow stripes of a bee, with wings upon his back quivering with every movement of his shoulders, his fine horseman's legs sheathed in vivid yellow hose, and tall black leather boots polished to a high gloss that caught the light of the candles. He swept Elizabeth up onto the saddle before him, extricating her from the buzzing hive of male admirers that surrounded her, all reaching out for her, calling her name, begging for her love and favour. But he ignored them all and cradled her close against his chest, his hand grazing her breast as he held the reins, and spurred his horse into a gallop, and carried her away from them all to a bed covered in heart's blood red velvet to make mad, passionate love to her, though his eyes never left the golden crown pinned tightly to her red hair the whole time. Even in the throes of passion, his eyes were still upon the glittering, golden prize.

I awoke then, screaming like one in mortal agony, clasping my chest, gasping and crying out to Pirto, who slept nearby on a trundle bed that during the day was tucked beneath mine. I had such a fearsome pain in my chest, like a sword being driven straight through me. There was a burning, aching tightness there, between my breasts, so bad it half made me want to die just to escape it; it was like an ever-tightening knot that needed to be untied in order to ease me.

As she perched on the side of my bed and held me and stroked my hair and back, Pirto said, with an unmistakable sniff of disapproval, that Mrs Hyde's cook was "over-generous with the contents of her mistress's spice cabinet" and that it was "no wonder that it had set my heart a-burning".

I let her hold me, dry my tears, and dose me with a soothing syrup "to cool the burn", then tuck me back into bed as if I were a little girl again, but I knew it was more than that. Nor was it just my imagination, my worst fears coming to life in the guise of a dream; it was *real,* and I *knew* it. My husband had forsaken me; his sights were firmly fixed on the crown and the woman who wore it, the woman who could make all his dreams come true—Elizabeth.

❧ 20 ❧

Elizabeth

The Dairy House at Kew, London
April 1559

I had given Robert a miniature mansion in London called the Dairy House at Kew as a New Year's gift. The first time he was to take me there was on a glorious April afternoon. He brought me a soft brown bundle tied up with string and bade me don this disguise and come down the private stair and across the garden to the river, where he would have a barge waiting. I did as he asked, and soon I found myself clad in a simple russet cloth gown with a white linen apron and cap such as a milkmaid might wear, while a disapproving Kat frowned behind my reflected image in the looking glass as she grudgingly did up my laces.

"Don't glower so, Kat!" I said, turning to hug her. "I've been so busy with one thing and another, Council meetings, and state papers, shoring up our defences, and being courted by foreign ambassadors for one prince, duke, or another, that I *deserve* a holiday!" I spread my brown skirts wide and spun gaily around her. "A day just to be free, just to be me!"

"With Robert Dudley," Kat said stiffly, the frown deepening upon rather than departing from her face.

"And what of it?" I shrugged. "He has been a good and loyal friend to me since childhood."

"He is a married man," Kat said sternly.

"I know"—I nodded—"and I thank God for it! I do not look to have him as my husband, Kat, and I would not even if he were free. I want a man's company, Kat, but I don't want to be a wife and have to surrender all I value into my husband's hands. Robert can take nothing from me but what I myself choose to give."

"You always did say you would never marry, ever since you were a little girl," Kat mused aloud, "but I always thought, I always hoped, you would grow out of it. 'Tis not natural for a woman to be alone, Bess . . ."

"And I don't want to be alone, Kat," I assured her, "and I will not be alone, but I do not want to be a wife either. For me, *that* is unnatural. I value my freedom far too highly to ever give it up; I want to be mistress of my own fate, not surrender it to a lord and master."

"If you only knew . . ." Kat grasped my hands tightly and gazed up at me with tears brimming in her old, faded eyes. "And you are *wrong*; there is one thing he *can* take from you without your consent—*your reputation*! *Please,* have a care for your reputation. People are saying—"

"Gossip!" I said with a disdainful shrug and a sour puckering of my lips. "People *always* must have *something* to talk about, even if they must embroider fancifully upon the bare facts or make it up out of whole cloth. *Please,* Kat, don't scold me. I have had *so* little joy in my life, and Robert makes me happy. Being with him is such fun . . ."

"Aye, love, I don't doubt it." Kat nodded grimly. "The kind of fun that can get a bastard in your belly or you branded a harlot forever!"

Stung, I gasped and leapt back as if she had just slapped me.

"Oh, sweetheart, I do not mean to hurt you!" Kat came and put her arms around me. "But you are Queen now, not a green girl like you were in the days of the Lord Admiral, and people take note of all you do, and already they have noticed how much you favour Lord Robert above all other men. They are even saying—"

I pulled away from her and ran to the door. "I don't care what they are saying!" I cried, tossing my head rebelliously. "Don't tell me any more!" I stamped my foot. "I'm going to have a good time today with Lord Robert, and damn all gossips and scandal-mongers—neither they nor anyone else can stop me!"

I was about to flounce out the door, when I stopped, seeing the tears trickling down Kat's face. I turned and came back to her and tried to explain. Kat had always been like a mother to me, and I wanted her to understand. I needed to know that she did not think ill of me.

"His wife doesn't love him, Kat, and he doesn't love her; they're estranged. The marriage has grown cold and bitter; they married young and repented as they grew older and saw how little they had in common. I could tell how much it grieved and saddened Robert when he spoke of it. She doesn't want to come to court. I intended to invite her, but Robert urged me not to; he said it would frighten and upset her, and she would cry and make herself sick, fearing that her refusal would offend me, and I might punish her for it by forcing her to come anyway. She wants to stay in the country. And you *know* Robert is not the kind of man who could ever be content to play the country squire, spending his days wading through barley crops and flocks of sheep. He was meant for greater and grander things, things that I can give him, as a reward for his loyalty and the pleasure of his company, all of which takes *nothing* away from Amy; rather, it *gives* him the means to indulge her whims, to let her stay content in the country and have her pretty gowns. Truly, Kat, we are not hurting anyone; we are more sinned against by the gossips' tongues than we are indeed sinners."

Kat sighed deeply and shook her head and then, with a little halfhearted smile, gave in and gave me a hug. "Off you go, pet," she sighed. "But *please,*" she implored me, "have a care with that handsome rascal; he sore reminds me of the Lord Admiral. Now, there was a man!" she sighed, her old eyes misty with memory.

"I promise, I will." I kissed her cheek. "You need have no fear on my account, Kat. I'm not a little girl any more, and Lord Robert is not the first handsome rascal I've met," I added brightly as I shut the door behind me and ran merrily down the stone steps to the barge where Robert was waiting to enfold me in his arms and cover my lips with his.

When the stately little house first came into sight, it glowed like a puddle of fresh-spilt milk struck by the sun. The lawn unfurled before it like an emerald carpet, dotted with white marble statues and cunning seats shaped like milk pails. I laughed and clapped my hands in sheer delight as I sprang from the barge, without waiting for Robert to help me, blessedly unencumbered by my heavy, ornate court finery, feeling free and airy in my plain cloth gown and but a single petticoat, and no stiff, unwieldy farthingale, and without the pinch and bite of stays underneath as a rigorous reminder of decorum. I ran across the lawn with Robert chasing after me, darting behind statues and trees, letting him catch me to steal a swift or sometimes lingering kiss before I laughed and darted away again like a dragonfly.

"The house isn't finished yet," Robert said, when we collapsed, laughing and panting, into one of the milk-pail seats. "I don't want you to see it until everything is perfect, but I have arranged something else, a special treat, for your delight, and mine, for your pleasure is my pleasure."

He loudly clapped his hands, and servants in his blue velvet livery with the bear and ragged staff embroidered on their chests and sleeves immediately appeared to erect a small gold-fringed tent of purple silk, and to furnish it with a Turkey carpet that was like a field of colourful flowers, bright, plump cushions the colour of the finest jewels for us to lounge upon, and a gilded table with short legs so that we might dine as we sat upon the cushions. And musicians came to stand outside and play for us as, hand-in-hand, dressed as a milkmaid and her swain, we went inside. After us came a tall, dark-skinned man costumed in a feathered cloth-of-gold turban studded with gems, baggy ruby satin breeches, full, flowing robes of yellow silk embroidered with exquisite red poppies, and golden slippers with curled-up toes studded with rubies. With golden bangles clacking on his wrists, he bowed and presented us with a large golden tray covered with exotic foods I could not even name. Robert told me he was a chef from Turkey, who had once served in the Sultan's kitchen. I would have liked to talk to him, to ask him the names and ingredients of the strange and exotic dishes he laid before us, but Robert swiftly dismissed him. There were rich, savoury spiced meats and delicious cheeses, and a confection, like jellied fruit, that tasted and smelt of rosewater, dusted with a generous powdering of white sugar, and a delicious, flaky, golden pastry comprised of numerous delicate, paper-thin layers drenched in sweet, syrupy honey with morsels of dates and nuts baked in between. Robert and I laughed as we knelt on the cushions and fed each other bites of this exotic banquet for two, pausing to lick each other's fingers or to kiss away a dribble of meat juice or a dab of honey from our mouths and chins.

After our meal, and after servants had come in to take away the table, Robert clapped his hands, and three beautiful, honey-skinned, almond-eyed women with hair like black silk came in. They were clad in exotic, baggy silk trousers and trailing diaphanous veils and wore gold bangles about their wrists and ankles. Each one carried a luxurious armful of rich fabric.

Robert stood up and walked to the opposite side of the tent and turned to face me. He motioned for the women to come to him, but even as they surrounded him, their beringed hands sliding sensuously over his body as they divested him of his garments, his eyes never once left mine. Proud as a prince, hands on hips, head held haughty-high, he stood naked before me, showing off his fine, firm horseman's physique, as two of the women poured a spicy scented oil onto their palms and massaged it into his sun-bronzed skin, while the third set upon his head a magnificent cloth-of-gold, jewel-encrusted, peacock-feathered turban. A smile twitched his lips, half-teasing, as his cock rose beneath their ministrations and pointed straight at me. One of the women began to massage it with the oil, and he reached down, coiled the long, thick, blue black rope of her hair entwined with pearls tightly around his fist, and pulled her up and roughly kissed her mouth. When they were finished and every part of him was oiled and scented, they fastened around his waist a jewelled belt set with large sapphires, amethysts, emeralds, and rubies as big as my clenched fist, and brought a magnificent trailing robe of royal purple silk embroidered with peacock feathers trimmed with thick panels of gold brocade encrusted with tiny brilliant jewels and seed pearls, and the third woman knelt and kissed each one of his feet before she slid them into sapphire-studded golden slippers with turned-up toes.

Then it was my turn. At his direction, they came to me. I was unaccustomed to being attended by such sensual and exotic handmaidens and to having my person handled in such a familiar, intimate fashion. Robert noted my tension and spoke a few words in an unknown tongue to one of the women, and she nodded and produced a tiny golden box, like a miniature treasure chest, and opened it and offered it to me, gesturing that I should take one of the little golden discs that lay inside. She opened her own mouth and pointed to show me that I should place it on my tongue and let it melt there.

"Like this," Robert said, taking one of the gilt candy pastilles and demonstrating.

It melted quickly in the moist heat of my mouth with a sweetness spreading sensuously, like a rich velvet blanket, over my tongue. Beneath the sweetness, there was a slight yet sharp bitterness, but I didn't mind it, and at Robert's urging I gladly took another. And then, when their hands again reached for me, stroking my milk-pale skin as they laid it bare, and plucking the pins from my hair, massaging my scalp and combing through the long, rippling cascade they released to unfurl down my back, the jewels on their fingers winking through the red waves, I arched my back and closed my eyes and purred like a cat, and at times I even giggled, giddy with the wanton, brazen novelty and delight of it all.

As they had done with Robert, two of the women began to massage a perfumed oil into my skin, a bold yet at the same time delicate spicy rose scent that also evoked thoughts of cinnamon and honey and the warm sun. A dusky hand caressed my cheek and slipped another golden pastille into my mouth as three sets of hands stroked and caressed every part of me. The fingers of one woman reached out to paint my lips, whilst another rouged my nipples, and the third the tender pink lips of my sex. Then they began to dress me. One of the women knelt at my feet, holding out a pair of loose, sheer white trousers spangled with myriad tiny silver stars. I gasped in surprise when she pulled them up and tied the silver ribbon around my waist, for they were open between the legs. I had never worn such an immodest garment before, but before I could find words to protest, a girdle with long streamers like liquid silver pouring down over me was fastened around my waist. Next I was laced into a bodice of tight white satin thickly encrusted with silver embroidery and diamonds and pearl flowers that lifted my breasts high but also left them bare. Silver slippers with turned-up toes adorned with diamonds and pearls were put upon my bare feet, and large rings blooming with pearl- and jewel-petalled flowers were slipped onto my fingers, and bracelets onto my wrists, and an opulent diamond and pearl necklace fastened about my throat that dripped a bouquet of jewelled blossoms down between my breasts. I slid my bare arms into a full, long, trailing robe of the purest white silk embroidered in silver and gold and jewelled flowers made of rubies, amethysts, and sapphires, with emerald leaves, and a circlet of matching jewelled flowers was set, like a crown, upon my head.

The handmaidens lit incense and then left us. Robert came to me and lowered me onto the cushions, and I lay back, loose and languid in his arms. His dark eyes cast a spell, mesmerising me, and his tongue flicked out, like a serpent's, teasing and lapping at my nipples, hard and rouged as red as cherries as I lay weak and docile beneath him.

"Tell me you love me," he breathed against my neck, and I did, again and again, clinging to him like a vine as he ground his loins hard against mine to show his ardour, wrapping my arms and legs tightly about him. "I love you, I love you!" I cried, my head whipping wildly against the ruby satin cushion it lay upon as he ripped away the silver tinsel girdle and his fingers plunged into the hot wetness of my sex.

"Now you are in my power!" he sighed.

At the triumph in his voice, I stiffened. His words had penetrated the opium fog and broken the spell completely. I thrust him from me and, hugging my robe tightly about me, ran out into the fresh air to escape the opium-scented incense. Dizzy and lightheaded, flush-faced and sweating, I fell to my knees and vomited hard beneath a tree, expelling all the rich, decadent foods I had eaten.

Robert ran out after me and urged me to come back inside.

"Bess, *please*!" he groaned. "I *cannot* live like a monk!"

I waited until my head had cleared a little, gulping in great mouthfuls of the fresh air, then, bracing myself, I plunged back into the incense-clouded tent and found my clothes, my milkmaid's disguise, and struggled as best as I could without assistance back into it. Robert came to me, begging me to sit down, but I pushed past him, back out into the fresh air, and ran for the river where the barge waited.

Cursing as he endeavoured to pull his breeches back on under his ornate robe to cover his nakedness, Robert ran after me. Suddenly he caught hold of me, grabbed my shoulders, and spun me around so I stood facing him. "Marry me," he said, staring straight into my eyes.

I turned my face away and felt the day grow suddenly grey. "*Please,* Robert . . ."

"Every day could be just as wonderful as this!" Robert insisted. "If you would but banish this endless parade of suitors, that pompous lot of strutting cockerels, preening and pining for a crown, and marry me instead, the *one* man in England who *truly* loves *you,* Elizabeth the woman, *not* Elizabeth the Queen!"

I sighed and pulled away from him. "You already have a wife, Robert. You are not the Sultan of Turkey, and you cannot take another . . ."

"But *you*—" Robert knelt before me and reached out to put his hands on my shoulders, staring into my eyes with a blazing intensity—"*you* have the power to set me free so we *can* be married!"

"No!" I said adamantly. *"Never!"* I pronounced each word clearly and decisively. "I told you before, Robert, I am *not* my father, and I will *not* abuse my power and twist the law to suit me. Your Amy shall not go the way of Catherine of Aragon, and I, Anne Boleyn's daughter, will not step into my mother's shoes as the centre and cause of a divorce scandal. And I have no desire to marry . . ."

"But Amy does not love me, and I don't love her. I love you!" Robert insisted. "I *never* stop thinking of you, wanting you. I am *mad* with love for you!"

"I am truly sorry, Rob. I remember well your wedding day, and the way her face *glowed* with love, the way she lit up whenever she looked at you; it saddens me to learn such a love has died and that light has gone out. However," I continued, in a tone much more brusque and businesslike, as though I were addressing my Council, "as you well know, love is very rarely the foundation of marriage. Many marry and live their whole lives without it, often well and contented with their lot. Life is full of hard bargains, Rob, but, sooner or later, we all must make our peace with it, else it drive us mad with torment, or we sicken and wither away for want of what we can never have; and so must you. Make your peace, Robert; it will go better for all of us if you do."

"But if I could persuade her . . ." he persisted.

"Oh, *really,* Rob!" I sighed in annoyance and threw up my hands. "There are no grounds that I am aware of, and I will *not* meddle in this! *I will not!* I am Queen and now must have even greater regard for my reputation, and I will not have it being said that I turned Lady Dudley out like Griselda in her shift so I could take her place! Now, I will hear no more about it! And I've warned you before . . ." Robert started to speak, but I silenced him with a furious glare. *"Not one more word,"* I warned, ice and fire in every syllable.

Crestfallen, Robert nodded and hung his head, and his shoulders slumped forward, as if all the fire had suddenly gone out of him.

"The sun is setting," I said. "We'd best be going."

Robert nodded and came to take my arm. "But first I want to show you something."

He led me out into the gloaming and waved his hand back at the house. Every window I saw was lit by a single candle.

"Every night I am in residence here," he announced as he stood before me, holding each of my hands in his, "I make this vow: a candle shall be left burning the whole night through, from dusk till dawn, in every window, in the hope that its light will guide you to my door and into my arms." Then he gently pulled me to him and kissed me with the utmost tenderness, the gentlest passion I had ever in my life known, that made me also feel aglow, as if lit from within, like the windows of the Dairy House at Kew.

"I love you," Robert whispered.

And I answered, and in that moment I meant it, "I love you too."

Then, hand-in-hand, we walked slowly back to the barge, and I returned to my palace, to reality, to doff my milkmaid's disguise, to plant my feet firmly back on the ground after my afternoon's flight of fancy, and resume my duties as Queen. But even as the French

Ambassador knelt at my feet and recited a poem of love one of Catherine de Medici's litter of royal princes had written for me, I could think of nothing and no one but Robert. And when I closed my eyes and pretended to swoon beneath the caress of his sonorous syllables, in my mind I was back in Robert's arms again, and his lips were on mine.

❧ 21 ❧

Amy Robsart Dudley

William Hyde's Mansion House in Throcking, Hertfordshire
April–June 1559

The next time I saw Robert, he asked me to set him free. Right there in the Hydes' best parlour where he had taken me to speak privily. He draped a pretty shawl about my shoulders and settled me comfortably upon the window seat, smoothing the full skirts of my yellow silk gown and placing my sewing basket upon my lap and watching me thread my needle with bright green silk and even complimenting me on the scene I was embroidering—a sly tabby cat crouched in a bed of wildflowers watching a red-breasted robin tugging at a worm. Then he went to stand before the fireplace. He stood with his hands clasped behind his back, rocking gently on his boot heels, as he calmly asked me for a divorce in the same voice he might have used if he were inquiring if we were having quails for dinner.

He would be generous, *"extravagantly* and *absurdly* generous," he assured me, as if money really mattered when my heart was breaking and he could see it clearly upon my face, as though I were a porcelain figurine of a woman he had just smashed with a hammer. As he knelt to gather up the contents of my sewing basket, which had fallen from my lap and spilled, scattering all around my feet, I sat there white-faced and wide-mouthed, my eyes staring without seeing straight ahead of me. But Robert went on speaking as if nothing was wrong, as if he were merely giving me directions on the best route to ride from Suffolk to Surrey.

Since there were no children or lands and estates to muddle matters and tie up the law courts, he continued, and he closed the basket with a pat upon the lid as if it were a good puppy and set it on the window seat beside me, it should be a very simple matter. I had only to agree and sign my name upon a document, and it would be done, our union would be dissolved, and we would both be free to walk away from a mistake we had made in our youth.

"Oh, Amy!" Robert sighed, still kneeling before me, grasping both my trembling hands in his, rubbing them hard to try to restore the warmth to flesh that had suddenly gone as white and cold as chilled milk. "Do it for England, if not for me! A weak and petty, spiteful, vindictive woman would want to hurt me by refusing, and making no end of scandal and trouble, but I *know* that *you* are *not* like *that*! You, with your good country common sense, know that England is in a precarious position and will remain so until the Queen marries and gives birth to an heir. But she dare not take a foreign consort after the example her sister set with Spanish Philip. But an Englishman . . . that is a *very* different matter, and would be most heartily approved of by her people, and this Queen listens to and heeds the voice of the people; she believes it is they who put her on the throne and keep her there. And if she will wed an Englishman, then who better than I? I have known her and been her friend almost all her life. We met in the schoolroom when we were eight years old, and I have been her staunch supporter in good times and bad; I even sold my property and lands to put money in her purse. And I am an educated man, and skilled in military tactics, and I know the ways of the court and Council chamber—my father taught me well—and I can parry with words as well as I can with a sword. There's not a man in England or the whole of Europe who can better or match me! My shoulders can take the weight Elizabeth's are too frail to bear! And I *want* to, Amy." He squeezed my hands so hard, I feared the bones would crack into little pieces that, like my heart, could never be put back together. "I *want* to! But, *first,* I *need you* to set me *free*!" He sat up higher on his knees and kissed and nuzzled my cheek and neck. "*Please,* my darling, say you will set me free to be the King I was always meant to be! Show the *true* nobility and saintly grace I know you possess, and step aside. Do it for England, for the good of the nation, and every man, woman, and child will revere and thank you for sacrificing your heart for their sake! And you can still be my mistress, for I am fond of you in my way, and if you do me this *very great* favour, I shall be fonder of you still. I shall like you all the more for it, and Elizabeth need *never* know. And if our little interludes together should produce any children, I shall recognise them as my baseborn issue—after I am dead of course—in my will, and leave them a token bequest, though they shall have no claim to the throne of course."

I felt as though he had just struck off my arm with a battle-axe, then, out of what *he* considered the goodness of his heart, offered me a jar of salve and a linen bandage. How could he think that I, like a modern-day Griselda, would smilingly renounce my respectable position as his lawfully wedded wife and become his secret, on-the-sly mistress? How little he must think of me! I had my pride!

With all the strength I could muster, I pulled my hands free and stood up, marvelling that my knees did not buckle and I did not fall as I stepped around him and walked out the door.

"Never!" I said without looking back. "Not so long as there is a breath left in my body!"

Too stunned to speak—no doubt he had expected me to instantly and smilingly agree like Griselda—Robert continued to kneel there even after I had gone, and it was several moments before I heard him running after me. By then I was already at the top of the stairs.

"I am your wife, Robert," I said, startled by the calm coolness of my voice—it sounded so placid and serene. "I am your wife, and so I shall remain until my dying day."

"Why must I be perpetually punished for a mistake I made in my youth?" Robert howled in fury as he hurled my sewing basket after me. It struck my back, and as the contents went flying all over the stairs, I whirled around.

"And the blame is not *all* mine that we have no children," I cried accusingly. "I cannot go out into the kitchen garden and

pluck up a son for you from the midst of Mrs Hyde's salad greens!
It takes *two* to make a child, Robert, but you so seldom have time
for me. You are *always* with *her*!"

"Don't you *dare* try to foist your failings onto me!" Robert bellowed back at me, his face a contorted red mask of fury. "Your
womb hasn't quickened *once,* not *once,* in all the years we've been
married, yet tavern wenches get tumbled every night by men they
scarcely know and find their bellies filled! It's more *your* fault than
it is mine, Amy, and I'm *glad* now that we have no child—it would
only complicate matters!" Then he spun round and stormed towards the door, but once there he turned back and thundered, "*I
will have my freedom! You* will *not* stop me or stand in my way! I
was born for better things, and a better woman than you, and I *will*
have them all—*you* will not keep me from them if you know what's
good for you! I'll see you damned, dead, or disgraced first! I have
the Queen's ear, she loves me, and all it would take is just *one* word
from me, just *one* word, whispered in her ear to send you to prison
to rot for the rest of your worthless life, so be forewarned, Amy, be
forewarned! You *cannot* win, so why bother to fight me? And I
withdraw my offer to keep you as my mistress; I would rather cut
off my own cock than let such a mule-stubborn bitch as you have
the pleasure of it! Mark my words, Amy, *I will have my freedom!*"
he repeated, and then he slammed out the door, leaving me pale
and shaken, slumping against the banister, clinging to it for support, as I struggled to breathe. I felt a terrible tightness in my
throat, as if a noose were tightening round it, but after a few
moments it eased, and I could draw a full breath again.

Perhaps I was haughty and wilful and let my pride get the better
of me. As the Scriptures say: *Pride goeth before destruction, and a
haughty spirit before a fall.* But I wanted to hurt him as much as he
had hurt me, and I wanted to hurt *her* too, the Queen who had
stolen his love from me. Perhaps there was a goodly amount of
spite mixed in, but I was *determined* to keep him, even though I
knew in my heart I had already lost him. Even though reason said it
was folly to try to keep someone who wanted only to go, stubborn-
ness and pride told me to stand my ground, even though both my
head and heart knew that no good could ever come of this festering

resentment that now infected Robert's heart like an oozing, fetid canker—only hatred and misery and a lust for revenge would result. Still, obstinate as a mule, I stood my ground.

And I knew I was being selfish too. If I gave in and granted him the divorce he so ardently desired, I would be making Robert's dreams come true, but what about my own dreams? They were all gone now, scattered like ashes on the wind. I had lost everything that mattered most to me. Even my home—Syderstone, with all the smiling faces of the common folk and servants, most of whom had known me from a baby and danced at my wedding, and the sheep, apple orchards, and barley fields—*all* of it sold to the highest bidder by Robert. He had promised *so much* and left me with *nothing*! And, without my husband, without my father, without love or the kindness, encouragement, and support of loving family and caring friends, I didn't know how to put the shattered pieces of my life and heart back together and build a new life or dream new dreams for myself.

"What a spineless little coward you are!" I hissed in utter contempt at myself as I entered my bedchamber and caught a glimpse of my pale, stricken face in the looking glass. I was *so angry,* I wanted to spit in my own face as well as Robert's.

I felt locked and frozen by fear, as if stricken by a horrible paralysis. I couldn't move, I could only stand still, stand my ground, and stay Robert's wife, and with feigned bravado face whatever Fate held in store. I would not give him a divorce—that was a certainty. I would not be like Griselda who obligingly, amicably, and smilingly stripped down to her shift and walked away barefoot to make way for a royal bride just because her husband asked her to.

"I am Amy Robsart!" I said aloud, though I was alone. Startled to hear my own voice calling me by my maiden name, I hastily corrected myself. "I am Amy Dudley, *Lady* Amy Dudley, *not* Patient Griselda!" And, running to my writing desk, I tore the pages I had filled with Griselda's story from the copybook and ripped them again and again and again, then flung them out the window, the pieces falling like snowflakes onto Robert's handsome black horse tethered below, waiting for him, and I threw the handsome, costly, leather-bound, gilt-edged volume of *The Canterbury Tales* out after it, listening with great satisfaction to the thud it made as it hit the ground. And then I flung myself, weeping harder than I ever had before, onto my bed.

The pain was so intense as my breasts pressed against the mattress that I gasped and sprang up, cradling my left breast tenderly in my hand. It felt as though a shard from my broken heart had pierced the tender flesh, like a splinter of steel or glass buried so deeply that, though I could not see it, I could most certainly feel it. It was bad enough to make the breath catch in my throat, and— just for a moment—chase all thoughts of Robert from my mind. But it only lasted a moment—one heart-stopping, breath-stealing moment—then the pain of Robert's cruelty and betrayal came flooding back full force, like a great wave crashing against me, knocking me flat, and I fell to weeping once more, for all that I had loved and lost, and the shattered debris of my life that lay, like a body ruined and ripped asunder by the force of a cannonball, upon the battlefield of Love.

"Over my dead body shall he ever have a divorce from me! I shall die before I agree!" I screamed at the top of my lungs. And this time I didn't care who heard me. *Damn and hang them all!* My heart was breaking and driving dagger-sharp splinters into my breast, and I didn't care what anyone thought of me.

In May I sent for him. Shamelessly employing some wordy chicanery, I wrote that I had to see him most urgently, that I had something to give him, and I hoped with all my heart that he would be pleased. Knowing full well that these words would lead him to believe that I had relented, reconsidered, and decided to grant him the divorce he desired so, and bring him speeding to my side, still I wrote them; in a bold and graceful hand well honed from countless copyings of the tale of Patient Griselda, I used my much-practised penmanship to lure him back to me. I knew he would not dally and make excuses as he normally did if there was reason to believe that there was something to be gained and that he would profit well by his haste; for that he would kiss his royal mistress adieu and make his excuses to *her,* for once, instead of to his wife. He would not want to risk my changing my mind. *Hurry, Robert,* hurry, *lest I waver in my resolve and my heart gain the upper hand again!* I wrote to better bait the trap, underlining these desperate words twice in bold black ink.

I had been busy in the weeks since I last saw him. I had ordered a new gown from Mr Edney, made to *very* precise instructions when normally I would have left all to him. And I had written to Lavinia Teerlinc and begged the very great favour of having her come to paint my portrait.

After she arrived, I smilingly waved aside her concerns that I had lost flesh—after Robert's last visit my appetite had also deserted me—and my face appeared thinner, almost gaunt, and my eyes were deep-sunken and dark-shadowed, and the lids swollen and puffy. She asked with great concern if I had been ill, or, with even greater delicacy, if I were perhaps expecting a child, and discreetly suggested it might be best to postpone the portrait until I was feeling and—though she was too kind to say it—looking better. But I insisted that we proceed, and as quickly as possible, lest my courage fail me. I *needed* this portrait for Robert to take away with him, to prove, every time he looked at it, the depth of my love for him, that I could be whatever he wanted me to be, that I was willing to change myself, to become someone else if I must, to make him love me.

When Robert arrived, I did not go down to him. I put a bridle on my emotions, and in strict defiance of my usual exuberant way, I did not race downstairs and throw myself into his arms. Instead, I bade Pirto bring him upstairs to me. There he found me, standing stiffly, with my back held straight and my stays laced so tightly I could scarcely draw breath, trying to look as tall and slender as possible. I held this tense and aching pose as I stood beside my gilt-framed portrait, artfully draped in red velvet and mounted upon an easel. One hand laden with golden rings set with rubies, pearls, and onyx rested lightly upon the cluster of acorns and oak leaves carved atop the frame, while the other lay across my waist, my fingers frozen in the act of playing with the long ropes of creamy pearls hanging about my throat and all the way down to my waist. But the face in the portrait was a stranger to Robert, and the Amy he saw standing before him was an Amy he had never seen before.

Despite the pleas of both Pirto and Lavinia, I had insisted that Pirto apply henna to my hair until it was a bold, bright, flaming red.

"Aye, pet," Pirto glumly said after, "there's surely not a redder head in England now."

When it was time for me to prepare for my portrait, I bade her pile it high and pin it tightly, sculpting it into a smooth mound, which she then crowned with a fetching little cap of black velvet spangled with pearls like tiny tears topped by a fluffy froth of palest pink, virgin white, and bright red ostrich plumes held in place by an ornate brooch set with a square of polished onyx, as if the stone itself were a dark canvas in a fancy gold picture frame. It was made to match the gown I had ordered, a gown that had caused Mr Edney to immediately sit down upon receiving my letter and write back, *Dear lady, are you* sure? I could picture the quizzical frown furrowing his brow as he wrote. Still, though I hated to disappoint him, I squashed down my qualms and stubbornly wrote back, *Yes, I am sure,* quite *sure,* and asked him to make the gown with all haste, as it was needed most urgently, allaying his concerns by asking him to *think of it as a sort of costume; I shall only wear it just the once,* and, enclosing sufficient funds for him to afterwards make me another gown, one of his own design—*something pretty,* I requested, *perhaps with butterflies.*

The gown I demanded was made of velvet dyed the brightest, boldest red imaginable, a fierce, angry shade that those who decided such things had dubbed "Migraine" after the fearsome headaches that assailed the Queen and the red rage any who accosted her whilst in the throes of one was likely to encounter. Wearing it made me feel awash in red, as if I were bathing in blood. The redness was relieved only by a smattering of gold embroidery like curling, swirling vines meandering aimlessly down over the gown, and the gold and onyx clasps that adorned the shoulders, sleeves, and waist. It was worn over a stiff farthingale, like a small cartwheel about my hips, that caused my skirts to bell out and billow and sway with every step and had the flattering effect of making my tightly laced waist seem even smaller. And about my throat, cradling my head, was a wide white ruff, the widest I had ever worn, trimmed with the most beautiful point lace, just like snowflakes cut in half and stitched along the edges. I *hated* the ruff and the way it made my head feel as if it were separated from my body and my chin itch, and several times I was sorely tempted to reach up and rip it from my neck, but I forced myself to let it be—if Elizabeth could bear it, so could I!—and the weight of the ropes of pearls, as big as beans, Pirto hung about my throat, and the large pair, like milky teardrops, pulling cruelly at my ears, making them ache, burn, and swell. Once, while I was posing for Lavinia, the stinging grew so bad, I reached up to feel, and my fingers came away stained with blood.

To mimic the marble white pallor of our gracious Queen, I had Lavinia apply a white paste of white lead, asses' milk, alum, borax, and powdered eggshells and alabaster to my face and hands, finished off with a glaze of egg whites. Even though I whimpered and complained that it burned, I would not let her stop and wash my face clean. And, to disguise the puffiness of my eyelids, she artfully added just a touch of paint there, then went on to rouge my gaunt cheeks, restoring them to their former round rosiness. And, at my insistence, she plucked my brows and blackened them until they arched like dark rainbows over my eyes and, as a final touch, rouged my lips until they were as red as my gown.

Before she moved to stand behind her canvas, I caught her arm and pleaded, "Please be kind; I am doing this for love."

"My dear friend," Lavinia sighed, "did it never occur to you that he is not worth it?"

"Many times, Lavinia, many times," I admitted, but still I took a deep breath and assumed my pose. Now that I had come this far, I must see it through to the end, whether it be as bitter as vinegar, sugar sweet, or a rage as red as my dyed hair and gown. "Use your magic, my friend, and help me become the queen of his heart again. Elizabeth has all of England to love her. Let me at least have Robert; he is my husband, and I have greater need of him, and love him more, than she does."

When the portrait was nearly finished, I sent for him, confident as a queen that he would come. And thus he found me, standing straight and proud, as near an approximation of the woman I now detested as it was possible for me to make myself. But Robert saw only a mocking parody.

"Elizabeth demands to be worshipped as a goddess; I just want to be loved," I said, breaking the silence.

It was like touching a flame to a keg of gunpowder. Robert

lunged for me, knocking the portrait from its easel with a great bang, slipping as his boots tangled in the velvet that had draped it. He caught hold of my wrist with his left hand as his right dealt two hard, stinging slaps, one to each side of my face, with such force that my ears began to ring, and for a few moments I was deaf to anything else, and blood began to trickle from my nostrils.

"Do you mean to mock me?" he roared, grasping my shoulders and shaking me so hard, the hat was dislodged from my head and fell back, hanging by its pins and pulling painfully at my hair.

"No!" I cried, my voice quavering as he shook me. "I meant only to please you and flatter the Queen by making myself over in her image! *Like* her but *not* her! *Me* you *can* have!" I sobbed and threw my arms around his neck. "I'm *yours,* Robert, *all yours,* and I always have been, from the moment I saw you! And I want you to love me again the way you used to! I want us to be the way we were—before Elizabeth!"

Robert thrust me from him, and I stumbled and crashed against the table, sending the wine and cakes flying and the golden platter, flagon, and goblets clattering to the floor.

I saw hatred in his eyes as he stared down at me. And I drew up my knees and inched back, huddling and cowering against the wall, fearing that he might kick me.

"There *never* was a time before Elizabeth!" he thundered down at me, his eyes and voice blazing hot enough to burn me. "I have known her better than anyone since we were eight years old, and I've been in love with her ever since! I love *her*! Do you hear me? I love *her*! I always have, and I always will! I love *her—not you*!"

He yanked me to my feet, then he was dragging me out, down the Long Gallery, and down the stairs, not caring that my feet could not keep up, that I slipped and stumbled and lost my red velvet slippers made specially with cork platform soles to make me appear taller, and caught my toes in my skirts and tore them, as my little hat, still hanging painfully by its pins, flopped against my back.

"*Please,* Robert, *please*!" I begged and cried. "I love you *so much,* I was willing to change myself, to become someone else, to win you back to me!"

"Don't be absurd, Amy! When you talk so, you show yourself

for the fool you are, and me for the fool I was for marrying you," Robert said without breaking his stride or easing his bruising hold on me. "You cannot be other than you are!"

Those who saw us—the Hydes and their servants—ignored my cries and pleading eyes that beseeched them to come to my aid. Rather than have Robert's fury turned upon them, they merely lowered their eyes, turned their backs, or looked the other way, pretending they had not seen our clumsy and brutal exit. After all, it was a husband's right to chastise and discipline his wife, so what right had they to interfere?

We continued thus across the pleasure garden, heedless of the flowers we trampled and tore up by their roots as Robert dragged me whenever my feet lagged behind, all the way to Mr Hyde's well-stocked fishpond. There Robert tore off my hat, not caring that with it he ripped several strands of hair from my scalp, then yanked out the remaining pins and roughly ruffled my hair, staining his hand bright red with henna. He snatched away the detested ruff, so he could get a better grip on my neck, and pushed me down, and plunged my head into the fishpond.

"Hold your breath or drown—I don't care which you do!" were the last words I heard before my head slammed below the surface.

Even as I struggled, he held me down. Then, by the back of my gown, he yanked me up, spluttering and gasping for air, before he shoved me down again. My lungs felt as if they were on fire as I tried to hold my breath.

The silver fish came to see what was disturbing the peace of their pond, and one of them became entangled in my floating, billowing hair, pulling it and frantically slapping its tail against my scalp and face as it struggled to free itself. It was then that I lost my own struggle to hold my breath, and water rushed in, burning my nose and lungs. I fought even harder then, pushing and flailing and kicking, and, just when I thought my life was about to swim out of my body, Robert jerked me up. He left me lying there, with my long hair trailing in the water, like drifting yellow orange seaweed, as I coughed and spluttered, my chest heaving, aching, and burning, within the tight confines of my stays, feeling as if my heart was about to explode, as I vomited the green pond water out of my lungs.

I don't know how much time passed before Pirto came running out to me. She told me later that when she saw Robert with his hands and shirt all stained red, she thought for certain he had murdered me, until she realised, to her immense relief, that it was not blood, only henna, the same diluted red orangey mess that now trickled down the sides of my face and the back of my neck and still streaked my waterlogged golden hair. Pirto knelt beside me and, with her apron, did her best to wipe it away lest it stain my skin, then used it to wrap my hair up in a makeshift turban before she helped me up and back inside the house.

"He's gone now, love, ridden back to London as though the hounds of Hell were nippin' at his heels," she assured me, as I leaned heavily against her. "It's all right, love, you're safe now; you've nothing to fear."

I stood in silence, the tears pouring down my face, washing the remnants of the paint away, as Pirto undressed me. The red gown was ruined, but I didn't care; it had accomplished nothing except arousing the kind of rage its colour was named for, and I never wanted to see it again. As I stood shivering in my wet, henna-streaked shift while Pirto banked up the fire, my eyes fell on the ropes of pearls and jewelled clasps. Furiously, I snatched up the gown, the red dye bleeding onto my hands, as it had onto my shift, and ripped the clasps away, letting the fabric tear and the pins pop and bend; then, scooping up the ropes of pearls, I ran from the room before Pirto could stop me. I plunged downstairs and burst out the front door and onto the road, running hard. I didn't stop even though Pirto ran after me, with a cloak fluttering from her arms, begging me to stop. I never slowed or looked back; I kept running until I reached the village church, where, panting and clasping my chest, even as coloured sparks danced before my eyes, I thrust the pearls and clasps into the poor box, then wrenched the rings from my fingers and threw them in too. "Let them do someone some good!" I cried, slouching in agony against the church's sturdy stone wall and praying God to bear me up and give me some comfort. "Let some good come of this!" I cried as, panting and flush-faced, Pirto caught up with me just as I slid to the ground.

"Look, Pirto," I said, half laughing, half sobbing, as she bundled me into the cloak, "I am barefoot and in my shift, just like Patient Griselda!"

"Oh, sweetheart!" Pirto cried, near tears herself as she sank down beside me and gathered me in her arms, holding me close and rocking me as if I were a child again.

We sat there for a long time, me torn between tears and laughter, while Pirto rocked me and stroked my sodden hair, which still dripped orange-tinted droplets like blood-tinged tears.

At last, when my laughter had ceased and my sobs had subsided, she helped me to my feet and gently led me back to the Hydes' house. I was too ashamed to meet anyone's eyes. When I caught a glimpse of Mrs Hyde peeping out of her bedchamber door, I hastily looked away even as she quickly closed it.

Back in my bedchamber as Pirto bustled about, laying out a fresh shift for me and preparing a hot bath, I stood staring, without seeing, out the window. I kept my back turned to the room, trying to hold back my tears and not give the wary-eyed servants who carried in pails of steaming water something more to talk about; I knew they thought I had gone mad.

When we were alone and Pirto came and gently put her hands upon my shoulders to turn me towards the steaming tub, my eye caught the tapestry depicting Griselda being turned out of her husband's kingdom in her shift. As Pirto lifted my ruined, red-stained shift over my head, I truly understood for the first time in my life why rage is sometimes called red. With a fiendish cry, like a demon escaped from Hell, I flew at that tapestry. My sewing basket was sitting in the fireside chair, waiting for me, as if it knew that my whole world had come apart at the seams and wanted to help, to offer me the means to sew it back together. I snatched up my silver scissors and lunged at the tapestry, stabbing into it and pulling the scissors down, tearing and ripping it, again and again and again, until it hung in tatters and gilt and coloured silk threads littered the floor and clung to my damp hair and skin. "*She* should be the one turning *him* out!" I screamed. "*He* is not worthy of *her!*" I didn't notice when Lavinia came in, but it took both her and Pirto to pull me away from the tapestry and wrest the scissors from my hand and prevent me from doing the same to the rest of the series.

I don't know how, but somehow they managed to quiet and calm me. They got me into the tub and let the warm water do its work and soothe and cleanse me. I remember the soothing smell of lemons and chamomile as I leaned back and closed my bleary, tear-swollen eyes and let them wash away the last lingering traces of the henna, restoring my hair to its natural golden glory.

Afterwards, clad in my night shift and wrapped in a rose-coloured velvet robe trimmed with tawny fur, with a goblet of hot spiced wine warming my hands, I sat propped up in bed with Lavinia beside me, like the sister I never had. Anna and Frances, my aloof, older stepsisters, always made me feel an outcast, an intruder upon whom the door of their special society of sisterhood was always locked and barred, and never did such things with me.

We talked far into the night; though she was loath to tell me and tried to change the subject whenever I asked about what went on at court, I saw the truth in her eyes. Though her lips wanted to lie to me, to be kind, to spare me the unavoidable pain, she could not deceive me. All my fears were well founded; my jealous, suspicious fancies and nightmares held more of truth than imagination. Robert and the Queen were in love—many said and believed that they were lovers in the flesh—and it was common knowledge that, had he been free, Robert was the man Elizabeth would have married. If not for me, he would have been the king he believed he was born to be. Only my life stood between him and his destiny, the power, and the passion.

And there was something else. Shyly, hesitantly, for I had never dared such a familiarity, I asked if I might show her something and have her opinion upon it. And when Lavinia readily gave her consent, I eased the robe from my shoulders and lowered my shift to reveal my left breast. There was a sort of dimple upon it that I had only lately noticed. For the life of me, I don't know when it first appeared, but I knew it had not always been there, else I would *surely* have seen it before. It was just a little spot, a tad tinier than the tip of my littlest finger, where the flesh dipped in when it used to, I was certain, plump outward, just a little dip that, though it was itself empty, filled my mind with worry.

With a warm smile, my friend embraced me, then, as she helped me right my clothing, spoke so reassuringly that I felt my fears floating away from me.

"You have not been worrying over that little thing?" she asked. "It is *nothing*! *Nothing*! Our bodies change as we grow older. I know a woman—in fact I know her very well, for she is me—who, after she passed a certain age, developed such dimples on her buttocks. Mother Nature and Father Time, they have their way of marking us, in ways we would not wish, but such is the natural way of things." She shrugged. "As we grow older, we sag and wrinkle and turn grey, and sometimes a dimple appears where there was never a dimple before."

She took the cup of wine from my hand and set it on the table beside the bed and urged me to lie down. "Sleep now," she said, bending to kiss my brow as she drew the covers up to my chin, as if she were my mother. "The day has been hard and most unkind to you, my friend, but tomorrow will be better." And her reassuring smile was the last thing I saw before she blew out the candle and I closed my eyes to sleep.

❧ 22 ❧

Elizabeth

The Queen's Summer Progress
May–August 1559

The glorious summer of 1559 will always live in my memory as the Summer of Suitors, when all at once they seemed to converge upon me like a great swarm of buzzing black flies on one tender morsel of white bread dipped in honey. The court's meandering course from one country house to another didn't deter them at all; the ambassadors and envoys simply packed their belongings and came along with us. What were a few more when there were already several hundred of us, thousands if all the servants were counted? It took 2,500 packhorses and 500 carts to transport all our luggage and provisions, and that not counting the more handsome mounts that carried my ladies and courtiers or the litters favoured by those aged, infirm, with child, or, for whatever reason, disinclined to ride. "The more the merrier!" I cried, extending a welcome to all.

It was *so* exciting! To play the royal marriage game while I was still young and pretty enough to do it, to have every eligible bachelor of royal and high birth vying for my hand, to enflame the carnal appetites and ambitions of so many men. And there was even more to celebrate as, just before our departure, we had made peace with France. They would not return Calais, but they agreed to pay us

500,000 crowns in recompense, and there were fireworks, banquets, and masques both indoors and out, tournaments, and hunting parties to celebrate it.

Before we took to the roads, in a long, winding procession of horses and carts, Robert staged a mock battle where 1,500 armed soldiers in coats of chain mail displayed their prowess on the lawn at Greenwich whilst silk banners flapped in the air and musicians played drums, trumpets, and fifes. And afterwards, those feigning death were resurrected and stood in neat ranks alongside the survivors as I walked amongst them, thanking them most heartily and telling them I could sleep easily in my bed at night knowing that I had such loyal and brave men to hold England safe for me. And I invited them all to sit, informally, on the grass and partake of a picnic with me, and afterwards the musicians played lively country tunes, and I danced with many a soldier until the stars came out in a blazing glory to rival the fireworks bursting above the Thames.

We also paused at Woolwich so I could christen and see launched a fine new ship named in honour of me, *The Great Elizabeth,* and enjoy a banquet and dancing with the sailors upon its deck that night as fireworks lit up the sky above us and coloured sparks showered down into the sea.

But best of all was the endless wooing.

From his deathbed, Gustave Vasa, the King of Sweden, sent a delegation of tall, handsome, smiling, blond Swedes, all of them eager and sweet; they seemed never to stop smiling, and I thought their jaws must ache abominably by the time they laid their heads on their pillows at night. They were a dear, bumbling lot, *most* endearing in their earnest awkwardness and the travesty they made of the English language. They wore crimson hearts pierced by "the arrow of love" upon their breasts and sleeves and trailed after me like puppies, promising me "mountains of silver, diamonds, sables, and ermine" if only I would promise to wed the wonderful Prince Eric, reminding me that as his wife I would also become the Queen of Sweden. And they distributed vast quantities of diamonds and silver coins amongst my ladies in the hope that it would encourage them to sing the praises of "the eternally loving Eric, who burns with the flame-haired fever called Elizabetha". In the privacy of my chamber late at night I would spread the Swedish prince's sables upon the floor and dance upon them in my bare feet, laughing all the while. Later, his younger brother, Duke John of Finland, would join us, to take the lead in this wooing by proxy. One night as we rowed upon the moonlit waters, sipping goblets of wine and lolling back against cushions of sapphire velvet whilst the moon played tantalising tricks with my silver gown, he took my hand and dared proclaim that he had fallen in love with me, and henceforth, though duty required him to woo me in his brother's stead, his heart would no longer be in it. "My heart is here," he said, boldly pressing a kiss onto the palm of my hand, then folding my fingers into a tight fist as though they were a cage meant to contain that captive kiss. The rivalry between this pair of handsome, fair-haired brothers would end a few years later when Eric, crestfallen over my refusal to wed him, married a common soldier's daughter instead and poisoned his brother John's pea soup as punishment for the treachery he displayed in declaring his love to me.

And the silky-tongued Comte de Feria was always there to remind me of his master's ardent interest. With Philip's counterfeited rubies about my throat I laid my hand caressingly upon his sleeve as we stood and watched the dancers and said in a voice low and sultry, "Be thou well persuaded that should I decide to marry outside my kingdom, my eyes and heart shall fix on none but Philip. But we find that we have no wish to give up our solitary and lonely state, though God in His inscrutable and infinite wisdom may at any time change our mind," I hinted tantalisingly as Robert caught my hand, pulling me away from de Feria, and swept me up in the dance.

And when Philip, later that summer, withdrew his suit and married a daughter of the King of France, also named Elizabeth, I pouted and in a fit of pique told de Feria that his master could not have been as deeply in love with me as he had led me to believe. In a fury, I tore his rubies from my neck and flung them at the Ambassador's feet. "His love is as false as his jewels! They are glass—just like his heart!" I cried and ran to my room, to muffle my laughter in the goosedown pillows, leaving de Feria and others to think that I was overcome with grief for the loss of the Spanish King's love. I kept to my bed the rest of the day and shunned the night's entertainments, enjoying some vastly welcome private time lolling abed with my favourite books. The next morning, with the curtains drawn so that my face was shadowed, so de Feria would not see that it was not swollen red from weeping, I sent for him and, sighing dolefully as I reclined weakly against my pillows, I extended my hand and bade him to "convey these most heartfelt words to your master: Although my heart weeps at the memory of the dreams that will never see fruition, that the 'someday' that was our shared dream will never come, like summer, love ends, and winter comes, but I cherish the hope that the friendship forged between us shall hold as an unbreakable bond and endure through all the seasons to come."

Overcome with emotion, de Feria flung himself to his knees beside my bed and kissed my hand and assured me that he and his master would stand my lifelong friends, that such bonds were not easily broken, and though he could never be my bridegroom, Philip would *always* be my brother, and the flame of fraternal love would burn forever bright inside his heart.

And in short order a new and even more magnificent necklace, this one of emeralds to stand symbol for the constancy of "my loving brother Philip's affection", arrived with a letter urging me to consider his nephews, the Archdukes Charles and Ferdinand, as prospective bridegrooms. They both found many supporters amongst my Councillors, as neither had a principality to govern and thus would be free to come and live in England and take from my shoulders the heavy burden of ruling. My Councillors and the Imperial Ambassadors, Count von Helfenstein and Baron von Breuner, aided by the suave Spaniard de Feria, did their best to persuade me, to emphasise all the Archduke Charles's best characteristics and minimise his flaws.

Whenever I voiced a concern, they were quick to allay it with answers as fast as a finger snap. Once I casually remarked, "He is said to be hunchbacked." At once they hastened to assure me, "It is *so small* as to be quite insignificant" and, "His tailors conceal it so expertly, it is hardly noticeable at all."

"But hasn't he a limp?" I then inquired.

"Yes," the Ambassador reluctantly admitted, "but it is *very* slight, and you will *never* notice it as long as he remains sitting or standing still and doesn't attempt to walk. And he cuts such a *splendid* figure upon a horse, Your Majesty!"

And to prove it, I was promptly presented with a handsome portrait of the Archduke Charles magnificently apparelled and sitting astride a pure white stallion.

"I don't know . . ." With mock seriousness I tapped my chin and cocked my head as I examined it. "I am told his head is uncommonly large and most ill-proportioned to the rest of his body." Inwardly I convulsed with glee at the storm of protests that followed, all assuring me that Charles's head was perfectly sized, "neither excessively large nor inordinately small." And then I could not resist . . .

"I am told his brother, the Archduke Ferdinand, has a very fine pair of legs. Have you a portrait of him?" I asked, knowing full well that the Ambassadors had only brought a miniature that showed just his head and shoulders. "Oh, what a *shame!*" I pouted. "His face is quite fine, but . . . oh, if only I could see his legs! The man I marry must be a fine dancer and horseman, and I find you can *always* tell by the legs." And so an envoy was immediately dispatched back to Austria, riding as though his very life depended on it, to procure a full-length portrait of the Archduke Ferdinand.

But when the canvas came and I stood before it, I heaved a great sigh and lamented that he was wearing black hose, as "Everyone knows black can be deceptively slimming." With an apologetic smile, I turned to the Ambassadors and asked if I might have another portrait of this handsome young man with his legs clad in white hose instead. "White is a much more honest colour," I explained above my coquettishly fluttering white ostrich feather fan. "Your wish is my command!" von Helfenstein and von Breuner said as one, and the whole process promptly began all over again. I daresay the portrait painters made quite a splendid profit during those wild days of wooing.

And then, as the lazy days of summer drifted by, one afternoon as I lay resting in the shade after an arduous day of hunting and vigorous country dancing at an outdoor banquet, the Ambassadors came, knelt down beside me, and presented me with a love letter from the Archduke Ferdinand, still busily posing for his portrait in a pair of white hose. I gave it one brief glance, then petulantly crumpled it and flung it away. "I *cannot* marry him," I announced, and I lay back, pulling the brim of my big straw hat back down over my eyes. "His handwriting is the *worst* I have ever seen."

As for his elder brother, the Archduke Charles, I found reports regarding the size of his head too contradictory to reassure me, and portrait painters were not to be trusted. Had my own father not learned that when he chose to wed Anne of Cleves after admiring her portrait? And my sister had come to no good end when Titian's portrait of Philip first aroused love in her heart. "I have taken a vow never to marry a man I have not seen in person," I declared. "I will not put my trust in portrait painters." So, unless the Archduke Charles would deign to visit me, that was the end of the matter; I would discuss it no further. And I imperiously waved his Ambassadors away and grandly bade them, "Trouble me no more; my mind is quite decided, and no pretty words or even prettier portraits can ever change it. I will not consider the Archduke again until he is standing before me."

Many deplored my highhanded ways with the Ambassadors and despaired of my ever taking a husband; they all thought me maddeningly capricious. One was even provoked to complain of me: "She behaves like a peasant upon whom a barony has been conferred. Since she came to the throne, she is puffed up with pride and imagines that she is without peer." But I laughed all the more when I heard and declared loudly and often that I would sooner be a nun than a wife. I flaunted my coronation ring before all and said, "Behold, I am married already—to England!" And more than once I heard Cecil sigh and complain of that heady summer: "Here is a great resort of wooers and controversy amongst lovers; would that Her Majesty would settle upon one and the rest would depart honourably satisfied."

And there were gifts aplenty, all luxurious and grand, and ardent envoys sent to woo me by proxy for the Dukes of Savoy, Nemours, Saxony, Holstein, Bohemia, and Bavaria, with each ambassador wearing a miniature portrait of his master proudly pinned upon his breast. I would have them all line up before me, standing at attention, straight as soldiers, and walk up and down viewing the portraits as if I were taking my leisure on a rainy day inside a portrait gallery and causing their hopes to rise or plummet by the comments I made and the questions I asked. One actually wept when I dismissed his royal master on the basis of his portrait as "a lady-faced lad" who would not do at all, as "I have a great liking for a strong, handsome, virile man." I would not squander even a moment's thought considering any dainty and effeminate lad, laughing inside at the way some of them winced, squirmed, and nervously shifted their eyes, being all too aware of their masters' unnatural predilections.

The Scottish Earl of Arran, Jamie Hamilton, the handsome, red-haired, and bearded Protestant claimant to the Scottish throne, came to visit me. He arrived concealed in a carpet, like Cleopatra for her fateful first encounter with Julius Caesar. When it was unrolled before me, he sprang up to dance a boisterous jig to the tune of bagpipers who had accompanied him disguised as merchants, the hem of his kilt bouncing and bobbing up to show off his fine, muscular, though quite hairy legs. And later he would speak words of tender love and vehement ardour that tried valiantly to penetrate his thick Scottish burr. He delighted me no end, and again and again I clapped my hands and cried "Dance, Jamie, dance!" until he fell down exhausted and beneath his silver-buckled shoes his toes bled and his band of bagpipers must carry him to bed and bandage them. But Cecil favoured the match, sagely noting that if I married him, it would bring peace and unite England and Scotland and prevent France—which had a foothold in that sparse and barbaric land through its Catholic queen, Mary Stuart, and her mother, the regent Marie of Guise—from using Scotland to mount an attack against us and financing further Scottish raids upon our borders.

And my English suitors were still buzzing around me, all ravenous for the honey of my attention and affection. Faithful old Arundel, who had taken to sporting a vividly gaudy and outlandish wardrobe far better suited to a much younger and more flamboyant man while leaning upon an elegantly wrought silver staff to ease his gouty foot, and telling anyone who would listen that my bravery during the reign of my sister had first led to the flowering of love in his heart for me. Shy, bashful, stammering Gooseberry was still tripping over his own tongue and feet in his eagerness to please me. And the debonair Sir William Pickering, who didn't try too hard because he knew he did not have to and had privately accepted my word that I meant to live and die a maid, but who was content to continue wooing me just for the pleasure of my company and to tweak Arundel's beard.

The Duke of Prussia's ambassador sent yet more falcons so that I might enjoy good sport with them while on progress, as he knew I delighted in hunting. He also brought a handsome miniature that might be worn as a brooch or a pendant depicting the Duke with a hooded falcon upon his wrist and earnestly implored me to wear it when I flew the birds so that in this way, "in spirit" we might hawk together until the day he hoped and prayed for arrived, when we could hunt together as husband and wife.

Robert was in such a *fury* over them all. I had never seen a man so flustered and feverish with jealousy; I fancied I could see the blood sizzling in his veins and feel the heat when I touched him. A perpetual scowl replaced his smile, and his mutinous dark eyes scorched me like embers on my naked skin whenever they turned my way. "*Any* man who advises the Queen to marry a foreigner is neither a good Englishman nor a loyal subject to Her Majesty!" he roared, boldly leaping up onto the banquet table, his eyes flashing a challenge to every man seated around it. And his band of liveried rogues, a surly bunch of cudgel-and-dagger-toting street toughs dressed up in blue velvet, often clashed swords with the retinues of our foreign visitors. He even tried, with money borrowed at enormous rates of interest from the London moneylenders, to bribe my foreign suitors to quit the field and sail away, assuring them with a grave mien and a serious and confiding tone that, "I have known her better than any man alive since the age of eight, and from that time forth she has always said, 'I will never marry.' She will go a maiden to her grave." I reminded him that it was treason to speak of the death of the sovereign and refused to see or speak to him for a week, during which I allowed the delightfully blushing Gooseberry or the dapper, unflappable Pickering into my bedchamber each morning to hand me my shift as I stood naked behind a screen, while Robert, who had been accustomed to performing this most intimate duty, fumed outside my door and had to be restrained from running them through with his sword. Sometimes I even sent him away. "Leave my court—you grow insufferable," I would say. "I cannot bear to have you near me," and he would ride off with his surly band and go I knew not where, or to the Devil for all I, in those heated moments, cared.

And to confound them all, my homegrown and foreign-born suitors alike, I lavished attention and favours upon the man I called my "Sweet Robin". I would, during plays or musical recitals, playing the absentminded and besotted woman for the ambassadors' avid eyes, reach out a hand and let my jewel-laden fingers toy with Robert's dark hair or tickle the back of his neck. And when the perplexed ambassadors, concerned about my morals and chastity, discreetly queried the affection I showered upon Lord Robert, I would reply, "Nature has implanted so *many* graces in him that, if I wished to marry, I would prefer him to all the princes of the world." Or I would tantalise them and leave them wondering just how far I had fallen by saying, "It is true, I am no angel, and I cannot deny that I have some affection for Lord Robert, for the many *fine* qualities he possesses." Then, to increase their confusion, I would add, "He is like my brother and best friend. I regard and honour him as my brother, for thus do I love him and will love and regard him my whole life long, for he deserves it." And sometimes I took an indignant stance, declaring, "I am insulted both in England and abroad for having shown too much favour to Lord Robert. I am spoken of as if I were an immodest woman." With a doleful sigh, a shake of my head, and downcast eyes, I would continue in a resigned tone, "I really ought not to wonder at it! I am young, and he is young, and therefore we have both been slandered! Though my life is lived in the open, and I have so many witnesses—a thousand eyes watch my every move—truly I *cannot* understand how so bad a judgment can have been formed of me."

It vexed Robert no end. He would sulk and sometimes storm red-faced into my room after having heard my words repeated, accusing me of using him as a tool, a toy, or ranting and raging because I said I loved him like a brother. But I would only laugh and, depending on my mood and whim, draw him into my arms and let the two of us be engulfed by passion, only pushing him away at the last moment, or else fling the nearest object at his head, stamp my foot, and order him from the room and banish him from my presence for several days to come.

I *loved* being the unobtainable object of desire for so many men, to encourage, then discourage, to change in an instant from hot to cold. I loved the power of holding all the power in my hand and beneath my skirts, to feel them yearn and burn but to refuse to grant them their desire, for my person or my throne. And Robert suffered the worst for my shifting whims and fancies, my mercurial moods, where one moment he held Aphrodite in his arms and the next was being pushed away by chaste Diana.

No one could understand why I took such pleasure in Robert's company. Indeed, at times, I could not understand it myself. Perhaps it was that he did not behave as one awed by me; with him I did not feel as one mounted upon a tall pedestal of ivory. We had known each other since childhood, when I was still thought of as a disgraced bastard of no real importance; he knew me when no one thought I would ever amount to anything. And there was such an *easy* camaraderie between us, though at times it did indeed border on the presumptuous or even pass that border, but I felt easy and relaxed in his company, free to let down my guard and just be myself, free to revel in bursts of passion like fireworks without the risk of being burned or singed or bound and chained in holy matrimony. In truth, had Robert been free, that might have tarnished his allure and attraction in my eyes; I felt in control with Robert. I, Elizabeth, the woman, not Robert, the man, was in command of our relationship, and that was *exactly* the way I wanted it.

Robert delighted in devising novelties and spectacular entertainments so that every day brought something fresh, exciting, and new for us. One evening there was an entire sugar and marzipan menagerie to delight my sweet tooth, with animals of every kind from beasts of the barnyard to the most exotic. There were lions, tigers, peacocks, sheep, camels, swans, ostriches, snakes, rabbits, elephants, rams, placid milk cows with swollen pink udders and teats, and fierce-tempered bulls, butterflies, pigs, bright-plumed parrots, lizards, leopards, turtles, sure-footed mountain goats and barnyard billies and nannies, strutting roosters and docile hens, stallions and mares, monkeys, frogs, giraffes, donkeys, flocks of ducks and geese, sharks, dolphins, great schools of rainbow-coloured fish, eagles and hawks, bears, graceful swans who mated for life, porcupines, porpoises, anteaters, wild boars, zebras, and walruses, even the fabled cockatrice, the monstrous manticore, the Kraken that was the sailors' dreaded peril, sea serpents undulating over blue sugar waves, and the mermaids that formed the stuff of the sailors' dreams during their long, lonely voyages at sea away from feminine company, the glorious golden phoenix rising resplendent from fire and ash, fierce dragons with gleaming scales, and magnificent snowy white unicorns garlanded with flowers and accompanied by flowing-haired virgins. Each one was painstakingly crafted, perfect down to the least little detail, by an expert confectioner and served to us by servants costumed as animals. Whilst Robert, splendidly garbed in a doublet of crimson and gold, his handsome legs sheathed in white hose that fit like a glove and black leather boots polished to a high gloss that came up to his thighs, smartly cracked a whip and danced, pivoting, spinning, doing high kicks and grand leaps in the midst of my ladies and gentlemen, all of them elaborately and sumptuously apparelled and masked as wild and exotic beasts that capered and leapt or snarled and showed their claws at each crack of Robert's black leather whip.

In another masque he arranged, all the ladies danced and swayed in gowns of leafy satin greenery adorned with red cherries, which the gentlemen, sauntering and dancing past with baskets of gilded straw slung over their arms, plucked until the trees were bare. And in another, most symbolic of those heady days of courtship unabated, I, with my eyelids painted gold, gowned in shimmering tinsel cloth of red, orange, and gold, with my hair stretched high and sculpted and lacquered over a tall wire frame, was a flame, and the gentlemen of my court danced about me dressed as moths being burned by me and falling dead at my feet. And at yet another banquet we sat down to eat off dishes crafted entirely out of sugar. I remember our Swedish guests were quite baffled by them, and at the next banquet one of them, thinking these sugar dishes were customary, cracked a tooth biting into a porcelain plate.

Once, like an alchemist transforming lead into gold, my Sweet Robin helped me change a looming scandal into a morning's delight. I was always slow to rise, liking to linger long in my nightclothes, in a state of loose dishabille, with my hair unbound and my body comfortable and unimpeded by the corseted confines and weighty layers of skirts, reading my beloved books, perusing state papers, walking in my private garden, and eating a leisurely breakfast before dressing and beginning the business of the day. I was not always as careful as I should be, and once, as I sat at my window early one morning, my pink dressing gown falling loosely about my shoulders as my elbow rested on the windowsill while I sat, with the morning sun warming my face, smelling the roses and listening to the birdsong, my night shift slipped from my shoulder and exposed a breast. A carter saw me and with an admiring whistle called up that he had seen with his own eyes that the Queen was *all* woman. I laughed good-naturedly as I adjusted my garments and tossed a coin down to him. But word quickly spread, no doubt due to my admirer gossiping in the alehouse, and the ambassadors were aghast, and my Councillors went about wringing their hands and worrying lest I be branded a woman of loose morals and my suitors desert me. Word had already spread by a volley of scandalised whispers that each morning when I dressed, Lord Robert always stopped in to hand me my shift, that most intimate of undergarments, as nothing lay between it and a woman's bare skin, as I stood modestly shielded by a screen. So one morning Robert decided that I should have them all—my courtiers and our foreign guests—come directly from their beds, still clad in their nightclothes, to partake of an early-morning breakfast with me. And we all sat about on cushions strewn across my bedchamber floor in our dressing gowns and slippers and disordered hair eating a hearty English breakfast and gossiping like old friends with the windows thrown open so we could smell the flowers and hear the birds sing. We had a fine time, and the ambassadors were soon assuring their sovereigns that all the lurid tales of me were naught but silly gossip based on titbits of fact outlandishly embroidered.

Our Progress ended with a splendid banquet at my father's great palace of Nonsuch, which my ageing but nonetheless ardent swain, the Earl of Arundel, was leasing from the Crown. It lasted until three in the morning, with music, dancing, and masquing, where I dared, masked in silver and mantled in diaphanous midnight blue spangled with silver stars to hide my hair and gown, lead my grey-bearded host into a fragrantly flowered and darkened bower and let him embrace and kiss me, just once, to keep his hope alive, and with it the belief that selling some of his lands to pay for this costly evening had been well worth it. And when I departed the next morning, he made me a present of the ornate silver plate that had adorned the banquet table, replete with an inscribed presentation cabinet to keep it in.

Our idyllic summer ended in August with our return to Windsor Castle, where I spent whole hot and humid days riding and hunting in the Great Park with Robert, tiring out, one after another, the strong and swift Irish hunters he chose for me and laughing, flush-faced and sweat-sodden, each time I called for a fresh mount. He gave me a gittern studded with emeralds, and often, after the banquets and dancing, where many shook their heads, sighed, and pursed their lips in disapproval of the intimacy with which Robert handled my person as we danced—the way he lifted, caressed, and held me, and even dared steal kisses—we would sail upon the moonlit river while I strummed it and sang to him. When Cecil came frowning into my apartments and told me that it was being said that I was "a wild and raving coquette insatiable in my lusts" and rumours were rife in London and spreading farther every day, even being carried across the sea by travellers, that I was carrying Lord Robert's child, I laughed defiantly and ordered my corsets laced even tighter to show off my board-flat stomach and tiny waist and danced with even greater abandon, leaping and kicking ever higher, shaking my hair free of its pins so that strands of it clung to Robert's sweat-glazed face as he lifted me high in the volta, and returning his kisses and caresses with equal fervour. I was *determined* to let no one spoil my pleasure. And the louder they grumbled, the more I gave them to grumble about. Wilfully, and rebelliously, I fed the flames of scandal. I was young and free, and I wanted to live while I was alive!

❧ 23 ❧

Amy Robsart Dudley

William Hyde's Mansion House in Throcking, Hertfordshire
Late May 1559

Lavinia had to return to court. I was sorry to see her go, but she had many commissions awaiting her, including miniatures of my husband and the Queen. Though coaxing the truth out of her was like pulling a tooth, she wanted so to spare me, in the end she confessed that these were gifts they meant to exchange; she would have his, and he would have hers. What had happened to my own miniature, the one Robert had ridden away from Hemsby wearing against his heart? I never saw it again. It was like a prophecy made in paint but fulfilled in flesh and blood. I had indeed become that melancholy, solemn-faced young matron, even though I didn't want to be her. I wanted to be that happy, smiling, loved and loving bride again, that radiant, confident, carefree girl with the wild, tumbling, harvest gold hair, who lay with her yellow skirts rucked up in a bed of buttercups by the river, safe in the arms of the boy she loved, watching the clouds roll by and dreaming of the future that lay before them. I wanted a beautiful, radiant, golden phoenix to rise from the ugly black and grey ashes of my life.

Soon after Lavinia's departure, I received a curt note from Robert, just a few terse lines informing me that the messenger who had delivered it, a young cousin of his called Thomas Blount, and the three liveried retainers who accompanied him, would escort me to Compton Verney, Sir Richard Verney's house in Warwickshire. I should make ready to travel at once, Robert instructed, and not inconvenience anyone by delaying. He went on to say that he liked the Hydes too well to further inflict my "mad, bizarre, and fantastic behaviour" upon them and subject them to gossip about harbouring "a poor, deranged madwoman beneath their roof".

I could hardly bear to face Mr and Mrs Hyde when the time came for me to take my leave. It was a strained and awkward moment, filled with lengthy, embarrassed pauses where words should have gone but no one could think of any, and averted eyes too ashamed and afraid to meet. Then young Master Blount came to my rescue, saying all was ready and, gently taking my arm, led me out and boosted me into the saddle of a gentle grey mare. As we rode away, I half expected to hear the whole house erupt in cheers.

"I daresay never has the sight of a horse's bum been so pleasing to them," I whispered to Pirto, riding beside me on a plodding white palfrey.

Young Master Blount—Tommy, as I came to call him—was very kind to me. He had apples in his saddlebag and passed them around, sharing them with us all.

"I know how well you like them," he said shyly as he handed me one, like a deep red ruby glistening in the morning sun. I accepted it gratefully, and, thinking of Syderstone and my father, I bit into it with relish, my teeth crunching through the peeling. As I savoured that first juicy, sweet bite, I smiled.

Whistling a tune as he rode alongside me, young Master Blount, who I doubted was a day over seventeen, smiled back at me and suddenly puffed out his chest and belted out a song:

> "I will give my love an apple without e'er a core,
> I will give my love a house without e'er a door,
> I will give my love a palace wherein she may be,
> But she may unlock it without any key.
>
> My head is the apple without e'er a core,
> My mind is the house without e'er a door,

My heart is the palace wherein she may be,
And she may unlock it without any key."

With apple juice glistening on my lips, I quite surprised myself
by joining in, and with great gusto I sang along with him:

"I will give my love an apple without e'er a core,
I will give my love a house without e'er a door,
I will give my love a palace wherein she may be,
But she may unlock it without any key.

My head is the apple without e'er a core,
My mind is the house without e'er a door,
My heart is the palace wherein she may be,
And she may unlock it without any key."

It had been *so* long since I had sung, or done anything except
mope and mourn, I was surprised to find that I still could, that I
could feel good again and enjoy being out in the sun on horseback
singing a song and munching apples with a comely and compan-
ionable young man beside me.

When the apples were all gone, I bought us cherries from a
woman selling them at the roadside and shared them with everyone. Robert's grooms smiled and thanked me and seemed to look
kindly upon such a gesture, which gladdened me. My husband's
men usually aped his high and haughty airs, taking great pride in
having been chosen to wear his livery, and often looked down upon
me—some even had the distinct appearance of common ruffians
dressed up in blue velvet and carried more weapons than I thought
was warranted—but these three were just as nice as they could be.

In no time at all, Tommy and I were fast friends; it was as if we
had known each other our whole lives, though we had scarcely met
before. I had caught an occasional glimpse of him and even nodded
politely or bid him good day once or twice as he was coming or
going on some business for my husband, but my mind had always
been preoccupied and distracted by other things.

Now I discovered to my immense delight that he was a collector
of tales who had carried over into his manhood, like a peddler's

pack full of wonderful things, a child's love of stories. At every tavern, alehouse, or cottage he stopped at, he added to his collection, stashing them away in the storehouse of his memory and writing them down in a battered old copybook he carried for this purpose. He blushed a little when he told me this and was glad, and surprised, I think, that I did not laugh at him or mock but implored him to tell me a story instead. And as we rode along, he regaled us all with wondrous, captivating tales of giants, mermaids, witches and wizards, talking beasts and vicious plants, sinister serpents of both the land and sea, unicorns, elves, fairies, and goblins, evil gnomes guarding treasures, valiant knights upon daring quests, fair princesses disguised in peasants' rags, and paupers who were really princes, bold outlaws with hearts of gold, Love's triumph over all adversities, fire-breathing dragons, perilous voyages, enchanted realms, and travellers' tales of exotic, faraway lands across the great blue sea.

I enjoyed myself so much that I was sorry to reach our journey's end, and not just because I had to bid farewell to Master Blount and all his wonderful stories . . .

❧ 24 ❧

Amy Robsart Dudley

*Compton Verney, Sir Richard Verney's manor house in
Warwickshire
June–September 1559*

The moment I caught sight of Compton Verney, the blood froze
within my veins. My skin crawled, and I felt as if my hair were
standing on end. There was such a sinister feel about that place! It
made me want to turn my horse around and gallop away, I didn't
care where, just as fast and far as I could. I knew it in my bones; this
was an accursed place. It was a bleak and ominous, frightening,
dark, medieval manor, with a moat and turreted towers and narrow, arrow-slit windows that kept more light out than they let in.
Even the garden seemed desolate and forbidding; nothing seemed
to grow there except thorns.

"How could Robert send me here?" I wondered aloud. "Has he
ever been here before? Does he *know* what it is like?"

Master Blount gazed at me with such sadness in his eyes, but he
had no answer to give me and was good enough not to try to fool
me with false cheer. He could see just as well as I could what a dark
and miserable place Compton Verney was and that happiness
could never flourish there.

As for the master of it all, Sir Richard Verney, never were a man
and his house more perfectly matched. Sir Richard Verney and

Compton Verney were two of a kind. Had he been a character in one of Tommy's tales, he might have been a man who, either by his own evil will or a witch's curse, could transfigure himself into a raven. When I saw him in profile, his nose was like a beak, as long and sharp as a knife. He dressed entirely in black except for his white shirts—I never saw even a spot of colour enliven his attire the whole time I knew him—and his hair curved back across his scalp like a gleaming blue black raven's wing. His eyes were small, dark, and beady, and he *never* smiled, at least not that I ever saw. His face was like a mask carved from marble, very hard, cold, and still, and it showed no emotion at all. He was tall and sallow and slim, but he had big hands—*a murderer's hands,* a little frightened voice in my mind said. And he had a voice that matched his appearance perfectly; very condescending and patrician, it dripped superiority and scorn like poison. And I *knew* instinctively that this was a man who would not hesitate to do me harm if it were to his own advantage.

When he came to help me dismount, I shied away from him—I didn't want him to touch me! I would have fallen over backward, tumbling right off my horse, if Tommy hadn't reached out and caught me. With gentle but strong hands, he eased me back up straight into the saddle. I had no choice then—I could not be rude and insist he step away and that Tommy or one of the other men come to assist me instead, nor could I give way to hysteria and cry and scream at him to keep away and slash at him with my riding crop—so I, most reluctantly and shivering with fear and skin-crawling revulsion, suffered Sir Richard Verney to put his hands on my waist and lift me down from the saddle and take me inside his gloomy abode.

I did not sup with the others in the Great Hall that night. I made my excuses, that I was too weary from my journey, that I had a headache, and wished only to rest.

The housekeeper brought me a tray with a tankard of ale, a loaf of bread, and a big bowl of savoury stew generously laden with chunks of beef and vegetables, and, for dessert, a beautiful cherry tart shaped like a heart with a great dollop of rich cream on top, which, she told me, had been "baked special" for my arrival, as "a lady likes such things".

In spite of the fear that I could not shake from me, I enjoyed this hearty repast, and, when she came to take the tray away, I thanked the housekeeper and asked her to convey my thanks and compliments to the cook. The words were sincerely meant, and I hoped they might be the first step towards a new friendship. I was lonely and felt the need for kindness and companionship if I must live within these stark, dark walls that already felt as if they were closing in on me. Had I actually glimpsed them moving and seen them sprout iron spikes, I would not have been at all surprised. And when I lay down upon my bed, I half expected to see a sword dangling above me, swaying from a fraying rope.

And later, whenever I passed the suits of silver armour that stood like sentries all along the Long Gallery, where the rushlights cast only little spurts of radiance that made me feel as though I were walking alone inside a long, dark tunnel, and the walls were hung with all manner of ominously glinting weaponry—swords, daggers, pikes, axes, maces, and shields—I quickened my steps and moved as far away from them as I could, even though it made me feel silly and scold myself, but a part of me feared that they might come magically to life and reach out to harm me. I would utter a little shriek and feel my heart leap if my skirts even brushed against one of them. Despite my best efforts, more than once I became careless as I hurried anxiously along, and my skirt actually caught upon one. The suit rattled and lurched towards me as I tried to free myself. I screamed in terror and leapt away—the way the arms were posed made me think it was reaching out to grab me—causing the whole thing to fall with a *tremendous* crash onto the stone floor, tearing my skirt as it fell, and I was sorely embarrassed when the servants came running and had to pick it up and put the whole thing back together again, all because of my carelessness and nerves.

The whole time I was at Compton Verney, my ears always expected to hear the moans and groans of tortured souls in rattling chains and agony, like denizens of a dungeon, though the servants repeatedly assured me that there was no dungeon and that which had been in bygone days was now a harmless root cellar, which I might at any time see for myself if it would put my mind at ease.

I was *amazed* there was not a ghost story attached to the house, for if ever a house deserved a ghost, it was this one. But there was

only a bloodstained white damsel who was said to run across the
park on moonlit nights, her mouth open wide, screaming silent
screams that no one could hear, and always running in a direction
away from the house, where, the servants assured me, she never
ventured. I wondered if the poor, damned soul were instead fleeing
from it. And there was also a tale of a woodcutter who had sold his
soul to the Devil for a sack of gold, but when he opened it, he
found it to contain only chestnuts.

Though I was bone weary and did indeed have an aching head,
I did not sleep at all my first night at Compton Verney. I spent the
whole of it either bent over a basin or squatting over a chamber pot
or lying back against the pillows gasping, clutching my aching
stomach and chest, as beads of fever sweat sparkled upon my brow.
I slept a little after the sun came up, but, after I sat up and accepted
a small bowl of porridge at Pirto's urging, I was plunged right back
into the agonies of the night.

Robert arrived three days later, riding like a prince on a white
horse, accompanied by a bevy of blue-velvet-liveried retainers and
a party of elegantly apparelled gentlemen, apparently friends to
both himself and Richard Verney, and a cook who had once served
a French prince. There was also a cart filled with food and costly
spices. But he did not stay long or spend much time with me or
even come to my bed. I doubt the time I spent with him that week
tallied up to even one hour. He amused himself drinking and gambling downstairs, behind closed doors, with Richard Verney and
the other men. And there were women there as well, the unsavoury
sort, the kind who sell their favours cheaply in dark alleys and low
taverns. I caught a glimpse of them, giggling and whispering with
their unwashed heads together, as Richard Verney's steward, grimacing with distaste and keeping his distance as if he feared fleas
would leap off their shabby, tattered finery onto him, discreetly ·
herded them into the room where his master was entertaining his
guests. Robert must have encountered a rare run of bad luck, for
three times he had to send Tommy Blount galloping back to London for more money, and when I saw him, he was unshaven and di-
shevelled, wearing the same clothes each time, though more stained
and malodorous and in a thunderous black mood so that I hardly
dared speak to him. I had had Mr Edney sew the gold Spanish but-

tons Robert had given me onto a russet velvet gown with a gold-fringed collar, but Robert didn't even notice them. He had not a word of praise to bestow upon me, nor kisses or embraces to give me either. I daresay the tavern trollops lifted their dingy petticoats and attended to his manly needs while I, his wife, slept alone, twisting restlessly beneath the sheets, reaching out for the husband who should have been but was not there beside me. Then he was gone again, back to London, back to the Queen.

The whole time I stayed at Compton Verney, nothing that passed my lips seemed to stay put inside me; it wanted out just as much as I did. Thank God and all His angels for sending me Tommy Blount; without him I would have surely wasted away and died. He always found some excuse to stop and pass some time with me on his ceaseless rides for Robert, whether he had a message, money, or some token from my husband or not. He would take me out into the fresh air and feed me apples and other treats, like a gingerbread baby or a mincemeat pie he had bought at a fair, which we would break in half and share, while he regaled me with tales a Gypsy woman had told him, or a more humble repast like fresh baked bread and a yellow round of cheese he had bought from a cottager's wife he passed along the way. These foods filled me; they stayed put and did me good. Tommy also helped me to make friends with the people who lived near-abouts, and often I received invitations to visit and sup with them, and *not once* did I *ever* suffer a single bout of sickness, not even a twinge of bellyache, after sitting down at table with any of them.

When I realised this, I became even more certain that something was *very* wrong indeed at Compton Verney. I wrote to Robert, but he didn't believe me. He just scoffed at me and my "foolish notions" and said it was just my imagination "running wild and too fast" and I should "put it on a leash and bring it to heel", or "bridle it and break it as though it were a horse".

He sent me spices to sprinkle on my food, to make it more palatable and calm my stomach, but they only made me sicker, and when he sent me more, I threw them into the moat. As further proof that it was all in my mind, he pointed out that Pirto, who shared my food, even eating from the same bowl as I, or even switching plates to try to allay my fears, never sickened, nor did anyone else when I deigned to descend from my room and eat in the Great Hall with the rest of the household. I was the only one who was ill, and I was making myself so by letting my imagination "cast a sinister spell" over my mind and cause me to see "malice and mischief everywhere and accuse innocent people of the worst evils".

Sir Richard Verney, my husband insisted, was one of the kindest, most tenderhearted men he had ever known, "one who would weep like a woman if he saw a stray dog run down by a coach," "one who feels far too much rather than nothing at all." But I didn't believe him; seeing Richard Verney, I just couldn't. I could not even begin to imagine this man crying over a dead dog, or shedding a tear over anything at all, not even if his wife or child died. And I *knew* I was being poisoned; I was *sure* of it! Yet everyone treated me like a child or a madwoman and refused to believe me; they only listened with half an ear, never taking me seriously, and dismissed all I said as foolish or brainsick fancy. But I *knew* the truth; I *was* being poisoned, I *was*! Why else did every bite I took at Compton Verney disagree with me and provoke an agony of the bowels and vomiting and pains in my chest, whilst all that I ate elsewhere pleased me and filled my stomach, lying peaceably within it like a cat curling up on a fireside settle, and did me nothing but good? But no one would believe me; they thought it was all in my mind, or something wrong with my insides, suggesting perhaps "they were all knotted up" by the "surfeit of melancholy" that afflicted me. Some days I was so upset, frightened, and frustrated by it all that I lay abed all day crying with Custard and Onyx snuggled up beside me, my tears soaking into their soft fur.

I was no fool. I *knew* my death would serve a purpose, and, to certain folk, it would be deemed most advantageous, as if Death's scythe had, in striking me down, cut a bountiful golden harvest for Robert to reap. It would free him just as surely as the divorce I refused to give him would. And without the taint of scandal sticking like shit to his shoes, it would allow him to play the grieving widower, then throw off his sombre mourning black after a year, don his purple and gold finery and peacock feathers, and strut like a vain and preening cockerel up the aisle to claim his royal bride, and the crown he would gain by her, while I slept eternally, my mouldering bones boxed inside a marble tomb.

In desperation, I sent to London, to an apothecary and, at great expense, procured a unicorn's horn, as it was deemed a sovereign remedy against poison. Some believed one had only to dip it in any food or drink suspected of being maliciously tainted, and it would render any poison therein harmless, whilst others thought you had to grind it up and swallow a little before each meal to derive any good from it.

But Robert, on his next brief, fleeting visit, caught me with it and took it away. He called me a gullible fool and said *everyone* knew that in London such fakes abounded and I might as well have thrown my money—*his* money—into the Thames. Had I put it into cold water to see if the water boiled and yet remained cold? Had I fed poison to a pigeon and then quickly dosed it with the powdered horn to see if it would save it? Had I used the tip to draw a circle and watched to see if a spider could cross it without perishing? Had I put the horn in a pot full of water with three live scorpions to see if it killed them? I shook my head and sheepishly admitted that I had performed no tests to try its authenticity; I had only had it a few days and had been trying both touching my food and drink with it and taking a little bit ground off the bottom before I ate to see which suited me best. Then I dared to ask the question that had just popped into my head: Would not the scorpions drown in the water, and then how would I know if the horn's magical powers were responsible for their death? Robert sighed and rolled his eyes and mumbled an oath beneath his breath, praying to God to give him patience.

"*Give that to me!*" he snapped, and he snatched the precious horn away from me, lest others see me with it and word spread about "what a fool of a wife Lord Robert is shackled to".

I later heard tell of him kneeling before the Queen and presenting her with the horn of a unicorn, shimmering pearly upon a purple velvet pillow balanced on the palm of his hand, to protect her "precious and most beloved person" from those "malicious and evil persons" who might seek to do her harm with poison. I wondered if it were my unicorn horn that he had given her, or had he merely been inspired by it and purchased another of indisputable authenticity?

In a few weeks' time he came again, accompanied by his rough and surly entourage and a number of gentlemen, just as before, again with the French cook and a cart full of fine foodstuffs and rich spices. Again he kept away, closeted with his friends and doxies summoned from the local tavern. They hunted, and when I smelt the roast venison, laid out along the length of a great table, waiting for them, hot from the spit and slathered with spices, it was as though its scent, wafting upstairs, were an invisible hand beckoning to me. My stomach rumbled, and my mouth watered for want of it. And, knowing that this was safe food, that it could not be poisoned, for it was intended for my husband and his friends, I followed like one entranced that bold, savoury, beckoning scent all the way downstairs and fell like a starving dog onto that rich feast of venison, ripping out great handfuls of the meat, not caring that it burned my hands, and ravenously shoving them into my mouth, cramming in yet more even before I had swallowed the last mouthful.

Robert and his friends came in and found me thus, with smears of grease on my face and in my hair, which hung loose about my face, my cheeks puffed out with the meat I had stuffed into my mouth, and my hands smarting red from the heat and greasy from the handfuls of meat I still clutched in each fist. Robert was across the room in an instant. He slapped me so hard, the meat I had been caught in the act of chewing spewed from my mouth, and I fell across the haunch of venison, staining my gown with grease and spices. He yanked me up by my hair and slapped me again and again and pushed and beat me all the way across the room and out the door, ordering me back upstairs to my room, bellowing again and again, *"You have made a fool of me!"* whilst the other men stood by laughing and smirking as they watched. "Robert has married a peasant wench—you can tell by the way she eats!" one man guffawed, and the others nodded and laughed along with him.

I didn't see my husband again after that except once when I peeped from my door to see him leading a giggling tavern wench with breasts already bared above her unlaced bodice to his room.

He kept downstairs, closeted with his friends, or to his own chamber, and left me, smarting with humiliation and my face swollen and bruised from his blows, without having further words with me or even saying goodbye.

To save myself, I knew I *had* to try again; I had to see Robert and, somehow, persuade him to stop all this and bring my would-be murderer and not my imagination to heel. I wanted him to give me a home of my own, or at least send me to a pleasanter place where fear didn't dog my every step like a yapping little lapdog always getting underfoot. If he didn't, I knew that I was doomed. I would die here; it was no hysteria-fuelled fancy, some evil toy that had taken hold of my mind. If I did not get away, Compton Verney would be the death of me, and I just might become the ghost it was missing, the restless earthbound spirit, a murdered woman everyone believed mad, felled by the poison of her own imagination, roaming its halls in an eternal but futile quest for justice.

Once again I enlisted the aid of Mr Edney. He came to see me, and I took him into my confidence, and I told him all. This time, we put our heads together and came up with something bold and new, a way to let Robert see me as he never had before, not as a frantic, frightened creature desperate to please in dyed hair and a gown that did not suit, but an Amy who could herself be every bit as alluring as the ladies of the court, without pretending to be someone else and aping their airs.

He asked me to put my trust in him and promised he would make for me a gown that would dazzle my husband and silence any complaints before they had a chance to spring from his mouth.

"Dear Mr Edney, I place myself fully in your hands," I said, a hopeful smile breaking like the sun through my sorrow.

"Let's get started, then!" Mr Edney smiled and, clapping his hands, called for his apprentice boy.

Apologising for the intimate tone this fitting must take but explaining it was vital for the gown he meant to create, Mr Edney asked me to strip down to my petticoats, leaving myself bare above my waist, and handed Pirto a piece of white linen, which he asked her to pin around me as though it were a bodice. When I was ready, Mr Edney, apologising for touching me so familiarly, took a stick of charcoal and made a series of swift markings directly upon the linen over and around my breasts, followed by a series of similar marks, like raindrops dripping down over my ribs and sides, then he turned me around and, lifting the golden weight of my hair, did the same on my back.

I had never had such a fitting before, and I felt like to die of curiosity, but Mr Edney would only smile and say, "Usually the phoenix rises reborn from the ashes, but this one shall come from the cold depths of the sea to reawaken your husband's passions and set them aflame!"

"Like at Hemsby, when we were so happy by the sea!" I cried, my face all smiles as joy coursed through my body, chasing away the tired lethargy, making me feel more alive than I had in I didn't even know how long. Oh, I could not wait to see the magical gown Mr Edney would make for me!

Before he returned to London, Mr Edney urged me to take heart. He told me, without revealing names, of course, of other ladies he had helped in the same fashion, women whose husbands had all, enraptured by their gorgeously gowned lady and the tableau he created, succumbed to their charms and come back to them more besotted and in love than ever. One gentle lady, a melancholy, violet-eyed, black-haired beauty still childless after five years of marriage and very much neglected, had greeted her husband gowned as a fiery red, orange, and gold phoenix, standing before a big gold nest lined with a mattress of red satin, and now he scarcely ever left her side; he had forsaken his mistresses, and she now had eight children to show as proof of his attentiveness and devotion. "They made a pair of twins that night in the nest I designed for them," Mr Edney smilingly confided.

When he came for the final fitting and unveiled his creation, it took my breath away. I was dumbstruck and dazzled by the sight of it. I had never imagined there could be such a gown. And, just for a moment, I feared I lacked the courage to wear it.

The bodice was sleeveless and made entirely of some gossamer-sheer, flesh-hued fabric with a multitude of shimmering crystal beads that covered my breasts, like tiny bubbles, and flashed rainbows of colour whenever I moved, and dribbled down, in a light spattering, like raindrops, over my ribs and back. And the skirt, the fullest I had ever worn, stiffened beneath by a farthingale to make it stand out about my hips and make my waist seem even smaller, was a beautiful, frothy concoction, a confection made of blue and green taffeta, all ruched and ruffled to mimic roiling waves as it flowed back behind me in a long, graceful train. The crests of these sumptuous fabric waves were covered in fine netting of either pale blue or green and sewn with tiny crystals, seed pearls, and little gold and silver shells. And at the front of it, right below my waist, was sewn a beautiful, shimmering-scaled, emerald green mermaid's tail, creating the illusion that I was a mermaid breaking the surf with my bare breasts all a-shimmer with sparkling beads of water. The skirt was cut shorter in front—to show off my pretty ankles, Mr Edney said—and embroidered all around the hem with branches of coral, crabs, and cockleshells, and in the blue sea on either side of the mermaid's tail swam beautiful fish of silver and gold. And there was a beautiful coral pink taffeta petticoat, rustling and crisp, that peeped playfully from underneath my full skirts to match the coral satin shoes festooned with golden cockleshells and seed pearls that Mr Edney had brought me as a surprise. The style was new from France, and they had petite heels, like little stilts underneath, that I had to learn to balance and walk gracefully upon. And though I stumbled often and feared I would end by breaking my ankle, Mr Edney patiently helped me, holding my hands and slowly leading me about my room like a tot learning to walk in leading strings. But our patience was well rewarded, and soon I was walking as if they were a natural part of my feet, and even dancing in them, spry and nimble as could be.

But Mr Edney was not done. He sat me down and showed Pirto how to dress my hair when the time came for me to greet my husband in this gown, arranging it so it poured down my back in a loose golden cascade woven with ropes of pearls and pink cockleshells and even a couple of combs, one on each side of my head, crowned with golden crabs twinkling with emeralds and sapphires. Then he demonstrated how to darken my lashes and brows and apply gold and silver paint, and just a touch of shimmering blue and green, to my eyes and coral pink rouge to my cheeks and mouth. I must, he said, look the part of a court lady about to swim forth to dance the lead role in a masque. "You are a mermaid,

Amy," he said, setting the scene for me, "who has captured the heart of a mortal man but must forsake her home in the tranquil blue kingdom of the sea to be with him.

"I can give you the means to captivate and enchant him, but"— leaning over my shoulder, he whispered softly in my ear—"only you, dearest Amy, can know if he is worth it."

Then I set to work bombarding Robert with letter after letter, making a real pest and nuisance of myself. It took over a month, my fingers grew sore from writing, and I spent a ludicrous amount of the money Robert sent me on paper and ink and messengers who went galloping off to deliver them two and sometimes three times a day. I paid them well to put themselves forward, to pester and accost Robert and deliver my letters no matter how inconvenient it might be for him, no matter where he was or what he was doing, waylaying him in palace corridors, at banqueting and gambling tables, upon the tennis court, and even when he was about to mount his horse to compete in a tournament, or being fitted with new clothes by his tailor; one brave man even barged in while Robert was relieving his bowels, until, at last, I *finally* wore him down, and, just to put a stop to my letters, he sent a curt note to say that he was coming.

And while I waited for my letters to do their work, I set about decorating my chamber with the things Mr Edney sent, following his instructions to the letter. I hung lanterns with blue, green, yellow, and pink glass, draped the walls with swaths of blue bunting sewn with pearls, and from the ceiling beams I suspended pretty painted fish and strings of pearls, coral, and crystal beads. I hired a fine cook, adept at confectionery, to prepare our supper, to prove to Robert that I could provide him with as fine a fare as the court could, and to create trays of colourful candies shaped like shells and fish and other creatures from the sea. And to play soft music for us, I hired a blind harpist to travel down from London, whom Mr Edney recommended for situations such as these, knowing that I did not want to show myself thus arrayed with my breasts all but bare beneath the crystal beads before any eyes except my husband's. And there was a new set of clothes for my bed too, made of green, blue, and coral pink satin, sewn with gold and silver fish,

and bed-curtains of a sheer, diaphanous blue and green overlaid
with another curtain that was like a fishnet woven of pearls.

The day Robert arrived, I awaited him nervously, pacing back
and forth across my chamber, my heavy skirts rustling, swishing,
and swirling with every step, sounding rather like the gently rolling
waves they were designed to mimic. I fidgeted my fingers and tried
hard to keep myself from gnawing my nails or playing with the
pearls clacking in my hair.

I had a speech all prepared, ready to recite to him:

"I know I made a mistake before," I planned to say in a voice
calm and sure but also humble. "I should not have tried to become
someone else. But I was *so* desperate to recapture the love that
used to be between us that I was willing to lose myself, to become
someone else, to win it back again. But I was wrong. Had I succeeded, what I got out of it wouldn't really be love, would it? Because when you love someone, you love them as they are, even
stripped bare of all artifice—paint, jewels, and fine clothes—
because *true* love is bare and mother-naked; it wears no clothes
at all."

In the happy, passionate fantasies of my daydreams, after hearing me speak these sincere and heartfelt words, my husband would
strip me, and himself, bare, and carry me to the bed, and make love
to me the way we used to, lying warm and naked in the cold, salty
surf at Hemsby.

This time, I wanted to show Robert that I could be me, but a
better, brighter, grander me, who was just as good as any lady of the
court, an Amy who loved only him and aimed to please.

But when Robert came in and saw me, dancing, swaying, spinning, and sashaying enticingly before him as the blind harpist
played, he burst out laughing as though it was the funniest sight
he'd ever seen. Bent double and slapping his knees, he laughed
himself breathless until he was red in the face and braying like an
asthmatic donkey. When he was able to speak again and stood wip-
ing the tears of mirth away, he said, even though I was "painted like
a whore, I looked just like a clown". And then, as abruptly as a sudden summer rain, his mirth turned to anger, and he denounced me
like a preacher thundering from the pulpit for my "lewd and

lascivious display". When I told him my intentions, he stared me down sternly, witheringly, making me feel as tiny as an ant, and informed me that "the court is not a brothel, Amy, and the ladies there do not comport themselves like painted bawds and whores, no matter what ignorant country bumpkins might believe".

My throat froze, and my lips quivered, too hurt and stunned to speak, as tears rolled down my face, ruining the carefully applied paint. No matter what I did, no matter how hard I tried, it *always* went wrong in the end. I just *could not* win! I wondered if it were my fate, written in the stars, to always be a disappointment and a failure. When I looked at myself in the mirror now, those words, *Disappointment* and *Failure,* seemed to spring ever more often to my mind. Sometimes I even felt as if they were branded upon my forehead and half expected to see them there, burned into my skin in charred-edged, angry red letters. It hurt *so* much, to want and try *so* hard, but to *always* fail to enchant and delight him, to make him smile and reach out his arms to me. That was all I *really* wanted. But when it came to my husband's love, I was a ne'er-do-well.

Then his back was turned, and he was walking away, leaving me once again, going back to court, back to Elizabeth.

I ran after him, in my furious pain forgetting that others might see me so immodestly arrayed, and on the stairs, from the upper landing, I shouted down at him: "I *hate* what you've become—the Queen's pet lapdog who is kept on a short, bejewelled leash! She yanks the chain, and *you* go running back! She holds up a treat, and *you* jump for it!" He stopped for a moment—but it was only for a moment—he never turned around; he just stood still for one long, lone moment, and then he started walking again, walking away from me, never looking back. "You don't *really* love her, you only love what she can give you, what she represents; once she's served her purpose, she'll be *nothing* to you! *Nothing!*—just like me! *I hate you, Robert, I hate you!*" I screamed through a hard rain of tears, raking my throat raw but too angry to care. *"Your head belongs on a pike, not on the Queen's pillow!"*

As the door slammed shut behind him, I suddenly became aware that there were others downstairs, staring up at me, their eyes and mouths agape. Sir Richard Verney was there, smirking, sneering up at me, his dark eyes telling me that I was nothing, and beside him stood Thomas Blount, who had apparently accompanied Robert, staring at me as though I were a freak in a fair. And there were servants.

I gasped in shame and horror and hugged my arms tightly over my bead-bedecked breasts. As I spun round in retreat, stumbling over my skirts and high-heeled shoes, I fell hard, barking my palms against the stone stairs as I instinctively reached out to break my fall. Tommy Blount was up the stairs and at my side in an instant, taking my arm, trying to help set me aright on my feet again, but, in my shame, I pushed him away, my face burning scarlet and hot beneath the streaks of tear-damp paint. I couldn't even bring myself to look at him, and instead of thanking him for his help, I lashed out at him, screaming at him to, *"Stay away from me! Don't look at me! Don't touch me!"* Then I ran back to my room, losing one high-heeled slipper in my haste and further impairing my gait, but I was too embarrassed to turn back and retrieve it. I only wanted to be back inside my room with the door locked so none could bear further witness to my shame and weeping.

I rushed about like a madwoman, pulling the decorations down from the ceiling beams and ripping the blue bunting waves from the walls, sending the trays of candy shells and fish flying; then I ran to the bed and yanked down the beautiful new bed-curtains, ruining them, ripping the fabric and sending pearls scattering everywhere, as I screamed at the blind harpist to *"Get out!"* before I fell facedown onto the bed, weeping a whole ocean of tears. I didn't know which was worse—that I had failed again or that others had seen to what desperate lengths I was willing to go to try to win back my husband's love yet had *still* failed. It was a great and awful blow to my pride, and I did not know how I could ever go downstairs again and face any of the Verney household, knowing that they had seen—and those who hadn't seen would soon be told by those who had—how I had got myself all hussied-up with my face painted and had brazenly bared my bosom under a smattering of beads. Soon everyone would know; they would be laughing about it in the alehouse and mayhap even calling me lewd names. In my rage, I had become my own worst enemy; I had let my private shame become a public one. Would I *ever* be able to look anyone in the eye again? Could I even bear to face myself in the looking glass?

I sobbed myself to sleep, but even in slumber I found no peace. I was tormented by a dream in which I found myself struggling in a cold blue green lake, weighed down by my mermaid gown and pearl-bedecked hair. I sank down, lower and lower, and as I kicked and fought my way back up, desperate for air, my arms and legs became hopelessly, terrifyingly entangled in the whirls and swirls of my billowing skirts. But somehow I made it to the top, and then . . . my fist struck *ice*! Hard, unbreakable ice! The lake had frozen over! And through the ice—it was like looking through a frosty window—I beheld a number of stern-faced priests circling the lake, solemnly chanting in a commanding tone words in Latin that I could not understand but somehow knew were meant to keep my soul imprisoned, trapped forever, through all eternity, within this lake. Even though I was underwater, I screamed—curious things can happen in a dream—as the folds of my skirt floated up about me, even as I fought to push the wafting, billowing layers back down, as if they meant to stifle me, the pearls and crystals twinkling like tiny bubbles, mocking bits of air I could not breathe. But no matter how hard I hammered my fists on the ice, it would not break, and no matter how loudly I screamed, no one would help me. And I knew that I was *trapped—forever*!

I sprang up in bed with a bloodcurdling scream that scared even me and shook the entire house out of their beds and sent them running to my room, certain that I was being murdered. And so—yet again—I had humiliated myself and exposed my shame and my pain to the scrutiny of others.

In his black velvet dressing gown and slippers, with a candelabrum in hand, his hair, only slightly mussed from sleep, hanging over his forehead like a sleek black raven's wing, Sir Richard Verney banged my door open without bothering to knock. He came to stand at the foot of my bed, condescendingly appraising me in my rumpled gown, the crystals over my breasts sparkling in the candlelight, and my face a red, bloated, tear-swollen mess covered with streaks and smears of blue, green, pink, gold, and black paint. He stared hard and long at me, with his cold and poisonous little serpent's eyes, before he turned and ushered his servants, who were crowding my door, peering in curiously with their annoyed and sleep-bleary eyes, back to their beds, telling them that, "Lady Dudley has suffered a bad dream—*again*," he added meaningfully, for it was not the first time a nightmare had jolted me awake with a scream that shattered the peace of the night.

Robert was already gone. He had ridden back to London immediately after he walked out on me. He didn't even say goodbye. He just rode away, in angry silence, charging down the road, back to the arms of Elizabeth, back to the cool, elegant, confident, and poised Queen, and away from his poor, pathetic, country-girl wife, all got up in beads and paint, pretending to be grand, pretending to be something she was not, trying—and failing miserably—to convince him—and perhaps herself as well—that she was every bit as good as the beauties on parade, dancing in the masques, at court.

As the harsh light of morning trickled in through the narrow, arched windows of Compton Verney, Pirto silently prepared my bath and unlaced me from my mermaid gown.

"It will make you feel better, love." She smiled, nodding towards the tub filled with steaming water, with dried rose petals, lavender, and chamomile bobbing on top.

As the beaded bodice fell away, I noticed that the dimple on my left breast had changed; it was now pointing out instead of in, like the tip of an accusing finger, as if the dimple had suddenly changed its mind about what it wanted to be and decided to become a nipple instead. It filled me with fear just to look at it. And, though there was no way to escape it—it was a part of my flesh—I turned quickly and stepped into my bath and sank down low into the steaming water, wishing I could scald that worrisome imperfection away.

Was that my punishment, I have oftentimes since wondered, for baring and flaunting my breasts beneath the dazzle of crystal beads, even though I did it out of love and desperation and intended the sight only for my husband's eyes? I had failed so many times in so many ways by the time I donned the mermaid gown, perhaps I deserved it.

I tried to tell myself it was nothing, just some sort of blemish that would get well in its own good time, though I could not resist slathering it with every ointment I could find or think of, hoping to speed it on its way. Every time I looked at it, I hoped to see some change; sometimes I tried to convince myself that I saw some sign of improvement, that it looked a *little* smaller, but I was only deceiving myself, it was only wishful thinking, and in truth, nothing did any good, and it was not getting even a smidgen smaller.

Instead, it grew and grew, and the more I tried to ignore it, the larger it got. But I was afraid to acknowledge it, to show or speak of it, and each time I changed my clothes, I shimmied hurriedly into or out of my shift, and when I bathed, I sank down low in the water and tried to hold my arm, even though to press upon it hurt, so it would not show.

Finally the fear got the better of me, and I broke down. Pirto found me weeping, and I blubbered and blurted out the truth to her.

With the practised and capable fingers of one who has spent a lifetime as first a nursemaid and then a lady's maid, she gently bared my breast and examined it.

"Oh, pet, an abscess is all that is! Have you been worrying yourself sick over *that*?" She hugged me close, kissed my cheek, and stroked my hair as I laid my head against her shoulder, still shaking with sobs. "My auntie had one of those, and it hurt like hell for a time, it did—pardon my words—but that's *just* what she said, but after it burst and healed, she was just fine and lived to the ripe old age of seventy-nine, she did."

"R-Really, Pirto?" I looked up at her.

"Aye, my love, sure as rain she did! Now"—she stood up briskly—"dry your tears." With the edge of her apron she began to do just that. "A hot poultice is just what you need—'twill encourage it to burst and take the edge off the pain after it does. I'll fix you the *very* one my Auntie Susan used—I'll go out into the garden and find a stone, and we'll put it in the fire to heat, then I'll lift it out with tongs and wrap it up tightly in a cloth, and you'll lie down with that, and we'll soon see the end of it." And she brightly set about doing just what she had said she would.

For many hours of many an afternoon afterwards I followed Pirto's instructions and lay with that hot stone upon my breast, but though the warmth felt comforting, it failed to have the desired effect Pirto predicted. It never burst. At times I thought the heat was only making it angrier, because it knew I was fighting back, trying to destroy it before it destroyed me. It grew even larger, until it was an angry, livid lump marring the pink roses and cream of my breast and causing a painful tenderness alongside, reaching fingers of pain beneath my left arm. And the day my nipple began to seep a foul perversion of mother's milk, sometimes tinted pink by my blood, I knew for the first time what *real* fear was. And I knew in my heart that, no matter what I did, what remedies I tried, I was doomed. This was no abscess; it was cancer, and it would take my life, sever my soul from my body, like a crab's claw clipping through a frail, fraying tether.

❧ 25 ❧

Amy Robsart Dudley

A Visit to London
The Dairy House at Kew
and
Richmond Palace
September 1559

While I languished at Compton Verney, suffering this increasingly painful malady of the breast, though none but Pirto yet knew of it, I received letters from my stepsisters scolding me about how I was being remiss in my duties as a wife. I should be at court, they said, smiling and "being a sparkling ornament at my husband's side". They wrote me of the handsome little house at Kew that the Queen had given him, a mansion in miniature called the Dairy House, as it had once provided butter, cheese, and cream for the royal household. They said that I should stop my spoiled and wilful ways, that I was not a little girl any more, being indulged and petted by my father. I should be in London living in grand style and presiding over that fine house as Lord Robert's wife. *If I were you, that is certainly what I would be doing!* Frances said. *I would not let my honoured and respectable place as his wife be usurped by another woman, even if that other woman is the Queen of England!* Anna added. They said that I was a disgrace to the name of Robsart, letting myself be hidden away in the country as if I were an object of embarrassment and shame like a dribbling idiot, a hunchbacked dwarf, or a madwoman. *I simply would not tolerate it!* said Anna. *Mark my word,* seconded Frances, *I would make a stand and put my foot down!* Clearly they had also heard the rumours from London that were spreading all over the country just like a plague and even being carried abroad by travellers. If you were there and a good wife to him, they implied, this would not be happening. It was all *my* fault; Anna and Frances had a way of *always* conveying that without actually saying it. Ever since I married Robert, either talking to them or reading their letters always left me feeling overwhelmed and exhausted and as if I could do nothing right at all. If I chanced to look in a mirror just after, the word *FAILURE!* would leap out at me, right into my face, like a blow from a fist struck unexpectedly and out of nowhere.

Only my stepbrother, John Appleyard, thought I was a proper wife, obedient to my husband's will, never forgetting my place or trying to put my own wants before my husband's, "a model of subserviency, *exactly* as a wife should be," he said of me, but then Robert always gave him money and cast-off finery and introduced him to influential people at court and had even seen to his appointment as High Sheriff of Norfolk. John prided himself on being one of Robert's followers and would *never* say anything against or contradict him. It might be crude and vulgar phrasing, but as the plainspoken country folk would say, John acted as if Robert's shit didn't stink. And that's the truth of it. Robert could have flayed my back open with his riding crop and turned me out in my shift and bare feet like Patient Griselda, and John wouldn't have uttered a word against it, only nodded his head and agreed that it was a just and fitting punishment. Robert knows how to buy loyalty—when charm alone fails, there are always gifts, money, lands, and titles—and Robert could buy John's soul for a cast-off pink brocade doublet, he's *so* eager to ingratiate himself with the right people.

Like a cat's claws, the written words of Anna and Frances kept tearing at my mind. And within me the resentment, like the cancer in my breast, kept growing and festering, giving me no rest. Until finally, after too many restless, sleepless nights and befuddled, dark-shadowed-eyed days, I could endure it no longer. I called up all the courage I could muster and ordered Pirto to pack a trunk for me and arrange for a coach. "To London I will go!" I declared. And when she tried to dissuade me, I stamped my foot and shrieked, "Damn the roads, and damn the weather, damn the risks, and damn this cancer—I am going to London to see my husband, and *nothing* shall stop me!" Though I had my concerns about Richard Verney, I kept them to myself and carefully timed my departure to coincide with a time when I knew he would be absent on some business for my husband, though I never quite understood exactly what it was he did for Robert. I only wished Robert would dismiss him, for that dark, sinister, perpetually black-clad figure had become the lead actor treading the boards of my nightmares. It scared me so to look at his hands, I always tried not to, but my eyes seemed drawn to them. I often dreamed of those hands around my neck. I would see myself lying on the floor, my skirts like a spreading puddle of blood at his feet, and I would jar the whole house awake with my screams.

One night I even bolted from my bed in terror and ran mindlessly, blindly out into the Long Gallery and crashed right into a suit of armour. I ran right into its open metal arms and slammed full force against its cold, hard, steel chest, and we fell together with a fearsome clang, with me screaming, striking out with my fists in a frenzy to fight off my imagined assailant, my would-be murderer. The servants and Sir Richard Verney found me in a tangle of steel armour, white night shift, and wild golden hair, with my fists, arms, feet, and legs all bloody from the fall and bashing at the armour. I had also split my forehead open, and there was blood dripping into my eyes, and I was sobbing from both the pain and the terror. And, to my great shame, in my terror I had lost control of my bladder, and my bare feet slipped in the yellow puddle I had left on the cold stone floor.

Without uttering a single word, Sir Richard Verney reached down and jerked me to my feet. My toes caught in the hem of my shift, and it ripped. With a terrified scream, I turned on him, my fear-addled brain taking him for another assailant who had been lurking in the shadows, striking out with flailing fists and kicking feet, but he simply drew back his hand and wordlessly slapped me hard across the face. Then a bucket of cold water struck me hard, thrown by one of the servants, to shock me back to my senses.

Then Richard Verney and his servants returned grumbling to their beds, leaving me sobbing and shivering hard, with my teeth chattering, my torn shift plastered to my body, showing every curve most immodestly. Pirto helped me back to my room, washed and dried me, salved and bandaged my wounds, put me into a clean shift, and bundled me back into bed.

"I'm going mad!" I sobbed as I lay there with Pirto clucking over me, trying to calm and quiet me. "It's this place, I tell you—it's driving me mad! It will be the death of me, I tell you—I *know* it will! It will steal my sanity, and then it will take my life! But by then it will be too late! No one will believe! They will think, poor, deluded woman, she did this to herself! *Please,* God, help me, deliver me from my desperation! Don't let them do this to me! *Please,* don't let them!"

To save my sanity, I felt I had no choice but to brave London and risk Robert's anger, to see him again and plead my case, face-to-face, as I had lost the chance to do when I made a fool of myself in my mermaid gown. My wiles had failed to win back his love and reawaken his desire, and he had left before I could broach the subject of a different, more pleasant abode. So now I must venture out, wearing no disguise, and just be plain, ordinary, everyday me and hope my words, fears, and feelings would be enough to sway him. I must convince him that Compton Verney would be the *death* of me. Perhaps, when he saw how pale and haggard I was, and the dark shadows shrouding my eyes, he would realise that it was not my imagination after all. *Have mercy upon me, Robert!* was my silent prayer, repeated over and over again, like a rosary, as the wheels of the coach turned, bearing me ever closer to London.

Suddenly the wheels ground to a halt, and Pirto and I were flung violently forward. As I struggled to right myself, a face appeared at the window, and I screamed. It was a death's-head, a bone-white skull, crowned by a jaunty, red-feathered hat, staring in at me. A powerful, red-gloved hand shot out and wrenched open the door and dragged me out, struggling and screaming, pleading for my life, and near fainting with pain when his arm squeezed my afflicted breast. When Pirto tried to help me, the opposite door flew open, and other hands reached out to restrain her. "You shut yer 'ole, or else I'll shut it fer you!" a voice growled, and Pirto's protests immediately subsided into meek little whimpers like a frightened kitten's.

My skull-faced assailant hurled me to the ground, so hard, the breath was knocked out of me, and I could only lie there stunned, gasping for air, my eyes wide with terror, as his dagger ripped my bodice open, cut through my stays and shift, and laid bare my breasts with the point just a hairsbreadth away from cutting my skin. Shame flooded me then, piercing through the terror, as his eyes fell upon the stained white linen bandage that covered my left breast. Sometimes the stinking, blood-tinged discharge seeped through to stain it. I *hated* the sight and smell of it, and it shamed me to the core to have anyone else see. I had always prided myself on being so clean, and now this stink that no perfume could ever entirely mask hung always about me, leaking from my once beautiful pink and white breast that had now become an ugly, distorted, sore, red, and mottled grotesquerie. Tears filled my eyes, and I turned my face away.

But my attacker showed me no mercy, straddling me, pinning me down between his strong thighs. He tore off the bandage, and I cowered beneath him in shame, turning my face away, squeezing my eyes shut tightly and tucking my chin into my shoulder. Even if he meant to rape or murder me, I did not want to see the disgust on his face and in his eyes.

"*Mon Dieu!*" he gasped, and there was something in his voice that made me tentatively turn my head and slowly open my eyes and look at him.

The death's-head mask, that ghoulish, grinning skull, was now hanging about his neck, and I saw beneath the wide red hat brim that my attacker was a very handsome, dark-haired man with sun-bronzed skin and a dashing moustache that curled up at the ends. To my astonishment, his dark eyes were full of tears, and as I watched, they began trickling down his cheeks. By his voice, I guessed he was French, for he gathered me up in his arms, tenderly cradling me against his chest, and kept mumbling something that sounded like "my *pauvre petite*", as he rocked me and stroked my hair and pressed kiss after kiss onto my brow. I also thought I heard the name *Marguerite* murmured in a tear-choked whisper. Then, just as suddenly, he stopped, and in a voice that demanded instant obedience, addressed his men, ordering them to stand down and cease their assault on us, return anything they had taken, and mount their horses and wait for him.

"It's all right, don't be afraid, I will not harm you," he said softly in his rich, velvety voice. As he spoke, he untied his red velvet cloak and wrapped it around me. And then he lifted me, oh, so gently, as if he were afraid I might break, and carried me back to the coach and put me back inside just as he had found me.

He settled me against the cushions and adjusted his cloak about me, drawing its folds closer, like a warm red velvet cocoon. Then he reached inside his shirt and took from about his neck what looked to be a miniature painted on ivory in a gold filigree frame dangling from a delicate gold and pearl chain. He pressed it to his lips, then, after one long, last look at it, draped it over my head and settled it round my neck, so that it lay over my diseased breast.

"This is *Sainte-Agathe*—St Agatha—she belonged to someone who was *very, very* dear to me. I loved her with all my heart—she *was* my heart—but . . . I lost her." He paused to swallow down his tears. "Women with your malady sometimes find comfort in praying to *Sainte-Agathe*. Please, you pray to her too, and I will pray that she will work a miracle for you."

I looked down at the painting and saw that it was of a lovely young woman with a halo about her golden hair and a beautiful smile upon her serene face. She was robed in red and white accented with gold, and in her hands she held a tray upon which lay what I, at first glance, thought were two cherry-topped cakes before I realised that they were actually her breasts, which had been cut off when she was tortured to try to force her to forsake her Christian faith.

"Thank you," I whispered. I was still shaking so hard, my voice trembled.

He reached out and stroked my face. "What is your name?" he asked.

"Amy," I answered.

"Ah!" His face broke into a smile. "*Aimee—beloved!* It suits you well; such a name is *always* given from the heart by one who *knows* they have just received the *greatest* gift of all."

Then he leaned forward, pressed the most tender, lingering kiss

I had ever received onto my brow, murmured some French words, which I just *knew* to be the most heartfelt blessing, and then he was gone, calling to his men, and I heard horses galloping away.

The coachman spared not a moment and cracked the whip, and the coach lurched forward, and we were on our way again. Through the open window I heard the coachman say in an awed voice to the man on the box beside him that we had just met Red Jack, *Jacques Rouge,* Bloody Jack, and by some miracle survived the encounter without so much as a scratch—"not a drop o' blood spilt, a skirt lifted, or a purse pilfered! God was watchin' out for us this day, 'e was!" he declared, cracking his whip and urging the horses to go faster. "I don't care if it rattles e'ery tooth in me 'ead loose, we'll see London before nightfall!" he vowed, cracking the whip again.

Once in London, I did not want to face my cousins in Camber-well. I knew they would have heard all the gossip about Robert and the Queen and would—whether they regarded me with pity or contempt—have much to say that would make me feel as if I were tied and bound and being spun round and roasted upon a spit, so I bade the coachman take me to a reputable inn instead. There I fell exhausted into bed and slept for two days straight. I didn't wake up until well past noon of the third, when a beam of sunlight, like a prodding, poking finger, penetrated a crack in the bed-curtains and made me stir myself.

As I halfheartedly pecked at a roll and sipped my breakfast ale, I lay back, near tears, against the pillows Pirto piled behind my back as I listened to the serving woman who had come in to tidy the room chatter on about the latest gossip from the court.

"Word 'as it that Lord Robert 'as given the Queen a fine, quilted red petticoat to 'ide the child they 'ave been a-makin'. And," she added, pausing to give me a nod and a knowing look, "I 'ave it direct from a groom at the palace that the Queen *never* goes on 'er Summer Progress but to be delivered. Some say she's 'ad *five* children by Lord Robert, the first bein' a bastard made when they was in the Tower t'get'er—'tis as good a way to pass the time as any, I trow, them both bein' prisoners an' not knowing if they was to live or die—but *I* think 'tis more like two, or per'aps three. 'Tis a right pity too, for I 'ear tell that 'e 'as a very beautiful wife waitin' at 'ome, pinin' fer 'im, but 'e doesn't live with 'er and visits 'er but seldom. Rumour 'as it that 'e 'as sent to poison 'er so 'e will be free to marry the Queen. May God preserve Our Gracious Majesty! 'E's a cad, Lord Robert is. 'Andsome is as 'andsome does, I always say, an' any man what would murder 'is wife to marry 'is mistress, even if she is Queen o' England, 'tis no man I want to share my bed an' board with! But bein' a queen doesn't save a woman from bein' a fool o'er a man; they say she ne'er lets 'im leave 'er an' visits 'im in 'is chambers day and night—right next to 'ers with a door connectin', they are. I saw the Queen once, I did." She patted her chest and nodded proudly, beaming wide to show the blackened stumps of her teeth. "Ridin' by on 'er coronation day. I ran out an' offered 'er a sprig o' rosemary, I did, an' she took it from me with 'er own white 'and an' tucked it inside the Bible she was 'oldin' on 'er lap an' thanked me right kindly for it an' said she would keep it forever to remind 'er of 'this *glorious* day'! Now, that's *true* majesty, it is, an' if it ain't, I don't know what is!"

The tears were pouring down my face by then, and, Pirto, seeing my distress, hurriedly pressed a coin into the woman's palm and shooed her out as I buried my face in the pillows and sobbed my heart out. So it *was* true about the poison, and Robert had known all along. Richard Verney had only been following orders! My husband wanted me dead! That was why the spices he sent only made me sicker, and why he had taken my unicorn's horn away; he didn't want me to get better!

I cried and cried as the last of my illusions died. But I knew I could not waste the whole day in weeping. I still had to see Robert. Even knowing what I knew, I had to find a way to dissuade him from this murderous course. I needed to get away from Compton Verney, to be somewhere pleasant and safe, where I could stop fearing what malice and evil lurked in the shadows and rest in peace for what little time I had left to live. Robert and his minions would not steal what was left of my life away with poison. I was fully on guard now, and I would not let them!

I forced myself to dry my tears and rise from my bed and give myself over to Pirto's ministrations.

"Please," I implored her, "help me; I need to look my best today. I need him to see at least a glimmer of the Amy he fell in love with. Help me be that girl again, Pirto."

"Time changes us all, love," Pirto said sadly, "but 'twas him a-changin' that made you change, broke your heart and made you sadder."

She applied salve and a fresh dressing to my breast and rose perfume to try to mask the fetid odour of the seeping discharge and helped me into a fine gown of buttercup yellow damask trimmed with seed pearls and frills of golden lace. She arranged my hair in shining curls, long, loose, harvest gold ringlets to remind Robert of the girl he had fallen in love with and been wild to wed and bed, instead of the wife he no longer wanted, with the wealth of her hair pinned up and hidden beneath her gold-bordered hood as becomes a respectable matron. And around my neck I fastened the black silk cord of the amber heart Robert had given me. "Here is my heart," he had said at the time. "Let this token stand as surety for my eternal, undying love." I wanted him to see it; I wanted him to remember that he had once given this most precious gift to me, not the amber heart, but the flesh and blood one beating within his chest and the love that it stood symbol for.

"God, give me strength!" I prayed. "*Please,* if I am to die, let God take my life, *not* Robert, or one of his or the Queen's minions. If he cannot love me like he once did, then let him like me enough to stay the poisoner's hand and let this cancer follow its course, and let me die a natural death."

Then I took a deep breath, squared my shoulders, and set out to confront Robert.

Hoping to meet him privately, rather than before the curious, scandal-hungry eyes of the court, I went first to the Dairy House at Kew, the small but stately milk white riverside mansion the Queen had given him, where the lawn sprawled emerald green and white peacocks paraded proudly amongst classical-style marble urns overflowing with meadow daisies, marigolds, pinks, cowslips, and gillyflowers, white marble statues of dairy cows, and chairs carved like wooden milk pails where two lovers might sit, embrace, hold hands, and converse most intimately. The whiteness of it all was so glaringly bright, I had to squint and shield my eyes. Like staring into the sun, it hurt just to look at it.

The housekeeper, a pleasant, moon-faced woman almost as round as she was tall, greeted me at the door and introduced herself as Mrs Margery Dowe. I asked if my husband were at home. To her credit, she tried to veil her astonishment. She fast recovered her wits and, though it was with a blush, averted eyes, and a stammer, she answered me, "N-No, M-My Lady, he . . . he . . . he is at . . . at . . . he is at court!" she at last blurted out. Then, as if rushing onward and changing the subject would make me forget her answer, she asked if I would like a piece of fresh-baked mincemeat pie or, she added, as my husband had just re-established the dairy, she could offer me some of his cheese or butter spread onto some bread that had also been baked fresh that morning. "Or per'aps some sweet cream slathered on a sugar biscuit would be more to m'lady's liking?" she asked, most anxious to please.

"No, thank you, Mrs Dowe," I said softly as I stood there in the stately entrance hall, gazing down at the highly polished oak floor peeking around a narrow carpet of red velvet, lest its lustre be lost to admiring eyes. Slowly, I turned in a circle, taking it all in. The carved and gilded ceiling and gleaming oak wall panelling were all acorns and oak leaves and bears holding ragged staves standing ankle-deep in red and white painted Tudor roses, and there were carved cameo portraits in profile of Robert and the Queen, their oval frames supported by cherubs and garlanded in roses, acorns, and oak leaves, everywhere with their initials—*RD* and *ER*—for Robert Dudley and Elizabeth Regina. And, if I looked straight ahead, where a beam of sunlight that poured in through a round clear and ruby red stained-glass window set like a jewel above the front door was pointing, my eyes were led to a life-sized portrait of she who ruled here, the mistress of the realm and this house, its gold frame all a-blossom with a garden of red and white enamelled Tudor roses.

I went to stand directly before it, to better scrutinise my rival. She was so regal and proud, within her confidence seemed to reign supreme. Her face, neck, breasts, and hands were as white as marble. She was like a statue all dressed up, like the statues in the churches in bygone Catholic days were sometimes given wigs of real hair and dressed up in embroidered robes with jewels to adorn them. The Protestant religion had banished the Holy Virgin from England's altars, and now Elizabeth was giving her subjects another virgin queen, this one of earth instead of Heaven, to venerate and adore. She was gowned in scarlet and white, all a-sparkle with ruby and diamond hearts—on her dress, at her wrists, ears, and throat, and in her vivid hair, like flames tamed to be docile and hold the jewelled hearts. Her head was tilted downward to contemplate something in her hand. It was a heart-shaped locket, attached to a long diamond chain she wore about her neck, with the golden halves open so she could gaze down upon the two faces inside. I stood on tiptoe and peered closer, squinting my eyes, the paintings within the painting were *so* tiny. And then, with a little thud, I sank down heavily onto my heels again, feeling altogether defeated, as if my errand today, though only just begun, was already a lost cause. Surely these two dainty likenesses were Lavinia's tiniest work—I knew they were hers by the telltale azure backgrounds. Each in one half of a golden heart, Robert and Elizabeth faced each other, so that when the halves were closed, their painted lips would meet.

"The Queen of Hearts and the Knave of Hearts," I said softly.

"Beg pardon, m'lady?" Mrs Dowe, now at my side, inquired.

"Nothing of any importance, Mrs Dowe." I feigned a smile. "I was just thinking aloud. I apologise for coming unannounced, but I wanted to surprise Robert."

Mrs Dowe's expression told me that, sure enough, had he been at home, Robert would have been surprised, and *not* in a very pleasant way, but she was too kind to say so.

"Would you—that is, if your time permits, of course—would you show me around? I would like very much to see the house. Robert has told me about it in his letters," I lied, "but—being a woman, I know you will understand—men don't always describe the details well enough for one to picture them, the way a lady likes to."

Mrs Dowe's lips spread in a wide smile, and she nodded vigorously. "Aye, m'lady, I know *just* what you mean, I do! Sometimes it's like pullin' teeth, it is, to get an answer out o' my 'Arry! 'E saw the Queen once, an' when I asked 'im what she 'ad on, 'e said, 'A dress,' Just that—'a dress'! 'Ad 'is own life been at stake, 'e couldn't 'ave told me the cut or colour of it or what kind o' trim-min's it 'ad! So I know *just* what you mean! Now, if you'll come this way, m'lady, I'll show you the best parlour first. You came at just the right time, you did; the murals were just 'ung up t'other day."

But at the door, with her hand hovering over the ornate gilded handle shaped like a naked nymph with long, flowing hair, she hes-itated once more. "Beggin' your pardon, m'lady, but are you *sure* you want to see?" She jerked her head back at the portrait of the Queen. "There's more o' that sort o' thing, if you take my meanin'."

"It's all right, Mrs Dowe." I gave a comforting pat to her arm. "I assure you, I am well aware of my husband's friendship with the Queen." The look on Mrs Dowe's face told me that she knew just as well as I did that *friendship* was not the best word for it, and, to reassure her further, I amended, "I mean, of course, his *intimate* friendship with Her Majesty. Now, please, if you would be so kind, I am most eager to see what my husband has done with the house."

Mrs Dowe nodded and gave a little shrug. "As you will, m'lady, this way," she said, and she turned the door handle, though I had the distinct impression that she thought I was only torturing myself and better that I go to the Tower and have myself racked rather than explore Robert's house any farther.

The best parlour was a sizeable room, "the largest in the 'ole 'ouse, m'lady, there not bein' a Great 'All," Mrs Dowe explained. The curtains and upholstery were done in a rich deep brown velvet trimmed with gold fringe and tassels, and the floor was carpeted entirely in a brown carpet woven in gold, tawny, and various shades of green with a pattern of acorns and oak leaves. I was *amazed* to see it. I had seen, and even owned, smaller squares of Turkey car-pet, but never one such as this that covered the whole floor, reach-ing from wall to wall. What it had cost Robert I could not even begin to imagine. The candles rose out of gilded sconces and can-delabra shaped like wreaths of oak leaves and acorns, and the carved oak ceiling and wall panelling continued the same pattern. But it was the murals covering every wall that took my breath away and left me reeling, groping behind me for a chair—and not a mo-ment too soon—as my knees gave way.

In the common clothes of a milkmaid and her gallant swain, the Queen and Robert cavorted through a series of bucolic, pastoral tableaux. In the first they shared a kiss over the back of a cow Elizabeth had apparently just finished milking, as its pink teats still dribbled drops of white milk into the wooden pail still sitting beneath, which a sly tabby cat eyed longingly. In the second, Robert lifted her over a stile, swinging her in such a way that her trim ankles and shapely calves showed. Next he crouched by the river, peeping through the reeds, to spy on her as she bathed, her nakedness barely veiled by the blue water and waves of long, rippling red hair. In the fourth mural they held hands and stared longingly at each other as they herded a flock of geese. And in the next, as a shepherd and shepherdess, they stole a kiss while minding the sheep. Then they progressed to lying together, embracing, in a haystack. And in the seventh—the one that tore at my heart most— they stood together beneath a mighty oak tree, gazing upon the ruins of a sprawling manor house where sheep grazed upon the overgrown grass and thistles as a rainbow spread over it all; from the looks on their faces, they were dreaming of the future and making plans. And in the eighth, and final, painting, they danced high-spiritedly together at their wedding, Robert lifting Elizabeth high in a white gown embroidered with golden flowers, surrounded by smiling faces and bountifully laden tables.

Lest I break down and fall weeping onto Mrs Dowe's shoulder, I sprang from my chair and hurried out.

"And now the other rooms please, Mrs Dowe," I said quickly in a miraculously steady voice.

Each successive room was like a shrine to Elizabeth, with her portrait prominently displayed.

In a yellow room decorated with gilded suns, she wore a golden gown with her hair like a sunburst rippling about her shoulders. In the next room, done in midnight blue adorned with pearly white moons and silvery stars, she was gowned in the same colours and emblems within a silver gilt frame, as chaste Diana with a silver crescent moon and diamond stars and ropes of pearls entwined in her elaborately styled hair, all coils and plaits and cascading curls, falling past bare shoulders as white as alabaster.

And in a room of deep forest green velvet and dark wooden panelling, with a plaster ceiling painted with hawks swooping after sparrows and other small birds, and wildflowers blooming on a

Turkey carpet beneath my feet, she was mounted, regal and proud, a commanding presence, sidesaddle upon a handsome bay hunter in a flowing-skirted green velvet riding habit and feathered cap, with a hawk on her wrist.

The next room was the library, lined with shelves of leather-bound books with the Dudley coat-of-arms gilded on every one; they were a bewildering assortment of works on mathematics, cartography, navigation, astrology, astronomy, alchemy, history, warfare, and geography. Even the ones in English seemed writ in a foreign language to me—I could scarce understand a word of them. And, presiding over it all, was a portrait of Elizabeth in a buff-coloured gown trimmed with gold and russet silk braid with a wide ruff edged in gold cushioning her chin, and a feathered hat set at a rakish tilt. In her leather-gloved hand she held the chain of a trained bear that stood up on his hind legs beside her, his paws reaching out as if he wanted to embrace her. It was as though Elizabeth's slim figure had replaced the ragged staff clutched in the Dudleys' bear's claws. On each side of the portrait hung a large framed chart, an intricate and elaborate horoscope, beautifully embellished with stars and other symbols. One was for Elizabeth; the other was, of course, for Robert. But I noticed one glaring error— upon each chart the date of birth was given as September 7, 1533, when I knew very well that my husband had been born in the same month and year as myself, though some days afterwards, on June 24, 1532. Had he spun a tale for Elizabeth about it being written in the stars that they were destined to be together? "We two are one—it was written in the stars at the hour of our birth." Truly I could almost hear him saying those very words, in a hot, velvety voice whispered into an all too willing ear that was eager to hear them. It was easy to imagine, because that had once been me, lapping it all up like a cat does cream.

Robert's desk sat in the centre of the room, and I saw that a letter lay upon it, as if Robert had been called away while writing it. Curious, I picked it up and read these words addressed to Elizabeth:

*I am your Ursus Major, your great bear, and forever
shall remain in the bond-chain of dutiful servitude,*

fastened to you above all others by benefits past and
your daily goodness continually showered upon me.

I let it fall from my hands.

"Shall we go upstairs now, m'lady?" Mrs Dowe asked anxiously, peeking curiously over my shoulder at the letter I had just dropped back onto the desk, and I nodded readily.

"There was a large portrait painted of me in my wedding gown," I said suddenly, turning to Mrs Dowe as we mounted the stairs, the posts carved to depict Robert and Elizabeth as various classical gods and goddesses, "with a goose beside me and a big bouquet of buttercups—my favourite flower—in my hand."

"Is that so, m'lady?" said Mrs Dowe. "Why, that sounds charming! Just charming! I 'ope to see it 'ung 'ere someday. Perhaps Lord Robert will 'ave it 'ung in the yellow room downstairs, with the buttercups you mentioned—it would look just *grand* down there, it would!"

"Perhaps he will," I said, though I would not have risked a penny bet upon it now that I knew for certain that there was no room for me in Robert's life any more, not even for my portrait in his house. There weren't even any buttercups—*my* flower— amongst the country blossoms blooming in his white marble urns. Heaven only knew what had happened to that portrait; I hadn't seen it in ever so long. I hadn't even been allowed to pack my own things when I moved first to the Hydes' house and then to Compton Verney. Had it been lost along the way somewhere, or did it languish forgotten in some musty attic, or had Robert ordered it destroyed because he did not wish to be reminded of me and our marriage and how happy, how much in love, we had once been? Did it even really exist, or had I only dreamt it? That radiant, happy bride I had been seemed so lost and distant these days, sometimes I thought she was only a figure in a fairy tale, a happily ever after story, not someone who ever actually lived and breathed. If *only* I could see that portrait again, if only I could take Robert's arm and lead him to stand before it . . . that portrait was the proof—the proof that it had not all been just a dream!

In a sky blue sitting room adjoining the master bedchamber

silver-framed portraits of Robert and Elizabeth, both clad in that heavenly hue, faced each other from opposite walls.

I hardly dared set foot in the bedchamber for fear of what I would find there, but I forced myself and crossed the threshold to behold a massive bed clothed in regal purple velvet edged with deep bands of ermine and sewn with pearls and embroidered with golden crowns set with tiny ruby, sapphire, and diamond brilliants. Draped over the back of a purple-cushioned and ornately carved and gilded fireside chair, which more than a little resembled a throne, was a red velvet dressing gown bordered with ermine, very like royal robes to be worn for some lofty state ceremony, and a gold-embroidered nightcap made in such a way that it mimicked a jewelled crown set with diamond and ruby brilliants. And, dominating the room, from over the mantelpiece, was a portrait of Elizabeth in her bejewelled gold and silver brocade and ermine coronation robes holding the sceptre and orb in her hands with the crown atop her flowing hair.

There was another door, and I crossed quickly to it and flung it wide and immediately wished I hadn't. A startled cry broke from me, my knees buckled, and I almost fell. Clinging to the doorjamb like a cluster of quivering grapes, I regarded what was obviously the nursery.

Robert and Elizabeth stood side by side in a portrait hanging over the mantel, smiling down upon a gilded cradle swathed in purple velvet and topped by a radiant golden crown that glittered blindingly when the sun poured in through the window and struck it. An ermine blanket was already turned back as if a prince would at any moment be laid down there for a nap. And there were shelves filled with all a child might desire and need, from cups and bowls to piles of linen napkins and a vast array of toys, including gold and silver rattles, some of them set with gems, that mimicked sceptres in their shape. And there were chests—I defied the pain that pierced my heart and opened one—filled with swaddling bands and beautiful little garments—exquisite tiny gowns, coats, and caps—embroidered with gold and silver threads and trimmed with the finest lace, and silk ribbons, and a magnificent christening robe of crimson velvet furred with ermine and trimmed with bands of gold. I let the lid bang shut and, with a hasty "thank you" to Mrs Dowe, I sped down the stairs, crying out in all my anguish, babbling hysterically: "He means to be rid of me, by divorce or death, he means to be rid of me, to have his minions poison me, murder me, so he can make *her* his wife! He will kill me to be King!" I rushed out the door, slamming it behind me, fleeing the house that was a monument to my husband's regal ambitions and the woman who was all he desired, and I flung myself into the carriage, calling to the driver to "take me away from here. I don't care where, just go! *Go! Go! Go!*" I screamed, pounding my fists and stamping my feet. *"Drive!"*

He took me back to the inn, but when he came to open the carriage door for me, I had composed myself sufficiently and stubbornly shook my head and sat up straight, like the lady Robert always wanted me to be.

"Take me to my husband; take me to court," I said grandly, in a calm, level voice. "Wherever the Queen is in residence, that is where my husband will be."

"Very well, m'lady, but you might 'ave said so before; your 'usband's 'ouse is right near Richmond Palace, it is," he said, heaving a sigh of weary exasperation as he closed the door and climbed back up onto his box, mumbling something about the minds of females being as stubborn and contrary as mules.

He drove me to Richmond Palace, and I stood for a moment stark still, gape-jawed and gazing up at the vast profusion of golden turrets, pinnacles, and towers shining in the September sun. When I heard someone laugh and turned to see them pointing at me, I hurried inside, flush-faced and flustered at having shown myself such a country bumpkin the first time I ever saw up close a palace. In truth, I cannot remember very much about it now, I was so frightened, except the urgent press and constant babble of the crowd within. There were *so* many of them—tradesfolk, commoners, and all those waiting to present petitions to the Queen, servants in a rainbow of varied liveries, black-gowned scholars, and statesmen with great golden chains hung about their necks, ambassadors from foreign lands chattering in foreign tongues and bearing gifts for Her Majesty, and the ladies and gentlemen of the court all dressed like colourful birds of paradise—all chattering and squawking as if the palace were a giant gilded cage full of parrots. I walked like one in a trance, dazed, befuddled, and terrified by all the constant and confusing colour and clamour, overwhelmed by the grandeur, all of it blurring together, trying and failing to make sense of it all, and feeling like running away and bursting into tears the whole time.

A beautiful young lady with high-piled auburn hair, dressed in an ornate gold-embroidered gown of vivid, brazen pink, with her bodice cut daringly low, detached herself from a group of gorgeously apparelled ladies and gentlemen and gently tapped my arm with her feathered fan and asked if she might be of some service. Up close, I was startled to see how young she really was beneath all the paint—surely not more than sixteen or seventeen.

"Would you be so kind as to tell me where I might find my husband?" I asked timorously, adding quickly so she would know whom I meant amongst the many gentlemen at court, "I am Lady Amy Dudley—Lord Robert's wife."

"Ah! So Lord Robert's wife is not a phantom after all! She really *does* exist!" the bold young redhead trilled, seizing my arm and pulling me over to those she had been conversing with. "This," she announced, "is Lady Amy Dudley—Lord Robert's wife!"

"Well done, Lettice!" a golden-haired girl in gold-spangled spinach green and turquoise blue applauded. "I was well-nigh certain Lord Robert's wife was imaginary, a figure of fantasy he had invented to keep the ladies at bay! Well, *most* of the ladies," she hastily amended, darting a knowing glance at a portrait of the Queen that hung high upon the wall as if she were looking down, watching over us all.

"Why, she isn't sun-browned at all!" another exclaimed, eyeing me up and down with amazement. "She's as pale as I am! I was expecting a nut brown wench, sturdy and broad as a plough horse!"

They all looked at me as if I were a freak in a fair. They made me so nervous, the way they stared and put their heads together and whispered and tittered behind their fans, that I wondered in horror if I might have some unsightly blemish upon my face. I even glanced down at my gown to make sure it had not become stained, torn, or wrinkled. Could they smell the stink of my bandaged breast? I wondered fearfully and nearly raised my arms and hugged them over my chest, but at the last moment I caught myself, fearing that would lead their eyes *exactly* where I wished they wouldn't go. I found it very hard to meet anyone's eyes and timidly touched the auburn-haired girl's sleeve and asked, "*Please,* do you know where I might find my husband? I have come to London expressly to see him."

"Of course! Forgive me. You have come a long way and are impatient, and I can see how tired you are." She smiled, showing teeth that were a little too sharp to be reassuring, and . . . there was just *something* about her that made me suddenly doubt her sincerity. "Come this way," she beckoned. "Follow me." And, being surrounded by strangers, I had no choice but to obey.

She led me through a lavish suite of rooms and out into a small walled garden.

"This"—she leaned in close and confided in a whisper—"is the Queen's *private pleasure* garden," placing a lascivious emphasis upon the words that called to mind startlingly vivid and lewd imaginings of Robert and the Queen romping and cavorting nude, frolicking with wild, wanton abandon amongst the flowers and trees like Adam and Eve. And my mind hurtled back to Hemsby, and the free and wanton way we had loved and played upon the beach, and it made my heart ache to think that he would share such pleasures with another.

It was then that I heard voices, a man and a woman's mingled laughter, and my memory bounced back to Robert and Mollie the milkmaid in the stable. My escort drew back, but with a wink and a mischievous waggling motion of her fingers, urged me onward. And, like iron shavings drawn to a magnet, being pulled ever forward, unable to resist the urgent, insistent tug, I followed the flower-lined path until I saw them sitting together on the grass beneath a shade tree.

They were in each other's arms. Robert's head was in the crook of her neck, kissing it ardently, while she, with eyes closed and lips parted ecstatically, clasped his dark head. Her hair was in disarray—somehow I just knew he had plucked the pearl- and diamond-tipped pins from it and left them where they lay, scattered on the grass—and her gown hung down, exposing one shoulder, so white against the black velvet of her bodice, it might have been carved of marble. To my horror, I saw that she wore a heavy, quilted crimson velvet petticoat thickly encrusted with pearls, diamonds, and silver embroidery, just as the gossipy serving woman had described.

Was it *true,* then? Had he given her a child? A child that should have been mine, as a balm against my loneliness, to fill my world now that he had left me, forsaken me for another. He had given her *everything*! *Everything!*

At my hurt, tearful gasp her eyes shot open wide, and she thrust Robert from her.

He whirled round to face me, and I saw the fury blaze up in his eyes as he leapt up and lunged at me.

I jumped back, away from him, and reached up and, without bothering to undo the clasp, ripped the amber heart from my neck and flung it onto the Queen's lap.

"Here is his heart, the one he gave to *me*! But *you* might as well take it too; you've taken everything else!" I cried, a sob mangling the last word.

I didn't look at her face. I couldn't bear to. I didn't want to see the laughter in her eyes, gloating and mocking me because I had failed at the only thing that mattered.

Then I spun round, only to see the brazen, pink-clad beauty called Lettice bent nearly double, laughing at me, cradling her ribs as if they ached within the tightly laced confines of her stays, with a giggling, dark-haired girl in milk-and-water silk beside her.

"*Poor* Robert!" Lettice blurted through her laughter. "She's *so far* beneath him!"

The brunette nodded, her dark ringlets bobbing in agreement, and added, "Even if she stood on tiptoe on the highest mountaintop, she still could not hope to even brush her fingertips against the soles of his boots!"

"Oh, how *low* can a man go?" Lettice crowed.

"For shame, Lettice!" The blonde in turquoise and spinach green approached and slapped her arm reprovingly with her fan. "And you too, Frances! I think you're being *awfully* mean to her!"

"Oh, Douglass!" What a curious name for a woman, I thought! Lettice groaned and rolled her eyes. "You were ever a tender-heart!"

"I sometimes think my sister is too soft a creature for court," Frances agreed. And that was all I heard as I rushed past them.

Blinded by tears, I ran on and on, pushing and shoving my way through the palace, not caring whom I blundered into or whose toes I trod upon, until I burst out the door and hurled myself back into the carriage, screaming at the coachman to *"Go! Hurry!* Take me away from here, back to the inn, at once! *Now!"*

I don't know how he found me, but Robert came to me later that day. The pain went so deep that I was almost numb. He said that I had made a fool of myself, and him, that I had embarrassed him and made of him a laughingstock. That was what this was *really* about, not his betrayal of me and our marriage vows, and his dalliance with the Queen—upon *that* subject he had nothing to say.

"Do you hear me?" Robert grabbed me by my shoulders and shook me so hard and fast, it was all I could do not to be sick upon his shoes. "You have offended the Queen! You fool, do you know how *serious* this is for me? I am the *most* important man at court. I am the Queen's Master of the Horse. *Everything* to do with the horses and transportation of the court is *my* responsibility. I am in sole charge of buying, stabling, training, breeding, and physicking *every* horse in the royal stables. I *personally* select the horses the Queen and courtiers and foreign visitors ride for leisure, hunting, and travel. I make sure each person has a mount perfectly suited to them, gentle palfreys for the timid, aged, or inexperienced riders, and fast, spirited animals for those who prefer and can handle them. I choose the packhorses and mules for when the court travels. I plan the processions and organise the routes and stopping points—*all* of that is entrusted *entirely* to *me,* and I have *full* responsibility for planning all the court entertainments—the pageants, tournaments, masques, banquets, and balls. It is *my* duty to be there whenever the Queen rides out, to ride immediately behind her, and to be there to help her mount and dismount. No one but *me* is to do it, *no one!* And now *my wife* has offended the Queen!"

"You mean by existing." I nodded knowingly. "I offend Elizabeth by the mere fact that I live and breathe and wear your ring upon my finger! It is easier to wrong a woman when she is buried alive in the country—out of sight, out of mind, as the old song says! For how can you hurt, how can you wrong, someone who doesn't even exist as far as you both are concerned and who doesn't know what is going on? I would imagine her conscience suffers fewer pangs that way, since she cannot see with her own eyes the pain she causes! Since I am not welcome at court and we live apart, far easier to pretend that we are estranged, so she can use that too as an excuse to steal my husband! And doubtlessly you lead her to believe that it is true! That we have parted amicably and willingly gone our separate ways, to each his own! Do you lie to her too, Robert? Do you tell her that I don't love you, that I am well content with my lonely state and don't want or need you? Do you lie *to* her as well as *with* her?"

Robert slapped me hard across the face, so hard, I stumbled and fell against the wall.

"I will not even dignify that with an answer," he said in quiet fury.

I turned away from him, rubbing my stinging, smarting cheek and the side of my head where it had hit the wall.

There were angry voices out in the courtyard: one foreign—French, I thought, that sounded strangely familiar—and the other English, and I thought I recognised it as well, so I glanced out. I instantly felt as if I had been slapped again. The foreigner *was* a Frenchman—the tenderhearted highwayman, Red Jack! And the Englishman was *Sir Richard Verney*!

In a flurry of furious, fast-paced French, Red Jack flung a purse at Richard Verney's feet, then spat on it and, with some last angry words that I was quite sure, by their tone, were a curse, turned on his heel and strode away, the red plume in his hat waving goodbye and good riddance behind him.

"Robert! Robert! Come look!" I cried, reaching behind me and groping for his sleeve. "Sir Richard Verney hired Red Jack to attack me—that purse he threw in the dust is proof! Look! Look!" I cried, forgetting that I had yet to tell Robert about my brush with danger on the road to London.

Robert slapped my clinging fingers from his sleeve and gave me a look of withering disdain. "*Really,* Amy, you *astound* me! What fanciful tale is this now?" With an exasperated sigh, he glanced out the window. "If you mean that fellow with the red feather in his hat, that is *not* Red Jack, the notorious highwayman, but a Flemish spice merchant. Richard Verney would piss himself from fear if he ever saw a highwayman, especially one with a reputation like Bloody Jack's, so the idea that he would consort with one is utterly absurd. Red Jack wears a necklace—he calls it his string of pearls—made from the teeth of the women he has raped and murdered, you know, so if he *had* attacked you, you would not be here now to tell this ludicrous tale you are spinning for God only knows what reason. If Richard Verney thought he was under the same roof as that man, he would flee like one escaping a burning building, screaming as if his hair were on fire. All you've witnessed is a quarrel over the cost or quality of spices, nothing more or less. Now come away, and stop hanging out that window like a gape-jawed slattern—you've embarrassed me more than enough for one day!"

"No, Robert, no, you are mistaken," I insisted. "I would stake my life upon it—that *is* Red Jack. I *know* it is! I would know him anywhere! And he does not wear a necklace of women's teeth—that must be just a story. It *was* a miniature of St Agatha on a chain set with pearls that he wore, but he doesn't have it any more—he gave it to me!" I fished it out of my bodice and showed it to him, ignoring Robert's disdainful dismissal of it as "cheap and worthless Papist frippery!"

"It was *all* Richard Verney's doing—I *know* it was!" I continued. "He is an *evil, evil* man, Robert. I *know*! When his attempts to poison me failed, he somehow found out that I was coming to London to see you, and he hired Red Jack to murder me along the way, to make it look like a random robbery, as highwaymen are known to lurk along the roads, but Red Jack spared me because Death's mark was already upon me!" I blurted it all out, forgetting that Robert didn't yet know about my breast. I had kept it a secret from all but Pirto; no one else knew but Red Jack, who had seen it with his own eyes when he ripped open my bodice.

Robert gave a weary sigh. "God, grant me patience. Amy, you do most sorely try me! Was ever a man more accursed in his wife than I am? You talk like a madwoman! People tell me I should have you locked away, but out of the goodness of my heart, I keep giving you chances, hoping you will snap to your senses and comport yourself properly as becomes a lady who has the honour of being my wife. *That*"—Robert pointed out the window, jabbing his finger at the man with a red feather in his hat, now mounting a handsome black horse—"is a Flemish spice merchant. I know that for a fact, as I bought some saffron from him a fortnight ago on Sir Richard Verney's recommendation to mix with my butter and cheese to give them a better colour and get a higher price for them at market. I have revived the dairy at Kew, since that was what gave the house its name, but I am not altogether satisfied with the quality of the goods produced. The milkmaids are a fat lot of lazy slatterns. I will lose my patience, and my temper, and dismiss the lot of them one day—I swear, they're good for nothing but gossiping!"

"But I could fix that!" I cried, a hopeful smile lighting up my face. "Oh, Robert, *please*! I have much experience in running a dairy! I can help you! I *know* I can! I know the *proper* way to make *good* butter and cheese! And, with me in charge, you'll have no further need for saffron! Oh, Robert, *please,* let me come to Kew, let me take charge of it. Please, let me do this, let me help you, let me show you how useful I can be, and I *swear* to you, your butter and cheese shall be the *finest* in all of London!"

"No," Robert said in a single, abrupt, clipped syllable. "Absolutely not. I will not hear of it."

"But *why not*?" I demanded, a petulant, desperate whine creeping into my voice.

"Because I said so," Robert said simply. "I will not be made the laughingstock of London by having my wife running around London playing at dairymaid."

"You just do not want me at Kew!" I accusingly retorted. "Elizabeth does not want me at Kew! She is the lady of that house, and there is no place for me in it, not even for my portrait!"

But Robert wasn't listening; he was already walking towards the door.

Suddenly he paused, as if he had forgotten something, and turned back to look at me, staring hard. There was something shrewd and calculating in his eyes that made me shiver as if a goose had just walked over my grave. Slowly, he came back to me, put his hands on my shoulders, and looked me straight in the eye.

"When you were babbling on, telling me that *ludicrous* tale about Red Jack, you said he spared your life because Death had already marked you. What did you mean by that? Are you unwell, my darling?"

I hung my head in shame and nodded, not daring to meet his eyes.

"Amy, dear," Robert said softly, his voice like a caress, and indeed as he spoke those words, he lifted his hand to stroke my cheek. "If there is something wrong, you *must* tell me. I am your husband, and in spite of our . . . difficulties, you are still very dear to me." He put his hand beneath my chin and tilted it up, making me look at him. "Tell me, my sweet, my darling little buttercup, tell me, so, whatever it is, we can make it better."

"I . . . I . . ." Tears pooled in my eyes. I *so* wanted to believe him, but his sincerity no longer rang true to my ears; every word sounded feigned and false, like poison hidden in honey. I *wanted* to believe, I *wanted* to hope, but I *couldn't,* and yet . . . *I couldn't stop!* "Th-There is a . . . a . . ."

"Come now, my darling, be brave, and tell me," Robert cajoled. "Out with it. Keeping it bottled up inside you only makes it worse—you know that, Buttercup. Remember what the Scriptures say—the truth will set you free."

I took a deep breath and let the words come rushing out. "I have a cancer in my breast!"

Robert just stared at me. "Is that so, my darling? Are you quite *sure* it is cancer, and not an abscess, or a boil, or some other bump or blemish? You know how excitable, imaginable, and prone to panic and think the worst you are."

"I am *quite* certain." I nodded. "It *is* cancer, Robert—I *know* it! If it were an abscess, it would have burst by now. Pirto's aunt had one, and we've tried all the remedies, but upon me, they all failed. The lump has only grown larger and more painful, and . . . there is a . . . a . . . an . . . unpleasant discharge that is sometimes tinged with blood."

"I see." Robert nodded gravely. "Well, then, you shall have the *best* doctor in London, my darling," he said, just as if he were promising I would have the prettiest gown at the next court ball. He leaned forward then and brushed his lips lightly against mine. "I want my Buttercup Bride to have the *very best* of care! I'll go at once and arrange it," he said, and he started for the door again.

"Robert, *please*!" I caught desperately at his hand. "Do not send me back to Compton Verney. It is a *terrible,* frightening place!

I *cannot* rest there! My food is poisoned, and I am sorely afraid that Richard Verney will murder me! *Please,* Robert, if you have ever loved, ever cared, for me, *please,* find me somewhere else to stay!"

"I have already made arrangements for you to leave," Robert said, reaching out to stroke my hair with a tenderness that now only terrified me; I couldn't believe it was sincere, it had come back all too suddenly. "Richard has told me how sorely jangled your nerves have been beneath his roof. In fact, they have been *most* disruptive to the peace of his household, and his servants have become wary of you; some even openly declare you are a madwoman and refuse to be alone with you. So I have already accepted, on your behalf, an invitation from my treasurer, Anthony Forster, to go keep his wife and children company at the house he is leasing, Cumnor Place. I shall take you there myself in November, before the Christmas festivities begin at court and I haven't a moment to spare even for myself. It is near Oxford, and only a day, or half a day's, ride from London, depending on which palace the court is staying at, so it will be much more convenient for me to visit you. You shall have your own wing, overlooking the centre courtyard on one side and on the other a beautiful park with fine shady trees, flowers, and a pond. Mrs Forster's children love the pond; I'm told they like to catch frogs there, so their antics should amuse you. It will be like having your own little household, and you needn't mingle with the others if you don't want to, but there are other ladies staying there as well, so if you want company, then you shan't be lonely. You see, my dear little buttercup"—he bent and smacked a kiss onto my lips—"your husband has thought of *everything*! Now, I'm off to find a doctor to make my Buttercup Bride all better!"

And then he was gone.

When the door closed behind him, I started shaking, trembling so hard, I had to take up Red Jack's velvet cloak and wind it tightly around me again. Why hadn't I thought to show it to Robert? It proved I had been telling the truth. I sat on the window seat and gazed out into the courtyard, contemplating all that had just occurred. I *knew* it was Red Jack I had seen having angry words with Richard Verney and throwing a purse at his feet. Surely it was not just a coincidence that it was the coach carrying me to London that he had waylaid? And why had Robert denied it, insisting that it was a spice merchant quarrelling with Verney? Whenever he spoke of Verney, he painted a picture of a sentimental and cowardly man that contradicted everything I myself had seen and experienced with him. Regardless of what Robert said, Richard Verney was *not* the sort of man who would weep over a dead dog or piss his pants if he ever came face-to-face with a highwayman. On the contrary, down there in the courtyard with Red Jack, he had seemed fully in command of himself; he had kept his back straight, and no wet spots had appeared in the dirt between his feet. I *knew* what I had seen. That was no quarrel over spices, and the purse of coins flung down into the dust had been for something far more unsavoury, that, to his credit, Red Jack had rejected. I huddled there, shivering in his cloak, and wondered what would become of me. I didn't trust Robert; his manner had been too cunning, too silky, when he queried me about my condition, calling me affectionate names he had not used in years. It made me wish I had not told him. My life had become like a maze I constantly blundered about in, taking wrong turns and coming up against walls, making mistakes that, by the time I realised they were mistakes, it was too late to undo them. And telling Robert that I had cancer felt like yet another mistake, one that could prove to be as deadly as the cancer itself.

"God, help me!" I prayed as I sat there, huddled on the window seat wrapped in the highwayman's red cloak. "*Please!* Deliver me from my desperation; I am *so* afraid!"

I thought I would be seeing a doctor soon, one of London's best and most learned physicians, that he would come to the inn to examine me and mayhap prescribe some remedy superior to those I had tried, but when Robert returned, he was alone. He sat down on the side of my bed, took my hand in his, and said that he had discussed my condition in great detail with the Queen's own physician and that the doctor had concluded that there was no need to insult my modesty with a personal examination. Instead, he had given Robert a vial of hemlock pills for me, though he advised that I wait until I was settled at Cumnor to start taking them, due to the deleterious side effects I was certain to suffer. Robert promised that he would arrange for a doctor to come from Oxford to visit me often and keep me well supplied with all the necessary pills and potions I would need, including the hemlock. And, he stipulated, I *must* obey him *completely* and do *everything* the doctor said, and take *every* remedy he prescribed *exactly* as instructed.

"But they will make you *very, very* sick," Robert cautioned as he placed the vial of green pills in my hand, "for that is how they work. They will poison the disease until it is dead and make you feel as if you are on the very brink of the grave, but you *must* take them just the same. Don't stop until you are *fully* recovered. Promise me to take them faithfully. *Promise me,* Amy."

Hemlock I knew was a deadly poison. My hand began to shake, causing the pills to rattle against the glass vial, as my eyes searched Robert's face. Were the pills he had just given me murder in the guise of medicine? I could not tell by his face. By his firm, unwavering gaze, Robert might as well have been playing cards.

"*Promise* me, Amy," he said again, "that you will take the pills, even though it feels like you are swallowing death itself; promise me that you will keep taking them until you are well, that you won't stop until the doctor pronounces you cured."

"I promise, Robert," I lied, just to put an end to it. I had no intention of taking even one of those vile, evil little green pills.

"That's my girl!" Robert smiled and bent to kiss my brow again. "My Buttercup Bride shall soon be well, and we will put the past and all our problems behind us and make a new start!"

I smiled and said I hoped so with all my heart, but I didn't believe a word of it.

After that he didn't linger; he said he would come to Compton Verney next month to fetch me and from there escort me to Cumnor. I nodded and smiled to please Robert and speed him on his way, whilst inside my heart pulsed and pounded with fear. I could only pray that Cumnor Place would be better than Compton Verney.

❧ 26 ❧

Elizabeth

Richmond Palace, London
September 1559

For the second time in my life I saw a woman's heart break upon her face. I saw the horror, the dawning realisation, the awakening, like a brutal slap or a pail of ice water thrown in her face, as she discovered that all her suspicions, everything she didn't want to believe, were true; her life and the love she held so dear were all a lie that, even as the shattered fragments fell about her, she wanted desperately to piece back together. As I watched Amy's heart shatter and tears drown her blue green eyes, in my mind I was catapulted back to the day my stepmother, Katherine Parr, discovered me on the staircase at Chelsea in her husband's arms. Tom Seymour was, just like Robert, another charming, handsome rascal who did not deserve his wife's love, but both Katherine, and now Amy, were too blind and wounded to see that.

As Amy fled, crashing blindly through the crowded corridors, Robert turned to me; he actually opened his arms to me, as if he thought I would run into them, but I stormed past him into my bedchamber and slammed the door. I ordered my ladies, who sat gossiping over their needlework, to get out, and Kat to sit outside my door and keep everyone away. I wanted to be alone.

For the third time in my life I had come between a man and his wife. In my giddy, green girlhood I had succumbed to the seductive, virile charm of Tom Seymour, and, to save my life, during the reign of my brainsick sister, I had flirted and dallied with her beloved consort, Philip, and now, as Queen in my own right, craving passion and excitement, to be a woman without being a wife, I had discovered that my trusted childhood friend was also a liar, that what I did, thinking I was hurting no one, had actually broken a heart.

I poured myself a goblet of wine and sat and stared into the fire and wondered just how much of what he had told me about his marriage was true.

Amy's eyes told me that Robert had lied. They were the eyes of a wronged and wounded woman. And that was not the face of a woman who no longer loved her husband and was content to bide apart from him. I saw the desperation and longing; I felt it, as if her angry, furious pain had reached out and slapped me. Amy's love was still alive, palpable, kicking and fighting, though Robert's had clearly died. Amy was fighting with all her might to hold on, to win back what she had lost, while Robert wanted only to put the past behind him and go forward, following the blinding-bright star of his ambition. No doubt when he squinted his eyes and tilted his head just right, that star looked just like a crown. And the pretty country girl who had worn a crown of buttercups on her golden curls on her wedding day must be put aside, cruelly, callously, and cold-heartedly, while Robert ploughed on, indifferent to her pain. Poor Amy! She was the sacrificial lamb to Robert's ambition.

She was much altered since I had seen her last. I wondered if she had been ill. She had lost weight; though by no means slender as a reed, she was no longer the round and rosy young girl of seventeen I remembered striding across the meadow with a bouquet of buttercups on that joyous June day nine years ago. Had the worry and fear I had seen eaten her flesh away? She was very pale, and it was not the work of fashionable cosmetics, and her eyes were deep-sunken and dark-shadowed. I myself was no stranger to fear, I had seen its mark on her, and I knew I had been looking at a *very* frightened woman. But what was she so afraid of? There was more to this than met the eye, and I would have the truth laid bare before me.

I shouted for Kat to send Robert in, but she told me he had

gone, in pursuit of his wife no doubt. I left orders for him to come to me the moment he returned and commenced pacing back and forth before the fireplace, the crimson petticoat he had given me rustling and swaying with every step, as I awaited him. I would have answers, even if I had to pry them from Robert like a tooth-drawer with his forceps, even if I had to wrestle them out and draw blood; when I was done, the truth would lie naked before me, exposed and vulnerable, without a shadow to hide it.

I was seated at my dressing table, tapping my nails upon the gilded wood, when Lettice boldly knocked.

"Come!" I called, thinking it would be Robert, my spine stiffening as I steeled myself for the coming confrontation. But it was only my cousin, Lettice Knollys, that brazen minx, and my spine eased, and I settled back against the cushions of my chair again and continued drumming my nails.

"I have brought Your Majesty's hairpins. I retrieved them from the garden," Lettice said with feigned solicitude; she was as transparent as the finest Venetian glass, and I knew she couldn't have possibly cared less about my hairpins. If curiosity hadn't driven her to come, she would have left them where they lay, to be ground into the dirt or ruined by the rain if their sparkle didn't prompt a thief to pocket them before the weather changed. I could see the greedy, hungry curiosity in her eyes begging to be fed and sated, just as I could tell she was bursting to talk, and I could easily guess what about.

I held my hand out for them before she could bend over to deposit the glittering handful inside the enamelled box that sat upon my dressing table for this purpose.

"Don't bother. I'm not a man, and I've no desire to see your paps, girl," I said in a voice tart and weary.

A moue of anger puckered Lettice's boldly painted mouth, and she bobbed a swift, straight-backed curtsy and let the pins fall into my cupped palm.

"Shall I brush Your Majesty's hair?" she asked, lingering behind my chair.

I stared straight ahead, into my looking glass, and fixed her with a firm gaze. "I'm not blind, Lettice, and you'll never win a fortune at cards; I can see the laughter squirming inside you like a piglet in a sack. Spare us both the pretence, and let it out."

"Lady Dudley!" she blurted out in a bubble of snickering laughter. "Wasn't she a sight? What a spectacle! Did you ever see such a pathetic creature in your life? She looked about to burst into tears the whole time; her lips and her chin trembled, and her voice shook. She is as gauche as a peasant in a satin petticoat; she doesn't know how to act like a great man's wife! Why, she talked to me as if I were a queen and she a servant, so soft and nervous, as if she were afraid of giving offence! No wonder Lord Robert keeps her hidden away in the country! He has every reason to be ashamed of her! Looking at her, I couldn't begin to guess why he married her! We all used to marvel that no one knew her—apparently she hasn't a friend in the world, and now I know why!"

"She has one," I said softly, thoughtfully, speaking more to myself than to Lettice. "She just doesn't know it."

Caught up in the throes of her laughter, Lettice didn't hear me and had to ask me to repeat myself, but I thought better of it and instead retorted, "And what impressions, I wonder, did *you* give Lady Dudley about the ladies of my court? That they are all ill-mannered gossips who paint their faces and dress themselves like strumpets and, to bolster their own sense of superiority and pride, though it already be bursting at the seams of their too tightly laced gowns, converge like a gaggle of pecking geese upon anyone who is different, timid, or nervous, and mock, ridicule, disdain, and insult that person? That is certainly what *I* would have thought if I were Lady Dudley! I am ashamed and appalled that she was given such a rude welcome, though I hesitate to call it that, as it was anything but welcoming, and sent her running away like a frightened rabbit pursued by a pack of snarling, barking hounds!"

Anger flared high in Lettice's eyes, and she rounded boldly on me, like a she-cat with her claws unsheathed.

"It was not *I* who sent her running! It was the shock of coming upon her husband and you—"

I picked up my heavy, ornate, gold-backed hairbrush and banged it hard upon the table. "Do not presume that the familiar blood we share gives you leave to dismiss with deference and respect in my presence and say and do whatever you please, Cousin Lettice. Your youth and beauty will *not* excuse or save you; remember our other cousin, Katherine Howard! Now, *get out!*"

"Very well, Your Majesty," Lettice said with frigidly feigned politeness, spreading her skirts wide and bending low in a much exaggerated curtsy, the better to flaunt the bosom that threatened to burst from her vulgar pink bodice, before, with a briefly flashed gloating and superior smile, she left me with her head held as high as if she were herself a queen.

I flung my hairbrush after her and rose to pace again, agitated and swift, back and forth across the floor, while I waited for Robert.

An hour passed, then two, before he came striding, with a broad smile and open arms, across my threshold.

I rose from my chair and went to the middle of my chamber, standing my ground instead of going to meet him, silent and grave instead of smiling and laughing as I usually was when he came to me. When he reached me, I slapped the smile right off his face.

"You have been lying to me all along," I said.

Robert stared back at me with wide-eyed amazement as he massaged the smarting red handprint I had left on his face.

"You hellcat—you have drawn blood!" he exclaimed as he lowered his hand and regarded the red smears on his fingers. And I saw that indeed my rings had cut him in two places, tiny slits in the sun-bronzed skin from which blood slowly welled and trickled. But I was not about to apologise.

"You have been lying to me all along," I repeated. "I saw the hurt in her eyes; I saw her heart break . . ."

Breathing like an irate bull, Robert rolled his eyes and snorted, "Amy never could curtail her emotions, damn her! She is a disgrace to herself and to me!"

"There is nothing new under the sun or the moon," I sighed, turning and walking away from him, resuming my pacing. "Philip used to say the same thing of my sister."

"And he was right, and so am I!" Robert insisted, as he plucked a white silk kerchief from his sleeve and pressed it to his bleeding cheek.

"A queen cannot let her heart control her mind, Robert. It is a *constant,* enduring, lifelong struggle to not let one's personal feelings run wild and unchecked, for the destruction and havoc they can unleash, the dire repercussions that can rebound upon oneself and one's subjects. My sister was, God rest her, living proof of what happens when a queen forgets or ignores this. But Amy is *not* a queen, Robert—she's a *real* woman, free to be herself, and unseemly as some might find such a show of emotion, it is also the truth unmasked and unvarnished, uncloaked by courtly manners and diplomacy." I sighed and turned from him and began pacing again. "Thrust, parry, deflect—it's like a duel, isn't it, Robert? This is not about Amy's conduct. In truth, she is not at fault. She has *every* right to be upset and, in the throes of pain, to forget herself and throw the teachings of the etiquette books out the window. You are simply trying to deflect and disown the blame, to assign it to another, to distract from the fact that you lied. You told me the love between you had died, that you had grown apart and gone your separate ways, Amy contentedly to the country, and you to court, and never the twain shall meet. But you are the only one who would have it so; you left her—with what lies and promises, I do not know—but she did not gladly let you go, this I know. I daresay she has done all in her power to bring you back to her. How many letters has she written imploring your return, beseeching you to come visit her? But it is an easy lie for you to sell, and you must no doubt account the circumstances fortuitous—an obedient wife of a timid and docile nature who is kept cloistered in the country, as a guest in the homes of men who are loyal to you, owe you favours, or want your patronage, without friends or family to speak up for her, to spread the word that she is being wronged. You have most effectively silenced her and made her invisible, imprisoned her in oblivion. You have fooled and deceived everyone, until today, when I saw the love still alive in Amy's eyes. Only *you* have consigned your love to the charnel house."

"So what if I have?" Robert shrugged. "She'll be there herself soon enough, and then we need never worry about her again, and never waste another moment talking or thinking of her either!"

"What do you mean?" I demanded.

"I mean she is dying," Robert answered, striding across the room and putting his hands on my shoulders as he gazed down intently into my eyes. "I've only just found out, she has a cancer of the breast. Darling, don't you see?" He had the temerity to *smile* at me, as if this were *happy* news, a *good* thing! "Now we have only to wait! She can't last long, and her death will spare me the expense and bother—and the scandal of course—of procuring a divorce. Hallelujah, God *is* good! Aye, my love." He would have pulled me close, but I put up my hands to stop him. "God is smiling down on us; this is a sign of His approval. He wants us to be together as man and wife, to fulfil the destiny that was written in the stars for us at the hour of our birth, and He in His infinite wisdom is removing the only obstacle that stands in our path. Soon He shall take Amy home to Him, and she shall bother and vex us no more! This cancer in her breast is God's judgment visited upon her; it is divine punishment for her refusing to be a reasonable woman and an obedient wife and give me a divorce when I asked her to. God is punishing her for her sins and blessing and rewarding me—and you!" he added as a brightly smiling afterthought.

"You lying whoreson, bastard, traitor, you insensitive brute!" The hellcat inside of me was unleashed, and I struck him again and again, slapping and punching him, kicking, clawing, and pummelling until his back was to the wall and his arms up to shield his face from my nails. "I can't think of anything bad enough to call you! How *dare* you *smile*? How *dare* you *rejoice*? *I* am a woman too, Robert. I have breasts!"

"*Beautiful* breasts," Robert affirmed, swiftly raising his arms again as I launched another onslaught of blows.

"How *dare* you act like this is cause for celebration? How dare you speak for God and say this is His retribution and reward? *Get out!*" I screamed. "*Get out!* I am mad enough to kill you with my bare hands!"

"At once, my darling. I can see you are overwhelmed by this news. It is as if the clouds are lined with gold and raining diamonds down upon us!" Robert said as he stepped around me, his smiling bravado marred by wincing groans as I continued to follow him, raining blow after blow, pummelling his back with my fists and kicking at his calves and buttocks. He made for the door that led to the rooms adjoining mine that I had recently awarded him as a sign of my great favour, an action that had both scandalised and titillated my entire court and, in the eyes of the foreign ambassadors, hung a dark cloud of suspicion over my morals. "I have some medicines I want to send to Amy . . ."

"Medicine?" I ran around in front of him so I could see his face. "What *kind* of medicine, Robert?" I demanded.

Robert shrugged. "I'm no doctor, sweet. They're just medicines to ease the poor woman's suffering; Tamworth is packing them now, I believe." He grabbed my wrist and drew me to him. "You have wounded me deeply, Bess. I am not a man without feeling, and you wound me to the depths of my soul by thinking I am, just because I am honest enough to admit that this is *good* news for *us,* for *our* future, and to be pleased about it. But that does *not* mean I do not care that Amy is being struck down by this horrible disease. How can you credit me with such coldness, such callousness, you who have seen me weep over the death of horses?"

"If you are waiting for me to apologise," I said coldly, "I would advise you not to hold your breath!" Then I rushed on past him, flinging the door wide with such force that it pulverised the painted plaster acorns carved upon the wall, and I stormed like a whirlwind into his bedchamber.

"Mr Tamworth!" I called.

Instantly the valet stopped what he was doing and fell to his knees before me.

"Mr Tamworth." I drew myself up regally before him, endeavouring to appear calm and in full possession of myself, for it was impossible that he had not overheard my frenzied attack upon his master. "I believe you are preparing some medicines to send to Lady Dudley?"

"Yes, Your Majesty." He gestured to the table, where some glass bottles sat alongside a box and some wads of wool and lengths of cloth he obviously meant to wrap and pad them with. "I have them here."

I reached out and picked up a bottle filled with a murky green liquid. Boldly, I uncorked it. The stench of it was enough to make my nose want to flee my face, but I kept a firm grip on it and stared Robert straight in the eyes.

"Will this harm her?" I asked, my eyes boring into his, digging for the truth.

"Of course not!" Robert cried. "Elizabeth, how could you possibly think . . ." His mouth dropped, gaping open in a wide, slack *O,* as I put the bottle to my lips, like an open-mouthed kiss against the cold, hard, glass rim. *"Elizabeth! No!"* He lunged, hurling himself across the room at me, knocking me down flat, and as we fell together onto the floor, to lie disordered and entangled like lovers, the bottle flew from my hand and shattered against the stone hearth.

"Liar!" I hissed, slapping at him, struggling beneath the weight of his body, panting and pale, his brow beaded with a sweat of guilt or fear.

"I *swear* to you, I am not," he said, gazing down at me, as he grappled to grasp my wrists and pin them to the floor above my head to restrain me, even as I continued to thrash beneath him. "But I *had* to stop you. You might have harmed yourself. You are not ill and have no need of such strong medicine, my love. I was afraid it might harm you, to take it thus, direct from the bottle, its strength undiluted, when it is meant to be taken a little at a time and mixed with wine to make it palatable."

I drove my knee into his groin, and as he rolled away, cradling his privy parts, grimacing and groaning, I struggled to my feet.

I stood with my back to him and took a deep breath to steady myself before I turned around again and stared down at him.

"Hear me now, Robert Dudley." At the icy strength in my voice he stilled, though his hands still clutched between his legs. "And commit every word I speak to memory. As Amy's husband you may be in the eyes of most her lord and master, but do not attempt to play God and decide whether she lives or dies. My father killed two of his wives, one of them my mother, the other my cousin, so do not imagine that I will take kindly to a man who does the same. If Amy is to die, then let her die in peace, and let it be by God's will and in His own time; do not seek to hasten it. And do not think to be King *ever*; relinquish those mad dreams *now* before they lead you to do murder. I have always told you the honest and plain truth that I will never marry anyone; I will *never* marry *you*! The games I play I play for my own reasons, for England first and my vanity and amusement second, but when I am dead and buried, the stonemasons will carve upon my tombstone: Here lies Elizabeth the Queen, who lived and died a virgin!"

"Elizabeth! *I love you!*" With pleading eyes Robert rose onto his knees, like a supplicant kneeling before me, and reached out his hands, like one begging the statue of a saint for a miracle. "*Please, do not deny our love!*"

But I held my ground. I didn't melt. I didn't waver or weaken. "I warn you, Robert, if *any* harm befalls Amy, if she dies by poison or any other foul or unnatural means, you *will* pay for it like any other murderer upon the gallows or the scaffold. My favour does not place you above the Law or entice Justice to turn a blind eye. You will not hide behind my petticoats. I will *not* shield you. Remember that." And I left him, this man who had lied to and betrayed two women who had both loved him, to ponder those words.

I was silent as Kat undressed me, but when I was alone in the darkness behind the closed velvet curtains of my bed, I let my tears soak my pillow. I had seen the ugliness that hid behind the handsome face of Robert Dudley, the callous granite hardness and the heart of ice that lay beneath the warmth and charm of the smiling façade he presented to the world at large. I had always known he had a ruthless streak, that Ambition was his guiding star, but I had also thought he had a heart. And though I eventually slept, rest and peace were both denied me as in my dreams the ghost of Tom Seymour stood beside me, his arm about my waist, his fingers roving and caressing, and his lips at my ear, singing in a soft, lust-dripping, voice intended just for me, of "Cakes and Ale" as we watched Robert's radiant and smiling "Buttercup Bride" walk barefoot across the meadow, blind to the warning presence of the sad-eyed, diaphanous white phantoms of Katherine Parr and my sister Mary floating alongside her like reluctant bridesmaids, frantic but powerless to stop her, as she walked towards a future, and a man, she should have been running away from. I also was powerless to stop her. I could only watch in horror as she went smiling with a loving heart and in good faith to embrace her fate—a handsome, hot-blooded youth who married her in rash and raging lust, only to afterwards punish and hate and blame her for his mistake when a brighter star rose in the sky, to tantalisingly and mockingly remind him of a destiny he thought should have, and could have, been his if only he weren't already married. And even as he leapt and grasped for the star, that looked from high above so like a crown, Amy was there, grabbing his ankles, to weigh and pull him back down. Would he shed her innocent blood to free him from this burden that impeded his rise? He was blinded by the halo of bright golden light that surrounded the crown; he could not see that he was reaching and grasping for something he could never have. If he killed her, Amy would die in vain.

In the cold darkness, still hours before dawn's first light, I sprang from my bed, feeling feverish and hot, desperate to escape from the clinging shroud of sheets that damply entangled my limbs, and the disturbing dreams that held me an unwilling prisoner and denied me rest. I shook back my hair and untangled the sweat-dampened white linen folds of my nightgown from my limbs and began to pace, my body as restless as my mind.

Weary but wide awake, I sank down at the table upon which my ebony and ivory chessboard sat. I lined up the pieces, positioning them ready for a new game, and sat back and stared at them, thoughtfully, intensely, tapping my chin. Robert, the man I had loved, in my own unconventional way, was my invisible opponent across this board, so different from real life in which there were many shades of grey betwixt the stark black and white squares. I had been born into this game of royal intrigue, playing from the start, for my life, my title—the triumphant *Princess* instead of the disgraced *King's bastard*—for this kingdom of England, and the crown I was born to wear. Even though I had won, that did not mean I could sit back, enjoy my laurels, and disdain to play any more. The game must go on, the pieces continually reset, my opponents ever changing, again and again, as long as my life endured, as long as it, and England, were worth fighting for.

I picked up the black king and stared at him intently. *"Robert!"* I felt the carved ebony bite sharply into my palm as I grasped it tightly, wanting to smash, to shatter it, but instead, after a moment, I set it down again. *"You shall not win!"* I said with a defiant toss of my head. *"I shall best you!* And I shall do it in such a way that you will think twice before you ever *dare* challenge me again! *This is war!"* And with my arm I swept all the pieces from the board. Then

I folded my arms over the black and white board, laid my head down, and wept as I waited for the sun to rise. I wept because, once again, I must fight against myself, the passion and desire that always simmered and sometimes boiled and even flared into flames inside me that reached high, trying to burn away my reason, to scorch out caution and make it flee from me like one who has awakened in the night to a burning house, desperate to escape the inferno, and the man who stirred and aroused that passion, making it leap into bright flame, a man who used passion to win what he desired, and what he wanted most was my crown. Desire my body and claim to love me though he might, had I been a beggarmaid or a squire's daughter like Amy, I would have been forgotten the moment his lust was spent. Robert Dudley's eyes were on a greater, more glittering, prize. He wanted to sit upon a throne; he was not a man to be content with a comfortable fireside chair.

One of the chess pieces had fallen into my lap, and I picked it up. A pawn, one of the weakest and most numerous pieces in the game. A white pawn—*Amy!* In my mind's eye I saw her, in her bare feet and wedding gown as I always pictured her, frightened and running frantically back and forth across the black and white squares of a chessboard, buttercups falling and scattering from her bouquet and crown as she tried to evade Robert, the Black King who was trying to capture her, to vanquish and get past her, as only she stood between him and the White Queen—*me*! *"You'll never win!"* I told him from where I stood, white-gowned and defiant, my feet planted firmly upon the black square beneath me. "I *promise,"* I whispered as I gazed down at the white pawn in my hand, "he will *never* win!"

❧ 27 ❧

Amy Robsart Dudley

The Spa at Buxton
and
Syderstone Manor in Norfolk
October 1559

Though I returned to Compton Verney, I had already decided that I would not tarry there waiting for Robert. I had made up my mind—I would not eat another morsel beneath Richard Verney's roof. I would return in time for Robert to escort me to my new lodgings at Cumnor Place, but I wanted to go my own way for a while. I had long heard of the miraculous cures wrought by the healing waters at Buxton, both by drinking the mineral-rich water drawn from St Anne's Well and from soaking in the sulphurous hot springs. Invalids and those troubled by more trifling ails had been flocking to Buxton since Roman times; it was especially renowned for its beneficial effects upon rheumatism, arthritis, gout, and all manner of aches and cramps, so I thought there *must* be *some* good to be had there. And I wanted to try it, to see if it might, if God or His saints be willing, burn the cancer from my breast, and then . . . even though it was no longer my home, I wanted to go back to Syderstone. I wanted to see it, just one more time. I wanted to say a proper farewell to my dreams. So Pirto and I each packed a trunk, and away we went on an adventure of our own.

As we rode away from Compton Verney, I felt giddy and free; I felt the excitement growing inside me, like a rose from a bud to full bloom. This time I mounted a merry-spirited bay, who pranced along the road and tossed her silky mane, instead of suffering the confines of a carriage that made me feel as if my teeth would be jarred loose every time the wheels dipped into a rut or went over a stone. And I laughed as the blue and yellow ribbons that trimmed my hat flew out and flapped behind me, as if they were waving farewell to Compton Verney and its malicious, murderous master. And at every inn we stopped at along the way, I ate so heartily, I laughed and jested that I was right glad that Pirto had brought along her sewing basket, for she might have to let out my gowns again before long, for "I shall soon be round as a partridge again!"

I was too ashamed, too fearful of facing the revulsion in others' eyes, to take the waters publicly in the daylight hours, when men and women of all classes freely mixed together in the bathhouse. But being Lord Robert's wife, I discovered, had certain advantages, and, for a fee, I was able to have the bathhouse all to myself during the wee hours when all the other guests of the spa were in their beds. And for twenty days, at two in the morning, wearing a sheer white bathing smock beneath my buttercup yellow brocade dressing gown, with my hair pinned high and tightly upon my head, as I had been warned the water might leech out its colour, I traversed the long white marble-columned walkway, following a yawning young boy, roused from his sleep by the kitchen hearth, bearing a torch to light my way. I always thanked him kindly and gave him a coin before he left me alone at the door.

I went into the torchlit white marble bathhouse alone. Columns, ridged up and down and crowned with carved bouquets of flowers, and statuary of women, both draped and nude, in the style of ancient Rome, circled the large steaming pool. The bare-breasted women, some missing arms or even their heads, made me shiver as they loomed out at me from the roiling mist, a sight made even more eerie by the flickering torchlight. The ones with heads seemed to stare at me with their blank and sightless white marble eyes. I always hung my robe over the most disturbing one, a headless, armless woman whose perfect breasts seemed to glow, rubbed shiny, one of the bath attendants had told me, by the hands of countless men who always caressed them for luck before entering the bath.

Carefully, I descended the sunken marble steps into the hot, sulphurous, healing waters, walking boldly into the mist. My bare feet slid upon the marble-tiled bottom as the full skirt of my smock floated up and billowed like a white flower about my hips, and the waters caressed my limbs, their warmth seeming to reach beneath the skin to burn the ache and chase any cold right out of my bones. There were several marble benches submerged beneath the water, and I waded across the pool to sit on the one that directly faced the door. I would rest there, up to my neck in water, the vapours caressing my face, until six o'clock, when, bundled back into my robe again, I would emerge into the pale morning light, pausing to listen to the birdsong, as I made the return journey along the marble-columned path back to the inn to fall into bed and sleep the best part of the day away.

The attendant physician visited me every afternoon at three to make sure I was following his instructions and drinking eight tall glasses of water drawn from St Anne's Well every day, even though I found it acrid and bitter, and it felt as though a snail leaving a nasty, burning trail were crawling down my throat, and to ensure that I did not remain sequestered in my room, "cloistered like a nun," he teased with mock severity, and walked each day for at least an hour in the pleasure gardens and joined the other guests for the evening's entertainments.

I did all that he required of me, though I shied away from too close an acquaintance with the spa's other guests. I was startled to find that in this place of sickness and desperate hope, where 'most everyone was praying for a miracle, a festive, holiday atmosphere prevailed. Everyone was trying to pretend that their ailment was a trifling one, that they had only come because this was such a jolly, fashionable spot to lose a few pounds after indulging overmuch in rich foods—"my decadence at the dinner table has cost me dear!" they would quip—or for a few days' much-needed rest away from life's hectic, merry whirl. The gaunt, hollow-eyed consumptives, pale as chalk beneath their flushed cheeks, would hide their bloody handkerchiefs, balling them into tight little balls squeezed tightly in their clenched fists after a coughing fit and say it was naught but a cold; they had been foolish and gone out in the rain or lingered overlong in the garden without a shawl after the evening cool set in. "It's nothing!" they would say with an airily dismissive laugh while two words hung invisible and unspoken after the exclamation point: *just death!* Yet all of them were grasping eagerly at life, like a hungry infant for its mother's milk-filled breast, trying to hold on to the one thing they didn't want to lose, even though they could feel it slipping away beneath their frantically grasping fingers. Saddest of all to see were the ones who realised that it was no use and, with a weary sigh, just let go.

Sometimes, as I left my room in the wee hours to go to the bathhouse, I would see their sheet-shrouded forms being carried out by servants tiptoeing in their stockinged feet so as not to disturb the other guests, wanting no one to come to his door and peep out and catch sight of the corpse. The next day, none of the other guests would mention the missing; it was as if that person had never even been there at all, and any who blundered and happened to speak his name would be greeted by blank stares, as if they had just mentioned a complete stranger.

Even though I did not encourage it, I did not lack for companionship. I had three beautiful new dresses: the first of glossy black satin embroidered with white snowdrops and trimmed with frothy snow white lace, and I wore ropes of pearls with it, and a white lace veil and jaunty curling white ostrich plumes and a brooch shaped like a cluster of flowers made of pearls with emerald leaves on my round black velvet hat; the second a shimmering apple green satin embroidered all over with a shower of pink and white apple blossoms trimmed with white lace and pink ribbons with a French hood to match; and the third a gown and matching hood of palest purple the colour of iced lilacs embroidered with pink and silver thistles trimmed with pink ribbons and silvery lace, and a long rope of pearls the palest hue of pink that looked beautiful with either of the latter two dresses. And whenever I went out to walk, it pleased my pride to see how many men there were so eager to make my acquaintance and squire me about the gardens. Sometimes I had three, or even five, and sometimes as many as *seven* gentlemen of various ages all wanting to walk and talk with me, vying to be the one to take my arm or bring me cups of St Anne's water and plates of dainty cakes and tarts to tempt my appetite and sit beside me at supper. And if I sat in the garden, even those suffering from gout were all too eager to hobble and limp away to fetch a shawl for my shoulders at the least little nip of chill in the air. Some of them even made so bold as to whisper into my ear when I danced with them or when they sidled close as we watched the acrobats, magicians, dancers, and puppet shows that entertained us at the inn each evening, that they would like to be my lover, to come to me that night, but I fled them all like a frightened rabbit. Though one night, as a display of fireworks, like an exploding rainbow, burst high above our heads in the darkened garden, I let a young man kiss me. But when his hands began to rove and his kisses to grow more urgent, I pushed him away and ran. I ploughed right into the chest of another gentleman, and he also stole a kiss before I whirled, laughing, from his arms. For just a moment I felt light, airy, and carefree, but my feet always, all too quickly, touched hard, solid ground before I too far forgot myself. Though sometimes, when I lay alone, restless and wakeful in my bed, missing a man's touch and warm skin over mine, the feeling of being full inside instead of empty, I would wonder, if it weren't for the cancer, would I have had the courage to boldly whisper back, "Come to me tonight; I will leave my door unlocked."

Though I said nothing of it to the doctor, lest he be shocked and think me a wanton woman with morals lighter than a feather, I suspected that the sultry, hot caresses of the water and the steaming, sulphurous mist against my face inflamed my blood and made it hotter, stirring the lust that had lain dormant inside me. As my smock bubbled up and billowed about my hips when I waded across the pool, I secretly revelled in the rare delight of the bubbling, hot water's teasing caress between my thighs. It made my knees weak, and I feared they would buckle and I would fall, crashing below the surface to bang my head on the tile floor and drown in waters that reminded me of Hell's fire and brimstone. And often as I sat upon the sunken bench, I gave in to the urge and let my thighs fall slack and open wide. And there were times, I blush to admit, when I squirmed and sighed and, hidden beneath the water, behind the curtain of swirling hot mist, I let my hand boldly bunch up my smock and my fingers delve between my legs, to probe and explore as Robert's had once done, though that seemed a whole lifetime ago.

In those days at Buxton I very often found myself stirred by carnal thoughts, and in my dreams, as I slept most of the day away, with the painted ivory medallion of St Agatha resting between my breasts, many a time the bold highwayman Red Jack would clamber through my window in his red velvet cloak and feathered hat to make mad, passionate love to me. When I awoke, I always felt guilty and ashamed, because it was not my husband who coupled with me in my dreams and because I sometimes dared to wonder what it would be like to lie with the men who told me they desired me. Would they be passionate and kind and gentle lovers who did not mind about my breast, or would the desire in their eyes turn to disgust the moment that they saw its ruined and rotted beauty, like a perfect fruit blighted, or would they be rough, hard, and selfish, intent only on their own pleasure? All I did was wonder, and yet I felt as guilty as though I had indeed sinned in the flesh.

After Buxton, I went back to Syderstone. I put on my wedding gown, hoping to recapture some of the joy of my wedding day, but I felt nothing but sorrow as I roamed the crumbling ruins of the abandoned manor, thick with dust and spiderwebs, saying goodbye to the past and farewell to my dreams, knowing that I would never be here again; Syderstone and I were both doomed. In the Great Hall, humming to myself, with a candle in my hand, I danced alone, my naked feet leaving their prints across the dusty floor, a solitary Candlestick Branle. When I glanced up at the gallery, I thought I glimpsed my father watching, smiling down on me, and I cried out, my candlestick clattering to the floor as I fell to my knees and wept.

Instead of feeling light and airy as a cloud, as I walked across the meadow, where the sheep munched clover and thistles, the dress now hung loose and heavy on me, as though its hems were weighted with lead.

I took Robert's letters with me, the ones he wrote when he still loved me, that I had kept all these years tied up in bunches with yellow silk ribbons. I went back to the bed of buttercups by the river and sat there, with his letters on my lap, remembering how it used to be. The lazy afternoons when I lay there, barefoot in my yellow gown, basking in the sun and the loving words that Robert wrote me, I would close my eyes and hug his latest letter to my heart and *savour* his tender words, reading them over and over again until I had committed them to memory and knew them as though each and every word was written on my heart. I would close my eyes and sigh and melt and ache and long for him as I dreamed of his bold yet gentle caresses and the promises he made that I never doubted then that he would keep.

He used to write me just to say he was thinking of me. He said that I was his life, his world, his heart, his everything, that I made him complete, that when he held me in his arms, he had all he ever wanted or needed. He made me feel so important, so special. He promised that we would soon be together. He marvelled at how blessed we were, to marry for love, to be able to spend the rest of our lives together blissfully happy instead of as indifferent partners in a marriage of convenience, a deal brokered for lands, riches, and titles by power-hungry, socially ambitious parents. We had been given the *greatest* gift of all—*a true love match*!

I felt like a fool now, and a discarded toy a fickle child has worn out, broken, or grown bored with and thrown away, but in those days, when I was young and seventeen, I believed every wonderful, joyous word he wrote or spoke to me. Even across the distance he could *still* touch my heart and make my knees feel weak and the whole of me so warm, and safe, and wanted, as if his words wove for me a cloak of love embroidered with hearts and true lovers' knots.

I untied the yellow silk, and as I unfolded each letter, my eyes fell on certain tender phrases that now stabbed like daggers into my heart and made the tears fall down like rain to blur the ink:

> *I promise I will <u>always</u> be there on your birthday so we can celebrate the day the love of my life was born.*

Another lie, another broken promise. I crumpled it tightly in my hand, squeezing it into a small paper ball, and flung it into the river and watched it bob and drift away, like a loving wife watching her sailor husband's ship sail out to sea, wondering if they would ever meet again.

> *I am holding you close in my thoughts, Beloved, until I can hold you in my arms again.*

> *I am thinking of you, my Buttercup; I never stop!*

> *Crumple, crumple*—more lies I consigned to the river.

> *I want to look into your eyes and see myself in them.*

I was too in love to realise that the person he saw reflected in my eyes was the person Robert loved best of all—*himself!*
I crushed the letter in my hand and let the river take it.

> *I long for your touch, I yearn to feel your lips pressed against mine, to lie naked with you, skin to skin, heart to heart!*

He could have felt them every day, if only he had chosen to make a home and a life with me as he promised! Damn him and his lies—let the river take them and drown the lying words as sorrow had my loving heart!

> *You are the bright star of my life, and you shine brightest when in my arms*

But never bright enough to compare to Elizabeth; I never shone as brightly as her crown. *Crumple!* Into the river. Reading these words hurt too much to keep them any longer. Words I once believed, that made me feel so warm and wanted, so important and adored—they were empty, but their hollowness filled me with pain.

> *You are never far from my thoughts or my heart.*

> *Our hearts are one, my darling Buttercup, and we will have a long life together.*

I <u>cannot</u> live without you—you make me complete!

*I <u>long</u> to be with you, to hold you, to kiss and caress
and touch every part of you!*

*Thinking of you, Buttercup, and wishing we lay
together, warm and naked in each other's arms, touching and caressing, happy and blissfully content.*

*When I hold you, I hold the world in my arms—every-
thing that matters and is dearest to me.*

Lies, lies! Lies! Lies! Lies! *Crumple! Crumple! Crumple! Crumple! Crumple!* Into the river to drown them all the way my heart
drowns in sorrow! *I hate you, Robert, I hate you!*

I love how your body feels against mine.

I am thinking of you all hours of the day and night!

*I was thinking of you last night as I closed my eyes,
wanting to feel the warmth of your body next to mine,
your breasts against my chest, and your fingers wrapped
around my big, thick cock, feeling it grow hard in your
dear little hand.*

Crumple! Crumple! Crumple! Sometimes words hurt worse
than broken bones; bones heal, but sometimes hearts don't, and
words *always* have the power to come back to haunt and hurt all
over again!

I knelt there in the bed of buttercups by the river and watched
the wadded and crumpled letters bob and float upon its surface,
forming a little flotilla of falsehoods sailing away from me. And I
left the yellow silk ribbons lying in the grass like yellow worms for
the birds to find, to weave their nests with. Everything he had ever
said that made me feel good was all a lie. I had never been special
at all. I never *really* mattered; even though he married me, I was
just a dalliance he could easily walk away from, crushing and

breaking my heart underfoot, never caring how much it hurt and bled.

A loving heart is the most beautiful and precious gift one person can give to another, and I gave him mine. How could he break it? How could he say all those things—those wonderful, heartwarming, and stirring things—and not mean them? I used to think that I was special, I thought I mattered, I believed I was loved, and that I was important to the man I gave my heart to. Now I knew that I was nothing.

Words are worthless when actions contradict and reveal the lies hidden within. When Robert started breaking promises, that was when the truth first started peeping through the cracks, even though I turned my face away and tried to pretend, to make excuses, because I didn't want to see its harsh and ugly goblin face. I didn't want to face the fact that everything I believed was false. How cruel of him to pretend, to make me believe!

And how *foolish* of me to waste my life away, loving and wanting such a one as he; he didn't deserve my heart, and I deserved better, a love that was true, not a wolf dressed up in sheep's clothing, a human chameleon, a charlatan selling lies and contradictions like the potions the nostrum peddlers sold, touting miracles and wonders inside a glass bottle.

I had been blind for so long, but now I had regained my sight, and I saw Robert fully clear, and yet . . . God, help me! *I still love him!* I don't know why, and I know I shouldn't, but I do, I do, I do! I want him back—but it doesn't make sense! I know it can never be as it was; the hurt goes too deep, perhaps even deeper than did the love, the dream of which I cannot let go. I know I can never trust him again; the fragments, slivers, and shards of too many dashed hopes, shattered dreams, and broken promises lie scattered in the ever-widening gulf that has over the years grown between us. But I *cannot* break the spell of the illusion he sold that girl of seventeen in a bed of buttercups nigh on ten years ago!

All I want is to wake up from the nightmare my life has become and find Robert in bed beside me, smiling into my eyes, calling me his Buttercup, as he takes me into his arms and loves me with all the passion and tenderness he used to.

Let go! Let go! I tell myself. Let go of the dream—it isn't real, and it never *really* was! But if I let go, what is left for me to hold on to? Air as empty as Robert's words of tenderness and love. I'm afraid of falling, but the truth is, I've already fallen. I'm still alive, and yet I'm already dead. He killed me. For what is life without hopes and dreams, something to look forward to, like a welcoming candle in the window on a dark, tar black night? I know all too well the answer to that question. It is a meaningless failure, pain, and nothing; it is waking up every day knowing that you have failed at the only thing in life that matters. Sometimes I laugh—even though it hurts me, and any who saw might think me mad—I laugh until I cry, when I hear the talk that Robert means to murder me, because he already has. I live and breathe, I walk and speak, but I am already dead.

I flung myself facedown in the buttercups where we used to make love and wept, angry with Robert and even angrier at myself, watering their roots with my tears. I cried until I had no tears left and the stars had come out; then I walked slowly back to the house, to make ready to depart at dawn, to return to Compton Verney, to be there, waiting for Robert, when he came to escort me to Cumnor Place, another house that was not my home.

❧ 28 ❧

Amy Robsart Dudley

Cumnor Place, Berkshire, near Oxford
November 1559–February 1560

Cold, grey, bleak, and *dreary* were the first words that sprang to mind when I first beheld Cumnor Place. It was like a large grey stone rectangle with the centre hollowed out to create a grey flagstone courtyard. Everything was so ... *grey!* I dearly hoped the inside was enlivened by some colour and that the Forsters and the others who lodged within wore cheery clothes. The roof was peaked with several sharp gables, like arrows pointing adamantly up to Heaven, and the windows were arched too. The whole place still retained the look of the monastery it had been for over two hundred years until King Henry dissolved the monasteries. Though a few refinements had since been made by the owner, Dr Owen, Cumnor had never become a *true* home and was instead like several separate households existing side by side beneath the same roof, linked only by the Great Hall and the kitchen, buttery, and chapel they all shared. Though it was not a sinister place like Compton Verney, coming to Cumnor felt like arriving at the end of the world to me—desolate, with nowhere else to go, I knew I had reached my journey's end. It did not help that it was a grey November day, drizzling rain, and so cold that it felt as if an invisible torturer were there beside me, sticking needles of ice into me that pierced right through my flesh and drilled holes into my bones that instantly filled with ice water.

I shuddered as we rode through the arched gatehouse into the courtyard, gazing up at the high, vaulted ceiling upon which avenging angels, with shields and swords of fire, did battle against a legion of demons.

There was that shivery, skin-crawling sensation again, up and down my spine and neck, making my hair stand on end. "A goose just walked over my grave," I whispered, but if Robert, riding beside me, heard, he decided to ignore it.

Instinctively, I reached out to touch his arm, forgetting for the moment that I no longer trusted him; I just wanted a little of the comfort and warmth a wife should have from her husband.

"This place frightens me," I confided in a quiet, tremulous whisper. "It's like a tomb, a grey stone tomb; I think you mean to entomb me here, Robert!"

"*Oh, for the love of Christ!*" Robert exclaimed, smacking his brow with his leather-gloved palm. "You're *never* satisfied, Amy! You didn't like it at the Hydes' and, by behaving like a madwoman, saw to it that you had to leave; you thought Richard Verney was trying to poison you and, when that failed, hired a highwayman to kill you on your spur-of-the-moment trip to London, which he knew *nothing* about beforehand—a neat trick that, I must say!—and *now*"—he sighed and waved a hand to take in Cumnor—"this place frightens you! It conjures up macabre fantasies of a tomb, and you think that I, your loving husband, intend to bury you alive here! What will it be next, I wonder. A ghost, an incubus to molest you as you sleep, a blood-sucking demon, or a whole coven of witches? God's teeth, if you weren't a woman, I would tell you to try your hand at writing plays; you've certainly the imagination for it!"

"I'm sorry, Robert . . ." I started to say.

"Yes, you are, Amy," he adamantly agreed with a vigorous nod of his head. "You are a *sorry* woman who is *always* sorry about something!"

Without giving me a chance to answer, he spurred his horse onward and raised his hand to wave as he called out a greeting to

Anthony Forster and his wife, who had just stepped out into the courtyard to welcome us.

I glanced back over my shoulder and saw Thomas Blount riding behind me, looking at me with his eyes full of pity. He looked as if he wanted to say something but didn't know what to say, so to save us both—him from struggling to find the right though futile words, and me from having to hear them—I hastily turned away and hurried to catch up with Robert.

Robert left it to Mrs Forster to show me to my rooms, while he went off to warm his hands and sit by the massive fireplace in the Great Hall and converse with Mr Forster.

The instant I crossed the threshold, I gasped; I had never been so cold in my life! I burned and shivered and tingled and felt so tense, afraid, and wary. It was far worse than Compton Verney, which looked as though it were built to instil fear and give a body bad dreams, whereas Cumnor, though grim and grey, did not look like to harbour terrors, and the Forsters seemed right friendly.

"Come, my dear." Mrs Forster took my arm and gave me an encouraging smile. "It's a cold, clammy place, I know. One would think it were carved from ice instead of stone, but you'll be glad of it come summer, you mark my word! And far too dark, I know! It's *so* difficult to light; no matter how many candles, torches, or rushlights we use, it never seems to be enough to cast out the gloom! It's as though the shadows think this is their home, not ours, and will not be cast out! It does take some getting used to, I know. I *hated* it when I first came here—I thought it was as cold and dark as the grave—but those feelings will soon pass. And your rooms are *lovely*. You have the best wing at Cumnor—I made sure of it myself—and your things have arrived from Compton Verney, and your *darling* cats, and there's a warm fire all ready and waiting for you. You'll soon be as warm as toasted bread and feel right at home with us, I promise. And, later, after you've rested, I'll introduce you to the other ladies who are lodging here, and my children. I do hope you like children, Lady Dudley; mine are rather a rambunctious lot. And I hope you are not afraid of frogs; they catch them in the pond in the park and make pets of them. They've a great bullfrog named Christopher; he jumped on my chest the other night while I was sleeping and nearly scared me to death! I thought the fright would turn my hair stark white!" She laughed and patted her sleek nut brown hair, pinned smoothly back beneath her hood.

She led me to a steep stone staircase that spiralled round a newel post, broken by a landing like a great grey slab of a tombstone in the middle.

As Mrs Forster started up the stairs, I saw a grey-robed figure descending them at the same time. How curious! A monk! I had thought them all gone in King Henry's time! I started to cry out, for both seemed oblivious to the other and certain to collide, but the words froze in my throat when I realised that I could see through the grey-robed friar as if he were formed of frosted glass. I was looking at a *ghost*! He walked right through Mrs Forster, and she never gave a sign of noticing, only a little shiver as she uttered another complaint about the cold and drew her shawl closer about her shoulders.

I hung back in fear, cowering against the wall, gathering my cloak close about me—I didn't want any part of me to touch him—as he passed me by, then . . . *vanished*! He just . . . disappeared, as if he had never been there at all!

"Now, you *must* be *very* careful of these stairs, my dear," Mrs Forster cautioned as she continued slowly up them. "Don't rush, take your time, even after you are used to them; do not let familiarity or haste make you careless. I don't know why Dr Owen doesn't have them replaced. They are original to the house; it was built in 1330, I believe. The leather soles of two centuries' worth of monks' sandals have worn them as slick and smooth as glass. And there's an awkward turn just here that seems to come out of nowhere . . ."

Mrs Forster glanced back and saw me still standing there at the bottom. I hadn't moved a step; I was frozen with fear.

"Oh, I've frightened you when I meant only to caution you. Come, come, my dear, there's no need to be afraid—just be *careful*, and you shall be just fine! I'm up and down these stairs *all* day, as they lead directly into the Long Gallery, where I like to sit by the fire and sew, and my children delight in running up and down when they cannot be outside. They climb these stairs like monkeys, and we've yet to break a bone!"

I swallowed hard and pushed myself forward and started up after her.

On the landing, I paused, took a deep breath, and forced myself to ask, "Mrs Forster, is there . . . is there a ghost?"

"A ghost, my dear?" Mrs Forster turned and stared at me with a wary, concerned look in her eyes. "Why ever do you ask?"

"At Compton Verney there was a tale of a ghost the servants used to tell, and I . . . I was just curious if there was one at Cumnor. I . . . I've a friend who collects stories," I rushed on, concocting a half lie to not make myself appear even more a fool, "so I always inquire at the houses I visit."

"Oh!" Mrs Forster breathed a sigh of relief. "I see! Well, I hope your friend can be persuaded to visit and share some stories with us one cold winter's night. It would be so cosy to cluster round the fire and listen. I know the children would enjoy it, and so would I. Yes, there is indeed a ghost said to haunt Cumnor, but it's just a tale the servants tell, I suspect; whenever we hire a new housemaid, the others like to sneak up behind and give her a good fright. It's said to be a grey friar with his hood drawn up, so no one can see his face; there's only a darkness there that no human eyes or earthly light can pierce. But it's *nothing* you need worry *your* pretty head about, my dear, for they say only the dying can actually *see* him. Fancy that! It's not much of a ghost, if you ask me! Though I can see how it would give a fright to any who thought he was creeping up on them; no wonder the servants make such sport of it!"

I gasped, and everything seemed to waver and get even darker, and I felt my body lurch and sway forward and start to fall, but then Mrs Forster was there, her arms tight about my waist, shouting for help as I hung, limp as a child's rag poppet, in her arms. I heard running feet, and then Tommy was there, gathering me up in his arms and carrying me the rest of the way upstairs.

"Oh, the poor thing!" I heard Mrs Forster exclaim, though her voice sounded as if it came from very far away. "Lord Robert said she'd been unwell—prone to melancholy, he said she was—and the journey must have tired her more than I realised. Come this way, Master Blount, and lay her on the bed. There, my dear." She sat down beside me and began briskly rubbing my cold hands. "You just rest . . ."

When I awakened, with Custard and Onyx purring beside me, I heard galloping hoofbeats. I sprang up and rushed to the window just in time to see Robert's black cloak billowing out behind him like the wings of Death. Once again, he hadn't bothered to say goodbye. The vial of green hemlock pills was on the table by my bed with a note from Robert reminding me of my promise to take them. In a frenzy of anger, I snatched up the vial and flung it against the wall, shattering it, sending shards of glass and pills flying. But as Custard and Onyx stirred and padded across the bed, I ran and frantically picked it all up for fear that my pets might be harmed by them. I threw the evil little green things into the fire, then ran back to the bed, gathered both my cats in my arms, and nuzzled and kissed them, letting their soft fur soak up my tears.

I kept to my room for a week. I didn't want to see anyone. I had no desire for company or food. Every time Pirto brought me a message from Mrs Forster or a tray, I shook my head and turned my face to the wall until she went away. I just lay there, listless against the pillows, watching the sun rise and set through the windows, sometimes sleeping for a little while and always trying to remember to sleep on my back and not roll over onto my left side and provoke an angry protest from my cancer-riddled breast. It was like the pain caused by biting into something very sugary and sweet with a rotten tooth, only *much* worse, and this pain echoed for *hours* afterwards.

But my solitude was soon to end. Mrs Forster's rambunctious brood would not be dissuaded, and soon they were pushing past Pirto and bounding up onto my bed, to introduce themselves to me and show me their toys and frogs, including the famous Christopher, who they boasted could leap farther and croak louder than any frog God ever made, a talent he displayed by promptly belching out a deep, sonorous croak whenever his belly was tickled. They entertained me with stories, songs, dances, and riddles, and enacted little dramas for me, including their favourite game of "Old King Henry and His Wives". The boys would each take turns portraying the mighty, murderous monarch, pointing and bellowing like thunder, *"Off with her head!"* as the girls, taking turns being either Anne Boleyn or Katherine Howard, fell to their knees, cowering before the King, hands clasped, begging for mercy, only to be dragged away bawling and screaming by another boy enacting the role of executioner to lay their head upon the block. They brought flowers to brighten my sickroom and treats like jam tarts and fresh-baked gingerbread to try to excite my appetite. The boys enacted battles around my bed mounted on their hobbyhorses and clashing wooden swords while their sisters sat round me with their dolls. And sometimes they played dress-up with my gowns and jewels. When their mother cautioned them to be careful and despaired that they would ruin my beautiful things with their jam-sticky fingers, I shrugged and said, "Let them. I have many gowns, but no children of my own."

A few days later, Pirto bundled me into a warm, fur-lined cloak, and, with Mrs Forster fluttering about and fussing over me, and the children holding tightly to my hands and crowding close, promising, "We'll protect you, Amy!" I carefully descended the stairs for the first time since I had arrived at Cumnor. They took me out into the park, to see the pond, though it was iced over, so there were no frogs to be seen, and settled me on a stone bench to be warmed by the frail wintry gilt of the afternoon sun. And Mrs Forster took the opportunity to introduce me to the other two ladies who lodged at Cumnor, each occupying a wing of her own.

First she introduced me to the imperious and formidable Mrs Owen, the ancient, white-haired mother of Cumnor's owner, Dr Owen. Her wits and tongue remained as sharp as newly-honed razors despite her years, and she expressed her opinions with such utter and adamant conviction, one would have thought God Himself had descended from Heaven to present them to her chiselled on stone tablets, as if they were as sacred and inviolable as the Ten Commandments. She prodded my hip with her cane and bade me turn round for her inspection, then gave a grunt that left the question dangling of whether she approved of me or not.

Then there was an ageing beauty named Elizabeth Oddingsells who emphasised her voluptuous charms to the fullest degree with dramatic and expert use of henna, rouge, kohl, tight lacing, and a skilful dressmaker with more than a touch of flamboyance in his or her needle. It was only just after breakfast, and she was wearing peacock feathers in her hair. She showed an amazing amount of bosom despite the cold, taking the court fashion for low bodices to a most daring extreme, which provoked Mrs Forster to lean in close and whisper into my ear that she was known to even rouge her nipples and on many an occasion had suffered the "accidental embarrassment" of having her breasts pop out the top of her gown. "But don't you be fooled by it, if it happens—and it will, if you stay long enough at Cumnor—she used to practise making it happen when she was a girl and by now has it down to an art. Some women are content to smile coyly and bat their eyelashes, but that's not enough for Lizzy Oddingsells—*she* has to burst out of her bodice. She even did it once while feigning to faint at my uncle's funeral and had every man there rushing to help her. One man forgot to watch where he put his feet and fell into the open grave in his haste to reach her."

I found Mrs Forster's manner towards Mrs Oddingsells curiously frosty, colder than mere disapproval merited, and after the introductions had been made and Mrs Oddingsells had retreated to sit some distance away with her peacock-plumed head bent over her embroidery, Mrs Forster confided their history to me.

"If I were you, my dear Amy, I would not get too close to Lizzy Oddingsells. She's a sly one and more like than not to smile in your face one day and stab you in the back the next; she has a habit of betraying her friends." She went on to explain that in their girlhood they had been the very best of friends. "We were so close, people thought us joined at the hip; she was like a big sister to me. Now . . ." She sighed and shook her head. "Well, let's just say that red bodice she is wearing is an apt choice. She's my husband's harlot, and there's no use denying it or trying to sugarcoat it; the truth is what it is."

The affair had begun when Mrs Forster was *"enceinte"*, she said delicately, patting her stomach to make sure I got her meaning, in case I did not know this fashionable French word that ladies now preferred to use because they thought it sounded prettier and more elegant than to say that they were "with child" or "pregnant".

"Men have their needs and are prone to straying, like randy tomcats, at such a time," she continued, and by the way she spoke and shrugged, so plain and matter-of-fact, I gathered that Mrs Forster was not overly troubled by this and simply accepted it as the way of the world and a woman's lot.

But what she could *never* forgive or forget was "that Lizzy Oddingsells's putting herself forward like the brazen slut she is and luring *my* husband into her bed! Afterwards, she tried to tell me she
had done it for *my* sake, and for my children, saying better that it
be her, my best friend, who had me and my babies in her heart,
than some other woman who would use her wanton wiles to put
money in her purse and jewels and silk gowns upon her person,
and take food out of our mouths and clothes off our backs for the
glory and greed of her own self. Humph!" Mrs Forster's exclamation showed just what she thought of Mrs Oddingsells's charitable
explanation. "If my children and I did not live in such proximity to
her, I would wish the plague upon her! If she fell facedown in a
mud puddle, I would not stoop to help her up; rather, I would
plant my foot on the back of her head and gladly hold her down
and watch her drown!"

After these harsh and heated words, Mrs Forster flashed me a
smile and patted my hand. "I *know* that you, my dear Amy, will understand *exactly* how I feel," she said in what was obviously a discreetly veiled reference to my husband's dalliance with the Queen.

I nodded and assured her that I did, though I was right sorry, I
said, to see what began as such a loving and happy friendship end
in such gall and bitterness.

The next person Mrs Forster introduced me to was a Dr Walter
Bayly, who had just set up his practice in Oxford. Robert had made
inquiries about the various physicians practising near Cumnor and
had settled on this promising young man as the perfect one to undertake my cure. He had even sent him potions prepared by the
Queen's own apothecary to give to me, including more hemlock
pills, explaining that I was "sorely heavy with an overabundance of
melancholy, but, like a naughty child, My Lady is reluctant to take
her medicine, and I hope you, good Dr Bayly, can persuade her to
do what is best for her; I am putting my trust *entirely* in *you*." I
know he wrote these words, as Dr Bayly gently chided me for my
recalcitrance and read me this snippet of my husband's letter, saying afterwards, with a cajoling smile, "Now, we must not let Lord
Robert down."

He was a very kind and comely young man, tall, lean, and red-
haired with eyes the pale green colour of gooseberries. And, accord-

ing to Mrs Forster, local gossip said that since his arrival many ladies had found need to consult him, for their own sake or that of their children, even for the most trifling ailments that they could have easily treated themselves with their own grandmothers' remedies: time, rest, and common sense. Even Mrs Oddingsells had consulted him because she always broke out in a rash after eating strawberries, and Dr Bayly had calmly advised her not to eat them.

Like a court gallant, he kissed my hand when we met and sat by my bed and exchanged pleasantries with me, putting me right at ease, before he inquired about what ailed me. But when I bared my breast to him, he went as white as milk. He stepped quickly away from me and went to stand by the window, staring out, bracing himself against the stone sill.

With his back still turned to me, he asked what had been done for me thus far. I told him of the remedies Pirto and I had tried when we first thought it merely an abscess, but when I mentioned the hemlock pills Robert had given me, prescribed by the Queen's own physician, he spun round abruptly with his whole body atremble and his eyes staring wide, like a man who had just been frightened out of his mind.

I felt a sudden coldness like a shawl of ice thrown over my shoulders and a prickling upon the nape of my neck and turned to see that the phantom grey friar was standing beside my bed, like a sentinel keeping watch over me. For a moment I wondered if Dr Bayly could see him too, but I knew better than to ask, lest he think me mad.

Dr Bayly made a valiant effort to compose himself. He swallowed hard, and in a jumbled rush of words spoken so fast I could barely make sense of them, he said, if I heard aright, that I had no need of the physick my husband had supplied for me. He thought the suffering the hemlock pills would cause would far outweigh any slight benefit that might be derived from taking them. With sorrow pooled within his eyes, he said that he was sorry, "so very sorry," but there was nothing he could do for me, that I was in God's hands and must trust Him to protect me and effect my cure if such was His desire. And then he was gone, rapidly mumbling something about rest, prayer, and fresh air.

And he never did come back to see me, not even when I worsened and Mrs Forster, wringing her hands and unable to bear my pain, sent for him and begged him to help me; still he declined to treat me, to interfere or risk being blamed for something that was none of his doing and that he wanted no part of. He was, after all, a young man just starting out in his profession, and if my death were laid upon his shoulders, it would be a burden he could never shake off. And if those higher placed so desired it, he might even pay for my death with his own life to disguise the misdeeds of others.

"No, Madame," he said adamantly to Mrs Forster, in a voice loud enough for me to hear through my half-opened door, which was as far as he would come, "better that I walk away *now* and have no part of this. I shall write to Lord Robert and tell him that in my opinion his lady has no need of the physick he recommends and that there is nothing I can do for her and that I must decline to undertake her treatment. If he disagrees, then with all due respect, better that he seek the advice of a physician with greater experience of her particular malady. And, in confidence, I tell you, Madame, I will *not* be hanged to cover another's sin!"

And in truth I could not fault him, and I readily forgave him. Why should he throw away his life and a promising career to be Robert's scapegoat? Had I been in Dr Bayly's shoes, I think I might have done the same, though it would have hurt my heart and weighed heavily upon my conscience to turn my back on a soul in the throes of so much suffering. But if I could do nothing to ease that suffering, *why* should I risk being blamed when the inevitable occurred, when it could mean the gallows or ruin for me and the loss of everything I had worked so hard to achieve? Dr Bayly was not a bad man. He did the right and honourable thing and walked away rather than let Robert buy and use him for his own ends.

The days came and went. Sometimes they passed so fast, I lost count of them. Sometimes they dragged by like convicts trudging along weighed down by chains and shackles. My once-rosy cheeks were now as white as chalk, and even my gums had lost their healthy pink hue. My whole body was sore and ached as though I had been beaten and was mottled with bruises I could not explain; I knew I had done nothing to cause them. I suffered fevers that waxed and waned without rhyme or reason. Some days I found the strength to walk; other days I crawled. Often I awoke feeling as though I had not slept at all. I tried to rise but instead fell back into the arms of Sleep. Some days doctors came, an endless procession of them; they came to bleed me, and I would lie and watch listlessly as my blood poured into a basin, and marvel at how watery pale it looked, as though the bloom had faded from my blood as well as from my rosy cheeks. But the doctors just smiled and said I must eat plenty of rare red meat, juicy and red, the bloodier the better, even though the very thought of it made me sick, and drink red wine, and stuff myself with all the red berries my stomach could hold, all red like blood to brighten and strengthen my own.

I preferred to be outside in the park whenever I could, for Cumnor Place itself, despite Mrs Forster's reassuring words upon my arrival, continued in a state of cold, perpetual gloom, which I could never grow accustomed to. Every time the wind rattled the windows, my heart felt as if it were trying to leap out of my chest and run away, just like I wanted to run away, but no matter how much I wanted to win back my life, to outpace Death, I could not run away from myself, from the disease and pain-racked body that housed my soul. There was no way to escape my fate and nowhere to hide from it. Death's hand cupped and fondled my breast like a lover, but His touch withered and rotted instead of excited, it festered and inflamed my flesh instead of my passions, and it gave pain in the place of pleasure.

Mrs Forster tried to help me all she could. I drank barley water until I feared my bladder would burst just to please her. And I tried every remedy she recommended and tested the skills of this wise or that cunning woman, even those reputed to be witches, who came on the sly in the night to dose me with mysterious tonics and elixirs, some sweet, others bitter, to apply poultices either hot or cold, and to smear ointments on my breast that smelt so bad they made me even sicker. In one form or another—salves, ointments, poultices, plasters, and gums—my breast was slathered with olive oil, turpentine, rhubarb, castor oil, quicksilver, bitterage of gold, sulphur, vinegar, licorice, tincture of lead, a paste made of fox lungs and tortoise livers, crushed coral, chalk, and boar's tooth, pulverised pearls, and alabaster, oil of roses, hemlock, cinnamon, deadly nightshade, treacle, mandrake, valerian, linseed oil, goat's dung, crab's eyes, and viper's fat. But most of them hurt more than they helped. I would lie in my bed, my breast stinging, burning, and throbbing, impaled by stabbing pains beneath the dressing, and tears would fill my eyes, I felt such hopelessness and despair.

Upon Mrs Forster's recommendation, I consulted a boastful Frenchwoman who described herself as a "wise wizardess". She thought the flesh of my afflicted breast had a look she described as *"peau d'orange"*, like the pitted skin of an orange peel, and she spent hours rubbing my breast with oranges and put me on a diet of nothing but the juice and flesh of oranges for a month, hoping to cure "like with like". But this "cure" only left me with a sore and burning throat and my skin sticky with the rancid odour of rotting flesh masked by the smell of oranges. Some even recommended charms that I should wear on my person or uttered spells over my body. There was a Cornish woman, whom I felt sure must be a witch, who burned seven crabs alive whilst she chanted and danced naked beneath a full moon, then mixed them with oil and rubbed the resulting concoction onto my breast with a heron's feather. Another tried to burn the cancer out by applying a coating of sulphuric acid; he and his assistant held me down as I thrashed and screamed. Afterwards, my breast was so very red, inflamed, and swollen that it bled at the slightest touch. Another told me to be brave as he touched a hot iron to the bulging, tumorous mass. And other doctors, both dubious and esteemed, travelling charlatans and nostrum peddlers, came and went, with their leeches and lancets, enemas, plasters, purges, and potions, all of them leaving me feeling more tired and spent and mired in even greater pain and despair than when they found me.

Mrs Owen, who had been a wife and mother to two fine doctors, did her best to recall remedies that might ease if not cure me, and swore by the efficacy of enemas for all human ails. She fed me licorice pastilles until the very sight or mention of them sickened me and served me weekly with a vile and nasty purging beer in which watercress, treacle, licorice, rhubarb, red dock, raisins, honey, rue, lime, garlic, liverwort, feverfew, sassafras, figs, sugar, comfrey root, aniseed, lavender, saffron, egg yolks, and mashed hazelnuts were blended into the strongest beer.

They all meant well, I am sure, but nothing really helped, though, to make them feel better, I nodded and smiled and thanked them and said I felt a little better even when I didn't at all.

But it was all to no avail. And many a night I woke up thrashing and screaming, my face wet with tears from a dream in which they all—Robert; his royal paramour, my jewel-encrusted enemy, the Queen; all the doctors and charlatans, witches and wisewomen I had seen; and Mr and Mrs Forster, Mrs Owen, and Mrs Oddingsells, the Hydes, and Sir Richard Verney—ran after me, chasing me, each touting a particular remedy and brandishing it high in the air—bottles of pills and potions, leeches, lancets, purgatives, charms, magical spells, roots and herbs they swore were a sovereign remedy—whilst I, in a stumbling, fear-blind panic fled before them, desperate to outrun them and these cures that were supposed to make me better but instead only made me more ill, running as fast as I could, encumbered by my full, heavy skirts, whilst Fear tugged at my hair, pulling me back, slowing me down, dragging me to the ground. And they all fell on me at once, forcing my mouth open wide, cramming and pouring their pills and potions down, forcing me to swallow, opening my veins to bleed me, putting leeches to suckle on my diseased breast, and lifting my skirts to inflict the immodest indignity of an enema. It was a *horrible* dream, and I *hated* it so much that if I wasn't so very tired, I would have been afraid to go to sleep. I always awoke exhausted and feeling as if I had been running for my life the whole night through.

I think my illness made Robert repent some of his former cruelty and indifference, at least a little, at times. He seemed to remember and think of me more often after I became ill. After I came to Cumnor, I began to regularly receive pretty parcels from London. One day it might be an elegant black velvet hat fringed with gold, a cloak and muff made of the most magnificent sables lined with golden satin very like the colour of my hair, a bolt of heavenly blue silk to make a new gown, or green velvet slippers the colour of the grass to remind me in winter of when I used to walk barefoot and carefree in summertime, a bed gown of buttery yellow damask festooned with ribbons and lace, a rainbow of embroidery silks or a cunning mechanical songbird that actually sang, with its feathers beautifully enamelled, and my wonderful green chair, soft as a cloud that an angel in Heaven might have envied, all abloom with a garden of embroidered flowers, and, though he had never given a thought to it before, now Robert *always* made sure there were fragrant apple logs for my fire, just like I always had at Syderstone and Stanfield Hall. They were all such kind and thoughtful presents, not something just snatched from a shelf in a shop or from amongst a peddler's wares; it was as though each one had been chosen carefully. And, for a time at least, I let myself dare to dream, and be deceived, that the cancer had done what I had been trying for so long but failed miserably to do—revive Robert's tender feelings and remind him how much he used to care for me. But, oh, at what an exorbitant price! Now, if ever he came to my bed again, I had a body that would turn his lust to disgust!

But there were other packages that were not so pleasant. I never knew where or when I would find them—if they would come by messenger, or if I would find them lying at my door or on my windowsill waiting for me. Sometimes I even found them on the bench in the park where I liked to sit, or inside the drawers of my writing desk, or in my sewing basket. They were vile, *evil* tokens sent by someone who wished the worst on me. There were little dolls made of wax, always with a thorn driven through the breast. The wax had a rough texture that I found was caused by nail clippings being mixed in, and each doll wore a skirt made from bloodstained linen, like that used to staunch a woman's monthly courses, and there was always a lock of golden hair just like mine glued to their heads. Pirto always tried to persuade me to throw them in the fire, but I was afraid to, nor could I bear to bury them, to put an effigy that was clearly intended to be me into the ground . . . it was too much like a grave. Another time a box arrived containing a gruesome wreath woven of prickly black hawthorn sprigs, black silk ribbon, desiccated toads, lizards, and rats with their tails braided together. Sometimes I found tiny wooden coffins with the little wax dolls inside, always with a lock of golden hair and a thorn impaling the left breast, and my name carved crudely upon the lid. And once, most cruelly, for it came masquerading as a beautifully wrapped gift from London, a locket, a rectangle of gold with black enamelled accents and a wreath of exquisite enamelled flowers, that opened to reveal a smiling, sapphire-eyed, ivory skeleton. Inscribed inside the coffin lid in bold black enamelled letters were the words:

"DEATH IS NEVER FAR AWAY."

With a cry of horror, I flung it out the window; I could not bear to have it near me. The attempts to poison me had failed, and now Robert, or one of his lackeys, had resorted to witchcraft, to try to scare me to death with these ghoulish little horrors. And as my fear and desperation mounted, entwining, plaiting together with the pain to keep me from resting easily in my bed, more and more often I fell to my knees and prayed to God to deliver me from my desperation, to deprive these dark, sinister spells being worked against me of their power. "I am already cursed with cancer; *please,* save me from these witches and devils who work their dark magic against me!" I begged. The phantom grey friar bent his cowled head and seemed to pray along with me, but that only increased my terror.

One day Tommy Blount came riding up with a saddlebag full of apples and a treasure trove of new tales to tell me.

Dear Tommy, he always made my heart glad. One night, as we sat late by the fire in the Long Gallery, resting on piles of deep red velvet cushions strewn upon the hearth, roasting apples sprinkled in sugar and cinnamon in the big stone fireplace, with cups of steaming Lambswool warming our hands—he'd gotten the recipe from Pirto and had it brewed special just for me—his eyes told me what his lips were too shy to say.

But I turned my face away, saddened by the thought of what he would become someday. I couldn't bear it. For I knew it was inevitable. A day *would* come when the riotous gingery curls would be cropped and tamed, subdued to lie flat, submissive as a wife, beneath a pearled and feathered velvet cap, and the sudden and sincere smiles would be replaced by false and affected ones, and those gentle, sympathetic eyes, windows a kind and sincere soul looked out of, would harden and see all through the stained glass of self-interest and regard the world as a great chessboard and everyone and everything on it as pawns to be manoeuvred, traded, bartered, and sold, and the child's love of stories would be driven out to make room for facts, figures, politics, and court gossip and intrigue. It might be a slow death, but that sweet sincerity *would* die, and the charm that remained would be like a shell abandoned on the beach by the ambitious crab it had grown too small and cramped an abode for. I had seen it all happen before, and I didn't want to see it happen again. I had once loved a kind and eager boy of seventeen and over ten years of marriage watched him grow into a hard and ruthless stranger who would do *anything* for riches, fame, and glory, to feed the always hungry flames of the ambition that burned within him where his soul had once been. I was glad I would not live long enough to see it happen to Tommy. It was too sad to mourn the death of a soul even as the body still lived.

Even though I turned away, he reached for me. I know I should not, but I let him kiss me. It had been *so* long since I had felt the tender touch of a man's lips and hands and been the one to light the flame of his desire and feel it flare inside me as well as him. With this disease, I didn't think I could any more. I thought the desires of the flesh were lost to the land of memory and dreams. I didn't think my damaged body could still feel, much less ignite, desire any more, but I was wrong. I was wrong; I knew that as I melted blissfully into the arms of Tommy Blount, savouring and returning his warm, ardent, apple-sweet kisses. I suppose I could blame it on the heat of the fire, the lateness of the hour, the beer in the Lambswool, or wanting to grasp Life with both hands and be pulled up by it even as Death dragged me down, but that would be dishonest. A good excuse doesn't always make a wrong right. The only intoxication was the heady sensation of being in a man's arms and feeling like a desirable woman again.

I closed my eyes and leaned my head back as Tommy's kisses blazed a hot trail down my throat. But when his hand rose up to cup my breast, my eyes snapped open wide. I came to my senses and remembered who and what I was—Lord Robert's wife, always faithful, loyal, and loving, even when he was not, and a dying woman likely to have to face God's judgment very soon.

I gently pulled away from him and got to my feet. He stayed where he was, half lying on the velvet cushions, leaning on his elbow, staring up at me with the sad and bewildered brown eyes of a spaniel who desires only to please but has instead in some way, mysterious and incomprehensible to him, disappointed his mistress.

I leaned down and gently stroked his face, letting my palm linger on his soft cheek, smooth like a baby's flesh instead of prickly like a man's.

"You've a good heart, Tommy," I said, "and someday you'll find someone worthy to share it with. But it *can't* be me—I'm married, and I'm dying."

"But . . ." He started to speak, but I silenced him with my fingertip pressed lightly against his lips. And even though it pained me—I had noticed lately the pain descending to encircle me like a corset, an invisible garment woven of pain that could never be unlaced—still I bent and brushed my lips against his brow. Then I rumpled his wild hair and, with a smile, said softly, "Good night, Tommy, and goodbye." I knew he would be leaving in the morning, and I did not know if I would ever see him again.

"Tommy." At the door to my room I impulsively turned back. "*Please,* if you ever look back and think of me someday, after I'm gone, *please,* remember me with kindness."

"*Always,*" he promised, "with *loving* kindness, Amy."

His heart was in his voice as well as in his eyes when he said it, and I knew he meant it.

"*Thank you.*" I nodded and closed the door behind me, leaning my back against it with my heart pounding like a drum within my breast, and some part of me—my head, my heart, my lust?—wanting to turn around, open that door, and call to Tommy. I wanted to take his hand and lead him to my bed and feel his lips and hands gliding over me and the warmth and weight of his body over mine, flesh to flesh, heart to heart; I wanted to feel like a woman who is loved and desired just one more time before I died.

But I didn't do it, though many a time since I've wished I had. I didn't dare; I was a coward. I was too afraid that the desire that leapt and danced like flames in his eyes when he looked at me would turn to disgust when he saw my cancer-ravaged breast, so I let the chance—my *last* chance—go by. And I was *always* a good, virtuous wife, even when Robert did not deserve my loyalty and love.

A few weeks after Tommy had gone, I received an unexpected visitor. Dr Dee, the Queen's astrologer and my husband's former tutor, presented himself at Cumnor and asked to see me. When I heard, I lost my head, I flew into a panic, and, I am ashamed to say, like a little child, I ran and hid, sitting on the floor, hugging my knees, cowering behind a curtain, wishing myself invisible.

Though he was esteemed as a brilliant scholar, and people said of him that what he did not know of mathematics, navigation, and the stars was not worth knowing, Dr Dee blackened his reputation by delving into more eccentric, esoteric subjects that flirted with deviltry. He dabbled in alchemy, trying to find the secret formula for turning base metals into gold, and was said to possess a magic mirror that revealed to him the future, and to be able to read one's destiny written in the stars above or even in the palm of one's own hand. And dark rumours of necromancy, magical rituals, dealings with the dead and devils, hung like a black cloak about his shoulders.

All my fears about Robert came flooding back the day Dr Dee knocked upon the door.

I was *terrified* that my husband had sent him to divine the hour of my death or work some terrible spell against me. Perhaps he was even the one who had sent the little wax dolls and other macabre and ghoulish tokens. I had not taken the hemlock pills, and surely Robert must know it, and Dr Bayly had written to Robert and re fused to administer the potions Robert had sent, so perhaps he had turned to his old tutor for advice and decided to dispense with medicine and deal with the Devil instead.

Though the Forsters tried to shield me, there were rumours wafting down from London that Robert was sorely afraid that the Queen would get tired of waiting for me to die and set Robert free and would marry one of her many foreign suitors instead. They never ceased to woo her with gifts and pretty speeches, they showered her with jewels, sonnets, and sables, and all her Councillors pressed most urgently, for the good of England and the succession, for her to choose one of them to be her husband. No one—except Robert himself—wanted Robert to be King, and everyone knew that as long as I lived, he hadn't a chance. Thus rumours abounded that he meant to speed the course of my illness to a faster end with doses of deadly poison disguised as healing drams. My life was nothing to what Robert stood to gain after I was gone. Now I understood all the better why he had pressed me to take the hemlock pills even if they made me feel as if I were lying on the edge of my grave, about to roll in. He *wanted* me in my grave; he wanted it enough to shove me in himself!

So when I heard Dr Dee had come to call, I fled screaming afore him. The breath caught in my throat; I panted and gasped and fell to my knees and crawled behind an arras. I cowered back against the wall even as a hand swept the velvet curtain aside and a kindly-faced man with long white-blond locks and a waist-length beard like gleaming ivory silk smiled down at me.

"Dear lady, you've *nothing* to fear from me!" he said. "Come." He reached down his hand to me, upon which was a ring set with a great ruby that glowed as if lit from within by an ember. "Sit and talk with me."

His hand drew mine like a magnet—there was *something* about him that made me want to trust him—but just as our fingers touched, I gasped, uncertain and afraid, and snatched my hand back.

"No!" I sobbed. "Robert and his mistress, the Queen, have sent you! You will look at my hand and see that I will be cast down into darkness or some such thing! You will make them happy and foretell my doom and leave me even more afraid! Have you brought your black mirror? I will not look in it! I won't, I won't, and you cannot make me!" I cried, crazed with terror.

"My dear child," Dr Dee said gently, "you are already cast down into darkness—the darkness of fear and despair—and I don't need to see your palm or gaze into a black mirror to know it. I can see it on your face and hear it in your voice. Fear is your constant companion; it never leaves you, not even when you sleep."

He looked like such a kind man, not at all the sort to consort with demons.

He chuckled softly, and it was as if he had read my mind. "You were expecting horns and a forked tail and cloven hoofs peeping out from beneath my robes, weren't you? And these robes"—he touched a fold of his gown—"to be all encrusted with moons and stars and other strange symbols instead of this plain scholar's black. I'm just a man, my dear," he continued with a most reassuring smile, "a man with a boundless curiosity about *everything,* and an *insatiable* appetite for knowledge of all kinds. Just because I delve into strange mysteries does not mean I am in league with the Devil. I promise you I am not, and there shall be no horoscopes cast, no scrying into mirrors, or scrutinising of palms or tarot cards. I had some business in Oxford and knew you were in residence here and thought I would stop and see you. Robert was one of my favourite pupils, yet I never had the pleasure of meeting his bride. Come now." He reached for my hand again, and this time I took it and let him raise me and lead me to sit beside him on the window seat overlooking the park.

"Y-You . . . You . . ." Fear still caused my tongue to stick. But Dr Dee just patted the back of my hand and smiled and nodded encouragingly. "I-I am . . ." I paused and in frustration pressed my hand to my brow and shut my eyes. I just couldn't seem to get the words out!

"You are no fool, my dear." Dr Dee very kindly spoke for me when he saw that I could not. "You know what they say in London, and you also know that I, being the Queen's astrologer and well acquainted with your husband, know it too."

I nodded gratefully and felt the knots in my tongue unfurl, allowing me to at last speak freely.

"I *am* dying," I confided. "I have a cancer here." I lightly touched my breast. "And they are *glad* of it, for only my life prevents their marrying. But I am not dying fast enough to suit them! Robert plans to poison me. He has tried before . . ."

I told him all about my stay at Compton Verney, the spices Robert sent that only made me sicker, and of the hemlock pills he had given me, prepared by the Queen's own apothecary, and Dr Bayly's refusal to administer these and the other potions Robert sent, trusting him to persuade me to take them. And I also told him of the little wax dolls with the thorn-impaled breasts, bloody skirts, and locks of yellow hair, and other macabre mementos that had been sent, or left for me to find, since I had been at Cumnor.

"Please." I gazed at him desperately. *"Do not hurt me!"*

"Never!" Dr Dee promised me, taking my hand in both of his. "Poor lady, I know you no longer trust anyone, and with good reason, but I *swear* I would *never* harm a hair on your head. And I will tell you something else as well, and I pray that you will believe me—you've *nothing* at all to fear from the Queen. I *know* this to be true. But, with regret, I cannot say the same of your husband. You must be strong here"—he tapped his forehead—"and here"—he touched his own heart—"even though you are frightened and ill and your heart is breaking. Many think there is *great* power in evil curses and magical spells, but that is not *really* so. The *true* power is in the belief itself; those who believe themselves the victims of such things suffer as if they were indeed; by believing, they give those who would curse them the power to actually do so. There is *great* power in fear; you *must* loosen its hold on you, for your own sake."

We sat and talked a little longer—I was *so* grateful to have someone listen to me who didn't scoff or belittle and took seriously all I had to say—until the sun began to set, and Dr Dee had to take his leave.

I accompanied him downstairs, and at the door I touched his arm and earnestly implored that if he saw Robert that he would not tell him that I had behaved so badly and received him so ungraciously.

"My dear"—Dr Dee smiled at me—"you are a beautiful and charming young woman, and you deserve so much better! Rest assured, I shall say nothing at all to Robert; he did not send me, and I am not his servant. I do not answer to him, and he need never know that I have seen you unless you wish to tell him."

"Thank you, Dr Dee," I said most gratefully. "I . . . I am glad you came to see me. You have helped me more than any other physician."

He reached out and cupped my cheek in his hand and leaned down to kiss my brow. "Though a cure for your malady is beyond the powers of medicine as we know it, someday, centuries after our

bones have turned to dust, there *will* be survivors." And from behind my ear, like a magician at a fair, he drew a pretty pink silk ribbon and looped it round my neck like half a figure eight with the
ends left dangling.

"No demons, just a little sleight of hand, my dear." He smiled
and bade me farewell.

I stopped him with a hand on his sleeve. "Dr Dee," I asked with
a tremor in my voice, "do you know how long I have left? Have you
seen my death in your magic mirror?"

He shook his head and with a sad little smile flitting across his
lips softly quoted a bit of scripture to me:

"To everything there is a season, and a time to every purpose
under the heaven: A time to be born, and a time to die; A time to
plant, and a time to pluck up that which is planted; A time to kill,
and a time to heal; A time to break down, and a time to build up; A
time to weep, and a time to laugh; A time to mourn, and a time to
dance; A time to cast away stones, and a time to gather stones together; A time to embrace, and a time to refrain from embracing; A
time to get, and a time to lose; A time to keep, and a time to cast
away; A time to rend, and a time to sew; A time to keep silence, and
a time to speak; A time to love, and a time to hate; A time of war,
and a time of peace."

And in his words I saw my whole life rush past in a series of
vividly painted pictures blurring together on the rapidly turning
pages of the book of my memory. My happy girlhood, and the un-
happy years of waning health leading to my inevitable demise; the
years when I had waded through fields of barley, watching the crops
grow, helping with and celebrating each harvest, and the birthing
of the lambs, the tending of the flocks, and the shearing of the
sheep; the days when Robert and I were so deeply in love, when we
danced and laughed and loved together; the day he made me his
Buttercup Bride; and the joyous days when we frolicked on the
beach at Hemsby; the few days we spent together and the many
days we spent apart; the happy days when we laughed together, and
those when I wept alone; the times we came together in love and
parted in anger, the ever-widening gulf yawning between us, and the
weeks and months of absence and indifference when I feared the
love was lost forever and might even have turned to hate; the times

when I kept silent out of fear and the times when I set my temper screaming free; the days I mourned and buried my parents and the dreams Robert and I once shared, dreams that never came true; the festering resentment I felt for the woman, the Queen, who took my husband away from me, the one he, on fire with ambition and lust, had cast me away for; my desperate attempts to sew us back together, only to be brutally torn and ripped apart at the seams; those days when I dyed my hair harlot red with henna and danced before him as a bare-breasted mermaid trying to lure him back to me but only succeeded in driving him even further away; the day he asked me for a divorce, and we went to war; the quarrels and long, angry silences; the poisonous days and nightmares that tormented me at Compton Verney; the wary peace and uneasy truce, the illusion of tenderness returned and renewed that came with the cancer. It was *all* there, flashing by in an instant.

And then, after bowing over my hand and uttering a fervent blessing, he was gone. I leaned in the doorway and watched him ride into the sunset on his little grey donkey, and then I turned around and walked slowly back inside bleak and shadowy, cold and clammy Cumnor Place. England was full of pleasant houses; why couldn't Robert send me to one of those? Surely he had friends or people who owed, or were anxious to do, him favours who lived somewhere nice and cheery, where the cold didn't creep and seep into one's bones.

As I started up the stairs, I saw the ghostly grey friar standing at the top, his hands clasped and folded at his waist, holding his rosary, the crucifix at the end of the wooden beads swinging to and fro like a shimmering silver pendulum. Though I could not see his face in the impenetrable black shadows of his hood, I *knew* he was watching me, waiting for me, and that the shivery, prickly feeling up and down my spine and the back of my neck was his sandalled feet walking over my grave.

❧ 29 ❧

Elizabeth

I was looking at a selection of embroidered shawls I had requested be sent from London for my inspection when Kat came in to tell me that Dr Dee had arrived.

"This one!" I breathed, holding up a beautiful, fringed butter yellow shawl embroidered in bright, vivid colours with a bountiful variety of flowers, fruits, birds, and animals. "She will like this one—I'm certain of it!" I nodded decisively and folded the shawl carefully. "Wrap it and have it sent to Lady Dudley at once please, Kat."

"Very well, love," Kat sighed, shaking her dear grey head. "I'll do it, but I don't understand it! *Why* do you do it, send these things to her? Ever since we heard the poor lady was ailing, you've not let a week pass without sending her something, and such costly things too, like that fine flowered chair—I doubt there's another chair in all your palaces even half so comfortable—and *always* in Lord Robert's name, never your own!"

"If I sent them in my name, it would only scare her," I explained. "She would shrink from these gifts in suspicion and fear rather than take any delight from them. If Lady Dudley must die, then she is going to die in peace, Kat, comforted by the illusion that she is still cared for. I *can* give her that. But I cannot trust Robert to create that illusion for her; if he were to go to her, she would see his impatience, he would not be able to hide it, and he might even be tempted to hasten her end. He can master horses, but he cannot master himself, curb his impatience, and break his own temper. I know him, Kat, and though I am the Virgin Queen, and many equate virginity with innocence, I am well versed in the ways of men, especially ambitious men. So it is best, and kinder, that he keep away from Lady Dudley, even if I must bear the blame for it. The gossip is already such that I fear she must already know how greatly he desires her death, and this is one way to contradict it. If her husband sends her gifts, such pretty things so carefully chosen, perhaps she will think that despite his absence—which she may blame me for—and what the scandalmongers say, he does *still* care for her. Now show Dr Dee into my private garden, Kat. We will talk there," I said, and, swathed in the Swedish prince's sables, I went out to confer with the wisest and most learned man in my kingdom.

I smiled when Dr Dee bowed over my hand. People always expected him to look evil and extravagant, like a wizard in robes embroidered with esoteric symbols, or to see the Devil's hoofprint blazoned on his brow as flagrant proof that he had signed his name in Satan's big black book of damned souls. They were always astonished to discover that this benign, serenely smiling man, gowned in plain scholar's black, with blond hair and beard so fair they were almost white, was the notorious Dr John Dee who cast horoscopes, communed with angels and spirits, caught tantalising glimpses of the future in a black scrying glass, and dabbled in alchemy, as well as many more mundane and ordinary scholarly pursuits such as mathematics and astronomy. He was a great man, a fountain of knowledge, a glutton ever hungry to know more, a man who would spend money to buy a book he didn't have rather than food. And, even more important for the delicate mission I had entrusted him with, he was a kind man with a benevolent and reassuring manner, which was why I had chosen to send him to visit Amy. While his reputation might frighten her, I knew the man himself would quickly put her at ease and encourage her to confide in him. And I knew I could trust his judgment.

"You have seen Lady Dudley?" I asked, twirling the sable muff around my hands as we fell into step together.

"Yes, Your Majesty." He nodded sadly.

There was such a weighty sorrow in his voice that I stopped and turned to regard him fully. "Tell me. Spare me nothing."

As I listened to his words, it was as though I were actually there in the room with her, looking at her through Dr Dee's eyes. I saw her cowering there, like a frightened rabbit cornered by a snarling wolf, and I could *feel* her fear as if it were my own, filling every part of me until it threatened to drown me, overflowing from my eyes in tears. It made me *so angry*; if Robert had had the misfortune to cross my path at that moment, I don't know what I might have done. I had learned what it was like during my poor, mad sister's reign to fear the poisoned cup, the assassin's dagger, the suffocating pillow, or a silken noose as I slept, so I could well understand Amy's torment and terror. I knew what it was like to live without peace of mind. I also knew what it was like to love, but to not be able to trust, and I knew all about betrayal and lust and the cost of defiance and surrender.

I had been sorely shaken by my ordeals, but I had survived them. Even though my health at times crumbled and gave way beneath them, I was always able to claw my way back up out of the rubble and rise again like a phoenix from the ashes. But I was made of sterner, stronger stuff than Amy Dudley; I liked to think it was the unique and formidable combination of Boleyn and Tudor blood blended together and coursing through my veins that kept me alive and gave me the wits and will to survive, to always see the bright glow of victory, like a candle held aloft by Destiny, at the end of the tar black tunnel to guide me through the hard, treacherous, dark times, to make me persevere and fight to go forward, tenaciously following that light. But gentle Amy was different, and my fear- and exhaustion-provoked ailments did not compare with this disease that, like a great, fierce crab, had clamped its pinching claws upon her life.

"This Dr Bayly who refused to treat her," I began as we resumed walking, following the gravel path winding through the bleak, leaf-bare rose garden with its thorns standing out starkly against the white snow and leaden grey sky, "being more concerned with safeguarding his own reputation than alleviating her suffering, could he have done anything for her?"

"No, Your Majesty," Dr Dee replied, "and, I implore you, judge him not too harshly. I spoke at length with Dr Bayly before I left Oxford, and he is not by any means a cold or indifferent man, as circumstances might lead you to believe. I can assure you, he was much moved by her plight; though his decision was not made lightly, it still weighs heavily upon his mind and heart. He is a young man who shows great promise; he is an honourable man and a fine doctor, with a particular interest in ailments of the eyes, and I think he will do much good before he departs this world. But Lady Dudley's malady is beyond the skill of any ordinary physician, and, given the circumstances, it took both wisdom and courage not to meddle. Many would not have dared refuse Lord Robert; their eyes would have been on the rewards to be reaped from their compliance. The golden nimbus of greed doth often blind common sense and outshine compassion."

"Well said, Dr Dee." I nodded thoughtfully and approvingly. "Well said. So . . . Dr Bayly is to be commended, then. Perhaps one day when I visit Oxford, I shall see this good and honest physician for myself. But, for now, my concern is for Lady Dudley. If her ailment is beyond the skill of any ordinary physician, then find me one who is *extraordinary*!"

"Majesty, if you will forgive the presumption"—Dr Dee smiled—"I foresaw the need, and I have already done so. May I bring him to you?"

I could not resist smiling at Dr Dee. Though I often despised presumptuousness in others, depending on my mood and the circumstances, this was one of those times when I welcomed it. "I think you can foresee my answer to that as well."

And within moments Dr Kristofer Biancospino was standing before me. A man of blended exotic blood, Italian and Arabic with Persian and Greek ancestry, he had travelled far and wide in his insatiable quest for knowledge about the human body and the ailments that are its enemies, the diseases that strike with or without reason and show no mercy. He harboured a similar passion for plants, and the ability they had to harm or heal, to do good or ill.

During his travels he always sought out aged wisewomen and coaxed them to share their secret knowledge, lest it die with them. He had written a most learned and detailed study of poisons and was pleased to present me with a copy for my library. He had studied tenaciously and tirelessly in every land he visited, seeking the weapons, surgical and medicinal, to attack and defeat disease. And cancer, he had discovered, was the *ultimate* adversary, the undefeatable nemesis, the unvanquishable foe. And of the insidious form of this disease that afflicted Lady Dudley, he had made a particular study.

He quoted the sage ancient Greek physicians Hippocrates— who had given the disease its name, *karkinos*, the Greek word for *crab*, because the tumours reached out to grab healthy tissue like a crab's pincers—and Galen—who thought it was caused by an overabundance of black bile in the body. He told me the stories of two ancient empresses. First, Atossa of Babylon, who had awarded a slave his freedom when he saved her life by cutting a tumour from her breast, then Theodora of Byzantium, the former harlot and dancing girl who had wormed and wiggled her way into the Emperor Justinian's heart and bed until he put the imperial crown on her head and invited her to stand beside him and wield the sceptre of supreme power. Theodora carried on bravely, as long as she could, donning her bejewelled vestments and crown and playing her regal role, but she had chosen to die young and beautiful rather than submit to the surgeon's knife. Amputation of the breast was deemed the surest cure, though rarely a permanent one, in the ancient world, Dr Biancospino explained. If the patient survived the bloody and brutal ordeal of surgery, it bought her time, though at *great* cost to her vanity and pride, and, in the end, time *always* ran out, and the unwelcome guest inevitably came back, his claws snapping until he again caught hold of some piece of vulnerable flesh. And, true to his word, when I asked him not to spare me, he recounted the many horrors he had himself witnessed in the world's convents where the disease was, for unknown reasons, particularly prevalent, to such an extent that doctors had dubbed it "The Nun's Disease", though in truth it afflicted women of all kinds and classes, rich and poor, chaste and wanton, pious and pagan, pretty and plain, queens and commoners, highborn and low—it snapped and clamped its claws at random and respected no one. He told me of many of the afflicted Brides of Christ that he had known, and my heart went out to each of them. One French nun, a beautiful, violet-eyed young woman only a few years older than Amy, was so ravaged and riddled with tumours by the time Dr Biancospino came to tend her that, through the dead and brittle blackened tissue, rotting and reeking all over her chest, he could glimpse her heart and saw the exact moment when it ceased to beat and her suffering stopped.

Beneath my sable cloak, I touched my bosom and felt faint and light-headed with horror and dread, wanting to block my ears from this exotic foreigner's vivid discourse, forget the words I had just heard, and flee them, hoping and praying that the disease they described would never come to visit me, to latch on to me with its tenacious and fatal crab claws as it had done to Amy Dudley. I could see her in Dr Biancospino's words, like Atossa hiding her body from the eyes of her waiting women, bathing alone and in shame, hoping and praying the lump would just go away. And I glimpsed her in Theodora, falling weakly into the arms of Sleep, a woman of once vigorous and boundless energy too tired to stir herself even to don her royal robes, jewels, and crown. And again in the humble nuns wasting away, their bodies rotting from within, lying upon wafer-thin mattresses in convent infirmaries while the smell of death hovered in the air above the rancid, char-blackened, necrotic tissue on their chests, begging God's forgiveness for whatever sin they had committed that had opened the door to the Devil and invited this disease into their lives, even if it were something so innocuous and slight as admiring her reflection in the convent's well, coveting the pretty dress a wealthy benefactress had worn, glutting her belly on blackberries intended for a pie to delight all the holy sisters and afterwards claiming that the branches had been all but bare to explain the few, paltry berries left in the pail, or the lasciviousness and grandeur of a former life, the last like a penitent Magdalene renouncing all and taking refuge behind cloistered walls. I could catch fleeting glimpses of Amy Dudley in all of those poor women, in the cascade of blond hair draped over her shame-hunched shoulders and the arms folded tightly over her full and ample breasts, the desperate, pleading blue green eyes hungry for life and a love she could not have, once vibrant but now dulled and sorrow-filled, as her mind incessantly uttered prayers beseeching God or perhaps even St Agatha, whom Dr Biancospino said these afflicted women often prayed to, believing that this centuries-dead Christian martyr whose breasts had been cut off, then miraculously restored, could well understand their suffering and might even intercede to grant them a miracle.

"*Stop!*" I held up my hand. "Don't tell me any more. I have always believed that knowledge is power, but pray God I *never* need to know this! Dr Biancospino, I am confident that you are the man I am looking for. There is in my realm a patient, a young woman of seven-and-twenty years, sorely in need of your care. I wish to retain your services for her, *but,*" I stipulated firmly, "under *no* circumstances is she to know this. You are *never* to divulge my identity nor to admit to having ever met me; if she even suspects that you have come from me, you will lose her trust. Say only that your services are the gift of a well-wisher sorely concerned about her welfare amidst this maelstrom of ugly gossip. *Help her,* Dr Biancospino, *heal her* if you can. Do only what is in the best interests of your patient, and let the rest be damned, and let *no one* interfere, not even the lady's husband. You *must* be impervious to all rewards and promises. Are you the man I am looking for, Dr Biancospino?"

The black eyes that met mine were firm and unwavering. "Majesty," he said, "I am that man."

And I knew he spoke the truth. Here was a man who would do all that was humanly possible to save Amy Dudley, for the sake of battling the dark knight of cancer to try to save the fair maiden; he cared *nothing* for the players and the prizes in this royal game. His holy grail was finding a cure, not aiding Robert's fool's quest for a crown he could never have. Like St George slaying the dragon, Dr Kristofer Biancospino wanted to kill the great crab called Cancer who preyed upon, ravaged, and took, more than any one dragon, so many lives.

❧ 30 ❧

Amy Robsart Dudley

Cumnor Place, Berkshire, near Oxford
March–September 1560

As the days drifted past, day after empty, pain-racked day, I grew weaker. I no longer had any desire to go outside, and there was little out there to tempt me now. This year, summer didn't seem like summer, it was so cold and wet, the skies more often leaden grey rather than heavenly blue, and the sun seemed rarely to exert itself to vanquish the rain—like me, she seemed to have fallen into lethargy. Some days I passed entirely in pain-shrouded slumber so that at night, while everyone else slept, I was awake and restless, lonely, and feeling the sharp, needle-toothed bite of the pain, when all I wanted to do was sleep, to pull the covers up over my head and hide from the sad reality of my life, to just let my ever-dwindling days float past until Time ran out for me.

Many nights I passed sitting up in bed, sewing partlets and yokes to fill in the low-cut square bodices of my gowns, so no trace of my malady would ever show. Sleepless, by candlelight I embroidered delicate flowers and sometimes even healing herbs upon the fine white linen, like feverfew and chamomile blossoms, but no more hearts—entwined, inflamed, or impaled by Cupid's dart—or true lovers' knots; that girl didn't exist any more.

Sometimes I did indeed pull the covers up over my head, even though I lay tense and wakeful underneath, until dawn, when I at last drifted off to sleep again. I was afraid that, as he often did, the grey friar would step out of the stone walls and come to me, to stand a watchful and alert sentinel beside or at the foot of my bed. Though I knew hiding from him was senseless; cowering beneath the covers wouldn't keep him away. I was apt to see him at any moment, day or night, and even when I hid, I could still feel his presence in the cold and prickly sensation up and down the nape of my neck and spine. But I was scared that one night he would come to stand at the foot of my bed and lower his hood to reveal what the darkness hid and show me the *true* face of Death.

Often I wondered who he was. Had he perhaps served in the infirmary and tended the monks who were ailing and dying, keeping an alert vigil by their beds, comforting and praying as they breathed their last? Or was he guilty of some heinous sin, some horrible crime that damned his soul and barred the gates of Heaven against him forevermore? Sometimes I wondered if I had gone mad, as I was the only one who could see him. To everyone else the phantom friar was just a legend, just another ghost story to tell while sitting round the fire on a dark night for the thrill a little fright can give. But, to me, he wasn't just a story; he was *very* real indeed.

And then *he* came to me, as though he had been blown in by the March winds, the only one who *might* have been able to save me— Dr Kristofer Biancospino. At first I was sorely afraid of him; he was a foreigner, born of an Italian father and an Arab woman, olive skinned with piercing, deep-set, obsidian black eyes, and raven-wing hair, sleek and swooping over his brow, and a sharp nose and chin. My mind always wanted to picture him in a jewelled and feathered turban, resplendent in oriental robes of jewel-coloured silk and damask—ruby, emerald, sapphire, amethyst, and topaz—with golden pointy-toed slippers that turned up at the tips, though I never saw him in anything but plain, elegant, but severe black. He looked, at first glance, dangerous and harsh, a haughty patrician medical man with a long list of impressive credentials who could never conceive of caring being a part of the physician's art. At first, he reminded me of a more exotic version of Sir Richard Verney;

they had the same dark hair and eyes and the same sharpness of features, noses as sharp as knives when seen from the side. But I was wrong, *so very wrong*. He never babbled or blundered, flushed or fidgeted, or stammered trying to find the right words, nor was he hard-hearted or brutally blunt but matter-of-fact; his honesty never faltered or hid like a bitter almond inside a coating of coloured sugar. His fingers never fumbled with embarrassment or incompetence when he examined and tended me. Nor did he use humour and jests to try to cajole and distract me and make the truth seem less grim. There was no nonsense about him; he was, in all ways, confident and steady, efficient and brisk. And yet . . . there was comfort in those hands, the way they moved over my body, so *sure* what to do, never hesitating. And instead of disdain, arrogance, or self-importance, I saw in his dark eyes deep wells of kindness. He was not at all the frightening and sinister man I took him for at first glance.

The first time he examined me, when I bared my breast to his scrutiny, I turned my face away, tears filling my eyes, and clutched a perfumed handkerchief to my nose, humiliated and angered by the stink of the vile, disgusting discharge oozing out to stain the linen dressing that covered it. It wasn't fair! People were supposed to rot *after* they died, whilst I had been condemned to have my flesh decay even as I still lived, and to smell always this foul, rotting rancidness that no perfume could ever fully conceal; it was *always* there, like a whiff of manure beneath the roses.

Gently, he peeled the dressing away and, taking a bottle from his bag, tipped it over a folded square of linen and began to cleanse my breast with a sharp-scented liquid that felt strangely good even as it tingled and stung. "A cleansing wash, an astringent," he explained. "I shall write out the recipe before I leave. Have your maid do this for you every morning and night, each time the dressing is changed, and apply a hot towel for half an hour afterwards."

"Yes, Doctor," I nodded and said softly, still avoiding his eyes.

He paused then and took my face gently between his hands and turned it so I had no choice but to look at him.

"Do not be afraid or ashamed," he said. "Do not turn away from me, or away from yourself." As he resumed his examination, he continued speaking as his fingers gently prodded the swollen, distorted lump, feeling it move like a rotting fruit trapped beneath my skin. "You are *still* beautiful. Do not be alarmed, I tell all my patients this—you are *more* than *this*." He cupped my breast carefully in his hand. "*Much more!* I have seen this malady *many* times, many, *many, many* times, afflicting women everywhere—rich and poor, young and old, slim and stout, virgins, wives, and whores, godless and devout—and I can say, with *complete* confidence, it is *nothing* you have done that has drawn this disease to you. Many women despair and in the throes of their suffering think that it is somehow their fault and search their lives for some sin or transgression to account for it, when there is in truth none. Some even look to point the finger of blame at their vanity, the low-cut dresses, or the carnal pleasures they enjoyed, but, in truth, it is none of that. I have seen virgin spinsters who spent their whole lives modestly covered in high-necked gowns and never knew the touch of a man succumb to it. It is a disease that strikes down some and spares others; it has no respect for beauty, wealth, titles, and prestige, nor piety and good works either. It is not like a man who prefers a certain type of woman; this cancer is random and without mercy. In France and Italy it is called 'The Nun's Disease'—though no one knows why, it is seen tragically often in convents. When I was a young man studying medicine in Italy, and also when I was in France, I attended many such cases. I have charted its course from its first appearance to the agony and devastation of its final stage. We are old adversaries—cancer and I."

"Did they . . ." The word *die* stuck in my throat, and I could not say it, so instead I asked, "Were you able to cure them?"

"In some cases I bought them more time. I was able to slow the disease's progress or banish it temporarily, but at *great* cost, and I do not speak of money, but . . ." He sighed deeply and closed his eyes for a moment. "For some it cost more than the cure was worth, some found the remedy to be worse than the malady, and, for those who survived the cure, the disease took a holiday and came back after a time, sometimes months, sometimes a few years, later; only one was able to live out her life without it ever revisiting her. But, for most of my patients, I could only give a respite from their pain."

When he had finished speaking, I could only nod. I did not trust myself to speak, and, in truth, I did not know what to say. I had known all along that I was doomed. So I nodded and murmured, "Thank you, Doctor. I understand."

"Come now, my beautiful patient, it is not time for tears yet." He reached up and with his own handkerchief wiped my eyes. "I do not give up easily, not without a fight, and neither should you. Now, shall we begin?"

"Yes." I nodded and added softly, "Thank you, Doctor."

He prescribed a potent white powder of opium poppies, to be mixed with wine to mask its bitter, burning taste, to help me with the pain, though he cautioned it might bring confusion and strange dreams, both waking and sleeping, and even as it dulled the sharp edge of pain, it would also dull my mind. He also prescribed an elixir for cooling fever, and recommended ginger suckets, which I already knew of and used, to help quell the nausea, both before and after eating. "The weaker you get, the stronger the cancer gets," he explained. "You *must* think of it as your nemesis, your foe, your enemy, a *very* powerful one who is the emperor of all ailments, and fight it with *everything* you have, armed with what weapons I can give you." He wrote out recipes and careful instructions for Pirto to follow in a daily regimen of treatment, and, when I thought he was done, paused and added a hot poultice for my ribs and back, when I told him of the sharp pains that now beset me in these parts, and he urged me to leave off my stays. "No more tight lacing," he admonished. He prescribed a strengthening tonic that I should take daily and forbade me strenuous exercise, absolutely no dancing or horseback riding, even if I felt like it, and if I *must* travel—"and I do not recommend it now," he said in a grave and serious tone—I must do so only by litter, carried by men at a slow walk, taking the utmost care not to jar me. "I do not wish to alarm you," he continued, "but you *must* know, as this disease progresses, it can eat into the bones, suck the life out of them, if you will, and leave them brittle and vulnerable to fractures and breaking. I had one patient whose spine snapped as she was walking across her bedchamber, and another who broke a finger opening a letter."

I gasped and felt dizzy and light-headed at these words, more afraid for myself than ever, trapped in a body that was apt to break all apart even as the cancer did its evil work upon my breast.

Dr Biancospino took my hand. "I know it is frightening, but I would be most remiss if I did not tell you. You are a woman formerly accustomed to leading a busy, vigorous life, taking an active part in the management of a large estate, I am told, and I know you must miss being that woman, but to try to ignore this, to go on as if nothing were wrong, you would risk doing yourself *great* injury."

I said I understood, thanked him, and promised to do *exactly* as he said. And when I told him of the hemlock pills Robert had given me, and still continued to send, along with other medicines, Dr Biancospino merely shook his head and said, "I think I have something better."

He took from his bag a mortar and pestle and various powders and asked Pirto to bring him water. While he measured out the powders, he cautioned me not to mix the remedies he prescribed with those recommended by others, even if they meant well and had only the best intentions; combining the wrong ingredients or ingesting too much of any one of them could be *extremely* dangerous or even deadly. "And no more bleeding and purging," he said firmly. "With this particular malady I think they do more harm than good and only increase weakness and lethargy." Then, as he added the water and began to stir the mixture, creating a thick white paste, he bade me sit, bare to my waist, on a high stool before him. And from his bag he took a brush, just like an artist might use—I had seen Lavinia Teerlinc wield similar ones, albeit more delicate and smaller—and, with slow, steady, almost sensual strokes, he began to paint my afflicted breast with the white paste. "It may sting a little," he cautioned, "or even burn—some ladies have more sensitive skin than others—but that is a good thing; that is how we know the medicine is working." As I watched it harden, hiding the ugly mottled flesh and drying up the seeping discharge beneath a shell that made me feel as if my breast were turning into marble, he explained that it was a mixture of lime, hemlock, and belladonna and said that he would instruct Pirto in its preparation so that she could apply it fresh for me each morning.

For the first time since I realised that I had cancer, I felt as if hope hadn't entirely forsaken me. But it was only, I think, that I wanted *so much* to believe. I tried to deny it, to pretend and ignore it, when I continued to worsen, to hide beneath the balm of the medicines Dr Biancospino gave me, bittersweet elixirs that made me feel as if I were floating just below the surface of a placid river, the water either warm or cold, whichever my feverish or chilled body most wanted, hiding from the pain that lurked above, waiting to lunge and grab and sink its fangs back into me.

It was getting harder and harder. Every day I felt my energy, my strength, slipping further away, and myself falling, fainting feebly into the arms of lethargy even though I *tried* to hold on, *tried* to fight it. Every moment I was awake, a part of me wanted only to sleep. The least little movement could bring an excruciating burst of pain, as if Death himself reached out his cold, skeletal hand to squeeze my heart and steal my breath away or land a hammer blow against my bones. I began to suffer pains in my shoulders, an aching, almost unbearable pressure, as if someone endowed with great strength were standing behind me, pressing with all his might, bearing down upon them. And sometimes I had similar pains in my hips, chest, and back. Sometimes I thought pain had stealthily, one by one, replaced all the bones that made up my spine; it seemed to be made of pure pain now. I was also often troubled by headaches, when I had hardly ever had them before. My eyes were now glad of the gloom inside Cumnor, as I shrank from the sun I had once so dearly loved to be out and about in; now it made my eyes ache as if it were piercing them with needles of molten light. I had to turn my face away, squeeze my eyes shut tightly, and fight with all my might the urge to sink down right where I was, weak and weary, and go to sleep even as the pain thrummed all along the length of my body from top to toe like a plucked lute string.

Some days getting out of bed was just *too* much for me, though I tried faithfully every day, as Dr Biancospino said I should, telling me it was good for me to sit up, put on my pretty clothes, and stir myself a bit. To lie abed would only weaken me more and invite bedsores, he said; it was better to keep moving, albeit with all due caution and care. And I always tried to do just that, to dress and be up and sitting in my beautiful flowered chair beside the fire on the days when Dr Biancospino came to call. I wanted him to see how hard I was trying, and the vain woman in me wanted him to see me looking my best. Sometimes I even dared to venture outside, to sit on a bench in the park, just to get away from the stale odours of the sickroom, the fever sweat, chamber pot, and medicines, and the perfume that tried to mask it all, though as time passed, those days became fewer and rarer, going up and down the stairs hurt so much, like knives of agony stabbing into my ribs and back, and by the time I reached the top, or bottom, I was breathless and exhausted, and it took all the will I had to go on.

Finally a day came when Dr Biancospino admitted it too, that all his remedies had been in vain, like a sliver of ice tossed into a pot of boiling water in an attempt to cool it.

It was a Saturday—I remember it well—a grey and dreary day that typified this dismal, cold, wet summer. I had declined an invitation to join the other ladies for cards; just the thought of their catty chatter and the thrusts and jabs Mrs Forster and Mrs Oddingsells aimed at each other was more than I could stand. I was sitting by the fire, just letting the day pass by. I had put on a pretty dress and hood of pale pink brocade shimmering with silver threads and frills of delicate silver lace, and I had a beautiful pale yellow shawl the colour of fresh-churned butter that Robert had sent, embroidered with brightly coloured fruits, flowers, birds, and animals, which I never tired of looking at.

When Dr Biancospino arrived, I was stroking the arm of my chair and admiring an intricately embroidered pale pink flower with a cherry red heart, embellished with golden and silver threads that glimmered in the firelight. Dr Biancospino drew up a stool and took my hands in his. He met my eyes and said that it was time for him to speak boldly of a more aggressive, but *very* dangerous way in which we might attack my cancer—a procedure most would consider more barbaric butchery than surgery, as it would result in lifelong pain and the most drastic and permanent disfigurement, if the shock of the knife cutting or an infection afterwards did not kill me. He described it to me, and I forced myself to listen, even though I felt sick and faint with horror. I wanted to run away from his words, I didn't want to hear them, I didn't want to think about what he was describing, but I hadn't the strength to run, and there was nowhere to run to. I had to sit, listen, and face the truth. And he was right, it made perfect sense; if the disease was to depart, so too must the infected breast. So I braced myself, my fingers digging hard into the arms of my chair, and forced myself to listen as he described the procedure. The patient was made to lie flat upon a table, bound with leather straps, then large, new, and well-sharpened fishhooks attached to a series of ropes, strung overhead as pulleys, were inserted into the diseased breast, and the ropes pulled to lift it up, off the chest. The surgeon then, as quickly as he could, cut away the diseased breast and cauterised the wound with hot irons. The pain was excruciating, even with a potion to dull it, and many never left the table alive; the pain caused their hearts to stop, and those who did live often succumbed to fever and infection within a few days' or weeks' time. The rare ones who survived had pain and disfigurement replace cancer as their constant companion until Cancer came back to take the life he had already staked a claim to when he first marked their breast.

"I have myself performed this operation but rarely, and only upon six women," Dr Biancospino said gravely. "Two died upon the table, one survived three days, the other a day short of a fortnight, only to die in an inferno of festering pain and fever. One lived for another four years before the cancer returned; the other is still alive—for now—but she lived to dance at her daughter's wedding and hold her first grandchild. I will not lie to you, Amy, if you agree to gamble with your life, the dice are not loaded in your favour, and I cannot predict—I cannot even hazard a guess—whether you will win or lose, or if you win time, how much."

"I understand," I said softly, grimacing as I levered myself up from my chair and walked across the room to stand before the beautiful Venetian looking glass Robert had sent me, its silver frame a-bloom with golden buttercups.

I stood there for a long time, staring at myself, so thin and pale and wan, remembering the Amy I used to be, rosy-cheeked, plump, round, and robust. I remembered a time when Robert had called me his "gold and pink alabaster angel" when I used to wait for him in bed, longing and ready for his embrace, with my golden hair spread across the pillows, and my nakedness tantalisingly veiled in a bed gown of pale pink lace. If I submitted to this surgery, I could never again take sensual delight in being a woman; I could never give or receive carnal pleasure, lest the lover recoil in horror at the sight of the ugly, scarred, sunken hollow where my left breast had once been, with the right one beside it as a reminder of the creamy pink-tipped dessert to delight a lover it used to be. This was my only chance to live, but was it worth taking—was it a life worth saving? The cancer had already ravaged my body, spoiled my beauty, stolen my flesh, and sapped my vitality. Was what Dr Biancospino's knife would do any worse? My sore and oozing breast was not fit to be seen; it was an object to arouse disgust, not desire. Would a scarred and sunken crater on my chest be any less so? But what did I have to live for? What did I have to hope for? Everything that mattered to me was already gone. Robert would never love me again; he would never renounce the Queen and come back to me; he wanted me dead or divorced. And what other man would have me as I was now or if I submitted to and survived the surgeon's knife? My beauty was gone, and I didn't have that magical, magnetic confidence like Elizabeth that sometimes allows plain or ugly women to attract admirers. I didn't even have a fortune any more. When Robert married me, I was a Norfolk heiress, with three manors and a flock of 3,000 sheep, apple orchards, and fields of barley. Now all I had left was me, a tired and damaged, disease-ravaged woman eight years past twenty who had failed at everything in a woman's life that matters.

I was so absorbed in my thoughts that I did not realise Dr Biancospino had come to stand behind me until I saw his face reflected in the glass behind me.

"If you choose to have the surgery, to fight and maybe even win, and defy Death, you will still be beautiful," he said, "and any man who thinks otherwise is a shallow fool."

"Thank you," I said quietly as the tears dripped down my face. I *wanted* to believe, I *wanted* to hope, but I couldn't. I just couldn't do it! But I didn't want to disappoint dear Dr Biancospino. "I . . . I need time to think," I said. "I am so very tired, I just want to lie down and rest for a while, and later . . . later I will think on all that you have said to me and . . . and then decide."

He turned me round to look at him, and his eyes burned into

mine, and I felt the fire of his soul trying to will me to live, to fight for my life, even at the cost of my breast. He raised his hand and caressed my tear-dampened cheek.

"Believe!" he whispered urgently. *"Believe!"*

He took me by the hand and led me to my bed. Gently, he turned me round and unlaced my pink gown, carefully easing it, and my petticoats, down over my hips to pool round my feet like an open flower. I was surprised that he didn't call for Pirto but chose to attend me himself, as though he had doffed the cap of physician and donned that of a lady's maid instead, but I said nothing, and, as I had always done before, trusted myself in his confident, capable hands. He held my hand as I stepped out of my skirts, and when I sat down on the bed, he knelt before me and removed my pink slippers and turned up the hem of my shift, up above my knees, to untie the pink silken bows of my garters and roll down my stockings. He plucked out the pins that held my hood in place, and then he helped me to lie down, lifting my cold feet as I laid my head upon the pillows. He covered me and came to sit on the side of the bed, gazing down at me silently, never saying a word, just looking at me, stroking my hair, smoothing it over the pillows in waves of shining gold. Then he turned away and busied himself with the medicines on the table by my bed. He poured some wine into a goblet and added the familiar bitter white powder, that harbinger of strange dreams, derived from a pretty red poppy. Oh, how much I *loved* it for dulling the pain and, at the same time, *hated* it for the way it muddled my mind and made it feel heavy and befuddled upon waking, laboriously trying to separate reality from the realm of dreams. This time he added more of the powder, to make it stronger, to give me a deeper and longer rest, and I was glad. I wanted and needed it. I reached for the goblet and drank it down, almost greedily, never minding the burn and bitter aftertaste, then fell back against the pillows and shut my eyes.

He sat with me a little longer, stroking my hair, as my eyelids grew heavy and I started drifting off towards sleep and went, like a woman in love, into the arms of Morpheus. Was that the name of the god of sleep? It seemed a century ago that I had read the book of mythology to try to better myself for Robert. And it didn't really matter any more; regardless of his name, the god of slumber I had found was both a cruel and tender lover, who, in league with the medicine, liked to play games with my mind and leave me hopelessly befuddled and afraid that I was losing my mind. But this day, I was too tired to care. Let them have their fun, let the god of sleep and the white powder play, as long as I got to sleep.

Dr Biancospino bent and pressed a chaste kiss onto my brow. *"Believe!"* he whispered again, and then he left me.

I slept long and deeply, dreams barely rippling, like a gentle breeze blowing upon the calm waters of my rest, so slight that I could not remember or be disturbed by them.

Morpheus, or whatever his name was, was kind that afternoon, but sometime late in the night I was roused by a persistent hammering that sounded as if it were coming from right outside my door. But I felt as if my head had been glued to my pillow, and my body to the mattress. I just could not rouse myself or even call out to Pirto. Surely no one was making repairs at this late hour? Surely no loose panelling or floorboard could be so urgent that it could not wait until day? It must have been midnight, the witching hour, or even later. And then it stopped, and I thought no more about it until the pressing need of my body to be relieved forced me from my bed. After I had availed myself of the chamber pot, before I climbed back into bed, I remembered the curious hammering and went and opened my door to look out.

My scream shattered the peace of what was left of the night, for there, nailed onto my bedchamber door, was a dried, wrinkled, and red sheep's heart impaled with several sprigs of hawthorn, and, beside it, a small clay figure of a woman, with a nail driven through the middle of her chest, pinning her tiny body to the wooden door, and a lone hawthorn sprig piercing her left breast. A lock of golden hair was stuck to her head, and a bit of stained and bloody bandage formed a skirt around her hips to tell me who it was meant to be—*me!* I slid to the floor in a dead faint, dimly aware of numerous people in nightclothes with concerned and alarmed faces clustering around me, leaning over me with lighted candlesticks in their hands.

I awoke hours later in my bed. Everyone tried to tell me that it had just been an evil dream, a nightmare, and that I should think no more about it, but even though they had been removed, I knew what I had seen—dark omens, the signs of black magic, a death spell, nailed to my door. If cancer and poison couldn't kill me quickly enough, then someone was determined to frighten the life out of me. And when, later that day, I thought I caught a glimpse of the dark-cloaked figure of Richard Verney walking in the park, deep in conversation with Mr Forster, I was *certain* I knew who it was. Mrs Forster tried to tell me that he had merely come on an errand for my husband, to deliver some papers to Mr Forster, who, as my husband's treasurer, managed all his accounts, as well as a purse of gold for my own expenses, and that he had already gone away again, but I refused to believe it was an innocent errand rather than an evil one. Richard Verney was my husband's creature, his most devoted minion, and he had already tried to take my life twice, first by poison and then by hiring Red Jack. Only my departure from Compton Verney had saved me, but now . . . now I knew that he and his evil, murderous intentions had followed me to Cumnor.

My anger almost gave me the courage to send for Dr Biancospino and agree to the operation, to let myself be strapped to the table right at that moment and sacrifice my breast, to try to save my life just to spite my would-be murderers, to keep Robert, the assassin of all my dreams, from having his come true. But my courage faltered, and then it fell and plummeted to the depths and shattered when it hit the bottom the day I received the book of poisons in a parcel sent from London, authored by Dr Kristofer Biancospino, with the telltale red hair stuck inside that told me that my enemy, the Queen, had sent it.

I was always a creature of feelings, prey to my own emotions, not cold and calculating and precise, and they knew it, and so I played right into their hands and did *exactly* what they meant for me to do. I let Fear take hold of me and dance me round fast until I was senseless and dizzy with it, overwhelmed and unable to think clearly. Thus I let her accomplish what she aimed to do—plant the seed of mistrust and make me turn my back on Dr Biancospino, shun and send away the man who might have been my saviour.

❧ 31 ❧

Elizabeth

When we departed for the Summer Progress, few, if any, of my court were in a tranquil state of mind. There is always an air of excitement and expectancy that hangs about a Progress, but this year there was a strong undercurrent of tension and alertness rippling through the great, snaking procession, making it seem more like an electric eel than a snake as it slowly undulated along the long, dusty, winding roads. Trouble was brewing in Scotland, and many of our men lay strewn, dead and broken, on the field of battle in a war I had never wanted but that the men about me had insisted must be fought, though my inner instincts cried out for peace. Because of this, and other factors, this summer I had chosen not to stray too far from London. And to further complicate matters, the passionate Prince Eric had written vaguely but vehemently that he was determined to come woo me in person, sailing to me in a ship filled with gold to lay this fortune, along with his love, at my feet, to pile it there before me piece by piece with his own hands, and no one could say for certain, not even his ambassadors, whether this was merely sweet lover's talk or if word might come at any moment that his ship had docked. And the weather was dismal, so cold, rainy, and foul, it was hard to believe this was indeed summer. I heard more than one of my courtiers grumble, and most aptly too, that he would rather sit in the hot and close confines of the noisy, busy kitchen than in the draughty Great Hall, which was far too large to ever heat sufficiently.

And Robert! He was like a man possessed! A whirlwind of infectious, frenetic energy that I found contagious; from rising to retiring it was a constant, unending race to see which one of us would weary first. But he was also drunk on the wine of power and glutted on the feast of folly. Incessantly he hinted and wheedled and pestered me to elevate him to the peerage; he had his heart and mind set on an earldom. He seemed hell-bent on making himself even more hated and appeared to take a peculiar pleasure in being the most detested man in England. Already he wore a vest of chain mail beneath his shirt, and his death was spoken of by many as an event they looked forward to with infinite delight, but these threats seemed only to feed his vanity and pride as seeds for the peacock. And when he rode out as my champion in one of the many tournaments he arranged, he wore a coat embroidered with a tall white obelisk entwined with ivy and blazoned with the words *You standing, I will flourish.* It was clear to everyone what he meant: as long as I ruled, he looked to reign supreme as the highest in my favour and, in time, perhaps as more. It was no secret that he longed to be King and thought himself the man amongst all my suitors most worthy of it. When I told him, *"Never!"* it was as though he didn't even hear me; his arrogance and vanity rendered him deaf to common sense and reason. He went about behaving like a little boy leaping up and swooping down to catch butterflies, just for the pleasure of pulling their beautiful wings off and leaving them to die maimed and ugly. And I found myself trying ever harder to ignore the qualities that tarnished the allure of this man, whom I had known and loved almost all my life. I was torn. I was being maddeningly contradictory, and I knew it. He was irresistible, yet at times all I wanted to do was resist and put him from me, banish him from my life, though at the back of my mind the nagging thought tugged that if I did, the words would scarcely be out of my mouth before I was issuing orders contradicting them and calling him back to me. He was just too much fun. As for Amy, we never spoke of her.

Wilfully and rebelliously turning a deaf ear and a blind eye to the rumours that branded me wild and wanton, I tossed my hair and told Cecil to deal with the Scottish situation himself, and I flounced off to play and amuse myself with Robert, to spend almost every waking hour riding and hunting with him, picnicking and dancing with him beneath the trees or the stars at open-air banquets. I was in such a strange state of mind that summer! Looking back on it, that Elizabeth sometimes seems a stranger even to me. I no longer trusted Robert. I was *furious* with him over Amy, I despised and deplored his ambitions, and I would *never* marry him—nothing on this earth or in Heaven could ever induce me to make him my husband—but I couldn't shake or break his hold over me. He was quite simply the most fun and exciting man I ever knew. I still wanted him, but only in *my own way, not* his. It was only when his way was also mine that we agreed; when we differed, it was like thunder and lightning, clashing and crashing. And often, in cruel little ways, always publicly, so there would be many witnesses, I would put him in his place. One day when I saw him coming, a delighted smile spreading across his face, as he strode across the lawn of one of the country houses we stopped at, to join me where I sat picnicking with my court beneath the trees, I smiled and waved at him and trilled merrily, "Ah, there you are!" I moved my full skirts aside and patted the warm green grass beside me. "I *cannot* live without seeing you *every* day!" I watched Robert's smile broaden. "You are like my little dog"—I paused to allow my courtiers to gasp and snigger as the smile fell from Robert's face—"as soon as he is seen anywhere, people know that I am coming, and when you are seen, they say I am not far off." And though Robert grumbled and glowered at being compared to a dog, I laughed and gave a playful yank to the Order of the Garter that he wore about his throat, saying, "Just like a jewelled leash!" I smiled. "All of my dogs wear such pretty collars!" And all the rest of the day I made a great show of dropping things—my fan, my gloves, my handkerchief, even surreptitiously pulling the pins from my hat so that it would be blown from my head and go skipping on the breeze across the wide emerald lawn—so that "my gallant puppy" might fetch them for me, and each time he returned be rewarded with a pat on the head and a "Good boy!"—a morsel of praise or a sweetmeat to nibble from my fingers, which I hastily snatched back, lest he nip them in his anger. And by the time I retired that night, the highest man in the land was feeling *very* low indeed.

And still I flirted shamelessly with Arundel, Pickering, and my dear Gooseberry. And when the eldest statesman in the land, Sir William Paulet, who at five years past eighty had served my father, brother, and sister before me, entertained us at his house in Winchester, I kept him constantly at my side, kissing and patting his withered cheeks and clinging to his arm, many times lamenting how I wished that he was not so old, for "I would have him to be my husband before any other man in England, for he is pliable like a willow rather than mighty as an oak, and I care for him most deeply!" Oh, how Robert fumed at that; he banged his fist down into a plate of salad, jarring all the tableware around him and up-setting a goblet of wine into his sister's lap. I cried out in mock alarm for my physician, and when he raced to my side, directed him to attend Lord Robert. "His face is so red, I fear he is about to succumb to apoplexy! Look at the way the veins in his temples pulse!"

I was selfish, though I would not admit that to anyone but my-self. I was young still, and after so many years of fighting for my life, of being a prisoner of fear or behind locked doors, I just wanted to be free. I told myself I had done all that was possible for Amy, that she was comforted and well cared for, and I cast off my cares to have fun with the only man who could keep up with me. Or maybe those are all just excuses designed to try to cloak, conceal, and justify the fascination and allure that held me in thrall to Robert Dudley.

Everyone tried to make me see reason. Sometimes I retaliated by sending the men off to Scotland, including the most prominent and powerful of Robert's enemies, the Duke of Norfolk. I even dis-patched Cecil to sue for peace. I didn't want to hear; I chose to stop my ears and blind my eyes to Robin's faults and follies. I wanted to kick Reason out of my life and just have fun. In moments of solitude and quiet, when I forced myself to face the truth—as a result, I tried to avoid too many quiet moments that might open the door to such honest introspection—I knew that there would not be many more summers like this; indeed, this might even be the last one. I was a woman nearly seven years past twenty. Many thought I had dallied overlong in eschewing the marriage bed and began to believe I would indeed die an old maid, a crotchety, sharp, and sour as a crabapple virgin, and though several still ran after me, some of my suitors had already given up, admitted defeat, and married elsewhere.

Before he departed for Scotland, Cecil warned me, "Madame, if you are foolish enough to marry Robert Dudley, it will be your undoing. One night you shall go to bed as Queen Elizabeth and wake up plain Lady Elizabeth the next morning! By courting Robert Dudley, you are courting disaster!" he shouted after me.

But I didn't listen. Instead, I shouted: "Since this is your war, Cecil, you can finish it; don't come back until you have achieved peace!"

He was back by July, having seemingly accomplished the impossible, but I was too proud to even tender my thanks; instead, I retreated to Kew, where Robert hosted a grand banquet for all my court. As we fed each other bites of the fat quails, re-dressed after roasting in their proud heads and plumage, stuffed to bursting with apples and chestnuts, and presiding over a nest filled with their own pickled eggs, we sat apart from the other guests, in the perfumed rose garden, lounging upon plump rose silk cushions, tantalisingly veiled from their inquisitive eyes by sheer rose-coloured curtains fringed with Venetian gold, through which all could see our shadowed forms embracing. Robert presented me with an enormous deep blue sapphire that had once belonged to my father, which he had had cut into the shape of a heart and ringed by peerless white diamonds. "Here is my heart," he said as he offered it to me in a blue velvet box. "Let this jewel stand as surety for my eternal, undying love, and the depth of its blue as testament to the depth of my devotion, bluer than the bluest sea, deeper than the deepest ocean."

I was silent as he fastened its diamond chain about my throat, remembering the amber heart that Amy, in anguish and pain, had flung at me. No doubt he had presaged that gift with a similarly pretty speech, but to my ears now the words rang hollow, empty, and untrue; there was no sincerity to fill them. And I wondered how many other women Robert had given his heart to with pretty, meaningless words and symbolic gifts of jewellery.

One night, during the early days of September, shortly after we had returned to Windsor in preparation for my twenty-seventh birthday celebrations on the seventh, I rose from my dressing table, where I had sat in my shift, staring at without seeing myself in the looking glass, during one of those rare, moody, and brooding sessions of introspection, and softly bade Kat to help me dress.

"And what will Your Majesty wear?" I started at the sound of her voice; it was like a sharp-pointed icicle hanging above my head. "Might I suggest the scarlet satin? It is, after all, the traditional colour worn by harlots."

Gasping, hurt, and appalled, before I knew what I was doing, I spun around and slapped her; then, just as quickly, I fell to my knees, grasping her hands, begging her to forgive me.

Kat burst into tears and fell to her knees, and there we were, kneeling on the floor, weeping and snivelling in each other's arms as Kat implored me to renounce Robert Dudley before my reputation was ruined entirely.

"I would have rather seen Your Highness strangled at birth than live to see the day when my lovely girl, my Princess, my Queen, is spoken of in the same tone as those bawdy women who lift their skirts for any man who has a coin! In God's name, *please,* my darling girl, marry *now*—marry a prince who is worthy of you, and put a stop to all this ugly, evil talk! Some say you are with child by Lord Robert, and it is not the first child you have borne him, and others say you are in league with him, conspiring to murder his wife so that he will be free to become your husband, that you are just dallying, making cruel sport of all the men who come from far and wide to woo you, until the deed is done. Oh, I *know* you mean the poor lady no ill and have been the very soul of kindness to her—you have protected and shielded her all you can—but the scandal will *never* cease until you are safely married to another man suitable to your royal estate! Already they say he behaves as though he were your consort already, and that you are as good as married by the familiar and intimate way you behave together. They say you are as sinful as adulterers, as the horsemaster has a wife already—a fine lady from whom he has had nothing but good! I tell you, it is not seemly conduct for a queen! Don't you see, my love? You are lowering yourself in the eyes of your people. Robert Dudley will cost you all the love and respect of your people, just like Spanish Philip did your sister Mary! If you continue on this path, soon they will withdraw their affection and allegiance and look to someone else to take your place, war and bloodshed will rage throughout the land as the claimants battle for your throne, and you will have no one to blame but yourself! Better that you had died in the cradle, that I had strangled you with my own two hands, than that I live to see the day when my dear lady is no longer deemed worthy to wear the crown!" And she broke down, clinging to me and sobbing hard upon my shoulder.

"Oh, Kat." I hugged her close. "I know you speak from your heart, that this babbling is the outpouring of a loyal and loving heart and the true fidelity that you bear me, but I assure you, I am innocent! And though I am willing to consider marriage, it is not something that can be undertaken lightly . . ."

"Oh, stop it! Stop!" Kat cried. "It's *me* you're talking to, your dear old Kat, and I *know* how skilled you are at speaking a lot of words yet saying nothing at all!"

In a fury, I thrust her from me and began to pace wildly about the room, my fingers tugging and combing distractedly through my wild, streaming hair. "Robert Dudley has stood my good friend these many years, and none can, with just cause, object to our friendship and the favour I have shown him. I live my life in the open, surrounded all the time, watched by a thousand eyes, so *all* can see and rightly judge whether there is any dishonour in my conduct or not! But, I will thank you and all others to remember *this,* Kat: I am Queen of this realm, and if I had ever the will or desire to lead a dishonourable life—from which may God preserve me!— there is *no one* who could forbid me, but I trust in God that none shall ever live to see me conduct myself such!"

"Bess, *please,* for all the love I have borne you and that you bear your dear old Kat, *please,* at least, put some distance between yourself and Lord Robert!"

"No, I cannot." I turned from her. "In my life I have had so much tribulation and so little joy, and he makes me happy, Kat—

sometimes I hate and curse him, and myself for loving him, for I know full well what he is, what he aspires to, but, God help me, he makes me happy, Kat! Truly, Kat, I do not look to have him, and I wouldn't even if he were free as the wind. I don't want the ordinary, mundane sorrows and quarrels and familiarity that breeds boredom in a marriage. I want fun and frolic, excitement, to live while I am alive and young enough to enjoy it. I am innocent, Kat. I am condemned only by the scandalmongers' tongues. No, Kat, I will hear no more of it. I will not give him up. I cannot." And I left her to weep and called Robert's sister, Lady Mary Sidney, and Lady Catherine Knollys and her irksome, provocative daughter, Lettice, showing off her high-trussed breasts again, plump as plums ready to be plucked, above a prune-coloured satin bodice laced breathtakingly tight. I bade them be silent, as my head ached, while they helped me dress in a gown of sapphire satin to match the sapphire heart Robert had given me.

When he came in, to escort me down the stairs and outside to dine beneath the stars, as musicians played and fireworks lit up the sky in myriad coloured sparks, I gladly gave him my hand and turned my back on Kat, who sat sobbing on the window seat with her back to me. I never looked back. But in my heart, I knew I was lying to everyone, including myself. I had to find a way to break Robert's spell, or else I was doomed. I had fought too hard for this crown to lose it to, or over, a man.

The next morning when we were out hunting, my horse shied, and Robert grabbed the reins, as though I lacked sufficient skill to handle the situation.

"Don't think you can snatch the reins from me!" I shouted, slapping at his hands with my riding crop. "I don't need your help! I know how to handle a horse as well as any man!"

"Yes, of course you do," Robert replied in a soothing and condescending tone that sought to stroke my vanity and make it purr like a well-contented cat. "And under my tutelage you will soon be even better, and people will say that their Queen is the finest huntress in the land!"

I glared hard at him. "If you reach too far, grasp too greedily, you will end up with an empty hand, smarting from being slapped down; remember that, Robert!" And with those words I spun my mount around and galloped away from him.

I fumed in silent fury, simmering within, fighting to keep from letting my temper boil over in the presence of my ladies as they divested me of my riding garb. I quivered and quaked, and it strained my self-control until I thought my skin would burst, splitting open like a suit of too-tight clothing at the seams, and the rage would come pouring out. But my ladies seemed oblivious to my mood and maddeningly slow as their fingers moved over the various buttons, aiglets, lacings, hooks, ribbons, buckles, and ties. I wanted to scream out my lungs, to slap, kick, and strike them, roaring out my rage, bellowing for them to get out. I don't know how I kept it all in, but at last I was alone in my bath, shrouded in billowing curtains of steam. I felt my hands, grasping so tightly to the edges of the tub that they shook, relax and unfurl and my chest ease as my breath escaped in a long sigh.

When I emerged from my bath, I snapped at my ladies to take away the finery they had laid out in readiness for the evening. Instead I called for my night shift and dressing gown as I plucked the pins from my hair, raking my fingers through it and shaking my head as it tumbled about my shoulders and down my back, complaining that I had an abominable headache and would keep to my room. I sent them all out except Kat. I felt like a little girl again, lost and alone, as I had felt when my mother disappeared from my life, and, later, when I discovered what terrible fate had befallen her. I stood in the middle of my room, in my bare feet, free-flowing hair, and light, sleeveless, gossamer-sheer shift, pale as a spectre, bathed in the moonlight that poured in through the windows, and watched Kat, slow, grey, and stoop-backed, her fingers bony and gnarled, seemingly unable to straighten, fussing over my favourite dressing gown, a lavish, gold-embroidered emerald velvet one with sleeves that flowed back from my arms and swept the floor as they trailed behind me, and wondered when she had grown so old; the changes had crept up so slowly, I had scarcely noticed them before. I had seen, but I hadn't really noticed. It made me wonder—what would my mother look like if she had lived?

"Kat!" I cried, tears suddenly filling my eyes when she came and held the robe up for me to slip my bare arms into. Instead, I fell to my knees before her, took her hand in mine, and kissed it. "I'm so sorry," I said. "*Please,* forgive me!"

"For what, love?" she asked, a befuddled frown further creasing her careworn brow.

"For everything, for ever giving you cause to worry, or to doubt, or be ashamed of me. This business about Robert . . ."

"My darling girl." Kat thrust aside the dressing gown she was still holding and reached for me. Tenderly, as the most loving of mothers, she took me into her arms and stroked my hair. "Bess, I could not be more proud of you if I had given birth to you myself. I am sorry if I spoke harshly to you, but that business with the Lord Admiral sorely rattled me. I was silly and foolish then, like a girl myself, when I should have known better; I was certainly old enough to know. I should have been more vigilant, as my position as governess to a princess demanded, but I fell under his spell, and when it all fell apart, it was a rude awakening indeed; it opened my eyes. I was wrong to have encouraged you with him; it was as though, even though I am so much older than you, we were giggling girls together in those days at Chelsea, and then, nigh overnight—it seemed to happen so suddenly—we had to grow up together. And I see so much of the Lord Admiral in Lord Robert, I just don't want to see you make the same mistake . . . or an even worse one, since there is now so much more to lose. You are young and beautiful and have endured much; of course you want passion, excitement, and love. You *deserve* to have those things. I was just afraid that the freedom and power of being Queen, and the wiles of Lord Robert—he's such a handsome, ambitious rascal, just like the Lord Admiral was—would go to your head. And that, while seeming to give, he might instead take it *all* away from you, and I don't want to see that happen."

"It won't, Kat. I promise you, it won't!" I cried as I clung to her. "The scales have fallen from my eyes. Don't worry any more, Kat. Don't let me or Lord Robert put another line on that sweet brow." I stroked her forehead. "Today was another day of the sort you described, like of a sudden growing up, going from child to woman within the blink of an eye. I've come to my senses now, Kat, about Lord Robert, and he shall have no kingly triumph. I realised today that things cannot go on as they are. His ambition has grown too tall; it has to be cut down. And I can no longer ignore his arrogance and presumptuousness for the sake of a few pleasant hours." I stood and picked up my dressing gown and fumbled my arms through the long sleeves, even as Kat tried to help me. "Everything is going to be all right now, Kat. Rest assured, your Queen now has full command of her head and her heart. Go now"—I kissed her cheek—"and send Cecil to me; then, to bed with you. I've been keeping you up too many nights lately."

I paced restlessly back and forth across my room, absently combing, raking my fingers through my hair, in what was fast becoming a nervous habit, letting the stray strands fall free, until Cecil arrived, willing myself to harden my heart against Robert. My dream for us was not his dream for us, and the two could never be reconciled—I saw that now. I also knew that Robert would never give up; he wanted to seize the power from me just as he tried to take the reins from my hands today. I wanted a lover, not a consort, but Robert wanted a crown above all.

"I must speak with you about Lord Robert," I said as soon as Cecil came through the door. "He grows too presumptuous; his manner is too lofty, he thinks to command all . . ."

"Indeed, Madame." Cecil nodded. "There is a party late every night in Lord Robert's chambers after Your Majesty has gone to bed, with drinking, feasting, gambling, and whoring, often lasting until cock's crow." He went on to describe how, regally attired in gold-embroidered purple velvet, like a king presiding over his own little court in miniature, surrounded by his surly-faced cudgel-, dagger-, and sword-toting retainers, who proudly wore the bear and ragged staff blazoned on their blue velvet sleeves, Robert entertained his supporters, men just as ambitious as himself who wanted to grasp tightly the coat tails of this man they saw as a rising, soaring star, hoping some of the stardust would rub off on them, and the harlots who sat upon their knees, allowing themselves to be kissed and fondled and hoping that, for them too, there were profits to be derived. Like the mighty Caesar, with a crown of gilded laurel leaves upon his dark head and a golden goblet brimming with blood red wine in his hand, Robert would lift his cup high and boldly, boastfully proclaim that I was *entirely* in his power, *com-*

pletely besotted with him, and would do *anything* he asked of me, even give him an earldom. "The patent is even now being prepared," he presumptuously and precipitously boasted. And always, mysteriously and cryptically, he would declare, "If I live another year, I will be in a *very* different position from the one I am in now!" which many took to mean that here was their future King and flattered and fawned on him accordingly, his loyal, avaricious, lascivious band of sycophants, who would be the first to desert him when he crashed and burned, like Icarus, when he flew too near to the sun."

"*How dare he!* The presumptuous knave, to think that *I* am in *his* power!" I shrieked. I could not believe the fool's audacity!

"Madame, there is more." Cecil interrupted my fuming outrage. "I fear that Lord Robert is now in the pocket of Spain. He has persuaded Philip to back his suit for your hand as soon as he is a free man in exchange for promising to rule England as Philip deems best." To prove it, he took from inside his doublet a copy of a letter Robert had written to Philip that one of his spies had intercepted and copied. *I am the best servant Your Majesty has here,* Robert had written, and he went on to promise that if Philip and his ambassador could persuade me that I could safely marry Robert without loss of or detriment to my crown, he would *serve and obey like one of Your Majesty's own vassals.*

"*Traitor!*" I screamed. "*Never!* Not so long as I have a single breath left in my body shall England be Spain's vassal! *My* England shall *never* be just another coin in Philip's purse, sold to buy Robert Dudley a crown. Before I leave this earth, I *swear* that my England shall be a power in its own right to be reckoned with. I shall make it so before I perish! I shall break him, Cecil, like one of his horses. I shall break him! I will show him who rules here. I shall show him whose hands hold the reins of power he dares try to snatch! I am mistress here, and I shall have no master, not Robert Dudley or through his mouth Spanish Philip, God blast and rot them both!"

"*Bravo, Elizabeth Regina!*" Cecil nodded approvingly. "And, if I may be so bold as to say so, it is high time, and I shall rejoice to see you do it! And if I may be of *any* assistance in the matter, as always, I am at Your Majesty's service."

"Good." I nodded and dropped down onto the window seat

and patted the cushion beside me. "Then let us put our heads together, Cecil, and devise a way that will allow Robert to keep that handsome head of his but cool the fever of ambition that rages within it. With his words and schemes and actions, Robert has declared war, and I am now fighting the man I loved dearly as my best friend, for my throne. And a life—an innocent life, Cecil—also hangs in the balance."

"Amy Dudley." Cecil nodded knowingly.

"Yes." I nodded sadly with a long, drawn-out, doleful sigh.

"I remember her on her wedding day, and how she *glowed* with happiness," Cecil mused aloud quietly. "Mildred and I still have the cup she gave us in a glass cabinet where we keep various mementos and curiosities. She had such a lovely smile, shy and timid; I remember wondering how such a gentle creature could have won the heart of Lord Robert. Mildred was quite taken aback by the cup when Lady Amy presented it to us; the shape was rather . . ." He paused tactfully, searching for the right word. ". . . unusual . . . and tragically ironic, considering her current illness. And the Lady Amy, seeing Mildred's surprise, and fearing that she had somehow given offence, hastened to explain the reason for their unusual design, how a story about Helen of Troy had captivated her father. We were quite touched by her sweetness and sincerity. She was a little unpolished by court standards, but she was by no means a crude or vulgar woman, or the sort of wife any man should ever have cause to feel ashamed of. Mildred and I quite liked her; we were surprised that she never came to court. If she had, I am certain Mildred would have befriended her. I always suspected that Lord Robert used her natural timidity against her, to frighten her and keep her where he wanted her, if she ever pressed the subject of coming."

I nodded in agreement; that was my assessment of the reason behind the lengthy separations during their marriage as well.

"I am Queen of this realm, Cecil, and I have *many* champions, but Amy Dudley hasn't any, so I, as Queen, mother and sworn protector of all my people, must enter the field on her behalf. Robert's ambition shall *not* be the sword that slays her!"

"Turn that sword on him then, Madame," Cecil advised. "Let the sword of Lord Robert's ambition that would cut down any who stood between him and his desires, including his innocent and ailing wife, puncture his dreams instead; his ambition shall bleed out, but not his life's blood. Let the rumours of his murderous intentions murder his ambitions instead of Lady Dudley!"

"Yes!" I breathed. "Icarus shall burn himself. He already has the wings—we need only supply a breeze to help him soar!"

Cecil and I sat up late into the night, and by the time the sun had replaced the moon, we knew what we would do.

"I thought he was safe, Cecil, because he is married. I thought, here is a man, a dear old friend from childhood, with whom I can laugh and play and *never* have to worry about his wanting more than I am willing to give. I can have the best of both worlds, passion and male company without the commitment and control of matrimony, without surrendering my independence or rule. I thought he was safe, and yet he has turned out to be the most dangerous of all; he has put both my reputation and my crown at risk. And I cannot allow matters to go on as they are. It *has* to stop, and stop now. This is the end, Cecil, my last summer of folly. I have been playing Blindman's Buff with the truth, trying to evade it for too long. Now I must stop and unbind my eyes and confront it before it destroys me."

Like a kind father, Cecil patted my arm. "You are young, Madame, and love often confounds our hearts and heads. But hearts heal, heads clear and grow wiser, and it is my daily and nightly prayer that God shall soon send Your Majesty a *good* husband, one who is worthy of you, who will give you children to safeguard the succession."

I glanced down at the weighty gold and onyx coronation ring glittering in the morning sun upon my left hand and shook my head. "No, Cecil, I am already bound unto a husband—England—and I want, nor shall I have, no other. As for children, every person, young or old, male or female, with English blood coursing through their veins is my child. And for me, that is enough. When the stonemasons come to carve my tomb, let them write that Elizabeth, having reigned such a time, lived and died a virgin."

I knew what I had to do. Things had gone too far for me to escape unscathed. I would suffer the stains of suspicion and scandal—

there was no help for it—and that would be my penance. But I would survive—that was the important thing. I had done it before, and I could do it again, but for Robert, it would be a different story.

"Dear, are you quite sure you wish to hunt today?" Kat asked, alarmed, as she helped lace me into my buff and russet riding clothes, fussing with the gold frogs, bugles, and aiglets that adorned the sleeves and bodice. "You're so pale!" She pressed a worried hand to my brow to check for fever. "You look as though you haven't slept at all!" As indeed I hadn't, but I forced a smile and assured Kat that all was well.

Cecil was waiting for me when I emerged from my chamber, pulling on my gloves, the plumes on my hat bouncing as we strode briskly towards the stairs on my way to the stables to meet Robert.

"I know what I have to do," I assured him. "I don't like it, but . . ."

"Remember," he said as we paused and faced each other at the top of the stairs, "Lady Dudley is going to die. *You cannot* save her, and neither can any doctor or medicine known to man—no one but God Himself can save her. The words we are each this day to speak shall do her no greater harm than the London gossips and Lord Robert have done already. For the little blemish that will, unavoidably, mar Your Majesty's reputation, you prevent a greater evil from taking place—the murder of a dying woman—and thwart her husband's ambition to be King—you put the knave back in his place. Lord Robert would not serve England well, as he will *always* put his own interests first."

"I know," I sighed, "and never fear, Cecil, I shall not fail to play my part well. There is Ambassador de Quadra now." I nodded down at the approaching dark-clad figure of Don Alvaro de Quadra, who had succeeded the Comte de Feria as our Spanish Ambassador. "You go ahead, Cecil, and speak your lines. I have, as we rehearsed, forgotten my riding crop."

As I turned and walked slowly back to my room to retrieve it, I knew the words Cecil would be speaking. In an anguished voice, accompanied by wringing hands, he would, in a seemingly unguarded manner, let spill some rash words that de Quadra would eagerly lap up, venting his despair for me and England, blaming Robert for keeping me from affairs of state, his own feelings of defeat. He would point the finger of blame right at Robert, accusing him of making himself "lord of all affairs, and of the Queen's person, to the extreme injury of the whole kingdom", claiming I cared only for pleasure and the company of my handsome horsemaster, who "leads her to spend all day hunting and all night dancing with much danger to her life and health". And in hushed tones he would confide that he was considering retiring from public life to live quietly in the country with his beloved wife, Mildred, as "it is a bad sailor who, on seeing a great storm brewing, does not seek a safe harbour while he can". Then, the coup de grâce, his eyes darting about to make sure no one was near enough to overhear, he would grasp de Quadra's arm and draw him nearer as his voice dropped to an even lower, barely audible, whisper, and confide: "He intends to murder his wife. He has given out that she is very ill, with a malady of her breast, when in truth she is not, and on the contrary is quite well. She has completely recovered from the malady of the breast that did afflict her, and, having heard the rumours, takes all precautions to protect herself from poison. But God would *never* permit that any good could ever result from so great and evil a business!"

When I reappeared at the top of the stairs, I took a deep breath and steeled myself. Then, like an actor stepping from the wings onto the stage to play before an audience, I became who I needed to be, letting the *real* Elizabeth sink below the surface of the giddy, heedless, frivolous, and light-minded young woman I must pretend to be for Ambassador de Quadra. Smiling, twirling my riding crop, and humming a love song, merry as a young girl on her way to meet her swain, I skipped down the stairs towards where Cecil and de Quadra stood with their heads together, conversing still. They broke apart, like a pair of guilty schoolboys caught at some mischief, but then Cecil leaned in again and whispered urgently into de Quadra's ear. I knew he would be imploring him to, with all due tact and discretion, speak to me, "for the love of God, warn her of these dangers, and persuade her to be watchful and wary and not to ruin herself and her kingdom! Lord Robert would be better off in Paradise than here!"

"You two look as thick as thieves!" I declared, inserting myself between them, to link my arms with theirs, like a trio of old friends, before Cecil made his excuses, disengaged his arm from mine, and left me alone with the Ambassador.

As we walked towards the stables, de Quadra wished me a happy birthday. I was seven-and-twenty that day, and it was time for me to put aside childish things and grow up and fully become the Queen I was meant to be. The time to play had passed, and there was no use mourning it—no good could come of it, only fond, bittersweet memories. And there would be diversions from time to time, many entertainments to please even the most capricious monarch, and pastimes with good company such as my father enjoyed and wrote of in his famous song by that name, and I could, and would, be content with that; it would be enough. Fleeting youth had passed, almost overnight, rushing breathlessly past in the blink of an eye, and now, on the morning of my twenty-seventh birthday, I was wide awake and saw clearly what I had to do. I smiled and gave my full attention to Ambassador de Quadra walking beside me. He was saying that he had brought me many fine gifts from Philip, my erstwhile brother-in-law, who, though he had since forsaken my hand to marry another, still loved me like a brother and remembered me with *great* and *most* tender fondness.

I could not suppress a smile at those words, for I knew quite well what memories Philip cherished of me—of the spy-hole he had drilled in my wall, through which he might watch me dress and bathe, and of the kisses and bold caresses we had shared, when I had thrown back my head as his hot kisses travelled down my throat to my breasts as I rapturously sighed, "*¡Algún día, Philip, algún día!* Someday, Philip, someday!" and clutched tightly his head, the jewelled rings he had given me glittering amidst the thick waves of his burnished gold hair—back in the days when I had needed his protection against my sister's jealousy and madness, when the passion of a Spanish prince stood between my life and the scaffold.

"Have you heard about Lady Dudley?" I asked casually as we stepped outside, slapping my riding crop against my skirts as we approached the stables where Robert awaited me. "Is it not sad? She is only a year older than I am. She is dead—or nearly so—but, *please,* don't say anything; you know how people delight in gossiping. Ah, there is my Sweet Robin now! Robin!" I called gaily, waving my riding crop in the air, and I slipped my arm from de

Quadra's and ran to meet him, lingering, clinging, a moment too long in his arms as I let him lift me into the saddle, before he swung himself up onto his own mount, gesturing to me and calling out to de Quadra, "Our Queen has such a *passion* for riding, she is *mad* for speed, and she says the geldings I provide for her are too tame and wants them while they are still wild and barely broken!" Then we rode out to spend yet another day riding in the Great Park followed by another mad and merry night dancing together. But, for me, it was tinged with sorrow, for only I knew that it was the end, that we could not go on this way. Somehow I knew that the summer that, despite the cold and foul weather, I would always remember as golden had ended and would never come again. This was the last breath of that summer, and I was determined to breathe it in as deeply as I could and savour it before I exhaled and let it go forever.

❧ 32 ❧

Amy Robsart Dudley

Cumnor Place, Berkshire, near Oxford
Sunday, September 8, 1560

Now here I lie upon my bed in Cumnor Place, perhaps or perhaps not drinking Death from a bottle meant to lull and soothe me, to dull and diminish my pain, and let my soul float away on the calm waters of sweet rest.

The house is cathedral-quiet with all the servants away at the fair, and I smile at the thought of apple cider, cinnamon cakes, and gingerbread babies—I can almost smell and taste them, and this time, strangely, it doesn't make me even the least bit sick—jugglers, acrobats, morris dancers, puppet shows, and fortune-tellers, performing horses, dancing bears, and learned pigs who know their sums and letters better than I, and a whole rainbow of silk hair ribbons billowing out from the peddler's booth, flapping and streaming in the breeze to catch the eye of a passing maiden and say, "Come hither!"

My mind is *not* at peace, and it hasn't been for a *very* long time, but my body *can* rest, and my mind *can* think in peace. By sending everyone away, I have made sure of it, by giving them a day of fun and merrymaking, I have bought myself one day of solitude and silent, undisturbed contemplation. I can try to make sense of it all, puzzle it all out, put the pieces into their proper places, and see them in the right light, and decide what to do, whether to fight for a life I am not sure is worth living any more. I *want* to believe it is, that every life is worth living, that there might *still* be something to look forward to, and yet I *cannot*; I fear I would only be deceiving myself with false hope, dashing my own hopes the way Robert always used to do for me.

The angels and demons in my head pull me every which way until I feel like I am playing Blindman's Buff with myself, while the demons laugh to see such fun and the angels sigh, shake their heads, and weep. One moment I want life, the next I desire death, and all the time I pray to God to deliver me from my desperation. I am *so* tired, so *very, very* tired. I'm tired of fighting, of being confused and afraid, of the hopelessness and despair, of every day feeling the sharp-fanged bite of the pain that saps the strength out of me, of not knowing whom to trust or what to do, of fearing poison or an assassin lurking in the shadows, and of loving and hating Robert, and knowing that he and his royal mistress are impatient and tired of waiting for me to die. I'm tired of it all, so very tired.

I reach out and lovingly caress the cracked leather cover of Father's old prayer book, lying on the table by my bed. I open it, and let my fingers trace over the words written on the day of my birth: *Amy Robsart, beloved daughter of John Robsart, knight, was born on the 7th day of June in the Blessed Year of Our Lord 1532.* I hope, wherever he is, that Father cannot see me now, and what I have become. He would be *so* sad and, I am afraid, ashamed to see me so wasted and worn, with all my hopes dashed to nothing, my dreams dead, and my spirit gone, I who used to be so exuberant, so full of life, as busy as a bee from morn till night, bustling about the manor, with a smile always on my lips, and often a song, and a kind word for everyone, taking care of everything. But now... *My days are like a shadow that declineth; and I am withered like grass.* I raise the bottle to my lips and drink deeply, swallowing hard, the way I used to my husband's lies and his seed, and I let my head fall back again onto the cloud-soft goosedown pillows as the comforting warmth seeps slowly through me, spreading from my head to my toes, making me feel almost as though I am awake and asleep at the same time, and I float further away from all the disasters and dilemmas that overwhelm each moment of my life, making it more Hell than anything remotely near a Heaven.

Dreams beckon to me, enticing and inviting me to sail away from it all to find something better. My eyelids grow heavy, and I let myself drowse.

Yesterday was the Queen's birthday. I see her in a pink gown dancing a smouldering volta with Robert. As the music pulses and thrums like blood within veins, he lifts her high, and her full skirts bunch up to show off her red stockings. I used to wear red stockings too. As he holds her high, lust hangs hot and heavy in the air, mingling with Elizabeth's rose perfume; sweat glazes their flushed faces; and her red hair slips its pins, falling down to tickle his face; and as he lowers her, oh, so slowly, her body presses and slides sensuously against his. Their desire for each other is so blatant, it is as though they are making love on the dance floor for all to see. And then the scene changes. I am on the beach with Robert; he brandishes a stick at a blue green crab that nips at our bare toes. But then the crab starts to grow until it is *enormous,* bigger than both of us. Robert drops the stick and runs, but I stand there, petrified, staring after him as he flees without a single thought of me. I feel a sharp pinch in my left breast and turn to see it spouting blood. In a fury, I launch myself at the crab, mockingly prancing on its many spindly little legs that seem too delicate to support the giant creature, and snapping its big fiendish claws in the air like a Spanish dancer's castanets, pummelling its hard shell with my angry fists, kicking and screaming at it, futilely pounding my fists upon the great pinching claw that closes around my waist with a pain that makes me feel as if I am about to snap in half. *"Let go of me!"* I scream as I feel my bones break. "This is *my* life; it's *mine,* give it back! I don't want to die!" Suddenly the claw opens, and I fall, breathless and shaken, to lie, huddled and gasping, on the wet sand. In the distance before me I see my father standing in an apple orchard, ringed in hazy gold and rosy mist and light, and the sweet scent of apple blossoms fills the air, and I breathe it in deeply and feel stronger for it. He smiles broadly, all wiry grey curls and apple cheeks, his eyes filled with love, just the way he used to be, as he stands in a shower of apple blossoms and beckons to me, "Come home, lass, *come home*!"

Suddenly my eyes snap open, and I am wide awake, alert and on guard, with such a tense, wary feeling, as though danger infuses the shadows that are crowding in on me as the sun sets. Someone is watching me! I feel the cold prickle of fear, like icy fingers, up and down my spine, and the relentless, unwavering pain. I want to run as fast and as far as I can, to outdistance it and leave it gasping and panting in the distance, to stop and laugh and wave back at it and go on my merry way, free at last from this most irksome and unwelcome companion. From the corner of my eye I spy a movement. Was it a sound I heard that awoke me? A footstep? A rustle of garments? A scrape of metal as of a dagger being unsheathed? Or am I being silly, letting my imagination and fear get the better of me again? Was it merely Custard or Onyx after a mouse? Frozen by fear, I am almost too afraid to turn my head and look, but I *have* to, even though the motion of my head moving makes me dizzy and I feel that strange sensation of there being a delay between my mind telling my body what to do and my head complying. I gasp and whimper as a pain, like a sharp crick in my neck, makes me instantly regret the movement.

There *is* a man, a dark man standing in the shadows! I see him! His nose like a knife in profile! Sir Richard Verney! He takes a step towards me. *Robert has sent him to Cumnor to kill me!* Poison has failed, so now he will use a knife or his bare hands!

I ignore the pain, even as it explodes like fireworks within me, filling and burning every part of me, as though my heart were dry tinder lit by the falling sparks, blinding me with a dizzying burst of coloured stars obscuring my sight, as the instinct to preserve life impels me to bolt from my bed and run, just run, heedless of direction, as fast as I can, to escape Death at the hands of Richard Verney. I fly, as though I had wings on my heels, out my door, and down the Long Gallery to the stairs. I feel fur brush my ankle, and I stumble as an outraged *Meow!* reaches my ears. But I cannot stop, I keep going, I glance back over my shoulder so swiftly, I cannot tell if he is coming in pursuit of me, though I know that he is, I *feel* it, though I cannot see through the dense dazzle of coloured sparks that crowds out my vision, making me feel as if I am staring down a long, dark tunnel, straining to see what is at the end, but if there is even a pinprick of light there, I cannot see it. As I turn my

head, I hear a *pop!* At the same time as I feel it, a pain in the side of
my neck, like that which comes from forcing it to turn suddenly
and hard whilst there is a terrible, aching crick in it, that makes me
gasp and my hand fly up, even as I try to glance back over my
shoulder.

I keep running, and in my haste and horror, I forget the awkward twist in the stairs where they turn, curving down towards the
landing. I have not left my room in so long, I remember it too late,
and then a scream—*my scream!*—pierces the quiet of Cumnor, and
I plunge down, headfirst, almost like a child turning cartwheels in a
daisy-strewn meadow, down into black-velvet darkness. The edge
of one of the stone steps gashes open the back of my head; I feel the
skin split. As my head strikes the floor, I hear a sickening snap, like
a foot coming down on a dry branch, and I see, through the
crowded haze of the dancing, drifting rainbow of specks and
sparks, my rumpled skirts and my feet resting on the stairs, higher
than my head, and realise to my horror that I cannot move them. I
try and try, but I cannot move my legs, my feet, my fingers—or *anything*! *I cannot move!* Not even a tremor, not even a twitch! And
past my feet, I see my blood glittering dark in the frail, flickering
candlelight, staining the steps where my head struck; it oozes and
drips down, moving like slow baby snakes, newborn and going out
to explore the world, and I think my blood, which can still move,
has more life left in it than I do. It is getting harder to breathe, another fireworks display bursts inside my heart, and the darkness is
crowding out the sparks that dance before my eyes, driving them
away, and they go, docile as a flock of sheep following their shepherd. And I feel a warm wetness beneath my head, being soaked up
by the golden sponge of my hair, and a stinging, a burning, in my
scalp, but I cannot reach up to touch, to feel it!

Am I awake or dreaming? I do not know! Oh, God, *help me!*
Oh, *please,* God, *please* let this be just another bad dream! It *has* to
be! It *has* to be! I *must* be dreaming! The Queen is on the stairs,
when I know perfectly well that she is at court and cannot truly be
here at Cumnor, so it *must* be a dream, it *must*! But I see her, plain
as day, standing there upon the landing, her white gown glowing
bright as a sun-struck cloud, radiant, near blinding white, spangled
with rubies, as if her dress were weeping tears of blood, and her

hair, piled high and curled and bedecked with pearls, and her lips as red as violence-spilled blood against the stark marble white pallor of her smooth, cold, hard, emotionless face. Her eyes are canny and shrewd, dark and knowing. She is at once the most beautiful and the most terrifying woman I have ever seen. She shakes her fist, rattling the pair of ivory dice she holds within, and hurls them down the stairs straight at me. They land upon my lap, just below the point of my embroidered bodice. I cannot see the dots, but I don't need to; her voice tells me what I already know, plain and matter-of-fact, devoid of emotion: "The winner takes all." A map— of England, I think—unfurls upon the landing beneath her, and a jewelled sceptre and a weighty orb of gold appear suddenly in her elegant white hands, and a gold and jewelled crown shines brilliantly upon her head. Then she is gone—or is it my sight that has gone?— all is darkness, the most stultifying, terrifying, breath-stealing blackness with no hint of light at all! The breath catches in my throat, as though a pair of strong, cruel, murderous hands were pressing, squeezing, hard and tight. I gasp and choke, but I cannot get my breath out! *I cannot breathe!* It is *all* slipping away from me. I cannot hold on to anything, not even my breath!

But then the veil of darkness lifts, as if it had lain over my face and been of a sudden snatched away in one quick whisk. And I see the phantom grey friar standing at the top of the stairs, staring down at me; though my eyes still cannot pierce the darkness inside his hood, I feel his gaze upon me.

And I realise something suddenly, as abrupt and startling as a sudden slap in the face coming unexpectedly out of the dark. Maybe I have not lost after all?

My death will *not* roll out a velvet carpet leading up the aisle of Westminster Abbey to a crown and a royal bride for Robert. That dream is as dead as I soon will be! My death, just like my life, will keep Robert and Elizabeth apart forever. Each time they kiss, it will be over my tombstone. My death is *my* victory, *not* theirs! That was what she meant when she said, "The winner takes all." Elizabeth is a survivor; she will outlive the scandal of my death, though my blood might stain her hem a little, but Robert won't; she will keep her crown, but Robert will lose all hope of his; and my blood will stain him forever, and he will *never* be washed clean of it. He won and lost what he wanted all in the same moment. He wanted my death to set him free, but the world will judge my death too opportune; there has been too much talk of poison and intent to kill; Elizabeth will *never* marry him now. Robert isn't worth risking her kingdom for; she will not suffer a bloodstained consort to sit on the throne beside her and try to snatch the sceptre from her hand.

The grey friar slowly starts to descend the stairs, coming towards me; then he is standing beside me, looming over me. The hands he formerly held clasped at his waist, entwined with his rosary, rise up. He lowers his hood, and, at last, I see his face, bathed in golden radiance. It is the kindest, most beautiful, compassionate face I have ever seen! He smiles as he kneels down and gathers me tenderly into his arms. As he lifts me up, I feel *all* the pain, the fear, the aching loneliness, the wearying weight of worry, anger, resentment, despair, tiredness, and sorrow fall away from me; it is as though I am rising, but all that stays behind, stuck down below me on the ground where it cannot touch me. I wrap my arms around his neck—I can move again! He smiles at me. And in his arms I am at peace. I feel so warm, safe, and wanted, and, most of all, *loved, truly loved,* more than I have ever been before. I could not have had a more easeful death.

❧ 33 ❧

Elizabeth

Windsor Castle, London
September 9–20, 1560

I was having the most peculiar dream when a hand, rough with urgency, reached out and shook me from the land of dreams, where anything is possible.

I raised my rumpled, sleep-befuddled head from the pillow, brushed back my hair, and blinked in surprise at the sight of Cecil standing beside my bed in his mulberry velvet dressing gown, slippers, and tasselled cap, a candlestick clutched tightly in his hand, which trembled so mightily, it caused the flame to waver and dip, casting an eerily flickering shadow upon the wall. Kat, who must have let him in, stood a few steps behind him, her once matronly plump and ample form now seemingly swamped, lost in the folds of her voluminous white nightgown, her long grey braid protruding fuzzily from beneath her white ruffled cap. She let out a little cry and—too late—clapped a blue-veined hand over her mouth to stifle it, when Cecil, with a solemn frown, announced that Amy Dudley was dead. She had died yesterday, though the news had not yet spread far; one of his informants had only just brought him word of it, wakened him from a sound sleep, and he had come at once to me. But, he continued gravely, he fully expected the news to reach London and be the talk of every tavern by nightfall, and we must be prepared to weather the storm of scandal like sailors at sea besieged by a mighty gale; we must hold on, and hold fast, and brave the wind and waves and not be swept overboard, nor let the ship of state capsize or be deluged and dragged down.

Astonished, I sat up in bed and hugged my knees. I had known that she was *very* ill, beyond the power of any but God to save, but I had not expected her to die so soon, so suddenly. And after we had decided to use the rumours in our favour, against Robert, to break his accursed ambition and douse the fire that burned so hot within him to be King. Only two days ago—*two days!*—I had told the Spanish Ambassador that she was dead, or nearly so, and now she was. What terrible, terrible timing! I clapped a hand to my brow and shook my head. I could scarcely believe this was happening!

"How did it happen? The cancer?" I asked softly. "Did she suffer greatly at the end?"

"Madame"—Cecil looked at me sadly—"it was *not* a natural death." I gasped, and my mouth fell open wide. "And suffer, I fear, she did," he continued, "though I pray I am mistaken and that the end came quickly. She was found dead at the foot of the stairs, with her neck broken, the hood on her head still in place and her skirts but little disarrayed, not immodestly as one would expect after falling head over heels down a staircase. That morning she had sent away all who would go—even her maid, Mrs Pirto, practically the entire household—to attend the fair at Abingdon, leaving her quite alone; they discovered her late Sunday afternoon upon their return. Mrs Pirto was about to mount the stairs to bring her lady a gingerbread baby and some hair ribbons she had bought for her when . . ." Cecil paused sadly. ". . . when the tragic discovery was made."

"Oh, no, Cecil, no, not like that!" I cried. Suddenly, I stopped, the wheels of my mind turning in a loathsome direction, and I flung my legs over the side of the bed and reached out and caught hold of his sleeve. "*Look at me!*" I ordered. "*Look at me,* Cecil, and *swear* to me that you had *no* part in this! I *know* you dislike Lord Robert . . ."

"Madame, I *swear*"—Cecil met my eyes—"I had no part, and no foreknowledge, of this dreadful deed. I am just as surprised as you are! I would not have my Sovereign's hands stained with blood through me, nor have her live always under a pall of suspicion. And someday I must meet my Maker, and though I am not without sin, Lady Dudley's death is not one of them."

I nodded. I believed him; I knew instinctively that he spoke the truth.

"But people will think that—" I began.

"Madame," Cecil interrupted me, "take heart, I implore you; it is not so bad as it first appears. It is true, your reputation has suffered a blow, but it is *not* a fatal wound, merely a stain on your hem compared to the tar and feathers Lord Robert will wear in public opinion for the rest of his life; many will always look at him and see his wife's blood on his hands, and such a man is not fit to be King. But you *will* survive; you *will* go on, past this; you are the phoenix that rose from the ashes of Bloody Mary's reign, and you *will* rise above this too. Like you, I wished Lady Dudley a gentle end to her suffering. After all the rumours of poison, even before we staged our little drama for the Spanish Ambassador, there would have been suspicion even if she had died quietly in her bed, with the cause conclusive and indisputable, but it would have been whispered, not shouted from the rooftops and in the city streets. But, nevertheless, with this unexpected tragedy, our work is done— Robert Dudley will *never* be King now, and Lady Dudley, God rest her sweet soul, is past her pains and has not died in vain."

"But did he do it, Cecil?" I demanded. "Did he do this?"

"Madame, in truth, I do not know," Cecil answered. "There must be an inquest, a full investigation . . ."

". . . a full and earnest searching out and trying of the truth!" I finished for him; Cecil and I understood each other so well, we could at times finish each other's sentences. "No stone must be left unturned to discover the truth! And if it is found that he had *any* part in it, Cecil, *he shall pay,* just like any other man in my kingdom so condemned. My favour shall not save him. And that is not just idle or angry talk, Cecil. Justice will not turn a blind eye for Robert. As Dr Bayly feared his name and medicines' being used to cover Robert's sin, nor shall my crown cover his crime if he has committed one. When I became Queen, I asked you, Cecil, to never spare me any truth I need hear, even if you knew it would be displeasing to or pain or anger me, and I meant it, and I still do. Though I know there have been times when I have seemed to ignore those truths and have vexed you no end, though I have been like a wilful, rebellious girl determined to go her own way, that girl has grown up, Cecil, and said farewell to her dreams and the follies of her youth. Now, find me the truth, Cecil—uncover it, lay it bare and naked, cold as a corpse, before me, and do not shrink from showing me! I *must* know!"

"Majesty, it shall be done," he promised.

"When my mother went into the Tower, she laughed when her gaoler sought to comfort her by saying that all subjects of the King have justice. In my reign, Cecil, none shall *ever* laugh when such words are spoken; instead, they shall *know* it for the truth, that even the most helpless and humble shall have justice in Elizabeth's England. I leave all to you, Cecil. I trust you to see that all is done *exactly* as it should be. Keep a watchful eye on Lord Robert; he must not be allowed to interfere. I know him, Cecil. He has charm and winning ways, but he must not be allowed to use them to—"

"Madame, we *cannot* stop him from trying, but we *can* prevent him from succeeding. Mrs Ashley, if you would be so kind as to bring Her Majesty's dressing gown." Cecil spoke softly to Kat, then continued, politely turning away as I stood, clad only in my thin summer nightshift, and slipped my bare arms into the proffered gold-embroidered tawny velvet robe, "I hope Your Majesty will forgive the presumption, but time being of the essence here, I have anticipated your desire, and I have already the *very* man to assist us, one who has Lord Robert's trust, whose duplicity he would *never* for a moment suspect; indeed, if it were even suggested to him, I think he would laugh. He waits now in your private garden, if Mrs Ashley will open the door . . ."

"Quickly, Kat." I nodded.

And a few moments later an ashen-faced, wild-eyed young man with a riot of rumpled ginger curls standing up like springs upon his head, and freckles standing out starkly against his pallor, was standing before us. I recognised him at once—Thomas Blount of Kidderminster, Robert's country cousin, the one he used so often as his courier, sending him riding back and forth across the country on one errand or another, that the lad hardly ever felt solid ground beneath his feet for long and felt ill at ease in polite society and at a loss without the body of a horse gripped between his knees.

"A *perfect* choice," with an approving nod, I murmured sotto voce to Cecil.

Belatedly, Thomas Blount executed a hasty bow, and when his lips brushed my hand, I felt their coldness. I caught his chin in my hand and stared intently into his face. His eyes were red-rimmed from crying, and the still-moist tracks of tears were even then drying upon his cheeks. Cecil had already imparted the sad news, and clearly young Master Blount was much affected by it; he looked as though he might be felled by the merest touch of a feather.

"Come sit down with us by the fire," I said kindly, taking his arm and guiding him to a chair. And once he was settled with a goblet of wine in his hand, I began to speak softly to him. "I am told you are a great collector of tales," and at his nod I continued. "Well, Mr Blount, there is a damsel, sadly now departed, but when she walked this world, much distressed, for whom you can, if you will, still render a *great* service."

"Amy . . . I . . . I still can't believe it." He gulped back a sob. He looked first at me and then at Cecil. "Are you *sure* she's r-really gone? She's dead? Not just injured from her fall?"

"Sadly, in this instance we are not mistaken," Cecil answered. "Lady Dudley is indeed departed from this world."

"But"—I reached out and touched his hand—"you *can* still help her, Mr Blount. And"—I gave him a long, searching look—"I think you want to."

"I do," he affirmed. "Oh, yes, Your Majesty, I do! I wish I had been there. I . . . But what can *I* do? How can I help her now?" Tears overflowed his eyes again and began pouring down over his cheeks.

"You can help her spirit rest in peace," I said. "You can help ensure that she has not died in vain, that her life is not a sacrifice on the altar of another's ambition, that his purse does not tempt Justice to look away, to ignore Amy as he so often did. Let us have it plain, Mr Blount. I know you have heard the rumours about myself and Lord Robert. Despite what they say, I *never* intended to marry him under *any* circumstances, certainly not over his wife's dead and broken body. Lord Robert refused to believe that; he was blinded by the glare of his own ambition."

"But, in order to help Lady Dudley, you *must* be the Queen's man *first,* rather than Lord Robert's," Cecil interjected. "I know he is your cousin, Mr Blount; are you capable of ignoring the ties of kinship? Can you do that, Mr Blount? Can you serve the Queen before Lord Robert? Can you serve Lady Dudley before her husband?"

"Yes!" He swallowed hard another sob and nodded his head emphatically. "I can. I can do that—*anything* for Amy, *anything!* I...I..." He shook his head hard and bravely fought back the tears that threatened to overwhelm him. "He didn't love her like he should—I could see that. I...I thought he was a fool. She was so...so sweet and good, I could never believe that he wanted her dead. I thought it was just mean and idle gossip. If I had known..."

I nodded and sat back in my chair, letting my spine, and my hands' grip on the arms of my chair, relax a little and dangled my gold-braided tawny velvet slipper from my toes. "I believe you, Mr Blount. My mother once said to my father, 'All that glitters is not gold.' Lord Robert, for all his glittering vibrancy, his fine looks and manners, is *not* gold. And sometimes gold doesn't shine as brightly as it should; sometimes its sparkle is hidden, obscured by the mud. And thus I think it was with Lady Dudley; she was like a diamond rough from the earth that lacked polish and shaping, but precious nonetheless, and I lament her loss, as I can see you do as well, Mr Blount."

Thomas Blount gave me a startled look. "You didn't know her, and yet you understand her, I think, better than he ever did. She tried so hard to please him, but..." His words trailed off, and he shook his head, the sadness and confusion plain upon his face. It was clear that Thomas Blount would never make a good card player, but, to serve my purposes, he didn't have to face his cousin over a card table.

"I am a woman, Mr Blount. Just because I am the Virgin Queen does not mean I know nothing of life; my father had six wives, and history, even one's own, is an *excellent* teacher. Now, then"—I leaned forward—"here is what you are to do. Doubtlessly, as he is so accustomed to doing, Lord Robert shall send you riding to

Cumnor Place quite soon, to be his eyes and ears, to discover all about this dreadful business that you can. And you shall indeed do just as he commands, *but*"—I held my finger up—"you shall do *nothing* to interfere with the workings of Justice. If Lord Robert bids you speak with the coroner and the jurors or give them money or gifts, tell him whatever nonsense you please, that the jurors are well disposed to him, that you have dined with the foreman, played cards with the coroner—write a *fine* story for him, Mr Blount, one that he will believe, one that I and my Lord Cecil will think credible when we read your letters—as we indeed will—but you are *not* to consort with or befriend the jurors, the coroner, or *anyone* officially or informally associated with this case. Invent out of whole cloth or embroider on the gossip you overhear in the street and tavern to fill your letters to Lord Robert, and relate whatever you hear at Cumnor—do not lie about that, as he will be in contact with others there—but do *nothing* that he tells you; you are my man now, Mr Blount, and you follow *my* orders, not Lord Robert's. And do not attempt out of any cousinly loyalty to warn Lord Robert of this or to secretly carry out any orders he gives that are contrary to my own; you *cannot* serve us both, and you *will* be watched, Mr Blount. Yours are not the *only* eyes observing this tragedy and awaiting its outcome, and if you do seek to put Lord Robert's desires before Justice, I *will* find out. If he killed Amy or paid the hand that did, his life will be forfeit like any other murderer's; do not become his accomplice or abettor after the fact, Mr Blount."

"Remember, Mr Blount," Cecil said, "that Her Majesty can do *far more* for you, or against you, than Lord Robert ever can . . ."

"Majesty." Thomas Blount dropped suddenly from his chair, slumping on his knees at my feet as heavy sobs convulsed him. He fumbled to take the hem of my robe and lift it to his trembling lips. "Your servant first, A-Amy's s-s-second!" he blurted.

"Exactly." I nodded as I met Cecil's eyes over the young man's sob-shuddering back, and we exchanged an approving nod. "You are Lady Dudley's champion, Mr Blount, a knight clad in the shining armour of truth, and I can see that you will not fail her."

After Cecil and Mr Blount left me, I lingered long by the fire, sitting alone as the sky lightened and the birds began to sing, pondering my peculiar dream.

I had been riding in the hunt, with a number of lords and ladies, crashing through the forest, the hooves of our horses tearing up clods of earth, the branches and brambles catching at our clothes, as the barking hounds bounded before us in pursuit of our quarry. I could smell the heady commingled scents of perfume, sweat, horseflesh, and leather. Leading the chase was my mighty, majestic, and fearsome father, ruddy-cheeked and red-haired in his prime and glory, a magnificent figure astride a great bay stallion. And then the doe was cornered; I could smell and feel her fear as though my own soul were trapped within her form, my brain inside her skull, my heart pulsing and beating fast with fear inside her chest.

Suddenly the deer changed form and became a female—a slender woman in a black velvet riding habit with her hair caught up in a net of pearls beneath a black velvet hat adorned with an elegant, gracefully arching spray of black and white plumes held in place by a diamond brooch. I recognised her at once—my mother, Anne Boleyn. And I remembered the poem that had made her famous, written by Thomas Wyatt, the poet who had loved her, in which he compared her to a hunted deer.

She was cornered; desperately she stood there, her back against a tree, surrounded on all sides by hounds and huntsmen, bared teeth, poised knives, and arrows. And then a rustle of leaves, the sharp, sudden snap of a twig, distracted my father, and he was off again, in pursuit of another doe, one that kept flickering between the form of a fleeing deer and a frightened, flaxen-haired female whom I recognised in my fleeting glimpse of her as Jane Seymour.

My mother turned and faced me, calmly twirling her pearls, from which dangled a big golden *B,* as she said, "It's all about the hunt, the chase, you know. *Never surrender!* Stand your ground, Elizabeth—hold your own, and let no man take it from you! You are Queen in your *own* right, Elizabeth, *not* a consort through a husband's whim and sufferance! Your crown is not just some pretty ornament with no more power than a feathered bonnet, but it *will* be if you marry Robert Dudley; he won't just share your throne— he will *take* it from you!"

My horse was gone, as was my mother, both of them vanished all of a sudden, and I was left standing alone in a clearing, when Robert, galloping astride a fierce black stallion, accompanied by a retinue of huntsmen clad in his blue velvet livery and a pack of spotted hounds, came thundering towards me. I ran for my life. I felt my heart pounding in my chest, and the pinch and bite of my stays, my limbs tangling in the skirts of my purple velvet riding habit and linen petticoats, slowing and impeding me. Then I too was cornered, just as my mother had been, with my back pinned against a tree.

I heard a horse's whinny as Robert's night black stallion reared high, his hooves kicking the air before they thudded down again, throwing up clods of earth. Sitting haughty and high in the saddle, Robert took an arrow from his quiver and raised his bow. There he sat, aiming straight for my heart, a killing blow. But he was distracted, and I saw a grimace of annoyance cross his face, like a dark shadow, as a cream-coloured mare broke through the brambles. A young woman, buxom, full-hipped, and petite, clad in a flowing-skirted butter yellow riding habit, leapt from the saddle and ran to me. It was Amy—I recognised her instantly—vital and healthy as she used to be. A cascade of golden curls poured from beneath the wide brim of a yellow straw hat adorned with silken buttercups and sky blue ribbons and frothy cream-coloured plumes to frame her face.

"You're not the one who dies," she said simply, softly, her voice, like herself, shy and vulnerable, with a faint quiver of her upper lip. Her blue green eyes, which dared to meet mine only for an instant, were as bright as jewels beneath a shimmering veil of tears. And then she stepped swiftly between me and Robert's arrow just before it struck.

With a gasp, she fell back, wilting into my arms, a scarlet flower blossoming on her left breast, around the wooden shaft.

I lowered her gently to the ground and sat there, cradling her in my arms. When I tried to reach for the shaft, my hand hovering indecisively, trying to decide whether I should attempt to pull it out, her hand rose to cover mine, and she shook her head, and a faint smile graced her lips just before her eyes closed forever.

"Elizabeth." I looked up to see my mother standing beside me, holding out a bow and a quiver filled with arrows. "Robert Dudley uses people like the steps on a staircase that he can climb to reach the top. The knave has grown too proud. Take him down, Bess, *take him down!*" she commanded, her iron will evident in every word.

Gently, I laid Amy aside, and I stood up. Swiftly, I plucked an arrow from the quiver, took the bow, and aimed right for Robert Dudley's heart. *An eye for an eye, a life for a life,* I thought. But, at the last moment, I altered my aim.

"You missed," my mother said calmly as we watched Robert tumble backward from the saddle, clutching his arm as he rolled to avoid being trampled by his horse's hard, crashing hooves as the startled beast reared.

"No, Mother," I said in a voice surprisingly calm, "I didn't. He has fallen and shall never rise again."

I turned and looked at her. Our eyes met.

"It is crueller to let him live," we—mother and daughter— spoke as one.

It was at that moment that Cecil woke me, so I never knew what—if anything—came after.

I appeared before my court gowned in black and silver brocade, long ropes of silvery grey and black pearls about my throat and twined within my hair, and calmly announced the sad news—that Lady Dudley had died the previous day; apparently she had fallen down a staircase and broken her neck. And in the appalled hush that followed, as all eyes turned to Robert, I offered him my most sincere condolences and gave him my permission—in a tone that showed it was an absolute command and *not* an option he might consider or not as he pleased—to retire from court. "We"—I said, adopting the royal we—"know you will want to be alone with your grief, to mourn your loss in private. You are excused from your duties at court, My Lord. We suggest you go to your house at Kew and there await the coroner's verdict." Then I asked my court to don mourning clothes as a show of respect for Lady Dudley, and, giving my arm to the Italian Ambassador, I pointedly turned my back on Robert.

I quickly excused myself from the Ambassador's company, claiming a headache brought on by this sad news, and went alone to my private rooms. But I was not left alone for long, as I knew I would not be. The door connecting my chamber with Robert's flew open, and there he was—a pulsing mass of fury, like a human volcano about to erupt.

"You are to go to Kew, My Lord," I said, calmly fluttering my fan, pointedly ignoring his anger. "Consider yourself fortunate that it is not the Tower. I could send you there pending the outcome of the investigation. No doubt there will be a great many who will think me remiss in not doing so; they will see me as blind—wilfully or foolishly—besotted, and indulgent. But I never forget a friend, and you stood by me when I had few; so I choose to remember, and reward, your loyalty now, so I shall spare you the Tower—for the time being—but *nothing* else."

"Elizabeth!" He rushed across the room and fell on his knees before me, grasping desperately at my hands. "Please, do not send me away! People will think it means that you believe me guilty, and I need you now, to comfort me . . ."

"To *comfort you*, Robert?" I asked incredulously. I pulled my hands from his and reached up and pinched and pressed my ears. "Did I rightly hear you say that you needed me to *comfort you*? For which loss—the crown you imagined could be yours, or the wife you may have had killed?"

Robert leapt to his feet. He clenched his trembling fists, raising them, rather menacingly, to let me see how they quivered and the knuckles stood out. "How dare you speak to me so? If you were a man, I would—"

I brought my hand up and dealt his face a ringing slap. "*I am not* Amy, so do not expect to see *me* quail and quake before the mighty Lord Robert Dudley!" I said scornfully. "*I am* Queen"—I watched with great satisfaction as each word made Robert flinch like another slap—"and *you* do *not* rule here, and *never* will, but *I* do. And I fear *no man, least* of all *you!*"

Robert flung himself away from me and began to pace before the great stone fireplace, pausing only to pour himself a goblet of wine. "She killed herself to spite me, to blacken my name, to try to ruin my—our"—he hastily amended—"chance, but don't you let her do it, Elizabeth. Show yourself to be the wiser, cleverer woman I know you are; don't let a spiteful corpse come between us! *Damn her!*" he fumed, tossing back his head and downing the wine.

"Damn her for the spiteful wench she so obviously was; only in death does she show her *true* colours at last! She was cleverer than I thought! She *knew* no one would ever believe that anyone would be such a fool as to try to take their life that way, by throwing themselves down stairs! Who ever heard of such a thing? It is too uncertain! People fall down stairs every day and just get up, dust themselves off, and go about their business while their bruises heal! To take one's life is to jeopardise one's immortal soul and damn themselves to lie for all eternity in unhallowed ground, buried at midnight naked at the crossroads with a stake through the heart. But she knew no one would ever believe it; they would rather think the worst of me, that I did it, and thus she would be spared unconsecrated burial. She *deserves* to be damned for what she did, but she has damned me instead! She is the martyr, whilst I am cast as the Devil, the fiendish murderer who took poor Amy's life! *Damn, damn, damn her!*"

"And you think she went to such desperate lengths, breaking her own neck, to blacken your reputation?" I asked incredulously. "I don't believe it."

Robert paused thoughtfully. "Maybe she hurt herself trying to get my attention, thinking it would bring me back, but it went horribly wrong—*fatally* wrong? Or maybe it was an accident; she was always very clumsy."

"How very selfish you are! To say nothing of unkind!" I exclaimed. "A woman is dead, a woman you once loved, or claimed to love, enough to wed and bed—or was it the other way around?—and you have uttered not one lamentation, not one kind or sympathetic word, only condemned her for the troubles her death shall cause you."

"I may have loved her once"—Robert shrugged as he refilled his goblet—"but that seems a whole lifetime ago. I was young and foolish then, thinking with my cock instead of with my head. I will not lie to you, Elizabeth, I am *glad* she is dead. *Glad!* She was a mistake I made in my youth, when hot blood overruled reason; now her death has corrected it, erased my youthful error. A part of me wants to ride straight to Cumnor and kneel down and kiss every one of those stairs for making me a free man!"

It occurred to me then that my father must have felt much the same way when he killed my mother, though he hid behind a farce of a trial, so that he could claim Justice had been done and let a French executioner's hands be stained with her blood instead of his own. He wanted her gone, and it was his lips that ordered his minion Cromwell to find or fabricate evidence to rid him of the grand passion he now regarded as his greatest mistake, and it was his own hand that signed the death warrant.

"Get out," I ordered. "I cannot bear the sight of you or the sound of your voice; I don't want you near me. Get out, and know that if you were behind this, you have killed her for nothing. I will *never* marry you, Robert; I never would have, even if there had never been an Amy or any other woman you took to wife. There is something I love more than any person, something I put before the wishes, whims, and caprices of my head and heart and the desires of my body—*England,* my *first* and *greatest* love! And none shall ever come between us," I said, glancing down at the heavy gold and onyx coronation ring on my left hand. "And you would not be very good for England, Robert; on the contrary, you would be a *disaster.* Though your ambition makes you think otherwise, you have let your dreams delude you and convince you that you were born to be King, just like a child who dreams of growing up to be a great knight to slay dragons or to marry a fair princess, but you would in truth make a *terrible* king. You would be detested by your subjects for your arrogance and condescension; though your charm is a formidable weapon, and it works especially well upon women, it is far too haughty and lofty to win and hold a kingdom's heart. You would be loved only by those who profited well by your favour— and despised the moment you refused them anything they desired, passed over them in favour of another, or behaved towards them in a manner they perceived as a slight. Oh, I know." I came and patted his arm with mock condolence. "Ironic, is it not? The *one* thing you thought would set you free to marry me is also the one thing that will prevent it forever; you killed her for nothing, Robert. Besides, I don't think you would make a very good husband; you were not very kind to your first wife. I pity the poor woman who would be fool enough to take a chance upon becoming your second."

With blazing eyes, Robert rounded on me, flinging his goblet into the corner with a great clatter. "I see now that the only way to clear my name is to find the real culprit!" he cried.

"Yes." I nodded. "And I can help you, and I will," I promised, again patting his arm soothingly. "There is the door," I directed, brandishing my fan at it, "and on your way out of it, if you will pause and look to your left, you will find the *perfect* instrument to aid your discovery." I indicated the round Venetian looking glass framed in a wreath of silver set with jewelled and enamelled flowers.

"*Damn you!*" Robert hissed at me. "I *will* go, but *you* will be sorry when I discover the *real* culprit, when the real killer stands in chains before you, and you see how basely you have treated me, accusing me falsely of killing a woman who is better dead than she ever was alive! And then . . . then *you* will fall on *your* knees before *me,* like a supplicant; you will crawl to me and plead with me, *beg me,* for *my* forgiveness, to grant *you* my hand in marriage! Then we will see who is sorry!"

I threw back my head and laughed. "Oh, what a proud and vain peacock you are!" I exclaimed, and I laughed until tears rolled down my face, and I had to fan myself to ease the hot flush that coloured my cheeks. "Robert, why ever should I beg to marry *you*? You are emperor only of your own vanity and *nothing* else! I am Queen, and as such *I* have *all* the power; it is *mine* by right of birth, God's will, and my people's; you are my subject, and I can humble you in an instant lower than I have raised you, and your manly charms are, I assure you, not sufficient to bring me to my knees like a Southwark whore dazzled by a coin. And while I readily admit that you are a very amusing companion endowed with many manly charms and graces, and you are the best dancer and horseman at this court, and the best at keeping pace with me, and your kisses and caresses are not without skill or merit, and, when your presumptuousness does not border on treason and you keep your ambition under your hat, I have taken immense delight in your company, at forgetting myself, perhaps more than I should, and revelled in just being a woman, a *passionate* woman, but . . ." I shrugged and spread my hands. ". . . you are not worth a kingdom! You are *not* indispensable, as you seem to think you are, for I assure you, without you, I shall not lack for company and interesting and pleasant diversion. Now, be gone"—I flourished my fan towards the door— "before I call my guards and have them escort you from the palace; if I must do that, methinks I shall amend your destination to the Tower instead of Kew. You can either sleep on a pile of dank straw with the rats and black beetles to attend you, or on a feather bed with a satin pillow to rest your head upon and Mr Tamworth to serve you as befits the great lord you think you are; it is *entirely* up to you, Lord Robert."

And when he lingered, daring me to do so, I clapped my hands, and instantly my guards appeared from where they stood always stationed outside my door, halberds in hand, ready to obey my command. But before I could give the necessary orders to escort Lord Robert from the palace, he barged past them, roughly shouldering his way between them, banging his elbows against their gleaming silver breastplates, and stormed out.

As I knew he would, Robert immediately sent Thomas Blount riding hard and fast to Cumnor, his first concern being not his wife's fate but "how this evil should light upon me. Considering what the malicious world shall bruit, I can take no rest. I have no way to purge myself of the malicious talk that I know the wicked world will use"—thus he bewailed his misfortune in a letter he sent a courier chasing after Mr Blount to deliver. Then he sent for his tailor, commanding him to come at once to Kew and fit him for an elegant new wardrobe of mourning black velvets, satins, and silks with discreet gold and silver embellishments. And his glover, hatter, furrier, cobbler, and goldsmith were summoned too. As a rule, Robert would rather go *too* far than not far enough.

Cecil had all his letters, coming and going, intercepted and copied, so we were well aware when, through Thomas Blount, the "grieving" widower reached out to the jury. "I pray you say from me," he instructed, "that I require them, as ever I shall think well of them, that they will, according to their duties, earnestly, carefully, and truly deal in this matter and find it as they shall see it fall

out. So shall it well appear to the world my innocency by my dealings in the matter." And I also knew when he sent a gift of fine cloth
to the foreman, one Richard Smythe, and asked to be remembered
to him, as he had once served briefly in my household during my
girlhood, though I had scant memory of him and could not conjure
the man's face in my memory. We also learned that Robert purchased a plough horse for another jury man.

Every night, after the business of the day was done, and I put on
my nightgown and Kat had brushed out my hair, I lingered long at
my desk, reading Mr Blount's many assurances to his cousin that
the jury was well disposed towards him, and the local gossip he recounted, including some petty spite directed at Amy's host, Mr
Forster, and speculation about Amy's despondent state of mind,
which led many to believe that her death might have indeed been a
suicide. Most disturbingly, he mentioned that her maid, Mrs Pirto,
had confided that her lady had often prayed, asking God to deliver
her from her desperation, and she was widely thought to be a
woman of a strange mind.

One night, Cecil showed me a letter Robert had written after he
paid him a visit.

> *Sir,*
>   *I thank you very much for your being here, and the*
> *great friendship you have shown towards me I shall not*
> *forget. I am very loath to wish you here again, but I*
> *would be very glad to be with you there. I pray you let*
> *me hear from you, what you think best for me to do. If*
> *you doubt, I pray you ask the question, for the sooner*
> *you can advise me to come thither, the more I shall thank*
> *you. I am sorry so sudden a chance should breed me so*
> *great a change, for methinks I am here all the while as it*
> *were in a dream, and too far, too far from the place I am*
> *bound to be, where, methinks also, this long, idle time*
> *cannot excuse me for the duty I have to discharge else-*
> *where. I pray you help him that sues to be at liberty out*
> *of so great a bondage. Forget me not, though you see me*

*not, and I will remember you and fail you not, and so
wish you well to do. In haste this morning.*

*I beseech you, Sir, forget me not to offer up the hum-
ble sacrifice you promised me.*

Your very assured,

Robert Dudley.

"And what is this 'humble sacrifice' he beseeches you not to forget to offer up?" I asked when I finished reading it.

"Lord Robert is most anxious to return to court, Your Majesty,"
Cecil replied, "and, if he cannot yet, he bade me most earnestly to
inform you, as if my words came from his own heart and lips, that
he keeps the candles burning in every window the whole night
through at Kew, hoping that they will lead you to his door."

"Only in his dreams, Cecil," I sighed, "the same dreams
wherein upon his head rests a jewelled crown, and a cloak of velvet
and ermine falls about his shoulders, and his hand wields a sceptre
as mighty as a sword."

Cecil could not suppress a smile. "Indeed, though I warrant it
shall be a very hard dream for him to give up."

"There comes a time in all our lives, Cecil," I said thoughtfully,
leaning my chin on my hand and staring into the fire, "when truth
stares us, or even slaps us, in the face, and we must say farewell to
our dreams, even our most dearly cherished ones of many years'
keeping, hoping, and treasuring; we must accept that they will
never come true and that continuing to dream them will only bring
us pain."

"Madame"—Cecil turned earnestly to me—"you are young
still, and many of us are disappointed and hurt by love in our
youth, but there are better, *far better,* dreams for you to dream than
Robert Dudley."

I smiled and, nodding, reached out my hand to Cecil, the ring
that wed me to England glittering black and gold in the firelight.
"There is England, Cecil—that is my dream, to build a greater
England than this world has ever known."

"That is a dream that I believe shall come true"—Cecil
smiled—"God willing, as I believe He is."

* * *

When it arrived, I sat up far into the night, leaning over my silver-topped writing desk, intently poring over the coroner's report, pondering and weighing each word, hoping to find some clue that would serve as the key to unlock the mystery and set the truth free.

Inquisition as indenture held at Cumnor on September 9 in the second year of the reign of Elizabeth, by the grace of God Queen of England, before John Pudsey, gentleman, coroner of the said lady Queen, on inspection of the body of Lady Amy Dudley, late wife of Robert Dudley, knight of the most noble Order of the Garter, there lying dead, which certain jurors, sworn to tell the truth at our request, were adjourned on the aforesaid ninth day by the selfsame coroner to appear both before the justices of the aforesaid lady Queen at the assizes before the same coroner, in order there to return their verdict truthfully and speedily on which same day the jurors say under oath that the aforesaid Lady Amy on September 8 in the aforesaid second year of the reign of the aforesaid Queen Elizabeth, being alone in a certain chamber within the home of a certain Anthony Forster Esq., in Cumnor Place, and intending to descend the aforesaid chamber by way of certain steps of the aforesaid chamber there and then accidentally fell precipitously down the aforesaid steps to the very bottom of the same steps, through which the same Lady Amy there and then sustained not only two injuries to her head—one of which was a quarter of a thumb deep and the other two thumbs deep—but truly also, by reason of the accidental injury or of that fall and of the Lady Amy's own body weight falling down the aforesaid stairs, the same Lady Amy there and then broke her own neck, on account of which certain fracture of the neck the same Lady Amy there and then died instantly; and the aforesaid Lady Amy was found there and then without any other mark or wound on her body; and thus the jurors say on their oath that the aforesaid Lady Amy in the manner and form aforesaid by misfortune came to her death and not otherwise, in so far as it is possible at present for them to agree; in testimony of which fact for this inquest both the coroner and also the jurors have in turn affixed their seals this day.

John Pudsey, coroner	Richard Hughes
Richard Smythe, gentleman,	William Cantrell
foreman of the jury	William Noble
Humphrey Lewis, gentleman	John Buck
Thomas Moulder, gentleman	John Keene
Richard Knight	Henry Langley
Thomas Spene	Stephen Ruffyn
Edward Stevenson	John Sire
John Stevenson	

When I raised my head, instead of Cecil standing beside me, waiting patiently for me to finish perusing the document, I saw in my memory's eye that radiant young woman on her wedding day, her golden curls crowned with buttercups, in a wedding gown as frothy as milk with lace and gilt-embroidered flowers, looking up at her husband with eyes full of trust and love, never even imagining that Robert would fail to keep every single promise he ever made to her.

With a wrenching sigh, I shook my head and let the coroner's report fall onto my desk.

"What do you make of it all, Cecil?" I asked.

"Madame, in truth, I do not know," he confessed. "Like you, I have weighed each word and questioned my informants at length, yet it remains a puzzle. The jury seems satisfied that it was an accident. And though her maid stoutly maintains that her mistress was a good Christian lady who would never take her own life, I think loyalty more than true conviction compels Mrs Pirto's words. She paints a most vivid picture of a woman most heavily laden with sorrows, to such an extent that we *cannot* rule out the possibility of suicide. She has reported that Lady Dudley oftentimes fell to her knees and beseeched God to deliver her from her desperation. And many of the household were of the opinion that she was a woman of a strange mind."

"A mind can buckle under fear, Cecil," I said softly, looking back to my own past. "I know—I lived my life under the shadow of the axe and the assassin's nefarious tools from the day I was born and all through my sister's reign—the poisoned cup, the dagger in the back or in the breast, the pillow pressed over the face in slumber, the silken noose. I know the fear only too well, and even now, there are many who deem me a heretic and a bastard, who doubt my right to reign and would prefer another in my place or a return to the Catholic fold, and desire me dead, so I know those fears only too well."

"Majesty . . ." Cecil hesitated. "There is yet another possibility . . ." He paused and looked at me, and I knew he was about to speak one of those truths I had insisted he never keep from me.

"Go on, Cecil." I nodded.

"We cannot discount the possibility that Lord Robert acted the beast and fulfilled the expectations of the world by sending assassins to rid him of the frail obstacle that stood in the way of his ambitions."

I nodded sadly. "In the end, the only clear and certain truth is that we shall never know for certain."

"I fear so, Your Majesty," Cecil agreed.

After he left me, I went softly into the deserted chamber adjoining my own where Robert was accustomed to lodge. I opened the chest at the foot of his bed, usually filled with shirts and other linens, and found it empty except for a copybook and a dark circle lying at the bottom. I lifted them both out. When I turned the circle over, I gasped, startled to find Amy's face staring back at me. My portrait was everywhere, on every wall; even little statues, marble, gold, and silver figurines of classical goddesses sculpted with my features adorned the mantel and tables and even formed the bases of the candlesticks, making me the eternal bearer of flame. There were also portraits of Robert's father and brothers, his mother and sisters, even vain Guildford and the luckless Lady Jane Grey, looking utterly unlike herself in a gown of regal purple velvet, but of Robert's wife, there was no sign. There was no place on Robert's walls for the shy and melancholy girl of the once-radiant smile and trusting eyes whose love for her husband had shone like a sunbeam. Instead, she was banished to a chest, usually buried beneath a mound of linens. There, like one smothered in her slumber, the lawfully wedded wife of Lord Robert Dudley, the lady who had been so pitifully slain, was laid to rest in the same anonymity and obscurity as she had lived.

I stood and stared hard at that sad, melancholy visage Lavinia

Teerlinc's dainty and skilful brushes had captured, comparing it to the happy, radiant bride glowing with happiness I remembered from that joyous June day ten years ago.

"Love, so kind to some, so cruel to others," I mused aloud. "Oh, Amy!" I sighed. "Did you do this to yourself, or did he order it, directly or indirectly, merely by speaking aloud his impatient wishes? Did someone, one of his lackeys, take the hint, or else discern his wishes, and take it upon themself to act on them, hoping to please him and share the glory and riches they thought it would bring? How else to explain so opportune a death?"

I opened the copybook. An awkward and childish hand that gradually improved covered every one of the tearstained and blotted pages from start to end, laboriously and repeatedly copying out "The Clerk's Tale" of Patient Griselda from Chaucer's *The Canterbury Tales* until every page was filled. Like a schoolmaster, he must have set her this task. And at the end of each recounting I watched her signature grow from a sprawling scrawl to a more hesitant, but tighter and neater, more elegantly formed script more befitting a lady—*Amy Dudley*.

As I scanned one page my eyes lighted upon the lines:

> *If I knew my death would ease you,*
> *I'd gladly die, simply to please you.*

Sickened and appalled, I snapped the book shut and flung it hard across the room. I heard its spine snap and break against the wall, and I thought of Amy's fragile neck. And, cradling her miniature on my lap, just as I had her arrow-pierced body in my dream, I sank down onto the floor by Robert's cold and empty hearth and wept for all that was and never would be again, and for all three of us and the dreams we had had to bid farewell to. Amy to her loving husband and happy marriage, the future that seemed to unfurl, shining like a golden road before them; Robert to the crown he coveted as King Robert I of England, founder of a great royal dynasty; and myself to the dream that I might someday be at once a woman and a queen who could know Love's passion without having to relinquish my power into the hands of the man who stroked and caressed me. *Farewell, farewell, farewell!*

❧ 34 ❧

Elizabeth

Windsor Castle
November 27, 1560

I prepared with great care on the day I was to welcome Robert back to court; every lock of hair, every garment, every pearl, *must* be *perfect*. I knew all eyes would be watching us and wondering what would happen next. Many thought this ceremony of ennoblement, meant to invest him with the title of Earl of Leicester, was a prelude to the crown Robert had always coveted, and that a marriage service would follow shortly after. Well, let them wait and see! Already rumours were spreading abroad that we had, like my own parents, been married secretly in a late-night ceremony with unseemly haste, before Amy was even laid to rest, with Robert's brother Ambrose and his wife, Anne, and his sister, Mary, and her husband, Philip Sidney, acting as our witnesses. It was pure nonsense of course, but the truth never stood a chance against a good story.

I found him in his bedchamber, staring at the new mural I had ordered as a gift to welcome him back. It depicted Icarus with Robert's own dark hair and fine features and handsome, sweat-slick, sun-bronzed body, his wings melting, dripping wax, and bursting into flames, raising his hands as if they could ward off the fiery red ball of the sun he had flown far too near to. And if one squinted and peered carefully at the sun, they might just discern my own fiery locks and features.

"You wear false mourning, Robert," I observed, my eyes taking in the elegant sable-bordered black velvet doublet embroidered with rich golden scrollwork and black silken hose. "You mourn your lost reputation, not your wife, and what you think her death has cost you, though that was ever a fool's dream that would never have come true."

Robert stiffened and frowned. "Have you come here only to mock and insult me and be unkind?"

"A man of your age and experience should have learned long ago that the truth is seldom kind," I said as I turned to go back into my own apartment.

He followed me, as I knew he would. "And you must not attribute such ... perceived slights—shall we say?—as mine alone," I continued, "for I've heard that you are rather a merry widower. And a rather boastful fellow too, bursting with confidence that you can, in time, infect me with your own boldness and temerity, as though it were the smallpox, and persuade me to give you my hand in marriage, and with it, of course, my crown, and my throne, and all the power that goes with it. I believe those were your words? Your Mr Blount—Ah, here he is now!" I smiled and held out my hand for Thomas Blount to kiss as he followed Cecil in through the opposite door. "As I was saying, your Mr Blount, who is *my* Mr Blount *first*"—I smiled upon seeing Robert's face blanch as white as an egg before me—"is an Englishman whose *first* loyalty is to his Queen, and he has told me in *great* detail of the celebrations in your rooms at Kew that have taken place almost every night, even before Lady Dudley was entombed. Indeed this modest young man blushed to inform me of the drinking and other wild and wanton doings of the man who would be King and his guests; I hope you have not been promising your Southwark whores positions as my waiting women when you are King." I turned and stared at him intently, narrowing my eyes. "You do look rather tired this morning, My Lord, perhaps due to the few hours you slept upon a hard floor beneath a table, though you had two buxom wenches whose bosoms you took turns resting your head upon, though I daresay a goosedown pillow would have served you better. I detect a certain stiffness in your neck, in the way you move it and wince each time you do. Shall we ask Dr Bayly to take a look at it?"

At the mention of his name, Dr Bayly himself came in and bowed low before me.

"Ah, Dr Bayly." I held out my hand to him. "I fear I have misjudged you. When I first heard of your refusal to treat Lady Dudley, I was most upset, but once I became fully aware of your reasons and the circumstances, I understood. I commend you for your wisdom; a less honourable man would willingly have dived into Lord Robert's purse. Dr Dee has given me a copy of your treatise on diseases of the eye, which I read with great interest. I trust you will do us, and our realm, great credit in the years to come. When next we visit Oxford, we shall attend one of your lectures."

"Majesty," he breathed, sweeping me a deep bow, "you honour me!"

Too stunned to speak, Robert stared first at me, then at Thomas Blount, then swept cursorily over the doctor, whom he had never even met and knew only by letter, then lighted upon his cousin again.

"You are my cousin, my man . . ." he began in an accusing tone.

But Thomas Blount did not let him finish. "Aye, My Lord, I am, but I am the Queen's man first. I serve none but God before her."

"What nonsense is this?" Robert exclaimed. "*Nothing* can be proved against me. I am innocent! Innocent! The jury declared me so! They said it was an accident! An accident! Is that not enough to satisfy anyone? Am I to be blamed for Amy's clumsiness and stupidity for the rest of my life?"

I sighed, shrugged my shoulders, and shook my head. "I am afraid we mere mortals are a fickle and suspicious lot! But I have a small gift for you to welcome you back; just a little trifle. When I was my sister Mary's prisoner, confined under house arrest at Woodstock, I once took a diamond ring from my finger and carved these words upon a windowpane: *Much suspected of me, nothing proved can be*. You might take that as your new motto. I give it to you freely, Robin—may it stand you in good stead in the years to come. I think it shall most aptly define your existence from now on."

Robert just stared at me. "Surely *you*—you who know me best, my beloved friend since we were eight years old—don't believe . . .

You *do*!" He emitted a wounded gasp at the look on my face. "You do! You think I killed her!"

I shrugged lightly. "Not with your own hands perhaps." I gazed down meaningfully at his strong, powerful fingers, adorned with several fine rings, including a large sapphire that had once belonged to my father that I had given him. They were rough and callous and long accustomed to gripping hard a horse's reins, but I also knew them to be gentle and most skilful at caressing, yet I could well imagine them closing around a woman's fragile neck and squeezing the life out of her. "But you may have paid someone else's hands to stand proxy for yours, to keep the blood off your fine lace cuffs, fastidious creature that you are, and even if you did not . . . there are *many* ways you can kill someone, as in a love affair or a marriage in which the love has died and the thoughts and affections have turned to another. So yes, Robert, *I do* think you killed her, though not in a blatantly obvious manner that can be legally defined as murder; so your neck is safe. But, I fear that, in the eyes of the world, you will ever be suspect, and you must accept and accustom yourself to that fact, make peace with it or go mad with frustration as you futilely rage against it, though you can never change it. As for myself"—I touched my breast—"I would be a *fool* to ever take such a man as my husband. I will not go to bed Queen Elizabeth and wake up plain Lady Elizabeth the next morning. You are not worth a kingdom to me, Robert, and the title of Lady Dudley is poor recompense for a lost crown. But I pray that you do not take my words as a *personal* slight, for no husband is worth England's loss to me. And if, perchance, some obliging friend of yours, or one of those surly brutes you have follow you around, armed to the teeth with weapons, thought to do you a favour by ridding you of the encumbrance of your unwanted and ailing wife, well . . . they have instead done you a *grave* disservice; no amount of polish can ever remove the tarnish from your reputation."

"No!" Robert insisted. "No! I don't believe that! You are mistaken; none of my men would ever harm me! *She* did this just to spite me, to ruin me! God damn her to Hell, as all suicides deserve, because she didn't just destroy herself, she destroyed *me* also! She took me down with her!"

"May God bless and keep her!" I retorted. "For she saved me—and England—from *you*!"

I paused before one of the many fine, silver-framed Venetian looking glasses that adorned my wall and patted my hair, woven through with ropes of creamy pearls, with long ringlets cascading down over my shoulders to my waist.

"Observe my gown, Lord Robert," I said, sweeping my hand down over the tightly laced bodice and full skirt billowing over a stiff, conical farthingale, the black satin adorned with jewel-encrusted serpents and ruby red apples representing knowledge and temptation, and a dense shower of pearlescent pink and white apple blossoms that wafted down over it from bodice to hem. "Mr Edney!" I called, startling Robert with another familiar figure, a man whose bills he had been complaining about for ten years. "Would you bring my mantle please?" In the silvered glass I watched Robert's face, almost laughing as Amy's tailor reverently draped about my shoulders a black satin mantle embroidered with hundreds of staring, unblinking blue green eyes, the *exact* same colour as Amy's had been, and a number of delicate pink-flushed ears, each wearing diamonds and pearls, each one like a milky teardrop. *"How beautiful!"* I exclaimed. "You do fine work, Mr Edney; we shall have another, in orange, perhaps, with eyes of many colours. You see, Lord Robert?" I met his gaze in the glass. "I am the eyes and ears of my kingdom; I know and see all." From between my breasts, I lifted the golden pendant that had fallen there and laid it outside my bodice. It was a conjoined *AB* that had belonged to my mother, worn, just as she had worn it, suspended from a rope of pearls, but I didn't tell anyone what it meant to me—that was my private secret. The *A* represented not only *Anne* but *Amy,* and the *B* stood for both *Boleyn* and *Beware*.

I turned from the glass. "Where is my fan?" I inquired.

"Here it is, Your Majesty."

Robert started and nearly jumped out of his skin, wincing and uttering a sharp "Damn!" as he whipped his head around sharply, forgetting his sore neck, to behold the stooped and aged form of Amy's maid, Mrs Pirto, emerging from the adjoining room to reverently offer me my fan of dyed green ostrich plumes.

"Thank you, Mrs Pirto." I smiled and rested my hand on her

arm for a moment as I accepted it. "I can see that your lady was well served."

Robert did not know it—and there was no reason he should; he had already informed Mrs Pirto that her services would no longer be required—but I had told Cecil to see that Mrs Pirto's service to Amy was well rewarded and that she was able to live out the rest of her life in comfort. Given her age, stiff knees, and gnarled hands— signs I knew all too well, having seen them creep up on my dear old nurse, Kat Ashley—she was likely to encounter great difficulty in finding another position, and also, given the infamy and notoriety attached to her last position, to be pestered and harassed by curiosity-seekers.

"Have you been reading your Chaucer while you were away, Robert?" I inquired of him, smiling as, bewildered by my question, he shook his head. "I know you are fond of him, particularly 'The Clerk's Tale'. I know you had your lady wife copy out the tale of Patient Griselda *many* times for your pleasure and her private instruction. There is a passage that I recall and find *most* fitting to your present circumstances:

> *"Scandals kept spreading, and by these rumours,*
> *he was defamed, until hate smote out love,*
> *For murderer is not a pleasant name.*
> *Still Robert—'*

"I mean *Walter!*"—I smiled apologetically at my blunder—

> *'pursued his shameful game,*
> *Deeply cruel, just as he intended.*
> *Never doubt his intentions; he did what he meant to.'*

"Is it not amazing how words written so long ago can be so apt in the present day?" I mused aloud as I headed to the door, to make my way to the Presence Chamber. "Oh, and, Robert"—I paused upon the threshold—"one more thing. I said I loved you, but I lied. Opium," I added pointedly, "plays strange tricks upon the mind."

"You don't mean that—" he began, but I did not wait to hear the rest of what he had to say; it would have made no difference anyway.

In the Presence Chamber, seated upon my throne, with my court assembled to see the much-despised Robert Dudley elevated to the peerage and invested with the title of Earl of Leicester, I had the patents of parchment brought to me and bade Robert come forward. But as he knelt before me, I suddenly bent and took from the scabbard at his hip his own jewel-hilted dagger and used it to slash the fine, creamy parchment to ribbons, whilst Robert's face, aghast and open-mouthed, his eyes wide and bulging with horror, went as white as the document I had just destroyed, and my courtiers, depending on their feelings for Robert, gasped, appalled or delighted, smirked, or endeavoured to stifle their laughter. "I shall not have another Dudley in the House of Lords, since this family tree has sprouted traitors for three generations," I announced. And then I leaned forward and patted Robert's cheek consolingly. "No, no," I said as though I were soothing a child, "the bear and ragged staff are not so soon overthrown!"

A verse then came into my mind, half-remembered from a dream, and, thinking it particularly apt, I shared it with my court as I sat back, well-contented, against the cushions of my throne and plied my fan:

> O Bess, the knave is grown too proud,
> Take him down, take him down,
> Such twigs must needs be bound,
> Take him down, take him down!

The chant was readily taken up, the men of my court, Englishmen born and bred and foreign visitors alike, stamping their feet or banging the ends of their staves upon the floor, and the women slapping their folded fans against their palms or clapping their hands as they recited it over and over again, the words rippling with malicious glee down the ranks as Robert, in a rage, too furious to speak—and what was there to say anyway?—stormed out. But he could not escape; the verse tauntingly followed him as he went, eagerly taken up by the servants and carried mouth by mouth through the corridors, formal rooms, and kitchens, then out the doors into the courtyard and on to the stables, where Lord Robert's horse awaited.

> *"O Bess, the knave is grown too proud,*
> *Take him down, take him down,*
> *Such twigs must needs be bound,*
> *Take him down, take him down!"*

As I watched him go, I wondered, did he do it? Did he kill her, by design or by an unwisely and impatiently uttered wish? I didn't know, and I had to accept the fact that I would never really know. I only knew that I would never trust him again. My subjects' fears were groundless, and they had been so all along; I would never marry him; I never meant to, not even in my dreams. And every time in the long years to come when I was tempted by loneliness or the human need to share, to confide and vouchsafe some small measure of trust to him, the pale spectre of Amy would always rise like a ghost in my dreams to remind me not to give too much, lest I be betrayed.

He stayed with me for the rest of his life, and when he died, I locked myself in my room and wept over his last letter. I sat for days upon the floor, huddled in a corner, just like my poor, mad sister had done after Philip left her and the babies she thought growing inside her belly proved to be only phantoms born of desperate hope. After three days, I dried my tears, got up, and changed my gown and put on my pearls and a vivid, flaming red wig to hide my balding pate and the short-cropped, feathery grey orange wisps that were all that was left of my hair by then, and went on for England; my people needed me, their Gloriana, Good Queen Bess, and, the name most dear of all to me, the one my loving people were so proud to call me—"Our Elizabeth". The passage of years had taught me, though it had never been an easy lesson, that that love *truly* was enough; it made every carnal passion pale in comparison. I was *England's* Elizabeth, *not* Robert's or any other man's Bess; I never could be. I was not a marble statue, though I painted my ageing face with a mask as stiff and white as one, but a woman of flesh and blood who lived and breathed, laughed, loved, raged, and wept, but I was also more, *much* more—I gave my people something to believe in; I gave them hope and courage; I fed and fuelled their pride and determination; when they kissed my hands or hems, they were touching the true spirit, the pulsing, beating heart of England. I brought them a little closer to God, through me in my white gowns and pearls, my hair as red as flame; I was for them the beacon of hope that burned brightly through every trial and tribulation that troubled this small but proud nation; I blurred the lines between majesty and divinity, between the Holy Virgin and England's Virgin Queen—Elizabeth—and that was enough. It was everything I ever truly wanted or meant to be.

EPILOGUE

Naked and soft as a velvet glove, her long-fingered, lily-white hand shed of its heavy burden of jewelled rings, caresses the great gilded bedpost, petting the life-sized carved lion with claws raised and mouth open as though emitting a mighty roar, ready to leap and tear her throat out. She lingers, just for a moment, to make certain that the purple velvet curtains fringed with Venetian gold are shut tightly. Then she draws up the hood of the dusky rose velvet cloak, her fingers plucking nervously at the satin bow at her throat, making sure the ribbons are secure; then, with her head held high, regal as a queen with Tudor blood coursing through her veins, she walks boldly to the adjoining door that leads into Robert Dudley's chamber and enters without knocking.

Bare-chested and restless in his sleep, he lies bathed in blue white moonlight, tossing his dark head against the silken pillows and moaning softly, the coverlet kicked down around his legs, virile charms on full display, his bare limbs entangled in the silken sheet, as he lies upon his back.

This is the man she has always wanted, ever since the day she saw him, the man she wanted to marry, to ride like a stallion every night, and be mounted like a mare by, though he laughed gently at her coquettish ways and spurned and looked past her with eyes only for her cousin, Elizabeth, the frigid, icy bitch-queen who lacked the courage to face her own desires, who didn't know how to submit to a man without being conquered by him—a secret Lettice knew all too well but was not prepared to share; instead, she would use it against her royal cousin to take the only man she truly desired. But there was another woman who stood in the way, his wife—that stupid-as-a-pumpkin country bumpkin, Amy. This was the man she had squatted naked before a roaring fire and black inverted cross for, pleading with Satan to *"Make him mine!"* when prayers to God failed her. For him, her delicate, soft, white fingers had touched the vilest objects, dead things she shuddered now to think about, and fashioned little wax dolls, filled with nail clippings, locks of hair bought from a servant with hair the same hue as Amy's, and her own monthly blood, and impaled them with thorns and put them in tiny wooden coffins. For him, she had stolen a book of poisons from her cousin's library and a single long strand of red hair from her brush, all to frighten a woman who was unworthy of him and did not deserve him, a woman who was taking too long to die but whose death might remove him from her reach forever if he attained the crown he so desired.

She stands at the foot of the bed and watches him for a long time; then she reaches up and slowly unties the satin ribbons and lets the velvet cloak fall down around her ankles. And a long white hand snakes out and pulls the sheet from him, letting it fall with a silken whisper to the floor as, stealthy, quiet, and nimble as a cat, she clambers up onto the bed, naked but for her white silk stockings and pink satin garters and slippers, and crawls up to straddle him.

His cock kindles to her touch, springing to life, and she slowly lowers herself, impaling herself upon the ardently upward-pointing arrow of flesh.

His eyes open wide. He smiles, eyes and lips radiating triumph. *"Elizabeth!"* he breathes, crying out her name in the utmost joy. "Oh, how I have waited, how I have longed and dreamed for this moment to come!"

She speaks not a word, merely smiles into the flaming curtain of hair that hangs down and caresses her cheeks as the ends trail down to tickle his chest.

Only when he explodes within her, grasping hard her slender hips as his seed gushes out, flooding and filling her, does she shake back her hair and bare her face.

With a startled and outraged cry, he tries to push her from him, but she grips him tighter with her knees and plants her palms hard and flat upon his chest as she moves, rocking as she rides him, selfishly intent on her own pleasure, determined to have *her* way at long last, white and triumphant in the moonlight, sharp little white teeth bared in a wicked smile.

"I am the unrepentant Magdalene, not the Holy Virgin who must be venerated and adored," Lettice Knollys says.

"Yes, you are, you little whore, you hot little bitch!" Robert Dudley says furiously as he savagely rolls her over onto her back with her legs high and straight in the air and thrusts hard inside her as if his cock were a dagger aiming straight for Elizabeth's heart. This "hot little bitch", her very own cousin, a woman unafraid of her own sensuality, is the *perfect* weapon to hurt her, and that is all he wants to do at this moment. Revenge really *is* sweet!

The next day Elizabeth sat by the fire and calmly played chess with Sir William Cecil, while Robert Dudley inspected the royal stables, and Lettice Knollys, in a low-cut emerald gown, sat and embroidered and exchanged gossip with the Queen's other ladies.

"When I find out," Elizabeth said softly as she scrutinised the board, "let it be a surprise; they think they are *so* clever, it seems a shame to disappoint them. Only when it is too late," she said, as her long white fingers closed around the black knight, "will they discover how much they despise each other for what their 'love' has cost them. They *deserve* each other!"

POSTSCRIPT

Elizabeth endured, a living icon, a flame-haired, pearl-encrusted, white candle of hope, to inspire her people's love and loyalty, the invincible and unobtainable "Virgin Queen" with the body of a woman but "the heart and stomach of a king", wooed and courted by many, wife to none, but mother to many—every man, woman, and child of English blood. She reigned for forty-five years and died in 1603, the last, and greatest, Tudor.

The mystery, scandal, and speculation surrounding Amy's death never really died. From time to time it would rear its ugly head, to the extreme dismay of Robert Dudley. Try as he might, he could never put it behind him.

Seven years after Amy's death, her stepbrother John Appleyard attempted to blackmail Robert, who had finally obtained the earldom of Leicester in 1564, his ennoblement being a prerequisite to Elizabeth's scheme to offer her "cast-off lover, the horse master who had murdered his wife to make room for her", as a prospective bridegroom to her cousin and rival for her throne, Mary, Queen of Scots. It was a choice calculated to offend Mary and drive her straight into the arms of the dissipated pretty boy Lord Darnley, just as Elizabeth had intended all along. John Appleyard claimed that he "had for the Earl's sake covered the murder of his sister".

He was speedily imprisoned in Fleet Prison and ordered to produce any evidence he had, whereupon he hastily recanted and announced that he was fully satisfied with the coroner's verdict concerning his sister's death.

In 1584 an anonymously authored and widely circulated book, a best seller in its day, known as *Leicester's Commonwealth: A Discourse on the Abominable Life, Plots, Treasons, Murders, Falsehoods, Poisonings, Lusts, Incitements, and Evil Stratagems Employed by Robert Dudley, Earl of Leicester,* revived the scandal and accused Robert of a whole catalogue of nefarious deeds, including paying one of his retainers, the staunchly loyal Sir Richard Verney, to go to Cumnor Place and murder Amy.

To this day, Amy's death, and what, if any, role her husband played in it, remains shrouded in mystery. Murder, mishap, suicide, and an underlying medical cause, sudden as an aneurysm or chronic like cancer metastasised to the bones, leaving them brittle and vulnerable to sudden, spontaneous fracture, all remain much-discussed and debated theories. An attempt in 1947 to examine her body for clues proved unsuccessful, as renovations to the church in the centuries following her death had disturbed previous burials and made locating her remains impossible.

In December 1560 Lettice Knollys married Walter Devereux, the first Earl of Essex, after Robert Dudley refused to marry her. The morning light brought a harsh dose of reason to dispel the hot, angry lust of their night together, and a resurgence of Robert's confidence that he could in time overcome Elizabeth's timidity and that the scandal over Amy's death would eventually fade and be forgotten. "If I were to marry you," he bluntly told the naked and raging Lettice, "it would utterly ruin me. The Queen's favour would be lost forever, and she would never forgive me!"

But Lettice had her revenge. After her first rendezvous with Robert—which she managed to coax him into repeating on several succeeding nights, when she crept into his room, dropped her cloak, and crawled naked into his bed—she adopted a rather lackadaisical approach to contraception and often forgot, or just did not bother, to drink her pennyroyal tea, rise from her lover's bed and piss hard or jump vigorously up and down immediately after coitus, or to insert a small sponge soaked in lemon juice or vinegar prior to the act, and when she married Walter Devereux, with her smiling parents and her cousin the Queen looking on as witnesses, a child was already growing inside her. For the rest of his days Robert Dudley had to live with the knowledge that his firstborn son and namesake—Lettice named the boy Robert—the handsome, dark-haired lad who loved horses and should have been his own legitimate heir would grow up in the eyes of the world as another man's son.

For several years following Amy's death, Robert endeavoured in vain to persuade Elizabeth to marry him, insisting that it was only fear and timidity that stayed her. In 1575 he hosted a series of spectacular entertainments for her at Kenilworth Castle during her annual Summer Progress. The grand finale was his last marriage proposal. As fireworks exploded in the midnight sky above them, Elizabeth sat on the rim of a great marble fountain, and a bare-breasted woman with pearl- and gilt-shell-bedecked golden hair clad in a shimmering green mermaid's tail swam across and presented Elizabeth with a silver oyster shell in which an opulent ring rested on a bed of pink velvet. Robert Dudley took it and knelt at Elizabeth's feet, offering her the ring, and his heart, as he asked, one last time, for her hand in marriage. Elizabeth rejected him. For Robert, it was the death blow to his most deeply cherished dream.

After indulging in a lengthy secret affair—and rumoured secret marriage—with another of Elizabeth's ladies, the beautiful and vulnerable Lady Douglass Sheffield, who bore him the boy he referred to as his "baseborn son", Robert Dudley succumbed to the seductive charms of the widowed Lettice Knollys, and the couple were secretly married at Kenilworth in 1579, with the bride wearing a loose silken gown to conceal her swollen belly. They managed to keep their marriage a secret from the Queen for a year. Gossips laid another death at the newlywed couple's door when rumours attributed the sudden demise of Lettice's first husband to poison administered in the guise of medicine. Walter Devereux, the first Earl of Essex, died in Ireland, officially of dysentery, insisting that there was "something evil in his drink" and cursing his wife with his dying breath; his last wish was that their five children be removed from her custody and be raised by his kinsman, the Earl of Huntington, to save them from being corrupted by their mother.

Robert Dudley soon found himself in the uncomfortable position of being an accused bigamist when the much-wronged Lady Sheffield insisted that he had married her in a secret, late-night ceremony with three of his retainers as witnesses. But she was dissuaded from pressing her claims when all letters and proof of their marriage disappeared—stolen, she insisted, by Lord Robert's henchmen. Fearing for her life and that of her son, when she began to suffer stomach pains, vomiting, and her beautiful blond hair began to fall out in clumps, Douglass became convinced that she was being poisoned and accepted a £700 bribe from Dudley in exchange for her silence and denial of their marriage to prevent his being persecuted for bigamy by the vengeful Queen.

Despite whatever personal triumph she may have felt at stealing her royal cousin's paramour, Lettice Knollys gained little from her marriage. Branded "that She-Wolf" by the irate Elizabeth, Lettice was permanently banished from court. Elizabeth made sure that Robert was kept so busy that he seldom had time to visit his wife. Theirs was a marriage based on candlelight and shadows, the same perfume and similar gowns as those worn by Elizabeth, and creeping away before the honest morning light reminded Robert that the head on the pillow next to his was not a queen's, only her whorish young cousin's, whose similarity to the object of his desire was not, he had discovered, really enough. The couple's only child, Robert's namesake and only legitimate heir, Robert Dudley, Baron Denbigh, "that noble imp", as Robert fondly called the boy, died of a sudden fever in 1584 when he was three years old. Rumours immediately erupted that the child had died of poison, given in the guise of medicine by Lettice, who wanted to ensure that her husband's earldom would be inherited by her eldest son from her first marriage, the handsome and hotheaded Robert Devereux, the second Earl of Essex.

Robert Dudley, the Earl of Leicester, died on September 4, 1588, at the age of fifty-six, surviving just long enough to witness England's triumph over the Spanish Armada. The cause of his death was variously ascribed to a malarial fever, poison administered by his own wife, the now middle-aged temptress Lettice, to free her to marry her handsome young lover, Christopher Blount, the couple's Master of the Horse, and as a final act of spite against her cousin Elizabeth—marriage hadn't entirely broken the bond between her and Robert, but death would—or cancer of the stomach; either way, many thought, remembering Amy, her cancer, and the rumours of murder and poison, that his death was justice in its most poetic form, and few truly mourned his passing.

After Amy's death, Robert Dudley gave lands in fifteen counties to Sir Anthony Forster, which allowed him to purchase and renovate Cumnor Place, to make it a fit home for a country gentleman and his family. Many believed that this was Forster's reward for having been a willing accomplice in Amy's murder. After Forster's death in 1572, Robert Dudley bought Cumnor from his heirs, though he never, as far as is known, set foot there. But time was not kind to Cumnor, and it gradually crumbled into ruin. Rumours abounded that "a beautiful woman, superbly attired" haunted the staircase, and in the nineteenth century an exorcism was performed, with nine priests participating, to confine her spirit to the pond in the park, where afterwards, curiously, the water never again froze. The desolate, roach- and rat-infested grey stone ruins were demolished in 1811, though after the publication of Sir Walter Scott's novel *Kenilworth* in 1821, which shifted the tragedy's setting to Kenilworth Castle to include the lavish entertainments Robert Dudley hosted there for Elizabeth, Victorians flocked to view the site where it had once stood.

Thomas Blount withdrew from court to lead a quiet life in the country. He died in 1568 after a fall from his horse; he struck his head upon a rock and never regained consciousness. Every year until his death he laid a single white rose and a shiny red apple on the plainly inscribed white marble slab of Amy's tomb. He always lingered long enough to tell her a story.

In the same year, Richard Verney died raving mad, grasping frantically in blind terror at the robes of the priest attending at his bedside, begging him to save him, claiming to already feel the flames of Hell burning him and the claws of the demons trying to tear him to pieces and drag him down to Hell. Repeatedly he pointed at the foot of his bed, exclaiming: "There she is! I can see her now, her hair shimmering like gold in the dim torchlight, running for her life, glancing back over her shoulder; I'll never forget the fear in her eyes. And the scream, surprised and terrified, as she missed the step, there where it veers suddenly, and fell, head over heels. I saw the flash of the gold embroidered on her gown and heard the sickening snap of her neck, the thud of her body, then silence. He was a great man, who deserved to be even greater, the only one to ever see greatness in me, and I wanted to help him achieve his destiny, but she was holding him back. I wanted to please him. I went there to kill her, God forgive me, but I didn't; I never laid a hand on her, so why does she *still,* after all these years, continue to haunt me?"

The honest physician Dr Walter Bayly, who refused to meddle where he could do no good and risk being hanged to cover another's sin, prospered in the years following Amy's death. In 1561 he was appointed Queen's Professor of Medicine at Oxford University, where during her visits Elizabeth always attended his lectures with great interest. He eventually became a fellow of the College of Physicians and one of Elizabeth's Physicians in Ordinary who attended her personally. Over the years he authored many books, including a well-received treatise on diseases of the eyes, and treated many illustrious patients. He ministered to both Elizabeth's toothaches and Robert Dudley's rheumatism as they gained in years and such ailments became the bane of their existence. One can only guess that the tragic spectre of Amy hovered tensely between the much-maligned widower and the good doctor who had refused to become enmeshed in his schemes when Dr Bayly accompanied the Earl of Leicester to take the waters at Buxton each summer. When the infamous book known as *Leicester's Common-wealth* was published and made public Dr Bayly's refusal to dose Amy with the medicines her husband sent, Dr Bayly retained a proud and honourable silence, never challenging or refuting the story. He died at the age of sixty-three in 1592, wealthy, respected, and esteemed, both as a doctor and a man, by family, friends, colleagues, and patients alike.

Lettice Knollys outlived them all, including her own son—the power-crazed Robert Devereux, Earl of Essex, who played May to Elizabeth's December in the last great romance of her life but lost his head when he tried to incite the people of London to rise against her and help him take her throne. He was beheaded in 1601, as was his fellow conspirator, his best friend and stepfather, Christopher Blount. Having long outlived her extraordinary beauty, Lettice died alone in her bed during the wee hours of the morning on Christmas Day 1634 at the age of ninety-three.

FURTHER READING

For those interested in the history of breast cancer, I highly recommend *Bathsheba's Breast: Women, Cancer, and History* by James S. Olson.

Chris Skidmore's *Death and the Virgin* provides the most detailed and thorough examination of the circumstances, mystery, and scandal surrounding the death of Amy Robsart Dudley and contains much information not found in earlier, previously published accounts.

A
COURT
AFFAIR

Emily Purdy

ABOUT THIS GUIDE

The suggested questions are included to
enhance your group's reading of Emily Purdy's
A Court Affair.

DISCUSSION QUESTIONS

1. Discuss the marriage of Robert Dudley and Amy Robsart. They married very young; both were only seventeen. Was their marriage doomed from the start? What, if anything, could they have done to save their marriage? Though our modern-day concept of domestic abuse did not exist in Tudor times, do you think Robert Dudley, as depicted in this novel, was an abusive husband? If you were a marriage counsellor and this couple was seated on your couch, what would you tell them?

2. Today Amy Robsart Dudley is mainly remembered because of the way she died, not how she lived. Very little is actually known about her, and the woman herself often emerges as a nonentity in both novels and nonfiction books; sometimes she is little more than just a name upon a page. How does the woman depicted in this novel compare with your previously formed ideas about the real Amy? Do you like or dislike her? Discuss her personality. What are her good qualities and flaws? How does marriage to Robert Dudley change her? How does her illness change her? How is the Amy of seventeen different from the Amy of twenty-eight?

3. Discuss Elizabeth's feelings about romance, sex, and marriage. How were these ideas formed? Her desire for passion without the commitment and compromise, the give-and-take, of marriage sounds very modern, and it even leads her to consider an affair with a married man as a safe way to find what she is seeking. What do you think about this? Every time Elizabeth lets Robert kiss and caress her, she stops him before he goes too far, leaving him frustrated. Do you think she is emotionally incapable of a sexual relationship because of her past?

4. Discuss Robert's relationship with Elizabeth. If she had not been queen, would he have still loved her? How great a role does his ambition play in their romance? Why is it so

hard for Elizabeth, even when she knows what Robert is really like, to give him up?

5. Discuss the tale of Patient Griselda and its theme of wifely obedience. Robert orders tapestries illustrating the story, reads it aloud to Amy, orders her to repeatedly copy it out, and even stages a play based on it for Elizabeth. Why is he such a fan of this story? What does it mean to him? And what do you, as a modern woman or man compared to a Tudor-era one, think of it?

6. Do you think Amy would have had a happier life if she had given Robert a divorce when he asked her to? How would her life have been different? What do you think of the manner in which he asked her, the reasons he gave, and his suggestion that Amy might still be his mistress? How would you have reacted if you had been in Amy's shoes?

7. Why does Amy dye her hair red and dress in imitation of Elizabeth? Discuss Robert's violent reaction to this. Why does Amy try so hard in so many ways—the dyed hair, the mermaid gown, etc.—to win Robert back? Is he *really* worth it?

8. Discuss Amy's illness and the medical treatments of the time. Medical science and our understanding and treatment of breast cancer have come a long way since Amy's lifetime. If this story were set in modern times, how do you think it would be different? Would Amy have still become the central figure in one of British history's greatest unsolved mysteries? Would she have had a more positive outlook and perhaps have become one of this disease's survivors?

9. Having breast cancer causes Amy to fear that no man will ever desire her sexually again, that their desire will turn to disgust when they see her undressed. Do you think this is a valid, realistic fear? Is this something modern-day sufferers still struggle with? What do you think would have happened if Amy had taken a lover? Should she have done so,

or was she right to honour her marriage vows to Robert even after he betrayed her?

10. While staying at Compton Verney, Amy believes that she is being poisoned, though Robert insists it is just her imagination. Both also see the master of the house, Sir Richard Verney, in remarkably different ways—in Amy's eyes he is a dark, sinister figure, but Robert paints him as a sentimental and cowardly man. Whom do you believe—Robert or Amy?

11. Certain characters appear in the book who may or may not be real, such as Red Jack the highwayman and the phantom grey friar who haunts Cumnor Place. Robert insists that the man Amy identifies as Red Jack is really a spice merchant, and the grey friar is supposedly a ghost that only the dying can see or just a story the servants tell to frighten the new housemaids. Do you believe these characters are real or only figments of Amy's imagination? What does each one represent?

12. Robert insists that Amy take the hemlock pills he gives her even if they make her sick to the point of death. Why does he do this? Is he trying to heal her or to kill her? Is this a real remedy or murder masquerading as medicine?

13. Discuss Elizabeth's dream about hunting in which both of her parents, Henry VIII and Anne Boleyn, as well as Robert and Amy, appear. What does this dream mean? Why does Amy take the arrow that is intended for Elizabeth? How would Elizabeth's life have been different if Anne Boleyn had lived and been there to give her a mother's guidance?

14. At the end of the book, why does Elizabeth stage the ennoblement ceremony only to tear up the patent? What message is she sending to her courtiers and to Robert?

15. For 450 years speculation has run rampant about the cause of Amy Robsart Dudley's death—was it an accident, suicide, murder, or an underlying medical condition such as cancer? What do you think?